'Like an illicit lover, I have been sloping off all week to snatch another hour's pleasure with *Almost A Crime*, Penny Vincenzi's terrific new novel' Jilly Cooper

'A super read that will keep you guessing right until the end' *Company*

Teeming with style . . . outselling Danielle Steel and Barbara Taylor Bradford . . . these are family sagas filled with tempestuous women, successful, sexy men and passionate plots . . . Readers will find every page irresistible' *Washington Post*

'Seductively readable . . . I carried on reading late into the night' *The Times*

'Penny Vincenzi writes with such flair and gusto that I defy any reader, once they've taken the smallest nibble, not to gobble it all down' *Sunday Express*

'With an unerring knowledge of the worlds she describes and the emotions that go with them, Penny Vincenzi has created another absorbing page-turner, packed with believable characters and satisfyingly extreme villains, eccentrics and manipulators' *Good Housekeeping*

Something Dangerous

The Spoils of Time: 2

Penny Vincenzi

headline
review

First published in 2001
by ORION

First published in this paperback edition in 2006
by HEADLINE REVIEW

An imprint of HEADLINE BOOK PUBLISHING

8

A format paperback 978 0 7553 3316 5 (ISBN-13)

B format paperback 978 0 7553 3241 0 (ISBN-13)

Typeset in New Caledonia by Avon DataSet Ltd,
Bidford-on-Avon, Warwickshire

Printed and bound in Great Britain by Clays Ltd, St Ives plc

Headline's policy is to use papers that are natural, renewable and recyclable
products and made from wood grown in sustainable forests. The logging and
manufacturing pro

For Paul. For an unfailingly pliant ear and an astonishingly absorbent shoulder. With much love.

'Yet I have in me something dangerous'
Hamlet, Prince of Denmark

Acknowledgements

A small army of people helped me get this book settled in a moderately tidy way between its covers: led once more by my agent and informant Desmond Elliott, walking research library that he is on the subject primarily of publishing, but on other crucial matters too, most notably New York between the wars. In that area I also have to thank Edna McNabney, who provided so many delicious anecdotes, and so much inside information and breathtaking detail about the city.

Many, many thanks to Mme Nicole Delava, who held me spellbound with her reminiscences of Paris before, during and after the war, and of her journey down some of the same road followed by Adele. And to Annick Salters and Laurence de Lasnerie for putting me in touch with her and for other hugely helpful suggestions, and to Noni Holland for acting so tirelessly as interpreter, translator and guide. For further assistance in Paris I have to thank my niece Rebecca Vincenzi and her friend Mathieu Lis, and for a particularly memorable evening at the Café Flore; and much gratitude also to Nina Salter and her colleagues at Calman Levy in Paris, which was the inspiration, but in no way a model, for Constantines, and also the wonderful *archiviste* at Hachette.

Hugh Dickens was not only an inexhaustible and patient military consultant but a most creative and imaginative one; and I am also deeply grateful to Beryl Thompson for her vivid and charming reminiscences of her war in the ATS and to Joanna Lycett for hers in the WRNS. And I owe a great deal to Matthew Parker for his knowledge of the battles waged by the flying aces, and indeed his book *The Battle of Britain*.

Special mentions to Helen Pugh and other archivists at the Red Cross in London; and to Kit Sparkes, Colette Levy and Sue Stapely, all of whom gave me their time and expertise most generously; to Clare Alexander who has been such a great support to both Desmond and me; and to my daughter Claudia who also acted as translator and researcher. And Maria Rice-Jones, who gave me a crash course in French, thus enabling me to do even a little translating of my own.

Several books were of great help to me: *The Week France Fell* by Noel Barber; *Swastikas over Paris* by Jeremy Josephs; *Occupation* by Ian Ousby; *London at War* by Philip Ziegler; *The Viceroy's Daughters* by Anne De Courcy; and *The Great Crash* by J. K. Galbraith.

As always, huge thanks to Rosie de Courcy, not only for her creative, inspiring and sympathetic editing, and her now legendary capacity never to so much as mention that the deadline has passed this many a long day/week/month, but also for her ability to stop me panicking and make me laugh.

Much gratitude to lots of people at Orion: to Susan Lamb, Geoff Duffield, Dallas Manderson, Richard Hussey, Jo Carpenter, and Lucie Stericker, who between them produced, packaged, marketed, sold and dressed the book up so prettily; Emma Draude and the team at Midas who told the world about it; and last but absolutely not least to Kirsty Fowkes who saw the whole thing through with awe-inspiring calm and good cheer.

And of course, and as always, to my family for putting up with me and the bookmaking process for yet another year.

In retrospect, it all looks quite easy . . .

Foreword

I always felt that writing *The Spoils of Time* was a piece of total self-indulgence. I had long wanted to write a trilogy because the worst thing about finishing a novel is saying goodbye to the characters; and I thought if I could carry on for two more books, I wouldn't have to. And it was marvellous, creating those characters, and watching them fall in love and get married and have the babies: who two books later were major characters in their own right. I loved the way the family grew, along with the story, and how a small decision or chance meeting in the first book could lead to a hugely important event in the second, and then the third. I enjoyed the tangled threads of the different generations, the criss-crossing of the different branches of the family.

And I savoured the great span of time I could cover, the Lyttons moved from the luxury of Edwardian house parties to the poverty-wracked slums of London, were involved in the suffragette movement, savoured the excesses of both the twenties and the thirties, fought in two World Wars, escaped from war-torn France, and throughout it all, carved out a success for their publishing company on both sides of the Atlantic.

Most of all I loved the Lytton family; and especially, of course, Lady Celia Lytton, the difficult, despotic glorious matriarch, her lovers, her children and her greatest love of all, the publishing house. I do not feel I invented Lady Celia; I felt she was there, waiting for me to write about her. From my first meeting with her when she was a young girl, to my last when she was a great-grandmother, she held me spellbound; fortunately, if I miss her too much I can pick up one of the books and discover her all over again.

As I very much hope you will do too.

Penny Vincenzi, London 2006

The Main Characters

Part One
1928–1939

Chapter 1

Venetia Lytton was extremely fond of telling people that the whole country had gone into mourning on the day of her birth.

This announcement, although historically accurate, and guaranteed to win her attention in whatever company she chose to make it, gave nonetheless a slightly erroneous picture; it was left to her twin sister Adele, naturally inclined to a slightly more prosaic view of life, to explain that their birth had coincided almost to the hour with the death of King Edward the Seventh.

'Oh – all right,' Venetia would say crossly, 'but it was still a terrifically dark day, Mummy said the nurses were sobbing harder and harder each time they brought in another bouquet of flowers and when Daddy arrived, the doctor actually greeted him wearing a black tie. So of course he thought something terrible had happened.'

Whereupon someone, usually one of the twins' two brothers if they were present, would inevitably remark that indeed it had, and that she and Adele had been launched upon an unsuspecting world, then Venetia would pretend to sulk, Adele would smile serenely, and someone else (usually another young woman in search of a little attention for herself) would endeavour to change the subject.

It was not easy to divert attention from the Lytton twins; not only were they extremely pretty and very amusing, they were quite extraordinarily alike. It was said that the famous Morgan twins, Thelma and Gloria (better known as Lady Furness and Mrs Reginald Vanderbilt respectively), could not be told apart unless you were close enough to detect a small scar under Thelma's chin, the result of a roller-skating accident when she was a child; the Lytton twins offered no such helpful clue. Venetia did have a small mole on her right buttock, and the twins had also observed, from the first moment such a thing was observable, that Adele's nipples were darker and slightly larger than her sister's, but since these were facts extremely hard to verify, and certainly of no use at all in normal social situations, most people had no idea much of the time which of the twins they were talking to, sitting next to, dancing with.

It was a state of affairs that the twins still found amusing to encourage. They had gloried in it at school, each claiming constantly to be the other, confusing and enraging their teachers beyond endurance until their mother discovered what they were doing and, being immensely – and most unusually for her class and age – concerned for their education, threatened to send them to different boarding schools, which frightened them into submission, so deep was their dread of separation.

At their coming-out dance earlier that year, dressed in identical white satin dresses, large white roses in their gleaming dark shingled hair, they had produced so strong a sense of dizzy confusion that several members of the older generation at least had felt themselves to be rather more intoxicated than they were; and it was even rumoured that when they had been presented at court, they had changed places. But those who knew them best said not even Adele (at heart more outrageous if less extrovert than Venetia) would have dared do so dreadful a thing.

They were enjoying their season hugely; their mother had chosen one of the early Easter courts deliberately, feeling it would be more memorable, more distinguished: 'By June it's getting so dreadfully busy, you're in danger of being just another dance.'

Not that the occasion, held at Celia's parents' London house in Curzon Street, was in danger of being any such thing: had the house itself been less magnificent, the guest list less distinguished, the champagne less fine, the music less fashionable, the very fact that it was a dance for the twins would have made it remarkable. They were, unarguably, two of the most popular and brilliant debutantes of their year, caught up in a heady haze of dances and parties and country house weekends, with all the excitement of the actual season – the Derby, Ascot, Henley and the rest – still ahead. Their photographs appeared constantly in the society papers, and they had even been awarded the great accolade of a whole page in *Vogue*, wearing their Vionnet presentation dresses. Their mother, while complaining ceaselessly that their season was absorbing too much of her time, was extremely pleased with their success. To launch one beautiful and popular daughter would have been gratifying, to be able to claim two was triumphal.

Today, their eighteenth birthday, there had been even more reference to the country-in-mourning than usual; so much so that Giles, their elder brother by five years, said at breakfast that he would withdraw from the evening's party if he heard any more about it.

'And then you'll be sorry, Venetia, because I shall tell Boy Warwick not to come either.'

'I couldn't be less bothered,' said Venetia airily, pulling out a compact from her pocket, dabbing more powder on to her small, perfectly straight nose. 'It was you who invited him, not me, he's your friend—'

'Venetia, darling, don't do that at the table, it is so dreadfully common,' said her mother briskly. 'Now of course Boy will be coming, I can't have the arrangements upset at this point. I will check with Cook that everything is in order for dinner this evening – we're only nineteen I think, now that Barty can't come—'

'Such a shame,' murmured Venetia to Adele, and then seeing her mother's eyes on her, smiled brightly and said, 'I was just saying what a shame that was. Still, I suppose it is a long way. From Oxford. Just for dinner.'

'Well, she would have stayed a couple of days,' said Celia, 'but her finals are looming, and she is very anxious about them. I think we must respect that, don't you?'

'Of course,' said Adele.

'Absolutely,' said Venetia.

Their eyes met over their coffee cups: then fixed with sweet innocence on their mother.

'We will miss her,' said Adele, with a careful, quick sigh. 'She's so clever, I'm sure she'll get her first anyway.'

'Absolutely bound to,' said Venetia.

'Absolutely nothing of the sort,' said Celia. 'I cannot understand how you two can still have so little grasp of the connection between hard work and success. No achievement is automatic, and especially no academic achievement. Your father got a first, but he worked unimaginably hard for it, didn't you, Oliver?'

'What's that, my dear?' Oliver Lytton looked up from *The Times*, frowning gently.

'Apparently you worked very hard to get your first, Daddy,' said Venetia.

'I really can't remember much about it,' said Oliver. 'I suppose so.'

'Mummy says you did.'

'As I hadn't met your mother then, I really think it's a little difficult for her to say.'

'Mummy doesn't find anything difficult to say,' said Adele, and giggled; Venetia echoed her.

Celia glared at them. 'I really have more important things to do than engage in extremely silly arguments. And if I'm going to be able to be home in time for your birthday dinner I shall have to leave for the office in half an hour. Giles, do you want to come with me?'

'I – think I might go on ahead,' said Giles quickly, 'if you don't mind.'

'Mind? My dear Giles, why should I mind? I'm delighted you're taking your work so seriously. What particular aspect of it is to occupy you this morning? It must be very urgent, that it can't wait thirty minutes? Nothing's gone wrong, I hope.'

God, she was so unfair, thought Giles; so awkwardly, arrogantly unfair. Putting him in his place, underlining his lowly position at Lyttons even here at the family breakfast table.

'Nothing's wrong, Mother,' he said. 'But I have pages of proofs to read and mark up on the new Buchanan book and—'

'It's not going to be late, I hope,' said Celia. 'It really is imperative it goes on sale in July. I would be very worried to think—'

'Mother, it's not late. It's absolutely on schedule.'

'Then why the rush?'

'Celia, do leave the boy alone,' said Oliver mildly. 'He simply wants to get on with his job before the telephones start ringing. Proof correcting is painstaking work; I always liked to do it early in the day myself.'

'I'm perfectly aware of the mechanics of proof correction,' said Celia. 'I've done a great deal of it myself. I simply wanted to—'

'Celia—' said Oliver quietly. His eyes met hers; she stared at him for a moment, then stood up, pushing her chair back loudly, throwing down her napkin.

'Well, clearly I must get to Lyttons myself,' she said, 'since Giles is setting such an extremely good example. If you will all excuse me.'

Giles waited a moment, looking miserably down at his plate, then hurried out after her. The twins watched him; then, 'Poor old Giles,' said Venetia.

'Poor old boy,' said Adele.

'I'm afraid,' said Oliver, 'I fail to see quite why Giles should be deserving of such sympathy.'

'Daddy! Of course you can see. Mummy never loses a single opportunity to put him in his place, make it clear she's boss, at the office as well as here.'

'Adele! That was quite uncalled for. I think you should apologise.'

She looked at him, serious, almost shocked just for a moment, then the small, beautiful face broke into a sweetly flirtatious smile.

6

'Daddy, don't be silly. I was only joking, you know I was.' She jumped up, went over to him, kissed him quickly. 'Of course Mummy's not the boss. You are, everyone knows that. But – well, Giles is so nervous about his new job. And Mummy going on at him doesn't exactly help. Does it?'

'She wasn't going on at him,' said Oliver firmly, 'merely making sure there was no problem.'

'Yes, of course. Sorry, Daddy. It's sort of hard for us to understand, I suppose. Not being part of Lyttons ourselves. How important it is that everything goes well.'

'Adele,' said Oliver, 'nothing would make me happier than for you to be part of Lyttons. Or at least to think you would be one day.'

'And maybe we will,' said Venetia. 'Let's hope.'

'Let's hope,' said Adele, echoing her, giving her father another kiss.

He smiled at them both and stood up, scooping up the daily papers. 'Well, we shall see. Meanwhile, you must enjoy yourselves as much as you can. Now I, too, have work to do. What are your plans for the day? Some important shopping, no doubt.'

'Desperately important,' said Venetia.

'Absolutely desperately,' said Adele. 'Big country house party on Saturday for a start. We need new shoes, we've danced all ours through. Bye, Daddy. See you later.'

Left alone at the table, they looked at one another.

'Poor old Giles,' said Venetia.

'Poor old boy,' said Adele.

Giles walked briskly along the Embankment away from Cheyne Walk, away from his parents, wishing passionately he was not going to see them again in little less than an hour's time. He had been working at the House of Lytton on Paternoster Row, unarguably one of London's great publishing companies, for almost two years now, rising in its hierarchy from post boy to clerk to the trade counter to junior editor; the rise had, of course, been swift, hardly a proper apprenticeship, but he had still had to go through it.

'It's important you do,' Oliver had said. 'You have to understand what every phase in the process means, how it forms the whole.' And of course Giles agreed with that, he had not expected to come in as Mr Lytton the Third, and start publishing his own list on day one. He had worked with a will, had enjoyed it.

He had made friends, had enjoyed the others seeing that he was not stuck up, did not consider himself too good for such lowly tasks. But this new phase was much more interesting. Spotting the typesetters' errors, the mis-spellings, the wrong placing of punctuation marks, and then copying the corrections from one master proof on to other secondary ones, was more like proper publishing, reading each new book as it came off the presses, discovering exactly what lay behind the titles in the catalogues, the endless editorial meetings, the discussions as to whether this or that cover might be more suitable, the growing excitement that accompanied a new publication.

He enjoyed it all; and he didn't mind working late, he didn't mind working hard, he didn't mind being told to do something again and again, he didn't even mind being told he had done something wrong. What he did mind, almost unbearably, was his mother and her overpowering presence, her interference in everything he did. When his father pointed out that he had sent a second proof down with errors still on it, he felt mortified, apologised and put it right; but when his mother leaned over his desk, watching him as he marked up the proofs, pointing out a mistake he had missed, when she had come into the sales office and said she would like to go over some invoices with him personally, 'just to make quite sure they're absolutely correct', he almost felt like crying. It did not seem to be her desire on those occasions to help him to do things right, rather to point out that he had done them wrong and to make sure that everyone in the place saw her doing it, saw her stressing her superiority over him, observed her making it clear that he was so frequently at fault, that he might be her son, but she was not prepared to tolerate his ineptitude.

Her own perfectionism, her attention to detail, her almost visionary capacity for predicting literary taste, were legendary in the industry at large, let alone within Lyttons; she was talked about, admired, adulated, a legend in her own time. And it was well-earned, that admiration, that adulation; the beautiful, brilliant Lady Celia Lytton moved among the great literary figures of her day, took her place alongside the greatest editors, the finest publishers, the most brilliant authors. And that was quite right and as it should be. But it did seem to him that she could afford to be at least a little generous in furthering the ambitions and supporting the career of her own son: rather than crushing them at every turn with something so fierce and ferocious he would have called it jealousy, had not the very notion seemed absurd.

'I think we're getting it,' said Venetia, bursting into the sitting room that she and Adele shared. 'Isn't that thrilling?'

'Don't tell me!'

'I am telling you. I heard Mummy talking to Brunson. She said to be sure to see he kept the area in front of the house clear this afternoon.'

'Does sound promising, doesn't it? Oh, how marvellous. Mind you, it is time. I mean—'

'I know. Her very own too. Just for driving herself up and down to Oxford.'

'Well, but we'd rather share, wouldn't we? I wonder what it'll be. I mean one of those darling baby Austins would be wonderful, wouldn't it?'

'Utterly wonderful. Of course, a sports car would be more – dashing. Bunty Valance has got an Aston Martin, can you imagine. You don't think we might—?'

'Not a chance,' said Adele. 'They're bound to give us something tame to learn on. Can't be very difficult, can it?'

'Of course not. Bunty said it's simply a matter of being able to keep going in a straight line, and learning which pedal to stop and which to go.'

'Well, there you are then. What heaven. I must say, I'm looking forward to tonight as well—'

'Me too,' said Venetia.

Adele looked at her. 'Especially seeing—'

'Well – yes. I mean – yes. Adele, you do think—'

'Definitely. Couldn't have been more obvious—'

'Truly?'

'Truly. And Babs says he's left—'

'But you didn't say—?'

'Of course not. Because she rather does—'

'Herself? I thought so.'

'But you're much more—'

'Do you think so?'

'Not just think,' said Adele. 'I know.'

'Goody,' said Venetia with great satisfaction. This was the kind of conversation the twins had all the time; a kind of verbal shorthand, phrases, subjects anticipated and therefore the need to actually speak them removed. It fascinated their friends, irritated their brothers, and absolutely enraged their mother, who could not bear to be excluded from anything.

'I wonder what Maud's doing?' said Adele suddenly.

'Still asleep, at this very minute I expect. It's only six o'clock over there.'

9

Maud Lytton was their cousin; born by some strange quirk of human biology exactly one year after them; they met only occasionally, but they were fond of her.

'Of course. One of these years we ought to spend the day together. She's such fun.'

'Bit of a long journey for a birthday tea. But – yes. It's time she came over again. We should suggest it. Mummy's a bit funny about her, though, isn't she?'

'Only because she's American. She thinks they're all common.'

'She's so ridiculous,' added Venetia with a giggle. 'Mummy, I mean, and to think she used to be a socialist. Come on, let's go. Now, shall we have the Marcel wave or not?'

Venetia hesitated. 'Not today. We might not like it and that would spoil tonight. Next time?'

'Next time.'

They arrived back just before lunch. The morning had not been quite absorbed by the hairdressers, they had made a trip to Harvey Nichols where they bought each other a birthday present, a tradition since they had first had their own spending money at the age of eight.

Today, the presents they bought one another were diamanté clips for their hair, Adele's an arrow-like shape, Venetia's a curving crescent moon; they agreed that they would wear them that evening.

Luncheon they were taking that day informally, in the nursery dining room with Nanny; they adored her, and felt for her, bereft as she was of charges during the day now that Kit was at school. Kit was eight; unlike Giles, he had not been sent away to Prep school; besotted with her youngest, Celia had refused to part with him, to subject him to the brutality and misery she knew Giles had endured. Time enough for him to go, she had said, at thirteen, and the headmaster of the school she had chosen, a small establishment in Hampstead much favoured by the intelligentsia, had said he was an absolute certainty for Winchester, and possibly even as a scholar; it was one of the innumerable sources of resentment Giles felt against his small brother.

'Darling Nanny, it's beautiful,' said Venetia.

'Absolutely wonderful,' said Adele.

They sat side by side on the nursery sofa, smiling at Nanny, holding her gift, a small but very pretty cut glass vase. She liked to give them one present between them for their birthday (although not Christmas), and their parents had very often done the same, one dolls' house, one dolls' pram (although twin style), one artist's easel and box of paints.

'It makes sense,' Nanny would say, 'only one birthday, after all.'

The twins never minded being turned into one in this way; they saw themselves if not quite as one, then certainly two parts of a whole. They still liked to dress identically, partly for fun, partly because, as Venetia had remarked, 'We always know exactly how we look. We don't need mirrors.'

Usually they shopped together; but if they were out separately, they always bought two of whatever they chose. 'Not so we can dress the same,' Adele would explain, 'but because we know the other will want it too.'

The hair clips they had bought that day were the occasional exception; deliberately chosen so that they could be swapped halfway through the evening; the childish fun to be had with that, begun in the nursery, was endless. They had always been sent to school with different coloured hair ribbons; amused and surprised that it should not have occurred to anyone that they would, they swapped them over whenever it suited them. It was a whole term before anyone discovered that their both achieving a distinction in their Grade One piano examination was not so much due to extra practice by the less musically talented Venetia, as to Adele entering the examination room twice. For such sins, they were punished, but they continued, with blithe disregard for such consequences, to exploit their situation.

The only thing they could not bear, and the threat of which ensured good behaviour, was separation.

'So, what are you doing the rest of the day?' asked Nanny now, heaping shepherd's pie (another nursery birthday tradition) on to their plates. 'Shopping, I suppose.' She sounded faintly disapproving; she felt the twins were over-frivolous. In this she was not alone; their mother, who had confidently expected them to go to university, or to take a secretarial course at the very least, and then to show some interest in working at Lyttons, was of much the same opinion.

'I find it quite distressing,' she said to Oliver at least once a week, 'that all those girls want to do is first buy clothes and then wear them. That expensive education, totally wasted.'

To which Oliver would reply that surely the purpose of education was to enrich the mind, rather than train it rigorously for some specific occupation. 'Their education will be valuable to them whatever they do. Even,' he added, looking wryly over his spectacles at her, half smiling, 'if they settle for marriage as their career. They're very young, let them have some fun. Plenty of time for them to develop careers if they want to.' And he would then endeavour to change the subject.

'No, Nanny darling, actually we're not going shopping,' said Adele now, 'because we've already done it. And had our hair done. So we're staying in this afternoon and – well, just staying in. Getting ready for tonight.' She looked at Nanny. 'You haven't heard any rumours about – about this afternoon, have you, Nanny?'

'What sort of rumours?' said Nanny. She sounded flustered. 'And anyway, you know I'm always the last to hear anything in this house. Now, Adele, look what you're doing, you don't want to get gravy on that pretty dress.'

The twins exchanged a look; Nanny's inability to deceive over even the mildest matter was legendary.

They were not too surprised therefore – although rapturously delighted – when Brunson called them downstairs in the middle of the afternoon, saying there was a delivery for them, and they opened the front door to see their parents standing in the sunshine, one on each side of a scarlet Austin Seven, and holding a banner across it which said HAPPY BIRTHDAY. The next two hours were spent weaving rather unsteadily up and down the Embankment, under the instruction of Daniels, the chauffeur; they came into the house at six, flushed with triumph and saying there was nothing to it.

'And we thought we'd drive ourselves down to Sussex tomorrow afternoon,' said Adele carelessly to her mother. 'So much less trouble for everyone.'

To which Celia replied that it would be a great deal of trouble for everyone if they had a crash and that they would not be driving themselves anywhere for several weeks.

'That's so unfair! Barty drove herself up to Oxford last term.'

'Barty had had hours of driving lessons and had to satisfy both your father and me that she was competent before we allowed that. Now, hadn't you better go and have your baths? Your friends will be arriving in less than an hour. Not to mention – yes, Brunson?'

'Telephone, Lady Celia. Mr Brooke.'

'Oh – yes, thank you, Brunson. I'll take it upstairs in my study.'

Celia picked up her heavy silver hairbrush and hurled it across her bedroom. It hit the wall above her bed and dropped rather ignominiously silently on to her pillow. She stood up and stalked over to the window, looked down at the Embankment. It blurred with her tears; the realisation that she was crying made her angrier still. 'Damn,' she said, 'damn damn damn. Filthy bloody manners. You don't treat people like that, Sebastian, you simply don't.'

She pulled her dressing-table door open viciously, took out her cigarette case and paced up and down the room, smoking, inhaling hard, trying to calm herself. It was absurd, she knew, to be so upset. But she was. And the twins would be upset too, when they heard he was going to be late for their birthday dinner, very late, possibly not arriving until it was over, simply because he had been delayed in Oxford, because of some ridiculous additional reading he had agreed to give at the last minute.

'Bastard. Bastard—' She had not realised she was speaking aloud; very aloud. Kit put his head round her door.

'Mummy? You all right?'

'Yes. Yes, I'm fine. Thank you, darling.'

'I thought I heard you shouting. You don't look fine.'

'Well, I am. Good day at school?'

'Yes, very. Where are the twins?'

'Getting ready.'

'What's that wizard car outside?'

'The little red one? It's their birthday present.'

'They've got a car! Lucky beasts. Can I go and sit in it? When can I have a ride, I want a go—'

Celia laughed, restored as always to good humour by his presence. The intensity of her feelings for Kit, her beloved youngest child, was so powerful it eclipsed almost every other emotion she knew. Not only beautiful, with his bright gold hair and his dark-blue eyes, not only brilliant – reading at four, writing stories and poetry at seven – but hugely charming, with the kind of social grace seldom seen in a child. At an age when most boys were able to converse only about cricket, model trains and the beastliness of school, Kit liked to talk about books, other people, adults as well as his own friends, and the events of the day. He read the newspaper every morning at breakfast, and for his last birthday had requested his own Gecophone radio, with its horn and neat wooden box, so much more convenient than a crystal set, so that he could listen to the news and to concerts in his own room.

The twins found this entirely baffling; their own preferred, and indeed only, form of home entertainment being the gramophone on which they played records of dance music, practising new steps with one another ready for the next party or nightclub. Fashion and society magazines satisfied all their literary requirements.

'You'll grow up dreary and boring like Giles,' they had warned Kit, 'or even Barty.' To which he would reply that he thought Barty was the jolliest of girls, and Giles not boring at all either; but in fact he was not in the least serious himself, and he loved to sit on the twins' beds listening to them chattering and giggling, asking them about their friends, most of whom made a great fuss of him when they came to the house, and where they were going that evening.

'You'd better be careful, baby brother,' Venetia had said one night, 'Mummy wouldn't approve of your interest in this sort of thing, you know. Far too frivolous.'

'Mummy approves of everything I do,' said Kit, with sublime self-confidence, and although he smiled as he said it, it was perfectly true.

'Kit, run along, darling,' said Celia now, 'go and get changed for dinner.'

'OK.'

'And don't say OK in your grandmama's hearing. Please.'

'OK.'

'Kit!'

She looked at him sharply; his face was innocently blank. Then he grinned at her. 'I won't. I promise. Hallo, Father, just going.'

Oliver frowned at Celia.

'I wish you wouldn't smoke in our bedroom, Celia.'

'I'm sorry, Oliver.' She so rarely apologised that she was surprised to hear herself doing it. 'I was – very annoyed about something.'

'Then perhaps you should try to be annoyed in your study. What is it?'

'Sebastian's going to be very late. Possibly not here until after nine.'

'Really? What's happened?'

'He's been asked to give a second reading. At the Bodleian. The first one was sold out completely.'

'Well, that's good for all of us.'

'You know perfectly well that's not the point. It's rude and unkind and extremely arrogant. Clearly being the most prominent children's author in the country has finally gone to his head. The twins will be so upset—'

'Celia, I don't really think they'll mind very much at all. They have their own friends here, they're going on to some nightclub, I don't really think the absence of one rather elderly gentleman—'

14

'Sebastian is not elderly, Oliver. He's our – your age.'

'And no doubt seems very elderly to them. Of course it's a shame, but I'm sure he'll do his best to get here. He's very professional. You of all people should respect that.'

Celia was silent. 'I'll go and have my bath,' she said finally. 'Someone has to be ready for this birthday party.'

Years of painful experience had taught her when to give in; when – and only when – Oliver had her in checkmate.

Chapter 2

'Celia, dear, you look tired.'

'Well, thank you for that, LM,' said Celia, slightly coldly. They were moving into the dining room after cocktails. 'Exactly what one wants to hear at the beginning of an evening. I'm not in the least tired, as a matter of fact.'

'Well, I'm delighted to hear it,' said LM. 'I envy you. I'm very tired myself.'

Celia looked at her: it was true. LM did look – well, not exhausted, but weary. She worked much too hard; her position as managing director of Lyttons demanded it to an extent of course, but just the same, LM wasn't very young any more: Oliver's big sister, as she always described herself, was fifty-four this year. The initials actually stood for Little Margaret, for she had been named after her mother; but no name could have suited her less and indeed nobody remembered it most of the time. She was a daunting figure: tall, very tall, over six foot, thin, with a deep voice and extraordinarily probing dark eyes in a pale face. She dressed with great severity, almost eccentricity, even now wearing the uniform of her girlhood, long skirts, tailored shirts and cravats, tailored jackets, and her mass of dark hair, greying now, was drawn tautly back into a rigidly neat chignon. But she was an acutely attractive woman, with an instant and rather surprising warmth and a quick, sharp humour; men still found her sexually attractive and women invariably liked her too for her directness and lack of guile. She was, Celia often said, her very best friend.

'How's Jay?' said Kit as they sat down. He had been placed next to LM at Celia's suggestion.

'He's very well, thank you. Enjoying this term. He's being tried out for the junior First Eleven already, and he's playing tennis for his junior house team. And then he's in the choir—' LM's voice had softened; her adoration of Jay, her only child, was legendary in the family, and the only time anyone had seen her cry had been when he had gone away to Winchester the term before. Indeed Gordon, her

16

husband and Jay's stepfather, had frequently said he would name Jay in any divorce petition he brought.

'No doubt at all about who LM loves best,' he would say cheerfully, his pale blue eyes twinkling at her, 'and it isn't me.'

A lesser man might have been genuinely jealous of Jay and of LM's passion for him; but Gordon Robinson was blithely unconcerned by it. He had fallen in love with LM and married her only six years earlier; to him, Jay had been a part not simply of LM's life but of her very self, and her love for him was essential to her own generous and passionate nature. The fact that she was too old to bear him a child of his own was of no interest to him; Jay, tough, cheerful, hugely intelligent, with a passion for the countryside and for wildlife that matched his own, seemed to Gordon an ideal child, readily assimilated into his life.

Gordon came into the room now, talking intently to Oliver; he towered over everyone, at six foot seven one of the few men LM could literally look up to. Celia adored him.

'My dear Celia, may I say again how lovely you look. Incredible that you should be the mother of all these grown-up children.'

'I'm not grown up,' said Kit, 'I keep her feeling young. Don't I, Mummy?'

'For now you do, Kit, yes. I don't want you growing up any more, though.'

Kit smiled at her. 'I'll try.'

'If you succeed,' said Oliver, 'I hope you'll share your secret with the rest of us. Now, Gordon, why don't you sit next to Celia, Sebastian is going to be late, and Venetia, you sit here next to me and then you, young man and—'

It had been a very good party so far, Giles thought; everyone was chattering away, no one sitting awkwardly silent – except for him, of course. He was used to feeling dull and awkward in company; but it didn't get any easier. His grandmother, the Countess of Beckenham, was delivering a rather technical lecture to anyone who would listen on the importance of keeping bloodstock pure and his grandfather was having a perfectly wonderful time with one of the twins' prettier friends, apparently listening intently to her account of all the dances she had attended that season, but his attention, Giles knew, was fixed entirely on her unfashionably full bosom. (It had been agreed beforehand with the twins that her personality was quite robust enough to withstand such an onslaught.)

Oliver's younger brother Jack and the lovely Lily – as she had been known on the theatre posters when Jack had first met her – were sitting rather unconventionally next to one another, being still rather engagingly in love after seven years of marriage. Giles was half in love with Lily himself; she was so absolutely gorgeous with her red hair and her extremely full white bosom. And Boy Warwick, of course, was charming everyone as usual: smooth bastard, thought Giles. God, he envied him. Most of his relationship with Boy was based on envy, he could never quite understand why they were friends. But for some reason, Boy liked him, had always liked him, from the first days at Eton, when Boy had seemed so glamorous and grown up, Giles so young for his age and homesick, through their years at Oxford (where Boy had arrived with his own servant, into a set of the best rooms, and proceeded to surround himself with the most glittering, the most brilliant of friends – and Giles); right up to now, when Boy paid the merest lip service to his job at his father's bank and spent most of his life spending his father's money, while Giles worked so earnestly and for such long hours at Lyttons, resisting for the most part Boy's invitations to luncheons, endless nights at nightclubs, and four-day country house weekends.

The reason was actually quite simple: for all his self-indulgent, almost hedonistic lifestyle, Boy was in fact a nice person, surprisingly loyal to his men friends (although less so to his women); Giles had several times covered up for him in scrapes at both Eton and Oxford, and perhaps more importantly, introduced him to his own family circle, with its own quite different sort of glamour, one which Boy was nevertheless fascinated by and enjoyed.

Celia had found him over-sophisticated, even when he was fourteen, and had said several times that he was clearly heading into exactly the same lifestyle as his twice-divorced, much-mistressed father. But she was extremely fond of him; he was amusing, with a fine line in flirtatious flattery that she found hard to resist, even while she could see through it. His most heinous crime, in her view, was not his extravagance, or his libertine ways, not even his occasional vulgarity of dress, but his idleness, his capacity for filling his days with nothing but pleasure, his apparent lack of any real ambition. It was, she often told him severely, a disgrace, for he had a brilliant mind, had come down from Oxford with a first in Greats.

The twins adored him: he was so good-looking, with his permanently amused dark eyes and slicked black hair, his extensive wardrobe, his stable of cars, his hyper-fashionable flat in the Albany, so charming, so amusing, so rich, and above all so unconcerned with anything more serious than the next party, the last race meeting, the latest fashion or piece of gossip. Giles, on the other hand, actually found him rather overpowering, however flattering his friendship.

The twins were terribly over-excited and telling increasingly risqué jokes egged on by Jack and Kit, but nobody seemed to mind; Celia had moved from her initial bad mood into her most witty and charming form, and was flirting alternately with Boy and an extremely handsome young man whom Adele had introduced as her absolutely greatest friend Charley. Oliver was almost silent, benignly enjoying the party around him while as usual not being quite at one with it.

If only Barty were there, Giles thought; it would be so much nicer. The family never felt complete without her: ironic, since she was not, strictly speaking, a part of it. She always made him feel happy, happy and at ease; just thinking of her now soothed his discomfort. He imagined her studying in her room at Oxford, quietly and methodically, setting her cool, calm intelligence to work . . .

Thank goodness, just thank goodness she wasn't there, Barty thought, pushing her books back, reaching for her cup of cocoa. She hadn't dared stop before, partly because she would lose concentration and start thinking about the twins' birthday dinner and partly because she knew she would realise how tired she was. And of course she did start thinking about the birthday party. Most years, even after she had gone up to Oxford, she had had to endure sitting and smiling till her face ached, trying to make the right sort of conversation with some poor boy or other put next to her, having to talk to her while not knowing quite what to make of her – was she a Lytton or wasn't she – oh, it was always horrible. This year she had the perfect excuse, no one could be upset. It was wonderful. One of the happiest days in her entire life, she often thought (though of course never said, never would say, to anyone), was when she went up to Oxford, and left the huge house at Cheyne Walk to make a new home for herself, for three years at least, at Lady Margaret Hall. As she waved Celia off – for of course she had insisted on coming up with her – she had felt only joy, and no regret of any kind, no nervousness even. Except for Celia's obvious sadness, of course: and at leaving dear Wol as she had always called Oliver. She had turned back into the building, climbed the stairs to her room, and sat there for over an hour, doing nothing at all, contemplating the pure pleasure of being, for the first time in her life, somewhere that was hers by right, where she felt she truly belonged.

And now it was nearly over; she would have to leave again and she was, as well as sad, anxious at where she could go next. Which could certainly not be Cheyne Walk: or not for long, anyway . . .

Dinner was very much over now; the conversation running down, the early brightness of the evening fading. Venetia stood up, smiled round the table. 'Well, shall we all go to the Embassy? It's getting late and the others will be there and—'

Adele stood up too. 'Yes, let's go. Mummy and Daddy, that was marvellous. Thank you—'

'Just a moment,' said Oliver, 'we've forgotten one toast. To Cousin Maud. Come along now.'

This was part of the tradition too: the family raised its glasses, the outsiders had it quickly explained to them.

'Happy birthday, Maud,' said Adele.

'Cheers,' said Venetia. 'Happy birthday, Maud.'

'What a dreadful expression that is, Venetia,' said Lady Beckenham. 'Where on earth did you pick it up?'

'What, "cheers"? Grandmama, everyone says it now.'

'That doesn't make it any better. Anyway, how are those relatives of yours, Oliver?' Lady Beckenham liked to make it clear to outsiders that any vulgarity in the family did not come from the Beckenham side.

'Very well, thank you, Lady Beckenham. Yes.' After twenty-four years of marriage to her daughter, Oliver was still unable to address Lady Beckenham by a more familiar name; as she addressed her own husband still as 'Beckenham', this was hardly surprising.

'We were saying, Daddy, it was time another visit was arranged. Either for us or them. I think we should all go, Giles as well. He ought to go anyway, visit the outpost of the Lytton empire. I'm sure Uncle Robert would be pleased to see us.'

'Venetia, Robert is just as busy as we are,' said Celia firmly. 'He certainly wouldn't have time to arrange all sorts of nonsense for you and Maud.'

'Mummy, Maud and us could arrange things on our own,' said Adele, 'you're so old-fashioned. I'm going to write to Maud and suggest it. Now look, we really must go. Come on, everyone. Boy, stop flirting with my grandmother – oh, Sebastian darling, you've made it. How absolutely lovely, and how dreadfully, dreadfully sad, we're just leaving.'

'Leaving? What for, work? Am I that late?' Sebastian Brooke stood smiling into the room. 'I'm so very sorry. Oliver, how good to see you. Celia, do please forgive me. LM, Gordon, good evening to you, and Lady Beckenham, how nice. What a gathering I've been unfortunate enough to miss. Lord Beckenham, what a delight, how are you—'

He moved round the room, easily, perfectly charming, giving the evening a new edge, fresh life. Old bugger, thought Giles, who was very fond of him, he could charm the birds not just out of the trees but into a cage, a glittering, golden cage where they would stay entranced with no need for anyone even to close the door. Only his mother appeared unimpressed; giving a cool nod, a frosty smile, and even those reluctantly.

'Sebastian,' said Adele, slipping her arm through his, 'we're going to the Embassy, do you want to come? Please do, you know how you love dancing and the Prince of Wales might be there, as it's Thursday and—'

'My darling, how could I leave so lovely a party when I've only just arrived?'

'But the party's over,' said Venetia. 'We're all going.'

'Not all,' said Oliver. 'Some of us elderly folk are staying put.'

'Well, I don't know why. Mummy loves to go out. Jack and Lily, you'll come, won't you, and – LM, what about you?'

'We might join you,' said LM, her long face very serious. 'Don't you think, Gordon? I'd certainly like to see the Prince of Wales, if you really think he might be there.'

'I really think, my dear, I'd rather not,' said Gordon Robinson. He sounded alarmed. 'I have a very busy day tomorrow and—'

'Well, I could go on my own with the young. I daresay one or two of these charming gentlemen would dance with me.'

There was a polite murmur of assent around the table; LM stood up. 'Good.' The twins stared at her, their eyes very wide.

She smiled, her sudden, brilliant smile. 'I'm glad chivalry is not quite dead. But it's all right, I won't come and spoil your fun. Another night perhaps. And we will leave now, I think. It's late and I, too, have a very difficult day tomorrow. You go off and enjoy yourselves. Gordon, you can stop looking so frightened.'

'No really, girls, I'll stay,' said Sebastian, 'and here, I almost forgot. Your presents. Now if you don't like them, Aspreys will change them. I shan't be a bit hurt. And they come with all my love.'

The twins unwrapped their parcels, drawing silver cigarette cases out of the Asprey packaging with cries of 'Oh, how lovely' and 'Utter bliss' and 'Sebastian, you shouldn't have' and 'As if we'd change these'.

'Phew,' said Venetia, piling into a taxi with Adele and Giles and Boy. 'That was close. LM, I mean. I really thought she meant it.'

'I think she's splendid,' said Boy. 'I would have danced with her. She's a very sensual woman.'

Adele stared at him. 'Sensual! LM! But, Boy, she's so old.'

'She's not old, she's mature. And you shouldn't confuse sex and youth,' he added. 'Giles, old chap, what do you think? Wouldn't you agree with me that your aunt is a very attractive woman?'

'I'm not – sure,' said Giles. 'I've only ever thought of her as my aunt. And she is quite old.'

'Well – she is,' said Adele thoughtfully, 'but I suppose she is a bit of a mystery. I mean, there's Jay for a start. I could never quite believe in the husband of only a few weeks being killed in the war . . .'

'Happy birthday, Maud, my darling. Sorry to be late for our tea. Here, present from your old dad—'

'Daddy! Tiffany's! How lovely. Oh, I love these boxes and the white ribbon so much – oh, Daddy! Thank you so much. Oh, it's lovely. Simply beautiful. Here, put it on me. Let me get to a mirror quickly. It's – oh, it's heaven. I shall never take it off again.'

'Darling, I hope you will. Diamond watches don't benefit from being put into the bath. Or taken out riding.'

'I know, I know. But it's ravishing. Thank you. Here, let me kiss you again.'

Robert Lytton sat back in his chair, smiling at her, thinking that every year made her so much more than a daughter to him, that she was also companion, confidante and best friend. Their love for one another was absolute, and remarkably untinged by any serious jealousy or possessiveness on Robert's part. He had brought her up alone from the age of two when her mother had died; they had faced the world together and made for themselves a very happy life. He had built the house where they lived for her, planned his social life round her, run his company with her always in mind. He refused to travel too much, or to work too late, turned down many social engagements so that he might be at home with her, and at all times endeavoured to encourage her interest in what he did. It was not difficult; Maud was as fascinated by the real estate industry as most girls of her age and social status were by clothes and boys.

Not that those things did not charm and engage her too. She was about to go into her last year at the Chapin school, an exclusive (and academically excellent) establishment in New York for girls; she hoped after that and after her debutante season – to which she had agreed without a great deal of enthusiasm – to go on to Vassar to study architecture. Most of her contemporaries thought she was quite mad.

'And you really don't mind having dinner alone with me and Jamie tonight?' said Robert now.

'Of course I don't mind. I'll love it. Here, have some birthday cake.'

'Mmm. Delicious. Dear Martha. She never fails. Amazing. She must be the oldest cook in New York.'

'And absolutely the best.' Maud licked her fingers one by one, then said, 'I wonder how the twins are. What they're doing today.'

'Driving their parents insane as usual, I expect. I had a letter from Oliver, saying happy birthday to you, and that he and, possibly, Celia are coming over next month.'

'I wish they'd bring the twins. It would be such fun.'

'Maud, those trips are—'

'I know, I know, business. Well, we'll just have to arrange something of our own. I really can't wait until you old fogies decide to have another big family party or wedding or something.'

'Well, you might have to.'

'Might not be that long,' said Maud, kissing him, 'there must be lots of weddings waiting to happen. When you think about it . . .'

Venetia looked at Boy Warwick, dancing energetically with Bunty Valance, and wondered if she'd been wrong and Adele had been wrong, and whether he was even the tiniest bit interested in her. He'd only danced with her once, and since then had done the Charleston with Babs Rowley, the foxtrot with Adele – well, that was all right, of course – and was now doing a very showy blackbottom with some other girl he'd met there, not even in their party. It was spoiling the birthday and – he came back to the table now, mopping his brow rather theatrically.

'That was hard work. Noël Coward's on the floor now, have you seen him, wonderful dancer he is. And yes, we were right, there's the Prince. And with Thelma.'

'I couldn't care less who he's with,' said Venetia sulkily, but she stared at the Prince of Wales and the beautiful Lady Furness in fascination just the same.

'Isn't she lovely?' said Adele, who had also been watching her, transfixed.

'Not as lovely as you, my darling,' said Boy, 'as either of you.' And he took both their hands, raised them to his lips and kissed them simultaneously. 'Come on, let me see if I can dance with both of you at once.'

Later, the band playing a waltz, Venetia danced alone with Boy, felt his smooth hand on her bare back, his warm body pressed against hers. She leaned just slightly too heavily against him.

'That's nice,' he said, into her ear. 'Very nice. You're very beautiful, Venetia. Very beautiful indeed. And in that dress, you look exactly like a print I bought the other day, by Lepape.'

She knew who Lepape was, of course, and was particularly familiar with his wonderful covers for *Vogue*: the twins might spend their days shopping and their nights dancing, but they had not grown up in their father's house without absorbing certain extremely important tracts of knowledge.

'Goodness. You've got Lepape prints?'

'I have. In my flat. Lots of them, many of ladies who look like you. You should come and see them some time. Both of you,' he added an almost imperceptible second later.

Venetia perceived that second and she recognised what he was saying. She took a deep breath.

'We don't always go everywhere together, you know,' she said, and smiled up at him. And then felt horribly shocked at herself. It was not so much the clear commitment to go to his flat, with all that it implied; it was rather the fact that for almost the first time in her life she had committed a betrayal of her absolute closeness and loyalty to Adele.

'Good,' was all Boy Warwick said.

'Well, Sebastian, do tell us all about your meeting,' said Celia. 'It must have been very well attended.'

They were still in the dining room but almost alone; even Kit had been banished, sent protesting to bed.

'It was,' said Sebastian. 'Which was nice for me. And for Lyttons of course,' he added, smiling at her. 'I sold a great many books this evening.'

'Splendid,' said Oliver, 'well done. I'm sure you did us proud, Sebastian. As always. And how is *Meridian Times Five* coming along? We will – I mean—' His voice tailed off; Sebastian laughed.

'Oliver, of course you will. Have I ever failed you? You shall have your new book, in good time for Christmas publication. And with luck, all the children are waiting for it; plus a few hundred new ones.'

'Of course. But I worry about the old ones these days,' said Oliver, 'that they will begin to grow out of the books.'

'I too. But if the reviewers are to be believed, and indeed our own letters, then they will not. Children as old as sixty-five read the Meridians. So perhaps we can assume that our first generation reaching double figures, or even their twenties, should not be deterred either.'

'Let us hope so,' said Oliver, reaching out, touching the table quickly.

'Indeed,' said Celia. 'But of course one cannot take these things for granted. Fashions come and go in publishing as in everything else. These new books of A. A. Milne's are extremely popular.'

'My dear, I hardly think some rather whimsical stories and poems about a toy bear can compete with Sebastian's elaborate time fantasies,' said Oliver mildly, 'angst-ridden publisher as I am.'

Celia looked first at him, then at Sebastian, her dark eyes unreadable. Then she said, 'Complacency is an unattractive quality.'

'We are not being complacent, Celia,' said Sebastian, 'merely cautiously optimistic. Now then, I would like to apologise again for my late arrival. And I – well, I have something to tell you both. I – I hope you will be pleased for me.'

'If it's good news, then of course we will,' said Oliver.

There was a silence. Sebastian stood up, walked round the table; they watched him, unsurprised. Sebastian's restlessness was famous. He was incapable of sitting through a meal, a play, a train journey without several interruptions.

'I – well, yes, of course it is good news. Very good news. For me.' He sat down again abruptly, drained his glass of port. 'I – well, the fact of the matter is, I have – that is, I would like to tell you about someone. Someone I have met.'

'Someone?' said Oliver, smiling at him gently. 'A female someone, are we to presume?'

'Indeed. Yes. A female someone. Someone very special, very – very – well, someone who has become very important to me.'

'This is rather sudden,' said Celia. She had become quite still; not only was her body totally motionless, but her face as well, quite expressionless, her eyes blank. 'Do tell us more.'

'I will. And yes, it is rather – sudden. I have known her for only – well, a month. I met her at another reading I gave. She works for the Bodleian.'

'Indeed?' said Celia.

25

'Yes. She is a librarian there.'

'A librarian!' said Celia. Her tone implied that prostitution might have been preferable.

'Yes.'

There was a long silence. Then Oliver said, 'Well, do go on, my dear old chap. Are we to know a little more about her, her name perhaps?'

'Her name is Pandora. Pandora Harvey. She lives alone, in Oxford, in a small house—'

'I imagine she would not require a large one,' said Oliver, clearly anxious to leaven the mood. Sebastian looked at him gratefully, and smiled.

'Indeed. I mean, indeed not. She is thirty-one,' he added, eager now to give as much information as possible, 'and very charming, and, of course, beautiful. I would have told you about her before, but I felt – what can I say – embarrassed. That I should have – that this should have – happened—' Sebastian hesitated, then went on, speaking faster with each phrase. 'Happened so unequivocally and so suddenly. At my rather advanced age.'

'You make it sound very – serious,' said Celia.

Sebastian looked at her. There was a long, a very long, silence. Then, 'It is – serious,' he said, 'very serious indeed.'

'Well,' said Celia with a rather slight, but gracious, smile. 'I'm sure she has every virtue. And of course we look forward to meeting her.'

'You will,' said Sebastian, 'of course you will. Very soon. Because you see – well, because we are to be married.'

There was an absolute silence. Then, 'Married!' said Celia, and the word cut through the stillness, so loudly it was almost shocking. 'You are going to be married?'

'Yes. Yes, I am.'

'I see,' she said, and it was as if Oliver was no longer in the room. 'Soon?'

'Yes, Celia. As soon – as soon as it can be arranged. We see no point in waiting.'

'I see,' she said again, and sat back in her chair, staring at him: and then she raised her hand to take a cigarette, knocking over the glass she was holding; the red wine spread slowly across the white table-cloth, sinister and somehow threatening, and looking horribly like blood.

Chapter 3

'Oh, my darling, congratulations. I couldn't be more delighted, or proud. It's wonderful news. You must be thrilled. I'm going to organise a big party to celebrate.'

'Oh no, please don't!' Barty felt the familiar panic rising. 'Honestly, Aunt Celia, I'd rather not.'

'But – why not? You deserve it and it would be fun—' She sounded hurt; Barty promptly felt mean. It would be the least she could do, really, to allow Celia to give her a party, small thanks for all her support, both financial and moral, through her three years at Oxford. She took a deep breath, forced enthusiasm into her voice.

'Yes. Yes, of course it would. I'd love it. Thank you. But – maybe not for a week or two. I'm awfully tired and—'

'Of course. Three weeks, perhaps? Summer is really more or less over here by then, I'm afraid.'

What she meant, Barty thought, was that the summer season would be more or less over. She smiled; the seriousness with which Celia still addressed the social calendar always amused – and astonished – her. There she was, brilliantly clever and innovative, wielding immense power over authors, books, editors, illustrators, indeed over the entire publishing industry: and she remained obsessed with all the nonsense of her upbringing, country house parties, the London season, race meetings, balls, court dinners, royal garden parties, titles, society gossip – it seemed to Barty, even after all the years she had known Celia, quite extraordinary. Well, it didn't really matter to her; although there had been the hideous time when she had said she really thought Barty should do the season, to have a dance, to be presented. Barty could never remember being so frightened. She had begged Wol to try and talk Celia out of it, but he had said he wouldn't have a chance; she had even started talking about dates and courts when Lady Beckenham heard of it and told her not to be so ridiculous, and that if she wanted to make both Barty and herself a laughing stock then she was going the right way about it.

'It's those absurd socialist principles of yours,' she said, 'and I absolutely forbid it.'

Barty, who had been called to the room by Celia while this discussion took place, found it difficult to see quite how socialist principles could be applied to a presentation at court, but she accepted Lady Beckenham's intervention with intense and silent relief. She knew better than to express any emotion of her own, for fear of misinterpretation; but she knew she was safe. Lady Beckenham was the only person in the world who could tell Celia what to do.

Anyway, this was different; a party to celebrate getting a First Class Honours degree in English Literature from Oxford would at least have some point to it. Again she took a deep breath and said, 'I think that would be lovely, Aunt Celia. Thank you.'

'Good. Let me have a list of people you would like to invite yourself as soon as possible, won't you? And Wol and I will take you out to dinner tonight to celebrate. I expect Giles and the twins and Kit will want to come too. Shall I tell Giles about your success, or would you rather do that yourself?'

'I'd like to tell him if you don't mind. Maybe when he gets home—'

'Oh, I think you should telephone him now. I don't think I can keep it a secret for long. What did the twins say? They'll be thrilled—'

Barty said the twins weren't up yet. 'But Kit is really excited.'

'Of course he is. Tell Cook to make a special lunch. Goodbye, darling. Congratulations again.'

'Thank you. For everything, I mean. See you later.'

She put the phone down, thinking sadly as she always did on such occasions how much her mother would have loved to hear about this, how proud, if uncomprehending, she would be. Billy would be pleased of course; she could tell him. And that was it; nobody else in her own family would understand what she had achieved, or care. There was no point in telling any of them.

It was at such moments that Barty felt truly alone . . .

'She's got her beastly first.' Venetia walked into their sitting room; Adele was painting her nails.

'Oh God, now there'll be trouble. Can't you just hear Mummy going on and on about it. Did she tell you?'

'No, Kit did. He's very excited. They want to take us all out to dinner tonight to celebrate.'

'Can't we find something to do?'

'Don't think so. Everyone's away, aren't they?' She sounded cross.

Adele knew why. Boy was on a cruise in the Mediterranean. He had asked Celia and Oliver if she and Adele could go too, but they had refused, on the grounds that there were no chaperones. Venetia had pointed out that Boy's mother and her latest lover would be there, but Celia had said briskly that Letitia Warwick was no chaperone for anyone and that her latest lover was no better than a gigolo.

'Moves from one rich divorced woman to the next. And he's a dago,' she had added, clearly feeling that entirely settled the matter.

The Lyttons were taking a villa in the south of France a little later in the year; 'Madly fun that will be,' Adele had said darkly, 'no one but the family, not even Sebastian. God, it's depressing.'

Their season over, the twins were extremely bored. Several of their friends had already put engagement announcements over moony photographs in the *Tatler*; for such stars in the social firmament, they had not done as well as either they or their mother might have hoped.

'Well, we'd better go. I mean it is rather clever of her. But I don't want to have to talk about it over lunch as well. Let's go shopping quickly. She's got Kit after all . . .'

Brunson came into the morning room; Barty smiled at him.

'Telephone, Miss Miller.'

It always surprised her to hear that. She had been Miss Barty to the servants for so long, until she had gone to Oxford in fact. Then by some strange social process, via Celia she supposed, she had become Miss Miller: more important, a grown-up, but at the same time awkwardly further removed from the Lyttons.

'Oh, thank you, Brunson. Who is it?'

'It's Mr Miller, Miss Miller.'

Billy! He never phoned.

'Billy? Hallo, what's wrong?'

'Nothing. Just wanted to say congratulations. Well done. You deserve it.'

'Oh, Billy, thank you. But how did you know and how—'

'Lady Beckenham come to tell me. Running into the yard, all excited. Said I had to come up to the house and telephone you.'

'Oh, Billy! That's really kind of her.' Barty's eyes filled with tears; she swallowed hard.

'Yeah, well, she is kind. I know that more than anyone. Anyway, pleased as punch she was. So am I. You got brains, Barty, you really have. Mum would have been pleased, wouldn't she?'

'Yes,' said Barty, 'yes, she would.'

'Barty, my darling, it's Sebastian. I just wanted to congratulate you. It's fantastic news. I'm so proud of you. Not that I have any right to feel pride, but – well, I'm thrilled.'

'Who told you?'

'Oliver. I went into Lyttons this morning. He and Celia are sitting there looking like cats that got a whole cow-full of cream. Can I buy you lunch?'

'Kit and I are having lunch here,' said Barty. 'Cook's already at work on a feast, I don't like to disappoint her. Why don't you come too?'

'Well – it's tempting. Will the Terrors be there?'

'No, they're going out.'

'Then I might. No, then I will. I'd love to see you.'

He arrived just before midday, with a huge bunch of roses in one hand and a bottle of champagne in the other. He handed the champagne over to Brunson and took Barty in his arms and hugged her.

'You clever, clever girl. It's so marvellous. Pandora sends lots and lots of love.'

'Thank you. Send mine back, won't you. Is she well?'

'Very well. Busy with plans for the wedding.'

'Which is to be in September, Wol said. At her house in Oxford. Lovely idea, it's so pretty.'

'I know. I think so too. I'm having the devil's own job persuading her to come down and live here afterwards though. She wants to stay there.'

'Why don't you?' said Barty.

'Because I love my house in London.'

'Well, why not spend half the time in each?'

'Oh, much too complicated. And where would I keep my books?'

'Well, you could keep one set in each place.'

'Have you been talking to Pandora?' said Sebastian suspiciously.

'No, of course not. It just seems quite – obvious to me. And it is so lovely, her house.'

'So is mine. Now come along, let's open that champagne. Kit, hallo, old chap. How are you? How do you feel about this brilliant creature in our midst? Something to live up to, eh?'

Kit grinned, shook his hand then gave him a hug; they were extremely fond of one another. Barty watched them as they sat together on the sofa, chatting easily, and thought how oddly alike they were. Both with the same golden looks, both so easily charming; two of her favourite people in the world.

For years she had had something of a crush on Sebastian; even now, she thought he was quite absurdly handsome. He hated his looks, said they were not in the least suited to a children's author and it was true, he looked more like a film star or at the very least some rather romantic poet. His hair was still dark gold, his eyes an astonishingly brilliant blue, his features perfectly sculptured; he resembled, everyone said, a blond Rudolph Valentino. He had been a fine athlete until an injury in the trenches early in 1916 had left him with a permanent limp – which of course added to his romantic image. Women found him irresistible. Even LM agreed he was extremely good-looking, and the twins were always saying he was swoon-making – their latest silly expression. Only Celia seemed impervious to his looks; the twins had once asked her if she didn't think he was the most handsome man in the whole wide world, and she had said quite crossly that she had never really thought about it and that she was a great deal more interested in whether his next book was going to be delivered on time and not be as late as the last one had been.

Barty sometimes wondered if Celia liked Sebastian at all; Giles had reported that she had been absolutely vile to him when he had turned up two hours late for the twins' birthday dinner: 'poor chap, he'd only been working as usual, giving a second reading because the first one had sold out', and that she'd been horribly awkward about meeting Pandora. 'But then she suddenly gave a big dinner party for her and was unbelievably charming and kept saying Sebastian didn't deserve her.'

Sebastian actually felt much the same about Pandora himself; and at finding her at a time when he had never thought to experience any such emotion ever again. Men of forty-seven, with a considerable past, containing one marriage and several love affairs, selfish, solitary men, set in their ways, with a breathtakingly successful career to absorb their attentions and their lives, did not, could not, expect to fall in love. And yet he had done so: helplessly, joyously and without any kind of warning.

It had been her voice that he had first fallen in love with; he had been sitting in the Bodleian library after a reading, signing what appeared to be an unstoppable flow of his books, smiling courteously up at his young readers and their parents as they came up to the table one by one, saying he was so glad they liked the latest, that it was most interesting that they still preferred the first, that no, he did not actually have a favourite of his own, that yes of course he would put 'To Freddie' above the signature, that no, naturally he would not mind signing an old copy of the first edition, when he had heard it. That soft, low, extraordinarily sweet voice, that nevertheless could be heard quite clearly above the hubbub, offering to fetch him more books from the pile of boxes in the corner; he looked up and saw a small heart-shaped face, a pair of large brown eyes, a gently sympathetic smile, and felt a pang of what he could only call recognition, but so violent it was like a physical blow, leaving him feeling odd, disorientated, slightly dizzy.

'That would be very kind,' he had said, trying to steady himself, to find normality, 'but of course only a few, or get someone to help you, find Mr Jarvis, he usually—'

She smiled again, and turned away; she was small, he noticed, very small, with a long snake of golden brown hair falling down her back, held by a large tortoiseshell slide, and she moved swiftly, gracefully, almost gliding across the room. When she came back with the books, and opened a few of them at the title page, ready for signing, he thanked her profusely and felt bereft when she left him; at the end of the function, he saw her carefully documenting what had been sold and went across to her.

'I was so grateful for your help,' he said, 'thank you.'

'Don't be absurd,' she said, 'it was nothing. I enjoyed your talk,' she added, and went back to her task; he felt at once dismissed and encouraged.

'I get so tired of it,' he said, and 'Of what?' she said, looking up after a long moment, as if distracted, and unwillingly so, from what she was doing.

'The talk. I do it so often, and it seems to me to be so boring. It probably is,' he added, 'but they seemed to enjoy it this afternoon, didn't they?'

'Oh, yes, I think so,' she said.

'And quite a good number of people, didn't you think?'

'Oh, I did. Yes.'

'It's always a strain, you know. Wondering if anyone will come, wondering if they'll laugh at the right moment, all that sort of thing.'

'I imagine, yes.'

'You never get used to it. Not really. Absurd, isn't it?'

'Yes. I mean no.' She looked at him very levelly. 'Mr Brooke – I don't want to be rude. And I did enjoy your talk and I'm sure everyone did. But I would like to finish this now, it's getting late.'

'Oh God, I'm so sorry. How self-centred and selfish of me. Do forgive me. And thank you again.'

'That's perfectly all right. Goodnight.'
'Goodnight Miss—'
'Harvey. Pandora Harvey.'

He had stayed the night in Oxford, having business to discuss next day with the manager of Blackwells; and then, drawn by what seemed some totally irresistible force, had walked into the Bodleian. She was actually walking out of it at precisely the same time, to go to lunch and then to stay with her mother for a week; he had often wondered since, and trembled at it, what might have happened if his conversation with Blackwells had lasted for even five minutes longer. He smiled and said how very nice to see her again, and might he perhaps take her for tea to show his gratitude for her kindness the night before, and she laughed and said that tea would be nice and perhaps even a sandwich since she was hungry.

After that, they went for a walk by the river and then he drove her in his motor car down to the Trout pub on the great wild flats, where she surprised him by asking for half a pint of beer and they watched the peacocks and discovered they shared a passion for (amongst a great many other things) the paintings of Modigliani, the music of George Gershwin and the literary works of A. A. Milne. 'If you wouldn't find such fondness for a rival author offensive,' Pandora added anxiously.

Sebastian said that of course he would not. And then she agreed to telephone her mother and tell her she wouldn't be arriving until the next day and he bought her dinner at the Randolph. They sat there talking until they were quite alone in the restaurant and the waiters were half asleep, and Sebastian said that he didn't suppose she would take it at all seriously, but he appeared to be falling in love with her and she said (with a glorious lack of foolish feminine guile) that she would certainly like to take it seriously, and also to think about its implications.

A week later, she telephoned him from her small house in Oxford and invited him to dinner on the following Saturday evening; Sebastian arrived with a bottle of very fine claret, a large bouquet of white roses and a signed first edition of *The House at Pooh Corner*. A few other friends were coming, she said, which disappointed him a little, but by one o'clock in the morning and after a very happy evening, and a wonderful meal which she had cooked, the friends had all left and she told him that she did seem to find herself also in love, and if he was still of the same persuasion, then she would be extraordinarily happy. Sebastian woke in the morning in her bed, her small body with its almost alarming capacity for pleasure coiled against his; he asked her later that day to marry him and she accepted.

That had been the simple, straightforward part.

Of course he had known Celia would be upset. He had expected it all: the icy disdain, the anger, the hurt. It was why he had put off telling her for weeks, why he chose to break the news on the twins' birthday, when she was in determinedly family mood, when Oliver would be benignly present, when he thought that with luck, LM would be there too, with her level, calm courtesy. He had not expected the party to be over, the house emptied so soon of distraction. But still – it had been done. Oliver's insistence on the celebratory champagne was unfortunate; but it had distracted attention, notionally at least, from the spilt wine and Celia's rage at having spilt it. They had somehow got through the hour or so it required for courtesy to release him again, and return, exhausted, to his own house. But he had discovered it had not been done quite as successfully as he had hoped.

'Of course I want to meet her,' Celia said, smiling at him brilliantly across her office desk a few days later. 'I can hardly wait. We must arrange it as soon as we can. I will talk to Oliver and see if we can find an evening when we are both free. It's just that we are extremely busy at the moment, the twins' season is so hectic, you know, I have a lot of extra entertaining to do, and a lot of country house parties, and then there's Ascot and—'

'Celia,' said Sebastian, keeping his voice level with an effort, 'Celia, a dinner, just the four of us, will do, so that you can—'

'Oh, Sebastian, don't be absurd. I would certainly not want Pandora to feel less than properly welcomed. I want her to meet the entire family, naturally, nothing else would be acceptable to me, and that inevitably requires organisation. Now give me a week or two and I will find a date.'

The week, and then two, passed; dates were even proposed and then cancelled, changed and then changed again. Pandora was first amused then irritated.

'It's absurd. I think I shall just walk into her office one day, and introduce myself. Then it will be done.'

'Please don't,' said Sebastian. 'Please, please don't.'

He looked genuinely anguished; she sighed.

'I am finding this – difficult, Sebastian. I really am. Whatever the reason. Please get it settled. Please.'

Sebastian said he would.

Finally he lost his temper: Celia had just cancelled a fourth firm arrangement, had asked Janet Gould to telephone him and express her great regret. Her mother was giving a court dinner, had asked her to step in at the last minute, she felt she couldn't fail her when she had done so much for the twins that season, she did hope Pandora would understand.

Sebastian put down the phone, looked at it thoughtfully for a minute or two and then called a taxi and went to Lytton House. He was in Celia's office for less than five minutes; that afternoon Pandora received a note, delivered by hand, inviting her and Sebastian to a family dinner at Cheyne Walk on the following Thursday.

'So, my little genius, what are you going to do now?' he said, refilling Barty's glass.

'Oh – I haven't thought yet.'

'I bet you have.' His dark blue eyes were on hers, thoughtful, probing.

'Well – only vaguely. You know.'

'Enjoy a bit of well-earned leisure?'

'Goodness, no. I like to be busy, all the time.'

'I know you do. But a few weeks wouldn't be a bad idea. Are you going to this villa of theirs?'

'I suppose so,' said Barty with a sigh. 'I really don't want to. But what excuse do I have, and—'

'Might be fun.'

'It won't be fun,' said Barty.

'What won't?' said Kit. He had left the room to get himself some lemonade.

'Oh – nothing,' said Barty quickly, 'just leaving Oxford, looking for a job.'

'Why do you have to look for a job?'

'Because she likes working,' said Sebastian, 'she's addicted to it. Like your mother.'

'But, Barty, you don't have to look for a job,' said Kit, 'you've got one already.'

'I have?'

'Yes, of course.'

'What is it?' said Barty, intrigued.

'Well, working at Lyttons,' he said, adding with all the simplistic logic of a child, 'everyone in the family does,'

'But I'm not—' said Barty and stopped.

'The Terrors don't,' said Sebastian, cutting into the conversation smoothly.

'I expect they will. Mummy – Mother – says they will one day. When they've grown up a bit. I heard her talking to Father about it.'

'You shouldn't listen to other people's conversations, young Kit,' said Sebastian. 'It's not the done thing, you know.'

'Oh, but I was there,' said Kit, looking hurt. 'Not listening outside the door or anything. They never take any notice of me, just carry on talking. Mostly about boring things. Anyway, that's what she said, Mummy, I mean. And then she said that of course Barty would too. As soon as she came down from Oxford. She said you should train to be an editor, that you'd be wonderful. Better than Giles, she said you'd be,' he added with a sweet smile. 'Mother says he has no idea.'

'But—' said Barty and stopped again.

'He could be,' said Sebastian quickly, 'a wonderful editor, but I know Oliver sees him moving into the managerial side. LM says he's marvellous with figures.'

'Well, there you are,' said Barty. 'Much more important than being an editor.'

'Anyway, she wants you to be an editor,' said Kit, 'so I expect you will be.' He smiled his seraphic smile.

Later after lunch, Sebastian and Barty walked along the river walk; she was quiet and seemed distracted.

'What's the matter?' he said.

'Oh – it's well – it's – you won't say anything to Aunt Celia, will you?'

'Of course not. I never speak to her these days without full written permission.' He grinned at her.

'It's just that I really don't want to work at Lyttons.'

'Because it would be too easy? Because of what people would say?'

'Well, yes. And—'

'And what?' He put his arm round her shoulders. 'Come on, you can tell me.'

'It's just that – well, it means more – more gratitude. More knowing how lucky I am. I'm so tired of it, Sebastian. So terribly tired of it.'

Later that night, safely back in Oxford with Pandora, Sebastian told her of Barty's problems. She listened intently, her large brown eyes fixed on his; then, 'Poor Barty,' she said, 'poor little thing.'

'Not so poor,' said Sebastian, feeling a rather surprising and disconcerting rush of defensiveness towards the Lyttons. 'She's had huge benefits from the arrangement. It wasn't all bad. Celia adores her and—'

'I fancy being adored by Lady Celia is not an undiluted pleasure,' said Pandora.

'Of course not. But it's better than not being adored by her, like poor Giles. And training as an editor at Lyttons is not exactly a bad way to start a career.'

'Of course not. But – it's what she said, Sebastian. I can so sympathise with that. About the gratitude. It must be so difficult.'

'Quite difficult. I have had to endure it myself to a small degree. Not now of course, but in the beginning. When Celia first bought *Meridian* and fought for it so hard, and against Oliver too—'

'Yes, yes. I don't think I want to hear too much about those days,' said Pandora. 'Come along, my darling, let us go to bed. I've been missing you rather dreadfully . . .'

Later – much later – Pandora lay in his arms watching him sleep, and thinking how much she loved him.

The violence of her feelings for him had not only taken her by surprise at the time, they continued to shake and even shock her. A great dynamic force for pleasure of every kind, emotional, intellectual, physical. She was not entirely inexperienced; she had been deeply in love on every level with her fiancé, and during the twelve years since his death had had one or two lovers – 'Well, two actually,' she said, laughing to Sebastian when he pressed her for accuracy, but she had been largely frustrated, her energies mostly suppressed. Now the places to which she travelled in Sebastian's bed, the experiences she shared with him there, were of a splendour and richness she had not imagined possible. Released by him, by his skill and tenderness and a considerable creative sexuality, her responses ran almost out of control at first; then she found she was able to offer him gifts of her own, a tireless sexual energy and curiosity, a clear, uninhibited delight. She could not have enough of him, would fall asleep finally sated and wake him, laughing gently at herself, a few hours later for more.

'I'm an old man, my darling, I need my rest,' he would say, but in truth was filled with joy and even relief that he could give her such pleasure.

She knew much about him, about his past, he had told her 'everything it is necessary for you to know', kissing her tenderly after a long night of revelation, some of it surprising, a little even shocking;

she sensed there might be still more. But she felt, curiously, content with what she had of him; and whatever had been left out of the telling, his most secret self, could wait to be revealed. Lying with him, as he led her on further and higher, exploring him slowly and sweetly, she felt she was making another journey, on another plane entirely; in time, she felt sure, she would have him all.

The holiday in the Cap d'Antibes villa was not a complete success; the twins were bored and irritable, refusing so much as to play tennis or get into the pool, Giles suffered so badly from the heat that he had to spend much of the time indoors, and Oliver contracted one of the stomach infections to which he had been prone since the war. On the other hand Kit and Jay, who had accompanied them, were blissfully happy, playing in the pool all day long, diving and leaping endlessly into it like rather noisy porpoises, Celia lay in a chair under the trees, oddly serene, reading manuscripts, and Barty surprised everyone, including herself, by becoming a sun worshipper, her face and body turning a perfect golden brown, her long tawny hair becoming streaked and lightened and her small nose developing pretty, tiny freckles. She was out by the pool early each morning, swimming energetically up and down with Celia, who was a most earnest disciple of the fashion for slimness and fitness.

The evenings were only modestly sociable; villas up and down the coast were filled with partying English and French, but Celia had decided (to her later regret) to take a small villa and very little in the way of staff. She therefore found herself unable to give the kind of large dinner parties that their neighbours were enjoying or to accept too many invitations; this made the twins even crosser.

Then, in the last week, Boy Warwick and a party turned up unexpectedly, having berthed for a few days in the Port de l'Olivette, and motored in to find them. Even Celia was pleased to see them and the twins were ecstatic, suddenly eager to show off their modest swimming skills, and showing a hitherto unrevealed passion for sailing.

But by the end of three weeks everyone, even Kit, had had enough.

On the last evening, Oliver announced that on the way home he was going to visit Constantine, the publisher in Paris with whom Lyttons had a reciprocal arrangement.

'I have been talking to Guy Constantine on the telephone this morning, and he has several books to discuss with me, as I do with him;

it seems foolish not to take advantage of being this side of the Channel. Celia, my dear, I imagine you will want to come with me; and Giles, it would do no harm for you to visit the Constantine offices and meet some of their people. Now—'

'Paris!' said Adele. 'Oh, how lovely. Daddy, can we come too? We can do some shopping, we're so behind with our winter wardrobes and—'

'Of course you can come,' said Oliver, smiling at her, 'and I fancy you would rather enjoy Guy Constantine's company. He's a very charming man, although his English is rather limited.'

'Oh, we wouldn't want to get in the way of your business,' said Venetia quickly, 'would we, Adele?' and, 'No,' said Adele, 'of course not. We'll just amuse ourselves, you won't have to worry about us.'

Oliver patted her hand. 'Of course we won't worry about you,' he said, smiling at her.

How do they get away with it? thought Barty, realising with a degree of relief that she and the boys would be travelling home from Paris on their own. The complete lack of effort they put into their lives, the nonsense they talked – 'behind with their winter wardrobes' for heaven's sake. It was not what she would have wanted, that idle, pleasure-seeking life: not in the least. Just the same, she still couldn't help feeling a little irked that no one seemed to expect anything more of them.

Of her own future nothing had yet been settled; Celia had talked about a job at Lyttons for her and, surprisingly, had accepted Barty's request for a little time to think about it. She was altogether not quite herself at the moment, distracted, and slightly subdued, although this evening, her tanned skin shown off by a narrow white silk dress, her dark hair gleaming in the candlelight, she looked particularly beautiful.

And many, many years younger than dear old Wol . . .

'Girls, I need your help.'

Oliver had come down to breakfast at the Georges V on his own; the twins, anxious not to waste a moment of shopping time, looked at him with a degree of anxiety. 'What with? And where's Mummy?'

'Your mother is not well. That's the whole point. And—'

'Mummy's not well! But she's always well.'

It was true; Celia's good health was legendary, her only physical weakness being a tendency to miscarry, a problem no longer in any danger of troubling her.

'Well, she is not well today. She had oysters last night as you know and—'

'Oh God.' Venetia shuddered. She had once had oyster poisoning herself and could no longer bear so much as to look at them on a dish. 'I did warn her off. Poor, poor Mummy.'

'I know. She feels perfectly dreadful; a doctor is with her now. Of course it's not serious, but I need a hostess for luncheon. I am taking Guy Constantine and his editorial director to Maxim's and I don't want to do it on my own.'

'Why ever not?' said Adele, genuinely puzzled. 'It's business, isn't it? Why do you need a hostess? And anyway, where's Giles?'

'He's at their warehouse. In any case, this is a social arrangement,' said Oliver impatiently. 'We will have been talking business all morning, and I want this to be a relaxing occasion, with some light-hearted conversation. So I would like you to join us. Preferably both of you, but certainly one.'

'But, Daddy—'

'Venetia,' said Oliver and his voice had an entirely different note to it, 'I don't often ask you to do things for me. Your mother and I devote a great deal of time and money to making life pleasant for you. You have just had an extremely good holiday and the next few months are not going to be exactly difficult for you. Now, which of you is going to be kind enough, generous enough even, to accompany me to Maxim's for luncheon?'

The twins looked at each other.

'Both of us,' they said.

They arrived at the Constantine building at twelve-thirty as instructed, having left their shopping at the Georges V and having looked cautiously in on their mother. She was asleep; the nurse in attendance put her finger to her lips.

It was a glorious place, more like a house than an office, set in a courtyard just off the Avenue de l'Opera. The great double doors opened on to a vaulted hallway and a magnificent double staircase; a rather bored-looking male concierge directed them to the first floor, where they were asked to wait. Five minutes later their father, Guy Constantine and a third man appeared from one of the rooms.

Guy Constantine was about forty-five, short, slim and neatly handsome in the French style, his dark hair greying, his skin tanned, his suit and shirt impeccable. The other man was rather different. Adele looked at him, and felt, as she expressed it to Venetia later, 'my insides sort of clutch at me'. He was dark also, but much taller than Constantine; his features were untidy, as if they had been somehow dropped haphazardly into place and left to be neatened up later. He looked, Adele thought, as if he might be Jewish; he was very dark, with extraordinarily penetrating, almost black, eyes, a large nose, a high forehead on to which a mass of thick black hair seemed to fall rather than grow, and a full mouth that would have looked girlish if the rest of his face had not been so strong. His smile, which was sudden and brilliant, revealed very white, albeit slightly crooked teeth; his hand, as he shook first Adele's and then Venetia's, was bony and very strong and warm.

'Luc Lieberman,' he said, bowing slightly. 'I am the editorial director of Constantine. *Enchanté, Mesdemoiselles*.'

'How do you do?' said Adele. She felt slightly dizzy, without quite knowing why. Luc Lieberman was absolutely not the sort of man she usually admired; his clothes left a great deal to be desired, being slightly crumpled and ill-fitting, the jacket sleeves just too short, the trousers just slightly too long. She waited for the feeling to pass; it persisted.

'It is very sad,' said Luc Lieberman, 'that your poor *maman* is ill. Is she feeling any better?'

'She's asleep,' said Venetia, 'we just popped in to see her.'

'Excellent!' said Guy Constantine. He gave it the French pronunciation. 'Sleep is what she needs. Now I thought you might like to see our rather beautiful building. Before we leave. Your father and I have a last few matters to discuss. Luc will show you around.'

Adele, who was normally quite impervious to the beauty of buildings, said she would adore to see around this one; Venetia nodded slightly less enthusiastically.

'And this is the boardroom,' said Luc Lieberman, throwing open the door with a flourish. 'Is it not beautiful?'

'Oh my God,' said Adele. 'Oh, it's – well, it's divine.'

'Almost, I think yes, it is,' said Luc. 'I think God might well have created it. If He had had a moment or two between dividing the light from the darkness and creating the beasts of the earth. And then I think He would have been pleased with His work here in Paris.'

The twins both giggled, slightly nervously. They could see he must be joking; on the other hand, his expression was very serious and they weren't really used to so intellectual a form of teasing. They felt foolish and inadequate; it was an unfamiliar sensation.

'I thought you would like it. Has your father not told you about this room?'

'Of – of course he has,' said Adele, and indeed she could dimly remember him sitting at the dinner table describing it, the jewel in the crown of this exquisite building, its art nouveau splendours, the perfect ceiling, the breathtaking fireplace, the Tiffany lamps, the elaborate wallpaper, the extraordinary table and chairs, seemingly carved out of glass; no doubt she had allowed her mind to wander as usual while he had been talking, into the more attractive country of dresses and dressmakers and whether she and Venetia should accept an invitation to this house party or that. She really must learn to be more – thoughtful – if she was to interest people like Luc. Well, interest Luc. She couldn't think of anyone she'd ever wanted to interest more in the whole of her life.

'Well, now. Shall we proceed to the archives?'

'I – I wonder if I might – well, sit this one out?' said Venetia with a dazzling smile. 'I hurt my ankle this morning, running up the stairs. Would you mind if I waited here, Mr Lieberman?'

'Do please call me Luc. I would be *désolé* of course. But I under-stand. I am so sorry about your foot. Is it very painful for you?'

'Oh, it's – nothing. Really. I'll be quite happy here. I'll see you in a few minutes.'

She smiled at him; her eyes met Adele's in absolute complicity.

'*D'accord*. Come with me, then, Mam'selle Adele. That is, if you would be interested in the archives.'

'Yes,' she said, 'yes, I'm sure I would. And, Luc, do please call me just Adele. There's no need to be formal.'

'Oh,' he said, and his voice was courteously surprised, 'oh, but I thought there was. Your father is, after all, my *patron*. I feel I have to show his eldest daughter some degree of respect.'

'How do you know I'm his eldest daughter?'

'Your mother told me.'

'She did?' said Adele. 'When?'

'Oh, the last time we met. She showed me some photographs of you.'

'Really?' Adele was astonished. Her mother was normally not the sort of woman to go round showing pictures of her children to anyone, let alone total strangers, and even less likely to impart rather intimate information as to which of her two twins had been born first. And yet – she could see why. There was something about Luc Lieberman that invited confidence, intimacy even; he drew you into his rather intense personality, and you found yourself – well, lost.

'I can't imagine why you should have been interested in learning

42

such a thing,' she said, fiddling with the clip of her handbag.

'Mam'selle Adele,' he said, and his face was very serious indeed, 'I would be interested in learning anything about you. Anything at all.'

Lunch at Maxim's was pure pleasure. The twins never tired of its splendours, the Lautrecs, the atmosphere, the lamps, the waiters with their long white aprons, the wonderfully chic Parisiennes pushing food delicately around their plates. Hair much longer here, they noticed, and skirts marginally so, and those dear little close-fitting small-brimmed hats; all important things to be taken back home.

But for Adele, sitting next to Luc, concentrating (in a way that was quite new to her) on everything he said, however complex, these were secondary things. She felt, still, slightly dizzy, shaken somehow to her innermost self; not the familiar Adele at all, but someone nervous, tentative almost, examining what she said before she said it, and quite often deciding to remain silent, lest she should sound foolish, and yet at the same time vividly, almost painfully happy.

'Now, we have a wonderful new book to publish,' said Oliver, smiling at his daughters across the table. 'A discovery of Monsieur Lieberman's. It's about the war, and it's called *Lettres tristes*. It's a novel, written in the form of a correspondence between an English soldier and a girl he meets as he journeys home wounded from the trenches. He arrives home, knowing he is in love with her, knowing he will never see her again and expected to marry his English fiancée. Very moving, very moving indeed, and I think exactly the right time to publish. With the war receding from us in time.'

'Indeed, Monsieur Lytton. And the author, Marcel Lemoine, is such a charming man. In fact, I was going to suggest that when you publish the book in England, if you were planning a little *reception* for it, then he could perhaps come to London himself. I'm sure the English would like him. He did fight in the trenches himself, it is a book based on real knowledge.'

'Indeed,' said Luc Lieberman, 'he is an exceptional man. The only problem as I see it is that he doesn't speak very much English, but – maybe Lady Celia could help. Her French is good, I believe.'

'Well, my French is quite good actually,' said Adele, 'and I would love to meet Monsieur Lemoine, I think it's a marvellous idea to have him over for the publication. And of course you should come too, Monsieur Lieberman, as the discoverer of this great talent.'

'That would be a delight,' he said.

'Well, well,' said Venetia, 'and when did you develop a talent for speaking French, Adele? You'll have to have some lessons pretty quickly.'

'Oh, shut up,' said Adele, 'I mean *tais-toi*. There, you see, I do remember quite a lot. It was one of my best subjects.'

'Which doesn't mean much. And views on publishing all of a sudden too. Oh, it's all right, I thought he was—'

'Isn't he? So – so sexy.'

'Yes. Terrible clothes, though.'

'Terrible. I thought that probably meant—'

'Possibly. Can't assume it, though. They're not all—'

'No Frenchwoman,' said Adele firmly, 'would let her husband go round looking like that.'

'What about her fiancé?'

'Don't think so. Do you? Anyway, we must—'

'I'll ask Daddy. Not Mummy, she'd guess. She never—'

'No, but she obviously liked him too.'

'How do you know?'

'She told him I was the oldest. Of us two.'

'How absolutely extraordinary,' said Venetia.

'I know. I just feel, Venetia, that he's well – that he's—'

'Important?' said Venetia.

'Yes. Very important.'

'Barty, my dear—'

His voice came from his study as she walked through the hall.

'Yes, Wol?'

'Could I have a word with you?'

Barty's heart sank; she knew what it was about.

'This is – difficult for me,' he said, sitting back in the big leather swivel chair at his desk. 'Sit down, my dear, sit down. Now then—'

She sat, silent, determined not to help him in any way.

'Celia tells me you have turned down our offer of a job at Lyttons.'

'Yes. Yes, that's right, I would have told you as well, but you were away—'

'I know, I know. That's not the problem. It's just that Celia is very upset.'

Barty felt angry suddenly. Celia had no right to be upset; emotion was irrelevant. This was a business matter, not a family one. She said as much to Oliver.

'I'm afraid that isn't quite true, Barty, is it?'

She looked at him steadily. 'Of course it is.'

'Now you know it's not. Celia loves you, she has worked very hard to help you over the years and—'

'Wol, please. That's not fair.'

He sighed. 'Isn't it?'

'No. You know it's not. I didn't ask to come here, I didn't ask to leave my family. I know it was a wonderfully generous thing to do, and of course I have had incredible opportunities, that I would never have dreamed of. But—' She stopped.

'But what?'

It was no use; she couldn't say it. Couldn't say how much of it had hurt, how much damage as well as good Celia had done; and besides, Wol knew that.

She took a deep breath. 'The thing is, Wol, I want to do things on my own. I think I'd feel this even if I was a Lytton—'

'You are a Lytton. In many ways.'

She allowed him that.

'All right. If I was a Lytton by birth. I don't want to have things handed to me on a plate, I don't want people saying, "Oh, she's only got that job because they brought her up."'

'Barty, they won't. You got a First Class degree in English Literature. From Oxford. No one can achieve that without extraordinary talent. And application, of course.'

'You should know,' she said, smiling at him, 'you got one too.'

'It's easier for a man.'

'Oh, Wol!'

'I'm afraid it's true. But anyway, we want you to come and work at Lyttons because we think you will help us. Not to do you a favour. I hope we are more professional than that. We think you will make a very good editor; we think you have great potential.'

She was silent; then she said, 'But there must be many other young people you could offer this job to.'

'I daresay there are. But why should we go out and find them? Why not just have you?'

'Because,' she said, and her voice was thick with exasperation, 'because I don't want you to. Doesn't that count for anything?'

He was silent; then he said, 'So, you want to apply to other firms for other jobs?'

'Yes. So it's – fair.'

'And do you think that these other firms won't know who you are? Barty, you have grown up with all these people. You have gone to children's parties at the Macmillans and the Murrays, you've danced with the Blackwood boys, you've dined with the Collinses. Do you really believe that they won't bend over backwards to accommodate you, give you a chance? Will that be fair?'

She was silent.

He looked at her. 'Tell me, Barty, if none of this was – an issue, which publishing houses would you most admire at the moment?'

'Oh – I'm not sure. Jonathan Cape, I suppose.'

'Because of the Sitwells?'

'Yes. Murrays. It's so – so scholarly. Macmillans, they're so innovative somehow, so commercially successful.'

'All very interesting. And what about Lyttons?'

'Well, of course.'

'I think we have a little of everything; a good base in poetry, equalled by none in biography, thanks to Celia's immense talent, a fine series of reference books, the Meridian books of course, a strong commercial list, look at the Buchanans, still going strong, a worthy rival to the Forsytes – if you knew nothing of us, wouldn't you want to apply to us as well?'

'Yes, of course. But—'

'And then we are still comparatively small. Small enough for you to make your mark. If you have the talent. If you don't, if we are wrong, then you will not survive with us for very long. I promise you that. As for making it easy for you, speak to Giles. See what he has to say.'

'I know, but—'

'Barty.' He leaned forward. 'Please come to us. I want you to, I know we can benefit one another. And there is something else . . . for reasons which I don't wish to go into, Celia is not entirely – happy at the moment. She's very brave, she always has been, she would cut her own tongue out before admitting to it but – well, I would like to do what I can to help her. And it would make her feel very happy indeed to have you at Lyttons. She sees it as a rejection, your refusal, a personal rejection. I can understand your feelings; she cannot.'

Barty thought this was highly unlikely, Celia was, despite her arrogance, immensely perceptive, but she said instead, 'I'm sorry she's not happy. Is there anything I should know about?'

'No, no, and you certainly shouldn't mention it. This is a conversation of absolute confidentiality. I know I can trust you.'

'Yes, of course.'

He looked at her. 'I have seldom asked anything of you, Barty. And as I told you that – that – well, on a particular occasion, you mean as much to me as my own children. And I hope I have given you whatever support you felt you needed in return.'

'Yes, yes, of course you have. And more—'

'I am going to ask you something now. Something I want you to do for me. In – I will not say in return, that would smack of emotional blackmail – in acknowledgement, perhaps.'

She nodded again, knowing what was coming, thinking it was still emotional blackmail, but forced to recognise that he had every right to apply it.

'Take the job, Barty. Come to Lyttons for a while – let us say two years. After that you will have made your mark, other houses will be after you anyway—'

She smiled again. 'Hardly.'

'Well, we shall see. But – will you do that? Please?'

There was a long silence; then she said quietly, as she had known she would have to, 'Yes, Wol. Yes, I will.'

'Good. And don't think your life will be easy. As I said, ask Giles. He hardly has a feather bed to lie on at Lyttons.'

'No. No, I know.'

He stood up and kissed her. 'Thank you, Barty. Thank you so very much.'

She kissed him back and left the room quickly; she felt horribly near to tears at the prospect of two more years at least of being indebted, of enforced gratitude. However Wol dressed it up, told her he was asking a favour of her, that was what it meant. And it wasn't fair. It simply wasn't fair.

Chapter 4

'I'm going out this afternoon,' said Venetia. She spoke casually; rummaging in one of her drawers.

'Where?' said Adele, but of course she knew.

'To Boy's flat.'

'Oh yes? More paintings?'

'Something like that. Yes. Damn. You haven't seen the new cream leather gloves, have you?'

'No, I haven't. Venetia, don't do it. Not a good idea.'

'What? Oh, where are the wretched things?'

'Venetia, don't. Please.'

'But why? I know what I'm doing.'

'Do you?'

'Yes. And that's why I'm going.'

'Well, be—'

'Of course I will. I'm not a complete idiot.' She looked at her sister; her face was flushed. She tried to laugh. 'Now I won't be long. Promise. And you can have the car. I'll get a taxi.'

'I don't want the car. And you are a complete idiot.' Adele picked up a copy of *Vogue*, started leafing through it.

She hadn't expected to mind about this love affair with Boy, had expected indeed to share it in all its excitement and discovery

They had each felt themselves to be in love more than once, had confided in and sought advice from one another, shared appallingly intimate revelations, and generally found any pleasure greatly intensified in so doing. They were still both virgins and their love affairs were of a highly restrained nature, but they were on the other hand very well-informed about how that innocence might be lessened or even lost. Several of their friends had crossed the great divide into sexual experience (and reported back on it in terms that ranged from the vague to the explicit), but the twins had felt no desire as yet to follow them.

'We will if we really want to,' Venetia said, as they sat dissecting an evening in the company of two particularly importunate young men, 'otherwise there's—'

'Absolutely none,' said Adele. And so it had been left.

And then Venetia had really wanted to; with Boy. And, moreover, declared herself to be in love with him. And Adele found herself, for the very first time in her life, experiencing a real and very harsh jealousy.

'I have to. Really I do.' Venetia had returned from a long afternoon with Boy, flushed, clearly upset.

'Of course you don't.'

'I do, I do.' Venetia suddenly started to cry. 'You don't understand. He makes me feel so – so silly. So young and naive. He says – well, he says he's so fond of me, he just can't understand me. Not wanting to.'

'But—'

'I know all that, but it's not quite true. Is it? Not these days. Everyone's doing it—'

'Everyone's doing it with Boy, you mean,' said Adele, 'or so he would have you believe.'

Venetia was silent. Then she said, 'But I do so adore him. And I'm going to. I really want to, and he really wants me to and I just can't see why not.'

Adele sensed defeat. She sighed, looked at her sister very soberly, and then got up, went over to her and hugged her.

'Does that mean it's all right?' Venetia said hopefully.

'No. But it means – anyway, you will at least – won't you—'

'Of course. I'm not that stupid. Made the appointment already, actually.'

'That's good. I might come with you. Sooner or later I'll need it too. I hope.' She smiled with an immense effort and said, her voice quite different, 'Now let's telephone the newlyweds and ask if we can take them out to lunch tomorrow. I promised we would.'

Pandora and Sebastian had been married quietly in early September; from Pandora's own small house in Oxford. Celia and Oliver had offered Cheyne Walk on the evening of the first dinner, but Pandora had refused.

'It's sweet of you,' she said, 'sweet and generous, but Oxford is home and I want our marriage to begin there.'

'Well, that's very understandable,' said Oliver, 'isn't it, Celia?'

49

Celia said that of course it was and enquired whether it might not be possible for Pandora to be married from her mother's home.

'Goodness, no. Even smaller than mine. Honestly a cottage. We don't want lots of people, just our families, of course you are Sebastian's, and my house will do perfectly.'

It did: on a perfect golden day, they became man and wife in the Oxford registry office – 'I always forget Sebastian was married once before, he doesn't look divorced,' said Adele, speaking for most of the family – and then over a wonderful, long, languorous lunch in Pandora's garden, the air scented with late roses, and the sunlight as golden as the champagne. There were only twenty people there, half of them Lyttons; it was a delightfully unconventional occasion. The bride looked quite extraordinarily lovely, in a simple white crêpe dress, her arms full of lilies, white roses in her hair, and the groom looked, as always, absurdly handsome. He was dressed in a dark grey suit and a cream silk shirt, and he looked like an illustration from one of his own wonderful books.

Oliver made a charming speech, Kit read a poem he had written for the occasion entitled 'The Wedding and Why', which brought tears to several people's eyes, including his mother's and the bridegroom's. Jay Lytton and Gordon Robinson played Mendelssohn's Wedding March as a duet on Pandora's piano while the cake was cut, Lily Lytton, in her last appearance before leaving with Jack for Hollywood, sang 'Mad About the Boy' quite exquisitely, followed by several other songs from her latest show by way of encore.

Pandora's mother, who was dressed rather unexpectedly all in white and bore a more than passing resemblance, several of the guests could not help thinking, to Miss Havisham, insisted on making a speech as well, and reciting 'Let me not to the marriage of true minds' rather badly, but it didn't seem to matter.

Celia, dressed dazzlingly in blue and looking exceptionally beautiful and young, was at her most brilliant and amusing; only Barty noticed that as Sebastian raised his glass a trifle unsteadily to toast 'my perfect bride' LM reached out for Celia's hand and held it tightly, but, as she had had a great deal of champagne herself, thought very little of it anyway.

They left at sunset in Sebastian's car for a honeymoon in Ireland.

'That was utterly wonderful,' said Venetia happily. 'Giles, race you back to London. Last one home's a cissy.'

'I'm going with you two,' said Kit, his eyes alight.

'You are not,' said Celia, 'you are coming with your father and me.'

'Oh, Mummy. It's not fair, I want to be in the race.'

'No one's being in the race,' said Giles, sounding (and hating himself for it) pompous, 'because I'm not racing. I've had a bit too much champagne.'

'You're all spoilsports,' said Adele. 'Well, we're going anyway. We have a party to go to.'

'Whose party?' asked Celia.

'A friend of Boy's,' said Venetia casually. 'And don't look so disapproving, Mummy, he's got three houses and a title. Bye, everyone. Lovely day.'

Celia, looking after them as the little Austin sped off down the road, felt anxiety join the other complex and violent emotions of the day; not just because they might drive too fast, or had had too much to drink, but because both of them, and Venetia in particular, had developed a certain studied vagueness about their comings and goings in the past few months. She knew what that meant; it was a device she had used herself in her own youth. It confused and diverted adult attention; in her case it had left her free to pursue and seduce Oliver. She must watch the twins more closely, she thought. And at least it would be a distraction from certain other matters.

'My darling, I'm so lucky to have you.' Boy Warwick lay back on the pillows of his extremely large bed and smiled into Venetia's eyes. She smiled back. She was beginning to enjoy the bed thing. The first time had been difficult, painful even, lacking in pleasure; but each one since had been better, and today, this afternoon, had been wonderful. She had climaxed properly, for the first time, had discovered its intense joy, the rippling, rising and falling, beginning deep within her, the great well of warm, dark intensity drawing her in; she had heard a strange sound as it happened, a wild, primitive cry, and only realised afterwards, as she lay panting, wet with sweat, in Boy's arms that it had been she who had made it.

'I'm lucky too,' she said, leaning over and kissing him. 'Wonderfully lucky, and so happy, you can't think how much. Oh, Boy, I love you, I really, really do.'

He replied with a kiss, settled her so that she lay sideways with her head pillowed on his shoulder. He hadn't yet told her he loved her; but she could wait. She could wait quite a long time . . .

❋

51

God, he was a disaster. In every way. Not just lousy at his job – he'd made a complete idiot of himself in the editorial meeting that morning, suggesting they did a biography of Prince Albert – 'Another one, Giles?' his mother had said with that hideous, half-amused politeness which could mean only one thing – and then there'd been his idiotic suggestion as well that they might consider reissuing the *Heatherleigh Chronicles*, Lyttons' first great success, the forerunner, it could have been argued, to the Buchanan saga.

'I don't think so, Giles,' his father had said politely. 'It's really very dated now.'

'Indeed it is,' said Celia. 'I think if you troubled to read it properly, even you would realise that.'

The words 'even you' hung heavily in the air.

But not only was he a failure at publishing, he was a failure socially as well; he'd asked three girls to go to a house party with him that weekend and they'd all refused. He couldn't blame them; he knew he was boring, a lousy dancer, even a hopeless shot. And he hated riding, so there was no question of his going out hunting either.

Here he was, almost twenty-four years old, still living at home with his parents, still not making a mark on Lyttons in any way, a social failure, and still – well, still a virgin. He'd never even come close to getting a girl into bed. Every time he even thought of it, he felt panicky. How appalling to be one of those chaps who did it for the first time on their wedding night. Not that there was anything really wrong with that of course. But these days, when everyone was doing it all over the place – look at Boy Warwick, dozens of girls. He'd better not be doing it with Venetia, thought Giles suddenly, feeling oddly alarmed. That was quite different. That was most definitely not on. No, of course he wasn't. People didn't do it with their friends' sisters. They just didn't.

'Giles?' It was Barty; she was standing in the doorway of his small office. 'Want to come and have a quick bite to eat?'

'Oh. Oh, well—' He smiled at her. What would he do without Barty; she was still the nicest girl he'd ever met. And jolly pretty now, although a bit different looking, with her shoulder-length hair and her unmade-up face.

She was wearing red today, a sort of long red jumper over a pleated navy blue skirt. It was like a very smart school uniform. A short skirt, of course, she wasn't old-fashioned, and she had the most terrific legs. So long and so – well, just terrific.

If only – and he hated himself for even thinking this – if only she wasn't so good at her job. He'd been so thrilled when she told him she was coming to work at Lyttons; but somehow, every time she came up with one of her wonderful ideas, every time his mother said, 'Barty, that's a very good thought', he felt himself wishing they were lousy ideas, terrible thoughts, and that she might appear at least occasionally as rawly incompetent as he.

But 'Yes,' he said now, pushing his work away, 'yes, I'd love to.'

'I've got a secret to tell you,' she said, taking a sip of the disgusting brown liquid that Lyons Corner House sold as tea. 'Something really exciting. Can you keep it?'

'Of course.' Perhaps his mother had given her a book of her own to edit, perhaps she had even commissioned her to write a book herself. Or—

'Giles, don't sound so gloomy. It's really nice. I've found a flat.'

'A flat!'

'Yes. All of my own, Giles, on the top floor of a house in Russell Square. Imagine, Bloomsbury. Isn't that romantic?'

'I – I suppose so.'

'It's much, much nearer here. I'll be able to cycle to work. Think what fun that will be. It's got a sitting room and a bedroom and its own tiny kitchen. I can just about afford it and—'

'So when will you move into it?' said Giles. He felt a leaden depression settle into his stomach.

'Oh – in about a month. Imagine, Giles, independence. Giles, what's the matter? I thought you'd be pleased for me. You don't look very happy . . .'

Adele had known, from the very beginning. On the day of the party at the Savoy for Marcel Lemoine and his book of French letters, as Venetia had christened it with shrieks of mirth; both the girls were going to the party. Adele was trying on, and abandoning, dress after dress, when Venetia came in looking bleary-eyed.

'Good morning. What do you think about this one? Oh God, isn't it just too sickening?' said Adele.

'What?'

'Venetia! You know! Such a bore, today of all days when I so wanted to feel my absolute best—'

'Oh – yes,' Venetia had said vaguely, not meeting her eye. And Adele had known. At once. They always got it together, always.

53

'Venetia, haven't you . . . ?'

Venetia met her eyes across another silence. And then looked down.

'Venetia?' said Adele.

'No. Not yet. So what? It's happened before.'

'Only once. When you'd been ill.'

'Oh, for heaven's sake. What time is our hair appointment? I'd better get dressed. Stop looking at me like that, Adele. *Please*.'

'But—'

'Adele, can I go and have my bath please? We'll be late at this rate.'

'Venetia—'

'Adele, stop it. There's nothing to worry about.'

But there was.

All day she worried about it. As the hairdresser crimped their hair into geometric waves; as they ate a lunch she didn't want; as she put on her make-up ready for the party; as she was sitting in the taxi, telling Adele not to be nervous, that she looked divine and of course Luc Lieberman would notice her, probably want to have dinner with her; as they walked into the party at the Savoy, and her father introduced them proudly to Marcel Lemoine; as she moved through the party, smiling, struggling to look interested as people talked to her about the book, about her father's publishing house, about her mother and how brilliant and beautiful she was; as she sat at the table in the restaurant that evening, next to Guy Constantine, watching Adele suffering because her mother was sitting next to Luc, watching Luc dancing first with her mother, then with Barty, then with her and finally with Adele; trying to sparkle, trying not to think about it, worrying, worrying: that she hadn't got the curse, and that although it was two days late now, that didn't mean anything at all, but because Adele had got it, it meant a great deal. In fact everything.

'Mam'selle Adele?'

'Yes. Who is it? Oh, Luc, how nice to hear from you. What a lovely party. I do hope Monsieur Lemoine enjoyed it.'

'He did. But for me it could have been even a little better.'

'Oh. I'm sorry to hear that.'

'Well,' his voice was less carefully charming, almost irritable, 'I would have liked to have talked a little more with you. And I had hoped to invite you to luncheon today, with Marcel, but it had been arranged that we visit some of the bookshops. And then there was a meeting with Monsieur Brooke. So – with great regret, I have phoned to say goodbye.'

'Goodbye,' said Adele rather dully.

'I wonder if you will be working for Lyttons more fully, like Mam'selle Miller? She is a most interesting person. I enjoyed talking with her very much.'

Wretched Barty. Why did she always win?

'Well – well, it might be an idea, yes.'

'Good . . . Well, *au revoir*, Mam'selle. It has been extremely pleasant to see you again.'

'*Au revoir*,' said Adele rather weakly.

And was left wondering if he had found it pleasant to see her in the very least.

Luc put down the phone. He had been fascinated by Adele.

Spoilt, difficult, silly as she undoubtedly was, he thought it would be interesting to observe the maturing of Adele, to assist in it indeed. Probably not yet; she was extremely young. And besides, he was running an extremely interesting affair with a young painter, called Colette deLisle, which would clearly not have a happy – or at least a neat – ending, but which for the time being was absorbing most of his sexual and emotional energies. But – later. In a year or two, maybe. Providing of course she didn't make some foolish early marriage . . .

'A flat?' said Celia. 'You want to move into a flat?'

She made it sound as if it was a brothel.

'Yes. Yes, I do. Please.'

'My dear Barty, there's certainly no need to ask my permission. You are over twenty-one, you are earning your own living, you must do what you want. If moving into some lonely flat seems nicer to you than living here in comfort, with everything done for you, then—' Her voice tailed away.

'Well – yes. I mean it does seem nice. Of course it's lovely here and I don't want to move in lots of ways, but I – well, I want to be independent. To feel free.'

That was a mistake.

'I am sorry you feel stifled here. Repressed.'

'Aunt Celia, I don't. It's wonderful here, I'm very happy. It's just that – I'm twenty-one. As you say. I think it's time I made my own way in the world.'

'Well,' said Celia, managing a smile, 'well, you can try it, can't you?

55

Now, where is this – this place you have found? Would I be familiar with the area? Probably not.'

There was no doubt about it. She was being more difficult than usual. Even Kit said she was being a bit crabby and he absolutely adored her.

'Barty wants to move into a flat,' said Celia to her mother. She had gone to see her in the house in Curzon Street where Lady Beckenham spent an increasing amount of time, especially in the winter. 'Extraordinary idea, don't you think?'

'Not at all. An excellent one. She wants to be independent. Most admirable. You should encourage it. That family is made of fine stuff. Look at young Billy, head groom he is now, entirely on his own merits. Mind you, the rest of the family don't seem to be up to much.'

'Well, we don't know that,' said Celia, feeling a perverse desire to defend the Millers.

'Of course we do. They'd come down to Ashingham, from time to time, see Billy, go to your place and visit Barty, if they had any proper feelings for them. Never mind, they've got each other, the two of them. Anyway, sounds a jolly good idea of Barty's to me.'

'I shall – miss her,' said Celia. Lady Beckenham looked at her.

'Of course you will. Not easy for you altogether at the moment, is it? But you have the satisfaction at least of knowing you did the right thing. Pretty girl. Beckenham's not too good,' she added, as if that was a logical sequence to their conversation.

'Really? What's the matter with him?'

'High blood pressure. Does all the wrong things. Eats and drinks too much and he doesn't take enough exercise either. Not since the doctor forbade him to hunt, after he broke his arm last year, and he can't really shoot any more either, makes it dangerous for everyone else. So he just does a bit of fishing and sits around in the library all day, writing letters to *The Times*.'

Writing letters to *The Times* was, rather surprisingly, a passion of Lord Beckenham's. They were only ever on one of three subjects; the abolition of compulsory income tax to be replaced by some other more voluntary, and as he saw it more equitable scheme, the continuing threat from the Hun and, rather unexpectedly, the abolition of capital punishment.

'Poor Papa. Maybe we should collect his letters and publish them. Does he have copies of any of them, do you think?'

'Oh, without doubt. He writes out each one three times, files one, gives the other to me. I just throw them away of course.'

'Well,' said Celia, 'tell him to get them together and send them to me. They're a bit of social history, I expect. They could go into the Biographica list.'

'Well, it would give him something to do, I suppose.'

'I should go home,' said Celia, standing up. 'Apparently Venetia isn't well. Kit told me. She keeps being sick.'

'I hope she's not pregnant,' said the countess, 'most usual reason for young girls being sick that I know. Never considered anything else with the housemaids, I can tell you that.'

Celia looked at her. She felt suddenly sick herself. 'Mama, really. I don't think—'

'Celia,' said her mother. 'You of all people are hardly in a position to be naive about such things.'

Chapter 5

'A little boy!' said Maud. 'Well, that's wonderful. Really wonderful. How exciting. What else does it say?'

'Um – let's see.' Robert looked at the cable. 'Name of Henry. Weighs seven pounds. Mother and baby both well.'

'Henry! That's very – English, isn't it?'

'Well – yes.' He smiled at her. 'What would you expect?'

'Nothing of course. Well – we were right, weren't we? Jamie and me? About them having to get married. About Venetia being pregnant.'

'We still don't—'

'Daddy, really. Girls like Venetia don't get married at four weeks' notice. Anyway, here he is, little Henry, born just under six months later.'

'He – might be premature,' said Robert. He found himself slightly embarrassed by this conversation.

'Oh sure. Weighing seven pounds. Anyway, what does it matter? I think it's wonderful and I'm sure Venetia's madly happy. I'm going to write and congratulate her this minute. And suggest we go over and see them all just as soon as we can fix it. You must want to meet this baby. He's your very first great-nephew!'

Maud ran up to her small sitting room to write to Venetia; they were at the house in Montauk, Long Island, which was, she often said, her favourite place in the world. Her father had built it himself, as he had the mansion on Sutton Place; she loved that too, but Overview, standing high on the dunes above the shore, was particularly dear to her. She loved the sea, simply being near it, loved the salt and wind in the air, the sound of the waves a background to everything; she and Robert often sailed together, and rode along the shore; a weekend spent in New York, especially in the summer, seemed to her a dreadful waste.

58

'Maud says she's coming over. Isn't that heaven?'

Adele smiled dutifully at her sister, said it would indeed be heaven. She found it hard to think in such terms at the moment; she was in a strange mood, not quite depressed, but dull, downhearted. Her sister's sudden propulsion into marriage and motherhood had shaken her; had left her not only jealous, but oddly bereft. She hadn't minded so much about Boy Warwick, because she knew she was still first in Venetia's life and heart. But with the arrival of Henry everything had suddenly changed. For the first time, Venetia told her, very clearly and almost cruelly, when she went to visit her the day after Henry had been born, that now she loved someone more than she loved Adele.

'Something has changed,' she said, lying back on her pillows, shaken by her baptism of pain, 'and you have to know about it. It's important I tell you. I – well, I seem to care more about Henry than I do about anything in the world. Even – even—'

'Me?'

Venetia nodded. 'Yes. Even you.'

'I understand. That's quite all right,' said Adele, almost formally polite. But it wasn't: she went home and wept heavy tears of grief and loss and something close to fear. She felt that the centre of her life had gone, that her heart had been wrenched out of her.

For a while she had dreamed of – in a foolish, almost schoolgirlish way – Luc Lieberman, had remembered the oddly strong feelings he had evoked in her, and had almost imagined him to be in love with her; but a few months later her father mentioned a woman, clearly his mistress, whom he had brought to a literary party in Paris, and hurt and angry – very angry – she had forced him out of her head.

She was in need of, if not marriage, something else; status, a life of her own. And she seemed unable to find it.

The obvious solution, work, with what seemed its inevitable consequence, a life at Lyttons, had no appeal for her. She felt no interest in books or their creation. Of alternative careers, other work, she had no concept. And so she moved fretfully through her days, bored, lonely, shopping and gossip the only outlet for her restless intelligence, wondering quite what was to become of her.

'What's the matter?' said Venetia to her now.

'Matter? Nothing. Don't be silly.'

'Dell! There is. Tell me. Come on.'

'Oh – I don't know. I'm a bit—'

'Lonely?' Venetia's dark eyes were tender, thoughtful. 'I'm sorry, Adele, so sorry.'

'Don't be silly.' She was not to be an object of sympathy; that did not suit her at all. 'I'm absolutely fine. But – well, bored, I suppose, not having a husband and all that sort of thing to occupy me, I want something to do. And I can't think what.'

'Not—'

'Absolutely not,' said Adele firmly.

'Good. I'd hate that. Let's think.' She stroked Henry's small head, smiled down at him; then hauled her attention visibly back to Adele. 'There must be lots of things.'

'There aren't,' said Adele. 'Really.'

'Of course there are. I mean you could do up people's houses, like—'

'Lady Colefax. Yes, well, I suppose so . . .'

'Such fun, she says. Or you could do flowers for people, like Catherine Mann.'

'She's getting married to—'

'I know. Just think, Catherine, a marchioness.'

'Let's not talk about getting married,' said Adele fretfully.

'You started—'

'I know. Anyway—'

'Or look at Constance Spry, she does flowers too. You'd be awfully good at it, I think.'

Adele looked at her and smiled. 'Mummy would be so cross. If I did something like that.'

'I know. All the more—'

'Wouldn't it. Huge rash of Barty-itis. Anyway you've had far more ideas than I have. Thank you.' Adele stood up and kissed her. 'I must go. Important appointment at the hairdresser.'

It couldn't last. It really couldn't. Common sense spoke out most firmly against it. And yet – yet it seemed to be going on for ever. This incredible rise and rise in the stock market, day after day, week after week. There had been no summer lull in Wall Street that year; in June Industrials had risen 52 points, in July another 25. Four to five million shares were traded on the Wall Street stock exchange daily. Endless new stocks were floated almost hourly.

Laurence Elliott, sitting at his desk in the fine building that was Elliotts Bank, on one of the endless stifling mornings that summer, reflected that Americans living in God's own country as they did, with all its great bounty of freedom and opportunity, had lately developed another, more dangerous belief, that of an inalienable right to ever-increasing prosperity.

Laurence wondered what his father and indeed his grandfather, the founder of Elliotts, would have made of it all; what view they would have taken of this heady, greedy era, of the dizzy rise of borrowing both by individuals and corporations, the near hysterical railing against anyone who expressed even a hint of concern over the situation.

No less a person than Chairman Mitchell of the National City Bank had several times expressed anger at anyone who dared to question the rise in brokers' loans – the most common cause for concern, rising at a rate of $400,000,000 a month.

Laurence felt fairly confident that his father at least would have erred on the side of caution; on the other hand he had had a famously cool head, had ridden out the great crisis of 1907 in a joint venture with JP Morgan and several of the other great banks, pouring money into the stock exchange and persuading his customers to leave their money where it was, rather than rushing in panic to get it out. Jonathan Elliott was a legend still on Wall Street, twenty years after his death; he had had more vision, more courage, more capacity for lateral thought than any of his contemporaries. Had he lived, everyone said, there was no limit to what he would have achieved; but he had died of cancer at the height of his powers.

Laurence, absolutely alone in the world, cut off ruthlessly and at his own instigation not only from his brother but from his stepfather and half sister, nurtured a savage and almost obsessive professional ambition; success and the recognition of that success was his prime, indeed his only, concern. To see Elliotts Bank rising ever higher in the financial firmament, to observe his own personal fortune increase hugely year by year, to be marked as one of the most brilliant and ingenious minds on Wall Street, served for him as substitute for family, for friendship – and for love.

He was, at the age of thirty-three, unmarried and unattached. He rejected any effort to be coerced onto charity committees, or into cultural circles, and went out of his way to inform the mothers of debutantes that he intended to remain single until he was at least forty, 'and probably beyond that'.

The only female company he courted was that of clever, married women bored by their husbands, but with no intention of actually leaving them; he had had several affairs with such ladies, and found them entirely satisfactory. Married women, he had been heard frequently to observe, were better in bed than their single sisters. They were less demanding emotionally and absorbed a great deal less time and trouble. 'You can't even buy them much in the way of gifts,' he said in a rare drunken moment (Laurence Elliott liked to remain absolutely in control), 'they can't wear the jewellery, can't use the cigarette cases, can't even display the flowers; the most you can get away with is underwear. And I don't mind buying that.'

Laurence did wonder from time to time if he was incapable of emotional commitment; and if he was, how much it mattered. Generally, he thought not at all; his only experience of love had been what he had felt for his parents, and particularly his mother, and it had failed him totally. He had no wish to risk his heart again. And until such time as he found the ideal woman – and he was increasingly sure that she did not exist – he was not prepared even to consider doing so.

After Adele had gone, Venetia rang for the nurse and told her to take Henry out in his pram. 'It's a lovely day, it will do him good.'

She was still very tired; tired and shocked. Shocked by the experience of childbirth, shocked by the extraordinary change in her own situation, shocked by the violence of her feelings for Henry, shocked perhaps most of all by the way her closeness to her sister had been affected.

She still loved her: far more than she loved anyone else – except Henry. But that there was an exception at all was quite literally astonishing. For the whole of her life, she had felt herself to be part of Adele and Adele part of her; no one else could begin to impinge upon that closeness. Even the intimacy of her relationship with Boy did not do that. Even after their marriage, it was still Adele she thought of every day, in relation to everything that happened to her, everything she did.

When she was back in London after her honeymoon, their daily life of shopping and chatting and giggling did not seem greatly changed and very often if she and Boy were at home for dinner Adele joined them, and then, through the long dreadful hours of Henry's birth, Adele had been with her almost until the end, holding her hand, comforting her, soothing her, sponging her down.

Venetia had refused to have her mother as companion and she and Adele had never been closer. And then, then this astonishing thing had happened and Henry was finally born and put into her arms and she had looked at him, and every other love, every other emotion had simply been cancelled out as if it had never existed.

The other shock had been Boy's behaviour, his attitude towards her. She had learned quite quickly that love, as she understood it, was not what he felt for her. He was fond of her, he found her an amusing companion, a beautiful accessory, a clever hostess, he was very glad, as he frequently told her, that he had married her; but that was about as deep as his emotions ran. As her pregnancy advanced, he was kind to her, but increasingly detached; sexually considerate, affectionate, but often absent not only from the house but also her bed.

She feared that she bored him, for he was formidably clever – indeed, when he was engaged with some intellectual argument with her parents, she found it almost impossible to follow – and so she tried harder to be amusing and better informed, reading the newspapers with some attention for the first time in her life, but it didn't seem to make any difference, he was still frequently out in the evenings, often until very late, and without Adele she would have been lonely.

While she was not exactly bored, and running the large house in Berkeley Square was surprisingly time-consuming, she found it difficult, especially having to direct and discipline staff who were for the most part considerably older than she was. Boy found it necessary to criticise her in this department more than once; mortified, Venetia tried harder and actually turned to, and began to rely a great deal on her mother, who (she now realised) was a surprisingly good housekeeper. Her constant deference to Celia in the matter went a considerable way towards healing the great rift that had opened between them in the period before and immediately after she had married Boy.

Celia had arrived back from her mother's house one terrible evening that Venetia would never forget, walked into her bedroom where she was lying down, struggling against a bout of nausea, without warning or even knocking, and asked her abruptly if she was pregnant. 'And don't lie to me, Venetia, it is absolutely pointless.'

Having established the truth and informed Oliver of it, she had astonished both the twins by telling Venetia there was to be no question of a marriage. 'We will have the pregnancy terminated; I know an excellent man, perfectly safe, and we can put the whole thing behind us.'

Venetia had protested that she had no desire to put the whole thing behind her, that she would not even consider such a thing, 'and nor would Boy if he knew about the baby. He will want to marry me, I know he will.'

'Venetia,' said Celia, 'I very much doubt that Boy will want to marry you. He doesn't love you, and even more important, you don't love him. You may think you do, but I can assure you that you do not. You don't have the faintest idea yet what love means.'

Venetia said she would marry Boy if she wanted to and that her mother couldn't stop her; Celia told her that unfortunately, since Venetia was only eighteen years old, she had every right to do so.

An appalling row followed, to which Oliver was a wretchedly silent witness; at the end of it Venetia, her voice frail with misery, telephoned Boy and asked him to come to the house. 'I've got something terribly important to tell you.'

Boy, who was nobody's fool, arrived with a very clear idea of what the important thing was and shook her dreadfully by implying (although not actually saying so) that he shared her mother's view that it might be better if the pregnancy was terminated while they had time 'to get to know one another better'.

'Of course I love you, my darling,' he said, tenderly wiping her streaming eyes, 'and of course it would be wonderful if we were married, I've thought about it a great deal, naturally, and about how happy we could be, but is a rushed wedding and a pregnancy really the best basis for beginning our life together? I'm not thinking of myself, of course it would be wonderful for me, but – well, you're so very young, you deserve a little more time to enjoy yourself before quite so much – responsibility is settled upon you. I do agree with your mother in some ways, a little diplomacy might be the answer in the immediate future.'

Venetia, shocked into silence, sent him away and spent the rest of the night sobbing in Adele's arms; the next morning, her father came into her room again, pale and exhausted-looking, and asked her what she really wanted. 'I can't bear to see you so unhappy, it breaks my heart.'

Venetia said what she really wanted was to marry Boy 'and I'm sure he wants to marry me, it was just a shock, and Mummy getting hold of him like she did before he came in to me, and telling him what he was to say, you know how she always gets her own way. I can't have this horrible thing done, I can't, I can't just – kill our baby, throw it away, I shall – I shall kill myself if you try and make me.'

Oliver was silent; sensing he was halfway persuaded, Venetia threw herself into his arms, gazed up at him, her great dark eyes beseeching behind her tears.

'Please, Daddy, I know you can make Mummy see sense, you're the only person she ever listens to, and Boy too, please try and do what you can for me.'

Oliver patted her head gently and said he would, told her to try and get some sleep and left her in Adele's charge; Adele, sent to reconnoitre, reported loud shouting from behind their parents' door, 'But I couldn't really hear a word and I was too frightened to stay for long.'

Oliver failed to change Celia's mind; two days passed; dreadful days of tears, recriminations, reproaches. Celia became more implacable by the hour; Oliver was increasingly miserable; Boy stayed away.

Then, on the third day, Lady Beckenham arrived to visit her granddaughters.

'Your mother doesn't know I'm here,' she said, 'but I was concerned for you. Silly girl. We never learn, I'm afraid,' she added rather unexpectedly.

'Who?' said Venetia, blowing her nose. She was very fond of her grandmother.

'Women. We go on and on making the same mistakes, generation after generation. Men as well, I suppose, but it's women who pay the price. What do you want to do?' said Lady Beckenham.

'I want to marry Boy, of course. And he wants to marry me. He said so,' she added, editing the truth with a skill that half her father's staff might have envied.

Lady Beckenham looked at her. 'I'm not at all sure he'd make you a very good husband. His father is a disgrace, the mother is no better, there's no real class there, and the money's new.'

'I know all that. And I don't care about class and new money and all that sort of thing.'

'Well, you should do. It's very important. Probably why your mother is so against this marriage.'

'No,' said Venetia, 'she says I'm too young and I don't know what I'm doing and she knows Boy isn't the right husband for me.'

Lady Beckenham looked at her, and then, suddenly and most unexpectedly, burst into her rather loud laugh.

'Well,' she said, 'that's rich, I must say. Very rich. Coming from your mother. Dear, oh dear.'

'What do you mean?' said Venetia.

'Oh – you'll find out one day, no doubt. I don't know what to think, Venetia, about all this. What would be best. I might have a word with young Warwick myself.'

'Oh please don't,' said Venetia, alarmed.

'Why ever not? I've known him all of his life. And his father. Dreadful man, bought his title you know. All that nonsense about services to his country is just so much poppycock. Services to the government's coffers rather more like it. He used to play cards with Beckenham, always cheated, and then tried to get out of paying his debts. Tried to diddle old Bertie Dunraven, who really couldn't afford it, out of two thousand pounds. Disgraceful, with all that money. Not many people know that of course.' She bent and kissed her. 'Now you try and get some rest. You look dreadful. Adele, go and make her some hot milk.'

When she had gone, Adele looked at Venetia. 'What was all that about?'

'What?'

'You know, all that about it being rich coming from Mummy stuff.'

'I don't know,' said Venetia, wearily. 'Oh God, I think I'm going to be sick again. Adele, could I have some water?'

After she had brought in the jug of iced water, Adele went out of the room and stood for a while on the landing, looking thoughtfully at her mother's study door. Then she took a deep breath and went in.

Ten minutes later, she hurtled into the twins' sitting room.

'Venetia, you won't believe – you just won't believe this.'

Venetia looked at her wearily. 'What is it?'

Adele was holding a large, parchment envelope; she started pulling out the contents. 'Just – just look at these. And think. About what Grandmama said. Mummy and Daddy's wedding certificate. See. And here, look, Giles's birth certificate. Dated just six months later. What about that?'

Venetia looked at her sister, colour in her face for the first time for days.

'Well,' was all she said. 'Just wait till she gets home, that's all I can say.'

Three days later, *The Times* and the *Telegraph* had announced the forthcoming marriage of Venetia, daughter of Lady Celia and Mr Oliver Lytton, and Mr Charles Henry Warwick, eldest son of Sir Reginald Warwick.

But how awful, Venetia thought almost sadly now, if her mother had indeed been right and she should not have married Boy at all. Which, in her most secret self, she was beginning to fear. Since Henry's birth, his absences from home had increased; he appeared very pleased with his son, visited him and Venetia several times daily – but that was what it felt like, she realised: a visit. After which he was inclined to disappear for several hours – not only from the room but the house.

She had tried taxing him with it, but he was infuriatingly and charmingly vague, insisting he was merely trying to give her time to recover; she felt frustrated, enraged even, but it was impossible to make any impression on his smooth, bland surface. She felt lonely and miserable much of the time, still too weak to re-enter the real world, go out, have fun, organise the life she was supposed to share with Boy; Adele was once again her main companion.

Adele, whom she had hurt so badly, she knew, and who had forgiven her so bravely and generously. Then she thought of Henry, the new beloved, with his dark hair and dark eyes, and the wobbly, difficult smile that he was beginning to master when he gazed up from her arms and her heart turned over and she knew that whatever Boy might not feel for her, and however unhappy and lonely Adele might be also, it was worth it. Anything was worth having Henry. Anything at all.

'There's trouble on the way. I mean really on the way. Getting close.' Dudley 'Duke' Carlisle sat back in his chair and looked at Laurence. They were lunching at the Yale Club, that bastion of tradition and privilege near Grand Central station; Duke was rather fond of Laurence. Twenty years his senior and with three wives to his credit, he was a stockbroker; richer by the day as well as being in possession of a vast private fortune, he had met Laurence at a Wall Street function and invited him to a reception at his recently purchased Fifth Avenue mansion, only a few hundred yards from Elliott House, where Laurence lived alone and in equal splendour. His patrician air and old-money Washington accent belied a total greed and ruthlessness more suited to a friend of Mr Al Capone than a member of the East Hampton golf club. His present wife Leila, an ice-cool blonde, had been rather taken with Laurence and had gone so far as to make the fact plain, but Laurence knew which of the Carlisles was of more value to him and had made it equally plain that he was not interested.

'You mean more than a recession?' said Laurence.

'I do. A crash, and a huge one. It's inevitable, the overheating is too great. The financial press is predicting it now as well. I had dinner with the editor of the *Commercial and Financial Chronicle* last night. He says Wall Street has taken leave of its senses.'

'Interesting. And – what would your advice be?' said Laurence.

'Sell, obviously. But quietly, day by day. Don't want to set any panics in motion. It could be, of course' – he looked at Laurence – 'a time when selling short should be considered.'

'Indeed? Well, I would obviously consider it. I had thought also – perhaps you could give me your reaction to this – that one might be a little, shall we say, ahead of the financial trend. When the collapse does actually begin. Offer to buy certain stock from certain clients at a fair price. To save them from serious difficulty.'

Duke Carlisle looked at him intently for a moment. Then he smiled. 'While supporting that stock temporarily yourself for a day or two? Inflating its price, exceeding your own estimates? So that the final price is – a little unfortunately for your client – higher than the one you paid him?'

'Exactly.'

'Very clever. Worthy of both your father and your grandfather, if I might say so.'

'Thank you.'

'And move your own money out of the country, Laurence. Fast.'

'I have already done that, to a large extent.'

Barty thought she had never been so happy. She had a job she loved, the independence she had craved, a home of her own – and now she had a friend in London, a true friend of her own age who was absolutely nothing to do with the Lyttons, and who Barty could claim as her very own. She was called Abigail Clarence and she lived in another flat in another house in Russell Square. Barty had entered her life by way of a collision of her bicycle and Abigail's as they both arrived home from work; Abbie was extremely clever and rather beautiful in an unconventional way; she had straight dark brown hair, cut into a Dora Carrington bob – 'I actually modelled it on Christopher Robin' – very large green eyes, and a rather hawk-like nose which somehow suited her high cheekbones and angular jaw. Her mouth was very wide, and when she laughed, revealed surprisingly perfect teeth; she was tall and rather athletically built and spent many of her weekends exploring the home counties on her bicycle.

She was the freest spirit Barty had ever encountered, astonishingly unencumbered by prejudice of any kind, class, intellectual, even racial.

Abbie was also a great advocate of sexual freedom; 'If everyone slept with everyone they wanted to, it would free women from the tyranny of marriage, and probably improve marriage altogether. After all, there's much more to it than sex; my way people would concentrate on the other, more important things. Women don't get all fussed if their husbands eat somewhere other than at home, why should it be any different with sex?' Barty felt this was a slightly impractical theory, but she didn't say so.

Abbie was the daughter of two Fabians – 'and don't ever let anyone tell you they're proper socialists, Barty, they absolutely are not. Obsessed with class, all of them' – and it was through this revelation that Barty's own history had come out. Not everyone, as Abbie pointed out, her green eyes dancing with amusement, knew about one of the most famous Fabian women of them all, Maud Pember Reeves; 'Come on, Barty, tell. I know there's more to you than meets the eye.'

And reluctantly, her head bowed with the old mortification, not meeting Abbie's eye from the beginning of the story to the end, Barty told. When she had finished, Abbie hugged her.

'I cannot believe,' she said, 'that you've come through all that and stayed so – so normal. Being practically stolen from your mother by some wicked lady bountiful—'

'She isn't wicked,' Barty protested, 'she meant it for the best.'

'They all do. It was wicked just the same. How terrible for you. Well done, old thing. Well done.'

Barty felt a sudden and unaccountable need to defend Celia. 'She was – very, very good to me, you know. My mother adored her. And Aunt Celia—'

'Is that what you had to call her?'

'Well – yes. Anyway, Aunt Celia took care of my mother in lots of ways: paid for doctors and so on, especially at the end of her life when she was so ill, arranged for me to go and visit them all the time.'

'Oh, how kind,' said Abbie, her voice sharp with malice.

'It was,' said Barty again. 'And if Lady Beckenham, that's Aunt Celia's mother, hadn't taken care of Billy, my brother, given him a job in her stables, no, don't look like that, he'd be out on a mat now, begging, like all the other poor wretches who came home without limbs. And I love Wol, that's Mr Lytton. He was so kind to me. So don't judge them all too harshly.'

'I don't,' said Abbie, 'not really. I can see they meant well. And OK, in lots of ways, you did benefit. St Paul's and so on. Even so, most people just would not have survived that. Bully for you, getting out too. Into the flat. Bet Lady Bountiful didn't like that.'

'No, she didn't. But only in a nice way, she said she'd miss me.'

'I expect she does. I would. Fancy her being sent to your mother by dear old Mrs P. R. I don't think that study of hers she presented to the government did any good at all, you know. However many statistics about poor families it contained. Still, a good effort. My parents adore her.'

'Aunt Celia was sort of expelled from the Fabians,' said Barty, 'for what she did to me.'

'I bet she was,' said Abbie.

Abbie was a teacher; the best school she had been able to get was a rather prim little girls' school in Kensington, but her dream was to become the headmistress of a large intellectual girls' school like the City of London, where she had been educated, and to instil in her pupils her dreams and beliefs about equal rights for women, which included not just the vote, but equal work opportunities with men and, even more incredible, equal salaries.

'One day, the decision of a woman not to marry but to pursue a career of her choice, in medicine, let's say, or at the bar, won't earn her derision, or worse still, pity, but admiration and a life of freedom and fulfilment. And if she does marry and have children, she will continue with her career, and continue to compete with her husband in the outside world. Doesn't that sound wonderful to you?'

Barty said slightly apologetically that it did, but that she had grown up with just exactly such a role model; 'And don't look like that, Abbie, I do happen to know she battled every inch of the way. It really wasn't easy for her.'

Defending Celia was a novel situation for Barty; so novel indeed that when she went into Lyttons the next morning she found herself looking at Celia with new and almost indulgent eyes. Only hearing her contemptuous dismissal of an idea of Giles's for Lyttons to endow a couple of scholarships restored her more usual view of her. So upset was she for him that she reversed her refusal to attend a family dinner at Cheyne Walk that night for Venetia and Boy, to mark the arrival of Henry. She knew her presence would be hugely comforting to Giles; he told her so repeatedly that he missed her, and that he found Lytton life unbearable without her, that she had ceased to find it flattering and found it irritating instead. Nevertheless, she was extremely fond of him; and told herself that attending the dinner would really do her no harm. Sebastian and Pandora were coming, and she adored them both; especially Pandora. She so admired her independence, her refusal to become a chattel; her insistence on keeping her house in Oxford, so that she could carry on with her job at the Bodleian, and that they share their time between Oxford and London seemed to Barty the most splendid thing.

*

Celia had not failed to notice Venetia's low spirits after Henry's birth; she grieved for her daughter; the fact that her instincts over the marriage had been proved right was absolutely no consolation. She longed to intervene, to speak to Boy, to discuss it openly with Venetia; Oliver, in a spirit of rare authority, forbade it.

'It is nothing to do with you, what goes on within that marriage; it is Venetia's, and she must cope with it however she sees fit.'

Celia said that Venetia was absolutely unable to cope with it and that she was not only inexperienced, but surprisingly timid; Oliver looked at her and smiled.

'You were inexperienced once, my dear, although most assuredly not timid; you handled your marriage in your own way. She must learn to do the same.'

'Our marriage, Oliver,' said Celia, 'not mine. And we handled it together.'

'If you say so, Celia,' said Oliver. 'I seem to remember some fairly uncompromising decisions. Anyway, our marriage is not under discussion. To interfere with Venetia's would be not only unwise, but destructive. Give her time; she is only nineteen. And quite clever really; I think when she matures she will be more than a match for Boy. He is extremely selfish, self-obsessed almost; that tends to lead to a certain blindness as to what is actually going on.'

Celia stared at him; he smiled back at her, the sweet, rather blank smile with which he ended discussions which he no longer wished to pursue. She knew what he was referring to; and it was safer left where it was, in their past, which however stormy and difficult, had at least led them safely to where they stood now – a couple, much admired and revered, long married, clearly happy. Such images worked their own magic, had the power to rewrite history; they were fractured at great peril.

'You're so very clever, Oliver,' she said, and went over to kiss him.

Boy was at his most charming that evening, smiling, chatting easily, flattering everyone, enquiring after Lyttons, discussing new books and authors with Celia – 'I thought Rosamund Lehmann's was one of the most interesting of the season, and as for Barbara Cartland, such fun and so pretty' – and Giles's golf, a new passion, rather than his job at Lyttons. 'I'll give you a game, old boy. Next Saturday, if you're free. And if my wife can spare me, of course.'

'And if I said I couldn't?' said Venetia. Her tone was light, but her eyes were hard; Boy blew her a kiss across the table.

'Then of course I wouldn't play.'

'You should go too, Venetia,' said Pandora, 'it's a lovely game, I used to play a little.'

'Now that is a marvellous idea,' said Boy, 'I'd like that so much, darling. Sadly though, no ladies on the course on Saturday.'

'Why not?' said Barty innocently.

'Barty, darling, the ladies can play any time. Saturday is for the boys. They wait all week for the chance.'

'Only the ones who work, surely?' said Barty, sweeter still. My God, thought Celia, she's developing claws. Well done.

Boy smiled at Barty. 'Well – yes, of course,' he said lightly. 'But it means us slothful individuals have more people to play with.'

'Boy's not slothful,' said Venetia quickly, 'he's very busy, managing his affairs and the gallery he has a share in in Cork Street, various charitable committees, boards he's on—'

'My darling, you're so sweet,' said Boy. 'I fear Barty has a point. I don't work very hard at the moment. Disgraceful, is it not, for a young man of today?'

'I have a friend who thinks that everybody should work, whatever their sex,' said Barty, 'and that in another generation they will. She thinks work is what gives life its purpose and gives us our individual dignity. Especially women.'

'Indeed!' said Boy. 'Well, it's an interesting view. Most interesting. I should like to meet your friend. Discuss her ideas. Anyway, I do have plans for myself—'

'Really?' said Celia. 'Do tell us.'

'Well, my father can't go on for ever. It was always understood I would move into the business when he was ready for me. I've been spending an increasing amount of time there recently, haven't I, Venetia?'

'Yes,' said Venetia, flushing, 'yes, of course.'

That was mean, Celia thought, that was unforgivable. To have presented her with that as an excuse for his absences in retrospect, announced it without warning; she looked at him now, steely-eyed herself.

'I'm very surprised not to have heard more about that,' she said. 'I saw your father only the other day, at a dinner. He didn't mention it.'

'Naturally not,' said Boy. 'He is a little – mortified by it. By not being able to carry the entire firm on his own slightly less young shoulders. Something which you and Oliver must surely have thought about yourself, Lady Celia? So wise to involve Giles in good time.'

Game, set and match to Boy, thought Barty: beastly man. She had no great love for Venetia; she had suffered too much at her pretty little hands. But she deserved better than this. She could bear it no longer, she felt Venetia's humiliation and it hurt; she stood up, smiled apologetically round the table. 'I'm terribly sorry, but I think I ought to go. I've got to get up early in the morning, lots of work to do, would you excuse me?'

'Of course,' said Oliver. 'We mustn't keep you. Do you have your car?'

'No, I came from Lyttons with Giles—'

'I'll drive you home,' said Giles. 'I'd like to.'

He had been quiet, almost morose, during the evening; refusing to be drawn even by Boy's attempts to charm him. Their friendship had virtually foundered on Giles's discovery of Venetia's pregnancy. Quite apart from a sense of outrage that Boy could have behaved so badly, he felt a greater one that his parents were so apparently willing to accept the situation.

'Absolutely no need,' said Celia now, smooth as ice, 'we don't want the whole party disintegrating. Daniels will take Barty, he's not busy. Goodnight, my dear.'

Celia lifted her cheek to be kissed. If I was Giles, Barty thought, kissing her dutifully, she'd be asking me what extra work, why, did I need help with it; in spite of her place in the sun at Lyttons, she felt sad for him.

It was a novel sensation to be in a happier situation than the family, but she seemed to be; oddly, she really didn't enjoy it. She supposed she must actually love them all more than she had thought. And wondered if she should take up Boy's suggestion that he meet Abbie: that would really be fun. She would make very short work of him.

Chapter 6

Sebastian was very, very angry. Pandora looked at him, dark, brooding, hostile, hunched over the morning papers, speaking only in monosyllables, refusing egg, bacon, toast, coffee even, and felt a pang of first remorse and then irritation in return.

It was an outrageous way for him to react to what she had told him. Childish, absurd, spoilt behaviour. But then he *was* childish, absurd and spoilt. Those things were all part of what she loved about him: uncomfortable as they were.

'Sebastian—'

'Not now, Pandora. I'm reading.'

'Well, I'm very sorry,' she said, 'to have interrupted you. But—'

'Pandora—'

'Oh really!' She was silent. They had never had a row. Unless you counted the odd argument over a house, a garden, where they should spend Christmas. She didn't know how to cope with it.

He looked up at her and scowled. 'I think I'll go out. For a walk.'

'Fine, I'm going to work.'

'Don't forget I'm lecturing tonight. In London.'

'I hadn't forgotten.' She looked at him, absorbing his hostile eyes. 'I think I won't come,' she said.

He stared at her. Then he said, 'Oh, for Christ's sake!' And got up and left the house, slamming the door behind him.

Pandora, half amused, half upset, went to work; he would appear, she was sure, at lunchtime, his arms full of flowers, apologising, telling her he loved her, that he had been wrong. He didn't. The afternoon ended; surely when she got home he would be there. Waiting for her, asking her to come to London with him. He wasn't. There wasn't even a note. Well, he would phone; he would arrive in London, stricken with guilt, would ring to say he was sorry, that he loved her.

She ate supper, listened to the wireless, read a book; no phone call came. She had a bath, then went to bed. She was beginning to worry now. At the silence. And of course at his reaction. So angry, so violently angry. As if she had done something terribly wrong.

Which of course, of course she hadn't. She had simply told him. Thinking he would be pleased. As pleased as she was. That she was going to have – that they were going to have – a baby.

'He is just heaven! Heaven,' said Maud. 'Truly the most beautiful little boy I ever saw. May I hold him?'

'Of course you may' Venetia smiled at her. The quickest way to her heart these days was through Henry. 'I hope he isn't sick or anything down you. He's just had a feed and – oh God, Maud, I'm sorry.'

'Don't worry!' Maud smiled, mopped at her dress with the napkin Venetia passed her. 'All babies do it, I'm told.'

Venetia looked at her, as she sat there, nursing Henry. She wasn't exactly beautiful, but she was terribly attractive with her red hair and green eyes, and her figure was wonderful, so tall and slim, yet with a full bosom. Her skin was exquisite, very pale, almost translucent, lightly freckled, and she had the most beautiful hands, very white and slender. She gave Henry one of her long fingers to hold; he gripped it tightly in his chubby fist and smiled at her.

'There now. I have a friend for life. Oh, it's so good to be here, Venetia. I should have come earlier.'

'How was your trip?'

'Quite wonderful. I do love those liners. I remember the first time Daddy brought me over when I was tiny and I thought I was in a palace floating on the sea. The terribly grand dining room, and the orchestra playing through dinner, and the steam room – goodness, I love the steam room – and – well, it was all just marvellous.'

'Did your father enjoy it?'

'Yes, but he always gets so seasick, poor Daddy. He said to tell you he'd be round, probably tomorrow, when he's recovered. But I couldn't wait. Adele said to tell you she'd be here by teatime. And your darling little brother, he is just so special, he said he would be coming to tea as well. Adele is shopping or something.'

'Shopping, I expect,' said Venetia. 'She's a little bored, I'm afraid. And lonely. We miss each other.'

'I can see she must miss you,' said Maud, 'but I wouldn't have expected you to miss her.'

'Of course I do,' said Venetia. It always astonished her that people didn't understand about twins. 'She's much more important to me than anyone. Except Henry of course.'

'Well, and your handsome husband, I imagine. Goodness, he is handsome, Venetia. Adele showed me the wedding photographs.'

'Yes, he is,' said Venetia. 'Very handsome.'

'Not as handsome as Giles, though.'

'Giles! You think Giles is handsome?'

'Terribly, yes. He's very like your mother, I suppose. Those wonderful dark eyes, and marvellous nose. And he's so charming and – and English.'

'You always did have a soft spot for him, didn't you? I'd forgotten,' said Venetia. 'When you were nine or whatever, you said you were going to marry him.'

'I did? Well, sadly, of course, I can't, as he's my cousin. In America that's not allowed. This house is superb, Venetia, I love it. Who did it for you? The interior, that is.'

'Gerald Wellesley.'

'I thought so. I recognised his style. All that silver leaf, so terribly chic. How clever of you to choose him.'

'Maud, how very well-informed you are,' said Venetia, laughing. 'I'm amazed you've heard of him.'

'Well, of course. You forget I aim to be an architect.'

'Yes, I did forget. Oh, hallo, Adele, how lovely to see you. Isn't it heaven to have Maud here?'

'Heaven,' said Adele, kissing her sister. 'Good afternoon, Henry, how are you today? Venetia, I've bought us the most divine blouses from Woollands. Silk and very long. You'll love them. They were just too much to resist.'

'Feeling better?' said Oliver, looking up at his brother as he came into the drawing room.

'Much, thank you. God, it's a curse, this thing. It really does cast a blight on visits here. It wasn't even especially rough.'

'Soon you'll be able to fly,' said Celia. 'Look at Mr Hinkler, flying to Australia. In fifteen days! It's amazing, however long would that take by ship, Oliver?'

'Six or seven weeks at least,' said Oliver. 'Yes, I'm sure there will be commercial flights to America before long, Robert. Tea? Or brandy?'

'Tea please,' said Robert. 'Now tell me, how are things at Lyttons?'

'Pretty good, I'd say,' said Oliver. 'Our own list is very lively, we seem to manage to keep up a pretty broad base. Funnily enough,

76

the educational books are providing a very solid foundation, aren't they, Celia?'

'Yes,' said Celia shortly. She didn't like the rather mundane list of school certificate literature, atlases and logarithmic tables; she had put Giles in charge and he managed it very competently. Inevitably this did not please her either, confirming her view of him as it did as a dull, uninspired editor.

'We're getting rather a lot of competition from Germany,' said Oliver. 'They are the new force out there all over the world. Ironic, really.'

'I hear from Felicity that the New York office is doing well.'

'Yes, indeed. Stuart Bailey is a very clever young man. But then everything in America is doing well, isn't it? This boom you're enjoying, quite extraordinary. I think I would feel a little cautious if I were you. Things are very hard here still, you know, we have dreadful unemployment, and that was triggered many years ago by our own post-war boom and the overheating of the economy.'

'Of course. But that was surely a direct result of the war,' said Robert, 'the sudden release of all those wartime bonus shares and so on. We've had years of stability and growth now. I think things will steady. The stock market can't go on rising like this, of course, but I feel reasonably confident there won't be a serious problem.'

'Is that the generally held view?'

'Well – yes, it is. There are a few scaremongers, but—'

'Well, we've had a few tremors here, you know.'

'What does your stepson think? From his rather privileged position on Wall Street?' said Celia.

'I have no idea,' said Robert. 'Laurence and I are still hardly on speaking terms. He'll never forgive me for marrying his mother and there's nothing I can do to change that. Jamie is a great joy to me, and I have my darling Maud. We're a pretty happy little family. Anyway, my own business is certainly booming. Slightly against the trend, I must admit but – well, John and I feel pretty confident.'

'How is he? And Felicity? Still the perfect wife, no doubt,' said Celia. There was a new edge to her voice.

'Oh, both pretty well. Her poetry sells to all sorts of people, and she's always giving readings to ladies' luncheon circles and so on.'

'How very satisfying for her,' said Celia. 'It must be nice for her to have an interest.'

'I think it's a little more than an interest,' said Robert, 'she's really rather successful. She won some award last week—'

'Oh, those poetry awards,' said Celia, 'so many of them, there seems to me to be one every week—'

'Celia,' said Oliver mildly, 'Felicity has done wonderfully well and we shouldn't begrudge her her success.'

'Of course I don't begrudge it,' said Celia. 'I discovered Felicity and her poetry, for heaven's sake, Oliver.'

'Indeed you did,' said Robert, 'and she has never forgotten it. Young Kyle is doing awfully well, incidentally. A senior editor now at Doubledays, really considered a great talent. John and Felicity have never forgotten what you did for him, getting him that first job. And neither has he, I might add.'

'Good Lord,' said Oliver, 'it was only a letter I wrote as I recall.'

'Well, there are letters and letters,' said Robert. 'Anyway, Felicity constantly says she wishes you would both come over to New York so that she could offer you some real hospitality.'

'Oh, I think it's far better for Oliver to go to New York on his own,' said Celia. 'We can't both leave Lyttons London at the same time after all.'

'Not even with LM there? And Giles, of course. How is he doing? He seems very competent to me.'

'I would like to agree with you,' said Celia with a sigh, 'but I'm afraid that, professionally, Giles is a disappointment. Unlike young Mr Brewer. He has no real – vision. No feeling for the creative side of the business. Wouldn't you agree, Oliver?'

'You know it is more than my life is worth to disagree with you, Celia,' said Oliver. 'Over anything.' His tone was light, but his blue eyes meeting hers were cold and very hard.

'My darling, please, please forgive me. I'm so desperately sorry. To have behaved like that, like an appalling spoilt child – I can't quite believe it of myself.'

'Well,' said Pandora coolly, 'that was exactly how it seemed. Really, Sebastian! Anyone would have thought I'd told you I was taking a lover.'

'But darling, darling Pandora, that's what it felt like. In a way. Oh, don't look at me like that, I'm trying so hard to be – good.'

'Well, I think you should try a bit harder. And you could start by getting me some warm milk. Expectant mothers need a lot of milk. And a lot of care.'

'Of course. And I didn't even ask you how you felt. Oh God, darling, how do you feel?'

'I feel fine,' said Pandora cheerfully. 'A bit tired, but nothing worse than that. Now go and fetch the milk and then perhaps we can talk about it sensibly.'

'I am trying to be sensible. I really am,' said Sebastian, settling on the bed beside her, his hands playing tenderly with her long golden-brown hair. She had arrived home from the library at teatime to find him waiting for her with an enormous bouquet of white roses, a bowed head, and an expression of dramatic contrition that would have put Henry Irving to shame. She had greeted him rather coldly and gone upstairs to have a bath and to lie down on their bed; he had come in to see her, having first knocked tentatively on the door.

'Well, you'd better try harder,' said Pandora. 'I cannot understand you, Sebastian. Most husbands are delighted when their wives tell them they're expecting.'

'I'm not most husbands,' said Sebastian, 'and please don't use that horrible expression.'

'Well, what am I to use? In the club? Preggers? That's what the twins call it.'

'They're all horrible expressions. The only one I can bear is the French. *Enceinte*, that has a passably attractive ring to it.'

'Oh, very well. I shall be *enceinte*. Now try to explain to me why you are so upset.'

'I don't want to share you,' said Sebastian simply. 'I love you too much. I want you all to myself, as you have been for the past year, I don't want you distracted, half your mind on someone else. I know it's foolish, but I can't help it. I'm sure I shall get used to the idea and learn to love the little sprog, but at the moment I just feel so afraid of losing you.'

'But, Sebastian, how can you lose me to a baby? This is your baby. Well, yours and mine, we've made it together.'

'Darling, I know. And I'm sure it will be beautiful and fascinating and all those things, although I must say I do find babies very unattractive. But they improve with time, I do admit that.'

'So, then, what—'

'It's because we agreed we wouldn't have any children. Well, not for a long time. Because we wanted to be together. Alone together, in our own – what shall I call it? – our own personal world. Pandora, ever since I met you, I haven't wanted to see anyone else, talk to anyone else, be with anyone else. I haven't even begun to discover enough about you. Every day still, I learn more and I love more about you. And now, it seems, I have to share you. With a baby.'

'Well, I'm sorry, Sebastian. I promise you I didn't do anything to scupper our birth control arrangements on purpose. If that was what you thought.'

'Of course not. Of course I didn't. But—'

'And I seem to remember you playing a very active role in the baby's creation. I even think I know when it was. That night in London, after the opera. After *Bohème*. I remember lying there, after you had gone to sleep, hearing *O care mio* in my head, thinking that it had been perfect, loving you was perfect, making love had just been perfect, more perfect even than usual. Darling, please try to be pleased.'

'I will try,' he said, leaning over, kissing her, 'I will try very hard. I think I felt just a tiny sliver of being pleased then, actually. And I remember *Bohème* and afterwards too. Anyway, the important thing now is to look after you. What do we have to do to keep you well and strong? I suppose now you really must give up work. That will be nice at least, we can have lunch together every day—'

'I'm not sure I want to have lunch together every day,' said Pandora, laughing. 'I like to read over lunch. Read uninterrupted,' she added, as he opened his mouth to argue. 'But yes, the doctor did say I should give up work. I'm quite old to be having a first baby. I have to get lots of rest. Eat lots of fresh vegetables, all that sort of thing—'

'When is it – going to be born?' he asked.

'Oh – May. Early May, the doctor thought. Now, I don't think we should tell anyone yet, do you? I'd rather keep it our secret. Just for now. I rather dread all the fuss. And I dread to think what Celia will have to say about it.'

'Yes,' said Sebastian, and his face was oddly sombre, 'yes, I think I rather dread that too.'

'Hallo, Barty. Remember me?'

Maud stood in the doorway of Barty's small office, smiling. Barty smiled back. She had always liked Maud.

'Yes, of course. How nice to see you.'

'Nice to see you too. Can I come in a minute, or are you too busy?'

'Well—' Barty hesitated; she was extremely busy.

'It's OK,' said Maud, recognising the hesitation, 'I'll come back.'

'Oh – I feel awful now. It's just that I am a bit pressed. I'll be all right later.'

'Don't worry about it. Listen, Giles and I are having a spot of lunch. Why don't you join us?'

'I can't. Really. I'm sorry. But after work I could – we could have a hot chocolate or something. If you weren't busy.'

Maud smiled. 'I'm not busy. And hot chocolate sounds just fine. I love it. Where do we get it?'

'The Corner House down the road. Ask Giles if he'd like to join us.'

'I will.'

And the hot chocolate became supper at the Corner House and then the three of them went to the pictures, which Maud called the movies, and saw *Broadway Melody* which had won the Academy Award that year, and after that they all went back to Barty's flat which Maud said she was just dying to see and then Abbie joined them for more hot chocolate and took a great fancy to Maud and they all talked for what seemed like hours until Maud jumped and said goodness, look at the time and that they really should be getting back to Cheyne Walk.

'Daddy still thinks I'm about four and a half,' and Giles told her she was lucky and that his mother thought he was nearer two.

'You should have parents like mine,' said Abbie. 'They hardly remember I exist, half the time.'

The next morning, after Giles had gone, Robert was mildly reproachful with Maud: 'What on earth were you doing until nearly midnight?'

'Talking,' said Maud, 'with Giles and Barty.'

'All evening?'

'No, of course not. We went to the movies and then we went back to Barty's apartment. It's so nice there, very small, but she's made it look just wonderful. I loved it and so did Giles.'

'What did Giles love?' said Celia, who had walked into the room.

'Barty's apartment. Pardon me, her flat. He says he goes there quite often after work, to have a chat and a hot chocolate. My goodness, that girl can make good chocolate.'

'Since Giles sees Barty all day long I'm surprised he feels the need to talk to her in the evening as well,' said Celia.

'Well, he does. They are obviously just very good friends,' said Maud. 'And you can't ever have enough time to chat to your friends. And there was this darling girl called Abbie there, Barty's best friend, she was just so nice, I expect you've met her?'

'Actually no,' said Celia. 'And some of us have to manage without time to chat. Now I must go, it's late and I have the most dreadful day ahead. I'll see you both this evening. Or are you disappearing with

Barty again, Maud? Of course you must do exactly what you like, but—'

'Aunt Celia, I'll be here.'

When Celia had gone, Maud looked at her father. 'I think I boobed there,' she said. 'I don't think I should have told her Giles went to Barty's apartment.'

'Oh, I don't see why not. I'm sure it's perfectly innocent,' said Robert easily. 'They're practically brother and sister after all.'

'Not quite,' said Maud consideringly. 'In fact, not at all. And I would say, Daddy, that what Giles feels for Barty is not very brotherly at all. He clearly adores her. Whatever she does, his eyes follow her.'

'You've been reading too many romantic novels,' said Robert laughing. 'And does she reciprocate this adoration, do you think?'

'I don't read romantic novels,' said Maud indignantly. 'And no, I don't think she does. He really is just a brother to her. And anyway, Barty's energies are all to do with her career. She is hugely ambitious, you know. I like her so very much. She's a completely original person.'

'I do agree she is very charming,' said Robert. 'Charming and interesting. Pretty, too. And if Giles is in love with her I can see why. However, all other things being equal, I think it would be better if you were mistaken.'

'I'll see you this evening then,' said Maud.

'Sebastian,' said Celia, her voice meltingly agreeable down the telephone line, 'I wonder if you would be kind enough to come in some time in the next few days. We really need to discuss the Christmas promotions for *Meridian Times Ten;* usually we've done it much earlier than this, as you know. It is really rather inconvenient your being in Oxford so much.'

'Well, I'm sorry if it inconveniences you, Celia,' said Sebastian. He sounded irritable. 'Perhaps we should consider moving more permanently to London to suit you.'

'Perhaps you should.'

'I wasn't entirely serious. Pandora loves her house and her job, as you very well know. Anyway, I'll see what I can do about coming up. It's a little difficult this week.'

He didn't want to leave Pandora; she had begun to feel less well, nauseous and terribly tired.

'Well, shall we proceed without you?' said Celia.

'Absolutely not. No.'

'Well, in that case' – her voice was less agreeable now – 'you're going to have to come down. I'm sorry. Is there some kind of difficulty?'

'No. No, of course not. It's just that Pandora is – well, having some problems and—'

'Problems? What kind of problems?'

'Oh – professional ones, of course.' God, he wished it were true, that the problems Pandora had were truly so simple, so well-contained.

'I'm sorry to hear that. They must be quite serious, if you feel it incumbent upon you to put them before your own work.'

'They aren't very serious, Celia,' said Sebastian, keeping his voice level with a considerable effort, 'but for the next few days, I want to be here with her. I'm sorry. Good morning to you.'

Later that afternoon, a letter arrived for Celia by hand from Foyles in the Charing Cross Road; would Sebastian like to be guest of honour at one of their famous literary luncheons in November? And could Lady Celia let them have an answer within twenty-four hours if possible . . .

Pandora was half asleep by the fire when the telephone rang; Sebastian had gone out to buy some of the salmon that was the only thing she could consider eating for supper. Slightly confused, she sat on the stairs, rubbing her eyes and yawning; it was Celia.

'Pandora? It's Celia. How are you? I'm extremely sorry to hear of your problems.'

'My – problems?' Had Sebastian told Celia about the baby?

'Yes. Sebastian is clearly very worried about you.' Obviously he had.

'Oh, really?' she said carefully.

'Yes. Refusing to come to London for what is really a very important meeting. Very loyal of course, but – well, is he there?'

'No, Celia, I'm afraid he's not just at the moment. He's—'

'Well, ask him to telephone me, would you please? Urgently. Tell him there's another matter that I need to talk to him about.'

Pandora tried to tell herself that Celia did not mean to be rude, that as Sebastian's publisher and editor she did have a genuine and regular need to communicate with him, and said that of course she would tell Sebastian. 'Would you like to be more explicit about whatever it is? So that I can give him an intelligent-sounding message?'

'Oh good heavens, no. Much too complicated. Just pass that on, would you? And I do wish you well with your – problem.'

'Celia.' Pandora heard her voice growing as cool as Celia's own, and felt a flash of anger with Sebastian, not only for telling Celia when they had agreed they would not, but for the way in which he had done so. 'Celia, whatever Sebastian may feel about the matter, I don't think having a baby should be described in quite such terms.'

There was an absolute silence from the other end of the line; then, 'A – baby?' said Celia. 'You're having a baby?'

'Well – yes. Isn't that what he said to you?'

'No,' said Celia, and her voice was very quiet. 'No, that isn't what he said, Pandora. I'm sorry, I didn't – I didn't realise. How – wonderful for you. You really must – must accept my congratulations. Good afternoon.'

Pandora put down the phone and sat staring at it. She felt even more sick. Sebastian hadn't told Celia about the baby; he'd told her some other, bland lie. Now everyone would have to know, which was exactly what they didn't want. And Sebastian would be cross with her: very cross. There was no doubt in her mind about that.

He wasn't cross: but he was clearly upset.

'How did she sound?' he asked, and Pandora said carefully, trying to be truthful, that she'd clearly been a bit surprised, but—

'And what did she say?'

'Well, nothing much. She congratulated me. As anyone would. Actually she said it was wonderful. So I don't think she was too upset by it.'

'I – hope not,' he said.

He walked over to the window, stood staring out into the dusk. Pandora felt a stab of violent irritation; for God's sake, why did it matter so much what Celia might feel or say about it?

'Sebastian—' she said, trying to keep her voice gentle.

'Pandora,' he said, 'please. I'm trying to think.'

He turned, looked at her for a moment, then walked out of the room. She heard him open the study door, heard it shut again, heard the telephone extension sound; she walked out into the hall then, unable to resist, heard him saying loudly through the door, 'Celia, please, please—' and then his voice became very low, the words unintelligible. Eventually the phone slammed down and a silence ensued. She went back quietly into the sitting room, sat in her chair once more.

He came in, and knelt in front of her, took her hands.

'Pandora,' he said, 'I'm sorry. But there's something I – that I haven't told you. And I think I really need to tell you now. And I'm so, so sorry—'

84

'Apparently Pandora's not well,' said Adele to Venetia. 'Sebastian's just refusing to come to London at all, and Mummy's absolutely furious and keeps shouting at him on the telephone—'

'Who told you?'

'Well, Daddy, that she's not well. And Giles about the shouting.'

'I wonder if Pandora's—'

'I know. That's exactly what I thought.'

'How lovely.'

'Absolutely lovely. Should we—'

'Not sure. Probably—'

'No, probably not.'

'Lady Celia, I have Mr Brooke on the phone—'

'Mrs Gould, I've told you already, I'm not taking any calls today from anyone.'

'But—'

'Mrs Gould, please—'

'Celia, this is Pandora, could I just—'

'Pandora, I'm sorry, but I really don't have time to talk at the moment. I'm extremely busy, a fact which both you and your husband seem to have difficulty understanding.'

'Giles, in the name of heaven, what are you doing with the promotional plans for your extremely modest list? Translating them into Arabic? I've been waiting for them for days. Just bring them in here, and if they're not complete I'll simply have to do it myself.'

'Celia—'

'LM, not now. I would have thought you of all people might have some grasp of how desperately busy I am. Why is it that not a single person in this company is able to do anything for themselves?'

'Aunt Celia—'

'Barty, I sometimes wonder if you listen to a word I say. I told you, I don't want to be disturbed. Now either you can deal with those authors' corrections on your own, as you assured me, rather too firmly, I thought, that you could, or you need help with them. Please make up your mind, and if you can't manage, give them to LM. Stop taking up my time with them. I would have expected better of you, I must say.'

'Celia, I wish you would talk to me about this matter.'

'Oliver, there is nothing to talk about. Absolutely nothing. And if there was, you are hardly in a position to make a contribution.'

'I beg leave to doubt that, my dear.'

'You can beg leave all you like, Oliver, it is nothing to do with you. Nothing whatsoever.'

'Oh, Abbie, it's terrible at Lyttons these days. She—'

'Who?'

'Aunt Celia. Who else? She's in a permanently dreadful temper, won't talk to anyone, shouts at everyone, and Giles says it's just the same at home. Poor old Wol, he really gets the worst of it. And he never fights back, it's so unfair. So terribly, terribly unfair.'

'Celia, I'm thinking of going over to New York, sailing with Robert and Maud next week. I could do with a change and Lyttons New York will, hopefully, benefit from my presence. I'm booking on to the *Mauretania* unless you have any objection, which I can hardly imagine you do.'

'Adele, Mummy's crying again. She won't talk to me about it. I really hate it, what can I do?'

'Nothing, Kit. There's nothing any of us can do. We just have to wait till something changes. It usually does. Want to come and see Venetia with me?'

'Oh – yes, all right. I'll bring my book, in case it gets really boring.'

Celia was sitting at the desk in her study early one evening when her mother arrived at the house.

'I was told you were at home. You're not ill, are you?'

'No. No, of course not. I'm never ill, you know that, Mama.'

'Not strictly true, but near enough. You look dreadful. What on earth is the matter with you? Venetia says you're upset, Kit says you're always crying, even Oliver, soul of discretion that he is, says you're not quite yourself.'

'I seem to have a lot of spies in the house reporting to you.'

'Just as well, it seems. Come along, you'd better tell me. You're not going to feel better until you do. Although I can perfectly well work it out for myself. It's this baby, of course.'

'Of course it's not.'

'Celia, I'm not a complete fool. And it's hardly surprising that you should feel as you do. Very difficult for you. And I'm sorry. But there's nothing to be done about it and you have to pull yourself together, you can't go on like this.'

'Oliver's going to New York,' said Celia, pulling viciously at a thread on her dress, 'and I can't blame him, I know. But it's the last – the last straw. I don't know, Mama, it seems so incredible I still – still—'

'There, there,' said Lady Beckenham, taking her daughter in her arms and patting her rather awkwardly on the head, 'of course you still do. And the best thing you can do is recognise the fact. One of your greatest virtues, facing facts. You're turning your back on this one as far as I can see, that's the trouble. Out of character. That's what's upskittling you.'

'Do you really think so?'

'Of course. It's perfectly obvious to me. You're running away from yourself.'

'But – oh, I don't know. I feel so – so pathetic.'

'Well, that's the last thing you are, Celia. You could claim all sorts of vices, but being pathetic is not one of them. Now you have a good cry, it'll do you good. And then you can come to Curzon Street and have dinner with Beckenham and me. You look as if you haven't eaten for weeks.'

'I haven't,' said Celia, blowing her nose.

'There you are. Very foolish. You do too much. And Oliver probably shouldn't go to New York just now, leave you to cope with everything. I should ask him not to, if I were you. He'll be pleased.'

'He won't,' said Celia, with a shaky smile. 'You've no idea how vile I've been.'

'Then be a bit less vile. Come on, blow your nose and go and wash your face. You look like one of the servants, all blotchy like that. Beckenham will be delighted to see you. He's working very hard on his letters for that book of yours. Given him a new lease of life. Not sure I'm entirely pleased about that,' she added, and smiled at Celia. Celia smiled back.

'Of course you are. You love him really.'

'Yes, I suppose I do,' said Lady Beckenham, sounding mildly surprised. 'Well, there you are. You'll feel the same one day.'

'Do you really think so?'

'Of course I do. Otherwise why should you mind so much Oliver going to New York?'

'I'm not quite sure,' said Celia wearily.

°

'Goodbye, dear Maud and darling Uncle Robert,' said Adele. 'It's been so lovely having you. Come again, won't you? I wish you the glassiest of seas, Uncle Robert. And, Maud, good luck at Vassar. I'm sure you'll love it.'

'I hope so,' said Maud. 'I'll write you and tell you all about it. Come on, Daddy, we'll miss the boat.'

'That's exactly what I'm trying to do,' said Robert. 'Still sorry you're not coming with us, Oliver. Don't make it too long, will you? And, Celia, please do come too next time. I'm sure Giles can hold the fort.'

'Maybe,' said Celia. She smiled. She looked tired, but very beautiful, Robert thought. She was an amazing woman. Not comfortable to be married to, but still, well – amazing.

'Now next time,' Adele said, 'bring Jamie with you. I'd adore to see him again. And even the wicked Laurence.'

'So, what is your view of the situation now, sir?' said Laurence. He always called Duke Carlisle 'sir', he responded well to such flattery.

Duke smiled at him. 'Did you move your money out?' he asked.

'Yes. Most of it's gone.'

'Good. God knows when this thing is going to explode, but the very fact that it's all so volatile makes it ever more likely. There are certainly alarm bells sounding in more than a few breasts. The banks are borrowing heavily from the Federal reserve to carry the speculation. Just last week the borrowing increased by $64 million. Well, you'll know that of course. That's the kind of information that – well, let us say disturbs people. And look at that advertisement in the papers today. I expect you've seen it.'

'You mean "Overstaying a bull market"? Of course. Very bold, I thought.'

'Well, of course it's a gimmick, it's been put in by an investment service. But it will contribute to the faint sense of unease; the pack of cards will be given a tiny push. Now at the end, when – not if – the crash comes, all the usual things will happen; there will be bankers' pools, as there were when your father so successfully stood against the tide, there will be foolish reassurances, there will be a rush to sell, there will be exhortations not to do so. People will be bombarded with advice, instruction, God and the President will be called upon to intervene, but the fact is that there is far too much stock out there worth far too little and the end result will undoubtedly be financial disaster on a huge scale.'

Laurence looked at him. 'What have you been advising your clients to do?'

Duke smiled; it was a rather ugly smile that Laurence had not seen before, almost a smirk, it sat ill on the handsome face. He was like an old buzzard, he thought, circling around, surveying the potential catastrophe below him, planning when and where to find the best pickings – and then to soar off, well-sated, with ample time to find new and better-stocked pastures.

'I have advised them in two directions at once. Naturally I have felt the only wise thing to do was to express caution at the state of the market, to urge restraint. They deserve that. And they will remember it.' He looked at Laurence, refilled his glass. 'But at the same time, I am a stockbroker. My business is trading; I make money out of buying and selling. If a client chooses to ignore my advice, given in good faith, that is of course up to him. I must act on his instruction. If he asks me my prognosis for a certain stock, I must answer truthfully. Steel reached 262 last week, General Electric was 396. Who am I to dissuade my clients from benefiting from such facts and figures?'

He reached out and patted Laurence's hand.

'I'm only telling you all this, my boy, because I like you, and I liked and admired your father.'

'Well, I'm grateful,' said Laurence, 'for your advice. Thank you. We must continue to talk.'

'Indeed we must. But only behind closed doors.'

The Atlantic was blessedly calm as Robert and Maud crossed it; Robert was able to join Maud in her five laps around the ship every morning that made up a mile a day, to play quoits and deck tennis with her, to sit on a deckchair in the autumn sunshine, a blanket round his legs, reading all the books Oliver had given him, and even to enjoy the magnificent food.

And after dinner, when Maud had gone with this or that young man to the ballroom, to talk to other passengers. There was much talk of the financial situation; of Roger Babson's address to the National Business Conference about an imminent and terrific crash; of the absurdity of that statement, notwithstanding the slightly ragged state of the market now, of still-rising dividends, of the foolishness of panic, of the great financial base and prosperity that America had created for herself and which would ensure, as the chairman of a Boston investment trust had recently prophesied, that if there was a downfall, then incorporated investors would 'land on a cushion'. God was in his heaven above America and all was right in the brave new world. That was Friday, 11 October.

On Saturday 19th, the secretary of commerce was finding it difficult to find the money necessary to pay for the upkeep of the yacht *Corsair*, presented to the government by Mr J. P. Morgan of the bank of the same name. The papers were full of stories of a weak market, with trading in decline; by the end of Saturday three and a half million shares had been sold. On the Sunday, *The Times* was reporting a wave of selling.

Next day, six million shares were sold; then at the end of the day the market rallied. Tuesday was altogether better; 'There, you see,' people were saying, 'just another of those setbacks. It'll be all right.'

On Wednesday, there were more heavy losses. Bluechip stock was going down like a plumb line; on Thursday, almost thirteen million shares went down. By eleven o'clock, sheer blind panic set in. Even the famous Jesse Livermore, known on Wall Street as 'the best man on stock-market speculation the world has ever known', was selling; such demonstrations increased the escalating panic. A crowd formed in Broad Street outside the Exchange and the police were dispatched to deal with it. At twelve-thirty the Exchange closed.

At midday, several of God's henchmen, in the form of the most important bankers in America, had met to agree to shore up the market. The panic eased; prices went into reverse and boomed upward.

There was a rush of relief; bankers and stockbrokers continued to assure people that the market was fundamentally sound, the great industrialists spoke complacently of stability and prosperity, and in church that Sunday, many sermons suggested that people should learn from the crisis of the past few days, now happily over, and recover a sense of spiritual values. There, people said, there you see, it's all right, it was just a panic, just a storm in a teacup. Laurence Elliott, who knew, with all the other grandees, that it was nothing of the sort, moved various pieces about the well-ordered chessboard that was his company, and waited in a state of odd excitement.

On the following Monday, flying in the face of all such optimism, even the bargains endured another disastrous fall; and on the Tuesday, there was a tidal wave of selling which broke uselessly on the beach of a Wall Street empty of anyone with the ability to buy.

In the Elliott mansion on Fifth Avenue, Laurence Elliott and Duke Carlisle raised their glasses to Duke's prescience and their own personal salvations.

Chapter 7

He could, at that moment, have committed murder. Murder: how appropriate under the circumstances. He could never remember being so angry. And with Barty, of all people . . .

'Giles, hallo,' she said, looking up from her desk. 'Whatever's the matter? You look awfully cross.'

'I am, awfully – cross,' he said.

'Why?' Her voice sounded less confident now.

'I'll tell you why, Barty. Because you went to my mother, privately, and put a proposition to her, an editorial proposition, not in a meeting, not through the conventional company channels, accepted procedures—'

'Goodness me! What is this?' She clearly still thought he was joking. 'I didn't know about any conventional company channels or accepted procedures.'

'Well, perhaps you should. They do exist.'

'But—'

'And without talking to anyone else in the company, she tells you to go ahead and start working on it. Your own list, more or less, as far as I can make out—'

'Oh dear!' She was flushed now, her large eyes brilliant. 'Giles, you've got it all wrong—'

'Have I really? I don't think so. Did you, or did you not, suggest a crime series?'

'Yes, I did. For the simple reason that crime novels are doing so well. Agatha Christie is selling like I don't know what and now Gollancz are launching a crime list, it seemed like a good idea to me.'

'And what about asking the rest of us, Henry, my father, LM, me, for that matter, what we thought? Well, I suppose you thought it really would be useless, asking me. Kiss of death, I am, to any idea in this bloody company.'

'Giles, please! It wasn't like that. I was just – just talking about it. As an idea.'

'Oh, really? And my mother didn't suggest discussing it with the other editors?'

'Well – no. I mean, it's such early days, she simply told me to go and do some work on it, line up some possible authors, work out costings and so on, work out how many and how often we might do them, nothing more—'

'Nothing more. Just plan out a complete editorial schedule, that's all. Without further recourse to anyone.'

She said nothing, started fiddling with the papers on her desk.

'And what's that?' he asked. 'Working on it already, are you? On your idea? On your – your list?'

'Giles, it is not my list, as you call it.'

'Well, it looks that way to me,' he said, and then, misery driving him stupidly on, 'The others aren't going to like this, you know, Barty. Edgar, Henry, they're going to see this for what it is.'

'And what is it, exactly?' she said, her voice cooler now, with an interesting edge to it that reminded him horribly, absurdly, of his mother. 'Do tell me.'

'It's bloody nepotism,' he said. 'Favouritism. She's always favoured you, always held you up as an example to the twins, to me, telling us how wonderful you were, how hard you worked at school. And now what a good editor you'll be, how creative and efficient you are, and I'll tell you why she says that as well, it's because she wants to prove how right she was, how clever, that it wasn't a mistake, like so many people said, taking you in, it was—'

He stopped, finally hearing himself, finally realising what he had said. She was white-faced, her eyes enormous, her lips trembling.

'Get out,' she said, 'just get out of here. Now.'

'Barty, I—'

'Get out.'

Giles got out; he turned just as he was shutting the door, and saw her bury her head in her arms. She looked suddenly like a small, unhappy child and he felt a pang of remorse so terrible it hurt him physically. He walked down the corridor to his own office and locked the door, wondering not only what he had done, but how he could possibly have done it.

'Venetia? Listen, I've just had the most marvellous phone call.'

'From? A new lover?'

'Sadly not. He's a fairy. At least, I think so. But he was at the party.'

'Drusilla's?'

'Yes. He's a photographer. Name of Cedric, Cedric Russell. Such fun, you know how wonderful they are to chat to, lots of gossip. Anyway, I said I thought we might have our hair done like Drusilla's and he said he was sure we'd look divine. And now he says he wants to photograph us. With our new hair. If we have it done, that is.'

'What for, *Vogue*?'

'Yes. You will do it, won't you? Yes, of course you will. I won't let you not.'

'Dell, I do feel terrible. Sick and so terribly tired, and I'm getting fat again already.'

'Oh, Venetia, you're not. You looked wonderful the other night. And it might take your mind off it. Please do it, please.'

A roar of rage boomed up the stairs, then a long diatribe, clearly accusatory in nature, punctuated by an occasional silence during which the accused was clearly endeavouring to defend himself. Or at least to speak. And then a loudly slammed door and then – blessedly – silence.

Pandora heaved herself over on to her side, and closed her eyes in relief. It was short-lived; the bedroom door opened and Sebastian came in.

'Stupid, moronic, incompetent man. And to think I'm paying him. Paying him! It's an outrage—'

'Sebastian,' said Pandora mildly, 'Sebastian, that is no way to increase my faith in my obstetrician.'

'I do assure you he's not your obstetrician. Not for a moment longer. Man ought to be struck off. I've told him so, in no uncertain terms.'

'Sebastian, that is outrageous of you.'

'Why?'

'I like Mr Cavanagh. I have developed a considerable faith in him. I think he's extremely – gentle. And reassuring. And he's *very* highly qualified, and has seen countless nervous ladies through difficult deliveries. And I want him to see me through mine. Don't you understand that? It's you who are being moronic, if you ask me.'

'I don't. And it's precisely because you are nervous that I have dismissed him. Why tell you it's going to be difficult? Why make things worse?'

'It doesn't make it worse. It makes it better,' said Pandora severely. 'I am nervous, naturally. Most women are. But I like the fact that he's been honest with me. I would prefer to know now that it's going to be a difficult delivery, because it's such a big baby and I'm so small. And that he may want to try and deliver it a little early, because of my high blood pressure. And that therefore he wants me to be in hospital for the birth. Even that I might have to have a Caesarean section. I would rather understand all that than be kept in some kind of absurd and patronising ignorance. It makes me much less nervous, not more. I respect Mr Cavanagh's knowledge and his skills. And I would be extremely grateful if you would telephone him immediately and apologise for what you said and ask him, beg him if necessary, to continue as my obstetrician. Sebastian, we've moved to London so I can be delivered by him. It's utterly ridiculous to change now, with only two months to go.'

'Oh, darling.' Sebastian picked up her hand, kissed it tenderly. 'I'm sorry. It's just that I'm so afraid for you. I can't bear to see you lying there, so uncomfortable—'

'Only uncomfortable, Sebastian,' said Pandora briskly, 'not in mortal agony. And there are worse things than lying in bed all day, reading and being brought delicious meals. The new cook is awfully good.'

'I've done something right, then.'

'Lots of things,' said Pandora, reaching up to kiss him.

'Oh, God,' said Sebastian, throwing back his head, 'dear God, I wish I could have this baby for you.'

'Yes, well, that would be very nice, I do agree. Unfortunately, they haven't advanced that far down the scientific road as yet. And in the meantime, what you can do is telephone Mr Cavanagh at his rooms now, at once. He should be back. And tell him I refuse to have the baby without him. And I think I'd better write him a note as well and you can have it taken round. I just hope we won't be too late, that's all. He's probably taking on another patient in my place even now.'

Barty had not appeared at the office that day; Giles, filled with remorse, walked constantly past her office, willing her each time to be there at the desk, giving him her quick smile as she looked up. The office remained stubbornly empty.

'Miss Miller's ill,' Edgar Greene, the senior editor, said slightly irritably, as he saw him looking in for the tenth time that morning. 'She has influenza, it seems.'

Giles went miserably into his own office, where he struggled to make sense of the overseas royalties for the rest of the morning. And failed miserably. Finally, at four o'clock, he could bear it no longer and left for Russell Square.

Adele sat in the photographer's dressing room, studying herself in the mirror while the hairdresser worked on her hair – the rows and rows of neat curls, exactly like the ones Drusilla Whittingstone had brought back on her chic blonde head from Antoine in Paris – listening carefully to the journalist from *Vogue* as she discussed exactly how she would like their make-up to be – 'lots of powder and quite dark lipstick and some of this eyeshadow, please' – wondering which of the white satin dresses that were hanging on a clothes rail in the corner she would most like to wear: and felt in some strange way she had come home. She and Venetia had been photographed a great many times right through their lives, and by some very well-known photographers; Cecil Beaton had taken a wonderful series of them when they were eighteen and doing the season; Lenare, the society photographer, had done some exquisite pictures of them in their court dresses, just before they left for the Palace to be presented to the King and Queen, and Dorothy Wilding had done a set of the two of them in their white dresses for Queen Charlotte's ball.

But this was different, in that it felt serious, important, more like work, and the most important thing today was not them, but their hair and making it look good for Fabrice who had styled it, and the beauty editor from *Vogue* who had commissioned the photographs for her pages, and Cedric, of course, who was supposed to be one of the most brilliant and revered photographers working in fashion magazines.

And although they were all very kind and polite, she felt less like Adele Lytton, and more of an object brought in to display the hairstyle and the make-up in the best possible way. And she liked it.

They were placed back to back on high stools, with white screens behind them, and told to wait while Cedric instructed his assistant to move the huge lights about while he looked at them through the lens of his camera.

The beauty editor said she wanted the lighting to be what she called very high contrast, 'a bit like the latest shots Paul Tanqueray did of Gertie Lawrence, really dramatic and high key', and Cedric clearly didn't like this, he said he would decide how he wanted the lighting, which the beauty editor, in her turn, clearly didn't like either. She kept wanting to look through the camera herself, which Cedric wouldn't allow; he got increasingly edgy and difficult as the morning went on. The lights were very bright indeed and Adele could feel her face getting hot and, she feared, shiny, and started worrying about poor Venetia who had already had to ask if she could go to the lavatory twice. Cedric was clearly irritated (while struggling to hide it), and started shouting at the hairdresser to resettle the curls and the beauty editor to repowder their faces. Poor Venetia: such bad luck getting pregnant again so soon . . .

'Right, girls, very, very still now, very, very serious, no smiles at all, please.' Cedric squeezed the bulb at the end of the camera's extension lead.

'Lovely,' he said, straightening up, smiling at them, 'perfectly lovely. And another one please – yes, very nice, and now—' He did a few more; it was all extremely slow, the assistant rushing about nervously, doing things to the camera, removing and re-fixing plates from the back of it, moving the lights infinitesimal distances. The hairdresser, meanwhile, tweaked at their curls and the beauty editor dabbed at their noses and Cedric examined the whole thing intently through the camera – and then Venetia said she was sorry, but she really did have to ask them to excuse her again for a moment, slithering off her stool and disappearing in the direction of the dressing room. Adele could see Cedric physically struggling to remain calm; to distract him, she said, not too seriously, that it might be fun if they had a mirror behind them. 'So that we'd be doubled up again.'

'Again?' said the beauty editor.

'Yes. So there'd be—'

'Four of you, not just two,' said Cedric. 'Quite wonderful. Beauty to the power of four. Let's do it, it will show more of the hair as well. It won't be easy making sure the camera doesn't get in the picture, but it will be infinitely worth it.'

Venetia had come back into the room, settled herself patiently on her stool; Cedric stood staring at the two of them, his head on one side.

'I just had this idea,' said Adele, rather apologetically, because she could see how tired Venetia was getting, 'for using a mirror. So there'd be four of us.'

Venetia stared at her. 'I can't see that, I'm afraid,' she said. 'There are only two of us. Surely that's the whole point about us being twins. We're not quads.'

'Unfortunately,' said Cedric, 'then we could have eight of you. My God, I wonder if we could use two sets of mirrors and do that . . . of course, we'd have to completely rethink the lighting. Michael! Michael, come back. Another thought. Fabrice, what does that do to our lovely hair – start with Mrs Warwick, would you?'

Barty opened the door herself; he felt a stab of relief. He had half expected the rather aggressive Abbie to be with her. She was wearing a very old and shabby jersey and a long skirt; she was pale and her eyes were dull.

'Hallo,' she said.

'Hallo, Barty, can I – that is, please may I come in?'

'I really don't think there's the slightest point,' she said.

'Barty, please – I only want to – to apologise.'

'Well, you don't need to come in to do that,' she said, 'do you?'

'No,' he said, 'no, I suppose not.'

'Well, then.'

Giles took a deep breath. 'I'm – I'm so desperately sorry,' he said, 'I can't tell you how sorry I am.'

'Well, thank you for that.'

'Please forgive me.'

There was a long silence; then, 'I don't think I can,' she said, quite calmly and politely.

Giles felt a stab of panic. 'Barty, please – I know what a dreadful thing it was, what I said. Well, all of it, but especially – well, you know – about – about—'

'Yes,' she said, 'yes, I do know what about.'

'Couldn't I just – come in for a moment? I didn't mean it. I really, really didn't mean it. It was cruel and terrible, but I only said it because I was upset.'

'I know,' said Barty consideringly, 'but it was true. I don't mean about me going to – to your mother, talking about my ideas. We could argue about whether I should have done that for hours. But saying – well, the other thing. That was true. And – well, I don't know how I can come back to Lyttons at all. Not now you've made me see that.'

Giles felt as if he might actually be sick. He put out his hand to steady himself, swallowed hard.

'Barty—'

'No, Giles. Don't say again that you didn't mean it. Whether you did or not, lots of people probably agree with you, probably say it all the time.'

'They don't. I swear they don't.'

'Well—' She sighed. 'They wouldn't actually say it, not to you. You're a Lytton, aren't you?' She made the word sound derisive. 'But, well, that's why I feel the way I do. Because you've made me see. Lady Celia Lytton's social experiment, that's what I am. And how clever of her, that she's made me turn out so well. Oh dear—' Her lip suddenly trembled, her eyes filled with tears. She swallowed, looked at him. 'How do you think being that person makes me feel? I – I really would like you to go, Giles. Please. Please go away.'

Giles left. He couldn't remember ever being so unhappy.

'Oh, that was just the best fun,' said Adele, smiling at Cedric, holding out her hand. Venetia had gone, exhausted. The session had taken almost all day.

'I'm so glad you thought so,' said Cedric. He smiled at her; the photographs taken and the beauty editor departed, he was quite restored to the sunny charm that Adele had so enjoyed at the party. 'Most ladies get terribly bored and restive. You were very patient. And wonderful. The mirrors – such a good idea.'

'Did you really think so?'

'I really thought so.'

'Well, I loved the whole thing. I suppose you use professional models most of the time. So you don't get people being tired and falling off their stools and things.'

'Sometimes,' said Cedric, putting a cigarette in a long ebony holder. 'But it's very hard to get the right look. To find the right girl. A lot of these professionals have rather – what shall I say – mundane faces. I do prefer to use real-life beauties, when I can. Like yourself.' He smiled at her. 'Of course, for the big fashion sessions, we do tend to use the professional girls.'

'How do you find them? Do you meet them at parties?'

'No, they usually come to us via the editors of the magazines. They know them all, of course, through seeing them at the fashion shows. But then they're not always photogenic. In fact, very often they're not photogenic at all. And sometimes we use young actresses, they can be fun. You can spend an inordinate amount of time just looking for a face, the right face. As, of course, looking for the right props—'

'Props?'

'Yes. Like your mirror today. We were lucky that we had something here. But it doesn't often happen. I like to use all sorts of objects in my photographs, small tables, vases, flowers, maybe an ashtray or a lamp – they lend a picture interest and character. But they all have to be found and it takes a lot of time. Tomorrow now, I'm taking another beauty photograph, more hair, not nearly as lovely as yours, I fear, and I want a figure – quite a small one, but very stylish – to stand on the table beside the model. Her hair will be straight, quite different from yours, and I want the figure to echo it. I just haven't had time to find it yet. In fact, you must excuse me now—'

'No need,' said Adele, smiling at him. 'I've got exactly the right thing for you. At least, I think I have. Bronze. Chiparus. Yes? Thought so.' Her voice was triumphant. 'I'll bring it in first thing tomorrow. Or later today, if you'd rather—'

'My dearest Adele,' said Cedric Russell. 'You seem suddenly to have assumed the proportions of a divine visitation. How simply wonderful. I would adore to borrow it. But not today. I would hate the responsibility of having something so extremely valuable in my studio overnight. And – would your parents be happy for you to lend such a thing? To someone they do not know?'

'Oh, absolutely,' said Adele lightly, 'they won't mind a bit. She just sits in the morning room, hardly looked at. Anyway, I'll bring her over in the morning. Don't give it another thought.'

She drove home rather fast, still excited by her day, and ran upstairs to the morning room where the figure stood – an exquisite creature in bronze and ivory, wearing a catsuit and cloche hat, poised mid-dance. She switched on the light, went over to the small table where she stood, and spoke aloud.

'Yes,' she said, 'yes, you would be just perfect.'

There was a cough from behind her; she looked round, saw Giles.

'Heavens! What on earth are you doing here, sitting in the dark, why aren't you saving the fortunes of the house of Lytton?'

'Fat chance of that,' said Giles, gloomily. 'I'm doing more for it staying away.'

'Oh, Giles,' Adele's face softened in sympathy, 'I'm sorry. Aren't you enjoying it better?'

'No,' he said, 'no, I can't say I am.'

And then suddenly he dropped his head into his hands. Adele looked at him, horrified, went over and put her arm round him.

'Oh, Giles! Poor old boy. Whatever is it?'

'I can't tell you,' he said, 'I couldn't possibly.'

'Of course you could. Whatever it is. Come on. All those confessions I used to make to you, watching Miss Davis sitting on the lav through the crack in the door, listening at the door while Mummy and Daddy were having their special talks, being beastly to Barty when Nanny wasn't looking—'

'Oh Christ,' said Giles, 'Christ, don't talk about being beastly to Barty.'

'Well, we were horrid to her. Both of us. But she's all right now, more all right than any of us, I'd say.'

'She's not,' said Giles. 'She really isn't. Far from it. And it's all my fault.' Adele looked at him.

'I think you'd better tell me what this is about,' she said.

God, oh God, thought Barty, he's come back. It could only be Giles. Abbie had been to visit her, had tried to comfort her and had left for the theatre with her parents; no one else would be here at this time of night. It was almost eight o'clock. She decided not to answer it. The bell rang again, and then again: hard. She'd get into trouble with her landlady if it went on. She sighed and went downstairs.

'Look,' she said, opening the door, 'look, just go away would you, I told you—'

But it wasn't Giles. It was Adele.

'Awfully nice, your flat,' she said, wandering round it, shedding gloves, hat, coat, smiling sweetly at her.

'Thank you. Look, Adele, I don't want to be rude, but I'm awfully tired and—'

'It's all right. I won't stay long, I promise. And Giles doesn't know I'm here. He'd kill me if he did. Cigarette?'

Barty shook her head, fetched an ashtray from the kitchen.

'Look,' said Adele, inhaling hard, blowing out a cloud of smoke, 'look, I know what Giles said to you. And it was awful. Awful.'

'You think so, do you?'

'Yes, of course.'

'It was true.'

''Fraid not,' said Adele cheerfully.

'What do you mean?'

'You mustn't be so – so touchy, Barty. Of course people aren't going round saying you only do well because Mummy took you in and took you over.' Barty winced at the words, but managed to remain silent. 'I rather wish they did. It would let us off the hook a bit.'

'I – don't know what you mean.'

'I mean that nobody thinks you're doing well because of that. Nobody at all. They think – well, they know – it's because you're so clever and work so hard. At Lyttons you have to prove yourself all the time. It's why I wouldn't work there for anything. Golly, then people really would be able to say it. Anyway, it's the same as your degree; I mean, a whole lot of old dons or whatever aren't going to give you a first just because – well, you know what I'm saying. I hope.'

Barty said nothing.

'Look,' Adele leaned forward. 'I probably shouldn't say this, but just think what it's like for Giles. I mean, he really isn't doing very well at Lyttons, and it must be agony for him, seeing you such a star.'

'I'm not a star,' said Barty fretfully.

'Well, a starlet, then. Doing well, having lots of ideas—'

'But—'

'Barty, don't be an idiot. Please. Let Giles see you. He's so sorry. And he does absolutely adore you—'

'I don't think that's true,' said Barty with a half-smile.

'Of course it is. You should hear Maud on the subject. She reckons he's in love with you.'

'Oh, Adele, honestly! That really is ridiculous.'

'I know. She's such a romantic. Just the same, he is terribly fond of you. And he just – well, he was hurt, Barty, just lashing out. He wanted to hurt you back.'

'Are you sure you haven't discussed all this?' said Barty, looking at her carefully.

'Good God, no. Of course we haven't. Do you think I could have said all this to Giles? Poor old chap. Anyway, I've got to go.' She picked up her coat. 'Venetia's on her own, bit down, not too good at being preggers, I'm afraid, poor her.'

She looked at Barty consideringly in silence for a moment. 'I know it must be quite – hard,' she said, 'to be you. Given the circumstances. But sometimes it's been quite hard to be us. Given the same ones. Think about that, Barty. 'Night.'

Barty stood there for a while, staring after her. Thinking back to another time, so long ago, when the twins had been uncharacteristically kind to her, when her father had been killed in the war. It had been all the sweeter then, for its unexpectedness; it felt much the same now.

Giles arrived early at Lyttons the next day; as he walked past Barty's office, he looked hopefully in. She wasn't there. He sighed, went along to his own office and shut the door.

He was sitting working an hour later when there was a gentle knock on his door; he looked up and saw her. She was pale and very solemn, but her eyes were softer, more friendly.

'Hallo.'

'Hallo, Barty,' he said carefully.

'I wondered if – well, if you'd like to have lunch,' she said, 'so we could talk.'

'I'd love it,' he said, 'I'd really love it, but I can't. I'm so, so sorry, I've got to go over to the printers with my father. Oh, God—'

She grinned at him suddenly and it was the old Barty, warm, friendly, fun.

'Don't look so tragic,' she said, 'it's not the end of the world. Tomorrow?'

'I'd rather it was today. Could I – well, could I take you out to supper?'

'Yes,' she said, 'if you like. That would be fun.'

Adele arrived at the studio holding her bronze figure. The atmosphere seemed even more strained than it had been the day before, indeed, it seemed to be open warfare, with the beauty editor insisting on a side parting, the hairdresser refusing, the model – one of the young actresses Cedric had mentioned – openly sulking and Cedric himself virtually in tears. He was so pleased to see Adele he drew her into his arms and kissed her.

'How wonderful to see you. And oh, what an exquisite thing. Exactly, *exactly* what I wanted. Let us go and set her up on the table while those terrible people continue squabbling.' He led her into the studio; a small round table, with carved legs, set with a dark velvet cloth, stood by a low chair. He put the figure down on it. They studied her.

'Perfect,' said Cedric, 'quite perfect. Don't you think?' There was a silence. Then he said, 'Only—'

'Only—?'

'Only the table's not quite right. Suddenly. Not right for her. Too—'

'Heavy? Dark?'

'Exactly. She needs something light – glass, perhaps.'

'Glass and chrome?'

'Yes. Exactly. I don't suppose you have one of those tucked away at home, do you?'

'Sadly not,' said Adele. 'But my sister has one. Glass and chrome. Quite small. We could borrow that.'

'Are you sure?'

'Oh, absolutely. I'll go now. It'll fit in my car. I'll be back before—'

'Before the battle has been won in the dressing room?'

'Oh, long before that,' she said and laughed.

Venetia was out when Adele got to Berkeley Square: the butler showed her into the drawing room. It was an extraordinarily magnificent room, a symphony in white and chrome; it had been featured twice in *Vogue*. The ultra-fashionable decorator Lord Gerald Wellesley had been commissioned by Boy to do it; he had covered the walls and ceilings with silver leaf, the chimney breast with mirrored squares. The furniture was all extremely modern, white leather sofas, glass and chrome tables, an exquisite maple sideboard; the new tubular chrome lamps. A portrait of Venetia by Rex Whistler, wearing white satin and standing in a rather improbably green woodland vale, hung on one wall, and a large white grand piano stood in one corner: Boy played jazz on it after dinner, rather well. There was a charcoal sketch on it, very well executed, of Venetia looking down tenderly at a newborn Henry; Boy had done that too, it was one of his latest hobbies. He had sketched Kit for Celia as well.

'Venetia's doing something terribly important at the dressmakers,' he said now, walking into the room, 'or something like that. Can I help?'

'You can lend me a table,' said Adele briskly.

'A table? Is Lyttons in such financial trouble that you are driven to borrowing tables?'

Adele giggled. In spite of disapproving of Boy dreadfully, she still found it impossible not to be amused by him. 'Not quite. It's for a photograph. For the photographer who was taking our pictures yesterday. He needs one. I thought the one in the window there,' she said, pointing. 'I wouldn't keep it for long.'

'I'm not sure I want to help him,' said Boy. 'He sent Venetia home completely exhausted yesterday.'

'That was my fault,' said Adele. 'I kept thinking of other things he could put in the pictures. Other ways he could take them.'

'And today you are running round London finding him props for his photographs. Is he paying you, this gentleman?'

'Goodness, no,' said Adele.

'Well, I think perhaps he should. From the sound of things. Yes, all right, I'll lend you the table. But how are you going to get it there?'

'In my car.'

'It won't fit in that silly little thing. I'll put it in mine. I'm rather curious to meet this gentleman. He obviously has great persuasive powers.'

Half an hour later, he was carrying the table into Cedric Russell's studio, and informing him that he considered both he and Adele should be paid for their work on his behalf.

'I hear she was being helpful yesterday as well.'

'Oh she was,' said Cedric, 'hugely.'

'Well,' said Boy. 'Talent should not go unrewarded.' He winked at Adele. 'I'm off. I'll send my car back for the table. You can telephone Venetia when you've finished. Goodbye, my darling.'

He kissed Adele briefly, waved and disappeared.

'What a charming person,' said Cedric.

'Sometimes,' said Adele.

'He's obviously terribly fond of you.'

'He's terribly fond of himself.'

'I see.' He smiled at her. 'Well, that is not such a bad thing. We all should be up to our own standards. Now, let me see—' He set the figure on the table, stood back, his hands clasped in pleasure. 'Wonderful. Absolutely wonderful. Now please don't go away, because I might need something else.'

'Oh, I hope you do,' said Adele, 'I'd adore it. This is such fun.'

Cedric looked at her thoughtfully. 'I don't suppose you'd like a bit more of this sort of fun, would you? On a slightly regular basis?'

Adele stared at him. 'Are you offering me a job?'

'Oh – nothing so vulgar as a job. Let us call it a kind of – commission. When I need something, I'll ask you to find it for me. Just now and again. And pay you. What would you say?'

'I'd call that a job,' said Adele. 'And I'd say yes.'

'That was a lovely evening,' said Barty. 'Thank you so much, Giles. What a nice place.'

'I'm glad you like it. I do too. Not too – smart.'

'No.'

She smiled at him; she had enjoyed herself enormously. Not the least part of her pleasure being derived from a new and totally heady feeling of self-assurance. She had kept hearing, even as she got ready, Adele's voice saying, 'he does absolutely adore you', and 'Maud reckons he's in love with you.' Of course it wasn't quite true, it was only Adele's usual nonsense, but just the same, she had always felt he did like her, enjoyed her company; now having that affirmed by what was really a rather unlikely source, she felt different, attractive, in control.

She even allowed herself to fantasise – very briefly – about what might happen if Maud was right and Giles was in love with her, and she with him; what an extraordinarily ironic situation that would be. Then she let her mind wander on to what Celia would have to say and do about it, and even the fantasy became alarming. But it wasn't going to be an issue. She was terribly fond of Giles in her turn, but she most certainly wasn't in love with him, nor did she find him – well, sexy. Barty was still a virgin, but she knew what physical desire felt like, and she knew she would not, in a hundred years, feel it for Giles. Giles would always be to her one of her best friends, her greatest confidants; for that very reason, she had absolutely no wish for him to become her lover. Just the same, it was nice to know he liked her so much.

She had cut off his apologies quickly, charmingly, saying it was quite all right, she had over-reacted, and expressed her own remorse at going to Celia about the crime list; for the rest of the evening they had chatted and laughed and talked more seriously about the matters of the day – most notably the growing problems of the Depression and the plight of the unemployed – as they had always done. And when Giles finally delivered her back to her door in Russell Square, she kissed him lightly goodnight and went up to bed, feeling extraordinarily happy.

Chapter 8

If you could see love, Barty often thought, it would look like Pandora and Sebastian together, in the room which had become Pandora's home that spring. Barty spent a lot of time there; she loved Pandora and had always adored Sebastian, they both told her she was, of all their visitors, the most welcome and indeed, as Pandora's pregnancy drew near its close, she would leave Lyttons occasionally as early as lunchtime at Oliver's instigation.

'You would be doing me a favour as well as them; I know Sebastian is so worried about her and worried about his work as well; if you are there, he's told me, Pandora is happy and he can go to his study without too much anxiety. Or indeed guilt. You can take some proofs with you, and work on them there if you like; would you mind, Barty? It isn't for very long and I would be so grateful.'

Barty said she would not mind in the least. She got the impression that Celia minded more than a little, while vehemently denying it.

The room was on the ground floor of what Pandora persisted in calling 'Sebastian's house' in Primrose Hill and opened on to the garden; the weather was exceptionally fine and very often the French windows, overhung with wisteria, were open much of the day. The room was always filled with flowers; Sebastian saw it as his mission and the one small thing he could do for her, to have the white tulips and narcissi and lily of the valley she so loved delivered freshly at least three times a week, great bouquets of them, that were then set into vases and bowls and jugs on every available surface.

It was not normally a bedroom at all, but a large sitting room, with a very pretty fireplace; the large double bed that had been moved into it still left room for several small tables, a pair of regency drawing-room chairs, and some of Pandora's favourite pictures, Victorian watercolours of the English countryside. Sebastian would lie beside her on a chaise longue and read to her by the hour, often far into the night when she couldn't sleep, or lie holding her hand, talking to her, arguing with her – they both loved to argue – regaling her with bits of gossip he had picked up from friends at the Garrick, where, at Pandora's insistence, he still lunched two or three times a week.

As much as talking to her, he was happy simply to be with her, reading quietly, listening to a concert on the wireless, or simply sitting with her, holding her hand.

It was an extraordinary thing, Barty thought, how Sebastian had changed himself for her that summer, had managed to be quiet for her, to curb his restlessness, rein in his impatience. She remarked upon it, laughing one afternoon when he complained only mildly to the daily woman, who had tidied his study and put the day's pages in a folder with those of the day before, a crime in Sebastian's eyes on a par with murder.

'But you will hear it again, my darling,' he said, 'I do assure you. When the little beast has been born, and Pandora is mine again, and I am no longer trying to be good.'

He always referred to the baby thus; when Pandora upbraided him for it, he would smile his most brilliant smile and say what else could he call anything that was causing her so much trouble.

Pandora was suffering considerably. The baby was very large, she was unable to get comfortable for more than a few minutes at a time whatever she did; her blood pressure was very high, her hands and feet swollen. She couldn't sleep, and she had developed a hugely irritating rash which plagued her, especially at night. But she remained astonishingly cheerful; she kept a chart, on which she ticked off the remaining days of her pregnancy, 'and at least I know it won't be any longer than this, because they're going to induce the baby on 20 May if it hasn't arrived by then. Barty, darling, pass me those cushions, would you? My two o'clock ones.'

She piled more cushions up as the day went on and she felt her discomfort more.

'But the thing is,' she said, 'I just want this baby so much, and I'll have it for the rest of my life and a few months of feeling horrid is really not important. I honestly think Sebastian minds more than I do.'

'And you call that a job?' said Celia. Her tone and her expression were totally contemptuous.

'Yes,' Adele said, 'yes, I do.'

'Running around London, borrowing things?'

'The right things. Yes.'

'I see. Adele, you have had a very good education. Not as good as you should have had, since you chose not to go to university, but you attended an excellent school, you gained your matriculation. You are hugely intelligent. And you plan to spend the rest of your life catering for the whims of some – some photographer.'

'She said "photographer" exactly as if it were "pornographer",' said Adele later, laughing, reporting this conversation to Venetia. 'She was terribly cross,' she added with a touch of complacency. 'Anyway, I said yes, that was exactly how I planned to spend it, although perhaps not quite all of the rest of it, and she just gave her snort, you know, and told me I was a great disappointment to her and Daddy, and walked out of the room.'

'And after that?'

'Nothing. It's not being referred to. But – well, it is my life. And I think it's going to be utter heaven. Tomorrow I have to find an absolute pile of Vuitton luggage, and some zebra-striped fabric. That was my idea, Noël Coward has it in his studio, you see, so—'

'It sounds terribly difficult,' said Venetia.

'Not really. You just have to think a bit. Vuitton will lend the luggage because the magazine, *Harpers Bazaar*—'

'I like *Harpers*. I think it'll do well.'

'So do I. Anyway, it'll give them a credit. That means they will put "luggage by Vuitton" under the photograph. And you can get the fabric at Swan & Edgar. So I shall just have to chat them up a bit.'

'Terribly clever, if you ask me,' said Venetia admiringly.

'It's not so much clever as having what Cedric calls an "eye",' said Adele. 'We share the eye, we like the same things. That's what will make it work. Touch wood. So if he tells me to get some flowers for a photograph, and tells me what sort of photograph, I know exactly what sort of flowers.'

'And you're just going to work for him?'

'Well, no. I mean at the moment, yes. But I'm hoping my fame will spread. You never know.'

'I'm sure it will.'

'Anyway, it's terrifically sociable, I'm always haring about seeing people, really good chums, some of them, I was chatting to Sybil Colefax the other day, asking her what she had got in the way of wallpaper, I hadn't seen her for ages. She's doing brilliantly, you know, working with darling John Fowler – anyway, this is the new me, career girl. Just as well, still not a prospective husband in sight and—'

'Maybe you could marry Cedric,' said Venetia, laughing. 'He obviously adores you.'

'Fairies don't get married, Venetia.'

'Some of them do.'

'Well, Cedric won't. He wouldn't want to marry anyone anyway, he just wants to have fun. Now listen—'

'It would be fun, being married to you. I'd like it,' said Venetia. She smiled as she spoke, but her eyes were sad.

She was not happy; in fact, she was actually unhappy much of the time. She had faced the fact – although not quite come to terms with it – that Boy was now utterly out of love with her and was, she feared, actually unfaithful to her. The fact that he was discreet, affectionate towards her and an exceptionally good father to Henry – not many men, after all, insisted on being present at bathtime every night and even on knowing how to change a napkin – was some comfort to her, but her sense of disappointment was acute. She was not quite sure how she felt about Boy herself; she was still extremely fond of him, even if she wasn't still exactly in love.

Of course they didn't have much in common. He was really rather an intellectual, she had discovered, he had read almost everything, he adored music and particularly the opera, and he was intensely interested in and knowledgeable about modern painting. She found the artists he brought home from time to time immensely tedious, all talking in terms she simply couldn't understand about things she couldn't begin to appreciate.

She wasn't even sure about having sex with him any more; she had enjoyed the whole thing very much in the early days, he was not only skilful and tireless in bed, but tender and imaginative as well, and she could still, when she allowed it, find herself taken to intense heights of pleasure. But such occasions now were rare; the spectre of a mistress, or mistresses, lay between them on the pillow, humiliating her and dulling her responses; increasingly, she liked to sleep alone.

It was not a happy state of affairs; but she could not quite establish in her own mind – particularly given the fact of her pregnancy – what she wanted to do about it, swinging between a desire to maintain the status quo of a highly luxurious lifestyle, considerable social standing, a secure home for her children and a longing to escape from the mesh of disappointment and humiliation that her marriage had become.

If she hadn't had Henry – and Adele of course – she quite often thought she would go mad.

Abbie had a new job; 'so much better than teaching all those snooty little girls, with their curls and their nursemaids and their closed-in, mean minds,' she said to Barty. It was not one of the august girls' establishments of which she had dreamed, but an elementary school in Brixton.

'It'll be awfully different. I asked what were the biggest problems, meaning things like, you know, none of them ever having seen a book or been read to, and the headmistress said nits and fleas and spotting the difference between a bruise acquired in the playground and one from a father's belt.'

Barty was silent; one of her earliest memories was of watching her father's belt swinging at her brothers, and of her mother lashing out at her with the heavy wooden tongs she used to pull the washing out of the boiler. That had not happened often and Sylvia had been driven to it by her own desperation, but it had directly led, she knew, to her being taken home to Cheyne Walk and the Lyttons.

'On the other hand, it's a wonderful neighbourhood, really close and – well, affectionate. The children grow up in this kind of huge family that's the street. And they're so sharp and clever and some of them at least do seem to want to learn; I'm so excited about it, Barty, I really am.'

Barty told Celia about it, knowing she would be genuinely interested; she promptly offered a large box of children's books for the school, 'and tell your friend if she wants more she has only to ask'.

Abbie was surprised, but, 'I keep telling you,' said Barty, 'she is a very kind and generous person.'

'Well, all right. I'll believe you. I must write to her and thank her.'

'You should come and thank her in person,' said Barty. 'She'd like that. The only thing is, you'd find yourself agreeing to write a book about your experience of teaching in the slums or some such before you knew it.'

Abbie looked at her thoughtfully. 'Well, that mightn't be such a bad thing, either. And I'd like to meet her actually, see if she's really as wonderful as you keep saying.'

Barty laughed. 'Wonderful in bits,' she said, 'not all of her. She's been in a foul mood lately, always quarrelling with poor Sebastian because his book's late.'

'I wonder if any of my children have heard of the Meridian books,' said Abbie.

111

'Well, if they have, I'm sure Sebastian would send some. Probably come down and do one of his talks. Children love them, I've been to a few. He brings the books absolutely alive, he reads and sort of acts out bits, so that when he's talking about the flying fish or the underwater horses or the king-children, there they are, in front of you.'

'It sounds wonderful,' said Abbie. 'Do you really think he would come?'

'I know he would,' said Barty, 'if I asked him. Not till the baby's born, though. Worrying about that is consuming him at the moment.'

'I'm not surprised. I can't imagine how anyone can live through that, can you?' said Abbie with a shudder. 'Having a baby, I mean.'

'No,' said Barty, 'I really, really can't. We'll have to though, won't we, one day?'

'As far off a day as possible,' said Abbie. 'In fact I'm thinking of adopting my children.'

'If you want any more you'll have to adopt them,' said Sebastian. 'I couldn't go through this again.'

'You couldn't!' said Pandora. 'Sebastian, I—'

'Only teasing you. I love making you cross. Anyway, one child is quite enough. I was an only child, absolutely loved it.'

'I expect you did. No competition. Anyway, imagine there being two of you, like Venetia and Adele—'

He looked at her in horror. 'Do you know, I hadn't thought of that. That the beast might be twins. It would explain the large size, wouldn't it? Dear God, how would you—'

'Sebastian,' said Pandora, 'the baby is not twins. Of course the doctor thought of it and he's as sure as he can be. He's listened endlessly for another heartbeat and there isn't one—'

'It might not always be possible. Celia would know, I might ask her—'

'Celia did know,' said Pandora, 'quite early on. She told me.'

'She told you? When?'

'Last time she came to see me. She said not too tactfully how enormous I was, that was her very word, and asked if this baby might be twins, and then told me all about having Venetia and Adele.'

'You didn't tell me.'

'I prefer not to talk to you about Celia,' said Pandora coolly, 'as you very well know.'

Sebastian said nothing, just leaned down and gave her a kiss.

'I love you so unbelievably much,' he said. 'It never ceases to astonish me, how much I love you, and how lucky I am to have found you. I don't deserve such happiness.'

'Probably not,' said Pandora. 'Now it's time for my eight o'clock cushions. My back hurts.'

'Badly?'

'Quite badly. But it's all going to be worth it, I do know that.'

'It had better be,' said Sebastian gloomily.

Absurd really, LM thought, to feel such passion. For a boy: a boy of just sixteen. To be reduced to this foolish indulgent admiration, just at the sight of him or the sound of his voice. Gordon teased her about it endlessly. So many husbands would have been jealous: just to have to share her with another man's child, never mind one she loved so uncritically. Thankfully, Jay hadn't been spoilt by the adoration; aware of it, she had fought it right through his upbringing, had been stricter with him than most mothers, certainly most mothers in her situation. So many war widows centred their whole lives around their sons, clinging to them, jealous of their friendships even, unable to discipline them or criticise them in any way.

Gordon had helped her so much; he genuinely loved Jay and they had, from the beginning, shared so many interests, wildlife, particularly birds, photography – and of course the Hornby trains. If anyone had told LM that when Jay was sixteen he and Gordon would still spend hours at a time in that room with the wretched railway layout, changing point systems, shunting trucks into sidings, racing through tunnels, putting up signals, she would not have believed it. It was all so – so childish; it irritated her almost beyond endurance. The weekends in the Highlands of Scotland, spotting the condors or the eagles, the endless plans – and the saving fund – to go to Africa big game hunting, the hours in the darkroom developing their photographs, all those things pleased her, seemed to her entirely suitable, fitting outlets for their intelligence and energies. But for two grown men – and Jay, already almost six foot tall, could be said to fit that description – to consider playing trains not only amusing but important – well, words, most unusually, failed LM.

'Hallo, Mother,' Jay called to her now, giving her his heart-turning grin as he jumped off the train. He was home on his half-term exeat from Winchester; he looked, she thought, more mature, was infinitely more handsome than any of the other boys. He ran over and gave her a brief kiss.

Every time she saw Jay these days she thought he looked more like Jago, with the same Celtic looks, the dark curly hair, the deep-blue eyes, the square jaw, and he had Jago's physique in many ways. Jago had not been so tall, shorter than LM indeed, but he had had broad shoulders and large hands and feet. And every time that Jay came home, she thought how proud Jago would have been of him, how disbelieving that a son of his could have been so academically brilliant, and yet so easily, so naturally mannered, so absolutely without affectation or conceit. She had done a good job: so had Gordon. Much of the credit must go to him. A woman could only do so much for a son; he needed a father. And from the time Jay had been six, Gordon had been there injecting his own gentle charm and humour and sense of fair play into the complex mix.

'How are you?' Jay said, linking his arm through hers. 'You look very smart.'

'Jay! Don't be absurd. When did I ever look smart? Every other mother on this platform is smarter-looking than I am.'

'No, they're not,' he said solemnly. 'Fashionable maybe, but I like your clothes. They're so – sensible. Some of these women look quite – embarrassing. Look at that one—'

LM looked: at a woman dressed rather as Celia would undoubtedly have been on such an occasion, in a slinky-slim dress, elaborately trimmed straw hat, long rope of pearls, and thought her clothes in all their dateless severity might indeed be sensible but that it could be quite soon now that Jay would be gazing at such women in fascination and admiration, possibly even be attracted to them.

'Well, I'm glad you think so,' she said. 'Now come along, I have my car outside—'

'No Barty?' he said, sounding wistful. He adored Barty.

'No, but she's coming to supper tonight. And so is Kit, I knew you'd like that. And Barty's asked if she might bring her friend Abbie with her. Do you remember her? She's a teacher.'

'Oh yes, that'd be really nice,' said Jay, 'I like Abbie. I was afraid you meant for a moment she was bringing a man.'

'Jay,' said LM severely, 'Barty is bound to have boyfriends sooner or later. You can't keep her all to yourself for ever.'

'I don't see why not,' he said with the quick self-mocking smile that was so exactly like his father's, 'she did save my life after all. Well, she and Sebastian. That seems to me grounds for keeping her to myself completely for ever.'

'Sebastian—'

'Yes, my darling?' He looked up from his book, smiled at her. It was eight o'clock, he had just closed the French windows. 'Do you need another pillow?'

'No. No, thank you. I thought I did, just for a moment, sorry. Go back to your book.'

'All right. Tell me if you change your mind.'

'I will.' She shifted in the bed; it had gone already, the niggling pain. Obviously cramp of some kind. She kept getting cramp in her legs now; it would wake her from her increasingly fitful, precious sleep, an agony of spasm. And then her stomach being so huge, she couldn't get at the particular leg to massage it. The pain had been a bit like that, only milder. Much milder. She picked up her book again; one that Celia had sent, one she was publishing in her new crime series. Pandora found herself increasingly addicted to such stories; sufficient to hold her attention, but not in the least demanding.

It always amused her, how commercial a publisher Celia was. Meeting her, talking to her, seeing her at a dinner table, you would imagine all her books would be seriously intellectual, on a par with her own beloved Biographica list. But she had an ear that was brilliantly tuned to public taste; it had seen her through the difficult publishing years of the war, the unashamedly popular and populist Letters series indeed had gone a large way towards saving Lyttons from financial disaster. And now there was a current fascination with crime fiction; all part, Celia said, of the need for escapism, escape from the Depression that was also sending people to the cinema in their hundreds of thousands, to lose themselves in the new glamorous, glittering musicals coming out of Hollywood – damn. Another spasm . . .

'What do you mean, she saved your life?' said Abbie, amused. 'Yes, please, Mrs Robinson, more of everything. I'm starving and this pie is so good.'

She smiled at LM, at all of them; Gordon was clearly very taken with her. She was wearing a white shirt and black jacket and trousers; with her Christopher Robin haircut she looked slightly androgynous and very attractive. They all like her, thought Barty, and she likes them. It made her feel very happy.

'Isn't it delicious?' said Jay. 'She's such a good cook, my mother.'

'Did you make this yourself, LM?' asked Barty. 'I thought you hated cooking.'

'I enjoy cooking greatly,' said LM, 'it's just that I have never had time to develop it as a skill. Except when Jay and I were living down in Ashingham after the war. But on Saturday nights, and especially if Jay is home, I make this pie.'

'And Cook sulks,' said Gordon, 'because my wife turns her out of the kitchen while she does the interesting part, and then leaves all the mess for her to clear up.'

'Sounds like Aunt Celia at the office,' said Barty, then blushed as they all looked at her and laughed. 'Sorry. Shouldn't have said that. Oh dear. You'd better not give me any more wine, Gordon.'

'On the contrary,' said Gordon Robinson, 'I think I should. I enjoy hearing your tongue so amusingly loosened.'

'Come on, Barty,' said Abbie, 'tell about the life saving.'

'I will,' said Jay. 'You see, I was in hospital, after Gordon ran me over with his motor. Well, actually, it was my fault, I ran right into the way of him. I'd been kidnapped, you see—'

'Kidnapped! This is the most extraordinary story I ever heard.'

'I'd run away,' said Jay, 'because I was so bored – this was when I'd been dragged away from the country I loved so much by my desperately cruel mother –' he paused, grinned at LM '– and this man said he'd help me cross the road and then he was dragging me along, God knows what would have happened in the end, and I finally escaped from him and ran straight under Gordon's car. He was doing about five miles an hour at the time, couldn't possibly be blamed. But anyway, I ended up in hospital and one night they really thought I was going to snuff it, and Barty arrived with Aunt Celia and Sebastian's book and she read it to me for hours and in the morning I was much better. That's about the size of it, isn't it, Barty?'

'Yes,' said Barty, 'that's about the size of it, Jay.'

She smiled at him; the drama of that night was etched into their joint personal histories, an absolutely unbreakable bond. It had been important to her for many reasons, and not only saving Jay; it had been the first time she had played her own part in the Lytton family, had become a proper force within it. Celia, who had been there, had always afterwards ensured that everyone knew about it; it had healed wounds for her that night, had helped her towards acceptance of her own situation.

'That's such an amazing story,' said Abbie.

'Isn't it? So Barty and I are very best friends. Only I've always had to share her with Giles.'

There was a ring at the door: a loud voice in the hall. Boy's voice. What on earth was he doing here? Barty wondered.

116

'Boy!' said LM, standing up, kissing him. 'How nice. To what do we owe this honour?'

'Venetia's found some new children's books she likes. She wants you to see them, LM. I was passing on my way to my club and said I'd drop them in. Jay, old chap, good to see you. How's school this term? Hallo, Kit, hallo, Barty. And now – you're not Abbie, are you? My word, I've struck gold this evening. I've heard about you.'

'Have you indeed?' said Abbie, laughing. 'And what have you heard?'

Barty looked at her sharply. Her voice had taken on an odd tone. Barty would have called it flirtatious if she hadn't known that was out of the question.

'Oh – now let me see . . .' He took a glass of wine from Gordon, raised it round the table, stopped at Abbie. 'Well, that you're fearsomely clever, of course. That you have very interesting parents. And ambitions to be headmistress of Eton—'

'Not quite,' said Abbie, 'although it's an intriguing idea. All those delicious little boys.' She smiled at him: a slow, rather sleepy smile. 'But no,' she said, 'it's a girls' school I've got my sights on. A good grammar, so I can get them young and open their horizons. See them all growing up into successes.'

'It sounds admirable. I'm full of admiration. And where do you teach at the moment?'

'Edge Street Elementary, in Brixton,' said Abbie, laughing, 'and not too much like a girls' grammar.'

'I would say as important. That's where the little girls will discover they want to go to a grammar school. Start working for the scholarship.'

'I'm surprised you know about the scholarship,' said Abbie.

'Oh, my father heads up a big charitable foundation. Giving children from poor families at least a start, offering bursaries and so on.'

'Really?' said Barty. 'I didn't know.'

'Ah, we're not entirely dissolute, we Warwicks, Barty, although I know you like to think so.'

He smiled at her, then returned his attention to Abbie. She was sitting looking at him, chin on her hands, her large green eyes very brilliant. 'If you wanted me to put in a word for your school as an outlet for a bursary,' he said, 'just let me know. My father is very open to suggestions. I mean it.' He smiled at her; he likes her, thought Barty, and he finds her attractive. He always did like clever women, of course; Celia often said so. Implying somehow that Venetia wasn't clever.

117

'Well – I don't know what to say. It's terribly kind of you. Perhaps – perhaps I could get back to you.'

'Please do. Barty will tell you where I am. Or – here. My card.'

'Thank you. Thank you very much.'

'Well,' he drained his glass, 'better go. Venetia will have a great deal to say if I'm much longer.'

A likely story, Barty thought, as if he cared in the very least what Venetia said.

'So – goodnight. Lovely to see you all. And it was – extremely good to meet you,' he said to Abbie.

She said nothing, just smiled at him; the new, sleepy smile.

There was a silence after he'd gone; then Abbie said, 'He was quite different from how I'd imagined.'

'He is extremely charming,' said LM. 'Even I can't help liking him.'

'He certainly is,' said Abbie, and then clearly anxious to change the subject, said, 'Your family is full of charming males. Look at Sebastian.'

'Not exactly family,' said LM, 'but—'

'He's an honorary Lytton, Barty said so. And I think it's wonderful the way he matches the books. He's an extraordinary and powerful creature himself. I was so afraid he'd turn out to be some puny little man and he's so – well, so beautiful, it's the only word for him, and so immensely charming too. His own personality is quite magical, I think.'

She looked at LM and smiled suddenly. 'You don't like him?'

LM looked back at her, her dark eyes very serious suddenly. 'I like him very much,' she said briefly, 'but you mustn't let yourself be carried away by him, Abbie. It happens rather easily, I'm afraid. His charm, as you so correctly say, is immense.'

'Did Mrs Robinson have a crush on Sebastian, or something?' said Abbie as they drove home. 'She seems to feel rather – strongly about him.'

'LM? Oh, goodness no. He's not the sort of person she'd have a crush on.' Barty's voice was slightly cool; she was still shocked at the intellectual, free-thinking Abbie's swift conversion to practised flirt.

'She seemed a bit – emotionally charged about him.'

'Well – probably I shouldn't be telling you this, it's Gordon's wine talking, but I've sometimes thought that – well, that Aunt Celia and he were rather fond of each other. Long ago, of course. And I suppose being Wol's sister LM disapproved.'

118

'Why ever do you say that? About Celia and Sebastian, I mean.'

'Oh – I don't know. It's really hard to define. But she was – different when he was there. Softer. Happier. Less difficult. And he was at the house a lot. Grown-ups always think children don't notice these things, but they do, just because they're there, with not much to do, a lot of the time.'

'Heavens! How exciting. Did you talk to Giles about it?'

'No, of course not. Anyway, she's his mother, it would have upset him dreadfully, even the very idea. He adores her. In spite of the fact he can't do anything right for her.'

There was a silence; then Abbie said, 'I thought Boy Warwick was just – wonderful. Truly the most attractive man I've met for ages.'

'That was fairly obvious,' said Barty.

'Was it? Oh dear. Barty, don't be cross.'

'I'm not cross. Well, only that you couldn't see through him.'

'Nothing to do with being attractive,' said Abbie firmly.

'Maybe not. But he's vile to poor Venetia.'

'In what way vile?'

'The usual way husbands are. He puts her down, doesn't treat her with any proper respect.'

'Maybe she doesn't deserve it. Is he unfaithful to her?'

'I – don't know,' said Barty, 'but certainly I wouldn't be surprised. He's dreadful, Abbie, I really don't like him.'

'It's his dreadfulness that makes him so attractive, I expect,' said Abbie. 'Don't look at me like that, Barty, let's change the subject. Tell me about Jay's father. What was he like?'

'I never met him. I was very little. And he was killed right at the beginning of the war.'

'When you were – what? Seven? And he never came to the house? Sounds pretty rum to me.'

'Abbie,' said Barty, 'when you know the Lyttons better, you'll find they're pretty rum altogether.'

The cramps were getting worse; Pandora heaved herself forward, swung her legs slowly and painfully over the edge of the bed. Sebastian looked up, still half lost in his book.

'All right, my darling?'

'Yes, I'm fine. Really. I just want to move about a bit.'

She smiled at him, then stood up; damn, her nightdress felt slightly damp. She glanced down, then felt a thud of clear, hideous terror.

'Oh, dear God,' she said. 'Oh, Sebastian. Oh, my God.'

He looked up slowly, half amused, half concerned; 'Darling, what—' and then he saw it too, and went as white as the sheets upon which she had been lying. And on which was a large and brilliant stain of bright red blood.

He would never forget the next few hours; not as long as he lived nor into eternity.

The fear, the heart-gripping fear of his own; the terror in Pandora's eyes, her struggle to remain calm; the cramps which turned swiftly to pain as they waited the seemingly endless ten minutes for the doctor to come; her muffled moans as they travelled in the ambulance; her hand clinging to his as he ran beside the trolley into the operating theatre; the sudden silence as the anaesthetic overtook her and she was taken away from him; the interminable wait then as he sat, head in hands, praying to a God he did not believe in for her survival; preparing himself for a life without her, the loss of the final, perfect love of his life; cursing the biology that had first created this unwelcome child and then its dreadful arrival in the world; longing for news, any news, of what was going on in that brilliantly lit world where life and death lurked hand in hand; and then the appearance finally of the surgeon in the doorway, his face unreadable, taut with strain and exhaustion, the endless silence before he spoke, said, 'Mr Brooke, you have a daughter. And your wife is well and as comfortable as can be expected.'

Chapter 9

'They are going to call the baby Isabella. Bella for short,' said Celia, 'because she's so –' she paused, clearly finding it difficult to finish the sentence, '– so beautiful.'

'Charming,' said Oliver.

'I'm surprised you find it so. I thought it rather common myself.'

'Well, as long as you don't convey that thought to her parents. And how was she, the little one?'

'Oh – like all babies. Ugly.'

'My dear, the twins were positively beautiful.'

'This baby is ugly. No doubt she will be very pretty, but at the moment she is ugly.'

'And Pandora?'

'Oh, she's very well. Absurdly smug of course. Nobody ever had a baby before. And Sebastian is behaving in the most ridiculous way, taking no notice of the baby, just sitting clinging to Pandora's hand as if she had been rescued from some terrible danger.'

'Well, I suppose it might be said that she had,' said Oliver mildly. 'Now, my dear, can we turn our minds to other matters? Such as publishing, for just a little while.'

'I shall be extremely pleased to turn my mind to other matters,' said Celia, 'it's only a baby after all.'

'Sebastian's wife has had a daughter, Beckenham.'

'Who's that, my dear? Who's had a daughter?'

'Pandora, Sebastian Brooke's wife. You must remember her, she—'

'Oh yes, of course I remember her. Pretty little thing. Lovely eyes. Well, that's good news. Better if it was a boy, of course, but—'

'Beckenham, not everyone has a title to pass down. And just as well Sebastian has not in my opinion. Anyway, Celia just telephoned with the news. I'm going to see her now.'

'What, the baby?'

'No, of course not. Celia.'

121

'Why on earth do you need to see Celia, just because Sebastian's wife's had a baby?'

'You wouldn't understand, even if I tried to explain. So I shan't. But I'll be back for dinner.'

'Oh, Sebastian, it's such lovely news. Adele and I are just so — so delighted and proud of you both. And girls are so much nicer than boys. Especially when they grow up. I do hope this new one of mine is a girl. Now, when can we come and see her? Tomorrow? Oh, good. Just say the time. And give her our best, our very best love till then.'

'Abbie, Pandora's had a little girl. Isn't that lovely? And they're both extremely well. I'm just so happy and so relieved. I'm allowed to go and see her later today, just for a few minutes. I'll send them both your love, shall I?'

'Superb news from England, my darling. Pandora has given birth to a daughter. Both well. Calling her Isabella Lily, after you. What do you think of that?'

'I think it's wonderful, Jack. As soon as this film is finished, let's go home and see her.'

'Fine by me.'

'Kit, old chap, do you want to come and see Pandora with me tomorrow? Pandora and her little baby. We could go after school, I'll get Daniels to bring you to the hospital, meet you there.'

'Yes, all right, Giles, that would be nice. I wish it had been a boy, though. More fun for me.'

'Daddy, there's a cable from Adele. Pandora, you know, that lovely girl who's married to Sebastian Brooke, she's had an adorable baby girl.'

'And how do you know she's adorable, Maud?'

'All babies are adorable. Oh, I'm so utterly delighted. I must send a cable back. Goodness, excuse for another visit, do you think?'

'Hardly, Maud. They're not exactly family. And—'

'I know, I know. Money's not as plentiful as it was. I'm only teasing. But you're wrong about one thing. Of course they're family. Sebastian is part of Lyttons, everyone says so. Oh, it's so exciting. I feel quite tearful about it all.'

✻

122

'She seems a dear little thing, Gordon. Not exactly beautiful of course, but quiet and good. And Pandora is well, that's the main thing. And Sebastian is – well, I can't quite describe how he looks. Isn't it odd, the happiness babies bring with them?'

'I can never remember being so happy. I never hoped to be so happy. Never. God has been too utterly good to me. Now, my darling, I want you to rest. Too many visitors by half, and I don't care if Matron did say it was all right. You look exhausted. Very pale. I want you to lie still and hold my hand. I'm not going until you fall asleep. And probably not even then. I can't bear to leave you. Now that I've got you back to myself again. Shut your eyes, darling, and just don't think about anything at all. The baby's right as rain, I've just been to visit her in the nursery. Let me give you a kiss. Sleep well, my darling. Thank you for being you.'

Celia was working late, when she heard the front door bell of Lytton House ring. She decided to ignore it. It couldn't be anything important. Oliver was at a dinner and the rest of the staff had been gone for over an hour. She loved being alone in the building; she felt time to be entirely hers. And she needed time: a great deal of it. Lady Annabel's biography of Charlotte and Emily Brontë was not as painstakingly researched as usual, requiring a lot of tactful and constructive editing. It wasn't going to be an easy task.

The bell went again: and then again. She frowned. A delivery, no doubt, from one of the printers. They knew it was not really allowed, after five. Presumably the typesetters, trying to rush something through before the weekend. She had spoken to them about it before. It would do them good to find no one answering, to have to take the work back again. It might make them take her instructions more seriously.

Another long, insistent ring. Very intrusive. She would have to go down. Another ring. Louder and still longer. It was too bad.

Perhaps it wasn't the printers. Perhaps it was a telegram. Or a personal missive from Lady Annabel, who had sensed her displeasure. She had sent her maid with handwritten notes before. On one occasion, even flowers. Yes, perhaps that was it. Although the knock would have been timid, she felt, diffident; the poor girl was very put-upon. The chauffeur perhaps: yes, that was more likely.

She opened the door. It was not a messenger from the typesetters; nor was it a telegram boy, or even Lady Annabel's unfortunate maid or chauffeur. It was Sebastian. Standing there, very still, just staring at her. Unable to speak.

'Celia,' he said finally, and his voice was strange, heavy, absolutely devoid of expression. 'Celia, let me come in. Please. It's Pandora. She's – she's dead.'

Chapter 10

'It's so terrible,' said Maud, 'so absolutely terrible. Those poor, poor people, they're starving out there, you know—'

'Oh, darling, not starving, surely,' said Robert. 'I know times are very hard but—'

'Daddy, they are starving. Their families too. There's just no hope for them, that's the worst thing. Do you know how long men stand in the breadline every day? Four or five hours. Can you imagine that?'

Robert was silent; he looked at her feeling faintly uncomfortable. It was certainly true; there was terrible poverty in the city. There was a famous photograph of the great line of men winding round Times Square, where one of the newspapers had set up a soup kitchen, while the world bustled on past them in shiny cars and smart clothes, a pitiful symbol of waste and degradation. Men were so desperate for work, they stood on street corners, with placards round their neck, begging to be given a chance.

'It is very – bad,' he said finally, 'I agree.'

'Well, we should do something about it,' said Maud. 'We could take people in, surely, give them work—'

'Maud,' said Robert, 'of course we can't "take people in", as you put it.'

'But why not? We could easily employ several more people, we've got two enormous houses, for heaven's sake. And you must be able to offer work, surely, labouring work?'

'No, Maud, I can't. I've told you several times. Things are hard for me as well, all my contracts have been cancelled—'

'Daddy, how can you say that? That times are hard for us. When we waste more food than lots of families live on—'

'Maud, when you are a little older you will be able to take a more realistic view of all this. All right, we are not facing real hardship. But I have lost a considerable amount of money. It would have been a great deal worse had I not been advised to move funds out of the country and to sell a little ahead of the real fall. We are living on the overseas investments I made and by a careful conservation of my assets. John is desperately worried about the immediate future, well, we both are, and far from taking extra men on, we've had to lay them all off. And this isn't confined to the United States, it's a global problem, that's half the trouble.'

'Yes, and in Europe, in England and Germany, they get money from the government. Here they just beg and starve. And I'll tell you what makes me angrier than anything, it's the thought of Laurence sitting there in that palace of his, apparently completely untouched by it all.'

'I believe he has lost a lot of money, Maud. Almost all the bankers did.'

'Well, that makes me feel truly heartbroken. Why didn't he warn people, he and all the other bankers? Why did they just go on and on taking their money? It's wicked, dreadfully wicked, all of it, but the bankers and brokers, people like Laurence, are the most wicked of all. I feel so – so ashamed of him. Of being anything to do with him.'

'*Meridian Times Ten* is – superb,' said Celia. She spoke with the kind of intense relief with which people relate an escape from a serious accident or the recovery from a near-fatal illness.

Oliver looked at her. 'Thank God. How he's done it, God knows.'

'Oh, Oliver, don't be absurd,' said Celia briskly. 'Work is the great anaesthetic.'

'Really?' He smiled at her, his deceptively vague, sweet smile. 'Well, I suppose you should know.'

She ignored this. 'What I feared, most of all, was that the book would be bad. I would have found it hard to publish, to have risked poor reviews. There has been a three-year gap, after all. Expectation is high. And it would have hurt Sebastian horribly.'

'Well, it doesn't have to. Have you told him it's all right?'

'Briefly. I've asked him to supper tonight. I hope that's all right?'

'Celia, if I said it wasn't, what would you do about it?'

She looked at him for a moment, rather oddly; then, 'But I knew you wouldn't,' she said.

'To *Times Ten*,' said Oliver, raising his glass.

'Times Ten,' said Sebastian. 'I hope to God it's all right.'

'Celia says it's marvellous.'

He was silent. Then, 'She could hardly say it wasn't. The way things are.'

'My dear Sebastian, when it comes to publishing, Celia is incapable of untruth.'

The faded blue eyes looking at Sebastian were very steady, with no amusement behind them; Sebastian was silent for a moment. 'You've been so very good to me, Oliver. Better than I deserve.'

'Well,' said Oliver, his tone lighter, 'we have to take care of our authors. Lyttons owes you a great deal.'

'I only wish—' said Sebastian, and then stopped. Oliver acknowledged the silence and lifted the bottle of port.

'Another glass?'

'Oh, I don't think – well, a small one.'

Oliver poured him a large one.

Sebastian had been drinking heavily ever since Pandora's death.

There had been dreadful days, weeks, months. For the first week or so he had lived at Cheyne Walk, never going to bed, sleeping briefly on the sofa, pacing the house, day and night, occasionally going out and walking with an almost savage speed along the Embankment and then returning to the house like some desperate, hunted creature in search of refuge.

Celia spent endless hours with him: Oliver would hear them talking behind closed doors, in various rooms, for Sebastian was unusually restless even for him, could stay nowhere for long.

Adele and Giles, afraid to be called to witness the agony Sebastian was enduring, stayed away from him as much as they could, only in Giles's case mumbling sympathy and in Adele's administering warm, but swift hugs and kisses and then withdrawing quickly and going to her room; Kit, however, was surprisingly and bravely forthcoming, went up to Sebastian the first time he saw him after Pandora had died and put his arms round him, and said, 'I'm so, so sorry.' Sebastian had stood for a long time, holding him, his great head buried in Kit's hair, saying nothing, and when he set him back and looked at him, there were tears of sympathy in Kit's dark-blue eyes.

After that, whenever they met, in the hall or on the stairs, or even on the front steps where Sebastian liked to sit, smoking, staring at the river, Kit asked him if he would like to be alone, or have his company, apparently equally at ease with either answer. He would sit with him quietly when he was with him, not speaking unless spoken to, occasionally shifting closer to Sebastian and resting his head against him. 'It's so sweet,' Adele reported to Venetia, 'he's rather like some adoring puppy when he's with him. Of course, they've always got on

127

terribly well. But Kit's only ten, it's amazing, really, that he seems to know what to do. I wish I did. Poor, poor Sebastian. I've never seen such misery, such absolute misery in anyone.'

The funeral was the most terrible day any of them could remember; Sebastian so brave as the coffin was carried into the church, sitting utterly still as the service was read, just staring in front of him, with Celia on one side and Kit on the other; he had said he wanted no music as he could not have borne it, but the silence was dreadful, pain incarnate.

He remained silent until the last moment, when the coffin had been lowered into the grave; it was a beautiful afternoon, and some-where in the churchyard birds were singing, and there was sunlight shafting through the trees, and even when he had cast the posy of the white flowers she so loved on to her coffin, he still kept control of himself. But at the dreadful finality of hearing her 'committed to the ground, earth to earth, ashes to ashes, dust to dust', he began to sob, loudly and horribly, and simply stood there, staring down at her, the last sight of her he would ever have, his great shoulders heaving and the tears pouring down his face like a small boy. And it was a small boy who took his hand then and kissed it very tenderly, and looked up at him with infinite anxiety, and then down again at Pandora, lying beneath her garlands of flowers, and rested his head against him, and they stood there, the pair of them, for a long time, Kit and Sebastian, holding hands while the birds continued to sing through the stillness and gradually Sebastian's weeping quietened and finally Kit was seen to very gently lead him away.

It had been a blood clot that had killed her: travelling swiftly through her frail body to her heart. She died suddenly and quietly, a week after little Isabella's birth, just as she had been told that in another week she might be allowed to return home. Sebastian had been with her, had gone over to the crib to pick the baby up at Pandora's request, when he heard a faint sound from the bed; by the time he had reached her she was gone from him. It was not unusual after childbirth, the doctor said, struggling to calm Sebastian and to defend himself against the rising and violent tide of his anger, nobody quite understood why, there was certainly nothing that could be done to prevent it, it was undetectable and untreatable.

And Sebastian, roaring and raging, had finally left the hospital, returning after a few hours threatening to sue, to commit violence, to take vengeance on the nurses, the surgeon, the midwife; only Celia had been able to calm him, to make him understand that nobody and nothing could have saved Pandora. The baby he had left in the hospital, refusing to have anything to do with her; he was literally unable to look at her. When finally he was forced to recognise that she must go home, that he had a responsibility for her, he sent the maternity nurse and the nanny that Pandora had hired in his car to fetch her, and when the small sad little party arrived at the house, he went out immediately and did not return for many hours.

'It's dreadful,' Celia said to her mother, after worried conversations with the nurse a few days later, 'he refuses so much as to be in the same room as the baby, he can't bear her near him. I can understand it, of course I can, but it can't go on, he'll go mad and the child will suffer.'

'The child won't suffer yet,' said Lady Beckenham, 'she won't know. Give him time, Celia, let him begin to come to terms with it all. There's no need to feel you have to solve it immediately. Tell the staff to look after the baby, that's what they've been engaged to do, not worry about its emotional welfare. Too much of all that these days, if you ask me. All a baby needs is food and warmth, it's no different from any other young animal. I always took a holiday away with Beckenham, after I'd been confined, for several weeks; you all seem to have survived. I think it's a great pity, myself, wet nurses are out of fashion. Now stop fussing about the child and devote your attention to Sebastian. The other problem will solve itself.'

But in that she was wrong.

Kit had taken to visiting Sebastian occasionally at tea time, the house in Primrose Hill being only a short distance away from his school. One particularly lovely early autumn day, while they were eating tea in the garden, the nanny brought Isabella out and put her in her pram. Sebastian made a great business of going into the house and fetching some cake for Kit; when he came out, Kit was holding the baby, who was smiling up at him and tugging at his tie.

'I hope this is all right. I wanted to see her properly.'

'Of course,' said Sebastian, 'put her back when you've finished.' He spoke rather as if the baby were a toy Kit was playing with.

Kit carried Isabella over to his chair, sat her on his knee. 'She's so pretty. Little babies look quite ugly, I think.'

Sebastian shrugged, picked up the paper.

There was a silence; Kit dangled his tie in front of Isabella's nose. She grabbed at it, he snatched it away, then tried again. This time she held on. She made the small-baby noise that is halfway between a gurgle and a laugh; Kit laughed too.

'She's going to be strong. Look, Sebastian, she's really hanging on to my tie. Look.'

'What?'

'I said look, she's going to be strong.'

There was a silence while he continued to play with her; then he said, 'She's getting hair. I suppose that's why she looks prettier. It's going to be like Pandora's, you can see, same colour.'

Sebastian nodded, scowling at the paper.

'Her eyes are like Pandora's too,' said Kit, 'exactly. That must be nice for you.'

Sebastian shrugged.

'Isn't it?'

'What?'

'Isn't it nice? That she looks like Pandora?'

'Not particularly,' said Sebastian. He fished into his pocket for a handkerchief, blew his nose.

Kit looked at him very seriously over the baby's head. 'I can see how bad you must feel about her,' he said, 'that Pandora would be here if she wasn't.'

'Kit, can we stop this conversation, please?'

'Sorry. But—'

'Kit, I said stop it.'

Kit got up, walked down the garden with Isabella, showing her the apples growing on the tree, pointing out birds singing in the branches; then finally he put her back in her pram and stood looking at Sebastian in silence.

'I would like to say something about it,' he said finally.

'About what?'

'About Isabella. Henry calls her Izzie, you know. I like that. Better than Bella.'

'Really?'

'Yes. I think I might call her that too. Anyway, like I said, I know she must make you feel bad. But you do have her, don't you?'

'I do, yes,' said Sebastian shortly.

'Well, I was just thinking that you might not even have her. I mean she might have died too.'

'Kit, please—'

'At least you've got something of Pandora. Quite a lot really. I think that's important.'

130

Sebastian suddenly stood up; his face was white, taut with rage.

'Shut up,' he said. 'Shut up, Kit, at once. I will not have this – this obscene discussion.'

Kit stared at him, half frightened, clearly determined still to stand his ground. 'It's not obscene. I was only trying to help. I—'

'Well, you are doing precisely the opposite. It is nothing to do with you and I find it appalling to hear you talking in those crass terms about something you can't possibly begin to understand. There is nothing of Pandora left to me, absolutely nothing. Certainly not in – in that child. Now if you can't stop this, please leave. And don't come back until you've learned a little sense.'

Kit met his eyes steadily. 'I'm sorry, Sebastian. Very sorry. Of course I don't understand. I couldn't. Maybe I should go now. But please let me go on coming to see you. I do love it here. I promise I won't talk about it any more.'

Sebastian sighed. Then he lowered himself into his chair very slowly and painfully as if he were an old man and said with infinite weariness, 'Yes, yes, of course you can come. I'm sorry, I shouldn't have shouted at you. Go and ask Cook for another pot of tea, will you?'

'And some more of that wizard cake?' said Kit hopefully.

That night the nanny came to knock at the study door as she always did at Isabella's bedtime.

'The baby is just going to sleep, Mr Brooke. I wondered if you wanted to say goodnight to her.'

He looked at her and said nothing at first; then, 'Nurse, I would be grateful if we could stop this nightly performance. I have no desire to say goodnight to the baby. I hope she sleeps well for your sake.'

She stood there, flushed, visibly shaken; quite unable to find anything within her training or even her own instincts that supplied an appropriate response. 'Well,' she said finally, 'well, goodnight, Mr Brooke.'

'It's just dreadful,' she said later that night to Mrs Conley, Sebastian's housekeeper, over a late-night cup of cocoa. 'I don't know what to do. I really feel I can't go on working here in this atmosphere. He appears to literally hate that child. It's dreadful – wicked, if you ask me.'

'It is dreadful,' said Mrs Conley, 'but if you'd seen him and Mrs Brooke together, seen how he loved her, you'd maybe understand. He simply worshipped her. Nothing seemed to matter to him except her; her and his writing of course. Thank God he's still got that.'

'It's all very well. But a child needs one parent at least. I dread to think what's going to happen as she grows up.'

'Maybe he'll come round,' said Mrs Conley. 'I don't know if it's going to help or hinder things that she's so like her mother. Extraordinary it is, same eyes, same hair colour, same smile. Anyway, please don't leave, Nanny. You're all she's got at the moment, poor little lamb. You and me of course. And young Kit, he seems to be very devoted to her. Funny in a small boy.'

Nanny said it was unusual but that Kit seemed to her wise beyond his years and of course she would stay as long as she could, but it was very difficult for her. 'It's like a household where the parents are quarrelling all the time – only worse.'

She sighed and went back up to the night nursery to check on Isabella. She was asleep on her back with one arm thrown above her head and the other wrapped tenderly round her own neck, her head nestled into her own hand. Sebastian could have told her Pandora had slept in exactly the same position . . .

Chapter 11

'She's called Helena. Helena Duffield Brown. She's twenty-five. Her father's a businessman. They live in Chelsea. Anything else?' Giles looked at his mother defensively.

'Darling, there's no need to sound so touchy. I only wondered who she was. As you seemed so very taken with her the other night.'

'Mother, I danced with her once or twice.'

'Five times, actually,' said Adele, her eyes dancing.

'Oh, shut up. I've got to get to the office, see Edgar about the crime list.'

'I thought Barty was in charge of the crime list?'

'The editorial content, yes. The sales projections, no.'

'And what are the sales projections, Giles?'

'Mother, I don't know yet. I have to talk to Edgar. Now please excuse me.'

'Oh dear,' said Celia when he'd gone, 'he is absurdly touchy.'

'You should leave him alone more,' said Adele quietly. 'Trust him to do his job.'

'Adele, when and if you work at Lyttons instead of running around after that photographer, you will be qualified to comment on how it is run. Until then—'

'Sorry. Let's talk about Helena. He's obviously quite taken with her. It's nice. First girl it's ever happened with. Except – well, yes, first girl.'

'Except who, Adele?'

'Oh – I was going to say Barty, but of course she doesn't count.'

'Of course Barty doesn't count. She's family – virtually. He couldn't possibly feel like that about her.'

'I don't see why not,' said Adele, 'she's very pretty. And she's not family, virtually or otherwise.'

'Well, of course she's not. And yes, she is pretty. But – well, it's absurd. A nonsense. Now that girl, Duffield Brown, she seems quite

133

suitable. Pleasant looking, although a little on the large size. You don't suppose her father's Leslie Duffield Brown?'

'I have no idea. Venetia probably would. Why?'

'He's a dreadful man. Made his money in the war out of scrap metal, still angling for a knighthood. I don't think we would want him in the family.'

'Mummy, Giles has only danced with the poor girl. Let's not worry about her father joining the family yet.'

'He is Leslie Duffield Brown, yes,' said Venetia. 'Dreadful man, really common, as Mummy would say, and a bit lechy by all accounts. Ouch, that hurt, I swear this baby's got teeth already.'

'She's sweet,' said Adele smiling at Elspeth's small dark head. 'Is it nice to have a daughter?'

'It's wonderful. I can't wait to start buying her frocks.'

'Poor little Izzie,' said Adele soberly. 'I wish someone thought it was wonderful to have her. It's a hideous problem.'

'Have you been there lately?'

'Not really. Sebastian is quite – odd about visitors. He doesn't really like us going to see Izzie, it annoys him, and he's at our house so often, I don't have an excuse to go. But Barty often pops in, she's got the excuse, with proofs and things, and she says Izzie's so sweet now, running about, chattering nineteen to the dozen, and Sebastian hardly speaks to her. She's just growing up without anyone to love her.'

'Pandora would be so—'

'I know. Absolutely. Oh dear. It's nearly her birthday, isn't it, and of course that makes it worse for Sebastian, what sort of a day will she have—'

'I'll ask her here,' said Venetia, 'the boys like her. I can give her a little birthday tea. I'm sure Sebastian would agree to that.'

'Sweet idea. We can have Kit round too. He adores her. He's always there, he's the only normal contact she has. Sebastian seems to allow him to bridge the gap.'

'She'll miss him when he goes to school next year. Roo, don't do that, the baby's not a doll.'

Her second son, christened William, but named Roo months before his birth due to his kangaroo-like tendencies *in utero*, removed his small hands from his sister's neck and walked over to the rocking horse and shook it violently.

'Off, Henry.'

'No.'

'Yes.'

'No. Stop it, ow, Mummy, he's hurting me, tell him to leave me alone.'

'Boys! Stop it. Adele, shout for Nanny, would you – oh, Nanny, there you are, can you take these boys for their walk? I can't stand this fighting when I'm trying to settle Elspeth. Thank you. Oh Adele! Whatever is it like to be just you, just a person, not a mothering machine?'

'Lonely,' said Adele briefly.

'It's quite lonely being me sometimes too, you know,' said Venetia, her large dark eyes heavy.

'How are things with Boy?'

'Oh – all right. I just don't feel – he cares about me any more. He doesn't realise how tired I am, or – I mean this evening, just for example, he asked me if I'd like to go to the opera. The opera! He ought to know that by now.'

'Of course he should. Anyway, it goes on for about five hours, if it's the Wagner. Mummy's going. Now I've got to find some candlesticks. See you this evening. If Boy's out I'll stay.'

She dropped a kiss on her sister's head; when she looked back, Venetia was alternately stroking the small Elspeth's head and wiping her eyes.

'I suppose it proves something,' said Oliver with a sigh.

'Only how the prize has become denigrated.'

'Oh really?'

'Yes.'

'And what would you say if Guy Worsley had won it?'

'What, the Nobel prize? For *The Buchanans*? Exactly the same thing. It's too absurd. When there is so much fine writing. I would have given it to Waugh in preference to Galsworthy.'

'Celia, I don't think the Nobel prize goes to satirical writers. But I won't argue with you. Certainly the Sitwells are more deserving, any one of them. Anyway, one day we'll win that prize. I did think, though—'

'I know. It's such a magnificent book. Never mind, it simply shows the judges up as fools.'

One of Lyttons' newly acquired authors, Nancy Arthure, a novelist in the Virginia Woolf mould, had written a superb multi-layered book, brilliantly reviewed, about a group of women in the war years entitled *Remember Them*. Oliver had seen Arthure as a serious possibility for the Nobel prize; he was bitterly disappointed.

'Another year,' said Celia, kissing him gently. 'Now I have to go home and change,' she said, suddenly brisker, moving away from him.

'Where are you going, in the middle of the afternoon?'

'Oh, Oliver, I'm sure I told you! To Covent Garden. It starts at 5.15. It was so very fortunate for me, that Cynthia Arden was indisposed.'

'Hardly fortunate for poor Cynthia. But yes, of course. *Götterdämmerung*. It should be very fine. I envy you.'

'Oliver, you slept through *Rheingold* last month. It would be very discourteous to repeat the performance. And no sympathy for Cynthia, she doesn't really like opera and hates coming up from the country. It's so hard on poor Bunny.'

It was a superb night at Covent Garden. It was the last night of the 1932 Wagner festival: the house was filled with the most discerning and determined of opera aficionados. Frida Leider was singing Brunnhilde, Lauritz Melchior Siegfried, Sir Thomas Beecham was conducting. Everyone who was anyone in society was also there; the audience was not confined to opera aficionados. It was an excuse to see and be seen, to meet and gossip, to entertain and be entertained.

It was a visual delight as well; in a world where increasingly men wore dinner jackets to the theatre, the panorama of white tie and tails, of long dresses, of fine jewellery, even – despite the warm weather – of fur wraps and stoles and jackets was a pleasure in itself to those who cared about such things.

Of course there was a Depression out there, although it was affecting the poor a great deal more than the rich; and not for nothing had *Vogue* advised, 'If you haven't lost money pretend you have.' Ostentatious wealth in the old sense was somehow unseemly and the most surprising people were working, most notably Lady Diana Cooper with her Berkeley Square flower shop.

But tonight, ostentation was the word.

Lady Celia Lytton, sweeping the glittering audience with her opera glasses just as the lights went down and Sir Thomas walked towards the rostrum, suddenly saw Boy Warwick slipping late into a box accompanied by a young woman in a white dress. She could see little more than that, and the fact that the girl had dark hair; no doubt Boy had assumed no one would notice them. In which case he was more of a fool than she would have suspected. It was an extremely crass thing to do, to take a woman who was not his wife to Covent Garden on such a night. She felt a swell of violent rage; discreet adultery was one thing, confronting London society with a mistress was quite another.

It was unlike Boy, in fact; very unlike him. Apart from his frequent absences from the house and Venetia's own instincts, there had never been any proof whatever that he was not a perfectly faithful husband. She would go and seek him out at the interval, and make her displeasure very firmly felt. The two of them were alone in the box, she could see that; and as the overture swelled, the girl leaned over to see better and a fine, rather strong profile was etched against the lighted stage. It was not a face she recognised, but . . . Celia turned her attention to the stage, settled herself determinedly into the pleasure of the music. Time and the interval would no doubt reveal a great deal.

Boy Warwick was not only a great opera lover, he found the audience extraordinarily interesting as well. As the audience settled into stillness and the first act, he took out his opera glasses to look around . . . What a night: everyone, everyone was here. It had been an act of madness to come. But – well, he had his reasons. And they had come in so late, he had timed it terribly carefully. No one could have seen them.

Suddenly, he saw his mother-in-law in the box almost opposite. Now that was bad luck. He had checked if she was going and she had told him she wasn't; it was one of the reasons he had dared to risk it. She must have been invited at the last minute. Well – either she had seen him or she hadn't, there was no going back now. And perhaps she hadn't, she did appear completely engrossed in the music.

Surprising – and indeed intriguing – was that her companion was Lord Arden, one of the Mosley set, a close friend of Oswald Mosley himself and an enthusiastic follower of his new Fascist party, and its promise of 'something new, something dangerous'.

The first act ended; Celia made an excuse to Lord Arden and moved round to Boy's box.

It was empty: and its occupants did not return for the duration of the opera.

Giles was working very hard at being in love with Helena Duffield Brown. She was very pretty, with curly brown hair and her large brown eyes, and she had a good figure: she might not be as thin and elegant as the twins, or as – well, as lots of young women, but he rather liked her style. She had an unfashionably full bosom and a small waist, and as a consequence, tended to wear slightly more womanly clothes, two-piece suits during the day with belted jackets or slightly waisted jersey dresses; even her evening clothes were shaped to her body, didn't sort of slither past it as the twins' dresses did. And then she was very intelligent; she hadn't been to university, but she had passed her matriculation very well, and did some translating work for her father, whose company sold its aluminium pots and pans all over Europe.

Even more important to Giles was the fact that Helena seemed to find him very intelligent. She was passionately interested in current affairs, read the newspapers carefully, and listened intently to the news on the wireless as well. She would often ask Giles what he thought about all the events of the day, the state of the economy, the problem of the unemployed, the wisdom or otherwise of having a coalition government, the growth of the Fascist movement in Germany, and made it clear to him that his opinions were of immense importance to her.

She was just a little younger than Barty, and he was constantly surprised and relieved that she wasn't married or even engaged. She was also rather old-fashioned, and the fact that she didn't have a job meant that she saw a more conventional role for herself than – well, than lots of modern young women. Indeed, she had told him, and rather earnestly, that she considered marriage and motherhood the true career for a woman. Giles, rather taken with this view, trembled to think what his mother might have to say about it.

He wanted to love someone and be loved by them in return more than anything in the world. He had been, he knew, a disappointment to his mother from early childhood, nice looking but not beautiful and charming like the twins, not brilliant like Kit, not interesting like Barty, a rather doubtful asset at the family dinner table, never amusing and full of gossip like Boy, certainly not noted for his sporting prowess like young Jay. Outside the family he was less confident still, aware that he did not live up to the Lytton magic, either their social success or their professional brilliance.

Finding himself in the Duffield Brown drawing room, then, or at their dining table, to be an object of interest and even of some glamour, was a considerable novelty. He was, moreover, rather uncomfortably aware that it increased his attraction to Helena, made him perhaps seek her out rather more than he would otherwise have done.

But then – he told himself – that meant he got to know her better and more swiftly, and that in turn increased his appreciation of and his fondness for her. By the end of that June, when Helena was planning her twenty-sixth birthday party and asking him if he might be able to join its celebration at a house party at the Duffield country house near

Dorking – 'Surrey, oh dear, the suburbs,' said Celia when she first heard about it – he knew he must make some kind of a decision about her. She was clearly in love with him and it was wrong to go on encouraging her if he did not reciprocate her feelings. He had tried, indeed, to tell himself that what he wanted was a closer, more long-term relationship; but there was something holding him back, something unresolved and impossible to set aside.

That something was what he felt for Barty.

If she didn't have her job, Adele thought, she would go quite mad; she despaired these days of finding love. It just didn't seem possible. In all her grown-up life – twenty-two years of it – she had only once met a man who seemed even close to being what she wanted and needed. She had met, flirted with, been charmed by, even considered going to bed with, literally dozens of handsome, charming, rich young men, but there it began and ended. She was looking for something deeper than charm, more important than looks, more demanding than flirtation. She did not even know what it was, only that it had so far eluded her. The one man who had seemed to promise it was Luc Lieberman; and he was certainly not available to her. Indeed, her father had reported meeting Luc's wife after his last trip to the Paris office: 'Lovely girl, simply beautiful, works for one of the couturiers, apparently', and, absurdly hurt and disappointed, Adele had resolved to remove him from her consciousness.

She was still a virgin, a fact which alternately amused and worried her. Like most girls of her generation she was intrigued by the notion of sex and impatient to experience it; also like many of them, she was nervous of the consequences. Venetia's pregnancy, which had happened despite her best efforts at preventing it, had been sobering; it was not something, Adele thought, to be lightly risked.

But Cedric at least kept her increasingly busy and distracted from her own personal inadequacies. He had become her best friend, devoted to her and her welfare, breathlessly interested in what she was doing, wearing, who she was seeing, how every new relationship progressed. He made her laugh, boosted her spirits, bolstered her morale and she would do the same for him; they would sit for hours chatting, dissecting one another's relationships – 'Not that one, not nearly good enough for you, Cedric, he's just a tart' – 'Oh, darling, no, dull, dull, dull, don't you go wasting a single moment with him.'

'An old maid, that's what I am,' she said to him one afternoon over tea at Fortnums, 'I shall retire soon to a little flat somewhere with some cats to whom I shall leave all my money and people will say poor old Miss Lytton, it's so sad, no one ever wanted her.'

'Nonsense,' said Cedric briskly, 'everyone wants you, Adele, it's just that you don't want them. As for retiring, don't even think about it, I need you far too much, and I simply loathe cats. Now then, for tomorrow we want a tea set, one of darling Clarice's would be best. And one of those lovely glass and chrome cocktail trolleys. By ten o'clock, darling, so no time for looking for your little catty flat today. Let's move on to the Ritz, in your mood champagne is the only thing. Come along, darling, keep that little chin of yours up. It's too pretty to start sagging downwards, it might double up on itself and then no one really would look at you.'

'Abbie, you are free to come to the Prom tomorrow, aren't you? It's the "Pastorale", and I've got two tickets. You said to get you one if I could—'

'Oh, Barty, I'm so sorry. I can't. I'm going out, I forgot all about the concert.'

'Abbie! That's too bad of you, you said you'd keep it free. Do you have to go out?'

'I do, yes, I'm afraid. I've got to see my parents, they're in London for a few days. You know how they spring it on me.'

'Yes, but – couldn't you see them afterwards?'

'Not really. Oh, dear, don't be cross.'

Barty sighed. Abbie had been a rather less than satisfactory friend recently, constantly cancelling arrangements, saying vaguely she was busy, had to work late. But not to come to a concert for which tickets had been bought . . .

'Well, I am disappointed,' she said, 'but I suppose if it's your parents . . . that's a lovely watch, Abbie, is it new?'

'Yes,' Abbie glanced quickly at the gold watch on her slim wrist, 'yes, it's nice, isn't it?'

'Present?'

'Yes. From – my uncle David.' The pause was infinitesimal; Barty wouldn't have noticed it if she hadn't felt so irritated.

'I didn't know you had an uncle. Certainly not a rich one.'

'Oh, Barty, don't be boring. What are you, a jealous husband or something?'

'Sorry. Well – have a nice evening.'

'Thanks. Enjoy the concert.'

She had intended to go straight out from work next day, but she had managed to spill some coffee down her sweater and decided to go home and change; while she was rummaging through her wardrobe, her phone rang.

'Is that Miss Miller? Miss Miller, you don't know me, but you're a good friend of my daughter. Abigail Clarence.'

'Oh, yes, hallo, Mrs Clarence.'

'I hope you don't mind us telephoning you, Abbie gave us your number once when I wasn't very well.'

'Of course not. But—'

'We're trying to get hold of Abbie. We're coming to London tomorrow and want to see her, but she's not answering her telephone and we thought she might be with you.'

'No,' said Barty slowly, 'no, she isn't, I'm afraid.'

'Well, look, if you do see her this evening, would you tell her to telephone us?'

'Yes, of course: Only—'

'Thank you. Goodbye, Miss Miller, I do hope we meet you soon.'

'Abbie,' said Barty to herself as she put down the phone, 'whatever are you up to?'

She sat at her window late that night, watching for Abbie's light to come on, half intrigued, half ashamed of herself. At eleven she went to bed, but she couldn't sleep. She was surprised at her own distress; that Abbie should have lied to her. She'd thought they were closer than that.

It was almost midnight when she heard a car in the street below; she got up, and went over to the window. Just too late; she could only see the rear lights disappearing round the corner, and about a minute later, Abbie's own lights go on.

The only thing she could be sure of was that the car had been a big one. Very big.

'Celia, good morning to you.' Boy was just arriving at his Cork Street gallery as Celia walked towards it. 'Come in and have a cup of coffee. I've got a present for you – it will amuse you so much.'

'I don't know that I want a present from you, Boy,' said Celia briskly.

'Why on earth not? What have I done wrong? Anyway, what on earth are you doing in this neck of the woods? Not calling on dear old Bunny, are you? He's got a pad here, I believe.'

141

'No, of course not,' said Celia irritably. 'And while you're making innuendoes, Boy, what on earth were you doing at the opera the other night with – with some woman? And who was she, anyway?'

'She works for one of my father's charities, and he asked me to take her. Venetia could have come, but she refused. As you know, she has no great interest in opera, and she's still recovering from Elspeth's birth. And I didn't want to waste the ticket altogether. Hardly my fault.'

'Possibly not. Although you could have stayed at home with Venetia.'

'Which I did. I left after the first act, handed over my charge to someone else. I'm surprised you didn't notice.'

'I – did,' said Celia. She felt slightly foolish.

'Well, there you are. Did you enjoy the opera yourself?'

'Very much.'

'And how much did Lord Arden tell you about his exciting new political party?'

'Hardly his,' she said, grateful for a change of subject. 'But yes, quite a lot, as a matter of fact. He's promised to introduce me to Tom Mosley. I find their ideas rather interesting.'

'Celia, don't even think about them. Those people are deeply dangerous. They believe in force when it suits them, they are violently racist and they all think that chap Adolf Hitler is the most wonderful man, when in my view he's a psychopath.'

'Absolute nonsense. Hitler is a visionary, and vision is what's needed at the moment. We could do with a bit of it here. All these wretched people out of work, hunger marches, the miners virtually starving and all the government can offer is reduced unemployment benefit. No imagination at all.'

'And what does Sir Oswald have to offer them?'

'He says control should be taken from the established authorities and complete reformation of the economy and society inaugurated.'

'By force if necessary, as I understand it.'

'Not by force, by persuasion. You know he's been approached by both major parties, they recognise how brilliant his ideas are. But he's bravely decided to go on on his own. To try to do things his way. His ideas are so exciting, you wouldn't believe it.'

'I haven't actually, no,' said Boy drily, 'and do I sense a new book coming on, Lady Celia?'

'I – well, it's possible,' she said, 'yes. I think more people should know about these things.'

'And what does Oliver think about that?'

'We haven't discussed it. Now, can we change the subject?'

'Yes. Open your present. Go on.'

She opened it and began to laugh. 'Boy, it's heaven. Thank you so much.'

'Isn't it? I knew you'd like it.'

It was a paper doll of Noël Coward, dressed in vest and underpants, complete with cut-out wardrobe. 'I adore it. I shall keep him in my bedroom.'

'Very appropriate. I have one myself, in my office here. He cheers me up.'

'Do you need cheering up, Boy?' Celia said. She spoke lightly, but her dark eyes were sharp.

'Oh – only occasionally.'

He would speak to her, Giles decided. Find out how she felt once and for all. After all, she had no real idea how he felt about her. It might be reciprocated. And then – well, then everything would be all right. More than all right, wonderful . . .

'Barty, hallo. How would you like to have supper with me tonight?'

'I'd love it. But I've got to get these proofs up to Sebastian, get his comments on the corrections. Could it be a bit later than usual?'

'Of course. Why don't we meet at – let's say, eight-thirty. Where would you like to go?'

'Oh – I don't know. Corner House.'

He looked shocked. 'Barty, I meant somewhere a bit special. I – well I want to talk to you about something. We could go to the Ritz.'

She looked at him just slightly anxiously. Then she said, 'Oh, Giles no. Not the Ritz. I feel so – uncomfortable in those places. What about that little place in Walton Street, we went a few months ago, that was lovely.'

'Oh – all right. Yes, I'll see you there.'

She was fifteen minutes late; she looked upset.

'I'm sorry. It's so sad up there, Giles. Little Izzie is so sweet and so exactly like Pandora, more every day. And she toddies about, chattering away, and every time she sees Sebastian, she goes up to him and raises her arms to be picked up and he just ignores her, walks past her, and she stands looking after him, her little face so sad. It's awful, it really is. I don't know what can be done.'

'Perhaps she could go and live with Venetia,' said Giles, 'one more would hardly make a difference.'

'Do you know, she actually suggested that? Venetia, I mean.'

'She did? To Sebastian?'

'A few weeks ago. He wouldn't hear of it, started shouting at her and saying Izzie was his responsibility and of course she had to stay with him. I'm surprised she didn't tell you.'

'Oh, it's just one other example of my family taking no account of me and my opinions,' said Giles bitterly, and then, seeing her face, half shocked, half troubled, 'Sorry, Barty.'

'Was that Boy I saw you with at lunchtime?' she said in an attempt to change the subject.

'Yes. He was trying to tempt me on to the golf course for the afternoon.'

'Oh, Giles, really! He is dreadful. His life is so – so pointless. When he sits and talks to me, I can see why everyone does like him. He has such charm, he always seems so really interested in what you're saying.'

'But he's not your sort of man, is he?'

She looked at him oddly. 'I don't know what my sort of man is, Giles.'

'You haven't met him yet, then?'

'I certainly haven't,' she said laughing.

That was encouraging. Or was it? God, this was awful.

'Let's order. And I thought we might have some champagne.'

'Giles! Whatever for?'

'Well – we don't often go out like this together.'

'No, we don't. Not often enough.'

'Boy, what's that?'

'Oh – a new table. Do you like it? It's japanned papier mâché. The top tilts to display the painting, see, like this . . . They were very popular in the mid-nineteenth century, these tables.'

'Really?' said Venetia, her voice glazing over.

'Yes. I was very excited when I found it. In a sale in Chelsea today. I really want to buy some more. Japanois-serie is terribly fashionable at the moment.'

'Is it?'

'Very. In fact, I'm going to go to a big fair next week, see what I can find.' He hesitated. 'Would you like to come with me?'

'Oh, no,' she said quickly. 'I wouldn't have the faintest idea what it was all about—'

'You could try finding out.'

'No, Boy, really. It just isn't the sort of thing that would interest me at all.'

'No,' he said, 'I suppose not. Venetia—'

'Yes, Boy?'

His eyes were thoughtful.

'Would you like to tell me what might interest you? So that we could – share it?'

'Well – to be quite honest, I don't know,' she said carelessly. 'I mean, we never did have much in common, did we? From the very beginning. We just don't share interests. We don't like the same sort of music, or shows, or – well anything, really. Except the children, of course, and our friends. Which reminds me, I was thinking of giving a big garden party at the end of the summer, just to celebrate Elspeth and being thin again. What do you think?'

'I think if you want to do that, then you will,' he said, and his tone was dismissive. 'Just give me a date and I'll be there. You must excuse me now, I have work to do. I'll see you at dinner.'

He walked out of the room; Venetia looked after him, her eyes filled with the easy tears. He was so harsh with her these days; he just didn't seem to love her at all. In fact, she could hardly remember a time now when he had been anything other than courteously affectionate towards her. Except in bed of course, that was still all right. When it happened, which wasn't nearly so often these days. But nobody stayed madly in love, surely. Her mother was always saying that. They had the children, and a beautiful house and a very good social life, everyone was always telling her how lucky she was to have Boy. That should really be enough for anyone. Anyone . . .

It was definitely going well. The champagne had been a good idea. She was laughing and chattering, talking about Abbie and how they'd joined a cycling club and went out riding on the Surrey Downs at the weekends.

'It's such fun. And we go to the theatre together a lot too, up in the gods, and to the cinema all the time. I love the cinema, don't you? The way you can just lose yourself in it. You ought to come with us sometimes.'

'I'd like that,' said Giles.

'And bring Helena too. I like Helena so much, she's—'

'Barty,' said Giles, 'that's what I want to talk to you about.'

'What, Helena?'

'Well – not exactly.'

'What, then?'

'Um—'

'This sounds rather serious,' she smiled at him, 'too serious for a restaurant maybe. Shall we have coffee at my flat?'

'Oh – yes. That's a good idea. I've got my car outside.'

'Come on then.' She stood up. 'Goodness, I feel quite dizzy. The champagne, I suppose. It was lovely. Thank you, Giles. It was all lovely.'

He looked at her. She was so pretty, no, that was the wrong word, so beautiful almost, with her great big eyes and her golden brown hair. She was a bit flushed with the champagne, and with laughing so much; she was wearing a navy-blue jumper with a low v-neck, and quite a short skirt, and her long, long legs were encased in shiny white stockings. She had wonderful legs, even the twins said they envied them. God, if only he wasn't a virgin. If only he knew how to approach a woman, what to do. He'd hardly ever kissed anyone properly. It was so awful. Suppose things went really well and Barty did say she – liked him, he'd hardly know what to say or do to her after that. Of course she wouldn't want to – to do it, thank God, but he would want to kiss her, hold her, caress her. He'd have to get some experience before he got married, he'd simply have to—

They reached her flat quite quickly; Giles sobered up completely on the way. It was mostly terror.

'Well come on,' she said, smiling, 'tell me what it is you want to talk to me about.'

'I – oh God, Barty. I don't know how to start.'

'At the beginning? In the best traditions?'

She pushed back her hair, smiled again; he leaned forward and said, 'All right. At the beginning. Barty, I've always – that is, I've always—'

'Yes, Giles? Always what?'

There was a long silence: then, 'Loved you,' he said and his heart was thudding so hard he felt she must be able to hear it.

'Well,' she said quickly, 'and I've always loved you. Goodness, what would we have done without each other, all those years? Certainly what would I have done?'

He felt sick; she hadn't understood. Or chosen not to understand. He must move on quickly, before he lost courage.

'Barty, that's not what I mean. Not love like that. I mean really love. I love you, Barty, so much. I think you're beautiful and clever and so, so good, and – well, I suppose what I'm saying is I can't imagine ever

146

loving anyone else nearly so much. I – oh God, darling Barty, could you – that is—' He moved towards her, reached out, took her hand. She allowed that, didn't snatch it away, he leaned forward, thought yes, it's going to be all right, I can kiss her, I can do that at least, I know how to do that, she seems to want—

'Giles, no! No, please. Don't spoil it, don't spoil what we've got.'

'Spoil it?' he said, leadenly confused. 'Spoil what, Barty, what do you mean?'

'I mean spoil our friendship.' She took a deep breath. 'Because that's what we've got. Such a wonderful friendship. I do love you, Giles, but only – only as a friend. I can't imagine my life without you, you mean more to me than anyone. But – but—' She stopped.

'But you don't – you couldn't—'

'No, Giles, I couldn't. I think you're clever and fun and I love talking to you, but I don't – well—'

'You don't find me attractive?' he said, suddenly angry, with her as well as himself. 'You don't want to kiss me. You couldn't imagine going to bed with me.'

That was awful; he shouldn't have said that. But she didn't seem shocked.

'No, Giles, I really couldn't. I'm sorry. I just don't think of you like that at all. I grew up with you, you were always there, like a brother, like Billy—'

'Have you been to bed with anyone?' he said harshly. He didn't know why, but it seemed to matter.

She met his eyes steadily. 'No. No, I haven't. Not yet.'

He wasn't sure if that was worse or better. Better, he supposed; she couldn't really know if she wanted to or not.

'But I – well, I have wanted to. With some people.'

Worse. Definitely worse.

'Giles, I do love you. Honestly.'

'Don't,' he said, still angry. 'Now you're patronising me. You like me, you think of me as a brother, as poor old Giles, not clever, not amusing, not a Lytton, just a poor oaf whom nobody admires or fancies. I suppose I should be grateful you like me even. If you do. You're probably only being kind, saying that.'

'Giles, I am not being kind. Not in the way you mean. If I was, I'd be lying to you, pretending, letting you kiss me. Only it wouldn't be kind, really, because I'd be taking the easy way out. Pretending I felt more – differently – than I do. Not being honest, which is what you deserve.'

'Deserve! That's rich.'

'I mean it. You do deserve it. You deserve someone lovely and attractive and – and warm, who wants to – to get married and have babies and things. I don't, Giles. However I felt. I don't want to get married for years and years, certainly not have babies. I want a career, I want to do really, really well in life—'

'My mother has done really well in life,' he said bitterly, 'and she was married and had babies.'

'Yes, and you never saw her. That's not what you'd want, Giles. But I do. When I do get married, I still want to work. Even when I have children, probably. Like – well yes, like your mother.'

'I wouldn't mind. If that was what you wanted, made you happy, you could do what you wanted – oh, God, this is ridiculous,' he said suddenly. 'You don't even want me to kiss you, now for some reason you're telling me how you want to work when you have children. It's absurd. Ridiculous. I'd better go. I'm – I'm sorry if I've upset you. Embarrassed you. It won't happen again.'

He stood up then somehow and got to the door; when he looked back, she was staring at him, her huge eyes wide with distress, her hands hanging limply at her sides.

'I'm so sorry,' she said and her voice sounded hoarse, almost a whisper. 'I'm so sorry, Giles.'

'Goodnight,' he said, and ran downstairs and out to his car. When he was safely inside, he buried his head on the steering wheel and cried, sobbing very quietly, as he had not done since he was eight and lying under the blankets in his bed at school, utterly wretched, when he had felt his parents had abandoned him and his sisters had usurped him, and the only person who cared about him in the whole world was Barty.

Then he started the car and drove very slowly home.

Chapter 12

'My darling, I want to take you to Paris.'

'Paris! How romantic. Can we stay at the Ritz? And will you buy me lots and lots of positively wicked negligees?'

'I'm not joking,' said Cedric, plaintively. '*Style* are sending me to Paris. There's a marvellous model there apparently, called—'

'I know, Muthe,' said Adele. 'She was spotted in the reception of *French Vogue*, feeding her baby by the editor, who said, "I have just passed the Virgin Mary suckling her child, go and bring her to me." Or something like that.'

'Exactly like that. Adele, you're such a star at gossip. Anyway, she has been booked for a beauty sitting for us, so will you come, darling?'

'I certainly will,' said Adele. 'Try and keep me away.'

'I'm going to Paris,' she announced to her parents at dinner that night, 'next week. Won't that be fun?'

'With your photographer friend?' said Celia.

'Yes. Of course. It's work.'

'Oh. That,' said Celia.

Adele sighed. 'Yes, Mummy, that.'

'I have to go myself next month,' said Oliver. 'We have a lot of books coming out this autumn. The explosion in the crime market over there is considerable. Georges Simenon is turning over a dozen a year; quite extraordinary. We are trying to find someone to compete with him, although not in volume terms of course.'

'Is Luc Lieberman still working for you?' asked Adele carelessly.

'Of course. I'd forgotten, you rather liked him, didn't you?'

'I remember him,' said Kit. 'I met him when he came over with that French author, I liked him a lot. He said when I was older I could go and stay with him, and he'd take me to see Josephine Baker dance. She—'

'What an extremely unsuitable suggestion,' said Celia. 'How old were you then, Kit?'

'Oh – I don't know. About eight.'

'I'm sure he didn't mean it,' said Oliver mildly.

'Whether he meant it or not, it was a stupid thing to say to a little boy.'

'Well I'm much older now,' said Kit. He looked at his mother, a gleam of malice in his eyes. 'I might just take him up on it.'

'I'll mention it to him,' said Adele, 'remind him. When do you go back to school, Kit?'

'Adele!' said Celia. There were times these days, Adele thought, when her sense of humour seemed to be completely failing.

'The twentieth,' said Kit, 'so there'd be plenty of time. April in Paris – wonderful. Excuse me, I've got work to do.'

He left the room; Adele smiled after him. He had been at Eton for over a year and loved it there. Kit loved everything. He had the blithest of temperaments, was never bored, never out of sorts, extremely sociable – the Lytton set was the one everyone in his year wanted to be in – and while formidably clever, had none of the characteristics of the swot, being apparently more interested in having fun than pursuing the academic glory that came his way with horrific ease.

He had endured at fourteen none of the adolescent horrors; the beautiful child had become a handsome boy almost overnight. He was tall without being gangly, and even the golden curls for which he had occasionally been teased at school had mercifully disappeared into thick blond waves. Celia had fretted over his angelic looks as he went off to school, fearing an onslaught of homosexual advances for him; it was Boy Warwick who had calmly and sensitively discussed the matter with him and how best to deal with it.

'Nothing can save him altogether,' he had said to Celia, 'but forewarned really is forearmed. I was very pretty and had a hideous time until I learned to box; that more or less stopped it. I'll advise Kit to do the same.'

Celia said she was more grateful than she could say that he would speak to Kit. 'Oliver and Giles are both completely incapable of it, he'll come away from any discussion more confused than when he went in.'

As time went on, Celia worried increasingly about Boy and Venetia. Boy was too clever, had too brilliant a mind, too broad a base of interest to be satisfied by Venetia's rather sweet silliness, her intellectual naivety. She still expected the marriage to fail; her hope was that Venetia would have found something else to absorb her and her energies before that time came.

150

But she did like Boy: she couldn't help it. He was irrepressibly good-natured, he was a most tender and loving father, he was generous to a fault, and an outstandingly loyal friend. There were innumerable stories of Boy Warwick lending large sums of money to friends in trouble, and then waving away any suggestion of repayment into the foreseeable future; indeed the loans were only so-called to spare pride and ease distress.

He arrived at Lytton House one particularly lovely spring day, uninvited, and asked if he might see Celia; he had acquired a painting by an artist she had admired, and brought it to the office to see if she would like to buy it.

'And I might take you to lunch, while you think about it. How would that sound?' It was a measure of her fondness for him that she agreed; normally an arrangement to lunch with Lady Celia Lytton was booked at least three weeks in advance.

'I prefer to eat at my desk in the usual run of things,' she said, picking up her hat and gloves, 'but I just happen to have a little spare time today. Where did you think we might go?'

'The Savoy? It's quite near . . .'

'Venetia is in the club again,' he said as they toasted her purchase of the painting with champagne. 'I expect she has told you.'

'She has, although not in such vulgar terms. Congratulations, Boy, although I personally think four is rather excessive in this day and age.'

'You had four children, Celia.'

'I did indeed. But only three pregnancies.'

'Ah. So you think it all looks rather, what shall we say – uncontrolled? Vulgar even?'

'I think Venetia will be worn out, Boy. No more than that.'

'Of course, you had Barty as well. So actually – five. Although Kit was something of an afterthought, was he not? And a great delight no doubt for you and Oliver.'

His black eyes danced; she met them very steadily.

'Yes. A great delight. As he has continued to be. And I do have to say, Boy, you are a very good father.'

'I like being a father,' he said rather unexpectedly. 'I like children, I find them fascinating and fun, not in the least tedious like so many of my contemporaries.'

'I wish – Sebastian was a better one,' she said and sighed.

'Yes, indeed. Poor little Izzie. She never goes near him now, she's

151

learned there's no point. We invite her to Berkeley Square as often as we can: she loves it there. But – she still has to go home at the end of the day.'

'Oh God,' said Celia, 'what on earth can we do about it?'

'I don't know, Celia. But if *you* can't do anything with Sebastian, nobody can.' He smiled at her: his most artless smile. 'You're such good friends. Tell me, how is Bunny Arden? I heard he and Cynthia dined with you and Oliver last week. Next time they come, do ask us. I'm longing to quiz him about the latest developments with Tom and his gang of roughnecks.'

Celia frowned at him. 'I wouldn't dream of inviting you. And I don't know why you're so hostile to Tom Mosley. He's doing extremely well, he has up to 40,000 members now and with good reason. I would personally like to see him in government.'

'I suppose you're going to his ghastly meeting next week.'

'Yes, I am. Why don't you come, it might change your mind.'

'It certainly wouldn't. Celia, those people are mad. Baba Metcalfe is having an affair with Grandi.'

'Well, I like Grandi. And the Italian Embassy is glorious. You'd love to see his paintings, he has Titians, and the most wonderful tapestries and mirrors from the Medici court.'

'Yes, and have you ever wondered how he acquired them? Or rather how Mussolini did? Oh, I know it's no use talking to you, Celia, you're a woman in love.'

'In love? Don't be absurd.'

'Not absurd at all. I mean with a new cause. A new ideology. Now then, I have to go, I'm afraid. More coffee?'

'No, thank you. Yes, it has been fun, thank you. But you're wrong about the British Union of Fascists. And where are you going now? Home?'

'Where else? When I've been away from my wife and family all day.'

'Give Venetia my love and tell her to rest.'

As she got into her car, she looked back and saw Boy hailing a taxi; he had quite a long conversation with the driver before he got in and the cab pulled away. Pulled away not down the Strand and therefore in the direction of Berkeley Square, but in the other direction, turning right across Waterloo Bridge. Of course it didn't mean anything; anything at all. If he hadn't said he was going home, she wouldn't have given it a moment's thought.

Celia returned to Lytton House in a slightly anxious frame of mind.

Foolish of Venetia to have allowed herself to become pregnant yet again: very foolish.

'I'm – moving,' said Abbie. She didn't quite meet Barty's eyes.

'Moving! Where to?'

'Well – well, it's rather exciting, really. To a house.'

'A house! Abbie, how, why?'

'Well – you know I mentioned my uncle David?'

'The one who gave you the watch?'

'Oh – yes. Well he died; and left me some money. So I thought I'd buy a house with it. Not just fritter it away. I mean it's an awfully good investment and—'

'It must have been a lot of money.'

'Yes. Well, quite a lot. It's not an expensive house. Not a Lytton house.' She grinned at Barty.

Barty wondered, rather bleakly, if she was lying. Ever since the night of the concert, she hadn't been able to properly trust her.

She'd told her about it, of course, mentioned the phone call, knowing that Mrs Clarence was bound to: Abbie had been vague, said oh her parents were so hopeless, she'd waited in the restaurant for ages for them. It was so obvious she'd been with someone else altogether.

Barty didn't mention hearing her return, or seeing the big car. There didn't seem any point.

But it had hurt. It wasn't as if she cared what Abbie did, or what man she might or might not have been in bed with. Why couldn't she just have told her? Abbie obviously didn't think she was as close a friend as she had hoped. She had, on the other hand, been wonderful over the business with Giles; had listened carefully, asking only the most relevant questions, comforted Barty, told her that she had done exactly the right thing, so brave and so honest.

'So many girls would have just gone along with it. Tried to persuade themselves they liked him really, or let him down lightly later on with a letter or something.'

She was very keen on honesty: in other people.

'So where are you going to live?' Barty said rather sadly. 'I shall miss you.'

'Well – in Clapham. It's near the new school and everything. And of course I'll miss you too. Anyway, you must come over all the time, there's lots of room, you can always stay.'

'Yes,' said Barty, 'yes, I'd like that. Thank you.'

Later that night, lying in bed, she felt unaccountably anxious. It was more than Abbie moving away; there'd been something – odd about her. Different. What was it? What?

Probably just Abbie being obtuse. Setting out to confuse her, stop her guessing the real reason she was moving. How she had really been able to buy a house. But why? Why couldn't she just tell her the truth?

Barty sighed; she really wasn't very happy at all at the moment. Everything was – well, not exactly going wrong. But not right. Not right at all.

She had asked, straight away, immediately after Giles's declaration of love for her, if she might be able to go away for a while, either to Paris or New York. It had seemed such a good idea, a sensible solution: but both requests had been refused. There was no job for her, and she could not and should not be foisted on them at a whim, Oliver had said almost sternly. She had been dismayed; continuing to see Giles every day, having to work with him, discuss things with him on a daily, almost hourly basis, meet him at family occasions, particularly as they had always been such friends and so close, was horribly difficult. She had been truly shocked by his outburst, not just surprised; wondered if she should blame herself, if she had encouraged him, spent long hours examining her behaviour towards him, wondering if the affectionate teasing, the kisses she gave him, however sisterly, the invitations to her flat, the acceptance of all his invitations to lunch or supper, the habit she had of taking his arm as they walked along, had all wrongly encouraged him, led him to think she felt more for him than she actually did.

If that were so, then she was paying a terrible price; he could scarcely look at her, never spoke to her except in the most formal terms, and went out of his way to avoid her to such an extent that she felt everyone must notice and be wondering why.

In the event, it was only Celia and Oliver who did – and assumed, wrongly, that they must have had a quarrel.

Barty was shocked by the speed at which Giles's engagement to Helena had followed his declaration of love for her; shocked and saddened that Giles should rush into a marriage with someone he didn't properly love. He was using Helena to ease his pain and lash out at her, and it was terribly wrong.

But there was nothing she could do. She had to smile, to pretend, to attend the engagement party, to kiss Helena, to say that yes, she would love to be a bridesmaid – and never suggest for an instant that she agreed with the twins about the dreadful mistake Giles was making.

Helena was all right; she was serious and unaffected and obviously loved Giles. But she was extremely self-absorbed and what could only be described as touchy, and, perhaps most importantly, particularly given the family she had married into, she lacked humour. A conversation with Helena was not a very diverting experience.

Barty had initially quite liked her, and was inclined to be on her side, but as time went by, she changed her mind and not only because Helena's attitude towards her changed. From a rather pressing affection in the early days she began to treat Barty with something close to condescension.

Frequent invitations to the house in Chelsea ceased – as much to Giles's relief, she felt sure, as her own – and Helena's eagerness to be her friend, to admire her and her achievements, her clear desire to co-opt Barty on to her side as a member of the Lytton opposition all faded. Moreover Giles did not seem happy; he was often morose at work, especially in the morning, jumpy and defensive in meetings, unreceptive to ideas, and reacted with increased hostility to the slightest criticism, not just from Celia but Oliver as well.

It all made Barty's own life rather difficult – and not much fun.

Helena was waiting impatiently for Giles to come home. To their dear little house in Walton Street. She had such wonderful news. Such very, very wonderful news. She was so terribly happy. At last . . .

At the very beginning, her joy at his proposal, at the discovery he loved her as much as she loved him, and then all the wonderful rituals of engagement, choosing the ring, telling their parents, putting the announcement in the paper, receiving all the letters of congratulation – it had been too good to be true.

The family dinner at the Lyttons had been a bit nerve-racking, she found Lady Celia terrifying, and the twins distinctly tiresome, and it annoyed her too that Giles was so in awe of his mother; but Oliver she loved, he was so kind and gentle, and she liked Boy Warwick too, slightly against her will, for he wasn't exactly the sort of man she approved of. And Kit was sweet and so good-looking, and of course Barty was charming. It was a bit of a funny arrangement, Helena felt, the Barty one, and her mother had been distinctly withering about her: 'She comes from a very poor family originally, as I understand, almost the slums. Of course she seems perfectly – all right now, quite PLU, but one does wonder—'

'PLU, Mother?'

'People like us, darling.'

Helena, half shocked, half amused by her mother's snobbery, felt bound to remind her at that point that her own grandfather had come from an area of London not too far removed from the slums himself: and since this was something Mrs Duffield Brown made a great effort to conceal and even to forget, along with the fact that she had married plain Leslie Brown and added her maiden name to his on their marriage, they exchanged quite heated words, culminating in Helena saying that that kind of snobbery was supposed to have completely died off after the war. She couldn't tell Giles of course, he would have been upset, but she did make a great effort to be especially nice to Barty, and to tell her mother at every possible opportunity about her first from Oxford, and how brilliantly she did her editing job at Lyttons.

In the event the dinner party saw her mother almost completely silenced; the combination of the dazzling presence of the Lyttons en masse, and her anxiety that Leslie might let his accent or his story slip for just a moment was almost too much for her. She sat between Oliver and Giles, speaking only when spoken to and then only briefly, her appetite so adversely affected that Lady Celia was driven to enquire graciously if she was perhaps feeling unwell.

'Oh, no, perfectly well, thank you – Celia,' she said, feeling that continuing to call her daughter's mother-in-law Lady Celia was a trifle obsequious.

'Did you see Mummy's face then?' Adele said to Venetia afterwards. 'Poor old Mrs DB obviously didn't know you dropped the Lady without invitation at your peril.'

'Well, how could she?' said Venetia. 'Pretty frightful altogether, though I—'

'So did I. Didn't mind—'

'No, he's a poppet. And—'

'Mm. Still not sure. She's changed a bit since—'

'Hasn't she? Not nearly so—'

'Never mind. Giles seems—'

'I hope he is. I do so hope he is.'

The wedding was held at the Dorchester, Celia having made it plain without actually saying so that she did not consider Dorking in any way a suitable venue for her son's wedding – 'It's the way she says Dorking,' said Adele, giggling, 'as if it were Sodom or Gomorrah' – and the Duffield Brown house in Kensington was far too small. Helena looked lovely in white satin, and a rather flat veil, she carried a wonderful spray of lilies, and the attendants all wore palest pink. There were six grown-up bridesmaids including Barty and Adele, and six small attendants, including Izzie Brooke and the tiny Elspeth Warwick, both of whom looked so exactly like their mothers that people never stopped remarking upon the fact all day. Which would have been worrying, as Barty remarked to Kit, if Sebastian had been there, but he had refused, as he did almost all invitations these days. Abigail Clarence, invited to the wedding as one of Barty's guests, had expressed great disappointment.

The reception was very lavish, with the Duffield Brown coffers open extremely wide, and Grandpa Percy, Leslie's father, was the surprise hit of the day.

'Who'd have thought it,' said Venetia giggling, pulling off her hat and collapsing on to a sofa, 'charming Grandmama like that, common as muck as they say, but she kept saying how marvellous he was, backbone of Britain and all that, and how he had such wonderful stories of his life at the steel works. Mrs DB was having a fit, apparently she was hoping he wouldn't come at all.'

'I think Grandmama did it just to annoy her. I think she and Mummy hatched it up on purpose,' said Adele.

'Quite possibly,' said Venetia.

The honeymoon was a bit of a disappointment to Helena; she was pretty sure Giles hadn't guessed, she'd worked awfully hard at being grateful and telling him how wonderful it had all been, especially *it*, but – well, maybe, she just kept telling herself, it would get better. Of course she had nothing to compare it with, but from everything she had heard and read, it should have been better than *that*. Quite a bit better. At least it hadn't hurt – or not much anyway – which some of the books had said it would; that had been a relief. And of course the kissing was lovely, with no clothes on. She'd really enjoyed it. And Giles had been quite good, hadn't just – rushed at her, had stroked her breasts and told her he loved her. But then – oh, dear, then. It had been over so quickly. So terribly quickly. A few sort of thrusts and then he had groaned and she'd felt him shudder a bit and that had been that. Of course she'd pretended like mad, said how much she'd enjoyed it, and so on; but apart from the wetness, and the soreness, she would hardly have known it had happened.

But then, they had both been totally inexperienced. Well, she was, and Giles had said he was almost. Which she'd loved him for really, but – maybe a bit more would have helped. And then they had both been very tired.

So – maybe, she thought through that long first night listening to him snore – she hadn't expected that and it was very loud snoring, not exactly romantic – maybe when they had both settled down, got used to one another, weren't so nervous and tense, it would be better. They had lots of time, in the next few weeks, to practise. Get better at it. But still – she had hoped for a bit better. And had been almost irritated by Giles saying hadn't it been wonderful next morning. Over and over again. Yes, she'd said, yes, of course it had; and again, 'It really was all right for you, was it, darling? You really – well—' And, 'Yes,' she'd said, 'of course. It was very nice. Very nice indeed.' She couldn't quite bring herself to say it was wonderful. She just couldn't. When it was, she would say so. And it would be: of course it would.

The holiday part of the honeymoon was very nice; they had been lent a villa in the south of France, and the weather was gorgeous. Helena read a great deal, and they had a lot of wonderful meals and went on long walks and Giles had told her how much he loved her and how happy he was and they had discussed their future endlessly, the big family they were going to have and Giles's success at Lyttons. Helena was quite sure he was going to be a success; anyone could see he was extremely clever and he worked so hard.

'You'll be Mr Lytton the Third after your father retires,' she said, 'and you'll run the most brilliant publishing house in London.'

Giles said he didn't think his father would ever retire and his mother certainly wouldn't; Helena told him that was nonsense.

'It would be wrong and selfish of them to hang on. Depriving you of your chance. We won't allow it.'

Giles didn't seem to take quite such a positive view.

Settling into their house in Chelsea was fun, and seeing her girlfriends from her new status of married woman, gossiping over long lunches. And learning to run a house and cooking for Giles sometimes – they didn't have a live-in cook, Giles said he couldn't afford it, just a cook-daily.

Helena didn't mind that at all at first; but as the year went by, it began to irritate her. Giles really was paid rather little, he was always saying they couldn't afford things. It was so mean when Lyttons obviously made lots of money and could afford to give him more. If she hadn't had the allowance from her father, she wouldn't even have been able to buy all the clothes she wanted. She was very keen on her role as wife and hostess, and for that you needed nice clothes.

She wanted to give lots of parties, but until the first Christmas she wasn't allowed to: for the same enraging reason. Giles's telling her they couldn't afford things was the cause of their first big row . . . and the second and the third. After a bit she told him he had to ask for a salary rise, but he said he'd had one when they got married and couldn't possibly ask for more.

'What happens when we have children?' she said and he said well then, obviously, that would be different. He didn't like the fact she still had an allowance from her father either, but she said she needed it, and if he wanted it to stop, he'd have to do something about it.

She just hadn't realised how much he was in thrall to his family; not just at work which was natural, but at home. If Celia said she wanted them at the house, they all had to be there; if she gave a party, they all went as semi-hosts. Except Barty, of course; she seemed to get out of all that.

After a bit, Helena ceased to think Barty was wonderful and began to resent her. Oliver obviously adored her, she had her own car which he and Celia had apparently given her when she won her place at Oxford, no reason why not of course, but still . . . and her job at Lyttons seemed quite important, she even had her own authors to look after now, 'not any of the important ones of course', Giles had said, rather defensively. He was more and more defensive as time went on and touchy too. Sometimes they would sit right through supper not talking because he was in a bad mood. And quite often she would find him staring out of the window, looking morose and refusing to tell her what the matter was. That really hurt: that wasn't what marriage was about.

And even Helena could see, without ever having spent an hour in the place, that Celia thought less of Giles than she should do. And Celia did treat her as if she were some kind of fool. That really annoyed Helena; she might not have a degree – if she heard once more about Barty's first she would scream – but she was extremely well read and she made a point of keeping up with modern fiction. Whenever she tried to talk to Celia about a book, Celia would look at her with that particularly cold amusement and make it plain that her views couldn't possibly be of any value whatsoever.

By their first wedding anniversary, Helena was not exactly unhappy, but certainly not happy. Demoralised at her failure to contribute to Giles's success, permanently resentful on his behalf, side-lined by his family. Kit was lovely, of course. But then he was away at school now – and then there was the baby. Or rather not the baby. Of course she hadn't wanted one straight away, that would have been silly, and she had been very careful to use her contraceptive; but after Christmas she had decided it was about time to start trying. And nothing happened. For month after month. She went on and on having her period and every time she felt more upset and got more tense when Giles was making love to her and worried that because *it* was still not very good, she wasn't getting pregnant. There was no one in the family whom she could confide in; finally she burst into tears in the company of a friend who recommended she see her doctor – 'a woman, frightfully outspoken and modern, nothing would shock her, honestly'.

The doctor, middle-aged and rather jolly, was very matter of fact, and said it often did take a while to conceive; she managed to establish that their sex life wasn't quite what it should be, and told Helena not to worry too much about that either.

'Shame you're not enjoying it, of course, but as long as he ejaculates, you should be all right. Just keep working at it. Most women who don't get pregnant don't have enough sex.'

Helena, half shocked by this frankness, half relieved, went home and set about having enough sex that very evening; two more disappointing months went by and then suddenly, just as she had begun to despair, she missed her period and almost at once started to feel sick . . .

'Mam'selle Adele?'

Adele nearly dropped the phone.

'Yes. Yes, that's right.'

She sat down on the bed, her legs suddenly weak.

'Luc Lieberman. You remember me?'

'Yes, of course,' said Adele.

'I heard you were coming to Paris. Why did you not let me know? I feel quite – quite *desolé*.'

'Well, there's no need for that. Absolutely no need at all.'

'But I would have liked to take you to lunch—'

'Monsieur Lieberman—'

'Luc, please.'

'Luc. I'm not here on a social visit. Or even shopping. I'm working. Busy every minute. So – no time for lunches or anything.'

'How extremely sad. Are you quite sure?'

'Quite,' said Adele firmly.

'And what is this so important work? May I be told?'

'Yes, of course. I'm a stylist. For a very famous English photographer.'

'I see.' There was a silence. This wasn't going very well. Perhaps she should have been more – more forthcoming. It was just that he made her feel so nervous, so keen to impress him, she wanted to appear busier and more important than she was.

'And how long are you staying in Paris?' he said finally.

'Oh – just four days.'

'Are you happy with your hotel?'

'Oh, very, yes. It's perfect.'

Cedric had booked them both into a small, delightful hotel in the rue de Seine; set back in its own pretty courtyard, surrounded by art galleries, small restaurants and an enchanting open-air market, Adele felt herself to be truly in the heart of Paris.

Another silence. 'Well,' he said finally, 'if you do not have time for a meeting, then so be it.' It sounded very final; she should have been more friendly, she thought miserably, after all, he had sought her out, offered to entertain her.

'Perhaps – perhaps coffee tomorrow?' she said.

'Coffee? That sounds a little – brief. I wonder – would you like to join me for *petit déjeuner*?'

'That would be – lovely,' she said quickly.

She heard his voice change again. Clearly he was not a man to be thwarted.

'Good. You are so near the Café Flore, do you know it?'

'No,' she said.

'You should. It is a serious gap in your education. Boulevard St-Germain, just a little way along from your street. I will meet you there tomorrow morning. At eight-thirty.'

'Tomorrow morning we start at seven,' said Adele. Oh dear, that would make him cross again.

But: 'Seven! I am very impressed! The next day then?'

'The next day,' she said. 'Yes, that would be – all right.'

'Good. At last. Eight-thirty. Le Flore. *Au revoir*, Mam'selle Adele.'

Why was she bothering? Adele wondered, as she put down the phone. He was married, he had found her foolish, he was much older than she was – and then there had been his terrible clothes. Now that was a

161

really serious drawback. She would cancel it, just telephone him and say she couldn't manage it after all. It would be much more sensible.

'Tomorrow,' she said to Cedric, as they ate dinner in one of the small restaurants near their hotel, 'I have a breakfast appointment. I hope that's all right.'

'A breakfast appointment, darling? With whom?'

'Oh – just a man.'

'A man? Should I come too, chaperone you?'

'Of course not. He works for Lyttons in Paris. He's much older than me and married.'

'Married! Well, my darling, don't think that means anything to a Frenchman. The French believe absolutely in free love. Before and after marriage. Is he attractive?'

'*You* wouldn't think so,' said Adele firmly.

'How do you know? I can tell he is. I'm jealous already. Where are you meeting him?'

'Le Flore.'

'Le Flore! I'm more jealous still. Those waiters, so *sympatique*. They know all the secrets of Paris. I think I should come.'

'You're not to come,' said Adele, 'I want to meet him on my own.'

'So selfish!' said Cedric.

They had had a difficult day. Mostly because of the model: not the legendary Murthe, who had been ill, but another exquisite creature called Villette, who could, Adele said to Cedric, have given Celia lessons in perversity. She refused to wear the sequin cape Adele had brought, or the white fox stole, or even the gold fabric which the beauty editor pronounced as quite perfect. After two hours of Gallic shrugs, interspersed with brilliantly animated conversation with the hairdresser, which had brought even Cedric's famous patience to breaking point, Adele had gone to one of the street markets and bought several metres of velvet in wonderful colours, deep blood-red and midnight-navy and dark fir-forest green; Villette had looked at it all disdainfully and then picked up the navy length and swathed it loosely round her lovely blonde head.

'There it is,' said Cedric. 'There is our photograph.'

It wasn't quite, since the velvet had wrecked the hair, and the hairdresser had a tantrum; but by four o'clock, with Villette looking rather like Diana Cooper in *The Miracle*, they had the studio shot and then, on her own suggestion, went out into the brilliant rain-washed

162

evening and set her against the fountains of the Place St-Sulpice, where she suddenly became sweet-natured and creative and stood barefoot and laughing on the edge of the fountains, her arms raised to the sky.

'Not a beauty shot, I fear,' said Cedric, 'but a wonderful image. If nobody wants it, I shall blow it up ten feet tall and put it on the wall of my studio.'

Next morning, she was sitting waiting at her table in the *terrasse* of the famous Flore, enjoying the people walking past, when a small car pulled up outside and parked right in the lane of traffic; Luc Lieberman hurried in.

'Mam'selle Adele! Forgive me, I beg of you, for being late. The traffic – *terrible*. How extremely good to see you. And you are looking quite different, so grown-up and *élégante*, I feel quite intimidated.'

He looked very much the same, a little thinner perhaps, his intense dark looks sharpened, the clothes definitely improved, a cream shirt under a grey suit, and a grey slouch hat. A waiter in his long white apron and short black jacket stood behind him, holding a silver coffee jug: it was an archetypal Parisian scene. Cedric would have loved it; she should have let him come. She smiled up at Luc Lieberman.

'If only it were true.'

'What, that I felt intimidated? Oh, but it is.'

'I'm sure you're not,' she said briskly, 'but actually I meant about my being elegant. Two days in Paris and I feel like a country bumpkin.'

'But how absurd,' he said, settling himself beside her, his eyes moving over her. 'Why?'

'Everyone here is so chic. London women just don't have that, it's an instinct, like singing in tune.'

'But you have so many great beauties, singing wonderfully in tune, Daisy Fellowes, Diana Guinness, Iya Abdy—'

'Well, there you are, one French, one Russian, only one English. Anyway, you seem to have a great knowledge of pretty London ladies,' said Adele.

'Well, of course. Now what are you going to have?'

'Oh – just coffee please. And croissants. Isn't that what you French have for breakfast?'

'No,' he said, smiling at her, 'it is not. Let me guide you to a truly continental breakfast.' He turned to the waiter, '*Deux jus d'oranges, deux brioches, de la confiture, deux cafés au lait, et pour moi, deux oeufs*. Would you like an egg, Mam'selle Adele? They are all ready and waiting for you, see.'

And indeed the eggs were, six of them, perfectly uniform in size, set in a round wooden egg stand on the table. Adele shook her head.

'No, thank you. I'm not a breakfast eater.'

'That's because of those terrible English breakfasts.'

'No, it isn't,' said Adele crossly, perversely eager to defend her country and its food. 'I just don't feel hungry in the morning. I'm like my mother.'

'Ah, the beautiful Lady Celia. Certainly an advertisement for not eating breakfast. How is she?'

'She's very well.'

'And your sister?'

'Not quite so well. *Enceinte*, I think is the word.'

'Very good. I did not realise you spoke French these days.'

'I don't. I just know a tiny bit.'

'Well, the tiny bit suits you. She has other children, your sister?'

'Indeed she does. This is the fourth.'

'Very good. We believe in large families in France.'

He said this with great satisfaction, as if Venetia's sole purpose in having so many children was to give pleasure to the French.

'Are you a Catholic?' she asked curiously.

'No, no. My mother is Jewish. But my grandmother is a Catholic. They both grieve over the fact that actually I am neither. In the religious sense.'

'And in other senses?'

'How nice that we are speaking of the senses already.' He smiled at her, his dark eyes probing hers; she felt the familiar sensation of being disturbed, almost troubled, deep within herself. She looked away; he said after a moment, 'But in answer to your question I feel a little of both. Which is uncomfortable at times. I suppose if I were to think very carefully about it, I would say I was Jewish. That is a more – consuming thing.' He smiled again. 'But my wife is not Jewish and that is a terrible thing for a Jew to have done. To marry out of the faith.'

'Is it?'

'But of course. When we have more time, I will try to explain it to you.'

'Are we likely to have more time, do you think?' said Adele. Now why had she said that?

'I would certainly like it if we did,' he said slowly.

She looked down, fiddled with the brioche she had picked from the basket. How did he do this, make her feel at once so disconcerted and so brilliantly, sweetly happy?

'So.' His tone was suddenly brisk again. 'What are your plans for the day?'

'Oh – we have to go into *Style* this afternoon. And Cedric, that's who I work for, the photographer, you know, wants us to spend a few hours just wandering round Paris, looking for locations, taking what he calls notebook pictures.'

'Cedric. What a charming name. Like Little Lord Fauntleroy, isn't that right?'

'How clever of you to know that. Yes. I suppose he's a bit like Little Lord Fauntleroy altogether. Awfully pretty.'

'I see,' he said, laughing. 'Well that answers one of my questions. I have no need to be jealous, is that right?'

'You have no need to be jealous, no,' she said, 'not of Cedric anyway.'

'Good. Of anyone else?'

'Maybe,' she said coolly.

'Well that is not fair. You must tell me, yes or no.'

'*Monsieur*—'

'Luc.'

'Luc, you are married. It's nonsense to talk of your being jealous.'

'Unfortunately – or perhaps fortunately – human emotion is not affected by the marital status. I desired you when I first saw you, when I was single, and I desire you still.'

'That's ridiculous,' she said.

'Why?'

'Well – you hardly know me.'

'What a very English remark.'

'Yes, well, I am English,' she said, confused by his conversation as well as his presence. 'And therefore rather given to making English remarks.'

'You sound cross. Don't be cross.'

'I'm not cross.'

'I think you are a little. But it suits you. I noticed it before. Your eyes become even larger and your colour more brilliant. Now stop glaring at me and have a piece of this egg.'

'I don't want any egg. I don't like egg.'

'You will like this egg,' he said, and scooped a piece out of the shell very gently and carefully, and ate it, and then did it again and held the spoon to her lips, his eyes absolutely fixed on hers. She resisted for just

165

a moment, then opened her mouth and let him feed her the egg. It was perfect, very soft and tenderly flavoured; she swallowed it slowly and then smiled.

'That was – lovely,' she said. It was a moment of extraordinary intimacy; the waiter watched them with interest. A most practised observer of human behaviour, he could recognise this instantly for what it was: the birth of a love affair.

Chapter 13

'You're having an affair with someone, aren't you?'

A long silence; then, 'Yes. Anything wrong with that?'

'No. No, of course not.'

'Well, why are you looking at me like a cross between my mother and an elderly nun? What gives you the right to be judgmental?'

'Abbie,' said Barty, 'I'm not being judgmental. Honestly.'

They were sitting in a café in the Strand; a twice-postponed (by Abbie) supper arrangement had become an after-work cup of tea.

'Well, it sounds like it,' said Abbie, stirring her tea viciously.

'I'm not. I'm just a bit – hurt – that you haven't told me about it.'

'Barty, why should I tell you about it, for heaven's sake? It's got absolutely nothing to do with you.'

Barty felt slightly taken aback; she had thought she and Abbie were so close that any such important happening would be shared between them.

'No,' she said, 'no, of course it hasn't. Sorry, Abbie. I – I didn't mean to pry. It's just that you've been so secretive. It's not like you.'

'It might be. You haven't known me for very long. Certainly not when I've been having a love affair. Actually I find it quite – surprising you should expect me to tell you. A bit pathetic, if you really want to know. Maybe you need a bit of love interest in your own life.'

She looked at Barty coldly, her green eyes hostile. Barty stopped feeling apologetic and felt angry instead.

'Maybe I should,' she said, 'but I'll tell you one thing, Abbie, I don't like being lied to. I felt an absolute fool when your parents telephoned me. After you'd told me you were with them. You could at least have told me the truth then. What difference would it have made?'

'I'd probably have had a grilling like this, that's why,' said Abbie. 'Just leave me alone, Barty, will you, to lead my own life.'

'All right,' said Barty, 'I will. I'm extremely sorry to have upset you, Abbie. It's probably just as well you've moved to Clapham. You won't have to bump into me in the street any more.'

Absurdly, she felt tears in her eyes; she blinked furiously, stood up, put down half a crown on the table and walked out of the café. Thirty seconds later she felt a hand on her arm.

'Barty, I'm sorry. That was beastly of me. Come back inside. I didn't mean to upset you.'

She was always like that; swift to apologise, eager to make up friends, as she put it. Barty smiled at her.

'Oh – it's all right. I was being a bit – snoopy.'

'Just a bit. Come on, sit down, finish your bun.' She looked at Barty very levelly. 'I was being secretive. You're quite right. It's because he's – well—' She stopped.

'Married?'

'Yes.'

'Oh,' said Barty, determined this time not to react wrongly. 'Oh, I see. Well – that's fine. Isn't it? You're just giving him a – a free meal? Like you've always said. Improving his marriage, even?'

'Exactly. Glad you've been listening to your Auntie Abbie.'

She grinned at Barty; her wide, engaging grin. There might be something in Abbie's views on sex, indeed she agreed with some of them wholeheartedly – like sleeping with someone you loved whether you were married or not was absolutely all right – but to blithely take someone's husband into your bed and clearly not even feel guilty about it – that was rather different.

'And I'll tell you something,' said Abbie, 'it certainly is improving his marriage. He says his wife's much happier than she's been for ages. He's not – making so many demands on her, you see. In every way, not just sex.'

'Oh,' said Barty, 'yes, I see.'

'Anyway,' said Abbie, 'I don't suppose it'll last long. But while it does – well, we're both having lots of fun. He buys me marvellous presents, look, like this bracelet, do you like it?'

It was gold, quite plain, clearly very expensive.

'Yes, it's lovely.'

'And he's awfully clever, we have really wonderful conversations. It's not just sex.'

A bit more than a free meal, then, Barty thought.

And then, because she had to ask, without much expectation of Abbie answering, 'So – who is this man, Abbie? Are you going to tell me?'

She was right; Abbie did not. Barty left her feeling at once comforted and more anxious. There was more going on than Abbie had told her; she was quite certain of it.

At least life was better at Lyttons now. Helena's pregnancy had eased a lot of tension; Giles relaxed, mellowed, they were even able to begin to become friends again, he and she; it was as if finally he had something that was his very own, an achievement that he could take full credit for, that gave him status in every area of his world. It was a lot for a little baby to have accomplished, Barty thought, smiling at him as he told her one of his stupid jokes before a meeting; and it hadn't even been born yet. Who knew what might happen as it began to grow up: Giles might even begin to get the better of his mother.

It took Izzie quite a long time to realise that all fathers were not like her own. She had had few friends; the only families she knew well were the Lyttons, and Wol was nearly always in his study, as her own father was, and the Warwicks and her visits there were confined mostly to the large nursery.

She could see life in that house was very different, but she had always supposed it was because there were so many children. When Uncle Boy, as she had been instructed to call him, did visit the nursery, and the children all leapt on him and climbed into his lap and demanded that he read them stories and he got down on all fours and pretended to be a horse, she assumed that was because the children had got the better of him. Had there been only one of them, then clearly he would have been the distant, aloof figure that her own father was.

But then she went to school, and was invited to other children's houses and met their fathers, and observed that they too read stories, played games, hugged and kissed their little daughters; and she would go home and look at Sebastian, reading in his study or working, and say hopefully, 'Good afternoon, Father.' And he would scarcely glance at her, would just say, 'Isabella, surely you can see I'm busy. Go up to the nursery please.'

And she would go up and find Nanny, worrying at the difference, and wondering why it was: then slowly but sadly coming to the conclusion that it must be her fault, that she must be doing something wrong, that her father so clearly didn't want to have anything to do with her: and wondering what, if anything, she could possibly do to put it right.

'Adele? This is Luc. Luc Lieberman. I want you to come to Paris again.'

'Well, I'm afraid I can't,' said Adele. She spoke lightly, but she felt so weak with emotion she had to lean against the wall where she was standing.

'Why not?'

'Much too busy.'

'Then I shall come to London.'

'But why?'

'Because I want to see you again.'

'But Luc, it's ridiculous.'

'I don't think so.'

'It is. You're married.'

'Not entirely happily.'

'Oh, no' – she half smiled – 'I'm not falling for that one. It's what all the married men say. That they aren't happy. That their wives don't understand them.'

'All of them? What a large number, and what a miserable large number, of men you must know.'

'You know what I mean. And I'm not—'

'Not what?'

'Not interested.'

'Of course you are.' His tone was almost complacent, full of suppressed amusement. 'You are very interested. I felt it when I saw you, and I feel it now even over the telephone wires.'

'Then you're feeling wrong,' she said after a moment. 'And that's not what I mean, anyway—'

'I know what you meant, Adele. And it is of course natural. But – I can only repeat: I want to see you. I need to see you. And if you don't come to Paris, I shall come to London. Now which shall it be?'

'I am not coming to Paris,' she said. 'And that is absolutely final.'

'I'm – well, I'm going to Paris again,' she said to Venetia the next day.

'To – oh, Dell, why?'

'He telephoned. He said he wanted to see me again. And I said I couldn't. And here I am going. I can't help it. It's as if some force was propelling me over there. All I can think about is seeing him again and being with him again, and how happy I shall be, and then I suppose how miserable I shall be. Venetia, am I mad?'

'No,' said Venetia, patting her hand tenderly, 'just in love.'

'Father, it's a girl,' said Giles. His voice was tearful and exultant at the same time. 'Quite big, seven and a half pounds.'

'Well done, old chap. Well done indeed. How's Helena?'

'She's well. She was incredibly brave.'

'They are brave, these women,' said Oliver, remembering Celia's own stoicism in childbirth. 'I can only thank God we don't have to go through it. Well, that's wonderful news. What are you going to call her?'

'Mary. Mary Alexandra.'

'How very regal.'

'Is it? Yes, I suppose so. I must go back to Helena, she's a bit – weepy.'

'I expect she is. Well, when can we come and meet our new granddaughter?'

'Tomorrow, I should think. Please tell Mother and the girls.'

'Of course. Send Helena our love.'

Giles sat by Helena's bed holding her hand, smoothing her hair, smiling into her eyes; she was pale and exhausted but clearly very happy.

'I'm just so glad she's all right,' she said. 'I was so afraid she might not be.'

'I was afraid you might not be,' said Giles soberly. 'Was it very bad?'

'Worse than I expected. But now – who cares? I just kept thinking it had to end some time – if I didn't die, that is – and then it would all be worth it.'

He nodded. He had sat outside the delivery room while she gave birth, refusing to take sanctuary in the waiting room or his club, like most husbands. He would have been with her, if it had been allowed; indeed he had tried to persuade them.

'Be with her!' said the midwife in astonishment. 'What a dreadful idea. Don't you think she has enough to worry about without having you there?' And, 'Certainly not,' said the doctor. 'Not a pretty sight, you know, and you'd probably faint. You go off and have a couple of stiff gins and when you come back it'll all be over.'

Only it hadn't been, it had gone on for hours and hours, and he had heard her groaning and crying out, and guilt had suffused him, guilt and fear, to think he had inflicted this upon her.

Only now, seeing her restored to him, and the baby lying in her cot at the side of the bed, did he begin to forgive himself and to dare to feel happy again. Very happy indeed that he, Giles, had finally managed to create something that was entirely his and that he could be truly proud of.

171

'I love you,' he said to Helena, and for the very first time he meant it. Meant it and believed it.

'I am taking you to dine at the Lipp. Have you ever been there?'

Adele shook her head. She might well, in fact, have dined frequently at the Brasserie Lipp; but at that precise moment, sitting with Luc Lieberman's hand on her knee, his eyes boring into her own, in the bar of her hotel, she hardly knew her own name; she felt absolutely confused, every emotion, every piece of knowledge she had ever possessed changed, made unfamiliar, lost to her. She knew only one thing: that she was with Luc. And that was enough.

'Well,' he said briskly, 'I think you will like it.'

'What?'

He smiled at her, recognising – dangerously – the depth and breadth of her disorientation.

'*Ma chère Mam'selle.*' He picked up her hand, ticked over the fingers with his own, then raised it to his lips. She felt it, that kiss, not just on her hand, not just beneath his lips, but dangerously, treacherously in other places she had scarcely known about and never explored, soft, secret places in the depth of her, stirring, starting into life. She took a short, almost fearful breath; he heard it and felt it and smiled.

'Oh, Adele. How – beautiful you are.'

She struggled to regain herself, her quick, sharp self, to laugh at, to mock what would usually have seemed nonsense, exaggerated nonsense.

'Hardly,' she said, taking back her hand, reaching in her bag for her cigarette case. She pulled one out, hoping he would not notice how it was shaking, how she was shaking altogether, not just with nervousness but something close to shock.

But, 'You are trembling,' he said, his voice very gentle. 'Here, let me help you.'

'I – don't really want one,' she said, 'actually—'

'You seem to be a little – confused,' he said.

'Oh – no, not really. Not at all.'

What was the matter with her? Who was this stumbling, trembling, stammering creature, sitting here, taken so helplessly and hopelessly apart? She sighed, almost frightened; then smiled, quickly.

'Sorry.'

'Don't apologise,' he said, and his eyes moved now from her own, down to her lips and then to her hair; he reached up and stroked her cheek, very gently. 'I like it. I like it that you are confused. You seem to me at your very best this way.'

'Oh – dear,' she said, stupidly, and then, smiling at him, trying to appear in control, nervously. 'Well, I shall go and get ready, shall I?'

'You could scarcely look more ready,' he said, 'or more beautiful. But yes, if you must. If you can bear it, the parting, then so can I.'

At that she did smile, almost laugh; and fled up to her room to change: into a dress she had bought on her last visit, long, narrow black crêpe, the hem flaring gently at her ankles, modestly high at the front, dipping into a cowl at the back, and trailing down in a long drift of chiffon almost to the hem. Rhinestone clips in her hair, dark brown on her lids, dark red on her lips: 'You look as if you know what you're doing,' she said aloud into the cloud of Arpege she sprayed around herself.

But she did not, of course. She did not know what she was doing in the very least and in every sense. She sat in the art nouveau tiled splendour of the Brasserie Lipp, drinking champagne, unable to eat anything but the smallest piece of fish, the tiniest morsel of steak, a merest taste of crêpe Suzette, oblivious to the dazzling people around her, *le tout Paris*, as Luc said, amused. 'Look, there is the famous Murthe, and there, Mopse, with her new lady-love, you must have heard of Mopse, she is German, she knows everyone in Paris and has two faithful husbands as well as her bisexual lovers, and there is Nancy Cunard, in the leopardskins, oh, and see, Adele, there is Michel de Brunhof, the editor of *French Vogue*, you must know him—'

'I do,' she said, smiling very directly into Luc's eyes, 'but I don't want to talk to him now, I want to be just with you. Good heavens,' she added, stirred from her daze just momentarily, 'is that a dog?'

'It is indeed. How very English you are. To remark upon only the dog and not the people. Yes, dogs are frequent guests here, provided of course their owners are acceptable to the owner. And they are very chic dogs of course.'

'I am very English,' she said. 'I keep telling you.'

'I am learning that.' He smiled at her, a wide, mocking smile. 'Your mother would like it here, don't you think?'

'I'm sure my mother would like it,' said Adele, 'but she is not here, thank goodness. Oh, my God, is that Henry Miller?'

'Quite possibly. Let me see, yes, indeed. Ah, I see I have aroused your interest at last.'

'You have indeed,' said Adele, leaning towards him, kissing him gently on the cheek, and had again the odd sensation that she really had no idea what she was doing.

And so little did she know what she was doing, that, in spite of her protests, passionately feeble as they were, that she would never, never do it, never allow it, never go to bed with a man who was married, that she disapproved absolutely of such a thing: in spite of that, she found herself at only eleven o'clock – disgracefully early, as he said – allowing Luc Lieberman, married as he was, to lead her to her room; and there to seduce her gently, tenderly, and most beautifully – having been acquainted of the fact of her virginity, through tears that alternated between laughter and genuine distress.

'I think it is very, very lovely,' he said, kissing her shoulder, 'that the honour of your *dépucelage* should fall to me. I will endeavour to make it beautiful for you.'

And as she lay there, as he entered her tender, hungry, fearful self, as he managed to hurt her only a very little, as he led her then into a series of first gentle, then more urgent and finally violent sensations, as she rose and fell into the sharp, sweet hunger of her first climax and then the piercing, fierce violence of her next, as she heard her voice cry out, as she clung to him, weeping in the pure, clean calm of afterwards: then she knew that she was absolutely in love with him and that whatever happened, she was in thrall to him now for the rest of her life.

'And now what are we to do?' she said, as the early light came pushing through their shutters, as she studied his face beside her on the pillow, as the memory of what she had done and achieved, memory fiercely physical and joyously emotional at the same time, mixed with remorse and anxiety and a sense of near disbelief at herself.

'What do you mean?' he said. 'Do we repeat last night's performance, do I just hold you here and tell you I love you, do we sleep some more, do we go out and find some *petit déjeuner*, we have many options, which of them appeals to you most, *ma chère, chère* Mam'selle Adele?'

'I do hate that name,' she said, half irritated, half laughing, 'it's so silly and it reminds me of when I was so young and—'

'And so divinely, wonderfully silly?'

'Was I? Silly?'

'Oh, extremely. You brought silliness to a fine art, and I fell in love with you for it there and then. Giggling and flirting and teasing and saying nothing remotely interesting the whole evening—'

174

'Luc, stop it.' She felt a pang of genuine hurt. 'I don't like that. I was very young, you know, and trying to please you and—'

'And you did please me, my very, very dear one,' he said, 'you pleased me so much I never forgot one moment of that evening.'

'Oh, yes. So much that you married someone else—'

'I know, I know. Well – we must not let that trouble us now.'

And although he leaned over and kissed her most tenderly and then lay back, his dark eyes on her, moving over her, and although she felt still frail and helpless with love, she felt a dreadful harsh pang of foreboding at what those words, uttered however lightly, might really mean.

Later, much later, as they sat in the Deux Magots, having breakfast – 'Not the Flore today, I don't want to become predictable for you' – she said, 'I have work to do now.'

'Work?'

'Yes. So, surely, do you. I didn't come to Paris just to see you, you know.'

'Of course you did.'

'Luc, I did not. Cedric wants me to go to somewhere called Drouot. Do you know it?'

'But of course. It is the most wonderful place. A salesroom like no other in the world. On the rue Drouot, just off the Boulevard Haussmann. You will love it. Five floors of wonders, books, paintings porcelain, *tapissseries*. What does the Little Lord want from it?'

'The who? Oh, Little Lord Fauntleroy. Some lights and some mirrors. For a still-life. Cedric says it's the best place. And he might buy a couple of lamps, he collects them.'

'He is right. It is the best place. And they are very charming and helpful, you will find. I think I shall like your Little Lord. When can I meet him?'

'Oh, Luc, probably never. This can't go on – can it?'

'Of course it can go on. What else could possibly happen? Eat your egg. I am delighted to have converted you to such gastronomic delights.'

'I was hungry.'

'It was the exercise,' he said, kissing her hand, pushing back her hair. His eyes were very intent on hers; her body clenched gently with memory.

'Yes, well, maybe.' She felt confused again. 'And I didn't eat much last night. At that lovely restaurant.'

'I noticed. I shall have to take you again.'

'Luc—'

'And shall we meet for lunch? It is not so very far from Constantine. We are also on the Boulevard Haussmann. You could meet me there, if you like.'

'Well, I—'

'Good. At one o'clock.'

She had a wonderful morning, roaming through the rooms at Drouot, her head still full of him, lending it drama and glamour.

She found exactly the sort of dressing mirrors Cedric wanted and left two bids for lamps for him, one for a Tiffany glass and bronze, another for an exquisite piece by Raoul Larche, one of the famous Loie Fuller series. Then she hailed a taxi and directed it to the Constantine building; Luc was standing outside.

'I wanted to come in,' she said, 'see your office and the lovely boardroom again.'

'I thought it best that you did not,' he said, 'I thought we should not exactly encourage gossip.'

'Oh,' she said. She felt hurt. It was the first, the very first, signal of what was to lie ahead of her in a love affair that was not only adulterous, but in time would become dangerous for other reasons as well.

'So you were at this – thing,' said Oliver. His voice was quiet, but his eyes were icy, his tone savagely angry.

Celia looked at him calmly.

'Yes. Yes, I was. It was – wonderful.'

'Wonderful! Celia, really. I am appalled at you. That you should fall for this – this thuggery.'

'Oliver, it is not thuggery. It was thrilling, marvellous. Tom Mosley came on to the rostrum, all in black, he's such a charismatic figure, compare him with the uninspiring fools we have in government here, Chamberlain and MacDonald and that dreadful little Morrison man. They were all young too, that's Tom's whole idea, you see, to throw off what he calls the tired old men of government. There were about ten thousand people there, all cheering him and—'

'Cheering Tom Mosley! For God's sake. Did you see nothing of the violence that went on last night? The way people who dissented were bundled out by your blackshirts? Celia, this wasn't a peaceable English political meeting. This was something quite different. Banners,

176

spotlights, uniforms, people saying, "Hail Mosley", and saluting him. *The Times* likens it to a Nuremberg rally.'

'And what's so wrong with that? Hitler is achieving great things for Germany, if you—'

'Great things! Celia, the man is a psychopath. Don't you understand, he's banned all opposition parties. Those work camps, do you not realise what's going on in them? The storm troops are bullies of the most appalling kind, arresting people, rounding them up for no good reason—'

'Oliver, those people are troublemakers, they need to be disciplined—'

'Oh, for God's sake. Who have you been listening to? As if, unfortunately, I didn't know. Thank God you hadn't met him a couple of years ago, you'd have wanted to publish that book of his, what's it called – yes, *The Greater Britain*. The Greater Mosley, more like it. And now I believe he's publishing some magazine as well.'

She was silent.

'Those thugs of Hitler's with their anti-Jewish campaign, calling on the German people to defend themselves against Jewish atrocity propaganda. Jewish atrocity indeed! The atrocities come from Herr Hitler himself and his own bully boys.'

'Ill-informed rumours,' said Celia. 'Hitler is restoring a sense of pride to the German people, and his country's return to its high position on the world stage. Of course there will be complaints, there always are of a strong leader—'

'Complaints! Celia, for heaven's sake. Haven't you read about Dachau? Where people are imprisoned and half starved and beaten to death by the SS—'

'I wish you would just meet Tom,' she said, 'and Grandi perhaps. Hear their side of the story. I think it would change your opinion to a degree—'

'I wouldn't be in the same room as those people, Celia. I certainly would not shake them by the hand or speak to them.'

'Then you must hold on to your prejudices,' she said coldly.

Oliver turned to her; his eyes were hard, but his face was very sad. 'I know how this has happened. It's through the wretched Arden. That whole set is enraptured with Hitler and his regime; I have even heard that Diana Guinness has been out there to meet him, I pray it isn't true.'

'It's absolutely true. She found him mesmerising. She—'

'Yes, Celia? She what?'

'It doesn't matter.'

'I do hope very much that there is no suggestion that you might go out there. Oh, I see there is. To attend one of the rallies, perhaps. God Almighty, Celia, I thought you had more wisdom. Well, I can only tell you if you do go, it will be the end of our marriage.'

'Oliver, don't be absurd.'

'Not absurd. I have been extremely tolerant throughout the last thirty years of your behaviour, accepted and endured things that most men would find – well, never mind. But I tell you this, if you continue with this dangerous liaison—'

'I am not having a liaison with Bunny Arden.'

'Not in the accepted sense, perhaps. But you are liaising with his hideous beliefs and his despicable group of friends. Be so good as to stop it, Celia. That is all I have to say. Now I must get to the office. Excuse me.'

Celia felt slightly sick. Not because of what he had said about her attendance of the Mosley rally, or even his forbidding her to continue with her relationship with any of the Mosley entourage. She could deal with that as she had with any of his strictures in the past: by ignoring it. It was the fact that she had agreed with Lord Arden – who had passed the news on – to commission a biography of Goering, and was in the process of arranging a trip to Germany, to interview some of the people closest to him, and possibly even the great man himself. He would be a marvellous subject. But she could see it might be more difficult than she had imagined to persuade Oliver into agreeing to the publication of such a book. Well, she was going to publish it; it would be an important book. It could do much to persuade people that the Hitler regime was not the dangerous thing that so many of them feared.

LM parked her car outside Sebastian's house, and sat looking up at it, gathering her courage for what she had come to do. She shrank from the pain she must confront, the hostility she might encounter, but she knew she had to do it just the same.

He expressed delight at seeing her.

'LM, my dear, how very nice to see you. Do come in. I've asked Mrs Conley to bring tea out to the conservatory. You've got the proofs, have you?'

'Yes, I have.' That had been her cover, the excuse for her visit; she wondered if he guessed there was another reason. 'I think they're fairly clean. So you shouldn't have too much work on them. Two of our readers are checking them also, of course.'

'Just as well. Attention to detail was never my strong point. Recently it's become one of my weakest. Old age, I suppose.'

'Sebastian, you're hardly old.'

'On the way, I fear. Forty-nine now, LM, I do find it so hard to believe.'

'Well, I'm nearly sixty,' said LM. 'And I don't like that at all.'

'Oh dear. Where is that gilded youth that once was us?'

'It's become our children,' said LM quietly, 'whether we like it or not.'

'I suppose so. How is young Jay? Got any plans yet for his life?'

'Not – quite,' said LM. 'I hope he decides on Lyttons, but – he does have so many interests, so much he wants to do.'

'Quite right. As it should be. I never knew what I wanted to do. Still don't, really. Cake?'

She shook her head. 'Sebastian, how can you say that? The most famous children's author publishing today—'

'Arguable, that one. What about Milne? Anyway, it's hardly a job for a grown man, is it?'

She smiled at him. 'It's very much a job for a grown man, and I don't like this conversation at all. What would Lyttons do without you, Sebastian?'

'Oh, you'd find someone else and—' There was a tap at the door; it was Nanny.

'Yes?' he said shortly.

'I'm sorry to disturb you, Mr Brooke. Isabella is going to her dancing class in half an hour or so, and we are invited out to tea after that—'

'Yes, very well. No need to bother me with that. I presume I'm not expected to come?'

'Of course not, Mr Brooke. I just thought you might—'

'I'm busy, Nanny. Please excuse us.' She shut the door quietly; he looked at LM and scowled. 'Irritating woman. Always bothering me with trifles.'

'Surely arrangements for Izzie can't be considered trifles.'

At least she had an introduction to her subject.

'Not you as well, using that ridiculous name, LM. It's all right for the children, I suppose, but—'

LM took a deep breath. 'Sebastian, could I talk to you about Isabella?'

'I'd much rather we stayed with the subject in hand,' he said and his face was hard.

'You see, I do know – a little – of what you feel for her.'

'I don't think so,' he said, 'and LM, I should tell you, I really don't want to continue with this.'

'I would like to. Just for a few moments. Bear with me, please.'

He was silent.

'When – when Jay was born, it is not an exaggeration to say I – disliked him. I had hated being pregnant, and I wanted only to be rid of him, he was a most unwelcome intrusion into my life. I was quite sure that Jago hadn't wanted him, he hadn't replied to my letter telling him about the child, indeed I thought he had died angry with me for – for conceiving it. His wife had died in childbirth and he was very – very opposed to any idea of our having a child of our own. As indeed was I.'

'Yes, yes, I know all this.'

'No, you don't, Sebastian. You have to understand, I refused even to look at Jay, certainly I wouldn't hold him or feed him. I told them to take him away. I had already made arrangements for his adoption. I just wanted him gone. He was a symbol of my – my grief, if you like.'

He was silent now.

'It wasn't until Celia arrived with – well, you do know this part of the story – until she arrived with Jago's letter, that I saw things absolutely differently. He had wanted the baby, he was intensely proud and happy about it. And immediately I felt my attitude towards Jay change. I wanted him too, I could feel proud and happy myself. I could see that by rejecting him, I was in a way rejecting Jago—'

'LM—'

'Please let me finish. Jay has been the joy of my life.' She flushed. 'I love him more than I would ever have believed possible. Sebastian, couldn't you try to accept Isabella just a little? I know how dreadful you must feel. I know you see her as the reason for losing Pandora but—'

'Please leave,' he said, standing up. His tone was polite, but he was white and trembling violently. 'Of course you don't know how I feel. It's outrageous you should even think so. And just to set the record quite straight, I don't *see* the child as the reason for my losing Pandora, as you put it, she *is* the reason. It's as simple as that. Your – Jay's father – died in the war. Very tragic, but it is hardly comparable to my own case. I'm disappointed in you, LM, I must say. I thought you of all people had more – sensitivity. Good afternoon.'

She stood there facing him; it was quite hopeless. But – she might as well say it. It could make matters no worse.

'Sebastian, have you not thought how much you are failing Pandora in this?'

'What? What did you say to me?'

His face was so white and so set with rage now that she could scarcely look at him, his voice shaking with the violence of his emotion. LM felt almost physically afraid at that moment; but she went on.

'How do you think she would feel, if she could see Izzie growing up lonely, unloved? What—'

'How dare you!' he said, and his own voice was a great roar. 'How dare you speak of Pandora to me, of what her attitude might be, of what she might be feeling. That is an outrage, LM, and one which you have absolutely no right to commit.'

'I'm – sorry,' she said quietly, 'very sorry. I did not mean—'

'I don't care what you mean.'

'Sebastian—' Should she go on? Yes, she had to. 'Sebastian, if you would only – only try to accept Isabella, she could be such a source of comfort to you. Have you never thought of that?'

He walked to the door, opened it, clearly ushering her out.

'I asked you to leave. And since you ask, no I have not thought of *that*. Frankly, it is unthinkable. Clearly, in spite of your sentimental little speech, you have no real concept of grief. There can be no comfort for me anywhere, LM, and certainly not – not from her. Absolutely the reverse.'

'I'm beginning to feel like Queen Victoria,' said Celia, 'all these grandchildren. Too ridiculous at my age.'

'Mummy, you're years older than Queen Victoria was when she first became a grandmother,' said Venetia. 'Anyway, you've only got five.'

'Five is quite a lot.' She looked at Venetia. 'It's nothing to do with me, of course—'

'Of course it isn't. And I know what you're going to say. So don't say it.'

'Venetia, I'm only thinking of you. Your life is completely given over to – well, to having babies.'

'I know that, Mummy. But I like having babies. Boy likes children and he's a wonderful father. And anyway, what else would I do? It's the only thing I'm good at.'

'Well, that's absurd,' said Celia briskly, 'since you have never tried to do anything.'

'That's unfair.'

'It is not unfair.'

'Mummy, I've got four children. I had Henry when I was nineteen. Amy is only six months old. How am I supposed to do anything else?'

'I had Giles when I was also nineteen. I seem to recall doing – other things.'

'Yes, well, you're not like most people,' said Venetia irritably, 'and I happen to think that what I'm doing is quite important.'

Her eyes met her mother's in a kind of challenge; Celia looked at her in silence for a moment, then said, 'I recognise what you're saying, Venetia. And of course I admit I had certain shortcomings as a mother. But I just think you could regret this rather – limited way of life you've chosen.'

Venetia sighed. 'I think I'd like to stop this conversation, Mummy. I thought you wanted to ask me about that ball.' She looked at her mother and grinned suddenly. 'Actually, I didn't think anything of the sort. Since when did you come round here to talk about something you would regard as so absolutely unimportant?'

'Well – I did want to ask you about it,' said Celia, 'but only if you'd like to get involved. I thought as you so clearly have time on your hands—'

'Actually,' said Venetia, 'I don't have much. And I like spending time with my children. How do I get you to understand that?'

Celia frowned at her. 'The trouble with spending time with your children,' she said, 'is that they grow up and move away from you. Then you have nothing left. Look at that dreadful Duffield Brown woman. Always round at Giles's house, trying to bring up their baby.'

'I bet you wouldn't tell Helena she ought to do something else with her life,' said Venetia.

'I wouldn't, because she hasn't got a brain to do it with.'

'Mummy, that's unfair. She's terribly well read, much more so than me.'

'Being well read is neither here nor there, Venetia. It's pointless unless it's backed by judgment. Anyway, your brain is three times as good as Helena's.'

Venetia sighed. 'Oh, Mummy! If Helena saved your life, dragged you from a burning building, you'd say she hadn't done it in the right way.'

Celia smiled. 'Is it really that obvious?'

'It really is. How's Daddy?'

'Worried about the business.'

'He's always worried about the business.'

'I know. But things aren't very good at the moment. And he's so resistant to change, to doing the sort of things that might help. Like the book clubs, for instance, you know the sort of thing, people buy books cheaply by mail order; it's such a good way of getting books out to the public, but he just says they'll take people away from the bookshops. That we'll lose business.'

'Really? Well, I can see his point, I suppose . . . oh hallo, Elspeth, my darling. I haven't forgotten, I said we'd go for a walk, maybe Granny would like to come with us.'

'I'm afraid not,' said Celia, standing up. 'I have to go, I'm terribly busy at the office. Hallo, Elspeth, that's a very pretty dress.'

Elspeth looked up at her, her dark eyes solemn.

'So is yours,' she said finally.

'Thank you, dear. Now think about what I said, Venetia; I really do think you'd enjoy doing some work of some kind.'

'I enjoy not doing any work of any kind,' said Venetia firmly. She kissed her mother goodbye. 'We're not all like you, you know. Anyway, Boy's working much harder now. He's thinking of founding some kind of antiques business. A bit like Sothebys, I suppose. He does know an awful lot about it.'

'He certainly does. How very – interesting.'

'Well, there you are. This family is not entirely idle after all. Now give my love to Daddy and do tell him not to worry. I tell you what, why doesn't Lyttons form its own book club? That way you'd win both ways.'

Celia turned to look at her daughter. 'Venetia, it really is too absurd to say you haven't got a brain. I shall suggest that to your father as soon as I get home.'

Venetia was actually feeling happier; she genuinely enjoyed caring for her large family, her social life kept her very busy and 'Boy seems to be settling down,' she said to Adele, 'he's home much more often these days, when he's not busy with his various things.'

'What is he busy with?'

'Oh – you know,' she said vaguely, 'the gallery, this new venture—'

'Do you think that's a good idea?'

'Well, I suppose so. I hadn't really thought much about it at all.'

'Well,' said Adele now, 'I think it's a wonderful idea. I was talking about it to him the other evening.'

'You were! What do you know about things like that?'

'Oh – a bit. Through work, you know. There are some wonderful salesrooms in Paris that I was telling him about, I said I'd get some catalogues and things for him—'

'Well, I suppose you've got time,' said Venetia.

'Maybe. Anyway, I'm pleased you're happier.' She smiled at her sister. 'He was flirting like mad with Freda Dudley Ward the other night, I have to say.'

'Oh, I know. Only because she's so down about the fearsome Wallis. The Prince has just – abandoned poor Freda. God, that woman's a nightmare. Wallis, I mean. Frightfully chic of course, but apart from that. She's making him give up hunting, you know, when he loves it so much, it's so cruel, he had his own flat at Melton Mowbray, just for the season, Grandmama was telling me about it. She said he always looked so wonderful, in his buckskin breeches and top hat. She said it was altogether like a little Mayfair down there, too marvellous, anyway, he's not allowed to do it any more, it's awful, I think.'

'Terrible. She's not even very nice to him. Mummy says she treats him like some kind of a lapdog.'

'Mummy sees quite a lot of him, I believe. Ever since she got mixed up with Lord Arden and his crowd. She actually attended—'

'I know. And she's on the committee of that ball Diana Guinness is giving to raise money for the BUF. It's all a bit—'

'It is a bit. Anyway, darling Dell, what of you today and the divine Monsieur Lieberman?'

'The divine Monsieur Lieberman is coming to London next week, to see Daddy.'

'Not to—'

'Of course not. You know he's married. Strictly business. But – there'll be a little meeting or two. I hope. It's so – difficult. I do so adore him though, you can't imagine.'

'I think I can,' said Venetia soberly.

Luc arrived the following week, and booked himself into a small hotel in Bloomsbury.

'It was difficult, my darling,' he said, kissing Adele tenderly as he led her up to his room, 'persuading your father that I could not stay in your beautiful house as usual. But – I said I wanted to be near Lytton House. And so I am. *And* the most beautiful Lytton.'

'I don't think that's true,' said Adele.

'Of course you are. Well, you and your other self, of course. I hope I shall see her.'

'Venetia? Yes, of course. She wants you – us – to have supper with her tomorrow. You can meet Boy, I'm sure you'll like him.'

She wasn't actually sure at all.

'I would enjoy that very much. Please thank her for me.'

'I will. But tonight, you have to come to Cheyne Walk. Three-line whip.'

'What is this whipping? It sounds exciting.'

'Oh,' said Adele laughing, 'not exciting at all. Not in the way you mean. It's an expression used in parliament. If you're an MP you get a notice underlined three times telling you to come and vote.'

'What a lot I am learning through our relationship,' said Luc, kissing her gently.

'Not as much as me.' Adele returned the kiss. 'Anyway, LM will be there too. And her son, Jay. He's down from Oxford, doesn't know what to do all summer. He's lovely, you'll really like him.'

'You are all lovely. *Toute la famille*. So – we have only a little time. Let us not waste it. Would you be so good as to remove that rather severe little suit, *mon ange* – here, let me help you.'

Sitting at her parents' dinner table only three hours later, somehow reassembled from the fractured, joyous, crying, clinging, abandoned creature she could scarcely recognise as herself even in memory, Adele tried to eat and to follow at least some of the conversation and almost entirely failed. She could think only of Luc, of the pleasure he had led her to, of the intensity of her feelings for him, of the words he had spoken even as she settled back into quietude and released him slowly and reluctantly from her.

'I love you,' he had said. 'I love you very much and very truly. Remember that, won't you, Adele. Always, whatever you do.'

She had been silent, afraid to speak a word, lest it break the spell.

'I am looking for something solid, something large to publish,' her father was saying. 'I want a work that will become a classic.'

'I fancy *Clochemerle*, the most important book in France this year, however amusing, will fit into that category,' said Luc.

'Indeed. I would have loved to have got that one. Anyway, we've been fighting the Depression with cheaper books, all the crime novels have been a huge success, but now we need something more – prestigious. A major novel, perhaps, successful both critically and commercially.'

'The holy grail, in a word,' said Celia. 'Oliver never stops searching for it.'

'And why not, what better thing to search for?' said Luc. 'I imagine your *Antiques Dictionary* will be much admired,' he added into the silence.

'Indeed,' said Oliver, 'but that is hardly a major innovation, however much Celia would like to think so.'

He looked at her; she met his eyes almost coldly.

There's something wrong between them, Adele thought, it's not the usual bickering, they seem really hostile.

'I have two very strong biographies coming out,' Celia said, '*Madame de Pompadour*, you would enjoy that, Luc, we will certainly want to publish that in France, and a book on royal mistresses. Nell Gwynn, Lillie Langtry, Mrs Keppel—'

'And Mme Simpson? I imagine she would give your book a contemporary flavour.'

'I'm afraid not,' said Oliver. 'She is, we are assured, merely a friend of the Prince of Wales. A most unlikely story, I grant you, but – there are strict laws governing publication of such matters. Not even the *Daily Mirror* has dared to speculate on the subject.'

'What absurdity,' said Luc, 'of course she is his mistress! In France a great deal has been written of the matter.'

'I know, I know. But—'

'I thought there was supposed to be freedom of the press in this country,' said Jay. He leaned forward, his dark-blue eyes brilliant. 'I can't understand this nonsense. Why should the Prince of Wales be allowed such treatment? He's carrying on with a twice-married woman and we're all supposed not to notice. It's a conspiracy, if you ask me.'

'It is indeed something of the sort,' said Oliver. 'The Prince has Beaverbrook as a friend, for a start. And as I understand it, he has persuaded the others, Rothermere and so on, to join him in his voluntary silence.'

'Jolly good of them. Think of the papers they'd sell,' said Jay.

'Jay, there is more to life than profit,' said Oliver mildly, 'even in newspapers.'

'Maybe. But there's also more to it than pussyfooting about someone, just because they're royal.'

'Oh now come along, old chap,' said Gordon Robinson, 'royalty has its own mystique, you know. Won't do to get rid of that. Very dangerous, I'd say.'

'I don't see why. So they're royal. So what. A lot of inherited privilege and wealth and non-existent power. It's medieval. I think they should be done away with.'

'If you do that, you only end up with something quite possibly worse,' said Oliver. 'Herr Hitler, for example.'

He glanced at Celia as he spoke; she was crumbling a piece of bread with immense savagery.

'Please do not speak of that man to me,' said Luc quietly. 'I tremble when I think what will become of all of us, if he gains any more power.'

'Indeed?' said Celia. Her voice was cool, touched somewhere with a slight derision. 'Perhaps you would like to tell us why.'

'He is a madman. There is no doubt in my mind of that. In anyone's mind. A dangerous madman. He has a mission, to clear the face of Europe of every party and people and creed of which he does not approve absolutely. To create his pure, Aryan race. He would have me off to one of his concentration camps, for a start.'

'You!' said Adele.

'But of course. I am Jewish. My mother was Jewish, there would be no hope for me.'

'But you'd have to give him cause to – well, to send you off, surely?' said Jay.

'Not at all.'

'That's clearly nonsense,' said Celia. 'There is no possibility that you would be sent to a concentration camp simply because you had Jewish blood. Those are just foolish, irresponsible rumours, I have that on the best possible authority.'

There was a silence; then, 'I do not know from where you get your information, Lady Celia, but it is erroneous.' Luc's face was sombre. 'Surely you of all people have read of the public burning of books by Jews, and by those whose views are not his own, people such as Freud, Brecht, your own H.G. Wells.'

Celia was silent.

'Have you not heard of the restrictions upon free speech in Germany, or that Jewish actors have been banned in Germany, or that Jews are being expelled from the army, and the civil service—'

'I had heard some of these – rumours,' said Celia. 'What you seem to forget, Monsieur Lieberman, is that Germany was in the most appalling, virtually bankrupt state, particularly after the Depression, and that Herr Hitler has done a great deal, everything, some would say, to restore its fortunes. And I would add that with most of the German people he is extremely popular, and with good reason. He—'

'Oh, Lady Celia, please! Do not be deceived by the cheering crowds, the pretty pictures of small children presenting him with flowers. Beneath the surface there are appalling things going on, and if he is not stopped, then not only Jews, but much of the civilised world will be in mortal danger. I shall hope very much to be proved wrong, but it seems – unlikely. And now, if you will excuse me, I think I must return to my hotel. I am very tired and we start early tomorrow. Thank you for a delightful evening. It was most kind of you.'

'Of course, of course.' Oliver glanced at Celia. She was flushed, her dark eyes brilliant. 'We understand. Let me see you out, get your coat.'

'What was that about?' said Jay, as the front door closed. 'He seemed upset.'

'He was upset,' said Oliver, coming back into the room. 'As you would be, if you were Jewish and found yourself engaged in such a discussion and in such company. I hope you were well pleased with your defence of your friends, Celia, and the offence it clearly gave. Goodnight.'

'It was too awful,' said Adele next day, reporting this to Venetia on the telephone. 'Mummy was so angry, just swept out of the room, and half an hour later I could still hear them. Daddy talking quite quietly in that cold, angry voice of his and her almost shouting at him. Poor Luc, I hadn't realised, you know, how – well, how Jewish he is. I mean how Jewish he feels. Or how threatened. And there was Mummy, practically waving the swastika. Oh dear.'

'Who was that, Adele?' said Celia; she had come down the stairs dressed to go to Lyttons. Adele studied her; she was looking very beautiful, in a black ankle-length dress, a large diamanté brooch on the lapel, and a wide-brimmed hat trimmed in black and white. It was a new look she had developed recently, harder, more obviously glamorous. Adele wondered what had inspired it: her new circle of friends, perhaps. It was certainly the style favoured by Mrs Simpson.

'It was Venetia,' she said. 'Why?'

'Oh I just wondered. You and Monsieur Lieberman are having supper with her tonight as I understand it.'

'Yes. Well, he was very kind to me in Paris, gave me lunch and so on. I thought—'

'It's all right, Adele.' Celia's eyes were half amused. 'You have every right to have supper – or –' there was a pause '– lunch with Monsieur Lieberman, if you want to. But a – closer relationship might not be in your best interest. He is married, he is much older than you and—'

'Jewish?' said Adele.

'That is hardly relevant.'

188

'I think it is. To you. I am aware of all those things, Mummy, I'm twenty-four now. I am perfectly capable of making my own decision about relationships. And I feel rather – upset, incidentally, that you should find his being Jewish in some way undesirable.'

'Adele,' said Celia. Her colour was very high now; her eyes a brilliant blue. 'That is outrageous. We have many Jewish friends. As you know. The Rosenthals, the Friedmanns, the Rothschilds—'

'Yes, yes, I know. So that's all right, isn't it? Very tolerant of you. But I did think that your telling him so clearly that his anxieties were nonsense was at best rude and at worst insulting. I was terribly embarrassed. And anway, how could you know?'

'I know, because I have access to some excellent information on the subject. As I said at dinner, I thought he was speaking irresponsibly.'

'In which case, it will be perfectly all right for me to be friends with him, won't it? If that's what you're worrying about. And I did wonder if I mightn't bring him to Diana Guinness's ball. I haven't got a partner yet.'

'A very bad idea,' said Celia, and her voice now had the steely edge to it that had set boundaries for her children all their lives, 'very bad indeed. There will be many people there who will – what shall I say – who will feel that he has some very ill-founded and foolish ideas. He could possibly be made to feel – uncomfortable. I would not wish to inflict that on any guest of mine.'

'How considerate of you,' said Adele. 'In that case he certainly wouldn't wish to attend. And neither would I. Thank you, Mummy. Now you must excuse me, I have to go to work.'

It always irritated her mother almost beyond endurance, to hear her talking about her work. It was a small but very sweet piece of revenge.

'I'm afraid I'm on Oliver's side,' said Sebastian, 'I think that new lot of yours are appalling. Appalling and dangerous. I'm surprised at you, Celia.'

He sighed, then smiled at her rather sadly. 'I suppose it's partly jealousy,' he said. 'I don't like all this talk about you and Bunny Arden—'

'Don't be ridiculous. Absurd rumours—'

'Are they, Celia? Are they really?'

She looked at him very steadily.

'They are, Sebastian, yes.'

'Well, I suppose that's something. He's very attractive. And Cynthia is distinctly—'

'Dull?' She laughed. 'I wouldn't be so sure about that. She has a very interesting sex life—'

'Not horses? Don't tell me.'

'No, but she likes grooms apparently: grooms and jockeys. And in their own habitat where possible.'

'What, in the stables? How – original. Whoever told you that?'

'Bunny.'

'Well, I suppose he should know. Husbands usually do.'

Another silence.

'Sebastian, come to dinner on Saturday. Please. Barty will be there, and Jay and Kit of course, the first thing Kit said when he got home was when could he see you.'

'Did he? Well that would be – nice.' He hesitated. 'Would LM—'

'No, she wouldn't. But she was very upset the other day, Sebastian, I don't know what you—'

'I was very upset too,' he said briefly, 'but I have written to apologise. And she has, I think, accepted that.'

'Sebastian, don't you—'

'No, Celia. Not you as well, please.' He was silent.

'Do please come on Saturday, Sebastian. If not for me, then for Kit.'

'For Kit,' he said, and just for a moment there was a gleam of amusement in his eyes, 'for Kit, all right, I'll come.'

'Barty my darling, you're very quiet.' Sebastian, who had been placed next to her, smiled at her, proffered the bottle of wine. She shook her head, covered her glass. She felt sick, physically dizzy, dreadfully shocked. Had it been any other occasion, she would have cried off, said she was ill. But Jay and Kit had both telephoned her, in her new flat – her new, smart flat in a mansion block just off Grafton Way – and said they were so looking forward to seeing her and she didn't have the heart to fail them. She'd been looking forward to it too, and to seeing Sebastian; it was only what fate had done to her that evening, pushing her into the revelation, the discovery that had changed her life for ever: pushing her into a dark mix of shock and indecision and fear.

Had she not seen the newly published *Handful of Dust* in Hatchards, where she had gone to see the manager; had she not thought how much Abbie would enjoy it and bought it; had she not realised that she had two hours to spare before she need arrive at Cheyne Walk; had she not found Abbie's telephone engaged for almost twenty minutes; had she not decided to break the cardinal rule of their friendship, one Abbie had made very early on, of never arriving at one another's doors unannounced; had she not then passed a flower stall on the way and decided to get Abbie some of the yellow roses she loved; and had she not therefore arrived in Abbie's street precisely when she did, just as another car, a rather horribly familiar car, a cream Audi convertible, arrived in the street and pulled up outside Abbie's house: then she would not have known, life would have proceeded along routes she knew and recognised and she would be feeling happy, enjoying herself. But she had been there in that moment, and she had seen the car.

It was then that she had begun to feel so frightened that she wanted to drive away, turn her back on it all, save herself from having to sit there witnessing it and therefore be able to tell herself that it hadn't really happened at all: and indeed she did put her own car into reverse and start to move backwards down the street. Only even then fate pushed her harder, more roughly still, for a van came up behind her, stopping her progress, hooting its horn, and she was obliged to pull forward and let it pass, and when it had gone, it was too late and she found herself sitting there, staring at the person who had got out of the Audi, holding a large bouquet of flowers in one hand and a large carrier bag from Fortnum & Mason in the other and who then walked down the path to Abbie's front door and push a key into the door of the house and let himself in.

The visitor was Boy Warwick.

Chapter 14

'If you don't speak to her I will. I mean it. It's outrageous, the whole thing. Now which of us is it to be?'

'I really don't see—'

'Giles.' Helena tapped her foot. 'Giles, it's not right. That you should be paid so little. It's insulting, both to you and to me. And if, as you say, your father refuses to reconsider, then clearly you must talk to your mother. And about your position at Lyttons.'

'My position?' said Giles. 'What about my position?'

'It's too – modest,' said Helena. 'You should have the title of director, a proper board director that is, and considerably more authority. Giles, you're thirty this year. My mother thinks it's quite absurd that you don't have more status in the firm.'

'Your mother doesn't run Lyttons, dearest,' said Giles. He was beginning to grow very weary of hearing what Mrs Duffield Brown thought about most things, but particularly about his own professional life.

'I know that. But you must speak to your mother and demand a salary rise and a promotion on to the board.'

'But, Helena—'

'No, Giles. You have earned it. It was you who saw through that deal with the *Daily Express*. And who deals with Associated Booksellers day after day, sorting out problems? Talking to that difficult woman there – what's her name, the one who calls publishers the enemy—'

'Hilda Light. Do you know, she once captained England at hockey?' he said in an attempt to divert her. He was not successful.

'You deal with her. And with the book token people.'

She was extremely well-informed on every aspect of Giles's day-to-day professional life, she questioned him closely about it each evening when he came home. It was not a time he always enjoyed.

'They take you and your input entirely for granted,' she said, 'and it's not fair.'

'Well – I'll think about it. But—'

'No, Giles, you must do it. And I do mean it, otherwise as I said, I shall do it for you.'

'Helena, that is absolutely out of the question,' said Giles, 'it would be completely counter-productive.'

'I don't see why.'

'Because you don't understand the business, you don't understand Lyttons, and you certainly don't have the authority to discuss with my parents what they should do about my position there. Now please, dear, don't even mention such a thing again. I will speak to them, I promise you. But when I feel—'

'No, Giles, not when you feel anything. By the end of the week.'

Giles sighed. He knew better than to argue with her on this subject. 'I'll speak to them,' he said, mentally crossing his fingers.

'Good.' She kissed him. 'You have serious responsibilities now, Giles. A family. You have to meet them.'

Later, lying in bed watching Giles as he undressed, smiling at her in the way that told her exactly what was coming, she sighed inwardly. His perfomance in bed still afforded her very little pleasure. On the other hand, it had produced Mary and, in due course – next year if she was lucky – would produce another. A boy, she hoped. She didn't like Venetia having the only boys in the family: or Celia's constant references to the fact.

So what did she do? What could she do? There was no obvious, right thing. If she told Venetia, or indeed any of the Lyttons, it would cause dreadful unhappiness; if she didn't, and they found out, then she was hideously implicated. Even though she disapproved so strongly of what Abbie had done that she felt hardly able to speak to her. Either way she had lost her friend, her best friend: a fine judge of human nature she had turned out to be too, Barty thought, remembering how pleased she had been to find someone who was nothing to do with the Lyttons, who she could claim as her very own. Abbie had not only betrayed Venetia, she had betrayed Barty too.

'Oh, for heaven's sake,' she had said in exasperation when Barty had confronted her with her discovery, 'stop talking like a betrayed wife, Barty. He's not your husband. It's nothing to do with you.'

'Oh, don't be so ridiculous,' Barty was shouting now, angry tears pouring down her face. 'Of *course* it's to do with me. Venetia is a Lytton, I grew up with her—'

'Yes, and she was vile to you. I'm surprised at this display of loyalty.'

'Abbie, for God's sake. I don't terribly like Venetia, but she's my family in a way. I work for her parents. They brought me up. And you've – you've stolen her husband.'

'Hardly stolen. Don't exaggerate, Barty. He loves Venetia, he told me so, he'd never leave her.'

'Funny sort of love,' said Barty.

Abbie shrugged. 'He's a man. Look, Barty, I know you're shocked and upset. I – well, I do understand really. I'm not specially proud of what I've done. But he made all the running. I didn't chase him. I'd never have seen him again if – well, if he hadn't telephoned me.'

'He telephoned you? I don't believe it,' said Barty. 'I seem to remember him giving you his card.'

'Well – yes. I did ring him. But only about the bursary thing.'

'Oh, Abbie.' Barty would have laughed if it hadn't been so serious. 'And then what? Did you accept his invitation to dinner when it came? Or did you tell him you couldn't even consider it not only because he was married but also to one of the Lyttons? Given my relationship with them? I wonder.'

'Oh, Barty, Barty, I'm so sorry.' Abbie was suddenly in tears. 'You're the only person I've been worrying about. Truly. I don't care about Venetia, spoilt rich creature with nothing in her head but clothes and the servant problem. No wonder Boy finds her boring—'

'How do you know that? Did he tell you?'

'He – implied it.'

'I see. Well, Venetia is rich and she is spoilt. But she's also rather vulnerable,' said Barty.

'Oh really?'

'Yes. She was married and a mother at nineteen, for God's sake. Boy has fooled around ever since—'

'How do you know that?' Abbie's voice was suddenly wary.

'I just – do. I thought he was behaving better lately actually. Venetia's seemed happier. Anyway, this isn't getting us anywhere. But you're all right, aren't you, Abbie? With your nice little house in Clapham and your Uncle David's money. I don't know how you could lie to me about it, I really don't.'

'It wasn't a lie,' said Abbie. 'I was left some money. I wouldn't take that sort of money from Boy. But he wanted me to move away from Russell Square for obvious reasons.'

'He might have bumped into me, you mean?'

'Well – yes. So he helped me get a mortgage. I didn't have quite enough. Nothing more than that.'

'On very favourable terms, I daresay.'

'Oh, shut up,' said Abbie.

'I won't shut up. I think it's despicable, what you're doing. Absolutely despicable.'

'But why?' Abbie's expression was genuinely puzzled. 'Venetia doesn't know, I'd never tell her, never break her marriage up, I'm probably improving it for her, keeping her husband happy.'

'Oh really,' said Barty, 'don't expect me to fall for that old line. Of course you're not improving things for her. You're helping Boy to cheat on her. God, he's such a rotter, such a selfish rotter.'

'I know he is,' said Abbie unexpectedly, 'it's one of the reasons it sort of seemed – all right.'

'And Venetia?'

'I told you. I'd never do anything to hurt her.'

'God help me,' cried Barty, 'except sleep with her husband. I would never have believed you were so twisted, Abbie. Or so – bad.'

Abbie suddenly dropped her head into her hands.

'Stop it,' she said. 'Please, Barty, stop it. I can't stand this any longer.'

She started to cry: heavy, wretched sobs. Barty felt no sympathy for her at all. Finally she said, 'I'm going home. I don't know what I'm going to do. You've made my life absolutely impossible, Abbie. I can't ever remember feeling so awful.'

For days she suffered, unable to think what to do. In the end, worn out, sleepless with indecision and despair and a sense of double betrayal, she found help from the most unlikely source: Sebastian.

He found her in her office one lunch time, asked her if she'd like to join him for a sandwich and was clearly distressed when she burst into tears.

'Barty, this won't do. You're the family rock, whatever is it?'

'I can't tell you,' she said in between sobs; he lent her his handkerchief, put his arm round her and when she'd finished crying, insisted she come out with him anyway.

'I suppose it's some man,' he said and Barty said yes, it was; he went on lending her clean handkerchiefs of which he seemed to have an inexhaustible supply – 'I used to lend them to Celia in the days when she cried' – and saying he really thought she'd feel better if she told him about it: and finally, desperate for advice and comfort, thinking he was the nearest to a dispassionate adviser she had, she did.

He was wonderful: calm, sensible and hugely pragmatic.

He told her that she should do absolutely nothing. 'You can bear no guilt, you have no moral responsibility. There is no point telling Venetia, she will be dreadfully unhappy. Time enough for that when and if she finds out. Which she may never do. You would be amazed how long it can take for this sort of news to arrive at what you might call its true destination. And I'm sure the relationship won't last very long anyway. I can see you feel betrayed by your friend, but there is little to be gained by berating her. She is a very selfish and self-indulgent young person, hugely attractive as she is.'

'You think so, do you?' said Barty, blowing her nose.

'Oh I'm afraid so.' He sighed. 'In another life, I would have found her intriguing enough to want to know as well.'

She was silent for a while: then, 'And Boy? Should I tell him? That I know?'

'Absolutely not. That would implicate you dreadfully.'

'And – how do you view him?' said Barty. She was beginning to feel better.

'Oh, Boy is not unlike Abbie in many ways, attractive, charming, selfish, looking for pleasure. Of course he's a renegade, but – well, in many ways he's not such a bad husband.'

'Sebastian! He's an adulterer.'

'Not the biggest crime in the book, my darling,' he said after a moment, 'really not. As perhaps you will come to appreciate one day.'

'But—'

'He takes care of Venetia. He's generous, he's a wonderful father, he's unfailingly good-natured. It could be worse. Anyway, it certainly isn't anything to do with you. Your best route, indeed your only one, is to keep quiet, and learn to live with it. It's a hard lesson to learn, that one, but a crucial one. And if it does come to light, ever, and anyone throws any blame in your direction, I shall make sure they understand and take it back pretty damn quick. All right? Now dry your eyes, I haven't got any more hankies. And you'd better be getting back to Lyttons, or Celia will be after us both like an elegant avenging fury. Come on, darling, one day at a time, that's my motto. Always has been.'

'Oh, Sebastian,' said Barty, giving him a kiss, 'I do wish—'

'No, don't,' he said, 'don't say it. Please, please, Barty, don't say that.'

Celia was trying very hard not to scream. It was driving her mad. The negativity and blindness, the refusal to face facts and see things as they were. She looked at Oliver, wearing the expression she had always most hated, that of vague superciliousness, his mouth folded stubbornly in on itself, his pale-blue eyes meeting hers in absolute defiance, and thought she had never been nearer to just walking away, out of the room, out of Lyttons, out of what was left of her marriage.

'Oliver, please, please at least think about it. Properly.'

'There's nothing to think about.'

'But there is, there is. Paperback editions are not a ridiculous idea. In fact, I thought of it myself as long ago as the war, when we were so up against it.'

'And you dragged Lyttons down by publishing cheap populist rubbish?'

'I—' Let that pass, Celia, don't rise to it, don't tell him yet again that actually you saved Lyttons. 'But the time wasn't right. Now it is. I think we ought to do it.'

'And I don't. I don't trust Allen Lane, I'm not at all sure he's the sort of person I want to go into business with.'

'Well, he's the sort of person I want to go into business with, because he's brilliant. What harm can these editions do?'

'Immense harm to our main business. Cheapening books, under-selling ourselves, we've got enough to worry about with this dreadful new book club, the Readers Union, or whatever they're going to call it, selling books on an instalment plan.'

'Oliver, please. Please just see Allen Lane. Do you really want to be the only publisher who won't go in with his scheme?'

'I won't be. Don't be absurd. Selling books for sixpence.'

'Well Jonathan Cape is going in with him, the publisher of the moment, as *The Times* called him, if you remember.'

Oliver looked away. There had been a time when Lyttons had been the publisher of the moment, widely acknowledged as such.

She saw the hurt and moved in on it.

'Do you want to be the publisher of yesterday, Oliver? Do you really?'

'I would prefer that to being a rash, foolhardy publisher, risking the fine traditions that we have always had. Penguin! What a name for an imprint. It's got nothing to do with books. Unless they are all to be on the subject of natural history.'

'Oh, Oliver! You're being deliberately dense. Look, why not just a couple of books? He's offering publishers twenty-five pounds for each title, and then a farthing royalty. He's going to be publishing ten each

197

month for an indefinite period. It's going to cause such a stir. And don't you see, it will introduce people to books, it won't alienate them.'

'For nothing. Or next to nothing.'

'Oh, please, Oliver. Please.'

'I'm sorry, Celia, no. And in case you think I haven't given it my full attention, I did discuss it with Edgar Greene. And Giles. They both thought it was a very dangerous notion.'

'Edgar Greene! He was born middle-aged. And I don't recall you using Giles's disapproval as a reason for not doing something.'

'Giles has a very sound business brain. As I keep telling you. Have you spoken to LM about the paperback books?'

'Yes.'

'And?'

'She said she wasn't convinced,' said Celia reluctantly, 'but she said she was open to persuasion. But Jay thinks it's a wonderful idea, she did tell me that—'

'Jay! A boy of twenty-one.'

'He's the future, Oliver. And I hope he's going to come and work for Lyttons too.'

'Well, maybe he is, but I don't think we need take a major publishing decision on the strength of his say-so.'

'And Venetia thought it was really clever. She suggested the Buchanans as a sort of set. I thought that was really interesting—'

'Celia, when did Venetia display the slightest interest in or instinct for publishing?'

'Actually,' said Celia, 'several times lately. In fact I'm beginning to wonder—'

'If you mean that absurd idea of a Lyttons book club, I have never heard such nonsense. Totally impractical.'

'Gollancz are doing one.'

'I am aware of that, Celia. Dreadful rubbish. No, I'm sorry, I can't agree to it. Now I have a great deal to do. If you will excuse me, my dear.'

Celia walked out of his office, slamming the door. She had been slamming that door for a great deal of her life; it seemed to sum up the vast and increasingly unbridgeable gulf between his vision of publishing and Lyttons' place in it, and her own.

Luc and Adele were walking hand in hand down the Champs-Elysées; it was autumn, and the leaves were beginning very gently to turn. The light, more tender and gentle than in the spring or summer, flattered Paris, softened it: not that it needed flattering, Adele thought, its beauty was extraordinary. She was in love with the city as much as she was with Luc, it had become her emotional home; she told Luc that as they sat down at a café, and he ordered her the grand café au lait that was still her favourite; she had been unable to convert to the small pot of blackness that was Parisian coffee.

He kissed her and said the city suited her and she suited it, they were equally beautiful; she smiled at him, rather helplessly.

She was absolutely and passionately in love with him. She had set aside all caution, all moral scruples, all her personal ambition, albeit modest; she did not care any more that he had a wife, a wife moreover to whom he must remain married for the rest of his life. It having been a Catholic marriage.

She knew there was no question even of any kind of discreet formal arrangement. As long as she remained with Luc and in love with him, she was agreeing to something that she would have thought quite absurd only a few months ago, and a situation that her sister considered incomprehensible, that her parents found distressing, and that caused her friends to doubt her sanity.

'What you don't understand,' she said to all of them patiently, 'is that Luc is what I want. All I want, all I've ever wanted. It's no use me demanding he divorces his wife and marries me, because he won't. So either I live without him or carry on like this. And I don't want to live without him.'

She was, to an extent, a victim of the French culture, and of love and she settled into making the very best of it; but when she was being most honest with herself, she also knew that Luc was taking advantage of her situation, of the unlikelihood that she would move permanently to Paris and make her home there, that an important part of her life was still based in London. She knew (and Venetia had underlined this) that she was hardly conducting her life as a modern young woman should, that she had apparently laid aside dignity, self-respect, independence even. It meant very little to her; the only thing she cared about was Luc, being with him, enjoying him, learning about him. That he was undoubtedly selfish, self-absorbed, duplicitous, mattered very little to her either; nor even that he was inclined to complacency, a quality which in other people she had always especially disliked. He was as he was, and she loved him, able to set aside his vices entirely, and consider only his virtues. She knew that from the time she had first set eyes on him, he had changed her in some strange, important way, she had become a different person, and he was essential to that person and to everything she thought and did. She supposed that might be one definition of love.

She tried not to consider the future; she had set aside the past. She was no longer Adele Lytton, famous beauty, adored daughter, social success, brilliant stylist, sought after by the finest fashion editors, the cleverest photographers, she was simply Adele Lytton who loved Luc Lieberman and all the rest was of no interest to her at all.

She did still work of course, would have found her situation harder to cope with had she not. She worked for Cedric, and for other London photographers and, quite often these days, in Paris, for the fashion and beauty editors of *French Vogue* and *Femina*. It was a fortunate time for her: the endless pages of fashion illustration so beloved of editors for the last twenty years were beginning to be replaced by photographs: Adele found herself working for freelance photographers like Horst and Durst, Hoyningen-Huene and the revolutionary Englishman Norman Parkinson.

Fashion had become altogether more accessible; the great Chanel had led the movement into real life, and now even *Vogue* began to cater for the mass fashion market, talking about such unthinkables as clothes for the working girl, and dressing on a budget. It was an extremely exciting time to be in her business.

Adele had no proper base in Paris, but stayed in hotels when necessary, spending a fortune on fares; in London she still lived in Cheyne Walk.

Despite their distress, her parents tried to be supportive when she explained how she felt; her father's reaction was sorrow rather than anger, and the sorrow reserved entirely for her. 'I'm sure he's very charming, darling, but what kind of future can he offer you?'

Her mother was more practical: 'Luc Lieberman is simply using you, Adele, and he has clearly no intention of ever doing anything for you whatsoever. You are making a complete fool of yourself.'

'I don't care.'

'You will care. London, the whole of England indeed, is filled with eligible young men, and while you're spending so much time in Paris with someone who is not only married but unable to be divorced, you're not even going to meet them, let alone find yourself in the frame of mind to marry them.'

To which Adele replied that she had met a great many of them and had no desire to marry a single one; that she loved Luc and she wanted to be with him and if he was unable to marry her, then that was unfortunate but not an insuperable obstacle to her happiness.

'I despair of you, Adele, I really do,' said Celia with a heavy sigh, 'and how you can have so little self-respect is absolutely beyond me. I hope when this – this business reaches its unhappy conclusion as it inevitably will, you'll remember what I've said.'

Adele smiled sweetly at her and said she would try. She was oddly serene these days; serene and self-confident.

'Don't ask me why,' she said to Venetia. 'I suppose at last I've found someone who values me for what I am, rather than who I am and what I look like.'

'I do see that,' said Venetia, gently, 'but isn't there just the slightest chance that he might ask you to – well to live with him? If he loves you so much and he can't marry you. I mean that would be a commitment of a sort.'

'You don't understand,' said Adele, 'it's not the sort of thing he could do. The French just don't see things our way. Anyway, if you really want to know, I'm not entirely sure he does love me. Not as I love him.'

'I thought you said he did.'

'Oh, he says he does. But I don't think it's quite the same.'

'Well,' said Venetia with a sigh, 'he is a man of course. And they do see life quite, quite differently. But—'

'I know, I know what you're thinking. And of course it would be nice. But it just isn't going to happen. And so I have to accept what I've got. The thing is, Venetia, I would die for Luc. I'm sure he wouldn't die for me.'

Years later those words were to come back to haunt her.

'So Barty has been given promotion and you haven't. That is truly absurd. The Lytton foundling. If we're not careful she'll end up chairman of Lyttons.'

'Helena, don't be absurd. Barty is not a foundling, she's part of the family—'

'Oh, how foolish of me. I'd forgotten what socialists all you Lyttons were. All right, she's part of the family. She just happens to have been born in a slum. And then to have been dragged out of it by her grubby bootlaces.'

'Helena, please!'

'Meanwhile you, the eldest son, the heir, continue to work in that poky little hole they call an office at a pittance of a salary doing a job not as good as the one she's just been handed. As far as I can make out.

It's just not right, Giles. And if you're too much of a coward to talk to your parents about it, then I will.'

'Helena, please. I beg of you. Don't do that.'

'Someone has to look after our interests, Giles. Particularly as there is to be another child.'

'Just wait a few more—'

'A few more what? Hours? Days? Years? No, sorry, Giles, I can't.'

'Helena, *please* – look – I will speak to my father. I swear. Tomorrow. Please don't go and see him, it will diminish my standing there so dreadfully, to appear to be – well to be hiding behind your skirts.'

Helena sighed. Then she said, 'Very well, then. But you must do it tomorrow. I really insist.' She got up and left the room.

Giles looked after her wretchedly. There was absolutely no doubt she meant what she said. And short of locking her in her bedroom, there was no way he could stop her. He would have to speak to his father next day. And – and maybe it would work. Maybe they had simply not thought of it. And he could use the news about Barty's appointment – to senior editor, rather than junior editor – as a sort of launching board. But he was very afraid: not so much of asking, but of hearing the refusal. And then of Helena's reaction. She really was so very strong in her views.

'I'm appalled,' said Celia, 'quite simply appalled.'

'I'm sorry?' said Helena.

'That you should come on your own, to see Oliver – not even, apparently, thinking to involve me, not that that is so important of course' – she paused here, staring at Helena, making it plain that it was very important indeed – 'about this absurd business.'

'It's not an absurd business,' said Helena staunchly. 'It's a matter of Giles's future in this company.'

'Which he discussed with us yesterday. A conclusion was reached that he would receive a salary increase with immediate effect, and we would review his role here in six months' time. I fail to see that there is anything more to be said. For the time being. Certainly not by you.'

'Celia, I have to tell you that I think there is more to be said. And actually, yes, by me, since Giles is too – gentle' – that was the most acceptable word she could find: the others, 'cowardly', 'weak', 'spineless', were scarcely diplomatic – 'too gentle to say it for himself.'

'Really?' The dark eyes were very hard. 'Surely you must see that it puts Giles in a very poor light. Implying that he is unable to speak properly for himself.'

'Not really, no. I don't. There are things that I can say that he could not, that he would be too modest or embarrassed to express.'

'Such as—?'

'Well, I think that his talents are considerable, for a start. And they deserve recognition.'

'Really? I had not realised that you had such a – clear understanding of the publishing business. Better than our own, in fact. Perhaps you would like to share it with us. We are clearly not entirely au fait with what we are doing—'

'Celia . . .' Oliver put up a hand. He had hardly spoken since Celia had walked into his office and found Helena there. 'Celia, I don't think that is quite necessary. Helena is naturally anxious to plead Giles's case. And impressed by his professional qualities, as a wife should be.'

There was the faintest edge to his voice, an edge of wry rebuke for his wife, that Helena recognised and which gave her courage.

'And where is Giles?' said Celia, momentarily diverted from her argument. 'Why is he not here at your side, Helena, does he know that you are here?'

'No,' said Helena, 'of course not. He is out of the office for the day.'

'Yes, indeed,' said Oliver. 'At the printing works. Overseeing the printing of the new catalogue.'

'You see,' said Helena, feeling her face flush, not caring, 'you see, I feel that is exactly the sort of thing he should not be doing. That is surely what clerks are for. It's hardly work on a par with – well, with an editor.'

That had been a mistake. She could see Celia's face change, watched her mind pounce.

'Ah,' she said, 'now we have it. This is pique, is it not? That Barty has been promoted and Giles has not.'

'No,' said Helena. 'Of course not. I'm – I was delighted to hear about Barty. But Giles is a Lytton. He is your oldest son. And he's thirty, he's been working here for several years now, he should surely be working alongside you, helping you shape the company. Commissioning books, directing authors, that sort of thing. Not overseeing the printing of some – catalogue.'

'Catalogues are very important, Helena,' said Oliver quietly. 'They are our lifeblood. And—'

'Helena,' said Celia, interrupting him, 'I think perhaps I should explain a few things to you. Publishing is a complex and very difficult business. It relies perhaps more heavily than most on instinct. All the best publishers have a kind of sixth sense, about what will do well, what

203

people will want, not now but next year, in three, five years' time. My husband has this to an extraordinary degree. It is what has put Lyttons where it is today. Now I am very sorry to have to tell you that Giles does not seem to have that instinct. Indeed I would say Kit shows more promise in that direction than he does.

'Giles is sound, of course,' Celia said. 'He has a good business sense and I have to admit that on the design side of things he has a certain flair. But he is no more able to take over any part of the actual running of Lyttons at the moment than – well, than you are.'

She brought this out in a tone of absolute contempt.

'I see. And did you explain this to Giles?'

'Of course. That his time has not yet come, that he must continue with his apprenticeship until his judgment matures and with it his confidence. You need great confidence to run a business of any kind, Helena.'

'I do know that. I also know there is more to a business – any business – than its creative side. I know that from my father.'

'Aluminium!' said Celia, in a voice that implied that aluminium could be best compared with pornography.

'Yes. Aluminium. And my father runs one of the most successful companies in England, selling it.'

'I hardly think you can compare selling –' she paused '– saucepans with books.'

Helena managed to ignore this. 'The business side of the company, its financial stability, is just as important as next year's products. Which are quite innovative, I do assure you. I don't imagine you would denigrate Miss Lytton's role in the company. To her face at any rate.'

'LM's role is not simply about financial stability. It is about the overall running of the company, areas to invest and proceed in, and requires every bit as acute a grasp of publishing as ours does.'

'It appears I don't understand anything,' said Helena. She suddenly felt rather near to tears; it kept happening, something to do with her pregnancy she supposed. She swallowed hard, met Celia's eyes bravely nonetheless. 'But the thing I find hardest to understand is how you can employ your own son as a glorified office boy. Giving him absolutely no status, no responsibility; Giles is extremely intelligent, well read, he has a very good head for business. I have heard what you said, but I'm afraid I quite fail to see how you can under-use those talents as you do. And undermine what he does do. As his wife, I find it hurtful. Extremely hurtful.'

'As his wife, Helena,' said Celia, 'your role is to support and encourage him, rather than to usurp his position here.'

'Usurp it?'

'Indeed yes. To imply it is of little importance, that he is indeed a glorified office boy as you put it. That more than anything implies a lack of grasp of the situation. And I find it, as I said at the beginning, quite extraordinary and rather shocking that you should come to us, behind his back, making it plain you consider he is incapable of speaking for himself. I can only hope that for his sake he never comes to hear of this interview. Now you must excuse us; we are very busy here, and I imagine you have duties at home.'

This last was delivered with a look so withering, so full of contempt that Helena felt the tears start again. She stood up quickly, afraid Celia would notice, would despise her further.

'I do indeed,' she said, 'yes. Good afternoon, Oliver, Celia. Thank you at least for listening to me.'

'Goodbye, my dear,' said Oliver. He looked uncomfortable, upset. 'Can I arrange a taxi for you?'

'No, no thank you, I have my car.'

She half ran from the room, hurried down the corridor, out into the street. Safely in her car, she cried for a long time, but the tears were as much of rage on her own behalf as outrage for Giles, mingled with a degree of panic. She had achieved nothing, except to bring down a great deal of opprobrium on her own head. She had, if anything, diminished Giles in his parents' view. And worst of all, she had had her own view of him diminished as well. That Celia should have managed to accomplish that was truly unforgivable.

But as she drove home, her mood changed, became steely calm, as steely as Celia's own. One day, one day, she promised herself, she would have her revenge on Celia. She would show her that she was not a silly, vapid woman with – what was it she had said – duties at home. So far she had felt only a certain dislike for her, mingled with admiration and a respect for everything that she had achieved. Now the admiration was gone, and what she was experiencing was something much closer to hatred.

Chapter 15

'New York! Would I like it! Oh, Wol, that is so exciting. Thank you, thank you. But – I thought you said—'

'I know, I know,' he said, patting her hand, 'but that was months ago. Now it seems they do have room for you. And if you're still of a mind to go, then you may. We shall miss you of course, but—'

Barty said she was absolutely of a mind to go. It was, without doubt, the best thing that could possibly have happened; it solved all her problems at a stroke. She wasn't sure, indeed, how much longer she would have been able to endure the situation. She had felt better for a while, after talking to Sebastian, but guilt, anxiety, and acute sympathy for Venetia dominated her feelings and affected her behaviour, especially at family gatherings. And there were, as always, several of those, including, most hideously, Venetia's and Boy's wedding anniversary.

She missed Abbie too; she had felt quite unable to continue with the friendship, but it was a huge gap in her life, and she remained horribly aware of her, haunting her, a dangerous, difficult entity.

They had had a stormy exchange, when she had told Abbie so; Abbie had accused her of misplaced loyalty, of placing what she called her pathetic pseudo-family ties against friendship, but Barty stood firm.

'I can't go on being your friend, Abbie, and if you can't see that, then there is no point my trying to explain.'

Abbie said she didn't want her to explain, that she and Boy were having a harmless relationship of benefit to everyone involved, including Venetia, and that she could only feel sorry for Barty if she found that difficult to cope with.

'I thought you were above such bourgeois nonsense,' were her last words; Barty left her and went home and cried for a long time, unsure what she minded most, Abbie's betrayal of her, or being called bourgeois.

And then Giles had been – very difficult again: not quite hostile, but not friendly either, arguing with her in meetings, avoiding her whenever he could. She knew why that was, of course: it had been her promotion to senior editor. She had worried about it at the time, when Oliver and Celia had first told her, knew it might cause trouble.

She was not to know quite the form of that trouble, nor its extent; nor could she possibly have guessed that in being able to send her to New York Oliver had solved one of his greatest problems also.

That of Giles and his increasing resentment towards Barty.

Stuart Bailey had written to Oliver, as he had promised he would, to let him know when he had a vacancy. He had met and liked Barty, and welcomed the idea that she might fill it. Of course he would not necessarily have done so, had she not been who she was: for perhaps the first time in her life, Barty recognised the benefits of inherited privilege and tried to ignore the guilt. The job was only that of junior editor, but she didn't care; she would have gone to clean the offices had it been proposed.

She could hardly contain her excitement as well as her relief. London was obsessed with everything American at that time; from the music to the cars, from the dances to the skyscrapers – and of course the films, the wonderful, wonderful films.

Jack and Lily had actually written to say that if Barty had time, she must go and stay with them in Hollywood: at that point she really did begin to think she must be dreaming. Hollywood: home of the movies, as they called them: Hollywood which Cecil Beaton, who spent a great deal of time there photographing the stars, had described as being 'very much what one was told Heaven was like when one was a child'.

If she had time indeed . . . it was all much too good to be true.

She was to go out in November, and initially stay with Maud and Robert.

'Winter in New York isn't exactly a delight,' Stuart Bailey had written, 'very, very cold indeed. The only thing I can say is it's better than the summer. But I hope you will be happy here.'

Barty was sure she would be; Maud and she had already exchanged letters, and Jamie, whom she had met and liked at Giles's wedding, had sent a funny card saying he would be happy to find her an apartment. Even Kyle Brewer, the son of Robert's partner whom she had met in childhood, and who worked for Macmillans, had written her a little note, saying he was looking forward to meeting her but that she needn't think she was going to publish a single book that he wanted.

Only Celia was predictably hostile to the idea.

'You are doing so well here, and when you get back, who knows what may have happened, we can't keep a job open for you indefinitely, and the Americans are a strange people, very pushy and vulgar. I hope you'll be able to cope with it.'

Barty, who had been assured by Wol her job would be waiting for her, said of course she didn't take anything for granted, and she hoped her experiences would benefit her work: and thought to herself that anyone who could cope with Celia herself, not to mention the twins and Lady Beckenham, could manage a fair amount of pushiness.

At her leaving party, she made a very pretty little speech about her gratitude to Celia and Oliver for the superb training she had received and how she knew it would equip her for anything New York might demand of her. Later, Celia kissed her with tears in her eyes and Sebastian gave her one of his bear hugs and said he had rarely been more proud and fond of anyone and that he hoped New York would properly appreciate her.

'I think they will,' he added, giving her the rather reluctant slow smile that had become his trademark these days, 'they know quality when they see it, Barty.'

Barty, already over-emotional and over-excited, burst into tears.

She went up to Primrose Hill the next day, as he had said slightly stiffly that she might, to say goodbye to Izzie.

She found her playing with the dolls' house Jay and Gordon had built for her; she jumped up and flew into her arms.

'Barty, Barty, hallo. I'm so glad you're here, can you stay for tea? Father is out, so it would be quite all right.'

That sad little remark seemed to Barty to tell a hundred stories.

Over hot anchovy toast, Izzie's favourite, she told her why she had come: it wasn't easy. Izzie set down her piece of toast and sat totally still, staring at her, her huge eyes filled with tears.

'You mean – really away, for a long time?'

'Quite a long time,' said Barty carefully, 'a year, but I will be back, I promise.'

'But – but who will come and see me then?' said Izzie.

'Well, Henry and Roo and Elspeth of course, and their mummy and Aunt Adele and Lady Celia and Wol—'

'Henry and Roo don't come here,' said Izzie, wiping her eyes.

'Sometimes I go there. If Father lets me. Please, Barty, please don't go.'

'I've – I've got to, Izzie. I'm sorry. I've got to work there. But I promise I'll write a lot and send you pictures—'

'Letters aren't any good,' said Izzie. 'Letters don't hug you. And anyway, I can't quite read.'

'Izzie darling, your father will read them to you. I'm sure.'

'He doesn't read to me,' said Izzie, her eyes heavy.

'Well, Nanny will. And I'm sure other people hug you, I'm not the only one who does.'

'You nearly are,' said Izzie and burst into tears again.

They were sitting in the drawing room, Izzie on Barty's lap, when Sebastian came home; Izzie was quieter, but still visibly upset, sucking her thumb.

'Isabella, it's time for your bath. Up you go to Nanny.'

'Oh, Sebastian, don't make her go. We're having – fun.'

'I'm sorry, Barty, but I like Isabella to keep to a routine. And it's not fair on any of us, including her nanny, if it's upset. Isabella, go on, do as you're told.'

She got off Barty's knee obediently, without argument, and walked out of the room, looking neither at her father nor at Barty until she reached the bottom of the stairs. There she turned and the expression on her face was of such adult resignation and control, Barty felt quite frightened. Suddenly she couldn't bear it any longer. She had nothing to lose after all.

'Sebastian.'

'Yes, Barty?' His face was sombre, almost harsh.

'I'm sorry if this upsets you, and I know it will, but I wish – I wish you could try to be more loving to Izzie. She's nearly six now, old enough to notice. She's growing up into such a sad little person.'

'Barty—'

She ignored him. 'It's not her fault, what happened. I know it was dreadful, but you can't—'

'Barty, I think it's probably time you left. I really can't listen to this sentimental twaddle.'

'It's not—'

'I said leave. Now. I am surprised that you of all people, who knew and loved – loved –' he stopped, then '– my wife, should be so incapable of understanding how I feel.'

'Sebastian, of course I don't understand – exactly. Nobody could. I know how dreadful it was.'

209

'Of course you don't.' His voice had risen; she felt quite frightened. 'You couldn't know anything about it. Now bloody well leave me alone. The child is perfectly all right. She is well looked after, she isn't mistreated in any way—'

'But, Sebastian,' said Barty, and it took every piece of courage that she had, 'Sebastian, she isn't getting any love.'

'Get out,' he said, 'just get out. And be good enough to remember, please, that neither am I.'

'All right, all right. I'm going. But – Sebastian, don't look at me like that. You are loved. Very much. By all of us, all of us who ever loved you. Nothing has changed, nothing at all.'

'Everything has changed,' he said quietly, and his face was ashen suddenly, and drawn with pain, 'everything has changed for me. Now goodbye, Barty. I hope you are happy in New York.'

Nanny, watching from the window as Barty drove away in her little car, turned to swaddle Isabella in a thick bath towel. She was silent, seemed almost in shock, sucking her thumb and gazing in front of her, apparently unseeing.

From downstairs came a dreadful sound; ugly and raw, going on and on. Nanny knew what it was; she had heard it before. It was Sebastian weeping.

Barty enjoyed the voyage to America even more than she had expected. In spite of the time of year, the Atlantic was unusually calm and, in any case, she enjoyed the thirty-six hours of rough weather they did run into, enjoyed the feeling of the ship riding the waves, never once felt in the least unwell.

She spent her days reading happily on the deck in the wintry sunshine, a thick blanket wrapped round her legs, swimming in the small inside pool and even playing deck tennis with one of the many young men who were intrigued by her solitary status and her air of serene independence. She even once or twice ventured into the steam room and sampled the other tortures of the beauty parlours, but found them as tedious as she had expected, and returned to the more natural delights of the sea and the wind. She did not find the scenery – or rather the lack of it – remotely boring, rather the reverse; the endlessly changing colours of the sea and the sky, from dawn to darkness, and the vast stretches of brilliant night sky and stars all seemed to her quite extraordinarily beautiful.

One day she saw a school of dolphins, leaping joyously out of the

210

water; they followed the ship for almost an hour, and she watched them, spellbound.

In the evening, she dined at her table, chatting politely to the other guests; they were not for the most part companions she would have chosen, being rich Americans, but they were extremely friendly and interested in her and what she did and still more so in telling her where they had been and what they had seen on their European tours. And every night she slept deeply, rocked in the cradle of the sea, her dreams untroubled by small, unhappy children or large, unhappy men.

And the arrival of the ship in New York harbour at dawn would fill some of her happiest dreams ever afterwards: the astonishing buildings etched into the grey mist, the Lady, as the Americans called the Statue of Liberty, holding her torch high to welcome them in, the famous, almost mythical, places she had read about, the Woolworth Building, the Empire State reaching to the sky and the delicate lace-work of the Chrysler etched out of it in silver.

It was magically beautiful; and as the sun tipped them all, dispelling the mist and turning the water from grey to blue, Barty felt as if in some strange way she had come home.

Maud and Robert met her in the arrivals hall, Maud flushed with excitement, kissing her rapturously, Robert hugging her with delight. Barty thought suddenly and rather sadly of her parting from Oliver, so increasingly thin and frail these days, and somehow shabby, despite all Celia's efforts, his golden hair wispily thin. Robert, stoutly robust, his grey hair thick and waving on the velvet collar of his superbly tailored coat, looked the younger brother, not the older by ten years.

Maud had become most unusually attractive, Barty thought, her red hair carved into a perfect bob, her green eyes somehow larger than ever under carefully plucked brows, her fair skin dusted with pale freckles. She was perfectly dressed too, in one of the new crisply tailored suits in black and white check and with high-heeled court shoes on her narrow feet. She would take some living up to, Barty decided.

'It is just so wonderful to see you, I can't believe you're finally here. Was your journey all right? Did you find any beaux to amuse you? Now the car is waiting for us and we'll go right on home to Sutton Place, it won't take long and we have quite a reception committee waiting for you, Jamie is there and so are Felicity and John, they couldn't wait till tonight, when we are all going to dinner with them, and you can see

Kyle as well. Oh, Barty, we are going to have such fun together. Such great, great fun.'

All through the day, as she was shown over the great house – another Lytton town house by the water, she thought – as she was settled into her room, next to Maud's; as she was kissed and embraced by Felicity, and given one of John Brewer's rib-cracking hugs; and given another, gentler, one from a beaming Jamie – an extremely handsome and charming Jamie, they were quite something these American relations – as they ate luncheon in the terrace-style dining room with its breathtaking view of the water and the Queensborough Bridge; as they walked in the brilliantly frosty Central Park; as they drove downtown along Park Avenue and then up Fifth, so that she could get a taste of the wonderland of lights that was New York City before arriving at the Brewer house on East Eighty Second: through all this, the feeling that she was home persisted. Somewhere in this wonderful, glittering place, however unlikely it might have seemed, was what she had been looking for all her life.

She just had to find out what it was. Or who.

As she walked into the Brewers' vast first-floor drawing room, and Felicity greeted her once more, and John offered her a cocktail, Kyle Brewer came into the room towards her, holding out his hand, all six-foot-two of him, broad-shouldered and long-legged, so handsome now in the American style, all long, floppy brown hair and deep blue eyes and perfect teeth. He was nice, really nice, she could imagine—

A small and rather beautiful creature, with sleek ash blonde hair and wide blue eyes appeared from behind him, pushed her arm through his and held out the other hand to Barty.

'How do you do?' she said in tones so drawly they could almost be English. 'It's so very nice to meet you. I'm Lucy Bradshawe, Kyle's fiancée. Welcome to New York.'

She smiled at Barty, slightly condescendingly.

'Thank you,' Barty said.

'Kyle told me all about your history, how you were adopted by the Lyttons from a really poor family. So fascinating! I'd love to know more.'

'Well, there's very little to tell really,' said Barty.

She disliked Lucy Bradshawe already.

'You see,' said Celia, 'what did I tell you? The first Penguins are a huge success. And—'

'Yes, yes, I did see. And I also read that the biggest order came from Woolworth. Woolworth indeed! I told you it was a cheapskate operation. What about the bookshops?'

'Oliver, the first batch of Penguin authors included Hemingway, Linklater, Agatha Christie and Dorothy Sayers. Doesn't sound very cheapskate to me. Well, we've missed one great opportunity this year; what are you going to find for 1936?'

'It's a lovely office,' said Barty, 'I really like it. Thank you, Stuart. I shall be very happy here.'

'And work hard, I hope. Although I am sure I have nothing to worry about there. Oliver tells me you work like a demon.'

'I try to. I think I do. It's funny, that expression, isn't it? And then people are said to write like angels.'

'And who do you particularly think has an angel holding their pen right now? Of American origin, that is?'

'Oh, well – Scott Fitzgerald, of course. Ernest Hemingway. Dorothy Parker—'

'Of course. Anyway, Barty, if you can find me a new Fitzgerald, or a new Dorothy, for that matter, I shall be a happy man. My ambition is to see Lyttons rise to rival Macmillan. Although, as Macmillan have offices in Chicago, Dallas and Boston to name a few, as well as New York, I think they don't have a great deal to worry about for the time being. But with your help, who knows. Meanwhile, I'm putting you on to our popular fiction list; the senior editor is Clark Douglas, and you will report to him. I'll introduce you to him in a little while, he's out with an author right now. I'll leave you to get organised; and there are a few proofs which need reading on your desk. See you later.'

Barty watched him go, thinking she wouldn't want to get on the wrong side of him. Very nice while he was pleased with you, but—

She looked round her small office; it was tiny, but utterly charming, more of a study than an office, rather like a small version of Celia's with a pretty fireplace and lots of bookshelves and an old-fashioned wooden desk. She looked at the books: the usual selection, lots of the Lytton books, a complete set of Meridian of course, they did wonderfully well in America, the Buchanans, which didn't – 'too English', apparently. She wondered suddenly if an American version, an American family saga, would suit the market. If she could set that up, well, it was a bit early to be thinking of that.

She liked the area where Lyttons was based: Gramercy Park. It was comfortable and in another world from the forest of skyscrapers. There were sudden small squares and tall brown houses (known as brownstones), mostly built at the turn of the century. And then its architectural treasures were so unexpected too, the famous Con Edison Clock Tower and the Stuyvesant Fish House. The Lytton building was actually a house, just south of what was known as The Block, beautiful, a brownstone with wide steps running up to the front door, and an ornate ironwork balcony set over it. Robert had found it for Oliver when the New York office had opened before the war, and still talked about it with proprietary pride.

The reception area, built in the wide hall of the old house, felt friendly and bookish, almost like a library; the receptionist, a woman called Mrs Smythe ('nobody knows her first name,' Stuart said to Barty), was twinkling and almost cosy, and the looking-out boys at the back of the reception were cheeky and fun. Barty sighed: a contented sigh. She was going to be very happy here. And best of all, nobody really knew she was anything to do with the Lytton family: no tedious explanations all the time, no self-justification, nobody thinking she was doing well because of being almost a Lytton. Or doing badly and yet surviving for the same reason.

'That must be quite a challenge,' Kyle had said to her after dinner on that first night, 'working at Lyttons and being part of the family.'

'Well, I'm not exactly—' Barty began and then stopped. It was always impossible to explain.

'Oh, but you are. Absolutely part of it, that huge, talented, terribly attractive mob.'

Barty wondered how Celia would feel at having her family described as a mob, even a terribly attractive one. It was becoming clear to her already why Celia disliked Americans so much.

'You know, I was too frightened of Celia to say almost anything at all to her when I came over. She is the *most* terrifying woman I have ever met.'

'Oh, Kyle, do have a little tact,' said Felicity. 'Celia has been like a – well, a very close relative to Barty. I don't suppose she finds her in the least terrifying.'

'I do,' said Barty simply. 'We're all absolutely terrified of her. All her children, all her staff. Even though we all love her.'

'And – Oliver?' said Felicity. There was an interesting note in her voice suddenly: softer, almost wistful. 'Is he terrified of her too?'

'No,' said Barty firmly. 'Wol isn't terrified of her at all. He's the only person she listens to. Or rather takes any notice of. Him and Sebastian.'

'Ah,' said Felicity, 'Sebastian. Is he still part of the family?'

'Not so much. Since his wife died he's become very reclusive. Poor Sebastian. Even Aunt Celia can't do anything with him. She used to go and see him quite often, she was really terribly fond of him, you know—'

'Yes,' said Felicity and her eyes were amused, 'yes, I did know. Oliver did tell me about him.'

'And he was always at the house. Now he hardly ever comes. It's horrible. I feel so sorry for him, and yet – it's so hard to help.'

'I like Sebastian,' said Kyle, 'I think he's terrific. And my God, I wish we published him at Macmillan. He must be worth his weight in gold.'

'Well, that really is unthinkable,' said Barty, laughing. 'Sebastian *is* Lyttons. We couldn't imagine life without him. Him and Meridian.'

'I wonder—'

'Well, don't.'

'Very well. And how is dear old Giles, and his new wife and family? Maud always thought, you know, that he and you—'

'He's very well,' said Barty, cutting into this smoothly, 'and very happy. And the baby is so sweet.'

'And how is he doing at Lyttons? I don't suppose Celia is allowing him to make a lot of headway there?'

'Kyle!' said Felicity. 'You really are outrageously rude.'

'Actually,' said Barty, 'Giles is doing very well at Lyttons. Celia and Wol are very pleased with him.'

It wasn't true of course, but she felt she owed them all, and particularly Giles, some loyalty.

'I'm glad to hear it. Now what about—'

'Kyle, if you don't mind, I think I'd like to leave now. I told you, I'm terribly tired.'

Lucy's pretty little mouth was just slightly turned in on itself, her eyes, as she looked at Barty's, very sharp. She's jealous, thought Barty, she doesn't like me being the centre of attention; she enjoyed that fact, it amused her. And it was certainly a novel experience.

She went to sleep thinking about Kyle and how very different he was from the shy, rather subdued boy she remembered from childhood; it was extraordinary how people changed as they grew up.

Jamie was lovely too, full of charm; the only person she now really wanted still to meet – and probably never would – was the wicked Laurence. That really would be interesting.

⁂

215

LM had given a great deal of thought to Jay's future and whether it might – or indeed should – lie with Lyttons. One thing was quite certain: Jay and Jay alone would decide. He was extraordinarily decisive about everything and strong willed with it; if he had made his mind up on a matter, nothing and nobody could change it. Just like his father, LM often thought.

He had left Oxford with an upper second in history and what he referred to laughingly as a first in rowing; he had been in the second eight and would have made the first had not a bout of influenza interfered with his training. He had also, Adele often said, got a double first in girls.

Girls adored Jay; it wasn't just his dark good looks, or his slightly jokey charm, it was his interest in them. In them and what they were doing. He could often be found at parties, not dancing, not drinking – although he did both with great enthusiasm – but sitting in a corner with some girl talking to her intently: and not about the sort of things girls expected to find themselves discussing with a man.

'It's not fairy talk,' Adele explained to Venetia, who had a specially soft spot for Jay, 'not clothes and stuff. But it's still a bit – different. For a man. Like what they want to do, what they think about things, whether they plan to get married, whether they want to have a career or just babies. He really, really wants to know. It's not a fake thing. And the girls *love* it.'

The girls did; they found it irresistible. If Jay had tried to evolve a formula for a successful sex life, he could hardly have done better. He had had several full-blown love affairs while he was at Oxford and had even considered marriage to one girl who had been there with him. He had no serious girlfriend at the moment, and neither was he sure what he wanted to do; as a result, he was working for Lady Beckenham at Ashingham. The house was being reroofed and she had told him if he was prepared to work hard and muck in he could join her team of labourers.

'But no slacking, and no rushing off to London for some party or other either.'

Jay said he wouldn't do any such thing and told her she wouldn't regret it; and in fact he did work extremely hard and he didn't rush off to London either; but he and Billy Miller, who had always been good friends, spent a great many very happy evenings at local dances and hostelries, and acquired a certain local notoriety when they both drank so much one night they passed out and were still on the bar floor in the morning.

'I don't know, Mother, I really don't,' had been Jay's last words to LM when she asked him about joining Lyttons. 'Publishing is all right, but I really like doing things with my hands. You know? But it does quite appeal, just the same – publishing, I mean. And I like the idea of a family firm. Continuity and all that. Let me think a bit more, Mother, there's a good chap. I'll decide as soon as I can. By – let's see – New Year? How's that?'

'Your Aunt Celia is very keen for you to come on board,' said LM.

'I know,' said Jay. 'It's one of the things that's holding me back. Just between you and me.'

LM knew what he meant; being one of Celia's favourites – like Barty – made for a difficult life at Lyttons. Given that Giles so clearly was not.

Helena's pregnancy this time was not so easy; she was not so easy either, Giles had observed. She was querulous, argumentative and critical of him, to the point where he would make some excuse to avoid sitting with her after supper if they were alone. Giles would have found it unbearable had he not been able to tell himself that it was simply due to her condition. When she had had the baby – obviously a boy since it was both larger and more active than Mary had been – she would revert to her usual, comparatively easy self.

Just the same, feeling incompetent and denigrated at home as well as at Lyttons was extremely demoralising.

Even the prospect of a new year, which he was usually able to pin rather childlike hopes on, failed to lift his spirits.

'Happy New Year, Barty. You look so extremely beautiful. And it's lovely to have you here.'

'It's lovely to be here. Thank you.'

'Do I get a kiss? I really want one.'

'Of course.'

She found Kyle attractive, but not dangerously so; he was not for her, he was too easy, too naturally charming.

'He wasn't always like that,' Felicity had said one day, when she remarked upon it, 'he was a shy child, a rather awkward young adult. Well, you probably remember him. But then, thanks largely to Oliver, he found what he wanted to do, which wasn't going into the family business, as we had wrongly assumed, and you know the rest. Oliver got him his first introduction, his first job, I suppose, and from the very first day, he did well. And we just watched him change and – and discover himself, and this extraordinarily confident and charming person emerged. So, if thanks are due to anyone, it is to Oliver.'

She clearly adored Oliver. She was always saying how kind he was, how charming, how thoughtful, how interesting; Barty often wondered how she would view the anti-social, deliberately obtuse, almost querulously stubborn creature they all had to live and work with.

Of course Wol was charming as well as those things, and she adored him, but he could be extremely difficult.

They were celebrating New Year at a charity ball at the Plaza. Barty, who usually hated such things, had enjoyed herself immensely, without quite knowing why. She had even allowed Maud to persuade her to buy a new dress – the grandest she had ever owned, black crêpe, very narrow, with long sleeves sliding off sexily bare shoulders; it flattered her long neck, her long, graceful shape. Robert had given her an exquisite gold and crystal pendant for Christmas; she was wearing it for the first time.

'It is at exactly the right length for you,' said Jamie laughing, 'settled there, just above your bosom. People can have a good stare, while pretending to admire the pendant.'

He had quickly become an elder brother to her; she enjoyed him immensely. She had even had her hair done: 'I know you always do it yourself, but you can't tonight, not with that dress,' Maud had said, and took her to her own hairdresser, who had swept it back into a mass of curls and studded it with tiny diamanté flowers.

'It can't be you,' said Maud, examining her as she joined her in the drawing room for champagne with Robert and Jamie before setting out. 'You look quite, quite different.'

'Oh, don't say that,' said Barty. 'I don't like not being me.'

'An astonishingly beautiful you, but you just the same,' said Robert. 'Don't worry about it. Now let's drink to the New Year. A good one, I hope. The country is turning around, I feel it, indeed I know it. Roosevelt has worked miracles and will work more. I think we should drink to him as well as to the New Year.'

They all dutifully drank to the President, but afterwards, Maud whispered to Barty, 'He does get a little carried away, dear Daddy. Hardly miracles, as we all know.'

Barty was continually touched by Maud's distress at the plight of New York's poor, used as she was to living with the Lyttons with their blithe ability to sweep such disagreeable things out of their collective consciousness. She was also mildly amused by the way in which Maud appeared to hold her stepbrother almost solely responsible for the crash; 'I know, I just know there must have been things he could have done, people he could have helped.'

'Well, maybe he did,' Barty said, but Maud shook her head vehemently.

'Not him. In fact, he laid off lots of his own people from Elliotts. But he's richer than ever, there was an article only last week saying he'd bought some new yacht. I hate Laurence, I really, really do. If ever, if *ever* he came to this house, I would get him up here on to the terrace and push him right off.'

Barty, knowing both events were equally unlikely, nodded sympathetically and even offered to help.

She was distressed herself at the poverty that lay beneath the glossy rich surface of New York; at the beggars on the street corners, the long, long breadlines, the faces of the desperate men who queued outside the factories and warehouses for a possible few hours of work. It was far worse than anything in England.

Maud, with her serious goodness, tried desperately to help in whatever way she could; she organised concerts and dances in aid of the unemployed and their families, collected discarded clothes from her wealthy friends and distributed them to the various charitable agencies, and even worked at the soup kitchens herself one evening a week. None of it properly appeased her conscience.

Barty was very impressed by President Roosevelt's 'fireside chats': regular broadcasts to the American people about his plans, his hopes and his sympathies with them in their plight. People found him absolutely irresistible; he was a natural broadcaster, and what he said went straight to the hearts of his listeners. Barty tried in vain to imagine Ramsay MacDonald speaking so easily and naturally to the English.

After the dinner, which was extremely lavish, there was dancing, first to a classic dance band and then a jazz one; after the midnight fireworks over Central Park, a swing band took over; Barty stood tapping her feet as they moved into 'Lullaby of Broadway'.

'May I have this dance?' said Kyle, bowing to her, and, 'Yes,' she said, laughing happily, curtseying, 'of course you may.'

Barty loved dancing.

'You dance so well,' said Kyle, 'really, really well.'

So well indeed, and so suited to him, that people stood on the edge of the dance floor pointing them out to one another, and as the number ended there was a small round of applause.

Flushed and embarrassed, laughing, Barty tried to walk away, but Kyle pulled her back, and they were just moving on to the floor when Lucy appeared. She was flushed and breathing rather hard.

'Kyle,' she said, 'that was the first dance of 1936. I thought you'd want to have it with me.'

'Oh, dearest – I – that is – well—' Kyle looked rather helplessly at Barty; she smiled with infinite sweetness at Lucy and said, 'Of course. He was only dancing with me because he couldn't find you. I want to go and talk to Jamie, anyway.'

But Jamie was not to be found; suddenly she could see no one she knew and felt slightly foolish. She decided to go to the Ladies' room, women's classic refuge in times of such trouble.

She studied herself in the mirror with some interest: she really did look, she decided, as unlike the Barty she knew and approved of as possible. Who was this glamorous, expensive creature, slightly flushed, brilliant-eyed, clearly affected by more than a little champagne?

Half amused, half shocked at the transformation, she smoothed her hair, renewed her lipstick and swathed herself in scent – 'My Sin' by Lanvin, bought for her and the evening as a joke by Maud – and returned to the dance floor.

'May I have this dance?'

Barty looked round; a man stood behind her, the most physically attractive man she had ever seen in her life. He was tall and athletic-looking, his shoulders were broad in his exquisitely cut tail-coat, he had dark red-blond hair and eyes that were almost aquamarine-blue; and a mouth that was – well, Barty had read of sensuous mouths and never actually known quite what it meant until that moment. This mouth was sensuous, it demanded and spoke of pleasure, even as it smiled slowly at her. His smile changed his face absolutely; his expression in repose edged on boredom, was supercilious, almost. When he smiled – a slow, oddly reluctant smile, that looked as if it had been dragged out of the heart of him – it warmed, eased, came alive. And she stood there staring at him, and feeling a little odd, and telling herself it was the champagne and knowing it wasn't just the champagne.

'Well? Do I have an affirmative answer? Or am I to assume from your silence that you mean no? Either way, I'd like it settled. If you don't mind.'

Barty shook herself almost visibly.

'Of – of course you may,' she said.

'Thank you. Come along, then.'

220

He took her hand and led her on to the floor and then took her into his arms, and began to dance with her with absolute assurance and musical sense and skill. The band was playing 'Dancing on the ceiling'; Barty moved into the music, joined him in it, and it was as if there were no one else on the floor, no one at all, and they danced again and then again, he didn't ask her, simply assumed, and was right in assuming it, that she would want to stay with him.

What seemed a long time later, she tried to pull herself away; not because she wanted to, but because she felt she should. He sensed it, looked down at her, and said, 'Is something the matter?'

'No,' she said, 'of course not, nothing at all, I just thought I should—'

'Should what?' he said, his eyes moving over her slowly and deliberately, as if studying some interesting object that he had found. 'If you want to sit down, we could go into the small bar over there. It's very hot in here. You do feel rather – warm.'

'Do I?' she said stupidly, and, 'yes,' he said, his eyes very serious. 'Really extremely – warm.' And indeed she did, very warm, almost feverish. 'So let us go and have a drink of something cool. And talk for a little while.'

'I really ought to—' she said and stopped again.

'If you mean rejoin your party, I don't think that's at all a good idea,' he said. 'I was watching you dancing earlier.'

'Were you?'

'I was indeed. Thinking two things. That you danced extremely well, and that your partner didn't deserve you. Besides, I happen to know he is engaged to someone else. Silly little thing, making that fuss on the dance floor. She was clearly jealous of you. With good reason. Mr Brewer was obviously enjoying you very much. As indeed he should have been. Champagne?'

'No, water, I think,' said Barty. 'I've had too much champagne.'

'How very unusual,' he said, 'for a girl to know such a thing. Very well, we will both have water.'

'You don't have to,' she said. 'I don't want to spoil your fun.'

'What an extraordinary thing to say,' he said. 'How could I be having more – fun? And how could drinking alcohol increase it? I have never found getting drunk particularly fun. A few glasses, then the palate is numb, don't you think? And then the other senses begin to follow it. Not a good idea. Particularly not at this moment. What about lemonade, would that be nicer than water?'

'No,' she said. 'I like water.'

'So do I. Another bond.'

'Another?' she said, amused. 'And what is the first?'

'Oh, there are several,' he said, his eyes moving over her again. The smile, the extraordinary smile, did not come very often, she observed. 'Several already. And no doubt we shall find more. We both dance extremely well. We find one another – intriguing. We're both tall. I like tall girls. Iced water,' he said to the waiter, 'a large jug.'

He showed her into a chair, sat beside her.

'Cigarette?' He took out a silver case.

She shook her head. 'I don't smoke.'

'Neither do I.'

'But you carry a case.'

'Of course. Tell me about yourself. You're English, are you not?'

'Yes, I am.'

'Staying over here?'

'For a year or so.'

'A year! What brings you here? A simple love of our city, or something more?'

'I do love it, yes. I adore it. I don't know quite why, but—'

'It suits you,' he said, 'that's why. You have an – originality about you. You are impossible to categorise. New York likes such people.'

'Oh,' she said, wishing she could find something as interesting to say, 'oh, I see.'

'And where are you living?'

'I've got a small apartment. In Gramercy Park.'

'There you are, you see,' he said, leaning back and looking at her with immense satisfaction, 'I was right. You are totally unpredictable. Who would have thought that you, chic, beautiful, accomplished, as you so clearly are, should have an apartment in Gramercy Park. Why, for God's sake?'

'I like it there,' she said, laughing at him. She was beginning to regain herself. 'I think it's wonderful.'

'And what do you find so wonderful about it? When it is moving down the social scale more swiftly every day. I know the Roosevelts and the literary elite – Edith Wharton for one – used to live there, but now – it's becoming really rather shabby.'

'Well,' she said, 'maybe that's why I like it. And that the houses are so pretty, and the streets are quite narrow and—'

'Has anyone told you about the Gramercy Park Speakeasy?'

'No.'

'It's a wonderful story. On the corner of Irving Place and

Seventeenth, now called Pete's Tavern, there was a flower shop. At the back of the flower shop they put a walk-in fridge and behind that was a speakeasy. A favourite haunt of politicians, that flower shop. Now then, I realise I don't even know your name. What is it?'

'It's Barty. Barty Miller.'

'Barty. What a wonderful name. I have never heard it before. Is it English?'

'It's a nickname,' she said. 'When I was born, my little brother couldn't say Barbara, and Barty I became.'

'And were you born into an immensely grand and important English family, Miss Miller? Are you an honourable, or even a Lady with a capital L?'

'No,' she said, 'nothing like that. A very humble family. Actually.'

'You don't speak as if you come from a humble family.'

'Well, I do,' she said.

'No further explanation?'

'Why should I give you one?'

'Because I want one.'

'And do you always get what you want?'

'Almost always. I work very hard on it.'

'I see.'

'And I also want an explanation because I find you extremely interesting. As well as extremely beautiful. It's a very potent combination.'

Barty was silent; she couldn't think of anything to say that wouldn't be crass. And more than anything she wanted not to be crass. She wanted him to continue to find her interesting: and unpredictable and unusual and all the other things he had already pronounced her.

He reached out a finger and traced the shape of her face, pausing on her chin.

'Even your beauty is unusual,' he said.

Barty stared at him; she felt frail, helpless, absolutely in his thrall. She shook herself mentally. This would not do; this was not how she behaved.

'I really think I should be – getting back.'

'Of course you shouldn't,' he said, and his voice was impatient again, almost rough. 'Of course you shouldn't be getting back. What on earth for, why should you?'

'Because – because they might be looking for me. Wondering where I am.'

'In that case, they could find you. We have not left the building, we

223

are not running away from the city; we haven't even departed from the ball.'

'No,' she said helplessly, 'no, I suppose not.' And then suddenly realising she didn't know his name either, she asked it.

He looked at her, his extraordinary eyes thoughtful. Then he said, 'My name is Laurence. Laurence Elliott. Absolutely at your service, Miss Miller. I am so very glad you came to New York.'

Chapter 16

'My darling, you're not going away again. How can I function, with my alter ego constantly leaving me? It's too bad, you know I have a desperately important shoot next week. Tallulah herself, and for *Vogue*. I wanted furs, rugs, tiger skins, everything. And acres of fabric, silk lace, velvet – I really need this to be successful, Adele, it's too bad of you.'

'Cedric, I'm sorry. But – I do have to go.'

'To see the wretched Mr Lieberman.'

'He's not wretched.'

'I didn't like him,' said Cedric, his face suddenly petulant. 'He does nothing for you, nothing at all. And aren't you jealous of his other admirer?'

'His other admirer?' said Adele, intrigued.

'Darling, he's so in love with himself, I don't think that you can possibly compete.'

Adele was actually beginning to find the constant criticism of Luc, and of her relationship with him, rather wearing. None of them understood in the least how it was for French men. Of course Luc loved her; he told her so constantly. And she loved him. Absolutely. She took no notice of what they all said to her, or what they thought. She had no trouble defending him and his behaviour to herself; it was just that to do so to everyone else was a little more difficult. Just the same, she did occasionally think he might say – or even do – something that indicated his appreciation of her and what she had given up for him. Willingly of course. But – maybe she should say something – something very gentle, when she saw him the next day. Just so he understood a tiny bit better.

'Sebastian, I've had a request from that girlfriend of Barty's. Abigail something or other. To donate a signed book which she can raffle at her school fête. I said you'd be delighted. That you'd probably give two, and that you might even draw the raffle.'

'Well, you had no right to speak for me, Celia. She can't have one.'

Celia stared at him. 'Oh, don't be absurd. Why ever shouldn't you sign the books for this girl? It's a perfectly reasonable request. She's doing something altruistic, I don't see what criticism you can possibly have of her.'

Sebastian glared at her. 'I don't like her.'

'Oh, really,' said Celia, 'you're just being awkward for its own sake. I find your attitude baffling, she seems a most admirable person, working for her school in this way. I'm not asking you to have dinner with the girl. Merely to sign some books which can then be raffled for charity.'

'Yes, yes, I know. Very well.'

'Good. I do like to see enterprise rewarded. I see from her card she gives piano lessons as well. I wish my girls would turn their lives to something half as useful.'

Abbie was marking exercise books that evening when her telephone rang. It was Sebastian Brooke.

'I just thought I should let you know that I've signed your books for you,' he said.

'Oh, Mr Brooke, thank you. That is so kind of you, I know—'

'I will not however be able to draw your raffle.'

'That's a shame, I—'

'And I would also like to say that if you make any further approaches towards the Lytton family, I shall personally see that you are extremely sorry. Good evening.'

He rang off at once, before she could say anything; she put the receiver down with a hand that she noticed was shaking.

So Barty had told Sebastian, had she? After swearing she wouldn't tell anyone. So much for friendship. It was as well for her that she was in New York, Abbie thought. Otherwise she'd be on the receiving end of some very frank speaking.

Boy had told her that Barty had gone; he had no idea of course that she knew of their relationship. The whole lot of them were so – so protected. From reality, from financial worries, from worries of any kind. Suddenly, she rather wanted to worry Boy at least. Drifting in and out of her life when it suited him, assuming she would be pleased to see him, that she would be sure to be free for him. She was always resolving to be busier, to tell him it was impossible, that the very next liaison he proposed was impossible; but somehow she never did.

The trouble was she was half in love with Boy; it wasn't just sex, not just the free meal she had defended so eloquently to Barty. He was so charming, so amusing, so interested in her – and so clever. She enjoyed talking to him almost as much – more, sometimes – as she did the sex. Although he was certainly the best lover she had ever had, imaginative, tantalising, and most gloriously interested in her and what she wanted. They would talk for hours, sometimes lying in bed, sometimes sitting in her pretty drawing room drinking the excellent wine he always brought with him: about politics (their views concurring more than she would have expected, but sufficiently different to inspire some fine arguments), about the rise of the Fascist movement in England, the dangerous international situation, about books (he was extremely well-read), about music (he had bought her a superb gramophone and often arrived with a present of a set of records that they would listen to together) and art, of course, about which he knew a great deal and was teaching her. He had even bought her a few pictures, by new artists who had come to his attention at his gallery, and her most cherished possession, a small abstract bronze which stood on her desk.

She looked at it now, thinking of him in a mixture of rage and fondness; thinking of Venetia with pure rage, no fondness at all. Boy was very loyal to her, made it plain he would never leave her, but at the same time she knew he found her boring. He had never said that in so many words, but often he would sigh and take her hand after they had nearly come to blows over some political nicety, or at the end of some symphony played on her gramophone and say, 'I do so enjoy all of you' or 'You really are a very satisfying companion' and she would know that there were serious limitations on what Venetia could offer him, and that she was not a very satisfying companion.

The very fact that Boy would sometimes say, 'Venetia's going to be terribly busy all week with some dinner party she's giving' told more about her than anything. She was spoilt, she was intellectually lazy, and she didn't deserve Boy. Maybe it was Venetia who deserved a little worry in her life, not Boy. And how could that be accomplished? Abbie wondered, at first idly, then more carefully. She was an anachronism; she should be brought into touch with the modern world. And maybe her husband's mistress was the person best placed to do that.

Jay had finally made up his mind about his future.

It had been a very difficult decision and he had changed his mind almost every day for weeks, even after his own personal deadline of the New Year had passed. In favour of joining Lyttons was that the business did absolutely fascinate him. Books, authors, publishing cycles, bookshops, were as much a topic of conversation round the Lytton table, and indeed the Robinson one, as politics and gossip or personal interest and ambition. He remembered once asking his Aunt Celia if she thought about books when she was on holiday or in bed, and she had looked at him with something close to astonishment and said, 'Of course I do, Jay. Of course. We all do.'

Not quite all of course; he hadn't observed Venetia or Adele devoting a great deal of attention to the subject, and he wasn't sure that Kit would do either; at sixteen his ambitions were rather un-Lytton, as Adele put it, he talked about becoming a barrister or even going into the Church.

But Jay did like books: a lot. And he liked, still more, the idea of doing what Celia did: discovering talent and nurturing it, turning ideas into books, turning raw young writers into bestselling household names.

'That's what editing is about, Jay; it's very like the gardening you enjoy so much. You pick out some interesting-looking, possibly sickly plant and care for it, nourish it, encourage it, and then see it grow tall and strong. Very satisfying. Of course it doesn't always work out, but if you have a nose for it – or rather an eye and an ear – and I suspect you do, then there's nothing more exciting.'

Jay had no idea how she could suspect any such thing; and it was precisely this tendency of hers to make judgments in his favour that worried him.

And then there was the problem of Giles: he had even discussed this with his mother, who admitted that Giles was not doing very well, but that in her view that was all the more reason for Jay to join Lyttons.

'You're the firm's future, you and Giles and possibly Kit, unless he becomes Lord Chief Justice—'

'Or the Pope.'

'Indeed yes.' She smiled at him. 'But if the firm is to prosper it needs all the talent available to it. To state you don't want to join us because one person is so far not displaying very much of that talent is ridiculous. Your non-arrival is not going to make Giles perform any better.'

'But my arrival could make things worse,' said Jay.

His dilemma was made worse by a proposition from Lady Beckenham who asked him if he'd like to run the Home Farm on the estate.

'I think you'd do it well and I know you'd enjoy it. You don't want to sit in some office day after day, surely. It would be a pleasure to have you down here, it's where you grew up after all, and I like your attitude, I know you'd work hard. What my daughter, and indeed your mother, would have to say I dread to think, but there's the offer, take it or leave it.'

That was a serious temptation; Jay loved the countryside, loved being out of doors, loved physical work. In many ways, farming looked the perfect career to him. On the other hand, working for the ninth earl meant in due course working for the tenth and, much as he liked Lady Beckenham, he didn't at all like James, her eldest son and the heir to Ashingham. He had an arrogance of manner that his parents entirely lacked, and no sense of style; he treated his servants inconsiderately, and he would clearly treat his farm manager in the same way. Lord Beckenham would not live for ever, his heart was not strong, and he had frequently said that it would be a close run thing whether he or King George would meet their maker first. When the old King won that particular race on a cold day in January, Lord Beckenham was visibly upset as he put on his black tie; he insisted on attending the funeral with Lady Beckenham which upset him further, not least, he said that night at dinner, because he felt the new King had no backbone.

'Nothing good to be said of him at all as far as I can see. Time he pulled himself together, stopped chasing pretty women all over the place and married someone decent. I've written to *The Times* several times about it but they haven't published any of my letters.'

Lady Beckenham said she couldn't imagine why not, but that he was a fine one to talk about chasing pretty women.

Finally, albeit with some misgivings still, Jay made his decision.

'Mother, I've decided. I'd like to join Lyttons. If they're still keen to have me.'

LM said rather stiffly that she imagined they would, but that she would have to discuss the final arrangements with Celia and Oliver, and then hurried out of the room and into the lavatory where she shed some sentimental tears and thought how pleased and proud Jago would have been of his son, who had proved to be not only clever and engaging, but principled as well.

'I'm sorry, Barty.' Maud's green eyes were very steady, full of determination. 'If you're going to – to see Laurence, then I can't have anything more to do with you.'

'But, Maud. Please, couldn't you – just—' Her voice tailed away.

'I couldn't just anything. It's your decision. Me or him. Us or him, actually. Me and Daddy and Jamie. Until it's over.'

Barty knew there was no point defending Laurence, making any kind of claim for him, saying what she knew to be true, that Laurence loved her, that it would not be over.

'Barty, he's – he's wicked. There's no other word for it.'

'Maud, I think there is—'

'No, there isn't. He spent thousands and thousands of dollars once, bribing people, trying to wreck Daddy's business. He's always refused even to speak to me. He made Jamie choose between us, when Jamie was just a little boy. He tried to have Daddy turned out of his house, his own house. I don't understand you, Barty, how you can have anything to do with him. I really don't.'

'Maud, I – well, I love him, I'm afraid. Please try to understand.'

'There's nothing to understand. Absolutely nothing. So – unless you come to your senses, stop having anything to do with him, I can't be your friend. Any more.'

'Oh Maud—' Barty put out her hand, tried to take Maud's; she pulled it away.

'Don't. I really mean it. I can't and won't have anything more to do with you. I – well, I just couldn't.'

'Very well,' said Barty quietly, 'I'm afraid we have to part. But, Maud, I wish you'd try to—'

'To what? To see him somehow differently? To say oh, it was all because of his unhappy childhood, that he's not really bad at all? Is that what he told you? Well, it's just not true. We all gave him the benefit of the doubt for a long time and he doesn't deserve it. Sorry, Barty, but no.'

Barty had been going to say that of course: to explain that anyone who had had to endure what Laurence had had to endure was bound to be – difficult. To find life difficult. He had spent hours talking about it, how dreadful it had been, watching his adored father die, in terrible pain, trying to console his mother, to look after Jamie as his father had told him: and then having to accept Robert into their lives, listening to her rather awkward explanations about how she felt, and then the announcement that she was going to marry him.

'Marry him! This man who wasn't half what my father had been, not so clever, not so wise, not so good. I'm sorry, Barty, I know he's your uncle but—'

'It's all right,' said Barty. 'I – I think I understand.'

'And then, you know, seeing her pregnant, can you think how that felt, to a boy of fifteen? Recognising the implications, thinking of them making love – it was horrible. We'd been so close, the two of us, she was such a splendid, wonderful woman, and here she was – well, I found it unbearable. When she told me that she was pregnant, I was physically sick. I threw up over and over again, trying to get rid of this horrible thing in my life. Well, that's what the shrink said—'

'The shrink?'

'Psychiatrist. I've had years of analysis. It hasn't helped much. And then she had the baby—'

'Maud?'

'Yes. And I looked at her, and I can't tell you how much I hated her. And then when my mother died, I really wanted Robert to die as well. Because it was his fault. She died having another of his – his children. I spent quite a lot of time thinking how I might kill him. I suppose you think that's terrible.'

'No,' said Barty gently, 'not in the circumstances.'

'It's amazing how you understand these things. Nobody ever did before. Not really.'

'Well,' said Barty, 'I had quite a difficult childhood myself. I told you.'

'Yes.' He smiled at her, his rare smile. 'Thank God for it.'

'I wonder which of us had the worse time,' she said, her tone not entirely serious.

'Oh definitely I did. No doubt.'

'We-ell. I'm not so sure. I mean my own family rejected me. Except for my mother, and my brother Billy.'

'I like the sound of Billy.'

'You'd love him.'

'I'm sure I'll like him at least.'

'Laurence, you are not going to meet my family.'

'Of course I am. I am going to come to England and meet them.'

Barty didn't argue any more. She had learned not to.

It had been an astonishing few months.

She had said goodbye to him as quickly as she decently could at the ball, and returned to her party, feeling shocked and physically shaken. To be so – well, so taken with the wicked Laurence Elliott, about whom she had heard nothing but bad. She had always imagined him ugly, disagreeable, not – well, not hugely attractive, and interesting and – well, sexy. He was without doubt the sexiest man Barty had ever had

231

anything to do with. After one hour of his company, she could think of nothing else. And he was so easy to talk to, and he made her feel so interesting and – well, so sexy too.

'Tell me your address,' he called after her as she made her sudden, flustered excuses and fled from him, but she pushed into the crowd, found Maud, said she didn't feel very well, and would it be all right if she left?

Maud, of course, had said she would come too, wouldn't hear of letting her go on her own; 'and you must come and stay with us tonight, no nonsense about going back to your apartment. Come along, let's go find the car.'

Sitting in the car, trying to calm herself, trying to appear more or less normal, longing to be able to talk to Maud about Laurence, about the acute effect he had had on her, knowing she couldn't, she was silent; when they got back to the house, she made an excuse and went to her room and lay on the bed, trembling, half with excitement, half with distress. Of all the people in the whole of New York, why couldn't she have met and fallen in love with someone suitable? It was like – well, it was like Romeo and Juliet. Two feuding houses. Impossible to continue with it, of course; and anyway, she thought, giving herself a shake, she was being terribly presumptuous. She'd probably never hear from him again.

But she did.

'I had a terrible time tracking you down,' he said almost brusquely, over the telephone next day. She looked at the clock on her desk.

'Really terrible,' she said, smiling in spite of herself. 'It's taken you at least a morning.'

'It seemed much longer. I had to phone half the organisers of the ball, ask them if they knew you, they all said no, they'd never heard of you. So then I thought of the Brewers, and I'm not on very good terms with them, for reasons which I need not trouble you with—'

'I – I do know the reasons,' she said.

'You do? Surely not. Anyway, then I thought of the Bradshawes. Lucy's people, you know. I thought they might help me. Mrs Bradshawe particularly is always trying to inveigle me on to her committees, terrible woman. So I rang her; she wasn't very pleased when she found out what I really wanted, but she told me that you worked there at Lyttons. For the family publishing company. I want to hear about that, Barty, tonight.'

'Tonight?'

'Yes. I want you to have dinner with me. I've booked a table at the Pierre. At seven-thirty. Shall I send a car to pick you up from your modest little home?'

'No,' said Barty, 'no, don't. And I can't have dinner with you. Not tonight, not ever.'

'Why on earth not?'

'Because – well, I just can't. I'm sorry.'

An hour later an enormous bouquet of flowers arrived for her, with an accompanying note; six hours later she found herself sitting opposite him in the restaurant and informing him that she was, to a certain extent at least and certainly in terms of family loyalty, a Lytton.

'It simply doesn't matter,' he said impatiently. 'Not in the very least.'

'Of course it matters. You hate the Lyttons. I know you do. Well, the ones here anyway. And they – well, they're not terribly fond of you.'

'That's true. But I don't see that it has anything to do with you. Or rather with you and me.'

'Well, in that case you are a great deal more stupid than you seem. The Lyttons are my family.'

'Not biologically.'

'That's irrelevant. Maud is one of my best friends. She and Robert have been incredibly kind to me, I work for Lyttons—'

'Leave.'

'What! Laurence, of course I can't leave. I wouldn't. My career, and the whole of my professional loyalty is with Lyttons.'

'Is your career that important to you?'

Barty looked at him. 'It's the most important thing in my life. There's nothing I care about half so much.'

'Only, I suggest, because you haven't yet found anything else. Suppose you were to fall in love, get married even.'

'It wouldn't make any difference.'

'Children?'

'Still no difference.'

'You'd carry on working even if you had children, would you?' he said.

'Of course I would. Aunt – Celia Lytton, she's worked all her life. And she had four children. Five, if you count me.'

'Ah,' he said in tones of great satisfaction, 'and look how unhappy you all were.'

'No, we weren't.'

'You said you were.'

233

'I was unhappy because of my circumstances. The others were terribly happy.' Not quite true, that, but he was not to know. Anyway, it didn't matter.

'If you had my children you wouldn't work,' he said, his brilliant eyes moving over her.

'Laurence, that is such an absurd statement.'

'Why?'

'Because I'm not going to have your children.'

'And how do you know that?' he said, leaning back, the sudden reluctant smile breaking. 'How on earth can you know that?'

So it began.

If she had hoped that no one at Lyttons would find out about it, she was swiftly disillusioned; he telephoned her several times a day, had endless flowers and gifts delivered to her, parked his car outside Lytton House at night, waiting for her to come out. He took her all over New York: to the smart restaurants and nightclubs, to the Stork Club, El Morocco, the 21, all filled with celebrities, which he pointed out with enormous and rather proprietory pride – 'Look, there's Sophie Tucker, and there are the Astaires, and look, Barty, Gloria Vanderbilt, would you like to meet her – no? Another time, then – and there are the Whitneys and, my God, the utterly dreadful Elsa Maxwell' – and sometimes he took her to quiet, small places on the Upper East Side, where the food and wine were just as excellent and which she actually preferred. They had driven up to Harlem several times after dinner, to the Cotton Club, with its superb jazz bands, and to the more conventional and romantic pleasures of the Rainbow Room. He had taken her to the Metropolitan Opera House and the Carnegie Hall and to the wonderful shows at Radio City, to *Anything Goes* and to Orson Welles's *Macbeth* at the Negro People's Theatre.

One of the things she most enjoyed about him was the diversity of his intense recreations and pleasures; he was as pleased to be in Harlem jitterbugging as in his box at the opera, to be relating the latest gossip (at which he was surprisingly adept) as discussing world affairs. His mind was brilliant and savagely fast and his views on almost everything strong and often unpredictable; he was outrageously elitist, and she found it hard to hold her own, to defend the more liberal views she had been brought up on. One of his favourite tenets was that the rich served society far better than the poor – 'They employ people, they pay vast taxes, they patronise the arts and commerce, it's hugely important that they – we survive.' Another was that everyone had their price: that everyone wanted something so badly they would do

234

anything, even if it was something against their own moral code, to get it.

'What about you, Barty, what wouldn't you do to become – what shall we say – the head of Lyttons? Or to become a noted member of that round table clique at the Algonquin, quoted in all the literary journals?'

Barty said firmly that there were many things she wouldn't dream of doing, but he laughed at her and said he would remind her of it one day 'when I find you on the horns of some moral dilemma'.

She struggled to remain independent, to escape this onslaught on her time and attention, but it was hard; one night she sat in her office determinedly until after eleven; when she emerged, he was there, waiting for her, reading.

'I've been reading one of those children's books Lyttons publishes, by Sebastian Brooke. Awfully good. What else should I read?'

'Oh, Laurence, I don't know,' she said wearily.

'You look tired.'

'I am tired. I've been working.'

'No, you haven't. You've been hoping I'd go away. No good, Barty. I'm here to stay.'

That was the night he took her to Elliott House. And tried to persuade her to go to bed with him.

'No,' she said fretfully, dazzled by this demonstration of his vast wealth, and of his taste and sense of style displayed, the magnificent white and silver drawing room, the paved courtyard in the centre of the house with its fountain and glass rotunda, the long gallery, its walls hung with Impressionist paintings, the library, built with curving walls – 'I'm told that was a challenge set by my grandfather to the architect' – the indoor swimming pool, his father's study, with its booklined walls, huge leather desk and even ticker-tape machine, kept exactly as it had been: 'My mother insisted, as of course did I. Look, here we all are. Probably the last time I was properly happy. Until now.'

She looked at a photograph in a silver frame of a handsome man, and a smiling, fine-looking woman in evening dress, hair swept up from her face, and two little boys, holding her hand.

'Please, Barty,' he said, 'please. Come to bed with me. I want you so much.'

'No,' she said again. 'No, Laurence, I won't.'

'But why not? Don't tell me you have moral scruples. About going to bed with someone who is not your husband. That would be very disappointing.'

'Of course not,' she said. 'At least not in the way you mean.'

'Are you a virgin?'

'Yes,' she said, her eyes meeting his steadily, 'yes, I am.'

'Why?'

'Because I haven't yet met anyone I wanted enough.'

'Until now.'

'Laurence, not until now. I still haven't.'

'I don't believe you,' he said, 'I know you're lying. But we'll leave it for now. I'll take you home if you like.'

Surprised and pleased by this, she said she would like it.

And then, inevitably, later than she would have believed possible, Maud found out. Or rather Jamie did: sitting with a prospective client over cocktails in the Palm Court, he saw her come in, look round, hesitate, and then as someone tapped her on the shoulder, watched her turn to him, smile, present her cheek to be kissed. To Laurence. His brother. The brother who had done so much to make his own childhood wretched, who had worked so hard to undermine his stepfather's business, who had set him against everything and everyone to do with the Lyttons. Saw his brother take Barty's hand and kiss it, saw him speaking intently to her, saw her listening, equally intently, saw her shake her head, then suddenly laugh and follow him outside.

When he told Maud she sat looking at him for a moment in absolute silence; then she dropped her head into her hands and began to cry.

In a way, Barty felt better after the confrontation with Maud; at least the need for secrecy was gone, at least she could be open and honest. With herself as well as with the family.

That was the night she went to bed with Laurence for the first time.

He had been surprisingly sensitive about her misery, had let her cry, listened to her protestations of remorse, didn't even try to argue with her, or tell her she was being foolish.

'You mustn't blame yourself,' he said. They were in his house, sitting in the courtyard at its centre. 'You've done nothing wrong.'

'I have, Laurence, I have. I've been disloyal to all the Lyttons and the Brewers too, they've been so good to me, I've deceived Maud, I should have—'

'You should have what?' he said.

'I should – that is, I shouldn't – have got involved with you, I should have stopped it right at the beginning when you first—'

'But I wouldn't allow that,' he said simply. 'It wasn't up to you, it was my decision, you have nothing to reproach yourself with.'

'Oh, Laurence, don't be absurd,' said Barty, blowing her nose, smiling through her tears, 'of course it wasn't your decision, I have a mind of my own—'

'It was my decision. I accept full responsibility.'

'But I could have just—' She stopped.

'Just what?'

'Sent you away.'

'I wouldn't have gone. And anyway, why should you have done that, missed out on all this – happiness?'

'Happiness!' She started crying again.

'Yes, happiness. And love—'

She looked at him startled. 'Love?'

'Well, yes. Obviously. What else is this about?'

'Well – I—'

'Oh, for heaven's sake,' he said irritably, 'of course it's about love. You're in love with me, aren't you?'

'I – don't know. I haven't said so.'

'I'm aware of that. But nevertheless I do know it. Know that you are.'

There was a long, long silence then; it took all her courage to break it at all, certainly to pose the question. 'So – are you in love with me?'

'Of course I am.' He looked at her as if she had asked a question so crass, so pitiful it scarcely deserved an answer. 'Why else do you think I've been behaving as I have? Out of some kind of distorted sense of social duty, perhaps?'

'I don't know,' she said. 'I just didn't think – think that you—'

'Didn't think what? That I was capable of love, is that it? The family fiend, the cruel monster, Laurence Elliott with the heart of stone, you didn't think he was able to love?'

'No, of course not,' she said quickly, half frightened by the anger in his voice, 'I just didn't think you would love – me.'

'Oh Barty, Barty, I thought women were supposed to have intuition about this sort of thing. Of course I'm in love with you. I obviously should have made it plainer. You have to forgive me, I haven't had much practice. What am I saying? I've never had any practice. I've never wanted to say it before.'

'Never?'

'Never. I've admired women, I've wanted them, I've enjoyed them. But it wasn't in the least like – this.'

Barty looked at him; he was sitting staring at her; his expression was of bemusement, almost surprise. His eyes meeting hers, his extraordinary blue-green eyes, were absolutely without guile; there could be no doubt of his sincerity.

They were sitting on one of the elaborate wrought-iron seats near the fountain; Barty suddenly stood up, held out her hand to him.

'Perhaps,' she said quite quietly, 'perhaps we should go to your room.'

And all next day as she sat at her desk, pretending to work, she felt as if she were existing in some remote space, isolated from everything, where the only thing she felt to be real was the memory, her memory of being in bed with Laurence, and the pleasure he had given her, the intense, undreamed-of, unimaginable pleasure. And even more than that, at the end of it, his voice telling her he loved her.

'It's too absurd.' Venetia sighed. 'Boy wants Henry to start having piano lessons. I'm sure he's too young.'

'Not necessarily,' said her mother. 'Barty was only seven.'

'Yes, but Barty was a dutiful little girl, she practised. Henry won't.'

'He might. With the right teacher. Actually, I've got an idea for you there. That friend of Barty's telephoned me the other day, wanted one of Sebastian's books for her school raffle, do you remember her, Abigail Clarence?'

'Yes. Yes, I do.'

'Nice girl. Highly intelligent. Anyway, she gives piano lessons. You might like to consider her. As a teacher for Henry, I mean.'

'Well – it's a thought. Why don't you tell her to come and see me? Or telephone me, anyway. Do you know where she lives?'

'Clapham, I think—' Celia rummaged in her bag. 'Yes, here's her card. Why don't you telephone her, have a chat? I really admire the way she's making the best of her situation in life. Enterprise should be rewarded, I do think.'

A rebuke hung, however lightly, in the air.

'And what is Jay doing at Lyttons, precisely?'

Helena's voice had its sharpest edge. Giles sighed. 'He's working as a looker-out on the trade counter.' Giles wasn't sure why, but it had always seemed to him a most satisfying part of the publishing process, collecting books from the great store in the basement of Lytton House and bringing them to the counter at the front of the building for the collectors, as they were called, from the various bookshops to take away. 'You know what they do, they—'

'Yes, yes, you've told me. You told me how much you enjoyed it yourself. And how long is he going to do that for?'

'Oh, Helena, I don't know. A few months.'

'And then? Senior editorship, I daresay?'

'Helena, don't be so absurd. Jay is doing his apprenticeship, as we all have done.'

'Even Barty? Did she do the looking-out?'

'No, of course not. It's not woman's work. But she did other, quite humble tasks. Writing out invoices all day, that sort of thing. Anyway, I fail to see what Barty has to do with this. And I don't think I can stand this very much longer. Please can we close the subject. Not just tonight but every night. I am doing my best at Lyttons. What I need from you is support, not endless criticism. In due course, when I have earned it, I shall attain the position at Lyttons due to me. Until then—'

'And what will that be I wonder? Chief Clerk?'

'Helena, shut up!' He heard himself with horror. He had never shouted at her, certainly never spoken to her in those terms. He looked at her, ready to apologise; but she was there before him, flushed and breathing heavily, her fists clenched.

'I think, Giles,' she said, and her voice now was full of menace, her face almost ugly in its anger, 'I think you should speak to your mother about your prospects at Lyttons. Then perhaps you will believe me.'

'My mother? What do you mean—'

'I mean she has views—' She stopped, clearly realising how much too far she had gone.

'Views on what, Helena? How do you know her views?'

'I – don't. I just worked it out for myself.'

'Helena,' he stood up, went over to her, grabbed her wrist, 'have you been talking to my mother? *Have* you? Answer me, damn you.'

And in a low, reluctant voice, almost in a whisper, she did.

'Oliver, I want to discuss something with you.'

'Yes, Celia? Is it professional or personal?'

'It could be both.'

'I see. Well – what is it? I don't have a lot of time, I've a meeting with LM in an hour about costings and—'

'I – I would like to go to Berlin this August. It's to visit the Olympic Games.'

'I had no idea you had an interest in the Olympic Games.'

'Well of course I do,' said Celia irritably. 'Anyone would have, they are an extraordinary event, a display of the very best of sporting prowess drawn from all over the world. And this year—'

'Yes, Celia? This year?'

'Obviously they will be unsurpassed. The opening ceremony will be quite extraordinary—'

'Ah, yes. Herr Hitler will be present, no doubt.'

'Well, of course. These games will be seen as a demonstration of his desire for peace, for cooperation with the rest of the world, they represent the sporting ideal at its very best.'

'Indeed? And who has explained all this to you? Lord Arden, perhaps? Your friends the Mosleys?'

'Oliver, I have been reading about it, for God's sake. As you would have been, if you weren't so hopelessly out of touch. There will be five thousand of the finest athletes in the world there, I don't see how you can fail to be – intrigued.'

'And I find it appalling that you are intrigued. Celia, what is the matter with you? Have you gone quite mad?'

She was silent, thinking of the outline of her biography of Goering, the introduction already written, the tentative publishing schedule already drawn up, of appointments she had made through Lord Arden coinciding with her visit to the Games, even, possibly, one with Herr Hitler himself – she had to go, she absolutely had to. Apart from anything else, she would lose such face if she had to cancel it now; the Mosley set were extremely gratified with this unexpected boost to their cause, and that of the Nazi regime in Germany, from so intellectually impeccable a source.

As always when cornered, she saw a possible route out; she smiled at Oliver.

'I – well, I thought, you see, we might do a book about the Games, there is an enormous interest in sport and health at the moment, look at the League of Health and Beauty, thousands of members, and everyone is dieting and exercising and there is the most marvellous woman photographer called Leni Riefenstahl going to the Games who—'

'Celia, no, you will not go to Berlin, as the guest of Lord Arden or indeed anyone else, and Lyttons will most assuredly not be publishing anything whatsoever about the Olympic Games. I hope that is quite clear. I have told you before, I find your continuing association with those people deeply distressing, not to say offensive, and I must request that it ends immediately.'

'Oliver,' said Celia, after a long silence, 'I find myself rather puzzled by your attitude. It seems to me to border on the autocratic. Well, you may be able to prevent me from publishing a book about the Olympic Games, it will only be one more publishing opportunity lost after all, but certainly not from attending them. And with whom I choose moreover.'

'Celia, I don't know what has happened to you,' said Oliver, and his voice was very low, 'but I don't like it. I don't like it at all. Through all our difficulties in the past, I have felt that you were willing at least to take note of my wishes and—'

'My God, your hypocrisy is breathtaking,' said Celia. 'Perhaps you might try to decide exactly the kind of person you are. You hide behind this façade of sweetness and reason, Oliver Lytton, the perfect gentleman, the liberal, always prepared to listen, while in reality you are deeply bigoted. You've brought it to a fine art, and I am absolutely weary of it. You aren't brave enough to argue with me publicly, no one ever has the faintest idea how extraordinarily unpleasant you can be. It's cowardice, Oliver. But then that's not so out of character, is it?'

'Celia—' said Oliver, and his face was very drawn, his eyes almost hollow in his thin face, 'Celia, I would like to say—'

'You may say whatever you like. I am going to Munich and I am going with whom I please. I do hope I make myself absolutely plain.'

She slammed the door and went into her own office and sat there shaking; Janet Gould, taking in first Celia's post and then Oliver's, often said afterwards, in the light of what happened, that it was impossible to say which of them appeared more upset.

'Miss Clarence? Good morning, Miss Clarence. It's Venetia Warwick here, you may remember me from my brother Giles Lytton's wedding. Yes, that's right. Look, my mother tells me you give piano lessons. My husband feels our little boy, he's just seven, is ready to learn. I'm not at all sure that he is, but I wonder if you'd be kind enough to come along and see him, see what you think. Henry's home this week, if you could manage it, it's half-term. I'd pay for your time, obviously, and we have a piano here of course . . . oh, yes, later this morning would be fine. About midday? Berkeley Square, number seven. Thank you. I'll look forward to seeing you.'

*

So there was a God, thought Abbie, putting down the phone; not in her wildest dreams would she have imagined orchestrating that. She wasn't quite sure what might happen next; but the thought of being able to study Venetia on her home ground, and of the severe fright Boy would get at the news she had been there, was quite gratifying enough. For the time being at least.

It was unfortunate enough that Jay should have been in Celia's office that morning when Giles arrived, still in a white-hot rage; still more unfortunate that he should have been leaning over her desk, pointing out something to her, and very much more that she should have been so clearly amused by it, that at the very moment that the door opened she should have been saying, 'How clever of you to—'

'Notice that,' she had been going to say, and what Jay had brought to show her was a request from a customer asking for 'a signed copy of Lady Celia Lytton' and what he had just said, laughing, was that if she could possibly oblige with such a thing, then that would be a very valuable promotional item. But it was very clear to Giles's eyes that Jay, the new favourite, the latest threat, was discussing something with Celia on a one-to-one basis, that their relationship was not the normal one enjoyed between apprentice and editorial director, that he had clearly said or done something that had earned her approval as well as her amusement, something that she was proclaiming as very clever. Giles tried and failed to think of one thing that he had ever done to earn such an accolade – and as a result, his request to speak with her urgently, in the boardroom and at once, sounded threatening as well as uncivil.

'Very well,' she said coolly, 'if it's really important. Jay, perhaps—'

'Of course,' said Jay, scooping up the papers from her desk, moving out of the office swiftly, smiling at Giles awkwardly as he left. Giles did not return the smile.

'Well, Giles,' said Celia, 'what is this private and urgent matter you need to discuss with me?'

'It's my future,' said Giles, 'that's what it is. And the fact that you have chosen to discuss it with Helena. How dare you, Mother, how dare you undermine me to my own wife, whatever your views might have been—'

'I was driven to it,' said Celia. She was flushed, her own eyes brilliant. 'Driven to it by Helena's stupidity. And lack of sensitivity, for that matter—'

'Sensitivity!' said Giles. 'Yes, of course, a quality you would appreciate and recognise very well, wouldn't you, Mother? I simply cannot believe that you could have said what you did to Helena. And Father, I gather he was there. And neither of you have ever had the courage to talk to me about my failings, as you see them. It's appalling.'

'Giles, you mustn't overreact,' said Celia carefully. 'I doubt if Helena related the conversation accurately. And her view of what was said will have been coloured by her attitude to you. As I recall, I merely expressed my doubts over a very early rise to board director level. Which is not—'

'No, Mother, that is not what you said. You said –' he produced a notebook '– here, I wrote it down, you see. I am "lacking in the publishing instinct", it seems. And "incapable of taking over any aspect of the running of Lyttons". I'm afraid I'm not able to perceive that as a simple doubt over the timing of my promotion to board level.'

Celia was silent.

'What's more, I think Helena's right. She feels my contribution to Lyttons and my position as your heir should be recognised formally, now. I'm sick and tired of scrabbling about, of struggling to earn your approbation, of being grateful for the smallest crumb of reward. When Father was my age, you and he ran this company—'

'Giles, we were—'

There was a silence; a long, agonising silence, then Giles said, 'You were what? Capable? In possession of the publishing instinct? Or simply in a position to do so, because Edgar Lytton had so conveniently died? I wonder. Well, I'm not prepared to wait for you to die, it's clearly a very long way off, or even Father, although that may be rather sooner from the look of him—'

And then everything blurred and telescoped into a hideous sequence, of realising that Oliver had come into the room, had heard at least the latter part of the discussion, of looking at him, ashen, dreadfully drawn, of him saying, 'Giles, please—', of Giles turning on him and saying, 'No, I've had enough, quite enough, of this wretched dictatorship you call a company, of waiting for recognition, of seeing people like Jay and – and Barty overtaking me, watching you take wrong decisions, did that occur to you? No, clearly it didn't. Did you ask me about the Penguin proposition incidentally? No, you most certainly did not, nor did you take any notice of my memo, my report saying we should have gone in and at once, and that we should most certainly cooperate with one of the book clubs. I think it's time you both came out of the self-satisfied cocoon you inhabit and looked hard at the profitability of this company. You're living in the past, especially you, Father, resting on the laurels of those wretched Meridian books, which are frankly not what they were, and the Buchanans, come to that, the same could be said of them. And unless you do give me some kind of proper hearing and recognition, I'm of a mind to leave Lyttons, go to another house, a more forward-thinking, democratic place which isn't run along the lines of the Third Reich which you and your appalling friends, Mother, so admire—'

And then Oliver's voice rising in an anger of his own and saying, 'How dare you speak to us like that, and in particular to your mother—' before he faltered and then collapsed entirely, his face grey, his lips etched in white.

He lay on the floor, absolutely still, staring up at them; then Celia spoke, absolutely calmly, and told Giles to phone for an ambulance, then she sat down by Oliver and took his hand and said over and over again, as if he were a small child, 'It's all right, Oliver, it's all right, everything's all right, there, there, lie still, it's all right . . .'

'Right,' said Venetia, 'Henry, come along, into the drawing room. Miss Clarence has come to see you and decide whether she can teach you to play the piano. Here's the piano, Miss Clarence, it's a very good one, I believe, my husband plays it.'

'This is a wonderful piano, Mrs Warwick.'

'Is it? Good. I'm not frightfully musical myself.'

'Lovely drawings,' said Abbie, indicating the set of charcoals on the piano, four of them now, of Venetia with each newborn child.

'Do you like them? Yes, my husband did them. It's a bit of a hobby of his.'

'He's obviously very talented.' Abbie smiled at Venetia. 'And is that marvellous portrait you? Do forgive me asking, but it really is so impressive and—'

'Yes. I was a bit younger then of course. It's by an artist called Rex Whistler.'

'I have – heard of Whistler.' The tone was slightly cool. Venetia felt embarrassed.

'Of course. I'm – sorry. Now, Henry, come along, sit down on the stool and—'

But at that moment, the door of the drawing room opened and Boy walked in. Walked in, saw Abigail Clarence and stopped. He stood so still, so absolutely still, and aware and wary, that it was almost a tangible thing. Venetia, looking up at him briefly, saw the expression on his face and felt something ease into her own consciousness. It was a sliver of fear: so raw and powerful a fear that she turned away from it, crushed it promptly and absolutely; and then she heard the telephone ringing and Donaldson appeared in the doorway looking quite shocked himself, to say that her father had collapsed and that she was to go to St Bartholomew's Hospital as soon as she possibly could.

Chapter 17

'Don't go.'

'I'm going, I've got to.'

'But I want you to stay.'

'I'm sorry, I—'

'Oh, for God's sake,' he said, 'you are being absurd. Some ridiculous appointment with a bookshop, what does it matter? When you know what I want to do with the rest of the afternoon . . .'

It was the first time she had seen him close to anger with her.

She faced him steadily and stood her ground; that much she had learned. 'Laurence, I have an appointment with Scribners. I have arranged to be there to see the manager at four o'clock. I'm sure you don't cancel appointments with the New York Stock Exchange purely on a whim.'

'That's hardly comparable.'

'I'm sorry, but it is.'

'Oh very well.' He glared at her. 'Go to your absurd meeting, if it's so important to you. I have to say I don't find it very flattering.'

Barty put her hand over his.

'Laurence, you have to understand. About me. I have a career, it's very important to me. I shouldn't even have had lunch with you today. I've got far too much work to do.'

'Well, I am so extremely grateful to you,' he said, 'but don't let me detain you any further.'

She stood up. 'Will I—' She stopped.

'Will you what?'

'Will I meet you as arranged?'

'You can hardly meet me as arranged. You'll be in some damn-fool bookshop. Oh, look, for God's sake, go. I'll leave a message at your office. I may have to cancel the whole weekend now.'

'Very well,' she said. 'Thank you for lunch. I'll wait for you to phone me.'

'Indeed. Possibly for some time.'

She bent to kiss him; he turned his head away. She looked down at him for a moment, then walked quickly out of the restaurant.

She was learning not to be too distressed at these outbursts; they were childish tantrums, no less. Tantrums which (his psychiatrist had explained, and he had explained to her) he had never had a chance to work through as a child, work through and learn to control.

'Because I had no proper loving discipline,' he had said after the first one, after he had apologised, kissed her, begged her to forgive him, 'just indulgence, pacification. I'm emotionally still about four years old, my darling. Trying to grow up. You'll have to help me.'

Barty had thought (but didn't say so) that at four or even five, he had had plenty of loving discipline, that his father had not died after all until he had been twelve; and then thought that he had been ill for a year before that, that Laurence would have been alternately neglected and indulged as his mother nursed his father and tried to come to terms with her own loss, and that perhaps even at twelve there was still a great deal of growing up to do.

But this was more than a tantrum; this was more serious. It had made her – what? Anxious? No. Thoughtful? Possibly.

Anyway, she had more serious things on her mind just now: her meeting at Scribners to discuss the possible promotion for a novel she was hoping to publish in the spring.

A wonderful novel, though: she was convinced it would do well. It was her own discovery and she was fighting hard for it. She hesitated to say it was in the Fitzgerald mould, that would smack of imitation, of passing off. Which it certainly wasn't. But it did chronicle the lives of the privileged in New York: the privileged and decadent. It was at once a saga and a thriller; a story of crime committed by a young member of a prominent New York family and the attempted concealment of that crime. It was exciting, stylish and very clever; Barty had been so excited when she had first read it that she hadn't been able to sleep. She had passed it to Stuart Bailey, without too much hope, for he was notoriously conservative. Reluctantly, he had agreed to meet the author: 'If he seems to have more than one story in him, I'll consider it. Solid bankable authors are what we're looking for, not single books that won't last.'

Barty had written to the author, a young man called George MacColl, and asked him to come in to meet her and Stuart Bailey. He was only twenty-six years old, charming, not quite good-looking, but very attractive, with floppy brown hair and grey eyes and rather girly-looking long black eyelashes; he was indisputably upper-class American himself, although clearly far from rich.

'My father lost a lot of money in the crash, my grandfather put me through Princeton; I'm the small white hope of the family.'

Stuart Bailey had clearly liked him very much and liked him even more when a long discussion about the book led to a longer one about other ideas he had. Two days later, he told Barty to make him an offer and to prepare a publishing plan. 'And I'd like you to edit it, it seems only fair. Of course,' he added firmly, 'I don't ever see him as a really big seller, but with the right publishing, he could do quite well.'

George MacColl was so excited he literally jumped up and down in Barty's office; 'I just never in my wildest dreams thought this would happen. Maybe a kind letter, rather than just a rejection slip. You really think it could do well?'

Years of living with Celia had taught Barty professional caution.

'We must hope so,' she said carefully, 'and of course we will be publishing only a very small number initially, let's say fifteen hundred at the most. That's far better, you see, than putting out thousands and running the risk of them all coming back.'

But George MacColl was not to be cast down; he begged her to let him take her to lunch and when she refused that, proposed tea. 'After all, if we are going to work together, we need to know one another well.'

Over tea, he asked her to call him Geordie ('not many people have nicknames longer than their real ones') and promised to do exactly what she told him with his manuscript. 'I'll cut it, lengthen it, make the beginning the end, whatever you want.'

Barty didn't actually think that the book – called *Brilliant Twilight* – needed any really serious editing, and her meeting that afternoon at Scribners was to present it to one of the buyers there.

She had been there several times now, to the beautiful building on Fifth Avenue. It was her favourite of all the New York bookshops, with its book-lined galleries, rather like a very grand library, set above the well of the main store.

James Barton of Scribners had read and liked *Brilliant Twilight*; he said yes, they would take ten and see how they went.

'Will you be doing posters, or anything like that?'

'Oh yes,' said Barty. 'Of course. Let me know how many you want and I'll supply them.'

'One, my dear, will be quite sufficient. Possibly two, in case of one getting damaged. I really don't think this book is going to be a big seller, good as it is. You'll have a lot of competition next year, you know. There's a new Steinbeck, *Of Mice and Men*, quite marvellous. And a Hemingway. And *Gone with the Wind* is still going to be selling very well.'

'Well—' said Barty, 'perhaps not as big as them. But not small either, Mr Barton. Now I have some other titles to discuss with you, if you have time.'

Oliver's condition had stabilised somewhat; he was in a private room, now at the King Edward VII Hospital for officers, breathing with some difficulty, and looking somehow pitifully small.

But he was unconscious, and had not moved or spoken since his collapse; he had had quite a minor heart attack, Dr Carter the specialist said, followed by a rather more severe stroke: 'Not so very unusual, but it's impossible to say yet exactly how serious the stroke was.'

Celia was sitting by him, holding his hand; Venetia and a horribly shaken Giles stood staring at him.

'He looks so – old,' said Venetia, her voice hushed, 'and as if he's not here at all.'

'Well – we must be grateful that he is,' said Dr Carter, 'and of course, at least fifty per cent of all stroke patients make a good recovery.'

'Really?' said Giles. 'Is that really so?'

'Oh yes. But – there are no certainties.'

'Could I – could I have a word with you? Privately?'

'Certainly, Mr Lytton. Lady Celia, Mrs Warwick, please excuse us.'

The look of absolute contempt Celia gave Giles as he left the room would have shaken a stronger personality than his. She knew what he was going to ask: and she despised him for it. She preferred to carry her own guilt and fear alone.

Dr Carter was as reassuring as he could be; the risk of strokes increased with high blood pressure and a narrowing of the arteries.

'I have to say that your father shows no sign of either of those conditions so far as we can tell; but a third risk factor is what we call atrial fibrillation, which is an irregularity of heartbeat, most common in a heart that has been weakened, in this instance, probably by the heart attack.'

Giles took a deep breath. 'And – could that be caused by stress?'

'The stroke no, the heart attack possibly. But of course your father is not strong, never has been since the war. Don't worry, Mr Lytton; he's holding his own so far. That's a good sign. We have to look for signs of what we call lightening, that is, his regaining consciousness, in however small a way; provided that happens quite soon, then the prognosis is good.'

Giles nodded and thanked him and went back into the room; Celia looked at him.

'Giles, I think you should get back to Lyttons. There seems no point all of us staying here. Venetia has spoken to Adele, she's going to fly back from Paris, and Kit is coming home from school this evening.'

'But—'

'There is nothing you can do here.' She placed a slight emphasis on the word 'you'; Giles flinched.

'Mother, I'm so – sorry. If – that is – if my – my outburst was a cause of this in any way.'

Celia looked at him; her face unreadable.

'Whatever the cause,' she said, 'it has happened. We can only hope and pray. Now do get back to Lyttons; and send a cable to Barty, please. She'll want to know, and possibly may even come back. Oh, and you'd better send one to Robert as well. And Jack and Lily, naturally.'

He did: one to Hollywood, two to Barty, at both her home address and at Lyttons, and one to Robert at Sutton Place.

It was still quite early in New York, so Barty might not yet have left home; she should get it very quickly.

He was not to know, of course, that Barty had not slept at her Gramercy Park apartment for two nights; or that she had left Lyttons at ten o'clock New York time for an appointment; and had then gone on to meet Laurence Elliott for lunch.

They lunched at the Colony Club. Barty very seldom agreed to lunch, because she couldn't spare the time; but today, with meetings running through the day, it suited her schedule to do so.

When Barty left him that day, he drank another coffee; then he signed the bill, asked for his coat and walked out into the street. It was a perfect day, a Friday; he had planned that after lunch they should go straight back to Elliott House and then leave for South Lodge, his house at Southampton, Long Island. He had taken Barty there only once and only for the day; her agreeing to spend the whole weekend there had delighted him. He had never known anyone like her before;

her fierce independence, and her refusal to do anything if it did not meet her own rather severe criteria baffled as much as it enraged him.

'You said you loved me,' he said irritably, the first time she refused to stay at home and in bed with him one morning. 'How can you rush off to that ridiculous office of yours when you could be making love with me?'

'I do love you,' she said, 'but I have to go to work. The two things are not mutually exclusive.'

'Of course they are. You don't have to work, you certainly don't need to work.'

'Laurence, I both have and need to work. I have to because I love it, and it matters to me and I need to because I have a salary to earn.'

'I could give you all the money you want.'

'Don't be ridiculous,' she said, laughing, 'I want to earn my money, Laurence, not take it from someone for nothing. You of all people should understand that.'

'I suppose this is all some nonsense about equality for women.'

'Partly yes, it is. Successful women – and there aren't many in publishing – are very important at the moment, simply in proving what can be done. When Celia Lytton speaks at a literary dinner, it gives a signal to other women, young, hopeful women, that they too can succeed. So don't try and divert me from my career, Laurence, please.'

He did: over and over again, and with mounting irritation. But with no success whatsoever.

He decided to take his car down to her apartment in Gramercy Park, and wait outside it for her return; she had said she would be there at six, and that way they would at least be able to leave for Long Island at the earliest possible moment.

It was already four-thirty; on a whim, he told his driver to stop outside the literally dazzling Harry Winston, the spectacular jewellery store on Fifth. He hadn't bought Barty much jewellery yet; the first piece – a necklace from Cartier – she had gently refused, saying it was lovely, but she couldn't possibly accept such a thing, it put their relationship on the wrong basis as she saw it.

She did accept a pair of diamond clips for her birthday and had worn them a lot; but today he wanted something more personal, to mark their first weekend. He regarded the two days as deeply significant, a commitment from her to their relationship and, for that matter, to himself. The house at Southampton was very special to him, he had built it himself, it was his own creation, not inherited, and as different as anything could be from Elliott House; he was longing to spend time with her there. He had never taken a woman there alone before Barty. Barty did not know that yet; but he planned to tell her that night, over dinner, to try to explain to her how much the house meant to him and how much he wanted her to share it. Giving her a piece of jewellery at that moment would etch the occasion still deeper into their lives.

Choosing jewellery for her was not easy; her particular brand of beauty demanded quality of an understated kind; after considerable deliberation, he bought a long double strand of pearls, one black, one white, with a diamond clasp. It would suit her absolutely in every way; he asked for it to be wrapped, put it in his pocket and went back to his car, dismissing his driver. He wanted to wait for her alone.

The meeting at Scribners over-ran; Barty realised as she left that it was too late to go back to Lyttons, they would all be gone. She hailed a taxi and directed it to Gramercy Park.

Robert was very distressed by the news of Oliver's condition. He had been shocked by his appearance the last time he had visited England, not only by the way he had aged, but by his look of permanent emaciated exhaustion. He looked at least fifteen years older than Celia, Robert had thought, Celia with her rich beauty, her almost visible energy, her restless pursuit of pleasure and success.

Robert telephoned Felicity Brewer that morning with the news; she was very upset. Very upset indeed, in fact; more than he would have expected.

'Oh, Robert, how dreadful. How serious is it? When will you know, could you telephone Celia perhaps—'

'I will, this evening. I need to know whether or not I should go over to see him. Maud will be so upset, she's very fond of her uncle—'

'Well – do please let me know the moment you have any news. Of whatever nature, please. Oh dear, Barty will be so upset. Have you spoken to her?'

'No,' said Robert shortly. 'As you know, Barty and my family are not communicating very closely at the moment. Well, not communicating at all.'

'I forgot, just for a moment. That is the most extraordinary relationship. And the most extraordinarily malevolent stroke of fate. That –

vile Laurence and dear, sweet, innocent Barty. Does she know all the dreadful things he did? Plotting against you and John—'

'Of course. Maud told her. Barty just said she couldn't believe it and if it was true, then his terrible childhood had to be largely to blame.'

'Classic Laurence. I'm sure he trades on that terrible childhood of his all the time. So attractive to women, that sort of thing.'

'Is it?' said Robert.

'Of course. It's a cause. We all like those. We think we can take it all away, the alcoholism or the cruelty or whatever, make it better by our love. Not always true, I'm afraid.' She sighed. 'Well, anyway, Barty will want to know about Oliver. I would imagine she'd be in touch immediately.'

'I hope so. Anyway, I'll cable Celia later in the day and ask for more news. And of course I'll let you know.'

But Barty did not phone Robert about Oliver; not by lunchtime, not even by the evening. Distressed, Robert telephoned Stuart Bailey to try and speak to her, and was told she had been out of the office at meetings all day so she wouldn't have got the call.

'But we did open the cable and it made clear that one had been sent to her apartment. So – she surely will have got that one. I'm sorry, Mr Lytton, I'll tell her the minute I hear from her.'

The house where Barty lived in Gramercy Park, just south of the park itself, was divided into three apartments; Barty's was on the first floor (which gave her a balcony), a young man lived on the ground floor and the top floor was the home of Elise Curtis, milliner (as she liked to put it) to the gentry. An insufficient number of gentry having become clients of Madame Curtis, she was obliged to make herself extra money by working for one of the downtown clothing factories; working the evening shift meant she earned more and had a little time during the day for her (almost) non-existent clients.

It was Elise who had signed for the cable for Barty that had arrived at about half past nine that morning; she had knocked on Barty's door several times but there'd been no reply. She'd obviously left already for work. Elise wasn't quite sure what to do: mail was always left on a table in the hall, but that seemed rather dangerous – for a cable. Barty might be missing some crucial piece of news. On the other hand, Elise could hardly go running all over New York looking for her. Besides, she was going away in the morning, to visit her sister for a week's well-earned holiday. It would be quite safe on the table, surely. And Barty would see it as soon as she got in. She had left it there, set apart from the rest of the mail, so that it was noticeable, and went back to her own apartment.

But when she walked past it several hours later, on her way out to her evening shift, it was still there. Elise sighed; she felt very responsible, having signed for it. She picked it up and looked at it, half tempted to open it: only that would hardly do any good. Maybe she should just push it under Barty's door and try to forget about it. And then she saw a car she recognised, a large black Packard parked in the small street below the house. It belonged to Barty's gentleman-friend. Elise had often seen the car (and its stable-mate, a white Studebaker), driven sometimes by a uniformed chauffeur, sometimes by an incredibly handsome man with reddish blond hair, had often watched Barty jumping into it, giving the young man a kiss, had occasionally arrived home from the factory at the same time as it dropped Barty off. There was no mistaking it, or indeed that day the handsome man: far better to give the cable to him than leave it to lie unseen in the house.

Laurence responded rather reluctantly to the tapping on his window.

'Yes?' he said, winding down the window.

'Forgive me,' she said, 'but I recognised the car, I've seen it before. You're a friend of Barty Miller's, aren't you?'

Laurence nodded.

'I'm Elise Curtis. I live in the house too. This came for her.' The woman produced a cable from her bag. 'I signed for it this morning. I just wanted to make sure she got it, I'm away now for a couple of days and there's no one else in the house and I don't like to leave it lying around. Could you be sure to give it to her, it just has to be important.'

'Yes, yes, of course,' said Laurence impatiently. 'Just give it to me and run along.'

He often spoke to people he considered his inferiors as if they were children.

When Elise had gone, he sat looking at the cable. It must be important; people didn't send cables in order to comment on the weather. He wondered if it was seriously bad news, if perhaps her adoptive mother, or whatever Celia Lytton was, had died or was even extremely ill. If she was, it would mean he would lose Barty for several weeks. She would go rushing off to England on the first boat; at best she would be anxious all weekend, distracted, wondering whether she should have gone, asking him constantly what he thought she should do. It would spoil the whole weekend; the precious, important weekend.

After a few minutes, Laurence, with infinite care and using a paper knife that he kept in the car, eased the envelope open. It was easy; these envelopes were not designed for close sealing.

He was half relieved at the message it contained: 'Wol in hospital after stroke. Not fatal, but please cable back. Cable also sent to Lyttons NY. Love Giles.'

Not so serious; not a death, not even a fatal illness. Oliver would almost certainly recover from the stroke. And even if he didn't make a full recovery, then he was clearly not going to die. So there was plenty of time for Barty to decide what she wanted to do. But – just the same. It would spoil the weekend. Laurence sat looking at the cable and thinking; until Barty appeared, smiling and flushed, tapping on the window.

'Still nothing from Barty?' said Celia as Giles came into Oliver's room. 'I don't understand it. Maybe she's away.'

'How could she be away? It's a working day in New York.'

He was almost relieved at Barty's apparently uncaring behaviour; his mother was clearly upset by it. Perfect Barty, behaving badly: relieving him of his role as the only villain of the piece.

He pulled himself together, shocked at himself: his father was what mattered, not his mother's attitude to him.

'How is Father?' he asked.

'There's no change,' said Celia. She appeared not to have moved, she was still sitting by Oliver, holding his hand.

'Would you like a rest, Mother?' said Giles. 'Would you like to go home perhaps for a while? I can stay here—'

Celia looked at him as if he had suggested she take a long vacation while Oliver lay in his coma.

'Of course I don't want to go home. I shall stay here until your father recovers consciousness. However long that may be. You could ask for some more tea for me, Giles, if you like.'

'Yes, of course. Where's Venetia?'

'She's had to go home briefly. She'll be back shortly. And she's going to bring Kit with her. Poor chap, he'll be so upset. And Adele should be here by about ten.'

'Helena sent her – best wishes,' said Giles awkwardly. He found it difficult even to mention Helena to his mother, when she had been – albeit unknowingly – responsible for the row that had brought about his father's collapse.

255

'How very kind,' said Celia.

'She would have come of course. To see Father. But I thought it better not.'

'Very much better. Yes, indeed.'

'Can I get you a cushion or something? Make you more comfortable?'

'I'm perfectly comfortable, thank you. Giles, do go and order that tea. I'm extremely thirsty. And then settle down and stop fidgeting, for heaven's sake.'

Giles sighed. It was going to be a long night.

Despite her fear about her father, Adele found the flight home from Paris fascinating enough to distract her. It was the first time she had been in a plane and she was enchanted by the whole experience. She felt she was taking part in some film: the walk across the runway and up the steps into the plane, being ushered to her seat, the apparent magic of the take-off, the effortless rise into the sky; and then the wonder and beauty of the great landscape of clouds they rode through. It all seemed to her rather surreal, and still more so when a waiter, dressed in short white jacket and black trousers, offered her a meal from a trolley, covered in silver salvers that would have been more at home in the Savoy or the Ritz than hundreds of feet up in the air.

The plane had landed in Croydon, the airfield that supplied London; she was standing rather dejectedly in the arrival hall, wondering quite how to get to central London, when she heard Boy's voice.

'Adele, darling, hallo. Lovely to see you. Come along, this way. I've got my car.'

'Oh, Boy, you're an angel.'

'I'm afraid not,' he said and his voice was surprisingly heavy; Adele looked at him curiously, but he smiled at her quickly. 'Come on. It's a bit of a journey, we'd better get going.'

'How – how is Daddy?'

'No change, I'm afraid. But they're hopeful.'

'Any news from Barty?'

'No, none, apparently. Everyone is very surprised.'

Maud put down the phone; she was very pale as she looked at her father.

'Apparently darling Barty was lunching with Laurence today. At the Colony. Long after she would have got the news. Someone saw her there and told Jamie. Obviously she's very upset indeed about Wol.

Come on, Daddy, let's see what we can find out about passages to England. That'll give us something to do. If only, if only one could fly. They say next year it might be possible.'

'Oh, Laurence, it's so beautiful here.'

Barty sighed with pleasure, looking out across the South Shore of Long Island at the great rolling breakers cutting into the white sand; the sun was dropping with dazzling splendour into the sea and behind them the stars were beginning to cut into the dark turquoise of the evening sky. 'You must love it so much.'

'I do. It's the one place in the world where I feel properly safe.'

'Oh, Laurence,' she said, smiling, reaching up to kiss him gently, 'you are a poor tortured soul. How can you possibly not feel safe? You with all your money, all your success—'

'Very easily. You probably can't imagine what it's like to have no one to love you. You always had your mother. You knew she loved you. And your Aunt Celia—'

'Aunt Celia didn't exactly love me. I don't think so, anyway,' said Barty carefully. 'Wol did, he was my only friend really for years and years, so sweet and kind and gentle. And one night – well, I don't know what I would have done without him—'

'What night was that?' asked Laurence curiously.

'Oh – I'll tell you another time. Maybe. When I know you much, much better . . . Come on, let's go in, I'm getting cold.'

They went upstairs quite soon after dinner, Laurence leading her by the hand, both of them equally impatient, longing to be in bed.

His room was huge, the full width of the great house: 'Have you ever thought of maybe doing things on a slightly smaller scale?' said Barty, looking round it in wonder, a great light space, with the bed set on a low platform at one side, the outside wall entirely glass, walls, curtains, linen, carpeting all white, the only colour some huge abstract canvases in blues and greens on the walls, echoing the colours of the sea. She went over to the window, looked out at the sea; Laurence followed her, slid one of the glass panels back and she stepped out on to the balcony. The moon was high now on the sea and there was a light wind, salty and sweet, and the sea grasses on the dunes sang and rustled through the silence: 'It's so beautiful,' she said, 'so lovely. If I were you I would never leave it.'

'Yes, you would,' he said, and this time his voice was light, amused. 'You'd be off to your wretched job the moment Monday dawned.'

257

There was a silence; then he said, 'Wait there' and came back holding a package.

'This is for you,' he said, 'to mark today, to mark your being here.'

Barty looked at him, looked down at the package and waited a moment, then slowly, almost thoughtfully opened it, pulled out the pearls and held them up in the moonlight.

'How lovely they are,' she said very quietly, 'how perfectly lovely. Thank you, Laurence, so much. I love them. Will you put them on?'

'On one condition,' he said, his face very serious, 'that I may take everything else off.'

It was this moment Barty loved: the intense anticipation of sex, when she was so hungry for him, so eager. She lay there in the great white bed watching him, waiting for him, her mind fierce, concentrated on him and the pleasure to come. She had been surprised, sweetly shocked, by how much she enjoyed making love with him, by the ferocious sensations, the sheer wanton greed of her responses. She had expected it to take time, to have to learn to respond, but it was as if he knew her body absolutely, every fragment and movement of it, as if he had been intimate with it always: the pure fierce joy he had evoked in her had been at once almost more than she could bear. But that night seemed somehow a new beginning and as she took him into herself she found new, dark, untravelled depths of sensation, opening, easing, ceasing, waiting, opening again for an endless time, and then the slow, sweet climb into a brightness and a brilliance and a great taut agony of pleasure and then, then the piercing, rippling, billowing pleasure, reaching through the brightness and into release.

And as she lay, wondering at it, held by him, looking out at the brilliant moonlit sky, she wondered how she could possibly have thought before that she knew what happiness was.

Sebastian's eyes as he looked at Celia were tender, anxious, filled with love.

'Dear Celia, you must go home. You can't do anything here.'

She turned to look at him, gaunt, somehow colourless in her exhaustion.

'I will not go home,' she said. 'I have to stay.'

'But – it could be days. Days more.'

'Then I shall stay for days. If need be. Sebastian, I would have thought you of all people would have understood that.'

He sighed. He had been summoned by Adele for that very reason:

'You, of all people, might be able to do something. She's absolutely exhausted, she won't even lie down. Apparently she fell of her chair in the night and the nurse was really frightened, thought she'd had a stroke as well. As if . . . not even LM can do anything with her. Please come, Sebastian, please.'

But he could do nothing; although she did agree to let him sit with Oliver for a few moments while she washed her face and did her hair.

'She wouldn't leave him with us even for that long. I think she doesn't trust us,' said Adele as he rejoined her later in the corridor, admitting failure.

'It's not that. It's that in the state she's in, she sees you as children, not adults. Where's Venetia?'

'She went home at about three. She was exhausted. She'll be back later.'

'You look pretty exhausted yourself,' he said, studying her.

'I am. But I don't have her responsibilities.' She sighed.

'Want a little walk? Fresh air might do you good.'

'Yes. Yes, it might be nice.' She slipped her arm through his. 'It's lovely to see you, Sebastian.'

'It's nice to see you too. London is not the same without you, you know.'

'Oh, Sebastian. If only. You look well.'

'I am well, thank you.'

'And – and how is Izzie?'

'She's perfectly well,' he said, his tone suddenly colder.

'I must come and see her. If that would be all right.'

'As you wish.'

There was a silence; then, 'And how is the dashing Frenchman?' he said, clearly with something of an effort.

'He's – very well. Thank you.'

'Will you be getting a flat in Paris?'

'No,' she said quickly, 'no, I'm not there enough for that. And besides—'

'Yes?'

'Oh – nothing.'

He knew what she meant: Luc Lieberman hadn't suggested it.

'Well,' he said cheerfully, 'it's probably not the best place to settle at the moment. France, I mean.'

'Why? Oh, you mean Herr Hitler and all his little games.'

'Yes. I'm very much afraid he means business.'

'Luc thinks so too,' said Adele soberly. 'And he says the Maginot

Line might as well be built of cardboard for all the good it will do. You know about it, do you?'

'Of course I do,' said Sebastian, amused. The ignorance of the twins on almost everything that did not concern them never failed to astonish him. They were both so clever, and yet their sharp little brains were like unexercised dogs, growing slack and useless.

'I suppose you would. Anyway, yes, all this re-arming of Germany, it is quite scary. But Mummy says it's all just part of Hitler wanting to make it strong and efficient and—'

'Yes, I have heard your mother's views on the matter,' said Sebastian drily. 'I imagine Luc would not share them.'

She sighed. 'No, I'm afraid they've fallen out quite badly. I can't bear those people she's so keen on, myself. It's so weird about Barty not being in touch. I can't understand it. She adores Daddy, we used to be jealous of her when he first came home, because she was closer to him than we were. She was always reading to him and playing the piano—'

'Maybe she hasn't heard.'

'She must have done. Giles sent two cables, one to Lyttons and one to her flat, so I don't see how she couldn't know.'

'No one's tried to telephone her?'

'Well – I don't think so. Maybe we should. Yesterday was such a nightmare, no one was thinking very clearly. Poor Giles is so upset, apparently he was having a row with Mummy and Daddy when he had the stroke. Maybe I should do that, book a call to her.'

'I think it would be an idea. Or I could, if you like. Is she still seeing this Elliott fellow? Robert's stepson?'

'I suppose so. She's very vague in her letters, just says she's met him and he's not nearly as bad as everyone thinks. But Maud isn't even speaking to Barty apparently, which seems a bit extreme. I think it's rather romantic, if it's true.'

'It sounds so extremely unlike Barty, to get mixed up with some wealthy ne'er do well,' said Sebastian.

'Well, of course she's much too sensible. That's why I'm sure it's all a storm in a teacup. I do wish she'd get in touch, though. That really is odd.'

Celia had resumed her vigil; she had no sense of being tired. Her emotions would not allow it; she had never experienced such guilt. And such fear.

For what no one knew, no one at all, was that when she had gone into Oliver's office, after the ambulance had left, she found lying on his desk, removed from her own, the outline of her book about Goering, some preliminary notes she had made and an introduction she had written herself, lauding the achievements of the Third Reich and its leaders, and the schedule of appointments she had made for her forthcoming visit to Berlin. Including possibly an interview with Herr Hitler himself.

It now lay in a small safe in her office where she kept especially valuable documents; clearly its publication would be postponed indefinitely.

It was that, she knew, rather than any angry exchange of words with Giles, that was most likely to have caused his heart attack.

Barty woke very early. It was a glorious day; the sun was just rising on the milky pale sea and the air was soft and mistily still.

She slid out of bed, pulled on a robe and tiptoed downstairs; the house was very still, there was no one about. Well it was only half past five. Not even Laurence's staff would be expected to be up that early.

Barty went into the kitchen and put the kettle on. She was still very English; she liked to start the day with a cup of tea.

She opened the kitchen door, walked across to what she had been told to call the deck and sat down on one of the wicker chairs, gazing out at the sea. The house was set, like most Southampton houses, quite high above the shoreline; the garden was level with the top of the dunes, and the view from the verandah, which ran round three sides of the house, was glorious. The walls of the lower storey were grey stone, Wiltshire stone, Laurence had told Barty proudly, shipped over from England, but the upper walls were clad in slate; a mass of wisteria and Virginia creeper climbed to the first floor, the colours mingling against the grey. Most of the windows were full length, and all the floors inside the house were all palest ash; the whole place seemed filled with sunlight, even on grey days.

'I told the architect I wanted to bring the shore into the house,' said Laurence, 'and I think we've succeeded.'

In another life, he told Barty, he would have liked to have been an architect himself.

The garden at the back of the house was simple, lawns, trees, a tennis court, but no pool: 'I don't understand why people would want to swim in a pool when they have the ocean. And I didn't want to disturb the view in any way.'

But the best thing about it all for Barty was the seascape in all its wonderful blues and greys and greens, always changing and present in

261

almost every room; her trip across the Atlantic, her first proper acquaintance with the sea, had been a crucial part of her love affair with New York, and to find it here, so important a part of Laurence's house, had seemed to her oddly significant. She sighed with pleasure now, and raised her face to the already warming sun; it was obviously going to be a perfect weekend. In every way.

'So – you're going back to the hospital?' Boy looked up as Venetia appeared in the doorway of the dining room. 'Would you like me to come with you? Kit's already gone, I sent him in the car. He's so worried, poor little chap, I don't think he's slept at all.'

'Poor Kit. No, I think it's better you're here with the children. Henry and Roo are upset anyway, they know Daddy's ill.'

'Very well.'

She hesitated, looked very steadily at him, then 'Boy—' she said.

'Yes?'

'I just wondered – well – I wondered whether you thought that that girl—'

'What girl?'

'Abbie Clarence, Barty's friend.'

'Oh yes.'

'Whether you thought it was a good idea for her to teach Henry the piano.'

'No,' he said, and his tone was absolutely level, 'no, I don't think so. I didn't like her very much.'

'Really? Why not? I rather did.'

'I think she's probably rather – neurotic.'

'Neurotic? How could you possibly know that?'

'I don't know it, Venetia. I said I thought it. She gives that impression.'

'In what way?'

'Oh, for heaven's sake,' he said. 'I can't define it exactly. I can only tell you that, on balance, I would prefer her not to teach Henry.'

'But, Boy—'

'Look, Venetia, you asked me what I thought. I've told you. Do we have to spend the morning discussing my reasons endlessly?'

It was unlike him to be so irritable. Of course they were all tired; but—

'No,' she said quickly. 'No, of course not. Well – that's settled then. Look, I must go. I'll telephone if there's any news.'

'Please do.'

Maybe she'd imagined it. The feeling of something – strange in the room. When Boy had walked in and seen Abigail Clarence. It had felt so strong just for a moment; and then of course she had heard about her father and – well, it was gone. Maybe it had just been Boy's inevitable reaction to an attractive woman. Which Abigail was; in a clever, Barty-ish sort of way. Yes, that was it. Of course. Anyway, it was hardly important: not when set against what had happened to her father.

But – she might talk to Adele about it. Try to describe it. Whatever it had been. That would help. It always did.

When she got to the hospital, Kit was sitting in the reception area with Giles. Giles had his arm round him; he was crying.

'I hate it so much. Seeing Father like that. It's as if he wasn't here already.'

'What do you mean, "already"?' said Venetia gently.

'As if he's gone. Left us. Even though he's still alive. As if he was on his way to – to not being.'

Venetia sat down on his other side, gave him a hug.

'Kit, try not to worry too much. He'll be all right. He's—'

'He's having some more tests,' said Kit. 'The doctors are worried, aren't they, Giles?'

'Well, of course they're worried, old chap,' said Giles. He looked appalling, Venetia thought; worse than any of them. 'But that doesn't mean—'

'Even Mummy was crying. She tried not to let me see, but she was. She looked frightened too. I've never seen Mummy frightened.'

'No,' said Venetia, soberly, 'none of us has.'

Barty and Laurence were having breakfast on the deck when the housekeeper came out.

'Telephone, Mr Elliott. It's Mr James.'

'James? Oh, very well. Barty, excuse me please.'

He was back in a moment; he looked at her oddly. Almost – she tried to define it – almost warily.

'He wants to speak to you.'

'To me? Why?'

'I have no idea. You'd better go and find out, I suppose. Only don't be long, I want to get over to the sailing club.'

'Of course. Where shall I take it?'

'In the hallway of course.' He sounded irritable. 'It's hardly likely to be private, is it?'

Two minutes later she was back, ashen-faced.

'I have to go. Back to New York and I must book a passage to England.'

'To England? What is this, Barty, have you gone mad, what on earth are you going to England for?'

'It's Wol. Oliver Lytton, you know. He's had a stroke. Twenty-four hours ago. And I didn't know. I never heard. What must they all have thought of me? I—'

'How could you possibly have known?'

'They sent me two cables, Jamie said. Thank God he phoned, he said it was just a hunch he'd had, they all thought it was so strange. Laurence, they sent me two cables, one to the office, only of course I was out all day, and one to the house. I never saw it, how could that have been, it wasn't on the table with the post, oh God, this is so awful, so terribly awful—' She began to cry, looking at him helplessly like a child.

Laurence suddenly stood up, put his arms round her.

'I have no idea what could have happened to your cable. Obviously. But thank God we know now. Of course you must go to England. As soon as possible. And if you like I'll come with you. In fact, I insist. No, don't argue. You'll have so much to cope with. I want to be there with you. Now stop crying and go and get your things. I'll order the car straight away. And I'll see if I can book a call to London if you like, so you can speak to someone there yourself.'

How could anyone possibly think he was wicked? Barty thought, giving him a quick kiss, turning to run up the stairs to the bedroom. How could they?

Chapter 18

'You've got to tell him. You've just got to. It's not fair on him otherwise.'

'But he'll be so angry. You don't understand. He won't be pleased, he can't be. He'll think I'm incompetent, that I'm going to be a burden on him and—'

'Adele! Stop it. What are you, some kind of Victorian miss? I'm ashamed of you. Look, you're pregnant. The father is Luc Lieberman, I presume—'

Adele looked at Venetia, saw the touch of amusement in her eyes, and smiled back reluctantly.

'Yes, of course he is.'

'Well then. He has to know, Adele, I will not have you rushing off to some clinic in Switzerland to get rid of a baby, without making sure that that's what Luc wants. If it is – well, then it's up to you, I suppose.'

'But it's so – so stupid of me,' said Adele, her eyes filling with tears again. 'I'm usually so careful. It was just that one time—'

'Oh, darling, we've all said that,' said Venetia cheerfully.

Adele ignored her. 'And then I was so worried about Daddy, and I thought that was what had held up the curse, you know, and it was only when I missed another, and started to feel sick – oh God, Venetia, what am I going to say—'

'Not many ways of saying it, really. If you mean in French, I have no idea.'

'I do,' said Adele, 'you say *"je suis enceinte"*. Oh well. Best get it over quickly. I'll go back tomorrow. I think I'll fly, I'm quite getting to like it, you know.'

It was very, very frightening. More frightening than anything Sebastian could ever remember. Except of course – well, of course. But this was so totally unexpected, that was the worst thing. Nothing could have prepared him for it. For going into his study every morning and being quite unable to find anything to fill the day's pages. Well, he could find something, obviously. He sat there right through the day, struggling;

that had always been his advice to other writers with the dreaded writer's block. He had always despised it anyway, privately declaring it an excuse for laziness. Just get back to your desk, and work through it, he had said over and over again, and in the lectures he gave; work through it as you would a cold. That's all you have to do. Drive the germs out, the demons away.

But his own advice was quite useless. And day after day the pages found their way into the waste-paper basket. Waste paper, wasted paper: that exactly described it. He had always known when he had written something poor, not up to standard; however much he had tried to ignore it, tried to pretend that it was fine, that he could move on tomorrow, he still knew, with a dreadful leaden certainty. It was like indigestion of the soul: that was how he had described it to Celia. And the only cure was ripping up the pages, quite ruthlessly. No use keeping them, in case: although he had done that a lot lately. Kept them until the morning, gone back to them after a restless night, telling himself he was worrying about nothing, that it would be fine, looked at with a fresh eye, that the new storyline was really rather good, maybe not quite so fresh, but then what could be after fifteen years?

But it was no good: day after day it was no good, the new storylines were feeble, sickly things, devoid of passion, humour, originality. For the first time since he had first begun to dream of Meridian, the impossible had at last happened and he had nothing to say. And the worst thing of all was not the fear that it would go on for ever, not that there was no one he could talk to about it: but that the one thing which had been his panacea, the drug in which he could take refuge for his grief, his loneliness, was suddenly quite useless and there was no escape from anything to be found anywhere.

'Barty, how is your friend Abbie?' Venetia was quite surprised to hear herself asking the question; it was over six weeks since what she always thought of afterwards as The Moment, since Boy had walked into the room where she and Abbie were and neither of them had said or done anything, anything at all and yet . . .

'I – don't know, really,' Barty said, her voice immensely casual. 'We've – sort of lost touch.'

'Really? But she was your best friend. You used to do everything together. What happened?'

'Oh – well, you know, I was going to America and she's always so involved with a hundred things, and we kind of drifted apart. Venetia,

I really wanted to—' She felt terribly sick. This was awful. Horrible. This was what she had gone to America to escape from. The quicksand, the dangerous, deadly quicksand.

'She came to see me, you know.'

Don't look at her, Barty, keep calm, just go on answering her questions, she can't know, she—

'Did she? Whatever for?'

'Boy wanted Henry to learn the piano. Mummy had heard that Abbie gave lessons and—'

'Your mother?'

'Yes. Abbie went to see her to get some more books for her school and it turned out that she gave lessons and Mummy suggested I get in touch with her.'

'Oh really?' She'd faint in a minute. Or be sick.

'Yes. But – Boy didn't think it would work.'

No, he probably wouldn't.

'Really?'

'Yes. So I had to say no to her. She seemed quite upset. Anyway, I just wondered if you'd seen her. More tea?'

Barty shook her head. 'No, thank you. I only came in to say good-bye, I've got so much to do before tomorrow. It's been so lovely seeing you all, Venetia, and I think your children are just wonderful—'

'You sound like an American.'

'I hope not. I still feel absolutely English.'

'Good for you.'

Better this: moving away from the quicksand now. She felt a wave of rage towards Abbie so powerful it hurt physically. She must speak to Sebastian, see what he could do. Venetia was still talking . . . she tried to concentrate.

'Now give my love to Maud and Uncle Robert and next time you come, bring the wicked Laurence with you.'

'He's not wicked,' said Barty firmly, 'he's – difficult, and a bit tortured and spoilt of course, but he most definitely isn't wicked. Do you know, when I first found out Wol was ill, he insisted on coming with me to England. To be with me. It was only some terrible crisis at the bank that stopped him. He's terribly generous and thoughtful and—'

'Those are lovely pearls. Were they from him?'

'Yes. Yes, they were. I'm glad you like them.'

'They're absolute heaven. And – is he truly disgustingly rich?'

'He is very rich,' said Barty, laughing, 'I don't know about disgusting.'

'How did he not lose it all in the crash?'

'I'm – not sure. He's very vague about it. He said it was best explained by asking if the royal family had lost all their money during the Depression here. I said no, of course not, and he said well, there you are.'

'I hope he doesn't liken himself to our royal family.'

'No, of course not. He meant – I think – that if you had that much of everything you could ride over any depression.'

'I'm sure he must be terribly attractive. Oh, Barty, it really is exciting. What a terrible pity Maud and you have fallen out over him.'

'It's only Maud falling out,' said Barty. 'I'd still love to be friends with her. I think if she'd come over to see Wol, I'd have been able to talk her round.' She sighed; Maud's flat refusal to come over as soon as she heard Barty was booked on to a ship on the Monday had hurt her dreadfully. Robert had come and on the same ship but she had seen little of him; the sea was extremely rough for the time of year; Barty had stood on the deck one particularly wild day, as the ship rode the great waves, her anxiety over Wol temporarily eased, thinking of Robert suffering in his cabin. When it was a little calmer, she had gone to see him, begged him to come outside and join her: 'It's so wonderful, it just takes hold of you and you feel part of it, part of the wind and the sea', but he looked at her in horror and closed his eyes again.

He had been touched by her concern for him, by her daily visits, and as the weather eased, and they had been able to talk, they had become friends again. She could see he was baffled and even shocked by her devotion to Laurence, and that nothing would change his view of him, but she also managed to convince him there was no need for the two of them to be enemies.

'I can't help how I feel about him, and how I view him, and nor can you, but if we leave him out of our friendship altogether, then it should be all right. Anyway, it's all much less important than Wol.'

'It certainly is,' he said, smiling at her weakly, patting her hand.

They were feeling more hopeful that day; a cable had reached them to say that Wol had finally recovered consciousness.

But nothing could have prepared Barty for what she found when she walked into Wol's room at the hospital; he was indeed conscious, but apparently little more. He could see and hear, Celia told her in a brisk tone that denied her own distress, but so far couldn't speak, and apart from his right arm, he appeared to be completely paralysed.

'The specialist has said I have to accept this, that the stroke was extremely severe and we are lucky Oliver is still alive. However, I've told him I have no intention of accepting it, and I'm already arranging to see several other specialists. In any case, there is an improvement every day, however slight. I am convinced it's just a question of time.'

Barty, looking at the fragile silent shell that had been her beloved Wol, found it extremely hard to believe her.

But the doctors had not encountered Lady Celia Lytton before; within two weeks, a rather grudging neurologist conceded that there did, after all, appear to be signs of Oliver recovering some movement in his left arm, and although he would not personally have described the patient's awkward grunting as speech, it was certainly encouraging that he could make any sound at all. Celia told him that what she had observed were not signs of movement, but actual movement, more pronounced each day, and that what might sound like awkward grunting to him were easily discernible words to anyone who cared to take the trouble to listen properly.

'Poor man, he was absolutely crushed,' said Adele to Venetia, 'left the room very quickly. And now Mummy's found some other specialist. She's having Daddy moved home, says he'll do much better in familiar surroundings. I tell you one thing, I don't envy the resident nurses he's going to need.'

There were times in the ensuing weeks when Oliver himself, as he told Venetia later, would have given anything to be back in hospital. He was moved home to Cheyne Walk and into the morning room on the first floor, converted into a nursing home. 'It has to be the front of the house so that he can see the river,' said Celia. 'He's always loved it and it will stimulate him. Stimulation is all, Dr Rubens says.'

Dr Rubens was a name they all came to dread; Celia had discovered him by chance through a friend and while he was a qualified neurologist, he was also and most unusually a committed naturopath and chiropractor. She regarded him as second only to God – 'and herself of course,' said Adele with a giggle – and quoted him endlessly, not only in what she insisted on calling the convalescent room, but over the dinner table and even in the office. Dr Rubens had prescribed a strict diet of entirely raw food; in the early days before Oliver was able to eat properly, Cook had to spend hours chopping and sieving fruit and vegetables into a juice which was then spooned into him, either by Celia or one of the nurses.

He also insisted on a regime of gentle spinal manipulation, essential to the health of the central nervous system – this again against the advice of the other specialists, who had told Celia repeatedly that Oliver's central nervous system was damaged beyond repair – and intense physiotherapy for several hours a day. 'The muscles must not be allowed to waste, Lady Celia,' Dr Rubens said. 'They must be exercised to preserve their strength and this in turn will stimulate the central nervous system.'

In the few exhausted hours when he was not having his limbs massaged, flexed, pushed and twisted, Oliver was given speech therapy, and quite literally taught to speak once more. Much of this task was undertaken by Celia herself, who was a most unforgiving practitioner.

'Not "nud", Oliver, "mud". Mmm. Push your lips together, that's better, and now make the sound. No, I couldn't hear you. Try again. No. Mmm. Mud. MUD, Oliver, you're not trying. Yes. That was better. Now again. No, don't try to tell me you're tired, plenty of time to rest later. This is much more important.'

The family watched, initially amused, then anxious, but finally awestruck as at the end of the second week, Oliver raised his left arm in a gesture of greeting as each of them entered his room, and by the end of the third, could stammer, albeit in rather strangulated tones, 'Kit' and 'Barty'.

'The two favourites,' said Adele lightly, winking at Oliver, but it was of course that those were the simplest names; 'Dell' followed and then 'Neesha' in another ten days. Only 'Giles' continued to elude him; Celia told Giles this was simply that it was the most difficult consonant, and that Oliver hadn't managed her name yet either, but Giles saw it as continuing proof of his guilt and his father's hostility, and carried his hair shirt home in anguish for Helena's inspection.

Helena was, perversely, rather impressed by Dr Rubens and his methods; amongst her earnest reading had been several studies on natural healing and what she called its near-miraculous results: 'It's all very well to scoff, Giles, but don't forget the doctors more or less wrote your father off for the rest of his life. This man has achieved absolute wonders for him in just a few weeks.'

Giles told her shortly that he felt the wonders would have been achieved anyway and that the twins and LM agreed with him: this fact alone confirmed the virtues of Dr Rubens' therapies for Helena.

'You must not be narrow-minded, Giles. An open mind is a very valuable thing.'

She had several times tried to visit Oliver, but so far without success. Celia had decided on a regime of absolute quiet in the few hours Oliver was allowed to rest, although the quiet was allowed to be disturbed at will by Celia herself, or by any of her friends she considered suitably positive in outlook ('although none of those Fascists, thank God,' said Venetia) – Jay Lytton, Sebastian Brooke, Venetia's sons ('Children are so stimulating, Dr Rubens said so himself'), and of course Lady Beckenham, who proved a surprisingly good extra pair of hands for the massage, after a crash course from one of the nurses. 'Can't possibly do him any harm, I've done a lot of work on horses after all, recognise tension and pain when I come across it.'

Whatever the reasons, at the end of another month, Oliver's recovery, while slow, seemed guaranteed; and Barty decided she must return to New York.

'If that's all right,' she said slightly apologetically. 'I do have a job to do, it's not as if I were just on holiday there.'

'Of course. We understand,' Celia said graciously. 'Although Oliver will miss your reading to him. He looks forward to it all day long, you know. I do my best but I really have to get back to my own desk now. Lyttons is falling into rack and ruin without me. Of course it just needs some concentrated work, getting people to organise themselves properly, but even Edgar Greene seems to have forgotten that our prime function is to nurture authors and publish books. He spends all his time talking to customers. At this rate there won't be any books at all on the shelves in a year's time.'

Certainly not a flattering biography of Goering; the outline of that was now at Cheyne Walk, placed with her jewellery and certain other treasures in her own safe – for she could not quite bear to part with the idea and the work done on it entirely.

She did not admit to Barty, however, her greatest fear: that Sebastian's latest *Meridian* book was dreadfully late and that while all her conversations with Sebastian had ended with the usual weary assurance that she would get the Christmas Brooke as usual if she'd only leave him alone to write it, she sensed an anxiety and tension in him that she had never met before.

'And what about this young man?' she said to Barty now. 'I presume the whole thing about his bad behaviour is largely exaggeration on the part of people like Robert and Maud.'

Celia had never liked Maud.

'Of course it is. He is difficult, I must say, but—'

'I rather like difficult people myself,' said Celia. 'At least they have something to say for themselves. It's the ones who just agree with one all the time I can't bear.'

This was so patently untrue that Barty found it hard not to laugh aloud; she fished in her bag for a handkerchief and blew her nose hard.

'And what does Felicity Brewer think of him?'

'She can't bear him either. It's all very sad, but—'

'Well, there you are. Silly woman, always has been told what to think by that vulgar husband of hers. And it's not as if he's interfering with Lyttons in any way, is he?'

'No,' said Barty, puzzled, 'no, of course not. How—'

'Good. Well, he sounds perfectly all right to me, Barty, but don't get too involved with him, it's never a good idea when you're young. And you have your career to think about, after all.'

Barty, stifling a temptation to point out that Celia herself had married at nineteen, meekly agreed that she had.

'And I've got a marvellous book I'd like you to read. It's called *Brilliant Twilight*. It's a thriller, a sort of society murder. It sounds a bit – brash, but it's beautifully written, and the plot is so clever. I just know it would do well here.'

'Send it as soon as you can. I'd like to see it. You should have brought it with you.'

'I know,' said Barty humbly, 'but I was so worried about Wol I just – came. It seemed a bit heartless to worry about books and things, anyway.'

'Oh nonsense,' said Celia. 'It's always a good thing to have something else to focus on, when things go wrong. Where are you off to now?'

'To see Sebastian. And Izzie of course. How are things there?'

'Oh – much the same. Poor child. And poor Sebastian, of course, she could be such a comfort to him. Still, she seems to be growing up all right. Very resilient creatures, children. Look at you, settled down with us perfectly well in a matter of weeks, didn't you?'

Izzie was at school when Barty arrived at Primrose Hill; a morose Sebastian greeted her on the doorstep.

'I'm not going to be good company, I'm afraid. Problem with the book. Nothing serious of course, but it's very late. Come along in, have a cup of tea, I suppose that's all you want, can't tempt you with champagne or anything?'

'No, thank you, Sebastian. I've only come to say goodbye. And to talk to you briefly about – about Abigail Clarence. It's so awful, Sebastian, apparently she—'

He listened to her carefully: then he said, 'My advice doesn't alter, Barty. It's nothing to do with you. In fact you could make matters worse, jumping in now. She's obviously in retreat. Boy's been alerted to her behaviour after all. He'll deal with her, he's a very skilful operator, you know.'

'So is she,' said Barty soberly, 'and I'm beginning to think a bit mad.'

'Maybe. Anyway, I'm sure he's as much in control of the situation as it's possible to be. Try not to worry about it. I'll miss you,' he said abruptly. 'It's not the same without you at Lyttons. When are you coming back?'

'I'm – not sure,' said Barty, and flushed.

He looked at her: 'In love, are you? With this Elliott chap?'

'Yes,' she said, 'yes, I am. But—'

'Well, I only met him once and loathed him. Arrogant little tick.'

'Sebastian—'

'Oh, I daresay he's better now. Grown up a bit. Giving you any trouble at Lyttons?'

'No, of course not. What do you mean? How could he?' Celia had said something like that as well.

'Perfectly easily I'd have said.'

'But how? Apart from trying to stop me working late and things like that?'

'How? Barty—' He stopped, stared at her, his dark-blue eyes genuinely puzzled. 'You must surely know, someone must have told you.'

'Know what? I don't understand.'

'Oh, God. No one has told you. I suppose everyone assumed you knew. Barty, Laurence Elliott owns forty-nine per cent of Lyttons New York.'

Chapter 19

'I don't believe you. You're making it up.'

'I'm not. I'm not making it up, it's true.'

'Prove it.'

'I – can't.'

'Liar, liar, your pants are on fire.'

'Stop it,' cried Izzie, and she burst into tears, ran from the classroom into the corridor, where she bumped headlong into Miss Parker, her form teacher.

'Isabella, whatever is the matter, why are you crying?'

'I – don't know,' said Izzie. Miss Parker, who was a perceptive young woman and very fond of Izzie, as well as saddened by her lonely, apparently parentless life, looked at her intently.

'Being teased?'

'Oh – no,' said Izzie, with a quick smile.

'You must tell me if you are. There are some quite difficult little girls in your class. They don't mean any real harm, but they – well, I need to know.'

'It's – not that,' said Izzie, and she burst into tears again.

Miss Parker led her gently into a classroom and shut the door.

'Come along. Tell me about it.'

Izzie told her.

'I see. Well, we must try and convince them, mustn't we? No use my saying anything to them now, they'll know you've been telling tales. As they would see it. But perhaps we could do something much more clever. Leave it with me.'

Two days later, Izzie was sitting eating her breakfast when the door flew open and Sebastian came into the room. He was clearly very angry, his eyes almost black and his face taut and white.

'Isabella, how dare you talk about me at school?'

'Father, I—'

'Telling people I'm your father, complaining when they don't believe you. Why should they believe you and why mention it at all—'

'But Father, I'm so proud of you—'

'Proud of me!' He was silent, staring at her, the rage evaporating and replaced by the usual cold distaste.

'Yes. Very proud of you. Everyone at school likes your books and—'

'I never, ever wanted to encourage this sort of thing. I don't want you mixed up with my writing life. Did you suggest I come to give a talk at school?'

'No, I didn't,' said Izzie. She put her cup down, stared at her father, feeling sick.

'Well, where did they get the idea from?'

'I don't know. I really, really don't know.'

'Well, you can tell them I won't. I'll write and tell them myself of course, that I don't wish to be taken advantage of like this, but – it really is very wrong of you. Do you understand?'

'Yes, Father,' said Izzie very quietly.

'I don't want to hear anything about this ever again. I've got enough problems without getting mixed up with some absurd school.'

Nanny, who had listened to this in silence, suddenly spoke.

'Mr Brooke, I'm sorry, I know this is nothing to do with me but—'

'You're right, Nanny, it isn't.'

'But I do feel it's unfair to blame Isabella for this incident. You are after all well known as a speaker at schools. I had heard of you long before I came to look after Isabella, you spoke at a school attended by two other little girls I cared for—'

'Look, as you yourself just said, this is nothing to do with you. Absolutely nothing. Now, Isabella, do you understand? I don't want to hear any more about this.'

'Yes, Father,' said Izzie, very quietly.

'Good. Now finish your breakfast and go to school. You'll be late. Good morning, Nanny.'

When he had gone, Nanny looked at Izzie; her eyes were filled with huge tears, overspilling on to her long lashes.

'Don't cry, Isabella. I'm sorry if I made things worse.'

'You – didn't,' said Izzie, swallowing, 'really you didn't. It's just that—'

'Just what? Tell me about it.'

They arrived a little late at school that morning; Nanny walked with Izzie to her classroom where Miss Parker was taking the register.

'I'm so sorry Isabella is late,' she said in her clear, calm voice to Miss Parker, 'but her father, Sebastian Brooke, the author, you know, had an urgent meeting with his publisher, and needed the car. We had to come on the bus.'

'That's perfectly all right,' said Miss Parker. Her eyes met Nanny's in absolute complicity. 'I do hope Mr Brooke was not late for his meeting. And that the new *Meridian* book will be out in time for Christmas as usual.'

'Oh there's no doubt about that,' said Nanny, 'I've seen the new cover myself. Good morning, Miss Parker. Thank you so much.'

Izzie would not have been human, had her eyes not met her tormentors' in a moment of absolute triumph.

Just the same, she knew something was wrong, that her father was behaving strangely, was even more bad-tempered than usual. She heard him shouting on the telephone, shouting at dear Mrs Conley, shouting at her of course when she made even the slightest noise on the stair – but she was used to that.

What was more worrying was that several times, recently, she had heard him making the awful noise; a noise that she had heard once or twice before. If a child had made it, she would have called it crying. She had also heard him moving about the house in the middle of the night; she had looked at her little clock and the small hand was still on two or three. And he looked awful, like a giant in one of her story books, really much older, with his hair all on end, and his clothes crumpled.

Izzie didn't exactly like her father, but she was concerned for him and she wanted to please him more than anything in the world; and without being quite sure why, she felt she must bear some responsibility for his misery. He didn't see many people after all, there was hardly anyone else who could have upset him. And when another night she heard him being sick, over and over again, while all the house was asleep, she began to be very worried indeed. She would have to talk to Kit about it; he would know what to do.

Kit was still her hero, the person she loved more than anyone else in the world. When he came to the house it seemed warmer, happier, and she felt safe and didn't worry about what she said or did all the time. Even now he was so grown-up, sixteen years old and as tall as

Sebastian, he still had lots of time for her, played games with her in the garden, read her stories – including, of course, the Meridian books – and was teaching her all sorts of fun things like card games and draughts and Ludo. Sebastian liked Kit too, he didn't get cross with him much, and didn't seem to mind particularly if they played noisy games in the garden, like hide and seek.

Kit had even managed to persuade Sebastian to let him put a swing up for her, in the old apple tree; she spent long hours on it, drifting backwards and forwards, gazing up into the branches and making up stories of her own in her head. Sebastian never joined in the games of snap and draughts, but he would occasionally stand watching them together, and once when she had missed a snap, he actually tapped her shoulder and nodded at the table so she saw it. She remembered that for weeks afterwards; it was the sort of thing other fathers did. And once or twice, when they were having tea together, he would come and sit with them; he wouldn't talk to them much, just read the paper and drink his tea, but still, he was actually there with them, not locking his study door and shutting them out. She sometimes thought if Kit could come and live with them, she might have a much more ordinary sort of life.

Adele faced Luc steadily. She had never seen him actually angry before; he could be irritable, he was certainly moody. But now he was white, his almost-black eyes hard under his thick brows, his mouth somehow folded in on itself. They were talking in the Luxembourg Gardens, sitting in the sunshine facing the memorial to Murger. He was one of Luc's favourite writers; and he had taken her to *Bohème* at the Paris Opera to explain to her why and for an evening of what Luc called romantic French glory.

Adele had hoped, therefore, it would be an auspicious meeting place; it seemed she was wrong.

'So,' he said, 'so you have known this for – what? Several weeks, I calculate.'

'Yes. Yes, several. But with Daddy being ill and—'

'You found yourself too busy to tell me this. This most important thing. Or perhaps you just decided it was not very important to you. Not important enough to impart.'

'Luc, of course I thought it was important. I told you. I was – very distressed about my father. For the first few days after he became ill, I didn't leave the hospital. None of us did. And then – well, I didn't come to Paris for weeks, as you know. I didn't want to tell you on the phone. Anyway, I wasn't quite sure. But it's perfectly all right. I can see you're angry about it.'

'I am angry,' he said and his voice was quite quiet, deadly in its rage, 'very, very angry. How dare you keep this to yourself, make decisions on your own about what you might and might not tell me—'

Adele suddenly lost her own temper. 'I have to do everything else all on my own,' she said, 'manage, within this – this relationship. If it deserves such a name.'

'I'm sorry? Our relationship doesn't deserve a name?'

'No, not really. Because it isn't a relationship. You give me nothing, Luc, nothing at all.'

'What? I give you nothing?'

'No. Nothing. Except a – a fuck, when it suits you.'

'Don't dare speak to me like that,' he said, his voice even lower. 'Don't dare use that word either. Or to say I give you nothing.'

'Well, it's true. A few presents, a dinner now and then. Apart from that, just – sex. You've hardly ever given me any time. When did we have a whole day and night together, Luc, when? Always you have to go back to your wife, I have to understand, that is the way it has to be. No promises, no discussions, nothing. Just your protestations of love. Well, I don't have the patience for that sort of love any longer, Luc, or even the stomach. I'm quite glad we're having this conversation, it's the nearest to being honest you've ever been—'

'I have always been honest with you, Adele. Always.'

'Oh really? Funny sort of honesty, if you ask me. You say you love me, you adore me. And then turn your back on me and go back to your wife. I wonder if she would see that as very honest? Does she know about me, Luc? I've often wondered.'

'She knows you exist. That I have a mistress. She accepts it. In the—'

'Don't say it again, Luc, or I warn you, it might be the last thing you ever do say. The bloody French way, that's what you were going to say, wasn't it? Well, I don't like the French way any more. I prefer the English. I'm only sorry I've seen so much of the French, you in particular. Goodbye, Luc. And don't try to contact me, because I don't want to hear from you or see you ever again. It's over, finished. You find yourself another – mistress. That's all I am to you, isn't it? A mistress, someone to go to bed with when you can find some time away from your marriage. Someone decorative and amusing, someone who makes your life more interesting. I think I deserve a better title than that. Goodbye, Luc. I'd like to say it's been wonderful, but it hasn't. It's been very upsetting quite a lot of the time. And I think I've been very patient. Very patient indeed.'

She stood up, and her head suddenly swam, the treacherous nausea overcoming her. Just for a moment she stumbled, and just for a moment she thought he would see her distress, come to her, help her. But he didn't.

Adele took a very deep breath, and walked slowly and as steadily as she could away from him. Him and his life.

'Is that Miss Clarence?'

There was no mistaking that voice: clipped, light, a bit breathy.

'Yes. Yes, that's me.' What did she want, had she—

'Good morning, Miss Clarence. This is Venetia Warwick. I don't know if you'll remember me.'

Just about, Venetia, just about.

'Yes, of course I do. How – how are you?'

'I'm fine. I just wondered if – if I could come and see you.'

'Come and see me? Well—'

Now what did she do? Boy had frightened her so completely that day, after he'd come in and found her in the house. Told her if she so much as dared to speak to any member of his family ever again, it would be the end of everything. She had behaved with absolute discretion ever since; unsatisfactory as their relationship was, she didn't want it finished. She supposed that might mean she was actually in love with him.

'It's nothing – nothing terribly important. In fact, you might think me a bit silly. But – I rather wanted to have some piano lessons myself.'

'Really?'

'Yes. I had hundreds when I was a little girl, never practised of course, and wasted what little talent I had. And my husband is so frightfully musical, he often says what a pity it is I'm so hopeless, I thought I might surprise him. And I could start all the children off with the piano myself, I thought, as well. I just thought it would be a good idea. But perhaps you're too busy—'

Abbie seized on this gratefully. 'I am. Awfully busy. I'm sorry. I just haven't got any – any spaces at all, I'm afraid.'

'Oh dear. Well, never mind. It was just an – an idea. You don't have any friends who teach, do you?'

'No, I don't, I'm afraid. I'm sorry. But thank you for thinking of me.'

Abbie put down the phone, shaking slightly. That had been close. Silly, stupid, spoilt bitch. God, she must be dense. She didn't deserve to have Boy as a husband: Boy with his brilliant mind, his wit, his fascinating conversation. They were a disgrace to the women's cause, women like her. Fifty years out of date. Venetia Warwick probably wouldn't even care if they took the vote away from her.

Well, it had been worth a try. She still wasn't quite sure why she wanted to see Abigail Clarence again. It was just the awful nagging, niggling feeling that something had been wrong that day: that moment. And that maybe if she saw her again, talked to her a bit, she could – pin it down. Probably she was completely mad. Almost certainly she was completely mad: had imagined the whole thing.

It was just that it had gone on and on nagging at her: the sensation that there was something between Boy and Abigail Clarence that she was excluded from. And he had been odd when she had talked to him about the music lessons. Nothing that she could pin down, just tense. And awkward. Boy was never tense and very seldom awkward.

Oh it was ridiculous. Absolutely ridiculous. Just as well her plan hadn't worked. She was like all jealous wives, imagining she'd seen things that simply weren't there. Abigail was hardly Boy's type, anyway; with her rather bohemian looks and clothes. He liked glamorous women. She'd do much better getting on with her life, putting it out of her head, being a good wife to Boy. They were going on holiday in a week, to a villa near Antibes; she and the children were going on the train and Boy was following in his latest toy, his own plane, landing on the tiny airstrip at Nice. She would instruct her maid to start packing for that today, tell Nanny to get the children's clothes and toys ready, cable the cook and butler there with instructions.

She really had far better things to do and worry about than premonitions about Abigail Clarence.

'Mrs Warwick!'

'Can I come in?'

'Well – I'm very busy. As I said.'

'You don't look very busy,' said Venetia briskly, and indeed Abbie realised she didn't, wearing a pair of wide-legged silk pyjamas (a present from Boy), a cigarette in one hand, a book in the other.

'No. But I am expecting someone.' God, this was frightful: suppose Boy turned up. But he wouldn't, he'd said he wouldn't be coming that day.

'This won't take long,' said Venetia. 'I would like to come in, though, if I may.'

She had no idea what she was going to say: she half wished she had never set out on this absurd mission. She was looking for reassurance as much as anything. Thinking that if she got to know Abigail a bit better, talked to her, observed her, she'd be able to convince herself.

And somehow, she felt she just had to explore it all further. She was never going to be able to settle down to enjoy her holiday with it unresolved. The worst that could happen was that she would look a bit stupid. And if Abbie didn't know Boy, that really didn't matter.

'What a pretty house,' she said, following Abbie into the small drawing room.

'Yes. I like it.'

'I thought you lived near Barty.'

'I did. But I was left some money and I thought I'd like to have a house of my own.'

'You and Barty, such independent spirits,' said Venetia lightly. 'I do admire you. I would never have thought of getting my own place.'

'Well – we don't all have husbands to look after us,' said Abbie. She smiled quickly and carefully.

She was very edgy, there was no doubt. She kept looking round the room: she's checking on things, Venetia thought, checking I don't see – what? Boy's photograph, a jacket he'd left behind? Hardly likely.

'Would you like some tea?' said Abbie. 'Or a drink or something?'

'Some tea would be nice. Thank you.'

Tea would take longer, give her a while to look around a bit.

But there was nothing to see: no incriminating evidence of any kind. No snapshots, no letters, although—

'That's very pretty,' she said, when Abbie came back into the room, indicating a bronze on the desk.

'Yes. I like it.'

'Where did you get it?'

'Oh – at a friend's gallery. In the country. In – Sussex.'

'Lovely. I wonder if you could give me the address, it's exactly the sort of thing I'm looking for.'

'Yes. I'll try and find it for you.'

She was more composed now; she handed Venetia her tea then sat down opposite her, smiled politely.

'Goodness,' said Venetia, looking up at the shelves, 'what a lot of books.'

'Yes, well, I love reading. Don't you?'

'Yes, of course.'

'Do you meet many of the authors Lyttons publishes?'

'Oh – no, not many. I'm a bit too busy to go to publishing parties.'

'I'd make the time,' said Abbie. She smiled again, but her voice was slightly barbed, the message very clear. That she considered Venetia foolish to forgo the opportunity to meet some of the great authors of the day.

'Yes, well, you don't have four children.' She could hear her own voice, sounding defensive.

'Of course not. Quite enough at school.'

'And what a marvellous gramophone. And such a huge collection of records.'

'Yes.'

'May I look?'

'Of course.'

It was indeed a very large collection. Boxed sets, of symphonies and concertos, whole operas. Some of them clearly still unopened. How did she have the sort of money to pay for those? On a teacher's salary?

'Er – Mrs Warwick, I don't mean to be rude, but perhaps you could tell me why you're here. I'm expecting friends, as I said, and—'

'Yes, of course. I'm sorry. It was just that I was passing' – as if she'd be passing a small Clapham street – 'and I thought I'd try again to persuade you to give me piano lessons. Is that the piano?'

'Oh – yes.'

Also very expensive: a Bechstein.

'It's lovely. I like the candlesticks.'

'Yes, it's pretty, isn't it? But, Mrs Warwick, I'm sorry, I really don't have any spare time.'

'You had the time to teach Henry,' said Venetia sharply.

An infinitesimal pause: then, 'Yes, but I've got some more pupils now.'

'Yes, I see. Well—' This was hopeless; the best thing she could do was leave, before she completely lost her dignity. 'I must go. Leave you in peace.'

She stood up, followed Abbie into the hall. Abbie was clearly more relaxed; Venetia looked round again, up the stairs. It was a pretty staircase with a half-landing. She saw Abbie's eyes following hers, nervous suddenly again.

Why, what could be upstairs? Boy perhaps? Even in her discomfort, Venetia felt the urge to giggle.

'I wonder – so sorry. Could I possibly use your lavatory?'

'Oh,' said Abbie, and for the first time she looked properly anxious, 'it's a bit of a mess.'

'Well, that's all right. I really would rather like to. So sorry—'

And she was ahead of Abbie, running up the stairs, calling from the landing, 'This door? On the right?'

'Yes, but—'

She went in. It seemed perfectly normal. No incriminating photographs, nothing like that. And certainly not a mess. Venetia came out again, walked into the bathroom next door to wash her hands. A very pretty bathroom: overlooking the garden, with a small table by the window with a plant on it. There was a mug on the wash basin, with a shaving brush in it. Well, that didn't mean anything; even though it was a very nice shaving brush, with an ivory handle. So Abbie had a boyfriend. A rich boyfriend who bought her gramophone records and books and possibly even bronze ornaments. That wasn't a crime.

She put the towel back, walked out on to the landing. That must be Abbie's bedroom; the door was open. She glanced in: a very big bed, a brass bed, piled high with cushions: more book shelves, and—

'Please don't go in there.' Abbie had come upstairs, was standing behind her. She looked more nervous now. Venetia smiled at her; by contrast she felt more confident.

'I just wanted to powder my nose,' she said, 'all right?'

'No. Not really—'

And there it was: opposite the bed. A large charcoal drawing, framed: not of Boy, as Venetia might most have feared, but of Abbie, a nude, very simple indeed, and very sexy, Abbie sprawled across the bed, her own brass bed, in a drawing style so horribly familiar to Venetia that she closed her eyes briefly, trying to shut it out. The same style in which her own children had been sketched, each of them, when they had been born; making up the set of charcoals that stood on the piano in the drawing room. The sketches Abbie had admired when she had come to the house.

Boy's style.

'I'm sorry,' he said. He kept saying it; it didn't make her feel any better.

'I don't really care if you're sorry, Boy. It doesn't help very much. What might help is if you explained a bit.'

He looked at her, his eyes heavily exhausted. 'What do you want me to explain?'

'Oh, you know, nothing much. Just how long it's been going on, what she means to you, how often you see her, a few unimportant things like that—'

'Venetia—'

'Boy, I want to know. Please. I think you owe me that at least.'

He got up, poured himself a second – or was it a third – glass of whisky.

'All right,' he said heavily. 'I'll tell you. I don't think it will help but—'

'It will help me.'

She wasn't sure afterwards if it had; it hurt so much, so terribly much that she had difficulty allowing him to go on. But she did.

It had been going on for quite a long time: a very long time for an extra-marital love affair. For almost four years. Four years in which Venetia had borne Boy two children; four years in which she had become convinced he had settled down; four years in which they had lived together, entertained their friends, dined together, visited Ashingham together, spent family Christmases – and she had had no idea.

He had known her for longer, he said, had taken her to some concerts, the opera even one night; but the affair had begun in earnest four years ago.

And gone on. And on.

'She must – mean a lot to you,' she said, forcing the words out with great difficulty.

He was silent.

'The gramophone, the records, the piano, the books, the paintings – I suppose you bought them for her?'

'Yes,' he said quietly, 'yes, I did.'

That hurt more than anything: that they obviously shared so much. It wasn't just sex, she could have coped with that. Anyway, that would never have lasted four years. If there was one thing she knew she was good at, it was sex. It was that Abbie was the sort of woman Boy clearly wished she was: clever, well read, cultured. The sort of woman he liked to spend his time with, the sort of woman who could talk to him about the things he cared about. The sort of woman Venetia was not.

How had it happened, Venetia wondered, as she wept and raged alone in her bedroom that night, how had she allowed such a thing to happen? And what if people knew? How appalling would that be, if they knew that Boy had been having a long-standing affair, had turned from his beautiful, socially accomplished wife, not to some dazzling star of the social firmament, or even some famous actress or singer, but to a schoolteacher, a middle-class, intellectual schoolteacher, who taught children from the slums and whose best friend had come from the slums herself, brought into the Lytton household so many years ago.

Barty, it seemed to Venetia, must bear at least some of the blame for this.

Chapter 20

Kit was having a pretty awful summer. Of course he didn't expect to be taken on holiday while his father was so ill, but the fact remained it was hot and miserable in London, and as he told Izzie one afternoon in the garden at Primrose Hill, he was unutterably fed up.

'I'd love to go on a holiday,' she said. 'What's it like, what do you do?'

Kit looked at her. She was sitting on her swing, her long, golden brown hair hanging down her back, her solemn little face just lightly flushed with the sun, her huge hazel eyes fixed on his in immense interest. She was such a jolly little thing; it was so sad she had such a rotten life. She was terribly grown-up too, for six, much more grown-up than Roo, or even Henry: he supposed that was because she had to be, and spent nearly all her time with adults, except when she was at school.

And what was more surprising was that in spite of everything, Sebastian's neglect, her own loneliness, not having a mother, in spite of a certain wariness and being inevitably shy and reserved, she remained basically sweet-natured. She must get it from Pandora, Kit thought; no one, however much they loved him, could call Sebastian sweet-natured.

'Well,' he said carefully, 'you go somewhere different, and do different things. Doesn't your nanny ever take you away? Nanny used to take us to the seaside every year. It was really –' he stopped, checked himself '– really quite nice.'

'No,' she said, sounding surprised. 'She never does. She goes away sometimes and then Mrs Conley looks after me. But she wouldn't want to take me with her. She needs a break, I heard her telling Father.'

Kit supposed parents had to organise these things. Nannies couldn't just decide what to do with their charges.

'What would be lovely,' said Izzie, 'would be if you and me went on holiday. Together. Wouldn't it? But I don't suppose Father would allow it, do you?'

'Probably not,' said Kit.

He was sitting reading that night when his grandmother phoned.

'Your mother there?'

'Yes, she's with Father.'

'I'd like to speak to her. In a minute. How are you, young Kit?'

'Bored,' he said before he could stop himself.

'You shouldn't be bored. Not at your age. Only stupid people are bored.'

'I know,' said Kit. 'But London in August isn't much fun.'

'Perfectly true,' said Lady Beckenham. 'Well, come down to Ashingham for a few weeks. Plenty to do here, we need help with the harvest, and Billy would be pleased to see you. You can amuse Beckenham as well, he's fearfully bored. Ask your mother, I'm sure she won't mind.'

'She'd be glad to get me out of the house,' said Kit. 'I – I think I'd like that. Thank you. Er – Grandmama, could I bring someone with me?'

'What, a friend? Of course you can. But he'll have to work too, some of the time, no room for layabouts.'

'It's not a he, it's a she. Oh, it's all right, she's only six. I just thought how lovely it would be for Izzie to come. She doesn't have much fun.'

'Splendid idea. Yes, of course she must come, poor little thing. If you have any trouble with Sebastian let me know.'

He did have trouble with Sebastian, who categorically refused his permission, saying Izzie would be a nuisance and it would disrupt her routine; Kit told Lady Beckenham, who snorted down the phone.

'The man's become impossible, begrudges that poor child any kind of pleasure. I'll speak to him, Kit, don't worry.'

Kit couldn't imagine what she could possibly say to Sebastian that would change his mind; but she telephoned him later to say that Sebastian had agreed to let Izzie come to Ashingham.

'How on earth did you manage that?' he said wonderingly.

'Let's just say I know Sebastian rather better than most people do,' said Lady Beckenham.

'Are you really determined about this?' said Venetia.

'Absolutely. I don't want to have a baby growing up without a father. It's not fair. I've booked into a clinic in Switzerland next week.'

'But, Dell—'

287

'No, don't. I've made up my mind. It'll be a relief, really. Then I can get on with my life.'

'Does Luc know—'

'It doesn't matter, does it? If he'd been a bit different, the least bit pleased even, or concerned about me, I'd have – well, I'd feel differently. But I told you, he was just vile. So that's that.'

'And you haven't heard from him?'

'No, nothing. He's an absolute shit, Venetia, I should never have got involved with him. It's just a relief that it's over, actually. I'd forgotten how it felt to be one's own mistress—' She stopped suddenly, burst into noisy sobs. Venetia took her in her arms.

'Adele, darling. Oh, poor, poor you—'

'No, it's all right,' said Adele, 'it was just saying that word. That beastly word. That's all I am to him, you know, his mistress. I thought he loved me, but no. Just a bit of – amusement.'

'Well, I know all about that,' said Venetia soberly. Only of course Abigail Clarence hadn't been a bit of amusement; she had been important to Boy, terribly important.

'Of course you do,' said Adele. 'Oh, Venetia, we're both in a bit of a mess, aren't we?'

'Yes. Yes, we certainly are.'

'Are you still absolutely sure about a divorce—'

'Absolutely. I couldn't go on like that. Knowing she—'

'No. No, of course not.'

'But let's not talk about that now,' said Venetia, suddenly brisk. 'Are you sure this clinic is a good one?'

'Marvellous. Lots of chums have gone there. Much better than some seedy place in England.'

'Shall I come with you?'

'Oh – no. You're sweet, but – no, I'll be all right.'

Venetia had never been more sure of anything than that she wanted a divorce. It seemed to her the only release from at least some of her pain. She could not even consider staying with Boy; or rather allowing him to stay with her. Every time she thought about him with Abbie, in that pretty house, with the pictures and books he had bought her, playing the music they both enjoyed, discussing things like – well, she couldn't even begin to imagine everything they might discuss. That was what was so awful. Abbie could give Boy something, a great deal, that she, Venetia, was incapable of, and the humiliation of that was appalling.

She had been terrified that people might have known, but it seemed they did not; he was clearly a most skilful deceiver.

Her mother, deeply shocked and distressed, surprisingly supportive, had counselled patience over the divorce, but Venetia was adamant.

'I can't even look at him, Mummy, without feeling sick. Sick and so – so stupid. How could I have let it go on and on, under my nose—'

'Sometimes, Venetia, what's under your nose is hardest to see.'

'Obviously,' said Venetia fretfully, 'and then to think I was so exactly what Boy didn't want, he must have found me so boring, so – so pointless. I can't help it, not being clever—'

'Venetia,' said Celia firmly, 'I can't allow that. You are clever. You just—' She stopped; Venetia glared at her.

'Don't start that. Just don't. All right, so I didn't go to Oxford like darling Barty. I wouldn't have kept quiet about my best friend having an affair with someone else's husband, either. Someone in my family.'

Celia was silent. Barty's possible involvement was one of the things that most troubled her.

Boy had come to her, begged her to listen to him; he had been surprised when she had agreed.

'But don't ask me to intercede for you, Boy. It would do no good, and in any case it would be very dangerous.'

'I don't want that. But I want to try and explain to you. Try to make you understand. At least a little.'

She understood to a surprising extent.

He was almost as wretched as Venetia: confused, remorseful, and feeling desperately alone.

Abbie had come to mean a great deal to him; indeed he would go so far as to say that in a way he did love her. She had filled a large part of his life – and a considerable need in it – for several years. She interested, intrigued and inspired him; sex was the least important thing they shared. He also loved Venetia; it was impossible not to. She was so engaging, so good-natured, so amusing, and – and this was important to Boy – so beautiful.

She ran his home perfectly, she was a marvellous mother – if there was one thing in which they were in total accord, it was the children – and she was also extremely sexy. Every time Boy thought about her and her virtues, he groaned silently; how could a man married to such a paragon need a mistress?

But he knew the answer, of course: he was, within his marriage to this paragon, very lonely. He could not talk properly to Venetia, he could only share a very few pleasures with her, she did not understand what he wanted to do, she had never shown any interest in helping him to find what that might be. Everyone thought Boy was a playboy, self-indulgent, self-seeking, but that was not quite true. He had been born to great wealth and yet to great emotional deprivation; his parents had never shown the slightest interest in him, or in helping him to develop intellectually or, indeed, in any way at all.

He was extremely clever, and very artistic, he could have turned his talents to many things; but without guidance in his early years, his self-indulgent tendencies had overcome any more worthy ones, and his charm and his gift for friendship, his talent for attracting women, combined with his large personal fortune, had dispatched him straight into the role of playboy. And then at the age of twenty-three he had found himself trapped in a marriage he would probably not have chosen and was certainly not ready for.

Boy's enemies, or rather his detractors, he had very few enemies, would have mocked the notion of a desire to find himself and to do something useful or at least interesting with his life; Lady Celia Lytton, despite her early disapproval of him, was one of the few people to recognise that. She had been opposed to the marriage for many reasons, but one of the more potent was that she knew Venetia was in no way a satisfactory intellectual companion for him.

She was saddened by Venetia's distress at the affair, but she was hardly surprised by it; indeed she was forced to admit that Abbie Clarence was a very compatible partner for Boy. It had been she who had encouraged him to open his auction house, she who had introduced him to several young artists for the gallery, she who had told him quite forcibly that a man of his intelligence and talents should not be spending his days on the golf course or at the races. She had been, in fact, and in many ways, more of a wife and certainly more of a companion to him than Venetia had; and Celia found it hard not to feel at least some sympathy for him. She was not prepared to admit it to him; but she did, in the end, agree to ask Venetia to reconsider her demands for a divorce.

'I've given Abbie up, of course, completely, I shall never see her again. I know it's probably too late, but if you could only try to persuade Venetia that I do love her. In my own way. And I don't want to lose her or the children.'

Celia said she would do what she could, while thinking there was very little prospect of the marriage continuing, and then asked him if Barty had had any idea of the liaison. Boy said he was absolutely certain that she had not.

'I'm so glad,' she said later to Oliver. 'I would really have hated to think she was party to it in any way. It would be so absolutely out of character.'

Celia was right: Venetia was adamant. She wanted a divorce and as quickly as possible and she refused to consider any alternative.

'If it wasn't for the children, I would like never to see Boy again as long as I live. I certainly never want him in my house again. I can't bear even to think about what's been going on over the last four years. He's an absolute brute and I hate him. I just want the marriage to be over. Fast.'

Celia had thought this might drive Boy back to Abbie Clarence; but it did not. He remained true to his word. That relationship was over for him as well.

'I feel desperately sorry for Venetia,' Celia said to her mother as they lunched one day, 'but I have to admit to a certain sympathy for Boy as well.'

Lady Beckenham smiled at her: an odd, rather cool smile.

'My dear Celia,' she said, 'I wouldn't expect anything else. From you.'

The night before they were due to leave for Ashingham, Izzie couldn't sleep. It was too hot and she was too excited. Her case, carefully packed, was in the corner of her room; the clothes she was to wear for the journey lay on the chair. Kit had told her – tossing the almost unbearably exciting information at her casually – that she would be able to ride the twins' old pony while they were at Ashingham, and Nanny had taken her to Daniel Neals and bought her some jodhpurs and jodhpur boots and some white cotton aertex shirts. She had also bought her some shorts, on Lady Beckenham's instructions, and some wellington boots – 'She needs to be able to muck about in streams and things, and her father will probably make a fuss if she spoils her nice things.'

Two whole weeks with Kit: in the country. She could hardly bear it, it was such a wonderful prospect. Playing outside, all the time, allowed to make a noise, and she would meet Billy, Barty's brother. Barty had told her all about Billy, he had only one leg but he could ride even the wildest horses. And one of the weekends Jay had promised to come down and see them. She loved Jay, he was such fun, and he'd promised to give her riding lessons too.

'And I'll show you how to drive a tractor. Only don't tell my Mother.'

'Of course I won't.'

They were to be driven down by Daniels, 'but when we get there I'm going to do some driving,' said Kit casually to Izzie, 'just around the estate. Grandmama says it's high time I learned. She's going to give me a couple of lessons. Only don't tell Mother.'

'Of course I won't.'

Heaven itself could surely not be as wonderful as the two weeks that lay ahead of her.

That afternoon her father had come to visit her in the nursery while she ate her tea.

'I hope you'll behave yourself at Ashingham,' he said abruptly.

'I will, Father.'

'Do exactly what Lady Beckenham tells you. And Kit of course.'

'Yes, Father.'

'And don't go falling out of any trees.'

'No. I won't.'

This was the first time he had shown the slightest concern over anything she did; she felt encouraged.

'Thank you very much again for letting me go, Father,' she said, 'I'm so looking forward to it.'

'That's perfectly all right, Isabella,' he said, and walked out of the room.

She looked now at the clock: the small hand was only at two. It was a very long time till morning; how was she going to get through it? She had once tried reading when she couldn't sleep, but Nanny had been terribly cross and told her she would ruin her eyes and she'd tell her father if it happened again. It was too much of a risk, they might even now stop her going if they were cross with her.

But she was so so thirsty. She would just have to get a drink. The water in the nursery bathroom was a bit warm, but it was better than nothing. Cautiously, she crept out of bed and opened her door; the house was in darkness and very still. She went into the bathroom: there was no cup there, not even a tooth mug. She tried drinking out of the tap but it was very unsatisfactory. Surely no one would mind if she went downstairs and got a cup from the kitchen?

There was a full moon; she could see easily on the wide staircase. She walked down it very quietly; and then in the hall stopped. There it was: the awful, dreadful noise. Her father. Crying. Quite quietly, but on and on. She stood there not knowing what to do. She couldn't go in to him, he would be so angry. But – it was so dreadful. Such an awful, sad noise. And then – it got worse. He said something. Aloud. Maybe there was someone in there with him. Maybe he had a friend after all. No one ever came to the house usually, no grown-ups, anyway, except Lady Celia, of course; but maybe they came at night. When she was asleep.

She stood there, hardly breathing, terrified to move; and then he spoke again, through the crying.

'Oh, Pandora,' he said, 'whatever would you make of me now?'

Not a friend, then: he was talking to her mother. Her mother, who had died when she was born. And then he started the crying again.

This was terrible. Awful. Izzie felt her own eyes fill with tears; sorrow for her father was suddenly stronger than her fear. Quickly, before she could lose courage, she ran across the hall, tapped on the study door.

'Who's that?' The voice was angry, rough.

'It's me, Father.'

'Go back to bed at once. What on earth are you doing up?'

'I was thirsty.' Another surge of courage; she pushed open the door. He was sitting at his desk, his arms folded in front of him. She could see he had been crying a lot; his face was streaked and his eyes looked red and sore. There was a glass half full of something, some grown-up drink, on the desk in front of him and a bottle beside it, in front of the photograph of her mother. She knew it was her mother although her father had never told her, of course, had never ever mentioned her; but Kit had, and Barty had shown her pictures of the person, the beautiful person whom she had never known and who they had told her she so exactly looked like and would have liked to have known so much.

'I said go back to bed.'

'I – heard you crying.'

'Oh, you did?' He was scowling at her.

'Yes. And I was sorry for you.'

'Indeed? Well—'

'And I heard you talking to – to my mother.'

'To your mother? Did you now? Well, sadly not, Isabella, I would have been talking to her in person, if it wasn't—' He stopped.

'If it wasn't what?' she said.

293

'No,' he said with a sigh, 'no, I won't say it. You wouldn't understand. Go back to bed, Isabella, please.'

'But—'

'I said go back to bed.'

She knew she was defeated. But she stood her ground. 'I'm very sorry, Father. That you're so unhappy.'

'Well – thank you for that,' he said politely.

Encouraged, she decided to go on: to say something that might please him, make him feel better.

'I do love the books,' she said, 'your books.'

'Really?'

'Yes. Kit reads them to me. They're so exciting and so special. And I love all the creatures.'

He was silent.

'The special creatures, I mean. The swimming cows I like best, and the flying fish. I wish I could see them really.'

Still no answer. But he was looking at her less angrily now; she went on.

'I was thinking, what if they came to this land? Just for a day? And met ordinary cows? How special that would be.'

'What did you say?' he said, and although he was still scowling at her, he didn't sound quite so angry.

'I said,' she said, only half aware that this was the first proper conversation she had ever had with him, 'I said how good it would be if your creatures came to England, and to our time, for just a day. And our cows saw your cows swimming. What they would think. If our cows would try to swim—'

He said nothing; she decided to go on.

'And the flying fish. What swimming fish would think of them. And then the two sorts of time, ours and theirs, I thought what if they got mixed up—'

There was a long silence; she felt quite frightened. Had she made him so angry he'd never speak to her again? She should have left at once, when he first told her and—

'Please go to bed,' he said finally. 'I need peace and quiet to work, not a lot of silly nonsense from you.'

She sighed. 'Yes, Father,' she said and turned to the door; and then, because she felt she had become just a little closer to him, and because he had been so very upset, and although it seemed unlikely that might be the reason for it, she said, 'Father, if you really don't want me to go to the country, I will stay here.'

He looked at her in complete silence, not moving; she stood there, meeting his gaze very steadily. And seeing it all fading away, the wonderful holiday, the two weeks with Kit and the pony riding and the streams and the blackberry picking and helping on the farm, all gone from her. She looked at it, and at him, rather helplessly, not knowing what to do, wondering what he was going to say, if the words 'yes, I want you to stay here' were going to come, and how bad it would be for her, if she had to hear them.

But, 'Of course I want you to go,' he said, and even through the flood of her relief she felt a twinge of disappointment that what he really wanted was to be rid of her, that he didn't want her with him. 'What on earth would be the point of your staying here?'

'I don't know, Father. I just thought—'

'Well, you can stop thinking. Now run along to bed. It's very late.'

'Yes,' she said, 'I know. It's about two o'clock.'

'You can tell the time?'

'Only half of it,' she said, 'only the little hand.'

'What a lot I don't know about you,' he said quite quietly, and then sat staring at her, and she could see he wasn't seeing her, he was looking past her into some sad, difficult place.

'Goodnight, Father.'

'Goodnight, Isabella.'

She went back to bed and lay awake for a while, thinking about him, about how unhappy he was and how angry and worrying that she must be the cause of it; and if there was anything at all she could do to make him forgive her. And finally deciding that there was not.

Chapter 21

She kept crying: on and on. She just couldn't stop. It was unlike her. Unexpected. She didn't usually cry at all. Certainly not uncontrollably, like this. She supposed it must be—

'Adele, what is it?'

Damn. Her mother.

'It's – nothing,' she said, sitting up, blowing her nose hard. 'Nothing important. Go back to bed, Mummy, I'm sorry I woke you.'

'You didn't. I was seeing to your father. Now come along, we'd better discuss this. Are you going to tell me about it or not?'

Adele was silent, feeling the tears begin again, unstoppable.

'Very well,' said Celia. 'I'd better begin, I think. You're pregnant, aren't you?'

Adele stared at her. 'How did you know?'

'Oh, Adele, really.' Celia sat down on the bed, took one of Adele's hands. 'Do credit me with a little sense. I'm your mother. Not a very maternal one, perhaps, but still your mother. And I have been pregnant a few times myself.' She sighed. 'I don't know quite where I've gone wrong. Both of you so unhappy. Not just one, but two of you getting pregnant out of wedlock.'

'Mummy' – Adele managed to half smile at her – 'we do know about you, remember.'

Celia ignored her. 'Anyway, what is to be done? I presume it's Mr Lieberman's?'

'Of course. And what's to be done is this. I'm going to Switzerland tomorrow. Not Paris, that was a lie. Sorry, Mummy. Anyway, it's to – to get rid of it.'

'I see,' said Celia quietly. 'And what does he have to say about that?'

'He doesn't know.'

'He doesn't know? Does he know you're pregnant?'

'Yes, and he was vile about it. Furious, no concern for me or the baby, just – horrible.'

'I'm not surprised,' said Celia.

'Oh, Mummy! That's a bit harsh. Why do you say that? Just because he's foreign, I suppose. And – and Jewish.'

'Adele, that is most unfair. I have absolutely no prejudice against either foreigners or Jews. I don't know where this – this idea came from.'

'Things you've said, I imagine,' said Adele briefly.

'Then you misunderstood me. Seriously. The only quarrel I have with Luc Lieberman, and it is a serious one, is his treatment of you. He has taken advantage of you in the most appalling way; he's much older than you, I imagine he is your first lover' – she looked at Adele quizzically; she nodded – 'so he seduced you. And then did nothing for you. Nothing at all. Just allowed you to squander your youth and talent on him, in return for a bit of sex. Which no doubt was extremely pleasurable.'

'Mummy, really—'

'Oh, come along, Adele. This is an adult conversation we are having. And an important one. Nevertheless, I cannot tell you how wrong I consider it for you to get rid of this child without his knowledge.'

'But why? He doesn't want it.'

'He doesn't think he wants it. He was no doubt immensely shocked. It's always a shock for any man, they never expect it, it's extraordinary. Your father was always absolutely astonished when I told him I was pregnant.'

'Really?'

'Really. But – however badly Lieberman has behaved, he does deserve to know what you are going to do.'

'He won't care.'

'Adele, he almost certainly will. The paternal instinct is surprisingly strong. The urge to protect the female and care for the young.'

'I saw very little sign of it in Luc,' said Adele and she started to cry again. Celia leaned forward and pushed back her hair, wiped her tears away. Adele, absolutely unused to any kind of tenderness from her mother, smiled at her rather uncertainly.

'I told you,' said Celia. 'He was shocked. Whatever he felt when you told him, it will have changed. He will be feeling quite differently now.'

Adele was silent; then she said, 'But, Mummy, he can't marry me. He won't marry me. I know that. He's told me so many times. And I don't want to have to bring up a baby on my own. It's not fair on anyone, least of all the baby.'

'Of course it isn't. And if he really continues to display a lack of concern and interest, then I might well advise you to have this termination.'

'You would?'

'I said I might. I have no moral objections to it. It's certainly the sensible thing to do. But I would warn you, Adele, you will be dreadfully unhappy. For a long time. And you will carry the guilt for the rest of your life. It's a very harsh thing for a woman to do, you know, to have an abortion. It's not a simple operation, not like taking out an appendix. That's a child you've got there. Don't think you'll feel fine when it's all over, that you can put it behind you, forget about it. You can't.'

Adele looked at her curiously. 'Did you – I mean was there ever—'

'I never did,' said Celia, 'but I came close to it. For reasons which I am not prepared to discuss. But I did have several miscarriages. One of which, possibly two, I could have avoided, had I rested, done the right thing. But in the case of the first, I was being foolish, more concerned about my career, and the second – well, that was a deliberate decision. Which I didn't regret, but still suffered for dreadfully.'

'What was it?' said Adele. This was the most extraordinary conversation she had ever had with her mother.

'Oh – you don't want to know.'

'Yes, I do. I really do.'

'Well – it was during the war. LM was down at Ashingham, she had just had Jay and she – well, she hadn't heard from his father. Actually he had been killed. She had assumed he didn't want the baby, she was preparing to have him adopted. Then a letter arrived at her house in London from—'

'Her husband?'

'The father,' said Celia. Her eyes met Adele's in absolute complicity. 'This is very – private information, Adele, I would not want it shared with anyone.'

'Of course not.'

'Anyway, this letter came. Telling her how happy and proud he was. I knew it was important she got it quickly. There were literally days, possibly hours before she signed Jay away. She was down at Ashingham. I had to get it to her.'

'So – you took it to her?'

'Yes. There was no one else, our chauffeur had joined up, few people could drive, you must remember. I drove down myself – in

298

premature labour. I knew what I was doing, and I thought LM was more important. Well, she was.'

'Oh, Mummy. What a sad story.' Adele looked at her mother, her fierce, tough, uncompromising mother, and realised she would never see her in quite the same way again.

'Not entirely. I got there in time. LM was overjoyed. And I – well, I—'

'Lost the baby?'

'Yes. Next day. It was a girl. And it took me a very long time – perhaps for ever – to get over that. I'm telling you only so that you know exactly what a serious thing you are doing, Adele. It's not something you can decide lightly; or that you can decide on your own. You must tell Luc about it. And remember, it's his baby too; it isn't just yours.'

Izzie was sitting with Kit on the steps at the front of the house, waiting for Billy to finish a conversation with Lady Beckenham, when the car pulled into the drive. The large grey Bentley. Her father's car.

She looked at it in terror; what had he come for, what did he want, was he so angry with her he was going to take her home, after only – what – four days?

'Hallo, Sebastian,' said Kit, standing up, walking over to him, holding out his hand, 'good to see you.'

'Good to see you,' said Sebastian shortly, and then, 'I hope Isabella's been behaving herself?'

'Of course she has. We've had a really good time, haven't we, Izzie?'

'Yes,' she said very quietly. 'Yes, a very good time.'

'Good. Very hot in London, you're lucky to be here. Is anyone about?'

'If you mean Grandmama, yes, but she's busy at the stables. Grandpapa's cleaning the guns. I can get him if you like—'

'No, no. Well, not yet, anyway. It's Isabella I've come to see.'

'I hope you're not going to take her home,' said Kit. 'She's starting riding lessons with Billy today. And this afternoon we're going for a picnic.'

'Of course I'm not going to take her home,' said Sebastian shortly. 'I just wanted to – well, to see her. Talk to her about something.'

This was such an extraordinary statement that Izzie felt quite shocked. Never in all her six years had her father said he wanted to talk to her. She must have done something very bad. Maybe the school had complained about her, or Nanny had said she didn't want to look after her any longer—

'I'd like to talk to her alone,' said Sebastian.

'Of course. Shall I tell Billy? He was going to give her a riding lesson.'

'No, no. It won't take long. Come along, Isabella.'

She stood up reluctantly, her legs felt rather wobbly. He set off briskly along the side of the house; then looked back at her.

'Come along,' he said, 'I thought you were in a hurry.'

'Sorry, Father.'

He led her across the lawn towards the meadow; when they reached the fence he climbed over it, and then turned and waited, clearly impatient while she wriggled under it on her tummy.

'Woods or meadow?' he said.

'I don't mind.'

'Never say you don't mind,' he said, 'it indicates a lack of interest. Express a view even if you're not sure.'

'Woods,' she said quickly.

He walked for a few minutes, and because it was such a narrow path, she had to walk behind him. Even with his limp, he walked very quickly, she had trouble keeping up. She wondered when he would start talking; this really was the strangest experience of her life.

'Right,' he said, suddenly stopping, leaning against a tree, looking at her, 'there's something I have to say to you.'

'Yes, Father?'

'I – thought I ought to come. I – well, that is, to thank you.'

'Thank me!' She felt the ground beneath her feet literally heave; she put out her hand to steady herself against the tree.

'Yes. I wasn't very – grateful the last time we talked.'

'Weren't you, Father?'

'No. Remember when that was?'

'Yes, Father. It was in the night when you were – when I said about your books.'

'Exactly. I don't suppose you realised it, but it was quite helpful.'

'Helpful? How?'

'It gave me an idea. I – well, I hadn't really had one before. For my new book.'

'I gave you an idea?'

'Yes,' he said irritably. 'Do stop repeating everything I say, Isabella, it's not necessary.'

300

'Sorry, Father.'

'Anyway, it was about the cows, do you remember?'

'Of course I do. I said what if they came to our time for a day and met our cows . . .'

'Exactly. Well, I found that interesting.'

'Oh, I see.'

'There was something else you said as well, about the time. Remember that?'

'I think so.' She hesitated. 'You mean about Meridian time and our time getting mixed up?'

'That's right. Well, anyway, it was a great help to me. And I thought you should know that. That's all.'

'I'm very glad, Father.' She stood staring up at him; and for some reason, although she was pleased she had helped him, she felt dreadfully sad, because he still looked so cross, with that awful face which made it so plain he didn't like her at all. She might not have noticed before, but it was so lovely at Ashingham, with so many people being kind to her and talking to her, it reminded her of how miserable she felt at home a lot of the time. It was going to be so much worse when she got back. She felt tears start, felt them beginning to spill over. She brushed her hand across her eyes.

'Oh, for heaven's sake,' he said impatiently, 'don't start crying. I thought you'd be pleased.'

'Sorry, Father. Sorry. Of course I am. I—'

And then it was no good, she started crying harder, proper crying, coming up from her chest; and she stood there, staring at him, longing so much for him to care that she was crying, instead of being cross with her.

Finally she managed to get it under control; and as she bit her lip, choked back the last sobs, she realised he was looking at her with a very odd expression on his face. Not cross any more, not smiling either; just rather – no, very – sad. And for a long time they both stood there, each of them confronting one another and each other's unhappiness. And then, awkwardly, slowly, as if it was very difficult for him, he reached out a hand towards her.

'Come here,' he said quietly, but she couldn't, she went on standing there.

'I said come here.' Still not seeming cross.

She took a step towards him then, and then another, expecting any moment for him to lose patience, to move away, and still he held out his hand.

And finally, and it seemed a very long journey, she reached the point where she could reach him, and then she put her own hand out and placed it in his. It was very warm, his hand, warm and firm; she had never touched him before, she realised. He closed his hand round hers very gently and stood looking down, down at their two hands in silence as if he had never seen them before. And then he looked down at her, looked into her eyes as if he was hoping she would understand something.

'I'm – sorry,' he said, and his voice was funny, deeper than usual, and a bit as if he was being shaken up and down. 'I'm very sorry, Isabella.'

She stood there absolutely silent, not moving, knowing without at all knowing why that anything she did or said might be wrong, might be dangerous. Another long silence; and then he gave her the funny almost-smile again. 'You're all right, are you? Down here with Kit?'

'Yes, Father. Thank you. It's really – really fun.'

'Good. I'm afraid you haven't had much – fun.'

He was staring past her again now, at that funny place beyond her; but still holding her hand. 'I'm sorry,' he said again.

'That's all right, Father.'

'Well, we'd better get back,' he said, sounding suddenly more ordinary, 'Billy will be waiting for you. I don't want to make you late. Come along.'

He released her hand and turned to walk away; she started hurrying after him. Then he stopped again.

'I don't suppose you remember, but you said something else that night. About the time. Remember that?'

'Not – not really.'

'You said you could only tell half the time. I thought that sounded like the name of a rather interesting book. Half the time. What do you think?'

'I suppose so. Yes.' She didn't really, but—

'Well, if you don't like it, I shan't call it that,' he said, sounding suddenly cross again.

She panicked. 'Oh, but I do. Really.'

'Good. Come along, keep up.'

As they reached the fence, he climbed over it, then turned as she was going to go underneath it and reached over to her, picked her up, then set her down and took her hand again. He smiled at her rather uncertainly. She smiled back.

302

'Next term, if you like,' he said suddenly as they reached the house, 'I'll come and give a talk at your school.'

'Father, you don't have to. If you don't want to, if it makes you upset.'

'Oh, but I do have to,' he said, and sighed, very heavily. 'I think I owe you that at the very least.'

Poor, poor Adele. It was today, today she was having the beastly thing done. It was so harsh, so cruel she had to go through it and on her own. Of course it was the right thing to do, especially as Luc had been so vile about it, but – she was so tender-hearted, it was bound to upset her. It had upset her already, dreadfully.

Venetia sighed. They were both so upset, both so unhappy. It was odd that it should have coincided, their unhappiness. She felt quite dreadful still, desperate at times. And so lonely. She had sent the children off to Frinton with Nanny and a nursemaid, thinking that some peace and quiet would soothe and help her and it didn't seem to be doing anything of the sort. The house seemed vast and echoing with her misery; she didn't know what to do with herself, just wandered about London, shopping, returning to the house feeling more lonely than ever. Every time she passed a mirror and saw herself, her white, exhausted face, her dull hair, her dark-ringed eyes, she wondered who on earth would ever want her now, what possible future she could have.

Well, tomorrow or the next day at the latest, Adele would be here, and she could look after her, nurse her. They could nurse each other: back to happiness.

And then Adele at least could begin again.

Only – she did love Luc so very much. Really, really loved him. It wasn't a schoolgirl crush, or just sex, or something amusing to do with her time, taking a married lover; it was love. Venetia did know that. Proper, intense, and very unselfish love. And getting rid of his baby would hurt her dreadfully. Horribly. Maybe it *wasn't* the right thing to do, maybe she should have tried to dissuade her.

The phone started to ring: on and on. Who could that be. Everyone was away. Her mother probably, asking her to supper. She kept doing that, and Venetia kept refusing. She couldn't face her mother at the moment: even though she had been so supportive and good to her. She knew that whatever Celia said, she felt that she had brought at least some of her troubles on herself. Well, maybe she was right, maybe she had. But it was a very hard thing to accept, just at the moment.

'Telephone, Mrs Warwick. Miss Lytton, phoning from Paris.'

Paris! What was she doing there? She was supposed to be in Switzerland—

'Venetia? It's me. Look, I won't be coming back to London, not for a bit, anyway. Luc is being absolutely wonderful and I – we – are going to keep the baby.'

'Come along, *mignonne*. A little more fish. We have to make you strong, able to perform this important task that you have been given.'

'What important task?' said Adele, laughing, shaking her head at the forkful he was proffering. 'No, thank you, Luc, really, the more I eat, the more I'm sick.'

'The task of bearing my son.'

'It might be your daughter. And it's not just yours.'

'Of course it will be a son. I feel it. And my grandmother says that even if you are sick, it is better to eat. I am going to order a little crème caramel, plenty of milk and eggs.'

'Your grandmother! Luc, you haven't told her?'

'But of course. I tell her everything.'

'Whatever did she say?'

'She was delighted.'

'She can't be delighted. You've committed a mortal sin, or whatever the Jewish equivalent is.'

'For my grandmother, I can commit no sin. Besides, she never liked my wife, she thinks this is far better for me. You must meet her, she will love you.'

'Luc, this is going a bit too fast for me,' said Adele. 'A week ago, there was no question of your leaving your wife, now you tell me I must meet your grandmother and that she will love me.'

'A lot has changed in this week,' said Luc soberly. His dark eyes were sombre, meeting hers. 'A week ago, I was a selfish, self-obsessed pig. Today I am to be a father, I have great responsibilities, I will think of myself no longer, only my son.'

'And me.'

'And you, of course. You, whom I love so very much.'

He smiled, raised her hand to his lips and kissed it; she smiled back. That Luc would cease to think of himself seemed hugely unlikely but she had no intention of saying so.

It was very strange, what this child had done to him: to him and their relationship.

She had done what her mother said, telephoned him, said she must see him; oddly subdued, he had said he would like that, had offered to come to London, if she felt too unwell to travel.

But 'No, Luc, I would rather come to Paris. Thank you.'

He had met her off the boat train, looking pale and drawn; had taken her to a small restaurant and sat her down and held her hand and without looking up at her had begged for her forgiveness for his behaviour.

'It was – *atroce*. Appalling. I cannot believe it even of myself. I am so ashamed, my darling, so dreadfully ashamed. I have no excuse – except perhaps the shock of it. I did not expect it.'

'I can't think why not,' said Adele irritably, hearing her mother's words, 'we've been doing all the necessary things to make a baby for months and months. Years, actually.'

'My darling, I know. But – well, just try to believe me. And then I thought you had decided not to discuss it with me, not to decide with me what was best—'

'No, no, Luc. It was only because you were so horrid—'

'And you said some very hard things to me. No doubt deserved, but still – upsetting. Very upsetting.'

'Of course. I'm sorry,' said Adele remorsefully, 'but I thought you didn't care about me, that you didn't want to know about the baby, of course I said some hard things—'

'Of course. Well, we have been at cross purposes. But not any more. Everything will be different from today. I love you and I am so proud of you. Now I have booked us into our hotel, in the rue de Seine, and tomorrow, well, tomorrow is the important day.'

'What sort of important?'

'You will see. Come along, *chérie*, I want to remove that extremely pretty dress and see if I am able to detect already any signs of our son's existence.'

Next day, he had disappeared early, leaving her alone (and grateful for it, for she still felt very unwell), but with instructions to meet him for lunch at the Closerie des Lilas, on the Boulevard Montparnasse; one of the prettiest restaurants in Paris with its trailing vines and enchanting *terrasse*, and one of their favourites, filled as it was with Parisian café society, writers, artists, journalists, all of whom seemed to know and love Luc. And after lunch, after the rejected fish and the uneaten crème caramel, he turned to her and said, very seriously,

'Well, if you will not eat, we may as well leave. But before we do, I have a present for you.'

'A present!'

'A present.'

She prepared herself to be pleased. Luc wasn't very good at presents. All the usual things that mistresses were supposed to enjoy, jewellery, lingerie, scent, never came her way. Not that she cared; she was too particular to appreciate someone else's taste: even Luc's. He brought her rare books sometimes, flowers quite often, but not anything she could set down on her bedside table and gaze at before she went to sleep.

'Here.' He handed her a small box.

There were none of the usual trimmings, no ribbons or even pretty paper, just a small brown cardboard box. Amused, she began to open it. Jewellery? Perfume? She opened it; inside was a mass of tissue paper, and well buried in it—

'A key? Luc, what—?'

He stood up, held out his hand. 'Come. I will show you.'

He hailed a taxi: gave an address she didn't recognise.

The taxi drove off: leaving the Boulevard Montparnasse, down the Boulevard Saint Michel, past the Luxembourg Gardens, down a maze of streets, before finally pulling up in a small street off the Place St-Sulpice.

'*Voilà*,' he said.

She got out, wondering: in front of her was a large door.

'Now,' he said, 'try your key.'

She put it in the lock: it turned slowly but easily. She pushed through the door. It was a *porte cochère* leading into a courtyard, quite a big one, cobbled and white-walled, filled with sunshine, and set with geraniums in tubs; across it was another door, slightly ajar.

'Push it,' said Luc and she did, and then on her left was a staircase. 'Now,' he said, 'we climb.'

'Luc,' she said, 'Luc, what—'

'Climb. *Ascendez!*'

She climbed. Three flights of narrow stairs and then at the top, immediately in front of her, another small door. Adele was silent; she hardly dared even breathe.

'Now,' he said, 'now is the moment. I will do the English thing. Come along.'

And he bent down and picked her up, and pushed the door with his foot very gently and it swung open and they were standing in a hallway so tiny it was the size of the cloak cupboard at Cheyne Walk.

Another door then: opening on to a room, a square room, with a low bed in it, and no other furniture at all. The shutters were closed and the room was in darkness, but she was afraid to turn on the light, for fear of spoiling the magic.

'Luc—'

He set her down, turned her to him, kissed her tenderly.

'This is our new home, *ma chère, chère* Mam'selle Adele. I hope you will like it and settle in it and be happy in it, my dearest one, together with our son. It comes with all my love.'

She woke early next day, when the Paris dawn was just breaking; he was awake himself, beside her in the big square bed, watching her, smiling at her.

'*Bonjour.*'

'*Bonjour*, Luc.'

'Did you sleep well?'

'Very well. Thank you.'

'I hope what took place last night did not disturb our son in any way.'

'I – really don't think it did,' she said, smiling at the memory of his great gentleness, his constant anxious questioning and concern for her.

'Good. Would you like some coffee?'

'I would, please,' said Adele, astonished to find that she did not feel even remotely sick.

He got up, walked out of the room and reappeared with two large bowls of steaming coffee; she sat up, drank hers gratefully.

'You are cold?'

'Not at all.'

'I fear in the winter you will be. Central heating was beyond my means.'

'I'm told that pregnancy raises the body temperature,' said Adele cheerfully.

'But I am not pregnant, I may be cold.'

'Luc,' said Adele sternly, 'you told me you weren't going to think of yourself any longer.'

'Well, I should have made an exception of how I would feel in the cold, perhaps. I detest it, it makes me miserable.'

'No exceptions. Sorry.'

'Very well.'

'And, Luc, is this really, really our home now?'

'It is really, really our home. It is not very large, I am afraid – but we will manage.'

'But of course. I adore it so.'

It wasn't very large; it was true. One large studio room, which would have to serve as dining room and living room, one large bedroom, and one tiny one *'pour le bébé'*, a minuscule kitchen and an even smaller bathroom, with a vast clawed-foot bath and an evil-looking water heater which emitted rasping, roaring noises and sent some yellowing water spluttering into the bath. But there was a balcony leading from the living room, with a wonderful view of the grey roof tops, the endless tiny balconies of Paris – 'and if you listen carefully, when it is quiet, you can hear the fountains of St-Sulpice' – and below them, the cobbled courtyard and three cats, sunning themselves in the heat.

'It's so beautiful. So absolutely beautiful. I love it.'

'I love it too. And I love it more because you love it.'

'And I love you, Luc.'

'I am *entiché*, my beloved Mam'selle Adele,' he said, taking her hand and kissing it, adding by way of explanation that *entiché* meant 'smitten'. 'I looked it up for you yesterday. Is it not a wonderful word?'

They ate their breakfast croissants, dipped into the bowls of coffee, sitting on the balcony; the sun was already warm. Adele stretched happily, then relaxed, smiled at him.

'I'm so happy, Luc. And I feel wonderful today, not sick at all.'

'Good. Now in a little while I have to go to work. I am a family man now, I have responsibilities.'

'Luc—'

'Yes, *chérie*?'

'Your wife? You've actually left her?'

'I have actually left her. Two days ago, as soon as I received your phone call.'

'She must be quite – upset,' said Adele carefully.

'Oh, not so much. She fell out of love with me long ago, as I have told you. She finds me a little – unsatisfactory. Dull, not successful enough. But still has our rather large and extremely warm apartment, she has most of my money, she has her mother, and she has a very handsome and satisfactory lover of her own.'

'Oh,' said Adele, 'oh, yes, I see.'

'It is the French way. I have told you before.'

'Luc,' said Adele, 'if we are to live together happily, there is one thing I never want to hear about again.'

'And what is that?'

'The French way. Please.'

'But it is such a good way,' he said, smiling at her. 'Look at us, the most happy result of it.'

There was such a profound lack of logic to this that Adele couldn't even begin to unravel it.

Chapter 22

For three weeks now she had refused to see him; had felt sickened by him, by his secrecy, his dishonesty, by the thought of how wrong about him she had been. He tried, at first, to humour her out of it, had used all his usual tactics, an avalanche of gifts, of flowers, all of which she had returned, of interminable phone calls which she refused to take, had sat outside her office and her house; finally she had told him that if he wouldn't leave her alone she would inform the police that she was being pestered. Then the letters began to arrive: cold, harsh letters, saying that clearly she had never felt anything for him, had failed absolutely to understand the depths of his feelings for her, had used him, taken what she wanted from him and now dared to think she could simply move on. And then finally, the emotional blackmail started, a low, shaken voice on the telephone, long, long letters berating himself, imploring her to think how desperate, how wretched he must feel, begging her forgiveness and for a chance to explain.

And finally, of course, she had given in; could stand out no longer against this assault, wretched and furious as she was with herself.

'Very well, Laurence,' she said, late one Friday afternoon when the prospect of yet another long, lonely, remorse-filled weekend proved finally too much for her, 'I'll meet you this evening. But not for dinner, not even for a drink. Just – meet you.'

'Where?'

'It doesn't matter. Central Park—'

'No, it's too hot and crowded there. What about the Russian Tea Room?'

She liked the Tea Room, liked its dark, exotic air, the all-year-round Christmas decorations on the lights, the many clocks all telling a different time.

'Oh – all right. But only for – for as long as it takes to explain.'

'Fine.'

She was dreadfully afraid that she was doing the wrong thing; but she lacked the strength any longer to do the right one.

Laurence was there already when she arrived, sitting at a table at the back of the restaurant; he looked dreadful, in spite of everything she felt a stab of remorse. He had lost weight, his face looked gaunt, his brilliant eyes dark now with exhaustion and everything about him, even his red-gold hair, was somehow colourless.

He stood up, reached out his hand. 'Thank you for coming. Please—' He gestured at the seat beside him.

'Thank you.' She sat down.

'I've ordered tea. Nothing – dangerous.'

'Good,' she said briskly.

'I've missed you so much.'

'Really?'

'Yes.'

'Well,' she said, 'there would have been no need for it. Had you been honest with me.'

'I wasn't – dishonest,' he said.

'Of course you were. Untruthful, anyway.'

'Not fully truthful. That's different.'

'Laurence, please don't try and tie me up in knots. I don't have the stomach for it.'

'I'm not trying to tie you up in knots,' he said, 'merely stating the facts as I see them.'

'Which is not how I see them. Or indeed anyone else.'

'Oh, for God's sake,' he said, and the touch of arrogance was somehow welcome, a return to normality, 'am I to be allowed to put my case? Or are you simply to be judge and jury and commit me without hearing any evidence at all?'

She looked at him; looked at him solemnly and for quite a long time in silence. Then she said: 'Very well, Laurence. Put your case. Succinctly, please.'

He looked at her and half smiled. 'Did you ever think of being an attorney,' he said, 'rather than a publisher?'

Of course, she should have known. That confronted by his apparently flawless, unarguable logic, interspersed with a little self-justification, and an emotional plea for clemency, she would have begun at least to see it from his viewpoint.

Which was what he had wanted to tell her from the beginning. How he had been afraid only of making her anxious, in those early days, at the realisation that he held enormous power, not just over her own professional life but the company for which she worked. How it would have seemed embarrassing, a form of showing off, to say look what I've got, half the company you work for – 'Yes, and I know how modest you are,' said Barty briskly – how he had resolved each time he saw her, in those early days, to tell her, and how each time it had seemed more impossible; how after a while, he had ceased even to think of it; how falling in love with her as he had, caring for her so desperately, it had seemed less and less relevant.

He reminded her of his record with Lyttons New York: that there was in fact none. That he had never been to the offices – apart from the annual board meeting – had never taken any interest in the company, hardly knew what books they published, or what (more importantly, he told her with a half-smile) profits it made.

That none of the editorial staff except the most senior knew of his connection with it – 'Why should they?' – that it was hardly his fault if Stuart Bailey had not told her. 'But again, why should he, how could he have known there was to be anything between us?'

He had, after all, only been left the company by his mother, he could hardly be blamed for that; he had never felt any interest in it whatsoever, had often thought of selling it but somehow never had.

And then that actually, in the early days of their relationship, had he been of a Machiavellian persuasion, he could have caused all kinds of difficulties and problems—

'How?' asked Barty feeling, reluctantly, a half-smile forming.

'I could have insisted you were dismissed. So that I could see as much of you as I liked. I could have demanded you were instated as editorial director. I could have had your superiors fired, your inferiors promoted. I could have had the offices moved into Elliott House; I could have interfered in the advertising, the publishing schedules, I could have bought up Doubledays and Brentanos, I could—'

'Yes, all right,' said Barty. 'I do get the idea.'

'And I did nothing. Just sat tight and hoped – absurdly – that you'd never find out. And then you did. And you thought badly of me for it. It seems a little harsh.'

'Well—'

'In fact very harsh. What harm has it done you?'

'A lot,' said Barty simply. 'It's made me realise you aren't who I thought you were.'

'Oh, Barty, really! In what way?'

'It's hard to explain. But – it is a very big thing. Finding out you owned half the company I work for. When I imagined – of course – you had nothing to do with it. When I thought my work was something completely independent of you. You know how important that is to me.'

'Yes. Although I don't know quite why.'

'Laurence,' she leaned forward earnestly, 'if you'd grown up like I have, needing to be grateful, feeling beholden, feeling less good than everyone else, you would know why. What I do, I do by myself.'

'Really?' he said, his eyebrows raised, his eyes on hers very sharp. 'Is that so, Barty? You have done it all by yourself? You'd have got that job at Lyttons anyway, would you? Without your family connections?'

She scowled. It was a sore point.

'Probably not. But having got it, I've made the most of it. And even more so here. That's why I'm so insistent on working hard, not missing days, never being late, not going out to lunch. Because I'm earning my place. This book I'm publishing—'

'Ah yes. The detective story.'

'Yes. I've discovered it myself, I'm persuading the bookshops to take it, I've had a big say in the jacket, Lyttons London are looking at it now – that's mine, Laurence, all mine. It matters so much to me, I can't tell you.'

He was silent. Then he said, 'Barty, you matter so much to me. I can't tell you either how much. I can't bear being without you. I'm desperately sorry I've deceived you as I have. It has all been a dreadful misunderstanding, I did it for the best possible reasons and I swear it will never happen again. Ever. Please believe me.'

She looked at him; wishing she could believe him, wanting to believe him. She had missed him – missed him a great deal. Life in New York had not been the same without him. He had been such a huge part of her life, ever since she had met him; hardly a day had passed without seeing him. And what he had done was only, perhaps, a further example of his damaged self: if he truly couldn't see how wrong it had been, then was she right to blame him? Probably not. Just the same, it had not been honourable of him; knowing how much she cared about her work, knowing that she was actually, if not by nature, then certainly by nurture, a Lytton, surely, surely he must have seen that he should have told her. And – suppose he did decide to start taking an interest in the company: what then? She could leave, she supposed, leave Lyttons, go and work for another company, for Scribners or Doubledays. She wasn't bound to Lyttons by chains after all.

She sighed.

313

'What was that about?'

'Oh – just a wish. That it hadn't happened. That I hadn't found out. That there hadn't been anything to find out. It's so sad.'

'Why sad?'

'Well, because it's spoilt things. For ever.'

'But Barty, why? What has it spoilt?'

'Oh, Laurence,' she cried in an agony of exasperation, 'it's spoilt so much. How I see you. How I feel about you.'

'I – still love you,' he said, very quietly. 'It hasn't changed anything for me.'

'That's not the point. It's changed a lot for me.'

'So – the love for me – which you swore you did feel – has changed, has it? At the first major hurdle? That's sad, Barty, that's very, very sad. It makes me think it can't have been very strong in the first place.'

'Don't,' she said fretfully, 'just don't.'

'Don't what?'

'Start confusing me, tying me up in knots. I can't bear it.'

'Look,' he said, 'what can I do to convince you, Barty? How can I make you believe that I meant no harm, that Lyttons is nothing to me?'

'You could – sell it,' she said. 'Just get rid of it.'

He sat there, staring at her, very seriously; then he began very slowly to smile. It was his triumphant smile, the one that heralded an idea: a big idea. Barty had seen it a few times, and it had amused her, the transparency of his delight in himself, the arrogance of his own absolute certainty that he was right.

'No,' he said, 'no, I'm not going to sell it. That would be rather a shame, I think. Not to keep it in the family. But I've got another suggestion, Barty, which might appeal to you.'

'What?' she said wearily. 'What's your suggestion, Laurence?'

'I want you to marry me,' he said.

Barty stared at him; she felt first very hot, then ice-cold. She felt her heart begin to race and her head to swim; she swallowed hard, gripping the table, desperately trying to keep reality within her grasp.

'Marry you?' she said finally, and her voice was so weak, she could hardly hear it herself.

'Yes. That's what I want. I want it more than I've ever wanted anything. I want you to marry me and—'

She took a deep breath. She had to say it, before she was swept away on this great rush of emotion and longing and fear and desire, had to get that at least set out, cleared out of the way.

'And give up work, I suppose?' she said, her voice stronger now.

'Give up work and be Mrs Laurence Elliott, taking care of you and your houses, commissioning interior designers, spending my days shopping and at the Elizabeth Arden salon, that's what you'd want, isn't it, Laurence?'

'Give up work?' he said, and his expression was astonished. 'Of course not. I know you better than that, Barty, I would hope. Nothing could be more guaranteed to see you off than that. No, of course I would expect you to go on working. I'd want you to. I'm proud of you, of how clever you are. And then, you see, and this is my idea, I could give you Lyttons New York, that is, my share of it, of course, as a wedding present. Now, isn't that a wonderful idea?'

Chapter 23

Kit looked at his mother and wondered why she was crying; it was hugely unusual, she hardly ever did cry. And – at *this* moment, on receiving this *news*, he'd have expected something a bit more – cheerful. He looked at his father; now he was certainly looking cheerful, setting down his coffee cup with the painstaking care with which he did everything these days, since his stroke, holding out his good hand for Kit to take.

'Well done, Kit,' he said, 'very, very well done. Not many people manage that, scholarships to both. But you've earned it, you worked very hard.'

Celia blew her nose and came over to hug him.

'Congratulations, dear, dear Kit,' she said, 'we're so proud of you. It's a huge achievement. Which will you choose, do you suppose?'

'I – haven't really been able to think yet. Too excited. But I imagine Oxford. Don't you? Family traditions and all that, you were there, Father, after all, and Barty of course, and Sebastian as well—'

'Of course. Yes, I think it would probably be best. Oh dear, I'm going to cry again—'

She reached into her pocket for her handkerchief, wiped her eyes, then looked at Kit and smiled rather unsteadily.

'We must tell Sebastian,' she said.

'What, both? Well done, old chap. Very well done. Can I take you out to lunch?'

'You certainly can. Mother's planning some celebration dinner tonight but today I'm at a loose end. Both the parents have gone to Lyttons of course.'

'Of course. Well, I'm at your service. Where would you like to go?'

'Oh – you choose. Could Izzie come too?'

'She'll be at school.'

'Oh, of course. Pity. Could I speak to her, is she there?'

'Yes, she is. We're just finishing breakfast. Don't keep her long though, or she'll be late.'

It was evidence of the great change in their lives, thought Kit, that Izzie and Sebastian now breakfasted together as a matter of course. No one had the faintest idea what had wrought the miracle, nor would they dream of asking; they were all simply thankful for it: that Sebastian seemed finally, and almost ungrudgingly, to have accepted his daughter and, moreover, to be prepared to enjoy her and her presence in his life.

He was still extremely strict with Izzie, still treated her rather distantly, but it was no longer in the least remarkable to see them walking together hand in hand, or seated across a table from one another, talking intently and seriously and even on rare occasions exchanging rather brief, but undoubtedly affectionate, kisses.

Izzie remained much the same, quiet and well-behaved, but with a new and very sweet confidence about her; the great change was in Sebastian. He was gentler, he had more patience, was less given to irritable outbursts and to making contentious statements, and as Venetia remarked, there was at least some point in issuing invitations to him; he did not often accept, but it was no longer a foregone conclusion that he would not.

Most importantly, his old restlessness and energy had returned; he and Izzie had taken to walking on Sundays, first on rather modest forays in the great parks of London, then further afield into the Surrey countryside, and there was even talk this year of a week on the Pennine Way.

'He might not in the end,' said Izzie to Kit, her small face earnestly concerned, 'you know how he can never quite make up his mind about what he wants to do. But I think he will, and it will be such fun.'

Strange fun for a little girl, Kit had thought, a long hard walk with a testy old man; but if it was going to make them both happy, then it was not for him to say so.

'That's splendid,' he said, 'absolutely splendid. I wish that I could come,' he added hastily, seeing her look of anguish, of torn loyalty, 'but anyway, I know how important these walks are to the two of you, I wouldn't dream of getting in the way.'

Sebastian raised his glass to him now; he had been waiting for him at the Savoy Grill, a bottle of vintage Perrier Jouet on ice at his side.

'Well done again, Kit. Very well done. It's an incredible achievement. I hope you're going for Oxford.'

317

'I think so,' said Kit, 'although I did like the people at Jesus very much. But Christ Church is so gorgeous, and Father was there and you of course—'

'And you're reading law? Or haven't you decided about that either?'

'Yes, I think so. I want to go to the bar. I still have a slight hankering after the Church, but I don't think I'm quite – humble enough.'

He smiled at Sebastian, a brilliant self-mocking smile.

'I don't think bishops and so on are very humble,' said Sebastian.

'No, but you have to start at the bottom, and they don't come much humbler than curates. I'd never have eaten that egg, you know, I'd have sent it straight back.'

'No, you wouldn't,' said Sebastian briskly, 'your manners are much too good. But I think you'll enjoy the bar more. And it'll make your parents happy, particularly your mother. Not that anyone should choose a career to please their parents.'

'No, but if it's going to anyway, it's a bonus. Poor old Father, I really don't think he can go on at Lyttons much longer. He struggles in every day, but it's such an effort for him. And he so hates having to be pushed about in that wheelchair, either by his secretary or my mother, he finds it humiliating.'

'Just the same, I'm sure it's better for him than sitting at home brooding. How's Jay getting on, by the way?'

'Really brilliantly,' said Kit, 'he just can't seem to do anything wrong. Any book he's involved with just flies out of the bookshops, all his ideas seem to work and you know it was him who pushed through that notion of Venetia's about the Lyttons Children's Book Club? Against Father's wishes of course, it being what he calls a gimmick.'

'I had – heard,' said Sebastian, who had heard the story at great length, not only from Jay himself, but from Venetia and Celia. 'It's doing really well, I believe?'

'So they all say. It's terribly hard on poor old Giles,' he added, draining his glass, nodding to the waiter to refill it, 'nothing ever goes right for him. And now this book of Barty's, the one that's had such a great success in America, that's being published here and Mother is working on it apparently, assisted by Jay. Which has upset Giles as well.'

'I'm sure it has. It's a marvellous book that, have you read it?'

'No.'

'You must. Now then, come along, what are you going to eat? The guinea fowl is delicious, so is the venison—'

Venetia parked her car outside Lytton House and ran inside. She was late; damn. For a meeting, an important meeting; her mother would be furious.

She was often late. It was all very well being a working woman, but it didn't exactly go with motherhood. Of course she had Nanny and the rest of the nursery staff, but that didn't stop them asking her a dozen times a day what one or other of the children should be doing, consulting her about their health or their manners or their social lives or their extra lessons. She supposed she ought to leave more of the decisions to Nanny, but she didn't want to, she liked to be involved still, and she also liked to be sure that the girls were at the best ballet school, the boys doing their piano practice properly. Roo particularly was very good at fixing Nanny with his large brown eyes and telling her he'd done his when he'd done nothing of the sort. A brilliant liar, was Roo; rather like his father.

Venetia switched her mind away from Boy and his talent for lying and concentrated on the meeting and its content. It was important, involving the publicity and sales people, and the studio, who were designing the latest manifestation of the book club, a newsletter.

'Which we can send to schools, I thought, as well as the bookshops and of course the existing members. There could be a token in it, that would entitle them to sixpence or whatever off the next book they ordered if they were joining—'

'Not sixpence, Venetia,' said Jay, 'far too expensive.'

'Well, all right, threepence then. Also, I wondered if we might do a paperback version of the last *Meridian*, which could be offered at a low price with the new one.'

'Absolutely not.' Oliver looked rather as if she had suggested they sold Lyttons books off a barrow in Cheapside. 'We will do a paperback of any of the *Meridian* books over my dead body.'

'But—'

'I said no, Venetia. There are some literary standards which have to be maintained: even in the abyss in which the book trade has found itself.'

'But, sir,' – Jay always called Oliver 'sir' in the office – 'you said yourself that the Penguins were proving a successful sampling device.'

'I am aware of that, Jay. I admit I was wrong in the first instance to refuse to go in with Mr Lane's scheme. And I agree we have had some success with them – the Buchanans particularly. But the Meridian books are of the very highest quality, I could not even countenance cheapening them in such a way. And they hardly need the help of –

what was it you said, a sampling device? Dear me. God preserve me from modern terminology.'

'Well, it was worth a try,' said Venetia to Jay when the meeting was over. 'Maybe we can find some other children's book to offer. Otherwise, I think it's all going swimmingly, don't you? I liked the designs and I thought the idea of a badge was awfully good. My children love things like that. Goodness, look at the time, I must fly. Thanks, Jay. Give me a kiss. See you—'

'Venetia, can I have a word please?'

'Mummy, I can't stay. I've got to get to Elspeth's school by two, she's in a play and I said I'd be there—'

'I'm sorry to hear that. You are supposed to work here, you know, it really might be an idea for you to remember that. It's not some kind of hobby you've found for yourself—'

'I'm sorry,' Venetia flushed, 'and I do know. But I did promise her and she's going to be the chief flower in the garden and—'

'Oh, go if you must. This time. But you really must get your priorities straight, Venetia. It isn't fair to your colleagues. How do you think they feel to have you constantly rushing off, when they have to spend the full nine-to-five or rather nine-to-seven-or-eight here in many cases?'

'Sorry. Yes, I know. But it is important, don't you think? To be there for the children?'

'It's a choice you have to make when you decide to work,' said Celia, 'I was always at the office, Nanny dealt with all your arrangements.'

'Yes and—' Venetia stopped. It would not help her cause to tell her mother how often they had all been distressed by her absences from concerts and plays, how inadequate had been Nanny's help with their homework: or even that she and Adele might have succeeded further with their education with a little more parental input. Her mother had been wonderfully supportive over the past two years; the least she could do was earn the faith she had shown in her.

It had been Celia's suggestion that she should come to work at Lyttons. She had been crying – again, saying how useless she was, how pathetic, wondering aloud if she would ever find anyone again.

'Probably not. I shall have to spend the rest of my life living alone, looking pathetic, everyone sorry for me. What do I have to fall back on now? More frocks, more lunches, I suppose, with a lot of other stupid women, half of them who fancy Boy anyway, whispering behind my back – poor Venetia, couldn't keep her husband, can't find another.'

Celia had looked at her and her voice had been quite sharp as she said, 'Venetia, please. Has it never occurred to you that there might be more to life than being someone's wife? Finding "another", as you put it?'

Venetia sniffed, blew her nose. 'Don't start that, Mummy. About how I ought to work, do something on my own account. I'm not up to it, and I don't want to and that's all there is to it. One of the reasons Boy left me was because I was stupid, I don't see why you can't understand that, instead of going on and on—'

'Venetia, Boy did not leave you because you were stupid. Far from it. He left you – or rather had his liaison – because he felt frustrated by you. He knows as well as I do that you are extremely clever. But for some reason, you have always refused to demonstrate the fact.'

'That's so unfair. I've always had children to look after. A house to run. I didn't have time to do anything else. And anyway, I didn't want to. And I don't now. Leave me alone, Mummy, I'm not like you and the sooner you recognise the fact the better it will be for both of us.'

'I think you're very like me in some ways,' said Celia, 'but I won't argue with you about it now.'

'Please don't.'

She said nothing more for a few weeks; then she arrived at the Warwick house one day to find Venetia raging, as she had never heard her, at Henry and Roo. Henry was staring at her in silent insolence, but Roo was clearly shocked, white-faced, tears rolling down his face.

'I want Daddy,' he said.

'Well, you can't have Daddy. He's not here. Just get that into your head, Roo. Daddy's gone.'

'Yes, he has,' said Henry, looking at her scornfully, 'and it's unfair to take it out on us. Come on, Roo, let's go and find the girls.'

'Oh, God,' said Venetia, bursting into tears herself as Henry slammed the door, 'he's right, that's exactly what I am doing. Taking it out on them. It's not fair. But I feel so lonely, Mummy, so lonely and miserable and useless. I don't know what to do.'

Celia looked at her. 'I wish you'd let me help you.'

'You can't help me. No one can.'

'I can give you a job.'

'A job? Oh, Mummy, don't start that.'

'Why not? It would distract you, get you out, stop you feeling so sorry for yourself—'

321

'Look,' said Venetia, 'it wouldn't work. I can't come and work at Lyttons just because my husband's left me, people would laugh at me. And I'd be useless—'

'No, you wouldn't. That's the whole point. You'd be very useful. Venetia, do you really think I'd want to have you working at Lyttons if you were going to be a liability? Do give me some credit.'

Venetia looked at her. It was quite true; her mother was far too professional to consider such a thing.

'Several times recently you've made some very good, commercial suggestions. The most recent being your suggestion of a Lyttons book club. And then there was the cookery book idea—'

'Daddy really loved that!'

'Your father usually comes round in the end. I think you have a good, hard business head, Venetia. I'm not suggesting you should start editing. But Giles is frankly not up to much, and LM can't go on for ever, we need more input on the commercial side. I would like you to think about it. This would be a strictly business arrangement, Venetia. If it doesn't work out, then I would be the first to want to end it.'

'And then I'd be worse off than ever. Everyone would know I was so stupid I couldn't even make a job invented for me by my own parents work—'

'Oh, for heaven's sake, Venetia. Don't be such a coward.'

'A coward!'

'Yes. You can't go on for ever not doing things in case they don't work out. You have to take risks, be positive.'

'I don't feel very positive. You don't understand. I feel dreadful, feeble and hopeless, you can't imagine, you've never had to cope with anything like this.'

'Venetia,' said Celia, 'I have had to cope with more than you might imagine. In what is beginning to seem like quite a long life. And in every case, having my work, having something to throw my energies into, absorb my unhappiness, has been an enormous help. Now please do consider this. For my sake as well as yours. I would love to have you at Lyttons. And I think you would love being there. Give it a trial at least. I'm sure you won't regret it.'

Venetia looked at her in silence for a long time; Celia knew what she was doing, visibly drawing together her courage, her will-power.

Finally she said, 'Yes. Yes, all right, I will. I can't go on like this anyway. And if you really mean it about wanting me. For your own sake, I mean.'

'I do. I really do.'

Venetia smiled at her. 'I hope you won't regret it.'

'I truly believe that neither of us will.'

'Well – thank you anyway. Mummy—'

'Yes?'

'I don't suppose you're going to tell me what you've had to cope with? That I can't imagine?'

'No,' said Celia, 'no, Venetia, I'm not.'

Venetia had started nervously, and in a modest capacity, but she learned fast and proved herself faster still. She began working as LM's assistant, writing out bills of sale and invoices to bookshops and libraries; at the end of two years she had her own office, and title: Manager, Lyttons Commercial Development. She discovered that her mother was right, that she did indeed have a sharp, shrewd brain; it not only recognised commercial opportunities but proved itself capable of creating them.

The publishing industry was becoming increasingly dependent on sales inducement; the Depression had hurt the book trade, people had less money to spend, bookshops, especially in the north, were suffering from rising rents and increased overheads. The book clubs, where people could obtain books at lower prices, and through instalment plans, the twopenny libraries, run through chains of tobacconists and stationers, the various book token schemes and the creation of the Readers Union, whereby readers were offered books in special editions at considerably reduced prices, all helped keep the public enjoying, and ultimately buying, books. It was Venetia who pushed through Lyttons' involvement in the Union, pointing out to her father and to Giles, both firmly opposed to it, that they had enrolled 17,000 readers in the first year.

Celia was fiercely proud of her, Oliver more grudgingly so, LM quietly pleased and Jay welcomed (as he put it) another positive Lytton 'rather than people like your father and poor old Giles who spend their lives saying no'.

But there was one person very unhappy with the set-up: Poor Old Giles.

Helena was outraged, pacing the carpet all evening when he first told her about it, proclaiming the unfairness, the injustice of it, Celia's autocracy within the firm, the complete lack of any true claim Venetia had to the job.

'It's monstrous, all she's ever done is have children and give parties, what does your mother think she's doing?'

'God knows,' said Giles wearily, 'showing me she's boss, I suppose, and less than happy with what I do. It's my area, it could be argued, that Venetia's moving into. But she's had all this trouble with Boy and—'

'I fail to see what that's got to do with it.'

'Well – she's got this wretched divorce, and I suppose Mother thought this would distract her—'

'I had thought Lyttons was a business, not an emotional convalescent home,' said Helena savagely.

Giles looked at her and, even in his misery, half smiled.

'That's awfully good,' he said, 'you ought to write something yourself, Helena.'

'Oh, indeed. And what a good chance I'd have of it being published!' said Helena.

'You could go to another publisher.'

'Giles, I don't want to write a book. Thank you. The very thought sickens me. Have you told your father how unhappy you are about Venetia's arrival?'

'Of course,' said Giles, 'and he simply said that he thought I had too much on my plate and that the educational side, which I am at least fully responsible for, needs developing further. He has a point, there's a fearfully nice woman called Una Dillon who's opening a bookshop for university students and lecturers in Bloomsbury. I think we can do a lot with her – providing it lasts, of course.'

Helena made the sound that meant she could stand the conversation no longer and went upstairs to the small room where increasingly these days she slept alone.

Not again . . . oh, no, not again.

Adele heaved herself out of bed and made the bathroom just in time. Five minutes later, she got wearily back into bed and collapsed on to the pillows. Three mornings running now: it had to be quite conclusive. God, it wasn't fair. Just when everything was getting a bit better, when she was managing to do a little freelance work for Cedric and other photographers, leaving Noni with kind Mme André the concierge. It helped pay the bills and she enjoyed it, the release from the near drudgery of caring for a baby as well as Luc, on a budget in a small third-floor apartment that didn't have central heating. Sometimes she looked back on her life at Cheyne Walk, with servants to attend to her every need, meals served in the dining room without any effort whatsoever, a chauffeur to drive her about if she didn't want to use her own car, her own maid to see to her clothes, and found it hard to believe in any of it. Of course she wouldn't have admitted it to anyone, that she found it so hard, and Luc thought she ought to be perfectly happy and of course she was, but he was out all day, doing his glamorous job for Constantine, lunching authors, meeting with editors, coming home exhausted to his *très chère famille* as he called them. While she had spent the day cleaning the apartment, shopping, cooking on the tiny stove, and of course caring for the small Oenone, washing her nappies with the help, or rather hindrance, of the evil geyser, sieving her food through the *mouli légumes*, pushing her in her perambulator through the Luxembourg Gardens.

'Of course I'm madly happy,' she said to Venetia firmly on a flying visit to London, the month-old Noni in a raffia carrycot, 'and Luc is quite marvellous, but it is – hard. Very hard. I do get terribly tired. And a bit of help would be awfully welcome.'

'I cannot imagine how you can possibly manage,' said Venetia. 'I remember needing a nanny and a maternity nurse even with Henry—'

'Yes, well, I suppose you need what you can have,' said Adele wearily. 'Luckily Noni is very good, otherwise I'd go mad. At least I get some sleep at night.'

'Poor angel. Come and stay with me for a few days, let Nanny take her over.'

'I can't this time. I might later on. I've come to cadge some stuff, some old cot sheets and things. I tell you, Venetia, my life now doesn't seem to have much to do with *le grand amour* Luc was always talking about.'

'Are you really hard up?' She didn't really need to ask this; she had seen the apartment, and even before Noni it had seemed unimaginably small.

'Quite. Well, you see, he still has to support his wife so there isn't much over and—'

'What about your allowance?'

'Luc won't let me touch it. We had quite a row about it.'

'Bit old-fashioned. Especially if he can't provide you with what you need.'

'He can provide me with what I need,' said Adele, 'just not what I'd like. But I do sympathise really. He's very proud and he wants to feel he's supporting me and Noni.'

'That's such a sweet name.'

'Isn't it? He wanted French, I wanted English, so we compromised on Greek. Only of course then I found out there's a character in *Phedre*, the nurse, called Oenone, so it's more French than I'd hoped. Sometimes I wish I was a bit better read. Barty would have known that, wouldn't she? Now I must fly, I promised Mummy I'd be at the house by six and she's gone home specially. I'm longing to see her, she was really marvellous, you know, when Noni was born, shouted at the French doctors at the Clinique Sainte Félicité, made them let her stay with me, and then made them give me gas. They said it wasn't necessary, that in France it was not the thing, and she said she didn't care about France, in England it was very much the thing, and that I was to have it. You do have to admit that when you really need her, she's always there.'

'True,' said Venetia.

But it was on that visit that Adele quarrelled, almost fatally, with her mother.

'Tell me, how is Luc, and how is his career? I believe Constantine are very pleased with him.'

'They are, he should be promoted to the board soon. He is extremely clever, you know.'

'I do know. I was always most impressed with him professionally. Is he getting on with the divorce yet?'

'He can't divorce his wife, Mummy, she's a Catholic.'

'Of course, I always forget, extraordinary really.'

'What?'

'Well, that someone so passionately Jewish should marry a Catholic.'

'I suppose it is a bit. But in a way the two religions work rather well, both very strict in their teaching, you'd be surprised. I like the Jewish faith, I must say, what I know of it, and their way of life, I've sometimes thought of converting.'

'Oh, darling, I shouldn't do that. I believe it's horribly complicated and you have to do all sorts of unpleasant things like fasting and not using electric light on Fridays.'

'Mummy, you don't know anything about it,' said Adele, laughing. 'Luc isn't an Orthodox Jew. But he does want Noni brought up one. He says one of the most important things about Judaism is that it exists, centres even, you could say, around the family.'

'Most religions do that,' said Celia, 'the Church of England is very family-oriented.'

'Mummy, it isn't. The Friday meal, the shabbat dinner, when everyone gathers together and says prayers, that's very special. I've been to Luc's mother's house for it, it's wonderful. And there's a special bond between all Jews, Luc says it's the shared history of persecution—'

'Oh no, not that again,' said Celia with a sigh. 'I hope he's not still obsessed with the Germans and their persecution of the Jews—'

'He's not obsessed with it, it's a fact,' said Adele. She could feel herself growing hot. 'I don't see how you can deny it. It's there, the facts are there.'

'Adele, you forget, friends of mine went to the Olympic Games in Berlin. They said there was no sign whatsoever of any anti-semitism. Sixteen Jewish athletes won medals, in fact. It's an absurd distortion of things. I do wish you would listen to me.'

'I am listening and I can't believe I'm hearing it,' said Adele. 'That was a very clever piece of propaganda on Hitler's part—'

'You're not listening, Adele. The German people are very grateful to Hitler. I do not believe he intends anyone any harm. He has a huge following from decent, normal people who want their country to return to its pre-war glory. He's a superb orator—'

'Have you heard him?' said Adele incredulously.

'I have, yes,' said Celia briefly.

'You didn't say—'

'I – that is, your father would have been very unhappy about it. I would still prefer that he didn't know of it. But yes, I was honoured to be invited once. It was marvellous, Adele, there were vast numbers of people there, and I cannot tell you how impressed I was with him. He speaks with passion about the love of their country living in the hearts of the people. What's wrong with that?'

'A lot,' said Adele, 'an awful lot. Haven't you heard the things he says about the Jews? That they are a disease. That disabled and mentally ill people should be – well, murdered is the only word for it. Can't you see what those floodlit rallies are that you admire so much, they're mass-brainwashing. People carried away on a tide of emotion. It's hideous.'

'Of course it's not,' said Celia. 'Tom Mosley says—'

'Oh, spare me Tom Mosley. What about that fight in London at the end of last year, with the blackshirts and the police at each other's throats—'

'You've been listening to the wrong people as usual. It was the Jews and the Communists who created the disorder—'

'The Jews! Mummy, there you go again. I can't listen to this any longer, I'm sorry. In fact I don't think I can stay here. Your granddaughter is half Jewish, I would remind you of that. When you extol Herr Hitler and his hideous carrying on, you're extolling the man who would have your granddaughter removed.'

She was crying now; Celia went over to her.

'Adele—'

'No, don't. I really mean it, I find all this truly offensive. I think I'll go back to Venetia for the night. Goodbye, Mummy. Please let me know when you change your mind about all this.'

But that was a long way in the future.

And now she was pregnant again.

They were to have a rare treat that night: Mme André was babysitting, and they were going to a ballet at l'Opera, and then out to supper. It didn't happen very often: Luc, who was out a great deal, taking authors to restaurants and cafés and even to the opera, liked to be quiet in the evening, couldn't understand her desire to go out and see people. But tonight he had acquired some tickets to see Serge Lifar and Solange Schwarz dance *La Sylphide*; she had been longing for it for weeks. It was a pity she'd be feeling sick, of course, but . . . and Luc would be in a good mood, he should take the news well . . .

'Pregnant! But that is impossible!'

'Luc, of course it's not. We haven't exactly been – abstaining—'

'But – you are always so careful!'

Her carefulness irritated him sometimes, he would complain that it destroyed spontaneity, that she could not possibly be as eager as he.

'Well – not careful enough. Luc, don't look like that, it's supposed to be good news—'

She smiled at him bravely: she didn't feel that herself, but—

'It is not good news, Adele. We have enough problems, Noni is only one year old, we don't have very much money—'

'Not my fault, Luc.' Adele could feel herself growing angry, tearful. 'Anyway, if you'd only let me spend my allowance—'

'Don't mention that to me.'

'But why not? When it would make all the difference.'

'I will not have help from your father. It is an insult.'

'Of course it's not an insult. It's just your absurd male pride.'

'I am sorry that you should find me absurd.'

'Oh, Luc,' said Adele wearily, 'this isn't doing us any good. I'm pregnant, we're hard up, it's not the end of the world, not the first time it's happened. Aren't you at all pleased?'

'Are you?'

She hesitated. He pounced.

'There, you see. It is not a good thing. For any of us.'

'Well, thank you for that, Luc.' Adele stood up, waving away the plate of food the waiter was proffering. 'Perhaps you'd like me to just get rid of it, this – this bad thing. I think I'll go back to the apartment. If you don't mind. I don't see any point sitting here talking like this. Please don't make a noise when you come in, Noni is cutting a tooth. I don't expect you to be troubled with such trivia, but if she cries all night it might disturb you, make you too tired to do your important work tomorrow.'

She cried herself to sleep and when Noni woke her at three, crying with pain from her tooth, Luc had still not come home.

Chapter 24

'The glittering society wedding took place yesterday between Mr Laurence Elliott, of Elliott House, Fifth Avenue, New York, and Miss—'

Barty hurled the paper into a corner of the room; she couldn't bear to read any more. Of course she was meant to, meant to read all of them, it was in all the papers, and he had had them delivered in a large parcel marked personal and confidential to her at Lytton House, Third Avenue.

Three months earlier, there had been the engagement announcements and he had had those delivered to her as well; not only the formal announcements in the papers, in the *New York Times*, and the *Times Herald* and even the *Wall Street Journal*, but the fuller stories in the social papers and columns, pictures of the radiant bride to be, beaming at her fiancé.

Well, they were welcome to one another, the happy couple, Barty had told herself then, and well-suited too; what fool of a girl would agree to marry a man after a six-week courtship who, except a man seriously emotionally disturbed, would ask her while professing himself still passionately in love with someone else?

It had been one of the many nightmare conversations between them: the last, in fact, or so she had hoped and prayed: when he had told her he was going to propose to Annabel Charlton that night, 'Unless of course you choose to stop me.'

She had no intention of stopping him, she said, and would have hoped indeed it would not be possible; but, 'Of course you can stop it,' he said, 'any moment. Just tell me not to, and that will be that.'

'Laurence,' she said, and it took every ounce of will-power she had, 'I wouldn't dream of telling you anything at all and certainly not what to do about your personal life. I hope that you and Annabel will be very happy. Good afternoon.'

But it had not been the last conversation; there had been another, the night before the wedding.

'I still love you, Barty. I will cancel this whole thing tomorrow if you say so. It's you I want to marry.'

She had put down the phone.

She stared at the wedding photographs, at Laurence, superbly handsome in what the Americans called his cutaway – his morning dress – and Annabel, simpering in a tiered concoction of lace, a tiara – what would Celia have to say about that? Barty wondered with a stab of malice – in her dark hair. The reception at the bride's home in Carnegie Hill had been a formal wedding breakfast for six hundred. The honeymoon was to take place in Venice.

Venice: that hurt. Laurence had promised to take her there, it was to have been their first stop on the European tour they were to share. She felt her eyes sting. She must cling to the thought that she was extremely fortunate never to have married him. That she had realised the full extent of his instability, and that the original instinct which had told her that to marry him was dangerous and wrong for her, had been correct.

But – it had all been very dreadful. Painful beyond anything she could have imagined.

She had refused to give an answer to his proposal for several weeks; dazzled by love for him, and – and she would hardly have been human had this not been at least a factor, however small – and the prize he had offered her. A half share in Lyttons New York! Even as she lay awake that first night, tossing and turning, absolutely unable to sleep, she remembered his words, his theory about everyone having a price. Was she really so mercenary, so ambitious, that she would accept such a gift? Could she accept it, what would the Lyttons say, Celia and Wol – and Giles of course? How could she face them, having become at a stroke their equal, or at least something close to it, in a position of power, not through earning it, but through marrying someone rich and powerful? Becoming the kind of person she least approved of? And then as the dawn broke, she found her mind reflecting treacherously on the undoubted and wicked delight of that: of Barty, the foundling, the poor little girl from the slums, come to possess such power.

But that was not the point, she told herself severely, setting it firmly aside, that was not the point at all, indeed, if she did marry Laurence, she would refuse the shares, refuse his wedding gift, she did not want it, she would not be able to live with it or herself.

She did not see Laurence at all for over two weeks; she told him she had to have time to think, to reflect on his proposal, away from the powerful insistent pressure he exerted upon her. He sent her flowers and presents daily, a huge beribboned box arrived, which she opened with some trepidation. Inside it was another box and inside that another and then another, until finally, her office overflowing with paper and ribbon and cards, she came to a tiny box from Cartier with a ring inside it, the diamond so big that it entirely covered her small knuckle when she tried it on.

'Don't you like it?' he said indignantly, when she telephoned him to thank him, and she said she did, very much, it was beautiful, but that it was not quite for her, too large, too ostentatious, she would be happier with something smaller.

'Absolute nonsense,' he said, 'no wife of mine will wear a small ring,' and she had said she was not his wife and nor would she be wearing it; next day another ring arrived, studded with several smaller diamonds, much prettier and more her style.

Finally, she decided; over dinner at the Plaza – 'well, it is our place' – she told him that she would like to marry him – 'Only "like"? That seems to lack passion, Barty' – and ignoring that, had gone on to say that she was not ready yet, would not be for many months, she needed time to prepare herself and her life, she didn't even want the engagement announced yet and if he went ahead, then she would insert another announcement the following day, cancelling it.

Sulkily at first, he had accepted the deal, then saw it as a challenge to make things more difficult for her, dropping hints to journalists, to people like Elsa Maxwell, that he might just conceivably and within the just about foreseeable future, cease to be a bachelor. Rumours began to fly about, paragraphs in the press; Barty confronted him with them, and he laughed and said he hadn't said a single word to anyone that she could contest or even argue with.

Finally, on New Year's Eve, 'our anniversary', she said he could go ahead and make the announcement.

'I love you and I want to marry you, so I don't quite know why I'm making all this fuss,' she said, and he said he had no idea either.

They were spending the night at South Lodge; he wanted to be alone with her, he said, in their special place, to celebrate the happiest year of his life.

'I want you to come to England, very soon now,' said Barty, 'to meet everyone. It's so important to me. I want them to meet you, know what you're really like, that you're not the devil incarnate that they've heard about from Robert and Maud—'

'And if they decide that I am—'

'Then I shall have to work very hard to change their minds.'

'But you won't change yours?'

'No, Laurence, I won't change mine. I can't think of anything that would do that.'

And then it had happened.

He had suddenly become rather pale and agitated; he said he would like to lie down.

'It's nothing, really, just one of my migraines, if you wouldn't be too offended, my darling, I would like to alone for a while. The effects are not always very attractive.'

She knew what he meant, she had witnessed one before; they were rare, only coming about twice a year, but savage, the intense pain accompanied by violent vomiting.

She had seen him up to bed, and left him obediently, slept in the guest room along the corridor; in the early morning she had got up and gone to see how he was. He was clearly in agony, and extremely ill.

'I think, perhaps, you should phone the doctor, when it's as bad as this, he gives me a shot, puts me out. I'm sorry, darling, not very romantic, oh God—'

She left him, hurried to the telephone; the doctor came within the hour and gave Laurence an injection.

'He'll be all right now. Poor man, dreadful, these things are. But he'll be out for a good twenty-four hours, you won't get a cheep out of him. I should go back to bed yourself.'

But in the morning, she decided to go home briefly; she had work to do on *Brilliant Twilight*, she was fretting over it and she could collect it and bring it back. She went to find Mills, Laurence's driver; he said he would be only too happy to drive her, with the wonderful new Triboro Bridge, it would only take three hours at the most, the roads would be clear, she could collect her work and he would bring her right back.

They were in Gramercy Park by midday; she ran in, collected her briefcase, checked the contents – proofs, original manuscript, cover designs – and then phoned South Lodge. Laurence was still absolutely unconscious.

She was just letting herself out of the door, leafing through the letters on the hall table at the same time, for she had not been there for forty-eight hours, when Elise Curtis appeared from her own small, rather murky apartment.

'Happy New Year, Miss Miller.'

'Happy New Year to you, Elise. Did you have a good time last night?'

'Oh – you know. So, so. I haven't seen you to talk to for months, Miss Miller. Course I've been working nights—'

'Yes, and I've been away a lot,' said Barty quickly, remorseful that whenever she did see Elise she avoided her, dreading the long rambling stories and the sickly odour that accompanied her everywhere. 'And then of course I had to go to England for several weeks. My – my uncle was very ill—'

'Yes, I heard you'd gone. That was the bad news in the cable, I suppose?'

Barty stared at her. 'What cable, Elise?'

'Why, the one that came for you. I signed for it, you know. The day before you went to England. Well, you must surely have got it? I gave it to your – your gentleman friend, he was waiting for you outside in his car, I told him to be sure he gave it to you. He didn't forget, surely—'

He had tried of course: to deny it first, and then when that proved impossible, to try to explain; she observed him, observed him in a mixture of disgust and rage, lying, prevaricating, jumping ahead of her in a series of the dizzying moves that she had come to know rather well. Lies about phoning London, about making sure Oliver was all right, about wanting to tell her himself after she had had a night's sleep: 'You were so tired, so overwrought, I thought it best that you should hear in the morning. You couldn't do anything that night—'

'I could have phoned,' she said and her voice was high, trembling, 'found out how he was. Started making arrangements. They would have known I cared. Instead of—'

'I did instruct whoever it was to make sure they knew you had phoned.'

'But I – oh this is ridiculous. Who did you speak to? No one mentioned it—'

'I have no idea. Some incompetent servant who clearly didn't pass the message on.'

'The butler at Cheyne Walk is marvellous, he would never have failed to do such a thing.'

He shrugged. 'Clearly not as marvellous as you think. Barty, come here, sit down, please let me explain. I know it was – remiss of me—'

'Remiss! You call that remiss. A piece of the most dangerous, wicked deception, while the person I love probably best in the world—'

'I thought that was me—'

'No,' she said quietly. 'No, it is not you.'

'Please. Let me try and explain. It was only because I love you so much. I wanted to—'

'Laurence, that was not about love. I'm afraid you don't know anything about love. I'm going to my room now, I can't ask poor Mills to take me all that way again. But I do warn you, if you come near me I shall scream and tell your servants that you're raping me. Goodnight, Laurence. I – I really don't think I want to see you ever again.'

He had thought – of course – that she would get over it, that it was a passing tantrum, that she would forgive him, that he could win her round. Convincing him otherwise was the hardest thing she had ever done. For weeks, as usual, he bombarded her with telephone calls, flowers, waited outside for her in his car, sat for hours in reception at Lytton House. Eventually she told him that she would inform the police he was pestering her.

'I don't want to marry you, Laurence. Don't you understand? I don't want anything more to do with you. Please, please leave me alone.'

And then the other, uglier assaults began, the near – suicide threats, the declarations that he was going to get in his boat and sail away in it, that he was unable to work and the bank was on the verge of collapse, that he was having investigations into a physical condition which might be fatal – all complete fabrications, designed to frighten her, to force her into submission.

Somehow she managed to hold firm, but it was quite extraordinarily difficult and disturbing.

Because, of course, she was still deeply concerned for him, and in a way, she was still terribly in love with him.

She was greatly comforted and distracted through this time, however, by the publication of *Brilliant Twilight*. With some misgivings,

335

encouraged by the modest orders of some of the more important booksellers – Brentanos had expressed great interest in it and ordered twenty copies and three posters – Stuart Bailey had decided on an initial print run of two and a half thousand.

'I don't think it will do three, but – well, if we're lucky, we should do over two.'

Publication date was 16 November – 'A week before Thanksgiving, it's a good time' – and although Lyttons weren't giving an official dinner for Geordie MacColl, Stuart and Barty took him to the King Cole Room at the St Regis on Fifteenth and Stuart ordered some Krug champagne to launch 'what I hope will be a vintage book'.

'I hope so too,' said Geordie. He was very nervous; Barty found it hugely engaging.

'I know so,' she said, 'and you should get your first reviews tomorrow.'

'I'm ready for them,' said Geordie gloomily.

Stuart Bailey smiled at him. 'They might be good. You never know. Anyway, even if they're bad, that's better than no reviews at all.'

Geordie said he found that hard to believe and Barty told him it was one of the oldest tenets in publishing and one of the truest.

'People buy it anyway then, out of curiosity. No review and they don't even know it exists.'

It had been a very rich literary year: *Of Mice and Men*, *To Have and Have Not*, A.J. Cronin's *The Citadel* and *The Hobbit* had all been, or were being, launched; 'So the competition will be stiff. But there's nothing really much like *Brilliant Twilight*,' said Barty, raising her glass to him, 'so we're in with a fighting chance at least. We've printed two thousand five hundred, you know.'

'Oh, God,' said Geordie, 'two thousand, four hundred and ninety-seven unsold.'

'Who are going to buy the other three?'

'My mother and my two sisters.'

Barty leaned over and gave him a kiss. 'I'll buy one. I promise. I'll stand in the middle of Scribners and ask for it very loudly. That was one of Celia Lytton's ploys, with every book she published. Only she did all the major bookshops. And of course she's so beautiful and so grand everyone stared and wanted to know what the book was.'

'Well,' said Geordie, with one of his shy smiles, 'you're very beautiful too. If not quite – grand. Imposing, though.'

'Oh, Geordie. You're very sweet, but I'm afraid it's not true. Anyway, I shall try it for you.'

There was no review next day, in a single paper; Geordie phoned Barty in despair.

'You see. Not even a bad one.'

'Give them time,' she said staunchly, 'they were all drooling over *The Late George Apley*.'

'I noticed. Should I fall on my sword now or tonight?'

'Wait till after the weekend.'

She did not tell him that she had gone into both Scribners and Brentanos and asked for it, and found it poorly displayed at the back of both shops. Barnes and Noble didn't seem to be displaying it at all. None of the bookshops were using the posters Barty had so carefully commissioned and overseen. She spent several near-sleepless nights, reflecting on the general hopelessness of her life, and wishing Celia was in New York.

In the *Sunday Post* there was a very nice, if small, review: 'Geordie MacColl writes like the proverbial angel, with his pen dipped intermittently in acid to give his tale a sharply etched edge . . . a most promising debut.'

'You see, you see,' Barty sang down the phone, 'and there's all this week, you should get some more.'

'I'm sure I won't.'

On Thursday, the *New York Times* said that *Brilliant Twilight* was a 'shimmering pearl of a novel', and described Geordie's talent as the 'piece of burnished grit in the oyster that created it'.

'Bit obscure, but nice,' said Stuart.

Next day he rushed into Barty's office with the *Post*. 'Look at this, Barty. This is extraordinary.'

It was so unlike him to display any emotion other than a rather weary caution that she was quite startled; she took the paper from him.

'It would be wrong to describe Geordie MacColl as the new Scott Fitzgerald, for he is an entirely new and fresh talent, but in that he covers some of the same territory with much of the same panache, it would not be completely out of order. A brilliant novel.'

'My God,' said Barty in awed tones.

The books moved forward to the front of the shops, the posters went up, and the reorders began to come in. Barnes and Noble ordered another ten, Scribner likewise, Doubleday fifteen and Brentanos an astonishing twenty.

The *New Yorker* hailed *Brilliant Twilight* as 'superlative' and both

337

the *Ladies' Home Journal* and *Harpers Bazaar* urged their readers to put it on their Christmas lists.

There were more orders, more reorders in fifties and then hundreds; when a store in Atlanta, Georgia, and another in Charleston, Carolina, both sent for ten copies, Stuart Bailey signed a print order for a further ten thousand.

'New York, Washington, Boston, you expect to do pretty well there. But when those kinds of places want to read you, you've made it in a big way.'

But what finally sent Geordie MacColl into the literary stratosphere was a superb review in the hugely influential *Atlantic Monthly*. Its issue immediately prior to publication had carried nothing, to Barty's secret disappointment, although she told Geordie that a review in it for such a novel was literally unthinkable; but the following month it told its readers that they would pass *Brilliant Twilight* by to their great loss.

'Once in a decade or so is a great new writer published. There is a moment when bookshops and libraries should clear a space on their tables and shelves, when not to do so would brand them as intellectually feckless, and when to do so would be to grant immense and rare pleasure to their customers. This is that moment in this decade; for an experience of excitement, tension, insight, emotion and carefully careless humour *Brilliant Twilight* has been given to us.'

Stuart promptly increased the print run again . . . and then again.

Articles appeared in all the papers about Geordie, about his old-money charm, his boyish looks, his personal history – 'Thank God it's so interesting,' said Stuart to Barty. 'I'm very sorry his family lost all their money in the crash but it's extremely good for us.'

Lyttons were suddenly on the map; from being a small, modestly successful publisher, which the big boys looked down on with affectionate but mild disdain, they had become a small, brilliant publisher that the big boys looked across at with alarm and envy.

And Barty, hitherto unknown in New York publishing circles, found herself fêted and quoted as well; Kyle wrote to her, congratulating her and telling her that if ever she wanted a job, Macmillans would be more than happy to offer her one.

She wrote back and thanked him, saying she was very happy where she was, but suggesting lunch; over a rather protracted one at the Colony – 'my treat' – she told him of the conclusion of, although not the reason for, her affair with Laurence Elliott. Kyle was very sweet: 'I'm sorry for you, because I know you must be sad, but I'm glad for the rest of us. He just wasn't nearly good enough for you.'

He then spent a great deal of time telling her all about his baby son, Kyle junior, known as Kip, and what a wonderful mother Lucy was; somehow, Barty managed to display the requisite enthusiasm. Felicity wrote a few days later, a charming little note, saying how sorry she was about Laurence and how much she knew Barty must be hurting; 'but I promise you it will get better, you must just live from day to day. And remember, you are always welcome here. We've missed you.'

Barty didn't feel quite ready to start associating closely with Laurence's enemies, but was touched nonetheless and rather surprised that a person who had been married for almost four decades should be able to remember what the ending of an affair must feel like.

There was still no word from Maud.

But as the year drew to a close and *Brilliant Twilight* was in every bookshop window and on every Christmas list, and she accompanied Geordie to yet another reading at yet another bookshop, Barty would frequently reflect, with something approaching disbelief, that she had not thought about Laurence Elliott for at least twelve hours.

But the engagement announcement and the marriage reports were almost beyond endurance. When he phoned her, to tell her he was going to become engaged, she had thought it was simply that: the thoughtful act of a past lover, had assumed that finally he was behaving with some kind of normality. It hurt but she managed to smile into the telephone and to say she was delighted and she hoped he would be very happy.

But 'Barty, I don't want to do this,' he said, 'I don't want to be engaged to Annabel Charlton, I certainly don't want to marry her. You have only to say you'll marry me, Barty, and I'll cancel the whole thing. Gladly. Joyfully. I still love you very much.'

She had managed to put down the phone; an hour later it rang again; it was Laurence.

'Now you've had time to think about it, Barty, how do you feel? Will you marry me? Or do I have to marry Annabel instead?'

'I won't marry you,' she said, hearing her own voice surprisingly calm, 'and if anything was necessary to make me sure I had done the right thing refusing you, this is it. Good morning, Laurence, and congratulations to you both.'

And then she dropped her head into her arms and sobbed for quite a long time.

She had thought she was used to it; to the pain, the loneliness, the disorientation, the sheer, frightful jealousy – that last had shocked her most, the thought of Laurence with, making love to, someone else.

But the wedding, the marriage, that was unbearable.

She went through the following seven days in a dream; during which she wrote a letter to Maud, apologising to her, telling her she had been right, and how much she had missed her.

Maud telephoned her next day, a tearful, sad voice, saying she was only sorry for Barty and that there was nothing to forgive.

'But what will you do now?' she said.

'Now?' said Barty, and suddenly as she realised what she could do, and wondered why she hadn't thought of it before, she smiled into the phone. 'Now, Maud, I'm going home.'

Part Two
1939–1942

Chapter 25

'We must get Adele home at once,' said Celia. 'This is quite appalling.'

She spoke more in irritation than in terror, as if the invasion by Herr Hitler of Poland and the subsequent declaration of war upon Germany by both England and France were inconveniences rather than events of world-shaking importance.

'I agree with you, my dear, it would be very – nice to have her here. But why should she come?'

'Because – oh, Oliver, don't be so ridiculous. Because we are at war with Germany. France is at war with Germany. France may be invaded—'

'She may very well be, I am afraid.'

'So Adele ought to be at home. With her children.'

'Celia –' Oliver looked at her in a certain amusement, '– Celia, Adele is at home with her children. She lives in Paris now, with the father of those children—'

'Most unfortunately.'

'I agree with you. But those are the facts. She won't even think of rushing back here.'

'Then we must make her think of it. Of the dangers. If Luc has any decency at all, he will agree with us—'

'I must say, I am very afraid for her,' said Oliver, 'for all of them. Luc being Jewish does put them in far greater danger—'

'Yes. I do know.' She had slowly and unwillingly changed her mind over the past two years as reports appeared in the papers of the persecution of the Jews in Poland and in Germany itself, of Austrian Jews being forced to scrub pavements while their Nazi persecutors looked on, of the looting and burning of synagogues becoming increasingly commonplace. But it had been the events of *Kristallnacht* – The Night of Broken Glass – the previous autumn that had finally convinced her, the wave of organised violence over twenty-four hours throughout Germany and Austria against the Jews. Twenty thousand men had been arrested as a result and sent to concentration camps, and stormtroopers had broken into Jewish homes to terrorise and beat women and children as well as men. Celia had sat reading the report of that in *The Times*, most unusually for her in tears; afterwards she had gone to her room and sat there for a long time, horribly shocked and chastened, not only that it had happened but that she and her friends could have been so wrong.

Some of them, including Bunny Arden, had clung to their support for Hitler, but: 'I can see I was wrong,' she said to Oliver. 'Dreadfully wrong. I – would like to apologise to you. And to Adele and to Luc, of course.'

She had gone to Paris to see them and to try to make her peace; she had never lacked courage of any kind, moral or physical, but she had never needed it more than sitting in Adele's and Luc's apartment and asking for their forgiveness.

It had not been granted.

'I was wrong,' she said simply, 'wrong and arrogant and extremely – offensive to you both. I'm very sorry.'

There was a silence. Adele, clearly confused over her own reaction, had looked anxiously at Luc, seeking guidance. But he, having sat ice-featured as she talked, nodded tersely and left the apartment, saying he had to meet some friends.

'I'm sorry, Mummy,' said Adele, looking after him, 'he's very distressed about it all. About what's happening. He sees any denial of that as an affront.'

'Of course. It is. I can understand that. Well, I hope in time he will forgive me.'

'I – hope so. But I still don't think you really understand how he – we – felt about your attitude. It is good of you to come, and I do appreciate it, but – well, I can see why Luc still finds it hard to accept you. Even after your apology.'

'Oh, Adele, really. What else am I supposed to do?' Celia felt a stab of irritation, in spite of her remorse.

'I – don't know.'

'Well, surely you and I can be friends again.'

Adele smile at her rather tiredly. 'I'd like us to be. I miss you.'

Celia decided to take advantage of this. 'You're terribly pale. And you look exhausted.' She looked round the apartment, at the mess of baby clothes and toys, at Noni's playpen occupying half the sitting room, at the nappies hanging on a line on the balcony. 'This can't be easy for you. Why don't you come home to have this baby?'

'No, Mummy, I can't. Really. I have to stay here and look after Luc.

I'll be all right. Anyway, it's not for another month or so. I do hope he arrives before Christmas.'

'He? Are you sure about that?'

'If Luc has anything to do with it, yes. He is determined, convinced rather, that it's a boy. Heaven help me if it isn't. I don't know why it matters so much but—'

'Adele, he's a man,' said Celia. 'They have to play their absurd games. One of those is perpetuating their own line. It's pitiful, but there it is.' She looked at Noni who was holding on to the bars of the playpen, smiling; she was a beautiful child, dark eyed and olive skinned, with a mass of gleaming black curls. 'She's sweet, Adele. Personally I rather hope you have another girl. Just to annoy him.'

'Oh, Mummy! That's not helpful. He's my husband—'

'Unfortunately he is not,' said Celia icily. 'That was a mistake.

Adele stood up, her face drawn and hurt. 'Please don't say that. It doesn't help. Of course he's my husband, in all but name, and—'

'And I suppose you're going to tell me again that it isn't his fault.'

'Yes. Yes, I was. I think you'd better go,' said Adele wearily. 'We're just going to start fighting again. I do appreciate your coming, but—'

'But what?'

'I can't cope with this hostility towards Luc. It's terribly hurtful.'

'Oh, Adele, don't be absurd. I'm merely stating facts.'

'No, you're not. Not merely stating them. As always there's a lot of opinion contained in facts as you see them. Distortion, even. I – I love Luc. And he loves me. And whether you like it or not, we are a – a family. I'm sorry, Mummy, but you've got to learn to accept that. For once your views aren't terribly important.'

They parted then. A letter came a week later from Adele, saying that she had been unable to persuade Luc to accept Celia's apology: 'and although of course I do, I do feel my first loyalty is to him.'

'Wretched, arrogant, disagreeable man,' said Celia viciously, stuffing the letter into her desk drawer. But she was very upset, not least that the estrangement from Adele had been for the most part her own fault.

Celia's wish that the baby be another girl was not granted: Lucas Lieberman was born on Christmas Day 1939: 'to the sound of bells ringing all over Paris,' Luc told Adele as he came to her bedside, with a bouquet of Christmas roses. '*Ma chère, chère* Mam'selle Adele, you have now made me perfectly happy.'

Oliver was right: Adele had no intention of going back to England.

'I'm sorry,' she wrote to Celia, 'but I wish I could make you understand, this is my home, this is where my children have been born and will grow up, and this is where I shall stay. Luc really doesn't think there is very much danger. If it gets worse, then of course I'll consider coming back, but I don't think it will.'

Nobody was taking the war very seriously: apart from the notices all over Paris calling for mobilisation 'because of the aggressive attitude of the German government' and the sight of a great many soldiers in uniform, life seemed almost unchanged.

'Paris will always be Paris' was the motto on everyone's lips; and indeed it seemed to be. As Adele pushed Lucas and Noni around each afternoon in the huge old perambulator which Lady Beckenham had delivered to her personally when Noni was born, she saw what she had always seen: people sitting in the sunshine at pavement cafés, drinking wine and smoking, and ignoring whatever might be going on in the rest of Europe. They went to concerts and to the cinema, listened to the *petits orchestres* in the *grands cafés* and in the Luxembourg Gardens; there might be sandbags on the steps of the Opéra but people flocked to it to hear *Madame Butterfly*; the cinemas were full, and so were the restaurants, the couture houses continued to work on the spring collections. It was as if the whole of Paris was resolved to show Hitler it had no time for him. There was no fear – or very little – in Paris.

'We have the Maginot Line,' everyone said. 'We have the shield of France. We will be safe.'

Sometimes, as Adele walked the streets of Paris with her children, she would catch sight of herself in a shop window, a dark thin girl, her hair grown unfashionably to her shoulders, wearing a printed silk dress, bare-legged, hatless, gloveless, pushing a very large, very old perambulator, and wonder where the spoilt, chic and extremely English Adele Lytton had gone.

'So what will happen, do you think? Will you have to enlist?'

Helena's face as she looked at Giles was troubled; irritating and ineffectual as he was, disappointing as a husband and a provider, she was still very fond of him, and fearful at the thought of what might become of him.

They had sat, Helena almost in tears, listening to the King's broadcast, to his brave prophecy that with God's help they should prevail; the next day, with all the banks closed and people unable to talk of anything but the war, had a strange almost surreal feel to it.

Draconian measures were immediately introduced: petrol was rationed, theatres and cinemas were closed, street lighting eradicated, and children from the cities, most notably London, were being evacuated to the country. Apart from that, not a great deal seemed to be happening.

'Of course I shall,' said Giles. He met Helena's eyes and smiled at her; he was surprised to find himself excited more than anything else by the prospect. He had become so accustomed to being in what seemed a terminally unsatisfactory situation that danger, pain, death did not at that moment properly occur to him; he saw only the chance of a glorious bid for freedom.

'I thought I would go into the army. They are asking for men between the ages of eighteen and forty-one. I actually don't see how any self-respecting chap could not go. I thought I would join Father's old regiment. It would please him—'

'I don't really see that pleasing your father has a great deal to do with the conduct of war,' said Helena.

'Not primarily, of course. But if I can please him at the same time, that would be a bonus.'

Oliver was touched by Giles's intention to go into his regiment. 'Splendid,' he said, 'well, I'm sure they'll be pleased to have you. I won't say I wish I could go with you, but if I was twenty years younger—'

'You'd be coming home from the last war,' said Giles soberly. 'Isn't that a fearful thought? Only twenty years ago, we were fighting Germany. Or rather had conquered it.'

'Yes, indeed. Not the war to end all wars after all. It's appalling, I do agree. But what else could be done? He's got to be stopped, this creature.'

'Well, I shall enjoy helping to stop him,' said Giles.

'Try and stop me,' said Jay. He grinned at his mother; she was white, her fists gripping the arms of her chair, her eyes huge and dark in her thin face. But she said nothing: even at this sinister, absolute repetition of Jago's own words. It was as if Jay had heard them himself.

'My father was off with the first wave, wasn't he?'

'Yes, Jay, he was. And—' She stopped.

'Yes, I know. And killed very early on. That's no reason to suppose I will be, Mum. I'll be fine. Lucky Lytton they call me, you know.'

'I – didn't,' said LM faintly.

'I don't think I can bear this,' said Celia. She sat down next to Oliver's wheelchair and put her hand in his.

'What's that, my dear?'

'What's that – Oliver, how can you be so – so calm about it?'

'Oh – you mean Kit.'

'Yes! I mean Kit. How can he go, how can we let him go—'

'My darling, he's nineteen. He's the right age, he wants to go—'

'The right age! He's a child. His second year at Oxford. Why can't he stay, finish that—'

'Celia, you couldn't expect that. Not really, not from Kit. Any more than from Jay. To stay out of it, safely continuing with their lives while their contemporaries risked theirs. It's totally out of both their characters.'

'You're not – not pleased about it, I trust.' Celia withdrew her hand, stood up, glaring at him.

'In a way, yes, I am. I'm proud of him. Proud of his courage, of his desire to serve his country. Of course I'm afraid for him as well, any father would be. But I would be more afraid for him if he was a coward, hiding behind some academic smokescreen.'

'But – the air force! It's so dangerous, more than anything else.'

'Nothing is more dangerous than anything else, my dear, in a war,' said Oliver gently. 'It can even be quite dangerous staying at home.'

'Boy, hallo. What are you doing here?'

Venetia looked at him; he was standing in the doorway of her office, looking slightly sheepish.

'I wondered if you'd let me buy you lunch.'

'Well—' She hesitated. She had a lot to do and she'd come in late anyway. 'What's it about?'

'It's about my joining the war effort. I wanted to discuss it with you.'

'Your joining – Boy, do you mean you're enlisting?'

'Yes. I do. I've thought about it a lot, and I think we all owe the old country whatever we can give it.'

'Oh, God.' She felt sick suddenly. It was one thing divorcing Boy, another seeing him off to war and the possibility of – well, of not seeing him for a long time. 'What did you think you might do? Which service would you go into?'

'Well, the army. I still remember my glory days in the corps at Eton. I'll go into the Guards, I think. If they'll have me. But of course we

348

need to discuss it, very carefully. I wanted you to be involved in my plans from the beginning.'

'Who will look after the salesroom? And the gallery?'

'God knows. Well, old Baker will take over the salesroom, he's perfectly sound. I shall probably have to move it out of London of course, away from the bombs. And then there's Henry and Roo. I was thinking that school of theirs, down near the Kent coast, is not the safest place. The front line, they're calling Dover. I think perhaps we should move them. There's a lot to talk about, you see.'

Venetia swallowed, fear seeping into her further, an awful, clammy, cold thing. 'Yes, of course, do let's have lunch. I'd love to. Oh, dear—'

Celia came in suddenly. 'Venetia – oh, good lord. What on earth are you doing here, Boy?'

'He's come to take me out to lunch, Mummy,' said Venetia, blowing her nose hard, 'and to talk about – about enlisting.'

'Oh, God,' said Celia. She sat down suddenly on the chair opposite Venetia's desk. 'This is dreadful. Everyone going. You. Kit. Giles. Jay—'

'Jay?'

'Yes. Into the Greenjackets. It's where all the Wykhamists go, or so he tells me. It's dreadful and for Lyttons as well, he's an absolute godsend to the firm, such talent, we shall miss him so terribly—'

Only Boy, standing by Venetia's desk, saw Giles in the corridor, waiting to speak to his mother; saw him, and saw that he had heard what she had said. About Jay's talent and how much he would be missed. And with a genuine ache of sympathy in his heart, watched him hurry away.

'I'm thinking of doing something useful,' said Barty. She was sitting in the garden of Primrose Hill with Sebastian; it was a golden afternoon, and they were having tea. Izzie was sitting on her swing, reading; every so often she would look up and smile at them and then return to it, pushing the escaped curls of hair behind her ears. She was so like Pandora now it was almost painful, with her wide hazel eyes, her small straight nose, the masses of brown hair, worn in a long plait hanging down her back. Sebastian no longer seemed to find the likeness painful, rather the reverse.

Barty, who had been away when the change had occurred, was warned she would find it surprising, but in fact she had found it almost disturbing.

Sebastian said nothing of it, indeed had never acknowledged it to anybody; the only clue coming in the dedication of the new Meridian (entitled *Half of the Time*), 'For Isabella'. He was still short with anyone who tried to discuss her with him, was more like a Victorian parent than one of the new modern school that Boy Warwick belonged to. He insisted on early bedtimes, few treats, and a strict adherence to homework and piano practice timetables; but Barty, observing for the first time the affection he clearly felt for Izzie, the careful attention he gave to what she said, the interest with which he observed her as she moved about the house and garden, was so touched, her eyes filled with tears.

'And what,' he said now to Barty, 'do you mean by "doing something useful"?'

'In the war, I mean. I might want to join the Wrens, or something. Helena is joining the Red Cross and—'

'God preserve us,' said Sebastian. 'I must remember not to get injured.'

'Don't be so horrid, Sebastian. Everyone's horrid to Helena.'

'She's horrid to everyone. Miserable girl.'

'That's unfair. Anyway, that's what I'm thinking.'

'So life at Lyttons isn't enough for you any more, is that it? Now that you've savoured life and literary success in the New World.'

She flushed. 'It's not exactly that. But – oh I don't know, Sebastian. It's difficult working at Lyttons, you know, Venetia is still a bit – odd with me and so is Giles. And I don't like seeing Boy either, and he's always coming in—'

'Well, you won't have to worry about him much longer,' said Sebastian, 'he's off to join the Grenadier Guards. Bloody typical. It would be far more useful if you stayed and look after Lyttons. Good God, there'll only be Oliver and Celia left soon; and LM and Venetia, I suppose. That'll produce a war all of its own on Paternoster Row. We shall need you as appeaser, our own Neville Chamberlain.'

She sighed. 'Well, it might not be enough. For me, I mean. Not at the moment.'

Sebastian looked at her sharply. 'You're not very happy, are you, Barty?'

'No,' she said abruptly. 'I'm not.'

And much to her surprise and embarrassment, she burst into tears.

At first getting home had been enough; the sheer pleasure of being in London, of seeing Wol and Sebastian and Giles, LM and Jay, even Celia, of settling into her old room at Cheyne Walk while she found a tiny mews house in Chelsea, and then settling into it, it had all been a wonderful diversion.

But there had been immediate problems, most notably with Venetia.

'You knew, didn't you?' she had said briefly to Barty, her dark eyes hostile. 'You knew, it was your friend having – mixed up with Boy, and you didn't tell me. I don't know how you could do that, Barty, I really don't.'

She didn't say very much: only that she had not known until it was too late, and then there had seemed no point; she did not say that Sebastian had counselled her against it, that he had done what he could on her behalf, she did not like to involve him. Venetia, pacing the room, had said finally that she supposed it was over now, and that it was foolish for them to quarrel, that it was hardly Barty's fault; but there was a shadow between them that would not lift. It might not have mattered so much once, but now that they met at Lyttons on a daily basis, it remained difficult.

She had been surprised to find her there, surprised and cynical; but she swiftly came to recognise that Venetia was actually extremely good at what she did, with her sharp mind and commercial sense.

The great joy of Barty's professional life was Jay; in him she found a true ally. He was still only a junior editor, but she found him more imaginative, more innovative and with a greater grasp of the broad publishing picture than anyone else in the firm, with the exception of Celia; the three of them could often be found talking in Celia's or Barty's office long after everyone else had gone home, and that in itself caused problems, with decisions inevitably taken, ideas floated, series launched, if only notionally, all finally having to confront the rest of the firm.

But if Lyttons was not comfortable, it was her grief over Laurence that really troubled her. She still missed him savagely. She had not expected to feel the dreadful lack of him in her life, day after day. For a year, he had filled every moment, every corner of it, with his passionate, difficult, demanding self; she had scarcely felt or thought or done anything without his involvement.

He had aroused her, angered her, amused her, made her think, and made her feel; now there was a vacuum in her, and she could not ever imagine it filling again.

She had half expected him to write, to continue to bombard her with details of his life, and his feelings, but he did not. Maud sent her a cutting (not realising how it would hurt) announcing the birth of his

351

daughter and after that there was absolutely nothing. Finally, clearly, he had decided to let her go. And that hurt more than anything.

'I thought I'd be better by now, it's a year since I came home. I still think about him every day, Sebastian, I can't believe it—'

'My darling,' said Sebastian, and his voice was very heavy suddenly, 'it's nine years since Pandora died, and I think about her every day. Contrary to popular opinion, I find that the passing of time and the dulling of grief have very little to do with one another.'

'Oh, God,' she said, staring at him in horror, 'Sebastian, I'm so sorry, how could I have said that, to you of all people? I—'

'Quite easily,' he said, patting her hand, 'and I'm glad you feel comfortable enough to do so. It's all right, nothing makes it worse any more. And I have learnt to live with it, learnt what to do with the pain. In that way at least, time does help, if not heal. But – yes, Isabella, thank you, put it down there. And then I think you should run along, Barty and I are still talking.'

'No, don't go,' said Barty, reaching out her hand to Izzie, 'it's nice to have you here. Your father and I have said all there is to say. How's school?'

'A big concern,' said Sebastian scowling, before Izzie could answer. 'I had planned for Isabella to go to St Paul's, hadn't considered boarding school. But with the war, I think she should be moved out of London. So I'm looking at places like Cheltenham Ladies'—'

'Father,' said Izzie, and her small jaw was set in a way that Barty found so reminiscent of Pandora she almost laughed, 'if it's dangerous for me in London, then it's dangerous for you, and I don't want to leave you here. In fact I won't.'

'You will do what you're told,' said Sebastian; his voice was harsh suddenly, but his eyes on Izzie were soft and concerned. 'I will not have you exposed to danger, and that is the end of the matter.'

'Perhaps she could go to Lady Beckenham's school,' said Barty lightly.

'What? She's starting a school? Good God, what next? What will it teach, horsemanship and the best way to treat servants?'

'That's not fair,' said Barty, who was eternally grateful to Lady Beckenham, after all that she had done for Billy. 'She's a marvellously wise person. But anyway, it's not her own school really. The place Henry and Roo are at is going to move down there. She offered it, said she knew they were looking for somewhere, and she wanted to do something for the war effort and couldn't face a hospital again.'

'Oh, my goodness,' said Izzie, 'oh, Father, do you think I could? I'd so love to go to school with Henry and Roo—'

'Of course you can't,' said Sebastian, 'it's an absurd notion, and besides it's a boys' school, they wouldn't have you. Now, it's time you were doing your piano practice, and you must do an extra five minutes, what's more. I timed you yesterday and you stopped too soon. You thought I wouldn't notice, didn't you?'

'No, Father,' said Izzie with a weary sigh; but she smiled at him as she got up. 'Goodbye, Barty, it was lovely to see you. I think it's a very good idea for you to join the army or something. You'd be marvellous.'

'I didn't think she was even listening,' said Barty, looking after her. 'Certainly not taking it in.'

'She takes everything in,' said Sebastian, with a note of grudging pride in his voice.

Inside the house, the sound of scales flowing rather gracefully up and down the piano was interrupted by the telephone; after a few moments, Mrs Conley appeared on the terrace.

'It's Lady Celia, Mr Brooke. She wants to speak to you urgently.'

Sebastian looked at Barty and raised his eyebrows. 'Proofs full of mistakes, I expect,' he said, and disappeared into the house. After quite a long time – the proofs must have been very bad, Barty thought – he reappeared, walking heavily, his face carved with unhappiness. He sat down and stared at the garden, then took her hand, started playing with her fingers, ticking them off rather distractedly one by one. After a while, he sighed, and said, 'Barty, don't you go off for a while, there's a good girl. We need you too much here.' He was silent again, then fished in his pocket for his handkerchief, blew his nose hard; when he looked at her, his eyes were full of tears.

'Kit's just got his papers. He's – he's off in a week to do his flying training, up in Scotland. Oh, Barty, I'm terribly frightened for him.'

She was too distressed by his grief even to wonder why he should have felt more for Kit than for Giles or Jay.

Chapter 26

It was a dreadful noise, a man crying. Helena had never heard it before; she listened in horror, horror and dread. Horror because she knew what it must mean, dread because she knew she must confront it.

She waited for another moment, then handed the children over to their nanny, took a deep breath and walked into the study where Giles sat with his head buried in his arms on the desk, a brown envelope beside him, marked 'The War Office'.

She put her arm round his shoulders. 'Giles, what is it? Whatever it is, you must tell me.'

He sat up, blew his nose, stared at her, his eyes red-rimmed in his white face; he looked like a small boy, afraid of some kind of retribution.

'I've failed my commission,' he said finally, as she had been so afraid he would. 'Failed again, Helena. My whole life is a bloody fucking failure. I failed my WOSB. Not officer material. Not material for anything, Helena, am I? Lousy publisher, disappointment to my parents, useless provider, oh, don't look like that, I know what you think of me and how you'd like more money and why not, for God's sake? And now, I'm not deemed capable of leading my men into battle.'

'But, Giles—'

'Don't "But, Giles" me. There were a whole crowd of chaps there, lots of them with only half my advantages in life, all passed.'

'You can't have been the only one who failed,' said Helena.

'No, of course I wasn't. I'm telling you that people who'd been to grammar school, for God's sake, from very ordinary families, they were obviously going to pass, and I – product of Eton and then Oxford, having spent the last ten years or whatever training to run Lyttons, I didn't. I must be bloody useless, Helena, absolutely bloody useless.'

'Tell me about it,' she said. 'All you said was that it was all right. Come on, Giles, I want to know what happened.'

'Oh – it's all so humiliating.' He wiped his eyes again, sat back, lit a cigarette with a shaking hand. 'There were three parts to it, a physical test, well, I did all right on that, not frightfully fit, but I can still thrash young Kit on the squash court, anyway, I passed that. And then there was a sort of psychological bit, had a kind of – oh, I don't know, an IQ test I suppose, had to do a presentation about myself in the mess, I think that was all right, I'm used to that after all.'

'So—'

'I'm pretty sure it was the leadership skills, the command task as they call it, that did for me.'

'What – what did you have to do?'

'Oh, they give you a test, you know, you have to get your men across a minefield. An imaginary one, that is, three planks and an oil drum sort of stuff. The irony is I think I might have passed it, I had quite a good scheme, but then there was another chap and he was so bloody persuasive, I gave in to his ideas. Which weren't as good as mine, they said at the time they lacked proper forethought, but I'd bet my life on him getting his commission.'

'How – terribly unfair,' said Helena. Thinking that that was precisely why Giles hadn't got his commission, because he was too easily persuadable, too lacking in confidence.

'Yes. Well, that's life. Or my life anyway. God, it's so humiliating. What on earth will my father say? As for my mother—' He stared at her, his eyes blank, almost fearful. 'Meanwhile, there's bloody Boy, straight into the Grenadier Guards as Captain, poncing round London on ceremonial duties; and young Jay, he's got his in a few weeks, no chance he won't pass.'

'So –' Helena hesitated. 'So what will you do? Have you been able to think yet?'

'Oh, yes,' he said. 'Yes, I've been able to think. I'm going to go in through the ranks. It's the only thing I can do, as far as I can see. Short of not going in at all, which isn't an option. What do you think about that, Helena? Married to a private, to one of the men, how does that make you feel? Pretty bloody proud, I daresay.'

'Actually,' said Helena quietly, taking his hand and kissing it, 'yes, actually it does.'

'You must be very – proud of him,' said Celia. She brought the words out clearly with an effort.

'I – I'm trying to be,' said LM.

'A commission in the Ox and Bucks,' said Oliver, smiling at her gently, 'jolly well done.'

'Yes. Yes, of course.'

'When does he go?'

'I don't know.' Her voice was flat, devoid of expression. 'He's doing his basic training now.'

'LM,' Celia went forwards, put her arm round her. 'LM, I know how awful you must feel. But—'

'No,' said LM almost coldly, 'no, you don't. Of course you're worried about Kit going into the air force. I appreciate that. But he even used the same words as Jago you know, about joining up. "Just try and stop me," he said. Extraordinary. And he says how he's always been lucky. Jago used to say that. I – I just don't think I can bear it, I'm afraid. I want to die myself.'

'LM! You can't talk like that. What would Gordon feel, if he heard you? Or Jay himself for that matter. We have to be brave for them, that's the one thing we can do.'

'I – can't be,' said LM, her voice low and shaky, 'I simply can't. I don't know what to do, Celia, I feel like screaming, begging him not to go. It just seems like so much stupidity, the waste of yet another young life. I love him so much, so very, very much. And all I can imagine is getting the telegram, standing there as I did last time, opening it, reading it, reading that Jay is – is – oh, God, help me.' She dropped her head into her hands, began to weep; Celia put her arms round her, stood looking down at her helplessly, biting her lip.

'LM, the best, indeed the only thing we can do for the young is set an example,' said Oliver slowly. 'I discovered that long ago. They don't listen to us, they find most of what we have to say at best tedious and at worst inane. We can influence them simply by what we do and how we do it. Now think about that. You can't send young Jay off to fight with an image of you crying helplessly, begging him not to go. He needs fine pictures, happy memories to carry with him, they are of immeasurable value. I should know.' He smiled suddenly at Celia; the old sweet smile. She smiled back, her face softening as she looked at him.

LM sat in silence for a long time; her head bowed. Then she stood up. 'Well, I – I still don't know how—'

There was a commotion along the corridor, shrieks and shouts of laughter; Venetia suddenly appeared in the doorway, her arm through Jay's. He was in uniform.

'Look what I just met in reception. Too thrilling. Home for forty-eight hours already. Our very own Lieutenant Lytton. Not even second lieutenant, isn't that marvellous? So dashing, don't you think? My God,

Jay, if we weren't related I could fancy you quite dreadfully. Well, I do fancy you quite dreadfully. LM, doesn't your son look marvellous, aren't you proud?'

LM looked at Jay for a long moment in silence; he looked older already, even taller, in his uniform, his face somehow thinner under his cropped hair. Then she smiled at him, the brilliant, rare smile that so transformed her plain face, and went over to him and hugged him.

'You do look marvellous, Jay. And I am terribly proud of you. How would you like to take your old mother out to tea at the Savoy, tell her all about military life?'

He bent to kiss her, took her hand and tucked it through his arm.

'Excuse us,' he said to the others, 'we've got a date.' And together they walked out of the room, LM smiling at him, fiddling with the buttons on his jacket. If anyone deserved the Military Cross, Celia thought, looking at them through rather blurred eyes, it was LM.

'Well done,' she said apparently inconsequentially to Oliver.

Telling his parents that he had failed to get a commission was one of the hardest things Giles had ever done.

He did it in the only way possible, simply and without fuss, making no apologies, offering no excuses, his eyes fixed firmly on his father's desk. But when he had finished, had said that in spite of it he felt he could still serve his country in as valuable a way as a private soldier, and looked up at them, he saw that his father was smiling at him, if rather sadly, and he reached out and patted Giles's hand, and instead of the contempt and disapproval he had expected to see in his mother's eyes, there was a certain softness and even pride.

'I think that's rather splendid of you, Giles,' she said, 'and in its own way extremely brave. Well done.'

She was nothing, Giles thought, smiling rather warily back at her, if not unpredictable.

It was terribly cold in Paris; it was cold everywhere, the coldest winter anyone could remember. The Channel had even frozen at Boulogne. There was ice inside the windows every morning in the apartment; Adele, struggling to keep the stove alight, fighting with the evil geyser, draping nappies over chairs, the window handles, anywhere they might dry, thought more longingly every moment of England, of Cheyne Walk, of warmth and comfort and – good temper. Luc was fearsomely bad-tempered; Adele was reminded every day of his warning that the cold made him miserable. She tried not to think of the warmth of his office at Constantine.

The children were miserable; little Noni had chilblains on her tiny fingers, and the daily trip out to the market had become a torment. Without Lady Beckenham's pram, it would have been far worse; but she tucked them both up in it, one at each end, and put the quilts from their cots over them, as well as an old mink coat of her own. She looked at it now, that coat, tucked in beneath them, and thought of it as it had been, wrapped round her spoilt self as she went on those other shopping expeditions, to Bond Street, to Harvey Nichols, to Harrods, seeking out some new dress or hat or pair of shoes, filling in her mornings until it was time for lunch, when she would leave it in the cloakroom at the Caprice or the Park Lane or Claridges, while she sat gossiping, toying with food she had not cooked or bought or even thought about. And then she would collect it, pull it round her again, hailing a taxi (in which she really did not need it) and returning to Cheyne Walk with it, where her maid would hang it next to the other two, the silver fox and the chinchilla, in her wardrobe. She could have done with those two now, to wear herself; she had a wool coat, which was quite warm, but there really was nothing like fur.

Everybody was far more obsessed with the cold than with the war and any possible danger from the Germans; people still for the most part persisted in saying there was no danger. There was the Maginot Line (work on which had been suspended because of the cold) and where that stopped, there was the Ardennes, a forest so thick it was virtually impenetrable, with one tiny road running through it. And beyond that, even supposing the Germans managed to get through it, was the vast, uncrossable River Meuse. No, they were quite safe. Everyone said.

Luc became hugely irritated with her when she tried to discuss any danger, when she mooted, however gently, that she and the children might be safer in England.

'You are safe here, Paris will never be invaded. And how will you get to England? Hitler will be bombing or torpedoing the ships.'

Adele found this rather at odds with his insistence that they were in little danger and said so: 'And anyway, no one's bombing anyone, Luc, everyone says it's a terrible anticlimax, the phony war, they're calling it in England, same as the *drôle de guerre* here, everyone rushing into air-raid shelters and gas masks, and then nothing happening.'

But Luc refused even to concede that she might be safer in

England; 'This is your home, you have French children, a French husband—'

'Not a husband, Luc. Sadly.'

A bitter row followed; ending in tears on her part, a mixture of self-reproach and remorse on his, and some rather distracted love-making: distracted on Adele's part at any rate, perpetually fearful as she was of another pregnancy and of one or both the children waking. But afterwards, lying in Luc's arms, warm for once, she thought that really she had a great deal to be grateful for. He did seem to love her and for some complicated reasons which she did not properly understand, she certainly loved him.

'So – are you enjoying military life?' said Venetia lightly, taking the cigarette Boy offered her. They were lunching at what was to become the bastion of London war-time life, the Dorchester, known to all its regulars as the Dorch: outwardly changed, the entrance covered by sandbags, the curtains lined with thick black cloth, the interior remained much the same. It was said to be the safest hotel in London, built as it had been of reinforced concrete; and the Turkish baths in the basement potentially a superb air-raid shelter.

Boy and Venetia's lunches there had actually become a regular occurrence, the excuse being that there was always so much to discuss: the reality that it afforded them both some rather perverse pleasure.

Of course, Venetia told herself, she was glad she had insisted on the divorce: and besides, this way she and Boy had somehow become better friends than they had been for some time. And he was clearly impressed by her job: not only that she was doing it but doing it extremely well.

'I might be enjoying military life if I was experiencing it,' said Boy slightly wearily now. 'I hadn't exactly expected to find myself changing the guard at Buckingham Palace—'

'As the song says.'

'Indeed. I can't see I'm doing a great deal for the war effort.'

'There doesn't seem to be much effort required; all that preparation and – nothing. No air raids, no bombs, all those trenches dug in the parks, all of us with our gas masks, and this ridiculous blackout, five more people run over last week, did you see – it's all quite a disappointment really.'

'I think when it does begin, you'll feel the opposite of disappointment,' said Boy. He smiled at her, but his eyes were heavy. 'Hitler is hardly going to lose interest in his scheme, say come on

359

everyone, settle down again, we've had our fun. I very much fear we shall hear a great deal of him yet.'

'Well – I suppose you must be right. But it is awfully quiet. Even the evacuees have come back to London. At this rate, Henry's school won't need to move.'

'It will. What's the latest on that?'

'The headmaster says they'd like to be at Ashingham for the spring term. Move over the Christmas holiday. But it won't be ready, Grandmama's fussing over the lavatories, and anyway, we agreed it did all seem a bit – pointless at the moment.'

'I think he's just trying not to alarm you. Nobody with any sense thinks this quiet will last for long. Champagne?'

'Yes, please. Well, it's hard to worry. Giles says they just sit in France listening to lectures on why they're fighting and wondering why they aren't.'

'At least he's in France,' said Boy gloomily. Venetia ignored him.

'And Kit's flying happily over Scotland, safe as a bird. It's wonderfully comforting for Mummy. She says she feels so much better about him now.'

'I'm sure if Hitler knew that, he'd forget all his plans,' said Boy lightly.

It was an odd Christmas; everyone felt guilty that they were not suffering more. The Lyttons were all at Ashingham with the exception of Helena who was with her parents. Venetia had gone down with the children and, at their passionate request, Boy, billeted firmly in the Dovecot by Lady Beckenham, who didn't quite approve of the arrangement. Barty, LM and Gordon were also there, and Jay, home on leave, and at the last minute Sebastian finally gave in to Izzie's importuning and joined them. The absence of Adele was felt; she had actually tried to persuade Luc to come over to England with her, but he had refused.

'It's all that nonsense with Mummy over the Jewish thing and her Fascist friends,' Adele wrote privately to Venetia. 'I'm afraid the hurt went very deep in spite of her apology. Have fun without me.'

They all raised their glasses to her, Venetia with tears in her eyes, and to her safety for which they were fearful.

There was much talk of Ashingham as a safe haven for the family as it had been in the last war.

'Although I have to say to you,' said Lady Beckenham, 'it is not as safe a haven as it was then. London has grown considerably nearer. And the bombing will undoubtedly be far, far heavier when it comes.'

'It's the safest we've got,' said Boy. 'And I think it should be pretty safe. The fact of the matter is there's no telling what will happen. We just have to – hope.'

'We got pretty good at that last time,' said Lady Beckenham, 'not much else to do really. Now about this school. The main problem will be the lavatories. There are only two on the nursery floor, which is where the dormitories are to be. And then another one down on our floor, but that's ours and Beckenham spends half his time in it anyway. We'll have to do a conversion, have some extra lavatories installed. I'm sure the school can afford it. Or would we get a grant from the government?'

'Either way,' said Celia, 'you won't be able to get it done. It's just like the last war, there aren't any useful men left.'

'Billy and I could do it for you,' said Jay cheerfully. 'When I was working here before, on the roof, we learned all about plumbing.'

'I doubt it very much,' said Lady Beckenham. 'It's a complicated job, not like putting up a few partitions or slates. Anyway, you won't be here. I can see the whole plan being scuppered. Damn shame.'

'No, wait. That chap – what was his name, Bill, the plumber?'

'Barber,' said Billy. He had joined the party for Christmas lunch as he always did when Barty was there. 'But he'll have joined up, surely.'

'That's the fellow. Anyway, Mrs Barber is a plumber as well, apparently. He told me, he sort of apprenticed her, taught her everything. She'll do it for you, I bet, if Mr Barber isn't around.'

'Jolly good idea,' said Lord Beckenham. 'Woman plumber eh? Is she pretty?' he added hopefully.

'Might have been once,' said Jay, winking at Billy. 'She's fifty now if she's a day.'

'It is possible to be fifty and not entirely ill-looking,' said Celia coldly.

'She sounds ideal,' said Lady Beckenham. 'Ask her to come and see us after Christmas, would you, Billy?'

Billy did; and not only Mrs Barber arrived to do the plumbing work in the New Year, but also her daughter, Miss Barber, who was as pretty as Lord Beckenham or indeed anyone else might have hoped. Rather more importantly, she was as competent as her mother, working long hours in the freezing conditions of Ashingham; by late February, the new lavatories had been installed, a neat row of six, situated next to the

361

vast bathroom on the first floor. 'The pipe run will be far easier than at the top of the house, your ladyship. And I would suggest a couple of showers could be fitted in without too much difficulty. Otherwise you'll never get them all clean.'

Lady Beckenham agreed that indeed she wouldn't, and commissioned the work; Billy Miller then suggested a second pair of showers be installed on the ground floor next to the utility room while they were about it, thus ensuring further opportunities for cleanliness for the small boys, further work for the Barbers and for Billy continued access to Miss Barber, whose name was Joan. By the spring, romance was definitely in the well-sanitised air.

Kit had never been so happy. Which was saying quite a lot. In a life which might have been considered charmed and had certainly been hugely agreeable, he had never found much cause for complaint. But as the freezing winter eased into early spring, and the skylarks and kestrels rose into the dazzling clear blue sky above the Scottish moorland he felt very close to heaven. Flying was all he had ever dreamed of, bestowing a freedom and a power which was quite literally heady.

As he took off for the first time, as his plane had slightly shakily lifted into the air, as the ground beneath him shrank away, as he looked ahead of him and saw nothing, nothing but sky, he couldn't help it: he shouted with excitement again and again, laughing with pure pleasure. And he never quite became used to it, the pleasure never even began to stale. Riding the clouds, swooping along the tops of forests and hills following roads and tracks (as sure a guide, once you got to know them, as any map), he felt inviolate, exhilarated, absolutely in command. This was his element, this great sweep of space, this was where in some way he belonged. On the days he did not fly, he felt odd, slightly bereft; restored to it, to his kingdom, he relaxed and came alive again.

It was glorious; even on rough days, bumpy days, he felt the same sense of ease and comfort, of being absolutely in the proper place. He gained his wings with absurd ease; he had a natural sense of navigation, found the instrument panel with its complex bank of information, simplicity itself; and he had a feeling for the plane, it was as if it were an extension of himself, he could guide it through storms, thick cloud, keep it steady in strong winds. On complicated exercises, switching suddenly from following in convoy to flying entirely independently using instruments, he found the transition easier, less confusing than most of his fellow pilots, seldom dived or found himself upside down

– except by choice. Nothing was more fun than that: looping the loop, turning full turtle, they all loved it, would have spent hours at it had they been allowed.

As the winter of the phony war went on, all of them longed for action; finally in March their squadron was ordered down to Biggin Hill near Bromley in Kent. The name meant little to them; they had no inkling that it would become as evocative and emotive as other famous stage-settings for the war, Dunkirk, Arnheim, and the beaches of Normandy.

Kit and most of his squadron were to fly the comparatively new Spitfire: the already legendary plane, with the same engines as the Hurricanes but with far less weight; it could climb with incredible speed – 'Twenty thousand feet in eight minutes,' Kit wrote proudly to Celia, 'and it can do 362 miles an hour. Marvellous in a dogfight. And don't worry, the cockpit is made of bullet-proof glass.'

Celia did not find this totally reassuring.

But Kit had another reason for wanting to leave Scotland, another reason for his intense happiness; he was in love. Catriona MacEwan was the daughter of the local doctor in Caldermuir, the nearest village to the base: not quite eighteen years old, dark-haired, blue-eyed, about to leave home to train as a nurse at the Edinburgh Infirmary, she had met Kit at a dance in the village hall. It had been love at first sight. He had had girlfriends of course, but they had been little more than that, friends who were also girls, whose prettiness and company gave him pleasure, whose hands he had held, and whose faces he had kissed. The extraordinary absorption of his head and his heart, the sense of absolute happiness in Catriona's company, the heady physical desire she created in him, had much in common with what he felt in his plane, a sense of rightness, of finding something he had been looking for.

They did no more than kiss and caress; they were young, virginal, respectful of one another and the mores of the time. Nevertheless, the kissing was passionate, powerful, hungry; and the caressing increasingly exploratory; as Catriona had said rather shakily one night, removing Kit's hand gently but firmly from the top of her thighs, they'd be in trouble soon if they weren't going to be separated. And then she had burst into tears when Kit told her the separation was only forty-eight hours away.

Luc was late again: it was really too bad, Adele thought, she had cooked dinner for seven o'clock as he had requested, indeed she had got the children to bed early, because Mme André had suggested they might like to go out, 'just for a drink perhaps, or to the cinema, *Carnet de Bal* is at the Odeon, so beautiful, you would enjoy it so much'.

Mme André was very fond of Adele; she worried about her lonely, clearly difficult life. She had observed the mink coat, the visits of her mother, the grand old pram; clearly Adele was born to better things.

Moreover she did not particularly like Luc; he had been charm itself when he took on the lease to the apartment, but since then he had scarcely troubled to pass the time of day with her. No doubt he thought she was a silly old woman; but like all concierges, Mme André prided herself on her ability to observe. And she had observed an increasing tendency in Luc to be home later and later at the end of the day, and once or twice, not until midnight or after. There could only be one explanation for such behaviour: she was very much afraid that Mam'selle Adele was being deceived.

Adele on the other hand was not in the least afraid that she was being deceived; for the simple reason that she knew Luc could not possibly afford it. There was no money available for courtship of the most modest kind. He had to support her and their children, and he had to support the demanding and petulant Suzette in her warm and comfortable apartment; any girl looking for more than the occasional *apéritif* was going to be extremely disappointed. If she felt any jealousy, any resentment towards a third party in their partnership, it was of Luc's work; if he was not at home, then he was to be found at the warm and comfortable offices of Constantine et Fils in the beautiful building on Boulevard Haussmann. That was his mistress, that was where he was unfaithful to her, it was for the warmth and comfort and interesting conversation there that he neglected his *chère famille*. Of that she was quite, quite sure.

Such conviction illustrated more graphically than anything the Englishness of Adele Lytton, and the lack of understanding she still showed of the French philosophy.

'I must leave,' said Luc with a sigh, looking at the clock on the bedroom mantelpiece, 'my dinner is waiting.'

'Only your dinner? You look tired, Luc.'

'I am tired. Very tired. It is not easy, working so hard, and then, the untidy apartment, the broken nights. I fear Adele is not quite the housekeeper I had hoped.'

'She is English. I could have warned you.'

'You could and you should. But – it is too late now.'

'Luc! It is never too late. You of all people should know that. Nothing is irreversible.'

'Not even two children?'

She shrugged. 'Of course not. Send her home to England, that is what she wants. She will be happier there.'

'But – I love those children. Very much. They are beautiful, charming, clever.'

Another shrug. 'Then I cannot help you. It is irreversible.' She moved her hand down, started to caress him, smiled as she felt the inevitable happen.

'Suzette—'

The dinner would have to wait; he abandoned himself to pleasure. It was extraordinarily good not to have to worry about children waking and crying, to be in this warm and charming apartment – he had forgotten quite how charming it was.

Finally he said he must leave, sat on the edge of the bed, lit a Gauloise; she put out a hand, took it from his lips, inhaled it and gave it back, returned to caressing his back.

'You are thin, *chéri*.'

'Well – life is difficult. For all of us of course, but particularly for me. Adele doesn't seem to understand how many sacrifices I have to make for her.' He sighed, looked down at her, at her naked body, started to caress her breasts. 'We should have had our own children, Suzette. As you often suggested. I should have been less selfish. It could all have been so different then.'

The day before Kit left Scotland, he had time off; he took Catriona for a walk over the hills at the top of the village. She was quiet, clearly upset; his own mood was more upbeat.

'You're excited, aren't you?' she said finally, clearly half resentful, and he said, almost shamefaced, yes, he was, he couldn't help it, at last he was going to be able to do what he had been trained to do.

'So am I. But I'd rather stay here with you. I suppose that's the difference between men and women.'

'I – suppose it is. I'm sorry – darling.' He used the endearment almost nervously; he hadn't said it to her before.

She smiled up at him, clearly moved; she slipped her small hand into his. 'It's all right. I understand. It's natural. Oh, Kit, when shall I see you again?'

'On my very first leave,' he said, ignoring details like the vast

365

distance between London and Edinburgh, the cost and time involved in travelling it, 'and I'll write to you every day.'

'Don't say that,' she said. 'You won't be able to, and then I shall worry more.'

He turned to her, touched by such tender logic.

'Well – I'll write whenever I can.'

'That's better.'

'I love you,' he said simply, looking into her blue eyes. 'I love you so much. And you're so beautiful.'

'I love you too.'

And then suddenly, because he loved her so much, and because parting from her was so suddenly and intensely painful, looking for some way to ease it, he said, 'I would like us to be – that is, I wonder if—' and stopped, and she looked up at him and smiled her sweet gentle smile and said, 'Wonder what, Kit?'

'You know what I think,' he said, 'you know, don't you?'

And, 'Yes,' she said, 'yes, I do know.'

'And – what do you say?'

'I say yes. Yes, yes, yes.'

'So – we're engaged?'

'Yes, we are. Unofficially of course.'

'Of course. I haven't even got you a ring.'

'It doesn't matter. I'll know. I love you, Kit.'

'I love you, Catriona.'

And so they parted, considering themselves promised to one another for ever, their only exchange of tokens being photographs and letters of love, identically worded and signed by each of them. Kit put his in the pocket of his shirt and told her it would be there always, next to his heart; Catriona, her blue eyes huge and dark with tears, said there would never be anyone else for her as long as she lived.

But as Kit flew south in the morning in a transport aircraft, his thoughts were more of the new life ahead of him than the one he had left behind, however sweet. It was the first of April. The war was about to properly begin.

Britain's first air raid had not been over London, or even Dover, but the Orkney Islands; a minuscule foretaste of what was to follow; then came Germany's invasion of Norway and Denmark. The British defence failed miserably and the whole affair was dreadfully bungled. As a result, Chamberlain's majority in the Commons was reduced to an unmanageable level; within days Churchill had become Prime

Minister and first the House of Commons, then the country listened for the first time to the extraordinarily powerful voice that was to drive it through the next five years. Brutal in its honesty, rough in its sincerity, but absolutely inspirational, it promised them 'nothing but blood, toil, tears and sweat in the quest for victory . . . however long and hard the road may be . . . Come then, let us go forward together, with our united strength.'

Celia, sitting by the wireless in a cold and growing terror, thinking of Giles in France, of Boy, at last preparing to leave, of Jay, waiting impatiently to go, and above all of Kit, all of them sucked into this dreadful, fearsome vortex, felt strangely comforted even as she wept.

Chapter 27

'I think, my darling, that after all you should go home to England. You and the little ones. I am growing afraid for you.'

Luc's eyes were tender, liquid with concern; Adele felt a lump rise in her throat.

'Oh, Luc, no. I – I couldn't. Not now. This is my home, our children's home.'

'But – a dangerous one. Hitler is on the move now. I think it is wrong of me to keep you here. Selfish and wrong.'

'But – you don't think he'll invade France? Get to Paris?'

'God forbid. No, of course not. But – I want you safe. And there may not be so much time.'

Adele sighed; it would be wrong, wrong to leave Luc, to take her children away from him. They were married in all but name; he was her home, her family now. She had to remember that and be brave.

'No, Luc. I'm not going. Sorry. You can't get rid of me that easily.'

It was 9 May 1940.

'Mummy? You've heard the news? Of course you have, what a stupid question. Hitler's invaded Holland. And Belgium and Luxembourg. Oh, my God. It's begun, it's really begun. Boy was right.'

'When is he going?'

'Oh – any day now. Dear God, I wish Dell was here.'

'No more than I do.'

'We should get the children down to Ashingham, don't you think? The girls, I mean.'

'Yes, I do. Any day now it could become very dangerous.'

'So – what are you going to do now?'

'Now?' Celia's tone made it very clear she thought the question absurd. 'I'm going to Lyttons. Obviously.'

It had got her through the last war, she thought, as she climbed the stairs to her beloved office; it would get her through this one. Here, within these walls, she could hide from reality, hide from her fears, tell herself that books, catalogues, bookshops, book tokens, were what mattered. As indeed they did; wars ended, life went on. You could not ease yourself into a vacuum, tell yourself that the only thing that mattered was the war. It didn't. It really, really didn't. Even when your youngest child was about to launch himself into the skies, into battle, in a plane that offered as little protection from the enemy and enemy fire as a motor bike. It wasn't the only thing . . .

Her phone rang.

'Celia?'

'Yes. Hallo, Sebastian.'

'You must be very worried. I just wanted to tell you I was here. Thinking of you. And of Kit. Holding your hand. Notionally.'

'You might have to come and do it literally,' she said.

It was 10 May.

'My darling! You're not still here.'

It was Cedric, looking dazzling, sitting near the fountains in the Place St-Sulpice in white flannels and white shirt, blond curls grown longer, accompanied by an equally beautiful, equally blond youth.

'Of course I'm still here,' she said, putting the brake on the pram, throwing herself into his arms. 'How lovely to see you.'

'And you. As beautiful as ever. This is Philippe. Philippe Lelong. Immensely talented photographer. We could have done with you today, darling. We've been working for *Style*. We needed six perambulators, and six miniature poodles to put in them. Not easy. You would have dealt with it in a trice.'

Not a trice, thought Adele, a pang of longing for her old life clutching at her, but she would have found them.

'It sounds wonderful. What fun.'

'It wasn't, it was quite dreadful. Anyway, absolutely my last job for *Style*. Or indeed anyone else in Paris. I'm bolting home, like a frightened bunny. I've been trying to persuade Philippe to come too, but he says I'm being foolish, that the dangers are hugely exaggerated.'

'Of course they are,' said Adele. 'I wouldn't dream of leaving. The Germans will never reach Paris.'

'I wish I had your confidence. But I'm playing safe.'

'Is English *Style* still running its letter from Paris?' asked Adele. 'I never see it these days.'

'It most certainly is. Philippe is their most valued contributor at the moment, so wonderfully good at gossip. Why don't you offer your services for that at least, my darling? They'd love it.'

'I'm afraid the only gossip I have is what I pick up in the children's playground at the Luxembourg Gardens,' said Adele. 'Not what they want. Oh, Cedric, it's so nice to see you. Are you really worried about the situation here?'

'Of course I am, darling.' He sounded stern, almost cross. 'So would you be, if you had any sense at all.'

'Well, maybe I haven't. Noni, not too near the road, my angel.'

'What an exquisite little creature,' said Philippe Lelong suddenly. 'May I take a couple of photographs of her?'

'Well, of course. Here, now? Noni, you wouldn't mind that, would you, darling? This gentleman wants to take your picture.'

Noni smiled at him, her rather slow, solemn smile. 'No.'

'*Bon*. Then let us have her over here, against the fountains. Smile, little one, that's the way – and again here, now—'

'I will send you a copy,' he said, when he had finished, 'Cedric will give me your address.'

'Of course. I live just along there, actually.' She pointed down the street. 'See on the left, big black door. But yes, Cedric has the proper address. Thank you so much. Now I must go. Cedric, give my love to everyone, and could you tell Venetia I'm perfectly all right, and don't, whatever you do, say you think it's dangerous. They all fuss so. So silly.'

'So sensible, in my view. But no, I shall be terribly bright and breezy about it all. Have you time for an aperitif, my darling?'

'Very sadly, no,' said Adele. 'Goodbye, darling Cedric. It was so lovely to see you, and to meet you, Philippe. I shall look forward to seeing the pictures of Noni. I'm sure they'll be divine.'

'They certainly will,' said Cedric. '*Au revoir, mon ange*. Look after yourself.'

'I will,' said Adele. She kissed him again, and felt horribly sad as she watched them walk off together across the street.

'I – thought I'd like to buy you dinner,' said Boy. 'I'm off tomorrow.'

'Tomorrow! Oh, God. Where to—'

'Somewhere in the north of Scotland. I've volunteered for some commando-type training. Can't tell you any more than that.'

'And what – what exactly will you be doing?'

'I don't know – exactly. Might even see some action quite soon. There's talk of raids on Norway. Needless to say, that is absolutely confidential information.'

'Of course.'

'It sounds pretty exciting, doesn't it?'

'I suppose so,' she said fretfully. 'Oh, Boy, I'm so frightened. For the children and Giles and Kit. And Adele of course, so terribly frightened for her, I wish she was home—'

'What about me? Aren't you frightened for me?'

'Yes,' she said, and was surprised by how much, 'yes, and for you.'

They had dinner at the Savoy; it was exceptionally busy, everyone dressed beautifully. Venetia was wearing a new beaded black dress – 'Probably the last new dress for a long time,' she said when Boy admired it.

He smiled at her, looked round the room. Everyone was chattering, greeting friends, dancing: no one who had not known would have dreamed there was a war on.

But Boy was quiet, slightly distracted; they danced a couple of times, then he said, 'Can we sit down?'

'Of course.' She looked at him, across the table, so immaculate as always in his dinner jacket, so unusually serious. 'So – how do you feel?'

'Oh – bit odd, really. Excited, in a way; relieved it's actually starting, that I finally can get a crack at the whip—'

'And – scared?' she said gently. 'Aren't you scared at all?'

'Oh – a bit,' he said, smiling at her, 'yes, of course. Only a fool would be otherwise. I might not come back, I might come back wounded, I might not conduct myself as I would like—'

'Of course you will,' said Venetia, 'you always do. I've never known anyone as in control of themselves as you are – with the possible exception of Mummy. She's terribly brave too,' she added. 'Probably the bravest person I know. Sebastian often says that.'

'Indeed? Well, he should know.'

'Why do you say that?' she said, intrigued, but his face became an immediate blank.

'No reason; champagne talking.'

'Liar.'

'Well, that I certainly am. As you know.'

'Yes. I suppose I do.' She pushed her fork round her plate; somehow she wasn't hungry.

'I'd like you to be out of London really,' he said.

'Oh, Boy, I can't. I've got a job to do. I want to do that, it's become important to me.'

'You're quite – brave too, I think,' he said, looking at her. 'It was one of the things I always – admired about you.'

371

'Me? Don't be silly. What did I ever do that was brave?'

'All sorts of things. Stood up to your mother for a start. Insisted on marrying me. Big mistake as it turned out.'

'Well—'

'And then you had all those babies.'

'All women have babies.'

'Yes, and a lot of them make a frightful fuss, I'm told. Not a squeak out of you, by all accounts. And then you were always amazing, out hunting—'

'Boy, when did you last see me hunting?'

'It may be a while ago. But I've never forgotten, certainly not the first time I saw you. At Ashingham, you've probably forgotten, you took one most incredible fence on that little horse of your mother's – what was she called?'

'Oh – must have been Butterfly. She did fly too.'

'Yes, that's right. I just watched you, open-mouthed, practically came off myself—'

'You never said—'

'Didn't I? Probably too overcome. Anyway, life rather overtook us after that, didn't it? All those babies, my bad behaviour—'

'Oh dear,' said Venetia. She brushed her hand across her eyes.

'What? What is it?'

'Oh – I don't know. So much time gone, so many mistakes – and now—'

'I—' He stopped, staring into his glass.

'What, Boy? What is it?'

'Oh – nothing.'

She was intrigued; she had never seen him nervous, at a loss for words. 'There must be something.'

'No – well, that is—' He took a deep breath, then began to talk, speaking very fast. 'There is something. Something I wanted to say. I don't know if you'll believe me. Or if this is what – what you want to hear. But I decided I couldn't go away maybe for – well, for a long time – without telling you that I still – still love you. It was important to me, Venetia. That's all.'

'Oh,' she said. She felt very surprised, shocked even. 'Oh, I see.'

'I know I've given you an awful time. I'm very ashamed of it. I wanted to say that too.'

Rage hit Venetia: hot, violent rage. It was so easy, so horribly easy for him. Behave badly all their married life, and then suddenly, because it suited him, because he was going away, tell her he loved her.

Just like that. And that he was ashamed of himself. As if it could negate all the wrong, that easily, that quickly. She stared at him, feeling her face flush.

'Look—' he said. 'I can see I've upset you. It was a bit crass, I should have gone off quietly, I suppose. I mean, I certainly didn't expect you to suddenly throw yourself into my arms, say you forgive me.'

'No,' she said, 'no, I should hope not.'

There was silence; finally he stood up.

'I'm sorry. Bad idea. This whole thing. If you want to go home, I'll quite understand.'

'I – yes, I think perhaps I would. I really can't cope with this, I'm afraid.'

'Of course not. I'm sorry. So sorry.'

When she got home, she went into her sitting room, and lit a cigarette; gradually her anger eased and she felt dreadfully unhappy instead. Unhappy and hurt, newly, freshly hurt. She looked at one of the few photographs that she had kept of herself and Boy, not on their wedding day, those had all been put away, but at Henry's christening, taken by Adele, both of them laughing, looking at one another and Henry's small, sleeping face between them. They looked so happy: but had they been? Happy memories; was that what happiness actually was, never now, only then, in the past where you could pick your time, say then, yes, that was it, that was safe?

There were happy memories with Boy, of course, some very happy ones; but they were fragmented, blurred with unhappiness. She remembered one sharply suddenly; when he had come to her, after Roo had been born, had sat down on her bed, and kissed her and said simply, 'Thank you.' She had felt happy then, terribly happy and so safe.

Safe: it was something none of them would be for a long time now. A precious, half-forgotten thing; danger would fill their lives, all of them, it would surround them, never leave them alone.

And then she thought of Boy, going away tomorrow into terrible dreadful danger, and in spite of everything, she wished she could keep him from it. She kept seeing him again, sitting at the table, so uncharacteristically nervous and quiet, saying the last thing she had expected, the last thing she would have wanted. Or would she? Was she really so angry, and if so, why? And would she be glad tomorrow she had sent him away crushed, unhappy, when he had so clearly struggled to say what he had, and had meant, at that moment anyway, everything he had said? What good would that do her, to reject him, rebuff him, send him away: how would she live with herself, come to terms with that, over the months and years ahead when he was in danger, when he might be injured, taken prisoner, possibly, quite possibly killed? And then she had the thought, and having had it, sat for a little longer, at first very serious and then smiling to herself; she crossed the room and picked up the telephone and dialled Boy's number in his flat in Pont Street.

He probably wouldn't be there of course, was probably finding comfort with someone else, comfort from his fear, it was ridiculous of her to even expect it.

But he was there.

'I just thought,' she said carelessly, as if he were a friend, someone she hardly knew, someone she was inviting to dinner, 'I just thought if you had nothing else to do, you might like to come round for a drink. Or something.'

'That would be very nice, yes, thank you,' he said, as if he were accepting an invitation to dinner, and she knew that he was absolutely aware of what she was actually saying. 'I'd like that very much. Very much indeed.'

It was extraordinary, what took place between them that night: everything was there, tenderness, violence, sweetness, familiarity, even discovery. She would not have believed it possible, that this man, with whom she had had four children, shared almost ten years of marriage, could possibly lead her into this new place, further, higher, deeper than she could ever remember; it was as if he wanted to reach, to explore, to savour every part of her, imprint himself upon her, and her on to him. And when it was finally over, and they lay holding one another, shaken, almost shocked by what they'd achieved and where they had been, she felt tears on her face, and realised they were his; and realised too that the terrible ghosts of unhappiness had been sent away and that whatever became of them now, they had this, this extraordinary physical memory to sustain them.

'I love you,' was all he said over and over again, stroking her hair; and, 'I love you too, Boy,' she said, and fell asleep, smiling.

In the morning he was gone: leaving only a note on his pillow that said, 'I couldn't bear to say goodbye again.'

And then it was Venetia's turn to weep.

Well, this was it. At last. Today. He was going. Over to France, to meet the Luftwaffe.

He had dressed carefully, absolutely according to instructions: in his blue shirt (Catriona's letter carefully tucked into the left breast-pocket), a spotted cravat into the neck – they all wore cravats, he'd told his mother, and she'd sent half a dozen, in silk, all different colours – thick trousers tucked into his boots – 'cold up there, never forget' – leather helmet and gloves – 'you'll need those, chaps, save your hands from being burned' – goggles, Mae West jacket: he slung his parachute pack over his shoulder, looked out of the small window above his bed at the blue sky, took a deep breath: and then, quite suddenly, had to run to the lavatory where he was violently sick. Again and again.

He emerged shaking, slightly groggy on his legs, walked back into the mess, hoping, praying, no one would have observed or heard him, witnessed this terrible rush of fear. But: 'Throwing up, were you?' said a sympathetic voice. It was one of the older chaps, twenty-five he was, an RAF regular, they'd done some of their training down here with him.

'Oh – it was nothing,' said Kit quickly. 'Bit too much beer last night, I expect.'

'Yes, I expect it was. Well, don't worry about it. It gets to us all – the beer. Come on, old boy, we're flying in convoy. Stay close to me, you'll be fine. All right now?'

'Yes, thank you very much,' said Kit politely.

Barty looked at Wol; he was sitting in his wheelchair, behind his desk, his blue eyes, faded now, fixed on her.

'Barty, my dear, I know you want to go and join one of the women's services.'

'Yes, I do. The ATS, I thought. It appeals to me most—'

'Well, I would ask you not to go just yet.'

'But, Wol—'

'No, let me finish. There is a – a great deal to be done here. We are somewhat bereft already and it will get worse. Giles is gone, of course, and Jay and—'

'Edgar Greene is still here. And you, and Celia and LM and Venetia and—'

'Of course. But the main strength of the staff is gone. And a challenge lies before us. To keep Lyttons going through the war. It won't be easy. Already there is the paper shortage, we are not to be exempt from rationing, you know, we're allowed exactly 60 per cent of last year's consumption. And costs are rising dreadfully, we have to pay for war risk insurance and—'

'Wol, I'm sorry. I do know all this, and of course I want Lyttons to survive. I'm sure it will. But I can't see it as being terribly important to the war effort. I'm sorry, I know that must sound like heresy to you. But I don't feel it's right for me to sit here, launching new titles and proofreading catalogues, while Hitler is advancing on us day by day. I want to go. Well I am going. I'm –' her lips twitched '– I'm not seven any more, Wol. Or even seventeen. I'm thirty-two. Just give me your blessing – please.'

He sat looking at her for a moment in silence; then leaned forward, his hands folded, rather as if he were in prayer, she thought.

'Barty,' he said. 'Please. Wait a little while. Do this for me. And for Celia. Please.'

'But—'

'Three of our children are in grave danger. Kit is flying now, Giles is somewhere in France, Adele is in Paris, God knows what will become of her. If you go as well, I fear for Celia.'

'For Celia!'

'Yes. She is afraid as I have never seen her. I would go so far, indeed, as to say I've never seen her afraid at all. But this time, she is in danger of breaking. I hate to do this, Barty, but I'm going to. Ask you to stay here with us, at least for a while. She – we love you so much. Don't give us further cause for fear.'

'Wol, I—'

'Barty, I beg you.' The voice was hollow with emotion. 'I am literally begging you. Do it for us, Barty, please.'

She turned and looked at Wol; his eyes were fixed on hers, pleading with her. It wasn't fair; he had done this before, used this emotional blackmail many times, and she wasn't going to give in this time. She had a task to perform, talents to offer, a love for her country and a desire to help defend it, far more important than the Lyttons and their demands.

And then he reached out for his pen, and he couldn't quite reach it, neither could he get his wheelchair any closer to the desk, and he sat there, looking helplessly at it, biting his lip, refusing to ask any more of her, even so small a thing. And suddenly she knew she couldn't do it, couldn't hurt him any more: not now, not for a while. 'All right, Wol,' she heard herself saying, to her own despair, moving forward, handing him the pen. 'I will stay. For a little longer, anyway. You can tell Celia I won't be going yet.'

It was 18 May.

'Luc, there is something I have to tell you. I – that is, I think I might be pregnant.'

'Pregnant!'

'Yes. I hope you will not be too cross with me. I—'

'Have you seen the doctor?' Panic gushed into his throat, he felt faint, he was going to be sick—

'Not yet. I wanted to tell you. But – what do you think, Luc? Are you pleased?'

'I don't know what I feel, Suzette,' he said, 'I really don't.'

It was a beautiful spring. The dreadful cold was an ugly memory: the city was alive again, smiling in the sunshine. Adele, pushing the children down the Rue de Seine, felt suddenly, fiercely happy. The chestnuts were out along the boulevards, the cafés were on the pavements again, pretty girls in flowered dresses sat sipping *citron pressé* or red wine, men pushed one another good-naturedly out of the way to sit with them.

She crossed the Quai Malaquais, heaved the old pram up on to the new Pont des Beaux Arts and pushed it across the river; it shone, a blue and silver ribbon, in the sunshine. She stopped, pointed out a barge to the children; the bargee saw them, waved up at them.

'He's nice,' said Noni, waving back, smiling. She spoke English to her mother, French to her father. Lucas still spoke very little of anything.

'Everyone in Paris is nice,' said Adele, foolish with optimism.

Of course there was worrying news. The invasion of Holland and Belgium was not good, there was talk of the Germans making their way through the Ardennes – but that couldn't be true, everyone said, they couldn't possibly, the French line would hold.

There were certain signs of change in the city; Cartier had removed a picture of King Leopold of the Belgians to mark French displeasure at the Belgian surrender and had inserted one of Queen Mary instead; large numbers of people were admittedly leaving Paris and moving south although the general view held by those who stayed was that there was no good reason for it, with no real place to go; there were a great many refugees arriving in the city every day from Belgium and Holland and then being moved on in their turn to the Loire district, and there were three meatless days a week in restaurants, three days when only wine could be served, nothing stronger, and three days without pastries. But food was still plentiful in the markets, the theatres were full, there was a new Cocteau comedy at the Bouffes which was a smash hit, a new production of *Cyrano de Bergerac* at the Comédie Française and chic audiences still went for champagne at the Ritz before curtain-up.

A hugely glamorous English and American colony lived at the Ritz: Mrs Reginald Fellowes and her family; Mrs Corrigan, the millionaire socialite (so rich that she put real Cartier lighters and cigarette cases in her party tombolas); Lady Mendl; the Duke and Duchess of Windsor were frequent visitors from their permanent residence in Antibes; Noël Coward attended the Molyneux Spring collection and *Vogue* itself had reported in its May issue that Paris was 'an attractive, comfortable, normal city'.

Adele clung to all this, along with most of Paris, and allowed herself to feel safe.

There were two new gardens of flowers on the embankments, filled with tulips; wonderful brilliant colours. Adele lifted Noni out of the pram, let her run over and admire them. She was such a good child, she would never try and pick them or pull the petals off; it was touching, her goodness, especially in the tiny flat, as if she knew it was required of her that she be as quiet and as untroublesome as possible.

Luc had been – odd lately. Not quite himself. Distracted, worried – he said it was about the war – but gentler, better tempered. He still kept urging her to go home, but she wasn't taking any notice. They were happier, doing better together; she wasn't going to be panicked out of her marriage – well, that's what it was really – by anyone. Certainly not Adolf Hitler.

'Mother? Mother, it's me. Kit.'

'Kit? Oh, my darling, how are you, what are you—'

'Absolutely splendid, thanks. Enjoying myself tremendously.'

'You really are? And not – not wounded, haven't been shot at or anything?'

'Of course not. Don't be ridiculous. We're giving them hell. Don't worry about a thing. Least of all me. Oh – got to go. Bye, Mother. Love to Father.'

The fact that 206 of 474 British planes had already been lost seemed absolutely irrelevant.

A telegram from the French Prime Minister Paul Reynaud had been sent to Churchill: 'The way to Paris is open. Send all the troops and planes you can.'

It was 20 May.

'These people are pathetic,' said Celia scornfully. 'Can you imagine our people behaving like this? Queen Wilhelmina, the Grand Duchess of Luxembourg, the government of Belgium, all running away, going into exile. While our Queen won't even send her own children away, says they must all stay with the King, and quite right too. They're an example to us all, the royal family. We're lucky to have them: them and Churchill of course.'

Oliver looked at her. She read the look.

'I know. I know, Oliver. You don't have to say anything.'

'I wasn't going to. Except that I see Tom Mosley has been imprisoned.'

'Yes,' she said and her voice was low. 'Yes. I know. Yesterday. It was this article in *Action* that did it, I've got it here, he offered to lead people into peace by cooperation. Well, prison is where he should be. It's appalling. Terrifying. And you know they say the Duke of Windsor was of the same mind. Which is worse. Supposing he were still King?'

'Well, we must all thank God that he is not. Tell me, what does your friend Lord Arden think about it all now?'

'Oh—' She looked back intently at the magazine. 'I don't really know, Oliver. I haven't spoken to him for months.'

'I see,' said Oliver.

It was 23 May.

'Do you – do you think Giles might be there?' said Helena.

She was working at Guys Hospital and had gone into Lyttons on her way home to see if Celia or Oliver had any news, her fear for him overcoming any other emotion; they were in Celia's office, staring at the paper, at photographs of men on the beach at Dunkirk – an aerial photograph, the men looking like so many flies. Defenceless flies. Being dive-bombed by German planes. The report was of the men cut off from the rear, of a long route march from Belgium, of abandoned vehicles, of the absolute unthinkable, the British Army in defeat.

'I don't know,' said Celia, and she did another equally unthinkable thing, and gripped Helena's hand. 'I suppose so, yes.'

It was 27 May.

It was several months before Helena heard the full story of Giles's experiences at Dunkirk; not from him, he gave her a rather modestly brief account, but from one of his men. In one of life's more determined coincidences Private Collins had arrived at Guys with a head injury; he was in one of the wards she worked on with her Red Cross trolley. Once he had recovered from the shock of the coincidence – 'Blow me down, that is, well, fancy you being Private Lytton's wife, blow me down, I can't ruddy believe it' – he gave her in close detail the story of the four dreadful days they had spent there.

'I don't know what we'd have done without your husband, Lits we used to call him, and that's the truth. Bloody marvellous he was, pardon my French, Mrs Lytton. Him and Sergeant Collingham kept us all sane. You know Sergeant Collingham, do you, Mrs Lytton?'

'I do now, yes,' said Helena.

It was Tom Collingham, one of the farmboys at Ashingham whom Giles had played with as a child, and who had later taught him to shoot rabbits, who had done much to ease his way into the difficult world of being an ex-Etonian private in the Wiltshires at the beginning of the war.

'Commanding officer, absolutely ruddy useless, young chap, one of the real toffs, still wet behind the ears, not much older than me. No end of airs and graces we had from him. OK when things was all right, used to come and give us pep talks, go on about king and country and all that baloney, but when it all began to go wrong – well, worse than blinking useless he was. I mean, your husband, Mrs Lytton, obviously he's a gentleman, what he was doing as a private, heaven only knows, but we didn't get none of that from him. Things had been pretty bad for days, while we were still supposed to be on the attack, we got the sense of no one knowing what they were doing, just wandering about, we seemed to be. Lits was pretty good then, Mrs Lytton, always cheerful, always brave, couple of times I saw him really taking one of the German soldiers on, face to face. Anyway, then came the order to abandon our vehicles and damage our weapons and dump them in the canal. We were retreating and it was bloody awful, I can tell you. Pardon my French again—'

'Corporal, I don't mind,' said Helena gently.

'Well, anyway, we were marching at night, not knowing where we were going, and morale was dreadful, you can imagine. A lot of the platoons seemed to have lost it altogether, no sense of order, but not ours. Sergeant Collingham was always there with us, bullying us if needs be, keeping us in line, talking to us, listening to us, making sure we ate what there was, telling us not to think about the tanks we could hear – we never knew if they was enemy or ours, you see. And your husband was one of the most cheerful, never down, used to organise little sing-songs, that sort of thing.'

'Yes, I see.'

'When we got to the beaches – well, it was hell. Not too strong a word, hell. The fire, the smoke, the noise, the noise of the planes and the bombs, men being hit, screaming with pain, nowhere to hide, just nowhere except in the sand and a fat lot of good that did. And we was hungry and thirsty too, after a bit. And the CO, he just went to bloody pieces. Started drinking, he was drunk all the four days, wandering about, talking rubbish. And our captain wasn't much better, we found 'im sitting in the sand dunes, hugging his teddy bear, crying. Well, Sergeant Collingham wasn't having that.

' "That's not doing anyone any good, sir," was all he said, but he really lost his temper, it was the only time I ever saw him do that. "Pull yourself together, sir," he said, and he snatched the teddy bear from him and hurled it away. It went on for days, four days we was there, I can't tell you what it was like; no food, precious little water, you heard awful stories of soldiers shooting one another for water; wouldn't have happened in our platoon, I can tell you. Each night, we'd ask Lits to organise one of his sing-songs, and after it we'd say the Lord's Prayer. That was him started that, he was just saying it to himself quite quietly one night and a couple of us joined in, and after that it got to be quite a habit.

'Another time I saw him with one of the men, he was real bad, poor chap, had the shakes, and he sat down really gentle with him, put his arm round him and talked to him like he was his mother or something.'

'His mother?' said Helena. 'Well, good heavens.'

'Anyway, finally it was our turn. You had to line up on the beach then start wading out to the little boats. We was so tired, so hungry, you can't think. And then there was a lot of fighting over those little boats, people trying to get too many in each one. Sergeant Collingham wasn't having any of that of course: "You try that once more," he said to one chap, who was pushing to the front, "and it'll be the last thing you ever do."

'Your husband was standing right by him, waiting for his turn. It was awful standing there, you were being shot at and bombed all the time, and some of the men were so tired they couldn't even climb in the

381

boats, had to be heaved in, and that was happening out at sea as well, the men were too weak to climb up the ropes into the big boats, and their clothes were so heavy with the water, they just fell down again. Anyway, just as we was nearly all in, into our little boat, a Stuka comes and strafes the beach. Sergeant Collingham got hit in the shoulder with a bit of shrapnel and goes under the water; he'd have drowned if it hadn't been for Lits. Still under fire, and weighed down with his rifle and pack, he dives under the water and drags Sergeant Collingham to the surface, heaves him into the boat in front of him, stands there calm and patient as anything while they settle him as best they can before getting in himself. I did hear he was recommended for the Military Medal for that; bloody shame he didn't get it. There's no justice in war, I can tell you that. But you should be real proud of him, Mrs Lytton, really proud.'

'I am,' said Helena, 'really very proud.'

Giles was still in England; the regiment had been posted to Salisbury to retrain. He had been made up to corporal to his immense pride, and was involved in training the new troops; that meant more to him than his (unsuccessful) recommendation for the Military Medal.

'Very sorry about that, Lytton,' his commanding officer had said, 'you should have got it. Typical of those bloody desk wallahs in London. Anyway, all the Dunkirk veterans think no end of you. Your day will come, I'm sure of it. Well done.'

When he came home now on leave, he was different, Helena noticed; less diffident, calmer, more authoritative even. She often reflected that if he had got his commission, he would have found it hard to cope, certainly at first, and the vicious circle of failure and fear of failure would have gone on. Their marriage was much better too; she felt a new admiration and respect for him.

How very ironic life was.

'Venetia? Venetia, it's me, Adele.'

'Adele – oh, God, are you all right, what's happening over there, why don't you come home, please, please, Dell, come home while you can—'

'I'm fine. I'm sorry I haven't phoned much lately, but it's so difficult, even to book a call. This is awfully crackly, can you hear me?'

'Pretty well. Now will you come home?'

'No, I can't. Honestly, I'm fine. Don't believe any of the nonsense you hear. Paris is going on just the same, it's perfectly peaceful, a few

382

people are leaving, well, quite a lot actually, but everyone says it's madness, they don't know where they're going or why—'

'But, Adele, you'd know, you'd be coming home to England.'

'Not very safe there from all accounts. Is Giles all right, do you know? And Kit?'

'Both fine. Giles was at Dunkirk, but he was all right, Kit's flying Spitfires and is winning the war single-handed.'

'And Boy?'

'Somewhere in Scotland. Adele, please – what does Luc say, surely he wants you out of Paris—'

'He – did seem a bit more keen. But the thing is, Venetia, we're getting on so much better, everything's fine, I just don't want to leave him or take the children away. This is my home now and I honestly feel perfectly safe. The news bulletins are all the same, nothing to worry about, the Army's holding its own. I'm sure the Government would warn us if there was a real danger. They're all still here, you know. I wish you could see Paris, it's all so normal, nothing's changed, well except for a few sandbags. Everyone's just getting on with their lives. Hallo – hallo! It's going. Give my love to everyone, don't worry, I'll be—'

The line went dead; Venetia burst into tears.

'*Mignonne*, I want you to go home. Very, very much. While it is still possible. The railways are becoming very crowded. I want you and the children to be safe.'

'Luc, it's absurd. You sound like Venetia, I managed to speak to her today. They're all fine, Giles was—'

'Adele, I want you to go. I am telling you, as your husband, that you are to go. I am going to get some tickets today—'

'Luc, no. Anyway, I'm sure it's too late, I'd never get across the Channel.'

'Not from Calais, no, you are right. But I could send you down to Bordeaux, there are still ships going from there.'

'Luc, have you looked at the railway stations recently? It's appalling, the battle every day for trains. Look, I'm happy here with you. I don't want to go.' She kissed him. 'Don't you understand? You should be pleased. Now stop fussing. It's such a lovely day. I shall take the children to the park or the river, have a picnic. Try to come home early, and we can go out for a walk, all of us.'

It was another perfect day. Paris was certainly very agreeable; there was far less traffic than usual, the roads were quiet.

Adele took the children for their picnic in the Luxembourg Gardens, wandered about the quiet streets, did some shopping and then went home again. By half past five both children were tired, ready for bed; it didn't look as if the walk *en famille* was likely to take place. Never mind; perhaps she and Luc would be able to go on their own. That would be even more of a treat. She would ask Mme André if she would come up, just for an hour.

It was a Friday; a good night for a drink. Friday, 7 June.

Luc was tired, very hot and extremely anxious. His life, always so orderly, had suddenly spun out of control. There was a very nasty war in Europe, the enemy was headed by a madman, and an anti-semitic madman at that, he had insufficient money, a wife who claimed she was pregnant, and a mistress with two children. Wherever he looked he was trapped. Whatever he did he was doomed.

Work was a nightmare too; Paris might still be buying books, but the rest of France was most certainly not. Constantine's profits were non-existent, its income decimated. Staff had been warned of redundancies. Not the directors – yet. But it seemed possible that in the foreseeable future he wouldn't even have a job.

He sighed, pacing the office; he had done no work for days.

If only, if only Adele had been less loyal, less courageous, had shown less of the damn British spirit. Then he could have got rid of her at least; she and the children would be safe, he could concentrate on Suzette and his problems with her.

Pregnant: how could she have done that to him? He had no doubt that it had been deliberate, the oldest trap in the book. He wasn't sure that he believed her, he was waiting for confirmation from the doctor. But if she was – he was a fool; an absolute fool.

Well, it had to be settled soon; he couldn't go on like this. Maybe he could order Adele home, assert his authority. But – she was right. It was too late. The scenes every day – at the Gare du Nord and the Gare de Lyon – were frightful, people fighting over seats, tickets, places; there were stories of children being separated from their parents, of old people being hurt in the crush, of women giving birth on the pavements. Her chances of getting even to Bordeaux were very slight. Maybe when this particular panic was over, he would be able to send her down to Bordeaux. And it would be over, most sensible people thought that. But—

Luc suddenly groaned aloud, put his head in his hands. It served him right; it all served him right. He was a fool and not only a fool, but an unpleasant one. He deserved all of it. He had seduced Adele quite ruthlessly – although he had always imagined she was more sophisticated, certainly would never have become pregnant. Or remained pregnant. He should have let her go to Switzerland that day, he regretted it now. But she had been so – beautiful. And so vulnerable. He had let himself believe he was truly in love with her. And then Suzette had always refused to have children, and the thought of a son – well, it had been irresistible.

But – going back to Suzette, allowing her to seduce him like that: it had been the warmth, the comfort, that had really seduced him, of course, the pleasure of being at home again, in his own well-ordered apartment. With no children crying, no washing hanging all over the place. But – again, it was too late now. His phone rang; it was Suzette.

'*Chéri*. Would you come for a visit? I am missing you, and Paris is a little empty, many of my friends have left, so stupid, I think—'

'Suzette, I don't think so, no.'

'But why not? What harm would it do? You can be back with – with her' – Suzette always refered to Adele as *her* – 'by nine. Just a glass of champagne. I have some perfectly chilled. Just right for this hot evening.'

Luc hesitated; then the vision of the chilled champagne, the quiet, luxurious apartment, was too much for him.

'Very well,' he said, 'but just for a glass.'

The children were asleep; fast asleep. Adele looked at the clock; only six. It could be an hour, maybe longer, before Luc was home; a waste of good child-free time.

Suddenly she had an idea; she would go and meet him. He never left the office before seven on Friday these days, Guy Constantine had taken to having a drink with the senior staff, discussing the problems they all faced, reassuring them, stiffening their courage.

She would go and meet him there, it would be fun, it was ages since she had experienced grown-up life.

Luc realised almost at once that he had left his briefcase behind: damn. He had to have it, he needed its contents for the weekend. He had a lot of work to do. He asked the taxi driver to go back and wait, ran up to his office, praying he wouldn't meet anyone on the stairs.

He didn't; but as he was leaving his office again, the telephone rang. Better answer it, it might be Adele. Or even Suzette.

It was neither; it was one of his authors, a neurotic novelist; had Luc liked his second draft? Which bits had he liked best? Did he think it was worth re-working the last chapter? By the time he escaped, the taxi driver was standing, shouting furiously at the concierge at the main door.

'Sorry,' Luc said, 'sorry, I'm here now, let's go.'

'I'm so sorry,' the concierge was most apologetic. 'Monsieur Lieberman has gone. About – oh, half an hour ago.'

'Oh. Oh, well—'

Adele felt absurdly dispirited, near to tears. 'Was he – was he with Monsieur Constantine?'

'No, Mademoiselle. Monsieur Constantine is still inside, would you like to see him?'

'No, no, thank you. I just thought – never mind. You don't – you don't have any idea where Monsieur Lieberman is, do you? If he was just round the corner, I could maybe find him—'

'No, Mademoiselle, not just around the corner, I'm afraid. He went in a taxi.'

'A taxi! Must have been to see an author, then. Otherwise he wouldn't run to such an extravagance.'

'Yes.' He smiled at her, shook his head at the memory. 'He made the taxi driver very angry, he had to come back and fetch something he had forgotten and was so long, the driver came in and started shouting at me, telling me to fetch him.'

'Oh dear. Well—'

'If it's any help to you, Mam'selle, he was going to Passy.'

'Passy!' She hadn't heard that, he hadn't said it, of course he wasn't going to Passy, it must be a mistake. 'Are you – sure?'

Anyway, there were other streets in Passy, other than the Rue Vineuse, it was quite a big area, probably that was where the writer lived.

'I am quite sure. The driver told me so that I could telephone some of the offices, find out who had hired him. Rue Vineuse, Passy. Anyway, Monsieur Lieberman had come back by then. Mademoiselle, let me telephone Monsieur Constantine, he will be pleased to see you, I'm sure.'

'No,' said Adele, and she could hear her own voice, dull, quiet with shock, 'no, really, it's all right. If – if Monsieur Lieberman comes back, don't mention that I've been here. Please.'

'Very well, Mademoiselle.'

❖

She got back at seven-thirty; she felt so tired she could hardly drag herself up the stairs. Perhaps it was all a dreadful mistake, perhaps he was home, perhaps she had simply missed him; but Mme André was waiting, smiling, in the apartment, telling her that both the children were still asleep, that neither had stirred.

'Good. Thank you so much, Mme André.'

'Are you all right, Mam'selle Adele? You look – very pale.'

'I'm absoutely fine. Thank you. Yes, just a bit – hot.'

She did feel hot: and cold, and sick and shaky and in a wild, terrible panic. So much explained, so much had become clear. Back with Suzette; no wonder he wanted her out of Paris. No wonder the sudden and complete change of heart. It was absolutely clear. Bastard! Bastard! And now, now she was trapped; she would never get home. And she could have gone, she could be safe by now, and her children too, they could go to Ashingham, like the last war, such a happy golden time it had been, all of them together, and little Jay too, and poor Billy and that stupid governess Barty had liked so much, and the poor men with their lost limbs and their shell-shock, that was how she felt, shell-shocked, she'd start shaking in a minute, she was shaking – she stopped, swallowed, took a deep breath. This was not helpful. Calm down, Adele, think. Think . . .

Luc came home some time after nine: desperately apologetic, carrying a bottle of wine. He had been with an author: where, she asked. Oh, in Montmartre, he said, silly fool, fussing over his book, they were all the same, authors.

She sat there, smiling, cool and controlled, saying what a shame, how tired he must be, no, it didn't matter at all, dinner was easy, just a couple of steaks; later they went to bed and she even managed to kiss him – he didn't seem to want to make love to her, thank God, he seldom did these days, and was that so surprising, now that he was back with Suzette?

She got through the weekend somehow; she went out a lot, with the children, he seemed grateful, he had work to do, he said. She met a few friends, at the pavement cafés, talked to them casually about the people leaving Paris, everyone said the same thing, that it was madness, the roads were all jammed; a few told her, laughing, that if she was thinking of getting home to England, it would have to be from Bordeaux. Adele laughed and said she was thinking of no such thing.

On Saturday night she and Luc went to the cinema, watched the newsreels of Hitler and Goering posturing about, listened to the reports of how they were making no progress, how they would never reach Paris, never conquer France.

On Sunday she went to church, leaving him with the children; he was annoyed, but she insisted.

'It's not a lot to ask. I want to go.'

'I thought you were going to convert to Judaism,' he said, his eyes half amused.

'Just now, I want to go to Notre-Dame.'

'Notre-Dame! Why?'

'Because it's so beautiful,' she said briefly.

She lit a candle for herself and her children, and knelt and prayed for a long time. Only it wasn't exactly prayer, it was a silent, solemn strengthening of her own will.

On Monday morning, 10 June, it was unbelievably hot. Paris was very still; Adele felt for the first time a sense of fear, allowed the thought finally that things perhaps were not as they had all been told. Although more than half the shops and businesses were open as usual, there was a listlessness in the air that was almost palpable, and a sadness too, tears trembling beneath the surface. More and more people were leaving, she saw people embracing one another, waving farewell, heaping possessions into cars. But the radio reports were as reassuring as usual. The French line continued to hold, Paris was still perfectly safe. There seemed nothing more to worry about than there had been the previous day. Or the previous week.

Well, she didn't have time to panic or to think very much; she had far too much to do.

She put the children in the pram, went to the bank very early, and took out all that she had in her own bank account. There was a very long queue; she had to wait almost an hour. Lucas became fractious and cried a lot; she didn't try to stop him, thinking they might be allowed to move up in the queue. They weren't. She had managed to bank most of her freelance earnings over the past two years: not a great deal, only a few hundred francs. But it would be enough. It would have to be enough.

Luc had a car, a rather battered Citroën; it was parked in the street, its near side wheels on the pavement. He only used it on Sundays; when she had returned from Mass the day before, after lunch, she had asked if they could go for a drive.

He had tried to dissuade her, saying it was too hot, but she had been insistent; 'The roads are so clear, it will be fun. Just for a little spin. We could take a picnic. Please, Luc.'

In reality, she had been making sure it started easily, that it was more or less in order. As they were loading up the car to go home again, she asked if she could drive.

'I'm afraid I will have forgotten how. It's months ago now.'

He smiled at her, handed her the keys.

'Of course. I seem to remember you were a rather good driver.'

'I was,' she said. She managed to slip the keys into her bag after locking it up.

He didn't use it to go to work, he would never notice.

When they got back from the bank, she went to see Mme André.

'I need your help, Madame. Will you care for the children for a couple of hours?'

'But of course. Are you all right, Mam'selle?'

'Perfectly. Just a bit tired. It's the heat.'

'I have just heard that the British have landed ten more divisions in France.'

'Oh, wonderful! That is good news.'

There were many such rumours that day; that the Americans had declared war, that the Germans had fallen into a great French trap and three panzer divisions had been decimated, that the German army was in retreat. All of them, combined with the official spokesman on the radio, in day-long broadcasts, reporting French victories, added up to the same thing: that Paris would be saved.

Luc had a journalist friend, Henri Thierry, who worked for the French newspaper *Le Figaro*; he had had an idea for a book, and came in to see Luc at midday.

'I'm going to need the work,' he said to Luc casually, 'no more journalism for a bit.'

'Why's that? Got the sack?'

'No. Serious news, Luc. We were called into the Clock Room on the Quai d'Orsay this morning; no more Paris newspapers after today.'

'God,' said Luc, 'what does that mean?'

'I think we know. Apparently there was an off-the-record announcement that the Government was leaving for Tours, but I was late, didn't hear that. I don't believe that. They wouldn't do it without some formal announcement.'

'It might still come.'

'Well, it might.' He grinned at Luc. 'Don't look so worried. So many rumours. Anyway, I'm going to be able to get on with my book in peace.'

'I hope so,' said Luc.

He felt very shaken.

He managed to get through the meeting with Thierry and then looked at his watch. One o'clock. This really didn't seem too good. Maybe he should go home. If Adele heard the news, she would be worried. But – what good could he do? It really was too late to send her away now. And she was unlikely to hear it, it was not a rumour that would reach the markets where she shopped. Even so—

Guy Constantine put his head round the door. 'Got a few minutes? I've got something I'd like to discuss with you.'

'Of course.'

Adele had about eight hours. Possibly more. Luc had said he might be late; she knew what that meant, unless she was very unlucky: he would be late. Even if he wasn't, she had until seven.

She moved the car as near the building as she could, went up to the apartment, pulled down a suitcase, and filled it with children's clothes, napkins, some soft toys, a couple of blankets, an old cot mattress to put on the floor. Lucas could sleep on that, and it would help with the noise and vibration of the rattly Citroën.

And then another suitcase, filled that with food: mostly tins, including some condensed milk. Remembering a tin opener. Some bottles of water and some fruit juice. Thank God Lucas was able to eat normal food now. She was just shutting that case when she saw two bottles of wine at the back of the cupboard: fine wine, Château Lafite Rothschild. Luc's pride and joy, a present from a grateful author, he had been saving them for over a year. They would be a great deal more use to her. Also in the cupboard was a small Gaz camping stove; she pulled that out as well, and some matches.

She took the cases down to the street, put them in the boot of the car. There was no room for anything else. She went to the market, bought three baguettes – no use getting more, they'd become bullets in days in this heat – and some fruit and hard cheese.

On her way back, she went into a shop and bought five packs of Gauloises and some more matches. She packed all this into the picnic basket, with some cups and plates and cutlery, and put it on the front seat.

Now for the most difficult task of all.

'Luc? Henri Monnet. How are you?'

'Oh – very well, thank you. A little worried.'

Monnet was another friend, a distinguished author, specialising in biography.

'I too. I phoned to thank you for sending me the cover proofs. Very nice. I particularly like the one showing the hall of mirrors at Versailles. Beautiful.'

'Good. That was my favourite also.'

'And also to tell you I've heard a rather disturbing rumour.'

'What was that?'

'Well, André Maurois, you know.'

'Yes. Of course.' Maurois was a captain in the army and a writer, recently ordered to fly to America for a propaganda lecture tour.

'Well, apparently he was phoned by a government minister this morning, who advised him to send his wife south.'

'Christ.'

'Yes. Worrying. I heard it on the journalistic pipeline. I thought you might have heard something, with your contacts.'

'Well – yes, I have. After today, no Paris newspapers.'

'Yes, I had heard that. Apparently the entire Parisian office of the *Daily Mail* are moving to Tours, to try and get the paper out from there.'

'Yes, well, there could be a reason for Tours. The press were told, off the record, that the entire French cabinet are moving there tonight.'

'Good God.'

'Quite. Have you heard any radio bulletins today?'

'Oh, yes, of course. The usual soothing claptrap. I don't know, Luc, I half wish I'd got out myself. But – what for and where to?'

'Well – exactly. Keep in touch. I'll let you know if I hear any more.'

'Are you staying there? In the office?'

'Oh – yes, I think so. More likely to get information. But I'll probably go home early. Adele may be worried.'

He put down the phone; he felt rather sick.

'Do you need help, Mam'selle?'

She turned round, pushed the hair off her damp forehead. She could feel the sweat under her arms. She must look really attractive.

'Well – yes. If you wouldn't mind.'

He worked at the garage down the street, she knew him by sight: a good-looking man, with black eyes and black curly hair. He was middle-aged, too old, she supposed, to be in the army, but very fit, brown and muscly.

He grinned at her. 'It would be a pleasure.' He had the pram on the roof straight away; she had been struggling to lift it for what seemed like hours. 'Pass me the ropes. Now take this end – that's right. Yes. There—'

In five minutes it was done: Lady Beckenham's Silver Cross pram was mounted most securely on to the roof of the car. It looked, oddly, even larger.

'Thank you so much. Here—' She reached into the car, pulled out one of the packs of Gauloises, and gave it to him.

'There's no need. But thank you. Be careful, Mam'selle. It's not so safe on those roads.'

'The roads are empty,' she said, surprised.

'Not once you leave the centre.'

She smiled at him; he obviously guessed where she was going. Well, it was hardly difficult.

'Thank you again. Goodbye.'

'Goodbye, Mam'selle. And good luck.'

Luc and Guy Constantine settled down at a pavement café; on the way they had passed a street vendor selling one of the favourite souvenirs of the moment, a porcelain dog with one leg cocked over a copy of *Mein Kampf*.

'They'll all be confiscated soon,' said Constantine gloomily.

'You really think they're coming?'

'I fear so. Finally today, for the first time.' He looked at Luc, hesitated, then said, 'I am sorry, my friend, I have some bad news for you.'

'Bad news?'

'Yes. I am closing down these offices. As of today. We are a publishing company. The Nazis do not like such organisations. They see danger in them. Quite rightly, for propaganda and so on. Do you really think they will let us continue to operate unchecked? And besides, we have strong Jewish affiliations, the company is registered as Constantine Friedman, you may remember, and you are not the only Jewish director. No, if they arrive, as surely they will, I think our time will be very short.'

'But what will you do?' said Luc. He felt sick and very cold. This was even worse than he had thought. He was about to lose his job.

'I have decided to move the company to Switzerland.'

'Switzerland!'

'Yes. I'm sorry, this must be rather a shock for you.'

Bastard, thought Luc, watching him closely, he's been planning this for weeks and not telling me. Bastard. Bastard!

Guy smiled at him, the smooth, charming smile that had beguiled a hundred authors. 'Please think about it. I would so like to have you with me. If I go, that is.'

'You mean when you go.'

Guy looked at him briefly, then into his glass. 'Well – yes. It is more when than if, I must admit. I had not expected to have to make a decision quite so soon. But the news is getting worse and – well, my wife and I, we feel we must get out quickly. What will you do about Adele? She has no French papers, no proper status. She should have gone home, Luc.'

'I know it,' said Luc gloomily.

The waiter was chatty, full of gloomy cheer.

'The Boches will be here within a week,' he said, setting down glasses, cutlery, bread.

'Oh, rubbish,' said a man at the next table, 'don't spread ugly rumours. I just heard the radio, the news is good.'

Luc felt better briefly; but common sense told him he had no right to feel so.

'I think I'll go home,' he said to Guy, 'I've got rather a lot to think about. And I fear Adele will be anxious.'

'Of course. Beer? Or wine? And an omelette. Let us fiddle just for half an hour longer, my dear Luc, while Rome burns.'

Luc looked at him, then stood up and left without a word.

It was three o'clock now: dreadfully hot. She locked up their apartment after putting a letter for Luc on the table. A brief, but carefully worded letter: explaining what she was doing and why. She owed him that; he needed to know.

The children were playing in Mme André's dark, stuffy sitting room.

'I gave them lunch, Mam'selle.'

'Oh, you're so kind. I'm sorry I've been so long.'

'It has been a pleasure.'

'Here—' She held out some notes. Mme André shook her head.

'Mam'selle, no. I could not take it. Not today.' Her eyes were filled with tears suddenly; her mouth quivered.

She knows, Adele thought, knows I'm going. 'Well – thank you. I'll – I'll go now. Thank you so much for – for everything.'

Now the moment had arrived, she felt suddenly terribly frightened; tempted almost, even now, to stay in the dubious safety of Paris. But – what then? Safety from the Germans, from the war, perhaps, for a little longer; but with Luc, Luc who no longer loved her, Luc who had gone back to his wife.

'Where are we going?' asked Noni, looking up at her, her dark eyes anxious.

'For a – a journey.'

'A journey! Where?'

'In the car.'

'And without Papa?'

'Without Papa.'

'I don't want to go without Papa.'

'I know. But he will – well, he will be with us later.'

'Are you sure?'

Adele smiled at her.

'As sure as I can be. Now come along. And you, Lucas.'

'He's got a dirty nappy,' said Noni. 'I can smell it.'

'Oh no! Oh, Lucas, what timing.'

She would have to change it; there would be others undoubtedly, but this one at least could be dealt with. She sighed. 'Noni, you stay here, I'll go and change him.'

Luc sat on the metro: only three more stops. It was crowded. He didn't know what he was going to say to Adele, what plans he could make for her. He was more worried about her, he realised, than about Suzette. Well, Suzette was a French citizen: she was not the enemy. And nor was she Jewish; he and Adele, they were both in great peril. Perhaps, after all, they should leave the city; take the car and go.

He looked at his watch: nearly four. They could pack the car up tonight and leave. But – where?

The train pulled in at Cité; he could hear shouting, a great commotion. What was it? Surely they hadn't arrived already?

He decided to get home as fast as he could. In five minutes, maybe ten, he would be there. Together they could decide what to do.

'There now. All clean.' Adele walked into Mme André's sitting room again, smiling. 'Come along, Noni, time to go.'

'Mme André is reading me a story. Can't we wait till it's finished?'

Another five minutes: what difference would it make? 'Yes, all right.' She sat down; Lucas began playing with some china animals which Mme André had on a table.

'Coffee, Mam'selle? Before you leave?'

'Oh – why not? Yes, thank you.'

Probably her last contact with a friendly adult for days; possibly weeks. She was very tired; she leaned back in the chair and closed her eyes briefly.

Mme André bustled about, measuring out coffee and water, then set the pot on the stove.

'I shall miss you, Mam'selle.'

'I shall miss you too, dear Mme André.'

They had still not discussed what she was going to do. There was no need.

Luc tried to push his way through the crowd on the steps leading up from the metro; it was very thick, very resistant to him. At the top, in the Place St-Sulpice, there was more shouting, panic, people pointing at something. Lots of things. What?

People were holding papers, reading them, showing them to one another; evening papers. There were none left at the stand; Luc found a small crowd gathered round a girl, all reading a proclamation by General Pierre Hering, commander of the city's forces, announcing that 'The capital will be defended to the last.'

It was true. The Germans were almost here.

Adele sighed, put down her coffee cup. She really must go. Lucas was half asleep in a chair, sucking his thumb, clutching a model cow; Noni was looking at a picture book.

The radio had been playing music; it stopped abruptly.

'Oh, the news,' said Mme André, turning it off, 'so tedious.'

She looked at Adele for a long moment, then opened her plump arms. Adele went into them; found herself surrounded with the smell of sweat and garlic. It seemed wonderful, she felt oddly comforted, safe just for a little longer. She was taller than Mme André; she looked down, smiled at her.

'You've been so kind.'

'It has been a pleasure, Mam'selle. Take care. Take great care.'

'I will. Of course. And if – when Monsieur Lieberman comes home, you don't know where I've gone.'

'Of course not.'

'I wouldn't be going if – well, if I didn't have to.'

'Of course. I understand.'

Somehow Adele felt she did. 'Thank you. For everything.'

'It has been lovely to know you, Mam'selle. You and the children. Here, let me come out to the car with you, help the children in.'

'Thank you.'

Home, he must get home. He started running across the square when a radio went on; and then another and another, in every café, from every open window. Very loudly. He stopped, walked over to the nearest café, as if pulled there by some strong, strange force. People stood stock-still, listening in silence: many in tears.

'Should the Germans reach Paris we shall defend every stone, every clod of earth, every lamp-post, every building, for we would rather have our city razed to the ground than fall into the hands of the Germans.'

Home: he must get home.

And then rippling through the crowd, passed from person to person, like giant snowflakes, being daubed on lamp-posts and walls and urinals, the leaflets came. *Citoyens! Aux armes.*

Luc stayed to read one carefully; so that he knew everything he could, before he reached Adele.

Noni and Lucas were in the car now, Lucas still clutching the toy cow.

'Lucas! Give that back, give it to Mme André.'

'Oh, it doesn't matter. He can keep it. Here, Noni, take the book. Maman can read it to you tonight.'

'Will you, Maman?'

'Of course.'

As if such a thing would be possible; probably they would still be sitting in the car, sleeping in the car. Well, that wouldn't stop her reading a story. She started the car, put it into gear, smiled out of the window at Mme André, blew her a kiss. She smiled back, tears now rolling down her cheeks.

'Wait! Take these.' She took two apples from the pocket of her pinafore, pushed them through the window. 'For the children.'

Behind them, in the Place St-Sulpice, Luc passed on the handbill and began to push his way through the ever-denser crowds; it was suffocating, like a nightmare. But – there it was, in front of him now, his street, his home, his children, Adele.

'*Au revoir, chère* Mam'selle Adele. You are going home to England, I suppose?'

It was the first time she had asked.

'Yes,' said Adele, firmly wishing she believed it. 'I am going home to England.'

Chapter 28

The trenches were quite deep: about six feet, and then covered in barbed wire. Any unauthorised person found in them was under threat of a firing squad.

'That's a bloody good defence we've got,' said Lord Beckenham, gazing from the one at the front of the house across the land towards Oxford. 'We can see the enemy coming from every direction. Well, I just hope they do, that's all. Give them a damn good hiding. Our men are ready for anything.'

Lady Beckenham was about to say that the opportunity for Lord Beckenham and his Home Guard troop to give the Germans a hiding could hardly compensate for an enemy landing and then thought better of it; the whole thing was keeping him wonderfully busy.

'Excellent,' she said. 'Now have you spoken to the headmaster about making the trenches out of bounds? Because they really are quite dangerous.'

'Of course. I told you. First chap in will be made an example of—'

'Beckenham, I don't think the boys believe you're really going to shoot any of them in the trenches.'

'Why on earth not?' His fine old face was puzzled. 'I would have, when I was a boy.'

'Yes, well, things were different then. What does the headmaster suggest as a punishment?'

'Oh, some damn fool nonsense about detention. I said at least a thrashing, but they don't even go in for that much these days. Anyway, I'm continuing to tell them it's the firing squad.'

'I think I'd better speak to them at my assembly.'

Her assembly had become a weekly occurrence; she spoke to all the boys after supper, usually on Sundays, about matters of discipline and other, more agreeable things. The boys loved them – she was such a game old trout, as Henry Warwick's best friend remarked graciously to him, she always had some jolly new idea for them – and she enjoyed them too, they had become a crucial part of running the school at Ashingham.

Originally, she had told the headmaster, an ineffectually pleasant man called John Dawkins, promoted when the young, forceful head had joined the army, that discipline was his area, as long as certain guidelines which they would draw up between them were observed. But she very swiftly came to regret this: and, indeed, her offer to take in the school. Fifty small boys, a teaching staff of five plus two domestics, combined with extra members of her own family and staff, added up to a lot of people. Of course Ashingham was big enough, it had been built for a household of at least a hundred, but the noise and administrative problems were considerable.

The boys were as good as could be expected and fairly well-disciplined; just the same, the heady delights of finding themselves in the middle of the country with unlimited trees to climb, streams to dam, livestock to get to know, had proved almost too much for several of them. The naughtiest ones – led inevitably by Henry and Roo Warwick who knew their way around – had already been severely punished for lighting fires, organising a (mercifully discovered) rabbit shoot, swimming in the river unsupervised, climbing up to the very top of the Home Farm barn and sliding down on the hay and, one dreadful night, indulging in a moonlit bareback riding session. It was this last that had almost resulted in an exodus back to Kent, such had been Lady Beckenham's rage, and John Dawkins had expressed immense horror together with a fear that the boys might have broken their necks.

'Their necks!' said Lady Beckenham. 'I'm not worried about their necks, much better broken if this goes on, I'd say. One of those horses is a mare in foal and the other is very nervy and inclined to break out. If he tried to clear that gate, God knows what might happen, last time one of them did that it broke its back, had to be put down. I think you'd better let me talk to the boys, Mr Dawkins. They don't seem to take a great deal of notice of you.'

Slightly reluctantly, Mr Dawkins allowed her to attend the next morning assembly, held each day in the ballroom; she stood up after prayers and told the boys that any more bad behaviour, 'and you know what that is, the rules are perfectly clear,' would result in expulsion from Ashingham.

'I shall get your parents down here and tell them you're going and why and that will be that. You'll find yourself back in Dover at the mercy of the Germans.'

At the same time, however, she did announce an impromptu games session every Sunday afternoon – 'sack races and an obstacle course, that sort of thing, and if anyone wants to help with haymaking on the farm, they can come and see me. And if anyone wants to learn to ride properly, they can write and ask their parents. Mr Miller, my groom, has been kind enough to say he'll organise that. Only don't think you'll be able to just arrive at the yard and mount; you'll have to learn to groom and muck out, all part of riding, you know.'

Lord Beckenham had responded to Anthony Eden's call on the radio for the formation of Local Defence Volunteers – later renamed the Home Guard – with great enthusiasm; within twenty-four hours the Ashingham Battalion had been formed, thirty-five men strong. He addressed them from the terrace of Ashingham wearing his rather elderly battledress – 'Far too big for him, I didn't realise how thin he'd got, poor old chap,' said Lady Beckenham – his medals pinned to his chest.

The younger ones leaned on their rifles, half amused, but the older men, many of them veterans of the First World War, Billy Miller included, found his speech moving and even distressing.

'Looking at him standing there, telling us to fight off the invader, and that the safety and freedom of our land could depend on us, took me right back to Flanders,' he said that night to Joan Barber in the village pub. 'I felt quite – quite upset. It was like I could hear the screams again, feel the mud and the cold—'

Joan patted his hand and told him she could see that, especially with his leg and all, but it must be nice for him to feel he could do his bit for king and country as Lord Beckenham had said.

'Don't know about king,' said Billy, 'don't have much of a feeling for all them, I'm with young Jay on that, but country, yes. I'd die before I let one of those buggers – sorry, Joan – get on to Ashingham land. Pity about the holes in the ground, but there you are.'

The holes in the ground were a source of some contention with farmers; Churchill's scientific adviser had recommended that in the event of a mass landing by air, now considered a serious possibility, large holes should be dug in the ground in all areas more than four hundred yards long and within five miles of an area of strategic importance. Even crop-bearing fields were not exempt; furthermore, large stakes were to be driven into the ground to give the invading enemy further discomfort as he dropped to earth. All this was, of course, also hazardous to the small boys. It had become a separate and serious offence to play anywhere near the craters and another matter for serious discussion at Lady Beckenham's assembly.

The Ashingham Battalion was rather more heavily drilled and disciplined than most – two sessions a week rather than one – and better equipped, admittedly with a rather odd armoury of weapons, ranging from Boer War rifles to Lord Beckenham's own beloved Purdeys – 'jolly good use for them, finishing off a few Germans' – and even a pearl-handled pistol which Lady Beckenham's mother had kept under her pillow all through her time in India. The neighbouring division was manned, it was said, with pitchforks and home-made clubs.

The Ashingham Battalion was also extremely zealous: in only its second week, a young courting couple found no less than three guns pointing at them as they lay in each other's arms in the long grass by the river and were taken off to Ashingham where they were rigorously questioned in the kitchen.

Rather to everyone's surprise, Lord Beckenham attended not only the requisite government course, but the two-day residential version organised by *Picture Post* magazine at Osterley Park, the home of the Earl of Jersey. He came back literally quivering with excitement from two days of crawling through smoke bombs, learning to explode anti-tank mines and firing at mock dive-bombers, and indeed begged so hard to be allowed to stay on that he was promised a further two days the following year.

'There's talk of the Home Guard taking over actual defensive duties if all the young chaps go to France,' he said to Lady Beckenham. 'Think of that, being back in the front line. God, I hope those bastards arrive soon.'

He was all for forming a cadet squad with the boys from the school and indeed held a preliminary meeting; it was only after Matron's report that several of the boys had woken crying with nightmares following Lord Beckenham's extremely vivid accounts of what could be done with a pitchfork, wielded with sufficient skill against the enemy, that the idea had to be scrapped.

'So tell me, what is your view of the chances of America coming into the war?'

Sebastian looked at Barty over the spectacles that he now wore. They aged him, made him less spectacularly good-looking, and he had resisted them for years: finally giving in after a rather painfully frank session with Celia when he returned the proofs of the latest Meridian virtually uncorrected, with the comment that typesetters were clearly becoming increasingly skilled as the years went by.

He had taken Barty out to lunch, telling her she looked pale and tired: 'and I know women don't like being told that sort of thing, but it's true.'

She felt pale and tired, she was sleeping badly and she knew the reason; not overwork, not the ache in her heart which still caught her by surprise at the most unlikely moments – when she saw a couple sitting, heads together, engaged in some intense conversation, when an American accent caught her ear – not even the news from France, which was very bad. It was a sense of resentment and injustice at having been emotionally blackmailed by Oliver; and of distaste with herself for having given in. She hated it, every day, the safe, dull backwater she found herself in; and it didn't suit her. It wasn't just the war and not being part of it; she had grown accustomed in New York, all through her time with Laurence, to living on the edge, every day a difficult ongoing challenge. And she missed that, as much as she missed Laurence himself, the difficulty and the danger. A new, tough challenge, a different sort of danger was what she needed, indeed longed for; and besides, she had not been brought up by Celia, been Billy's sister, without developing a fierce desire to help defend her country.

She had been deeply moved by Churchill's speeches, his exhortation to courage, to duty; she longed to respond and every day she resolved to tell Oliver that she couldn't stay any longer, that she was going to enlist, and every day she looked at him, so frail and aged, so clearly fearful for Kit and Giles, and put it off a little longer. Celia could have borne her absence, she knew; Celia, with her huge courage, could bear anything; it had actually been on his own behalf that Oliver had made his plea. And she loved him too much to refuse it; but it was making her very unhappy.

It was still surprisingly easy to imagine the war away: in London that summer of 1940 the Houses of Parliament might be surrounded in barbed wire, there might be sandbags in every doorway, and large signs saying 'Shelter' dotted about the city, there might be food rationing and talk of clothing coupons, and a sense of intense patriotism everywhere, but within the reassuringly unchanged inner sanctums of the Mirabelle and the Caprice, the Dorchester and the Savoy, there were few clues. The waiters were all rather elderly to be sure, and a lot of the male clientele were in uniform, but you could still order gulls' eggs, salmon trout, lobster and, 'Oysters!' said Barty joyfully. 'Oh, Sebastian, how lovely.'

'I'm surprised you like them. With your rather conservative tastes.'

'I became a bit more adventurous in New York,' she said, 'I learned to like all sorts of things.'

'Well, that's the first good thing I've heard about that young man. If he could corrupt your purist tendencies . . .'

She was silent, thinking of other corruptions, other delights Laurence had led her into; then, 'Why talk to me about the Americans?' she said.

'Oh – simply because you were there quite a long time, you must have got a feel for the psyche. And how pro- or anti-British they might feel. It would be marvellous to have them on our side.'

'I don't really know. I mean, I left two years ago, don't forget. But – I'd say the East Coast people, the old-money set, they had a strong pro-British inclination. An upperclass American is terribly like an upper-class Englishman.'

'I don't think you'd find Celia agreeing with you,' said Sebastian, laughing.

'No, I know. But you'd be surprised, they're bothered with all the same things, traditions, marrying into the right families, keeping up standards at all costs. Anyway, they might be on our side, but I know Roosevelt isn't in favour. And I'm very much afraid most of America wouldn't be.'

'And of course that slimy bastard Joe Kennedy, he's a well-known admirer of the Nazis. Nasty piece of work, if you ask me, how he got to be Ambassador to Britain, I'll never know. Well, it says a lot about the Americans – sorry, Barty.'

'It's all right,' she said, smiling, 'I can cope with it now. I'm really beginning to be over it. I think.'

'Really?' he said, his fierce eyes probing hers.

'Well – I said beginning. Actually more than beginning.'

'Good. Now I want to ask your advice about something. I really think I might send Isabella down to Ashingham. She can go to that school there, well, Lady Beckenham says she can, and as far as I can make out, the headmaster does what she says, poor chap. I don't envy him. And she'd be safe. I worry about her being up here. The bombing is bound to start soon. And she's too young to go to boarding school. What do you think?'

'I think it's a wonderful idea,' said Barty truthfully. 'Really wonderful.'

'You think she'd learn something?'

'Of course. It's a very good little school, I'm told.' She sighed. 'I had such a lovely time down at Ashingham during the last war. It was the first time I really felt truly happy.'

'Well, I may do it, then. I'm getting very worried about her being here.'

'I think you should. Oh, Sebastian, I wish we knew something about Adele. The telephone lines are completely dead to Paris now, there's no news of her at all. I do hope and pray she's all right.'

'Of course she is. Right as rain.'

'But the Germans are almost at the gates of Paris.'

'I know, I know. But she'll be all right. Survivors they are, those twins, both of them. Like their mother. I'd back them against Hitler's army any day.'

Adele woke up with a start; there was a sword, or was it a knife, sticking into her side. She sat bolt upright, pushing the cushion she had used as a pillow on to the floor of the car. What was it, who had got in? She had locked the door so carefully, only leaving a tiny crack of each window open to let in some air. She had even worried about that, afraid that the Germans, or more likely some predatory French, less well-equipped for this journey than she was, might force a window further down. But otherwise they would have suffocated.

Still, a sword, she hadn't expected that – only it wasn't a sword, of course, she realised gratefully as she eased herself out of her cramped position, it was simply an agonising stabbing pain, from lying cramped up all night. She felt terrible, though: hot, sick, thirsty . . .

She turned round, looked at the children. They were still asleep. They hadn't stirred once she had finally got them settled, some time after midnight. She wasn't too sure what the time was now – it was obviously very early, dawn had hardly broken, but her watch had stopped. That was horrible: not knowing the time. She had heard somewhere that it was one of the ways in which tortured prisoners had their spirits broken: by having their watches taken away, so that they had no idea what time of day or night it was and became totally disorientated. She must find out the time, and remember to wind her watch every night until she got home.

Until she got home; she kept saying it to herself. Not if, but when. She had already learned a hard lesson in that.

The journey had begun fairly well; they had moved quite easily through the city streets, which were for the most part wonderfully empty and clear; she had decided to leave by the Porte d'Italie on to the main road south. Every time she passed a main railway station, they were held up by the milling crowds and queues trying to force their way into it, dreadful, shocking scenes, reminiscent of some medieval painting of hell, she thought, people pushing and shouting at one another, tall men manhandling their way through the crowd, children held aloft, crying, often screaming, for the parents they had been separated from, old people literally panting in the heat, here a woman fainting, there a man collapsed, calling for a doctor, everyone ignoring him. And there were no trains; or almost no trains. It was the first time she had witnessed this particular horror; it increased her fear.

Her own children watched fascinated, staring out of the windows unmoved by the suffering, intrigued by such strange behaviour on the part of grown-up people.

'That man is horrible,' said Noni, pointing out a huge man at the back of a crowd, who was elbowing quite brutally two old women out of his way. 'Why is he doing that?'

'He wants to get a train,' said Adele briefly.

'Well, he should wait in the queue. Stupid man. I'm glad we've got the car.'

She was less glad later on: as they sat in the great crawling line of people leaving Paris for the south, lurching along in first gear, making so little speed the speedometer didn't register it. The evening sun beat through the windows; first Lucas, then Noni began to grizzle and whine that they were hot, thirsty, they wanted to get out.

'I can't stop now,' said Adele, struggling to keep her voice calm and good-natured.

'Why not?'

'Well, because if we stop, we'll get behind in the queue. Other cars will overtake us and—'

'Doesn't matter. It's so slow anyway. Look, that old man is pushing the lady on the cart. Where do you think they're going?'

'Oh – to see some friends,' said Adele, 'like we are.'

There were many such sights. The most fortunate were in cars; others were on bicycles, in carts, on motorbikes, in wheelbarrows, a great many were on foot, women carried babies, while children trailed behind them, crying. The men carrying suitcases, packed hastily with the few possessions they had felt they could not leave behind. All

405

looking frightened, bleak, hopeless, a long, snaking line of human misery, stretching before her as far as she could see.

She felt horrified, shocked at the scale of the exodus; she had expected to see a lot of cars, buses, lorries, but not this desperate, frightened army. It must be so very much more dangerous than she had thought; why had they been told so little? And had Luc known and kept it from her? No, surely not, they had all been the victims of the same conspiracy, the same cowardly foolish deception; she was not to know that at that very moment the French Government was leaving Paris in a fleet of large comfortable cars . . .

'We ought to help that old lady,' said Noni suddenly, looking at an old woman sitting weeping in the gutter, holding her head, 'she's upset, what do you think's happened?'

What had happened was easy to see: the old woman's husband had fainted in the heat, lying stretched out on the pavement, with a couple of battered suitcases at his side. Possibly, Adele thought, he had had a heart attack; he would quite possibly die here. And no one could or would help him.

But, 'Darling, I'm sorry, we can't,' she said, and indeed she knew they couldn't, she was going to need every resource at her disposal for her own small group of refugees. 'Their friends will be here soon.'

'How do you know?'

'I just do.'

Lucas started crying again.

'He's thirsty,' said Noni.

'Well, give him a bit of that apple Mme André gave us. Not all of it, Noni, he'll choke. Bite a bit of it off and give it to him – that's right.'

Lucas looked at the apple derisively, hurled it on the floor of the car and went on crying.

'Don't cry,' said Noni, sweetly maternal. She took his hand, stroked it. 'We'll soon be there, won't we, Mummy?'

'Yes, of course we will.'

By dusk they had only travelled a very few kilometres southwards; they were on the secondary road, it seemed slightly quieter and in any case the main ones were reserved for the army, and official vehicles. She had spent hours poring over the map late on Sunday night, after Luc had gone to sleep, plotting a route.

She had decided to go down via Chartres, it seemed the most direct way. Map reading was not one of her skills to put it mildly; she had never been able to work out which direction roads went in, how to relate the real one she was on to the winding line on a map. But desperation had driven her on; she had finally gone to sleep with her route fairly clear. Chartres, only about 100 kilometres from Paris, Tours, 240 kilometres. A hundred and fifty miles. They should do that easily in twenty-four hours. And then on down to Bordeaux in another – well, she would worry about that when she got to Tours. She had not, however, reckoned on sharing the route with countless thousands of others . . .

It was a little easier to move now, they had even made second gear. The children had been squabbling and were now in a state of strange, dull tranquillity that would, she knew, presage a fresh storm of protests. Then she would have to stop; they were hungry, thirsty, Lucas needed his nappy changed, Noni said repeatedly she wanted *faire pipi*. She always used that phrase, whether she was speaking in French or English. Adele was beginning to wish she had brought the potty; but it had seemed just one thing she could manage without, an unnecessary demand on space in the overpacked car.

Finally, at half past eight, she pulled off the road on to the grass verge. It was heavily occupied.

'Come on then, darling, out you get. Good girl. You too, Lucas. I'll change you. And then we'll have some supper—'

'Out here on the grass?'

'No, in the car.'

'But, Mummy, why? It's so hot and it's much nicer out here.'

She hesitated; reluctant to explain that spreading food out on the ground was clearly reckless, an invitation to loot. There were several people near them who looked already desperate, hungry, sharing one tin of beans, one glass of water. They might find her carefully prepared picnic irresistible.

'Can we just go for a little walk? I'm tired of the car.'

'Well – yes, all right. Just a tiny way. Come, take my hands.'

They walked slowly along the verge, keeping pace with Lucas's toddling steps, but still only a little more slowly than the traffic. Normally, the three of them walking along together, the pretty mother and the small, enchanting children, would have attracted attention, smiles, friendliness; not now. They met only with sullen indifference, as families rested, exhausted, or struggled back to their feet to continue their journey. There was no sense of camaraderie, of kindness even; it was horrible, a frighteningly unfamiliar experience. For the first time, Adele realised that if they needed help for any reason, they would find none.

407

'Come on. Let's go back to the car,' she said after a while, reluctant to leave it unattended, even though it was carefully locked up.

'Don't want to,' said Noni sulkily.

It was unlike her to be difficult; Adele frowned at her.

'Noni, we have to. We have to get on.'

'But why? What for? Where are we going, when will Papa be here?'

And suddenly she couldn't answer any of those questions, she had no idea why or what for, she had left Paris on an impulse, an impulse born of misery and humiliation, had thought it was the right thing to do. Now in this crawling, wretched mass of humanity, travelling to a destination that now seemed as distant and as unfamiliar as the moon, exhausted, with her head throbbing, hot and frightened, she suddenly panicked. They would never make it, never get there, it was impossible, so far to travel, such an unbelievable distance, hundreds of miles, she had been mad, mad to do this, to subject her children to this, this misery and danger, it was hopeless, wrong.

She sat down on the grass, holding Lucas, staring up at Noni, crying helplessly; Noni stared back at her, clearly frightened, and then Lucas picked up on her mood and started crying too.

People looked at them, not pityingly, but with a complete lack of interest; that made her cry more, at her sense of isolation and terror. She felt the panic growing, beginning to engulf her: and then Noni said, very gently, 'Don't cry, Mummy, it'll be all right.'

Her words calmed Adele; not because she was able to believe them, but because of the sweet unselfishness of the child uttering them, and she realised in that moment that her only hope of getting through was to believe: no, not just to believe, but to know. She must not even consider the alternative: she must justify Noni's faith in her.

She stood up, fished a handkerchief out of her pocket, wiped her eyes. 'Of course it will, darling. Of course. I'm sorry. Mummy's just a bit tired. We'll be fine, we'll get to this place by the sea, and then we'll get a boat to England. And you'll have such a lovely time there, I promise you.'

'And – will Papa come too?'

'I – yes, of course he will. When he's finished his work in Paris. Come on now, back in the car, let's have our picnic, and I tell you what, we'll cook some eggs on our little stove' – suddenly it seemed worth the risk to raise the children's spirits – 'and then I'm going to read you that story of Mme André's. And after that, I'm going to drive a bit further and then we'll stop for the night and we'll all go to sleep.'

'Where?'

'Well – I had hoped we'd find a room somewhere. But we won't. So – in the car, I'm afraid.'

'In the car!' Noni's eyes shone. 'All of us! How exciting.'

And now it was morning; God knew where they were. The last sign had read 'Chartres 65 k', but she couldn't begin to work out how far back that had been. She only felt horror at how long this was taking. She had been so exhausted, she had fallen asleep twice at the wheel. And then pulled off the road again, put some blankets over the children who were already asleep and slept herself.

God, she felt awful. She ached all over. She was stiff – and her mouth tasted horrible, sour and dry. What she would give for a coffee. Perhaps if she came off this road, tried for an even more minor one, they would do better. Make more progress And she might find a village, where she could buy, or beg, some coffee. And change Lucas again. He certainly needed it.

She pulled out the atlas, began to study it. It must be possible to do better than this . . .

In Paris, Luc woke up alone in the apartment. Alone with his misery and rage; he wasn't sure which was the greater.

At first it had been rage: rage and outrage. That she should dare to do this, leave him, take his car, take his children, without even saying goodbye. He had seen her pulling away, seen the car move down the street, with the pram strapped to the top – making her intentions clear as nothing else, could. He had run after it, all the way to the Boulevard St-Germain, shouting her name, baffled, furious, raging; but it was hopeless of course, he would never find her, never catch her.

He had gone to the police, asked if they could help, if he gave the number of his car and a detailed description of Adele and the children; but they literally laughed at him.

'There are over a million people on those roads, Monsieur. We would never find her. And besides, we have more important things to do.'

He had walked back slowly to the apartment; Mme André was nowhere to be seen. He climbed the stairs wearily, went in – and saw the letter on the table. It seemed to need reading over and over again, in spite of its brevity: he found it difficult to absorb properly what it said. Not just that she was leaving, going to England, taking the children: but the reason for it, that she had discovered he had gone back to Suzette, that she found it impossible to stay with him on that basis. There was no reproach, no anger even; it was just cold, simple, a statement of a few facts. That made it far worse. He could have done with a bit of flagellation.

He debated getting a car to try to follow her; but he knew she would be impossible to find. Reports were coming through now of the massive crowds on all the roads south, of the impossibility of moving at all, let alone overtaking people, of finding anyone. And he had no idea which way she would go, what road she would be on. How had she found out? How? He had been so careful: no one had known, he was quite sure. Would Suzette herself? No, surely not. It was a hideous thought; that she could have committed an act of such betrayal. Added to his rage now was fear: conditions on the road were frightful, it was said; people were fighting over bottles of milk and water. How would Adele fare on her own with two tiny children? His children: how dared she, how could she expose them to such risk? It was outrageous: outrageous and terribly, dreadfully wrong. When he finally saw her again, he would make sure she realised that, the enormity of the wrong she had done. Then he thought that it was quite possible he would never see her again, and he started to weep.

He got up, made himself some coffee and switched on the radio. It was full of warnings that people must prepare for a siege, for street fighting. It was frightening.

He went down to the *tabac* to buy cigarettes and found it closed; a lot of small shops were shuttered this morning. But the *boulangerie* was open, and full of people, talking, shouting, arguing. It was all rumour; there was still no real information. The Germans were at the gates of the city; they had already entered it, raping and looting; a rebel army had already been formed; de Gaulle was still at the Ministry of Defence; General Hering's army was holding the city; nobody had any real idea what was going on. Paris was still, waiting, frozen in impotence. Some shops were being looted, a few hotels had been taken over and were being held by a bunch of *poilus*, the veterans of the First World War, hospitals were turning people away, even women in labour, if they did not have identity cards. But there was nothing organised, no plan by those in charge to care for the city and its citizens.

Luc decided to go for a walk; no point staying at home. Half the telephone lines were dead, Adele could not phone even if she wanted to. And work would help, would help to distract him from his fear. Not only now for Adele and his children, but also for himself.

He walked slowly back to the apartment; as he pushed open the big door from the street, he saw a young man hailing him. Very handsome, very well dressed, probably a homosexual, Luc thought; well, he was out of luck.

'Monsieur Lieberman?'

'Yes,' said Luc.

'Philippe Lelong. I met your very beautiful wife a little while ago. I promised to give her these – here.'

He handed Luc a large envelope; Luc opened it slowly. And found himself staring into the face of his daughter; several faces, several photographs of her laughing, jumping, and in one, just staring at him solemnly against a background of the St-Sulpice fountains. His eyes filled with tears; he stood looking stupidly at Philippe Lelong.

'Monsieur? Are you all right? Is Madame all right?'

'Oh – yes. She has gone to England.'

'Gone? But I thought – oh, well. She changed her mind.'

'Yes,' said Luc shortly.

'I think she may have been wise. I wish I had left Paris myself, but – where would I go? Foolishly, perhaps, I am hoping for the best. As you are, Monsieur?'

'Yes.'

'What else can we do? I am sending some photographs and an article of mine to England today. In great haste, before it is too late. To *Style* magazine, through our courier service.'

'Really?' said Luc. Did this tiresome young man really think he was interested in such details?

'Yes. It may be the last I am able to send for some time. I should have given them to your wife, their arrival would have been better guaranteed.'

'I doubt that,' said Luc.

Philippe Lelong looked at him. 'You have not arranged a safe passage for her?'

'I don't think that is anything to do with you.'

'Forgive me, Monsieur. Goodbye. May I give you my card, in case you would like more copies of the photographs?'

Luc took the card without thinking, stuffed it in his pocket. It was the easiest thing to do: although it seemed to him extremely unlikely that he would want to communicate with some arrogant homosexual.

'You must excuse me now,' he said shortly. 'I have work to do.'

He sat staring at the pictures of Noni all the way to l'Opera on the metro, wondering how he was going to endure life without her. Her

411

and her mother. And how he was going to be able to live with himself without them.

Adele decided to move on, while the children were still asleep and it was still cool. They would have to get out later, have a break. But for now—

She took the next turning right, a very small road; there was still a line of refugees, but fewer cars, it was possible to actually make some progress. The countryside looked beautiful; amazed that she was even able to notice it, she stared at the golden cornfields, the brave scarlet poppies, the swoops of land, studded with trees, and felt comforted.

A village. Good. She might be able to get some coffee here, perhaps even a *petit déjeuner*. Thank goodness she had some money.

As she pulled into the village, she realised there was little hope of coffee. Or of anything. A vast queue of people stood patiently at the village pump, holding cups, jugs, anything that would take water; a man stood there operating it, charging ten sous a glass, two francs for a bottle. Bastard, thought Adele: she wasn't going to give him any of her precious money. How dared he take advantage of all these poor people at the pump, where water should be free? He deserved the arrival of the Germans, that was for sure. She wondered how near they were and shuddered. And drove on.

Two kilometres further down the road, she saw a farmhouse. A perfectly normal farmhouse, not very big, just below the road, down one of the tracks around which French rural life revolves. Was it worth it? Should she try? It would be marvellous. They might even let her use the lavatory, wash her hands. You never knew . . .

An old man came to the door: with a gun. He looked frightened. He had thought she might be the Germans, Adele realised, and hurriedly explained: that she was from Paris, trying to get south with her two children. She didn't say she was English; that might upset him too, arouse nationalistic notions.

'I wondered if, Monsieur, you could – sell me a cup of coffee? Just a small one. And—'

She was shocked to see him start to cry, tears rolling down his wizened brown face. So shocked that she stepped forward, put her arm round his shoulders. 'Monsieur, don't cry. It will be all right, I promise you.'

He wiped his eyes, began to explain, in a French so guttural that she could hardly understand it, that he was alone, that his son had left to join the army, and his wife had died, only a week earlier.

'It was the shock, Madame, the shock of all this—' He stopped.

'Oh dear. Well—' It seemed awful to continue to press for coffee; perhaps she shouldn't. But then—

'What do you want?' It was a woman's voice: hostile, harsh. Adele turned round; she was quite young, white-faced, holding an old rifle.

'Get out, go on—'

'Nothing, I don't want anything, well, only coffee, or even some water, and I would pay for it—'

'Get out, I said. We don't want your money. What use is money to us? When the Germans are nearly here?' She waved the gun at Adele. 'Get out of here.'

Adele left.

A little further on, they found a stream by the side of the road; miraculously there was no one else there. The children were awake now and fractious; she got them out, washed them as well as she could, changed Lucas, let them play while she made breakfast. She spread the last of the bread with apricot jam, gave them some juice, heated some water for coffee on the little stove, which she had set rather precariously on the running board of the car. It tasted like nectar.

Her spirits rose: they would get there. Of course they would.

But she decided just the same to rejoin the other road. At least that way she didn't have to worry about the route.

Halfway through that morning, Philippe Lelong was just packing up his pictures and captions to take to *Style* magazine to catch the courier when his phone rang. It was the unpleasant man, married to Cedric's friend, the one who had been so ungracious to him that morning. He was tempted to cut him off; but something in his voice was different, less hostile, there was a note of pleading in it. Slightly against his will, he found himself agreeing to meet Luc Lieberman at the *Style* offices: 'But don't be more than thirty minutes, Monsieur. Then it will be too late.'

He had a nerve: asking such a favour of him after he had been so rude. But this was a very special circumstance. They all had a common enemy: a dreadful one. They had to remain united; or the enemy would become twice as strong.

'Beware the Hun in the sun.' It was a well-known saying among pilots. They literally seemed to come out of the sun at you, you were dazzled;

what was more, you were confused, not sure if it was actually an enemy or a friendly plane. Above them, looking down, you could tell from the wing shape, but blinded by the sun, it was almost impossible, it could be a Messerschmitt or a Stuka. Or it could easily be another Spitfire or Hurricane.

The Germans had been playing a cat-and-mouse game that early June; 3228 Squadron was sent out to patrol the French coast, to 'show they were still in being', as the order was phrased. It seemed to them all after a bit to be a bad idea: the Germans would watch them flying past and then wait for them to come back before pouncing. It meant people were being lost unnecessarily. Those patrols were being stopped now and the raids were beginning in earnest . . .

Kit was supremely confident now; reaping the benefit of his long, careful training. Such training was becoming a luxury; months had become weeks, and, it was rumoured, would soon be days. But it was the new boys who were far more likely to be shot down; it was said if you could survive three weeks, you could survive. Not quite true, of course, but still. It was a thought to hang on to. There was another saying, slightly at odds with it; that there were old pilots and bold pilots, but no old bold pilots. Kit knew he was a bold pilot; confidence gave him courage, enabled him to take risks. He just tried not to think about being allowed to grow old, or even its likelihood.

The great fear was of being burned; they all felt it. Death, hopefully, was quick; but the living hell of fire haunted them all.

The worst thing was the waiting; waiting for the phone to ring, the order to scramble. It remained for Kit an absolute purgatory; he never got used to it. He had just about learned not to throw up, but he shook quietly, biting his nails to keep his hands still, smoking hard. They all smoked.

It was all so incongruous; one moment you were half lying in a deck chair in the sun, playing chess, pretending to read, fooling around, the next the phone would go. It didn't always mean scramble either, it could be a time check, a change of duties. That made it worse, the prolonged agony. But then it would come – 'Squadron scramble' – the ground crew would ring the bell and that was it.

'We run to the aircraft,' he wrote to Catriona, 'the ground crew start the planes, and we just put on our parachute packs, and get in. While we're being strapped in, we put on our helmets. And then that's it, we're up and away. All very exciting indeed.'

That wasn't quite true; but he knew it was what she would want to hear, would find less worrying.

What he found harder to describe was the change in his mood once he was up: the sense of absolute concentration which drove every other emotion away. But knowing that was to come didn't seem to help him through the waiting.

Catriona was enjoying her nursing training; her great ambition, she said, was to go and nurse abroad. 'Or in London, that would be grand. Anywhere the action is. But the rate I'm going, the war will be over before I finish emptying bed pans at the Infirmary. Although it's a lot faster than the usual nursing training; the older nurses, sisters and so on, are rather shocked by it, keep telling us we're having it easy and we're not properly trained.'

All their letters to one another ended the same way: with the words 'Love for ever and ever'.

'Look, I know it isn't very important. In the larger scale of things.'

'No, Oliver, it isn't.'

'But, Celia, we still have a publishing house to run. And if this bill goes through . . .'

The bill was one proposed by Kingsley Wood, the Chancellor of the Exchequer, to subject books to purchase tax, it was seen as a death knell by the trade.

'I honestly don't care if it goes through. And I don't see how you can either.' Celia glared at him across the breakfast table; she seemed even to herself to be in a perpetual bad temper these days, driven to it by anxiety for her children, three of the four in dreadful danger. She was surprised by how powerful and invasive the anxiety was; she had felt just as terrified for Oliver in the last war, but somehow she had managed to set it aside, at least while she was at Lyttons. But now, not even work could distract her; everyone noticed it, the uncharacteristic lack of opposition, the nod of slightly uninterested approval at anything she was asked to approve and, most notably, the lack of inspiration emanating from her office. Barty noticed it most and hated it, it added to her general depression; Celia's perfectionism was what most inspired her at Lyttons, made her struggle to match it. Suddenly life as one of Lyttons' major editors was absurdly easy; the taut wires of command and communication from her office had gone slack. And it was not a happy thing.

'I can't believe it,' Barty said to Edgar Greene, walking into his office after what she had imagined to be a long confrontation with Celia and which had lasted for all of ten minutes, 'she's agreed to the lot. I don't know what to do.'

415

'Make the most of it,' said Edgar, 'it won't last.'

But it seemed it would.

Celia was aware of it herself and hardly cared; she went through the days in an odd state, her mind only half on what she was doing, the other half listening for the phone, for the ring at the bell which would mean the telegram, or Brunson coming in with the post. They were good, the boys; Kit phoned regularly, brief, confident calls, telling her of the fun in the mess and the greater fun of flying. It was odd, she thought, that no one in his squadron was ever killed or even injured; did he really think she was that stupid? Well, he was only twenty: a child still. Then she would reflect that he was actually taking his life in his hands every single day, along with the controls of his plane, and moving out into the skies and enemy fire, all in order to defend his country; and realised he must be further beyond childhood, beyond carefree, thoughtless, self-indulgent time than she would ever be. Oliver could accompany him notionally into that life; he could understand. And when Kit did come home as he quite often did, for twenty-four hours, when he sat at the dinner table, telling tales of incredible courage and unimaginable skill, talking of the comradeship of the squadron, the terrific decency of the other chaps, the bond that had formed between them all, she would see Oliver's eyes on him, proud, smiling and then suddenly sad, and felt alienated by the shared bond between them, the bond of death faced, over and over again, faced and avoided, and the shadow of it over every victory, every escape.

Giles was safe for the moment: training with his battalion in Wiltshire. He was doing rather well. She would not have believed it possible, the triumph of her dull, dry, nervous son, his recommendation for the Military Medal after Dunkirk. After his failure to get a commission she had expected an indifferent war. But Helena had come in person to tell her about Dunkirk, in an odd mixture of pride and hostility. I know you never thought it of him, she was clearly saying, never thought he was worth anything, and here he is, so brave, so fine a soldier that in the first months of the war he has been recommended for one of the highest military decorations. And Celia listened to her, equally proud, but suddenly ashamed of herself, not only of her attitude to Helena, but to Giles as well, her impatience, her condescension, her near-contempt.

'I'm – sorry, Helena,' she said suddenly, 'very sorry.'

Helena looked at her, clearly surprised. 'What for?'

'For failing to recognise Giles's sterling qualities. And I made that rather clear to you, I'm afraid. I feel badly about it now.'

Helena, recognising the enormity of this concession, still couldn't quite bring herself to kiss her; but she went over to her and smiled and said, 'Of course, Celia. Thank you.' And when she left, a very short time later, she did offer Celia her cheek.

Later, the shelling started; and that really was like being in hell. Out of nowhere it began, another clear blue sky, another hot, hot day: and then suddenly low-flying planes swooping down on them and then fire dropping from the sky, people screaming, diving for cover, in ditches. How could they do this, Adele thought, sitting helplessly in the back seat of the car, trying to soothe her children, holding their heads against her, how could they bomb defenceless people, who had done them no harm, threatened them with nothing, helpless old people in horse-drawn carts, little children, exhausted mothers? This was not an army to be defeated, this was a mass of unarmed, passive people.

They saw some dreadful sights, a girl screaming by her injured mother, a dead woman lying on top of her baby, which was nonetheless alive, and scooped up by another woman who had been with her. The woman stood there, holding the baby, covered with its mother's blood, shaking her fist at the planes, foolishly defiant, but nonetheless an emblem of courage for them all.

The cries were not all of '*Les Boches*'; '*Les Italiens*' were also blamed.

The attack passed; shaking, she climbed back into the driving seat and drove on; there was nothing else to do.

When she got home. When she got home . . .

And then, that evening towards sunset she saw the wonderful sight of the twin spires of Chartres across the flat plain; she recognised them at once, she had been to Chartres once before, Oliver had driven them there, via the fields of Flanders which he'd wanted them to see, and she felt a lift of triumph, as if she were already home.

'Look,' she said to Noni, 'look, we're nearly there.'

She had spoken unthinkingly; it was a dreadful mistake.

The small face, filthy after two days and nights now in the car, tear-streaked with misery and fear, looked up at her, the black eyes alight with joy. 'In England? And is Papa there?'

'Oh, my darling,' said Adele, and burst into tears, Noni's misplaced joy affecting her as the shelling and her own growing hunger had not. How could she have done this to her, her beloved little daughter, who until forty-eight hours earlier had been playing happily in her home in Paris, safe, contented, how could she have dragged her into this hell of shellfire and heat and hostility and danger? To which there was no certain end?

In the cramped sleeplessness of the nights she faced that over and over again. Why did she think that there would be a boat waiting for her at Bordeaux, with a cabin neatly labelled 'Lytton'? It was madness, a dangerous, reckless madness that she had dragged them all into: simply because she had discovered her husband had gone back to his wife. Suddenly that seemed utterly inconsequential, a passing injury inflicted upon her, of no account at all set against what she had done to her child, a grown-up quarrel, a source of hurt pride, that she should have set aside, dealt with in a grown-up way.

She pulled over, signalled to Noni to climb into her lap, sat kissing her, cuddling her, making reassuring noises. Lucas slept on; he slept more and more, clutching his toy cow, dulled with misery and boredom.

They were on the outskirts of another village; they had parked the car beside a signpost. On it were pasted the now-familiar notes, heartbreaking, dreadful cries of pain: '*Madame DuClos, chez l'Hotel Reynaud, demande nouvelles de ses fils Bernard et Jacques, 4 et 5 ans, perdu près d'ici le 10 juin*'.

It kept happening; the children got lost in the crush, in the crowds, climbed unnoticed on to carts or trucks, their small legs too tired to walk further, without their parents realising they had gone, and in ten, fifteen minutes in the huge crowd it was too late. They were lost, for ever it seemed, while their parents continued to search, to ask, running up and down the line of people. Frantic mothers or fathers often banged on the window of her car, showing her pictures, desperately crying, '*Avez-vous vu cette fille, Madame?*' All she could say was, '*Non*'; but faced with that notice, thinking of the tiny Bernard and Jacques, lost to their mother probably for ever, imagining her panic and anguish as she waited so futilely in the hotel, Adele considered her own position and felt calmer. She had her children; they were all together; they still had some food; and they were nearly in Chartres.

On the other hand, it had taken two days to travel fifty miles – fifty miles as the crow flew at least – they were running out of petrol – and, it seemed days – it was days – since she had spoken to anyone, other than a fractious child or a hostile French adult.

When they got home . . . when they got home . . .

Chapter 29

'Home! You're home. But you can't be,' said Venetia. 'It's impossible.'

'Well, I'm sorry if it's unwelcome news, but I am.'

'Of course it's not unwelcome, it's marvellous. But why – how—'

'Well, you know I'm doing this course, para training, in Warminster. I've got a twenty-four-hour leave. I'd love to see you.'

'Jay, of course you can see me. I'll – I'll take you out to dinner. How would you like that? Oh, no, you've probably got someone much more glamorous and younger than me to spend the evening with—'

'Well, not in London,' said Jay, blithely tactless, 'and yes, dinner would be splendid. But of course I'd like to see my mother—'

'Of course you would. But she's at Ashingham, Jay. She's gone down with Gordon for a few days. She's been so tired lately, she collapsed last week, nothing serious, promise, and the doctor prescribed a week of country air. So she's in the Dovecot.'

'The dear old Dovecot. My first home. Are you sure she's OK?'

'She's absolutely fine. But she can't sleep, worrying about you and everything, and she's been working like a demon. She'll be broken-hearted to have missed you. Could you get down for the night?'

'Maybe on the way back. Not tonight, have to catch the dawn train. I'll telephone her.'

'Well, ask for Gordon first, otherwise the shock'll finish her off. Only joking. So – dinner, then?'

'Dinner it is. Thanks.'

'I'll take you to the Dorch.'

The Dorchester was in good form that night; filled with glamorous people, all beautifully dressed, the women in long dresses, the men in dinner jackets. Several of its regular set were there, the people who regarded it as their second home, a sort of clubhouse, the Duff Coopers, Loelia, Duchess of Westminster, Emerald Cunard, Lord Halifax – 'And look, there's Maggie Greville,' said Venetia. 'See, in her wheelchair, she's always here, holding court, she gives the kitchen masses of cream and eggs from her home farm and – oh, there's Hutch,' Venetia pointed out an extremely handsome and elegant black man, 'you know, the piano player, I think he was playing at the Savoy when we were there for Mummy's birthday last year, if you remember, anyway, they say he's having an affair with Edwina Mountbatten – oh, sorry, Jay, you probably don't want to hear all this silly nonsense.'

'Oh, but I do,' he said, grinning at her. 'It's a marvellous relief, and I knew I'd get it from you, silly nonsense, I mean—'

'Thanks,' said Venetia coolly.

'Oh, don't be stupid, you know I don't mean that. Have some more champagne, for goodness' sake. Get some roses in your cheeks, you look a bit pale. I wanted to see you terribly. Most of all because I knew it would be fun. Bit short of fun we are, down there in Somerset.'

'I expect you are. Oh, my God, Jay, time to hide behind the menus. One of Boy's fellow officers has just come in, nice but frightfully dreary, I really don't want to have to talk to him.'

'Where – oh, yes. Right-oh. It's all right, he hasn't seen us.'

'Good. Now, how is it all, Jay, what are you actually doing?'

'Well, I'll give you an edited version and then we won't talk about it any more. I'm doing a para training course, as I told you. Frightfully exciting.'

'Don't tell your poor mother,' said Venetia with a shudder, 'she really will never sleep again.'

'Of course not. I've actually told her I'm doing a code-breaking course. I couldn't think of anything much safer, except perhaps catering. And I didn't think she'd believe that.'

'Probably not.'

'What news of Boy? And Adele?'

'Oh, Jay, I wish there was some. Of Adele, I mean. As far as I know, she's still in Paris. It's a nightmare. An absolute nightmare. I can't sleep either. I feel – oh, it's hard to explain, permanently churned up. Odd. Distressed. If only, if only she'd come home earlier. Now it's too late. And the most terrifying thing is, with the Germans actually on their way to Paris, she's the enemy. God knows what will happen to her. It's appalling. I could kill that bastard Luc Lieberman.'

'Have you tried to make contact with her?'

'Of course. We've phoned and phoned, but the lines are dead. We've sent cables, but nothing happens. Do you know, Luc actually tried to make her come home in the end, and the stupid girl refused, told him she felt she should stay with him. Did you ever hear anything so stupid?'

'Oh, I don't know. You'd do the same. If Boy asked you. Well, perhaps not Boy any more,' he added hastily, 'but someone. You're like that, I know you are.'

'Well,' she sighed, 'I don't know that I would. Anyway, we can only hope and hang on.'

'And – Boy? Any news of him?'

'Yes, he's fine. At the moment. He's up in Scotland doing some kind of training. He's adoring it. He writes quite often.'

'I'd forgotten how you two were still friends,' said Jay, 'jolly clever of you, I'd say. Whenever I end a relationship, I can't wait to see the back of whoever it is.'

'Yes, well, we've got four children to worry about,' said Venetia quickly, 'so we have to keep – talking.'

'S'pose so. I'm in love at the moment,' he added, leaning forward. 'Super girl. I really think this might be it.'

'Jay! Really? How exciting.'

She smiled at him fondly; this was actually not the first time Jay had thought someone might be it, indeed it seemed to take place on an almost monthly basis. 'Tell me about her. And why aren't you with her tonight, instead of your old cousin?'

'You don't *look* old,' said Jay earnestly, 'you look marvellous. I like that dress. Although you are a bit thin, Venetia. Come on, you're not eating.'

'Oh – I'm not terribly hungry,' she said quickly, 'it's the worry about Adele. Tell me about your new lady love.'

'Well, she's in the WRNS. Posted down at Portsmouth. We'd have been together now, but she's on duty, couldn't get away. Bloody awful, but still—'

'What's her name?'

'Victoria. Victoria Halifax. Tory for short. She's an absolute stunner, so beautiful, look, I've got a picture here—'

Venetia looked: Victoria Halifax wearing her WRNS uniform smiled at her, a perfect, even-teethed smile. She was indeed, if not beautiful, extremely pretty, blonde, with a heart-shaped face and very wide eyes; she had signed the photograph 'With my fondest love – Tory' in a rather florid hand. Venetia smiled at Jay.

'She's – lovely,' she said.

'Isn't she? We met just before I went off. At the Blue Angel. She's a marvellous dancer, could be a professional, I should think. Anyway, she's doing awfully well in the WRNS, she was training to be a legal secretary before the war, she's frightfully clever, and funny too, she tells the most marvellous jokes, you'd love her, Venetia, I know—'

'I'm sure.' And then because she felt suddenly dreadfully lonely, and missing Boy more than she could have imagined, and felt so fiercely jealous of these two beautiful young people, she suddenly found her eyes filling with tears; Jay stared at her in horror; and she brushed them away quickly, horrified too at herself for spoiling his one lovely evening in London that he had so touchingly entrusted to her.

'Sorry,' she said, 'so sorry. Darling Jay, I'm a stupid old woman. Let's go and dance while we wait for our lobster.'

They were both already quite tipsy on the champagne; and both emotional, with their heads filled with other people. And somehow, partly in search of comfort, partly because of the champagne, but also because they were extremely fond of one another, they found themselves dancing rather closely.

The big hit that summer was 'A Nightingale Sang in Berkeley Square'.

'How appropriate,' said Jay, drawing her closer to him still as the band moved into it, and, 'Yes,' she said, thinking of that night, that last night there, in Berkeley Square with Boy, and resting her head against Jay, 'terribly appropriate.'

Across the room, Mike Willoughby-Clarke, the fellow officer of Boy's that Venetia had been so anxious to avoid, who was due to leave with his battalion the following day, pointed them out to his wife.

'That's Venetia Warwick. I was going to take you over, introduce you to her. But she's obviously pretty occupied with that young chap. New boyfriend, I suppose. She and Boy are divorced, you know. Damn shame. Lovely girl. Still, these things happen nowadays . . .'

It was on the third day, the Wednesday, that they ran out of petrol. Ten kilometres out of Tours. There were cars parked all along the road now, abandoned; petrol was becoming more precious than food. She had seen several fights at pumps; she had managed to get a few gallons the evening before. At a village, she had seen a petrol station just closing, an old man filling up a car, and then shaking his head at the next car behind, locking the tank, hanging a cardboard sign reading *Fermé* on it. The next driver and the next ran over to the old man, shouting at him, threatening, waving money; he spat on the ground, shook his head, pulled out a Gauloise and lit it. And then disappeared into the house.

She had waited, until everyone had lost interest, driven on. And then she got out of the car, brushed her hair, put on some lipstick, sprayed herself liberally with *Joy*, hoping rather vainly it would disguise the smell of sweat that she knew hung about her, taken one of the two bottles of Luc's Lafite Rothschild from the suitcase in the boot, and walked slowly and as provocatively as she could over to the door.

She never knew afterwards whether it was the provocative walk, the Joy or the Château Lafite Rothschild that did it; but she drove on with twenty litres of petrol in the tank and a sense of triumph as great as if she had won the war single-handed.

Absurdly, wasting time, risking losing the car, everything she had, she drove into Chartres, parked as near the cathedral as she could and led the children into its vast cavernous beauty; she went over to the candles, bought two, and lit them, gave them each one to hold.

'Should we say prayers, Maman?' asked Noni, accepting this new surprising scenario with placid sweetness.

'Yes, we should. We should thank God for looking after us all this time and ask Him to help us the rest of the way.'

'All right.' She closed her eyes, put her hands together. 'And say to bless Papa. Don't forget that.'

'Of course not.'

And then she took the children by the hand and walked them slowly round the cathedral and its velvety darkness, behind the high altar, pausing at each side chapel, lighting candles at another *prie-dieu*. And then panicked at the thought of what might be happening outside to the car, the precious car which had become at once their world and their refuge against it.

But it was quite safe.

She had been right to stay on the bigger roads; the villages were becoming dangerous, shuttered against the invader, and at the same time vulnerable to looting. She had heard talk in Chartres of tables and chairs in ransacked cafés hacked to pieces to make firewood, even of small churches being broken into and treasures taken.

But the greatest terror was of the German army, appearing from no one knew where . . .

She knew at once why the car had stopped: it had been overheating, in its slow progress, but she had managed to keep it ticking over. But it wasn't that; the dial had been jammed on empty for over five

423

miles, and now, finally, it gave up its gallant struggle and spluttered to a halt.

Oddly calm, she got out. She had been prepared for this; it was why she had brought the pram. Thank God for it: thank God.

'What are you doing, Mummy?'

'Getting the pram down, darling. We have to walk for a while. No more petrol, I'm afraid.'

'Goody. I'm so tired of the car.'

'Me too.'

As long as it didn't rain; the second night it had poured. She unpacked her cases with great care; the pram couldn't carry much. The Gaz stove would have to be left; probably just as well. She had shuddered at the thought of what would happen if it caught a bit of flying shell. She'd need the nappies – running low now – the tins of food and the tin opener, the bottles of water – only two left – the last bottle of wine, the precious Gauloises. She had given away two packs, in exchange for water, they had proved excellent currency.

She slung her own rucksack containing her money and her passport over her shoulder, then lifted Lucas on to the pram.

'I want to walk,' said Noni.

'You can. But you must hold on to the handle, I don't want to lose you.' Leaving the car was dreadful, like abandoning a stalwart friend. '*Au revoir*,' she said aloud, patting it, '*et merci*.'

'Who are you talking to, Mummy?'

'The car.'

'You're silly,' said Noni, a hint of slightly bossy reproof in her voice.

'I know.'

It was much more frightening; they had no protection now against anyone or anything. And the crowd was becoming increasingly unpleasant, any early camaraderie lost in the desperate struggle for survival, for food, for water. It was slow, painfully slow. After a while Adele's legs began to throb and her heels became sore. And they would have no shelter against the shells; but then there hadn't been an attack for two days. The children were happier, Lucas sitting, beaming at her, Noni running alongside, asking for rides now and again.

'This is much better,' she said. 'Are we nearly there?'

'Nearly.'

Four painful hours later, they arrived on the outskirts of Tours.

°

They spent two hours trying to find somewhere to stay. It seemed impossible. Every hotel, however tiny, was full, barred; no pleading, no indicating of her exhausted children, Noni crying bitterly, Lucas white-faced, lolling against her, silent with misery, no waving of her wad of money, helped her. There was simply no room. Anywhere. Finally, as they trudged through the streets, they found a schoolroom, its doors still open; the *directeur* had been about to lock up, but as she stood there, staring, almost hopeless by now, he suddenly nodded to her, gestured to her to come in. There was a mattress she and the children could share.

It was the first comfortable night they had spent; it was only a small mattress, but it was soft and they could stretch out. She pulled the blanket she had brought from the car over them, kissed them goodnight; Noni smiled, grateful for the sudden luxury, said sleepily, 'This is nice.'

It wasn't nice; she found a filthy lavatory, a cold tap hardly trickling, the air was fetid, and it was appallingly hot. But she fell asleep at once: only to wake after an hour or two, hearing children crying, women sobbing, men swearing; and in the terror of the solitary small hours, she looked her chances in the face and found them pitiful. She was still only halfway to Bordeaux. How could she ever get there, like this? It would take weeks. It was impossible. What could she do? What on earth could she do?

The Germans had arrived; after three days of eerie silence, of shuttered shops and closed doors and people talking in whispers, of appalling rumours of children's hands being cut off and women raped, of waiting and waiting in the deserted city, they were there.

It had been a desperate week, each day more nightmarish than the one before; no buses, an occasional train in the metro. Gas and electricity supplies were fitful; the great hotels, the Ritz and the Crillon, were shuttered and barred and on the Wednesday morning a hideous acrid smell hung over the city; the French had set fire to the vast oil supplies outside the city, rather than let the Germans have them. The huge crowds outside the stations had finally disbanded; shops were being ransacked for food.

Afterwards, Luc always wondered why he had not fled along with the rest of Paris; at the time, in his emotional confusion and misery, it had seemed quite simply unthinkable. Besides, there was Suzette; he could not abandon her now.

It was eight o'clock that Friday morning; Luc heard them first: the awful sound of motorcycles and trucks, and most agonising of all, summing up as nothing else could the conquest of the beautiful city, the sound of caterpillar tanks on cobbled streets.

There was a sudden beating on the door; Luc started. Was it possible they had come already to find him, the Gestapo, the Nazis, apprised of his Jewish blood? He took a deep breath and went to open it; but it was not the Gestapo that stood there, but Henri Monnet, grinning cheerfully.

'Come and watch. It's a tremendous spectacle.'

'But – is it safe?'

He shrugged. 'Probably not. But half Paris, or what is left of half Paris, is out there. Come along.'

They walked to the Champs-Elysées; they were not alone, groups of people stood all along the route, watching. And it was worth watching; he would not have missed it. It was a superb display, not only of military force but of theatrical know-how, Hitler's greatest gift, passed on to his generals.

There were two formations: one heading towards the Eiffel Tower, the other the Arc de Triomphe. They goose-stepped their way in, this seemingly endless army, preceded and followed by a great motorised phalanx, in perfectly pressed uniforms, gleaming boots, shining helmets, dazzling in the brilliant sun.

Hour after hour it went on. Cars arrived, patrolling the small streets with loudspeakers, warning that 'No demonstrations are permitted while our troops march in. Any hostile act will be punishable by death.'

The German flag went up over all the city, above Les Invalides, the Arc de Triomphe, the Hôtel de Ville, the place de la Concorde, even the Eiffel Tower; there had been a struggle there, the first had been too large, it had filled with wind like sails, and then begun to tear, and the Germans had had to climb the tower again (the evacuating French troops had put the lift out of commission), with a smaller one.

The Hôtel Crillon bore one as well, and the Lutetia; the Ritz had already served breakfast to General Bock, Commander of the Army, the Crillon its finest vintage champagne to General von Studnitz, the General Officer Commanding.

But in the outer reaches of the city, nothing seemed as brutal; and when Luc finally reached Suzette's apartment on foot towards the end of the day, he found her surprisingly calm and cheerful.

'It's not so bad,' she said, pointing to one of the posters of a handsome smiling German serving out biscuits to a group of children, holding the smallest in his arms, and holding out the biscuits.

426

'You can't believe that rubbish,' said Luc. But, 'I can,' she said. 'In the shop this afternoon, a convoy stopped and we were all so frightened, but you know, they bought chocolates and the charming young soldiers shared them among the children. They are saying now that we have made peace, the war is over. And they will settle the English very quickly.'

Luc was silent. Thinking of his own English, praying she was not yet 'settled'.

'And this is where we keep emergency rations. Chocolate, biscuits and so on. In case the Germans come. So if you get sent any by your father, you have to hand over half. All right? That way, if there's a siege, it won't be too bad. OK?'

Izzie nodded earnestly. 'OK. But I don't suppose Father will send me any, sweets aren't the sort of thing he thinks about.'

'Well, if he does. Thing is, I've heard Great-grandpa talking about what rations they've got for the siege and they don't sound much fun. Powdered egg, condensed milk, it'll be awful.'

'Does he think there will be a siege?'

'Oh, yes. Any day now, apparently. The Germans are going to arrive by parachute. Oh, and that's another rule. If you see one dropping into the garden or something you have to ring that bell, over there, see, by the terrace. And then Great-grandpa will get his gun and shoot him.'

'What – straight away?'

'Well, of course,' said Henry. 'They've got to know we mean business. No use asking him in for a cup of tea or something. After that, someone has to leg it down to the village to get the church bells ringing. To say there's an invasion.'

'Oh, I see,' said Izzie. She was beginning to feel a little nervous. No one had suggested the Germans would drop into the garden at Primrose Hill.

'The other thing is, they might be in disguise. So you have to suspect everyone. Specially nuns, Great-grandpa says, it's a very popular disguise. The thing in that case is to get them in conversation, see if they sound different. If they do, then ring the bell. But not till then.'

'But surely an ordinary nun wouldn't be dropping into the grounds by parachute?' said Izzie. 'You'd know that was a German, surely.'

Henry looked disconcerted; he clearly hadn't thought of that. 'Well – perhaps not. Anyway, use your common sense. They haven't got much of that, being foreigners, Great-grandma says. It's jolly good fun here,

Izzie. The only thing is, we still haven't had an air raid. It's so unfair. We keep thinking we've heard the siren, but it's always a practice. It's going to be so wizard, living down in the cellars. When they really start, we'll have to sleep there. The other thing that's fun is the dogfights. We've had a few of them over here, but not nearly enough.'

'Dogfights? Are there a lot of dogs here?'

'In the air, you dope. The planes, fighting, the Germans and our chaps. It's really exciting. We keep hoping for one to be shot down in the grounds, but that hasn't happened yet, either. If we were still in Kent, we'd be seeing them all the time, it's so unfair. Still, fingers crossed. Don't look so worried, Izzie, we'll look after you.'

Izzie found this only slightly reassuring.

Celia appeared in the doorway of Venetia's office.

'Venetia, have you got those costings yet?'

'What costings?' said Venetia.

'What costings! Sometimes I wonder if you're with us at all at the moment. For the new crime series.'

'No,' said Venetia. She sounded sulky, the little girl she had once been caught out in some omission.

'But why not? Venetia, this is important. We can't afford to get behind, we'll—'

'I don't care,' said Venetia in a low voice.

'What did you say?'

'I said I don't care.' The voice was less low now, with a throb of latent tears in it; Celia stared at her.

'Venetia, I know you're under a lot of strain. But you can't just let things go. When the war is over – and it will be – what happens to Lyttons will matter again. It matters anyway, we have a duty to supply people with books, the troops are ordering large numbers. Besides, I have always –' she corrected herself '– usually found that distracting myself with work is extremely helpful.'

'Well, I don't,' said Venetia. She stared at Celia, her face flushed, her eyes brilliant. 'I don't find it at all helpful. I can't even think about work at the moment. I'm so worried. About Boy and Adele and Kit, of course, and Giles and Jay. I know they're all right at the moment, but it won't last, Giles could have been so easily killed already. And – and the children, down there without me, suppose something happened—' She stopped, dashed her hand across her eyes.

Celia sat down suddenly, looked at her across the desk. 'And?'

'And what?'

'There's something else, isn't there?'

'No.'

'Venetia, I think there is.'

'Mummy, there isn't.' She looked wary suddenly, and surprisingly calm, as if she had been frightened out of her panic. 'Now please leave me alone. Look, I'll do the costings today. I promise. Sorry about that little outburst. I know everyone's just as worried. You must be desperate about Kit.'

'I am,' said Celia, 'absolutely desperate. This is far worse than the last war, then I only had your father to worry about. Now there's half a dozen of you. I'm finding it horribly hard to work myself. What's the latest from Boy?'

'Oh – training still in Scotland. He says it's huge fun.'

'It is hideous, isn't it?' said Celia. 'The fear. It's always there, like toothache, or some dreadful insistent noise grinding in your head. You can't get away from it. And it's going to go on and on, I'm afraid, it's not like some mercifully brief illness. And I have to tell you, I feel appalling about Adele. If we hadn't had that quarrel, she'd quite possibly be safely home. So I have guilt to add to my worry.'

'Oh Mummy, that's—'

'No, don't say it, you know it's true. Look, why don't you and I go out to lunch, and work on those costings between us? We could go somewhere nice, Simpsons, perhaps—'

'I'm sorry, Mummy, I really don't feel remotely hungry.'

Celia looked surprised. 'Hungry? When did that ever have anything to do with lunch? Lunch is an occasion, Venetia, not a meal. Still—'

'Oh – yes, all right. Thank you.'

'It must be lonely in that great house without the children,' said Celia suddenly. 'Why don't you move into Cheyne Walk?'

Venetia considered this for a moment; then, 'Do you know,' she said, 'I think I'd rather like that.'

'Good. I don't know why I didn't think of it before. Now, are you quite sure there's nothing else worrying you?'

'Mummy, I'm absolutely sure.'

But there was.

Kit had been given ten days' leave. Things had been a bit quiet since Dunkirk; there were still patrols of course, and the escort duties, but everyone seemed to be waiting for something. It was – odd. The calm before a storm. And there must be a storm soon. Especially with Paris being invaded.

429

That was a nightmare; he could only hope and pray that Adele was all right. If only she'd come home when it had been possible: if only. But there'd been that stupid row with their mother over her appalling Fascist friends, and – well, it hadn't been the same since. She must be in danger, she was English, she was the enemy. And besides, Luc was Jewish. Kit didn't give much for his chances. Not if Hitler was taking over Paris. As he was.

Anyway: however worried he was about everyone else, he was off to Scotland. To see Catriona. It was a glorious prospect.

'Apparently he's got some girlfriend up there,' said Celia. Her voice was ice cold. 'Extraordinary.'

'I don't see why,' said Oliver mildly. 'He's twenty, he's a very red-blooded young chap, I would think it extraordinary if he didn't have a girlfriend.'

'Oliver, he's too young. Far too young. I can only trust it's not serious. Or rather, that he doesn't think it's serious. I'm sure she's quite dreadful.'

'Now why should she be dreadful?'

'She's training to be a nurse. Not just for the war, but as a career. Not the sort of girl we'd want Kit to be mixed up with.'

'Celia, really! Why ever not?'

'Well – it's such a worthy career. So dull. And so – second-rate. Why not fly higher, why not be a doctor?'

'My dear, you really do talk the most appalling nonsense,' said Oliver, 'and I might remind you that you were only eighteen when we met. I hope you aren't suggesting that was all a bit of youthful folly.'

The family was all gathered round the lunch table at Ashingham on Saturday 15 June when the news came. Venetia, pale and tired, had insisted on going down to see her children. Sebastian said he would go with her to see Izzie and offered to drive her down. He had always been an appallingly dangerous driver; with his deteriorating eyesight, he was lethal. Venetia, who was in the process of moving into Cheyne Walk and disbanding her household, said she would get her chauffeur to drive them. 'He's joining up on Monday, but we might as well get our pound of flesh out of him. Then you can sleep on the way home, Sebastian. You know you always have too much of Grandpapa's port.'

Celia said she would join them. 'Oliver, you can stay here. I'll get Barty to come and sit with you. It's Brunson's afternoon off. You can't be left alone, the raids might start.'

'You don't think Barty might have something better to do?' said Oliver.

'Of course not. Why ever should she?'

But Barty said with unaccustomed selfishness that if they were all going to Ashingham she would like to join them 'and see Billy. I haven't set eyes on him since Christmas, and I'm longing to meet his Joan.'

'You could surely go another time,' said Celia coldly, but Barty said firmly that it seemed too good an opportunity to miss.

So in the end, Oliver was bundled, protesting, into the car and driven down as well.

Lunch was noisy: the Warwick children, never well disciplined, were over-excited at seeing their mother and at showing off their new country skills. 'I can skin a rabbit,' said Henry proudly, 'it'll come in jolly useful for the siege.'

'And I can bake a hedgehog,' said Roo, 'Great-grandpa showed me. You do it in clay. They taste really delicious, he says.'

Elspeth was proving as plucky and talented a rider as her mother: 'Have her out with the hounds in the autumn,' said Lady Beckenham proudly, watching her taking the fences in the paddock, her small face a study in fierce concentration. And even little Amy insisted on their going to admire her dam: a small but impenetrable barrier to the stream below the home meadow. As a result, the water had formed a deep muddy pool below it and a new tributary; she was flushed with pride.

'Great-grandpa says when the Germans come, we can drown them in my pond. Or the nuns.'

It was left to Izzie to explain about the nuns.

As a result of all this, lunch was very late; Lord Beckenham came in looking rather agitated.

'Just been listening to the news. The Germans are getting to work in Paris. Already arresting people, confiscating radios and so on, and they're bombing those poor devils on the roads down to the Loire, the injured are lining the roads apparently, and they're blowing up bridges. I wish I was there, could show them a thing or two—'

'Oh, Papa, don't,' said Celia. She had turned very pale. 'I'm glad you're not there. Tell me – tell me more about Paris.'

'Well, the government have left, apparently. Bloody cowards. Typical. Just abandoned their people in Paris. And the army's in full retreat. Just running away, can you believe it. De Gaulle's in London with Churchill. God knows what's going on. Rommel's advancing on Cherbourg and—'

'Yes, but – what else did it say about Paris?'

'Not a lot. I told you. There's talk of looting Jewish property, and a lot of Americans are being questioned but—'

A strange sound cut through his voice: it was Venetia, her voice loud, almost a scream. 'Stop it. Just stop it. They can't be, not yet. It's out of the question, how would they know where the Jewish people were, they can't, or the Americans either. It's obviously just rumour, stupid ill-informed rumour—'

''Fraid not, Venetia, it was the BBC.'

'It could still be rumour. It must be, I won't listen to this nonsense—'

The children all stared at her, their eyes large; Elspeth began to cry.

'Venetia, do calm down.' Celia's voice was cold. 'You're upsetting the children.'

'Don't tell me to calm down!' cried Venetia, turning on her. 'Just don't. If it wasn't for you, you and your – your dreadful ideas and your ghastly friends, Adele would be home now, with us, instead of over there in danger of her life. What do you think will become of her, in Paris with the Nazis? She'll be taken away, interned, probably has been already, we'll never see her again. And it's all your fault, yours, I—'

Shepard, the Beckenhams' extremely elderly butler, appeared in the doorway.

'Not now, Shepard,' said Lord Beckenham, clearly relieved nonetheless for the interruption, 'not a good moment.'

'But, my lord—'

'Shepard, what exactly is it?' said Lady Beckenham impatiently. 'If it's luncheon, it can wait.'

'It's not luncheon, your ladyship. It's a telephone message.'

'Well, that can wait as well. The vicar, no doubt, wanting to know how many boys will be at church tomorrow. Why he can't—'

'It's not the vicar, your ladyship. It's Mr Brunson, telephoning from Cheyne Walk.'

'Oh, how inconsiderate,' said Celia. 'He told me he was taking the afternoon off, now he's bothering us with telephone messages. What was it about, this message, Shepard?'

'It was about Miss Adele. Mr Brunson has had a call from France.'

There was a very long, fierce silence; the entire room stared at him. Venetia, who had been standing up, shouting at her mother, sat down abruptly, glassy pale, put out her hand and grabbed Sebastian's who

432

was sitting next to her; Celia put her hands to her throat, swallowed hard.

'What – what about Miss Adele?' she said, and her voice was scarcely audible. 'Is she – that is – tell me, Shepard, what—'

'She's in Bordeaux, your ladyship. She wanted to speak to you. She's going to try to telephone here apparently, but it's very difficult to get through. She's all right and she has the children with her, but—' He paused, his old face moving oddly with some unreadable emotion; Venetia, assuming he was about to cry, stood up again, still gripping Sebastian's hand.

'But what, Shepard, it's all right, you must tell us whatever it is, but what—'

Shepard looked at her and, his face under control once more, addressed Lady Beckenham.

'But she asked me to say, your ladyship, that she's very sorry, she's had to abandon your pram.'

Chapter 30

'It was like some kind of mirage,' said Adele.

'What was?'

'The hotel. The one in Bordeaux. After the dreadful time on the road, being so frightened, the danger, the hardship and everything, it was bizarre. And I was filthy, absolutely filthy, you wouldn't believe it—'

'You're not exactly in pristine condition now,' said Venetia, smiling at her. She had driven down to Portsmouth to meet Adele and the children off the ship nine days after her extraordinary phone call.

'This is nothing. I hadn't washed, literally, for five days. Except in cold taps or village pumps. None of us had, had we, Noni?'

'Lucas's bottom was disgusting,' said Noni cheerfully. Her ordeal didn't seem to have greatly affected her.

'It was. Not too good now, terrible nappy rash.'

'Nanny will see to that.'

'Nanny! I'd forgotten such wonderful creatures existed. Venetia, you don't know you're alive!'

'I know. But *you* are, thank God. Go on, finish your story. What was so bizarre?'

'Well, being in the Splendide in Bordeaux. Everyone behaving as if nothing untoward was happening, all the reception rooms full of palms, great thick carpets, waiters rushing about with silver trays. They didn't have a room, but they let me sit in the foyer, and use the telephone—'

'And you got there in an ambulance?'

'Yes. Well, from Tours. I got that far on my own.'

'Oh, Dell. You're so brave,' said Venetia helplessly.

'No choice. Anyway, I wasn't being very brave then, in Tours, I mean. I was crying, we all were, pushing Grandmama's pram through the rain, absolute chaos, you can't imagine, all the roads jammed, planes roaring overhead, I know now Churchill was actually arriving that day. Anyway, Lucas lost his cow—'

434

'A cow! You had a cow with you?'

'A toy one. A real one would have been long since stolen, I can tell you. Anyway, it was his lifeline. And Noni ran after it, didn't you, angel?'

'Yes, and I slipped, fell down and cut my knee—'

'She didn't just slip, she totally disappeared under a car and . . .'

Adele had screamed; and gone on screaming. Even after the driver, who had been virtually stationary, had hauled Noni and the cow out, checked her for injury, the only visible one being a gash on her knee, bleeding profusely, and handed her to Adele.

'She's perfectly all right, Madame. But it could have been much worse. You should keep your children under control.'

Adele stopped screaming. She looked at him. And then raised her hand and slapped his face.

'You bastard,' she shouted at him in English, 'you arrogant bloody bastard. How dare you tell me how I should control my children, how dare you, you arrogant bloody fool—'

'And the irony of it was,' she said, laughing, 'that if I hadn't lost my temper, forgotten to be French – and I'd been so careful, thought I'd be safer that way – the girl driving the ambulance wouldn't have heard me. It felt like some kind of a miracle, she leaned out and just said, "Are you English?" You have no idea how wonderful it was to hear an English voice.'

They had taken her in, heaped her into their already overloaded ambulance – overladen not with injured soldiers, but redundant English nurses from a makeshift hospital in Alsace Lorraine.

'But they couldn't take the pram. I was so worried about it for some reason, Grandmama's precious third-generation Silver Cross. The last I saw of it was an elderly couple leaping on it, piling their own possessions into it. Poor old things.' She was silent. 'I've seen so many dreadful things, Venetia, I'll never forget it, any of it.'

'Like—'

'Oh, not now. *Pas devant les enfants.*'

'*Pourquoi pas, Maman?*'

'Oh, Noni. Sorry, angel, how silly of me. Here, come and sit on my knee in the front. Lucas isn't going to wake up till we get to London. Poor little boy, he's been so terribly upset.'

'More than me,' said Noni. 'He kept crying and crying, didn't he, Maman?'

'Well, he's very little. You're almost grown up. She's been so wonderful, Venetia, I can't tell you. So good and brave and helpful.'

Venetia smiled at her; at this beautiful, rather solemn little person she hardly knew.

'How lovely for Mummy to have you.'

'What I want now is to see Daddy. Is he here yet?'

'Not – yet,' said Venetia carefully. 'But I'm sure we'll hear from him soon.'

'Good.'

They drove on; Noni became sleepy, sucking her thumb, curled up on her mother's lap. Adele smiled down at her.

'Poor little thing. She's had an awful time. They both have. God knows what harm it's done them.'

'Possibly not much. They're very resilient, children.'

'I know but – well, anyway. I'll finish the story. The ambulance was going to Bordeaux too. It seemed so amazing sitting there, travelling at what seemed like high speed down the road. We got there in twelve hours. Twelve hours! Unbelievable. It was taking me that to travel twelve miles. Anyway, we got there and I suddenly realised I had no idea what to do next. The girls were all going home courtesy of the Navy, but I had nothing arranged at all. Obviously. I'd just focused on getting there, couldn't think further than that. And there was this place, teeming with people, all trying to get away. It was another nightmare.

'The one thing I knew was I had a lot of money: I'd hardly spent any. So I got them to drop me near the centre of the town, and then asked someone where the best hotel was. And just walked in, head held high, and asked to see the manager. You know how Mummy always says breeding shows. It seems to be true. I mean, there I was in my filthy frock with these two little urchins, and it was quite easy. I showed him my passport and told him I was Lady Celia Lytton's daughter and that my grandfather was the Earl of Beckenham and he just believed me. He spoke English, he let me use the phone, and – well, I might still have been in trouble without Mummy's friend Lord Arden. You know, she told me to ring him after I got through again?'

'Yes. I'm extremely surprised you did,' said Venetia briskly.

'Why? Because he's a Fascist? Venetia, when you've been through what I had, you'll do anything. Anything. To survive. Believe me. It's the one thing above all this whole thing has taught me.'

'But – being one of Mosley's best friends, knowing what they all said about Hitler—'

'I know. But you just have to believe me. I just didn't even think about any of it. He was English, he could help me. That was what mattered. At that moment.'

'So – what did he do? He wasn't there, was he?'

'Yes. He's got – had – a house there. All that lot do, Somerset Maugham, Daisy Fellowes, you know, the best-dressed woman in the world, the Windsors were actually there, at La Croe, their house in Nice, entertaining Maurice Chevalier, of all people. They'd suddenly realised they were trapped, and actually asked if they could have a battleship to get them home. Can you believe that? They were told no.

'Anyway, Lord Arden was quite sweet, I must say, clearly adores Mummy. He was going home the next day on a boat, and he said he'd do what he could but he knew it was already terribly overbooked. They all were. There were even some English journalists trying to buy a boat of their own. Anyway, he invited me to dinner; I said I had the children with me and he said bring them to his house, his housekeeper would look after them. So – I decided to go. And I went to one of the shops in the Cours de l'Intendance, that's like Bond Street, they were all open still, selling wonderful clothes, and scent and chocolate and stuff. It was like another mirage, I just couldn't believe it. After seeing people fighting over cups of water on the road. So I spent nearly all my money on the most divine dress and some new shoes, and when I got to Lord Arden's place, I had a bath and bathed the children, God, it was heaven, and got all dressed up and off we went. Me still thinking I was hallucinating, I must say. We went to somewhere called the Chapon Fin, the Maxims of Bordeaux, and had dinner and Lord Arden said he'd arranged for the captain of the boat he was going on to come and have a drink with us. I mean, really sweet.'

'Mmm—' said Venetia. She looked at Adele doubtfully.

'He arrived, he was revolting, fearfully smarmy, kept kissing my hand and everything. And he said he was *désolé*, he couldn't possibly take us. Absolutely no room.'

'So what did you do?'

'I slept with him,' said Adele.

She had had to share a cabin, a third-class cabin for two, with five other people; they had taken it in turns to use the beds. Adele had slept on the floor most of the way, so that the children could have her turn in the bed. She kept them out of the cabin as much as she could: partly for their sake, partly for the sake of her fellow travellers.

Lord Arden had paid for her ticket; she had told him she would pay him back.

'I wouldn't dream of accepting it,' he had said, flicking an imaginary

437

piece of dust off his exquisitely tailored linen suit. Even he had to share with two others; the linen suit looked considerably less exquisite at the end of the voyage.

Theirs was one of the last ships to leave France; it was an endless journey, lasting nine days, zig-zagging all the way up to England. At first they were all afraid of shells and mines, but after a while they settled into an entirely false sense of security. Adele and Lord Arden talked a great deal, sitting out on deck when the sun shone, and in one of the desperately crowded bars – which quickly ran out of everything – when the weather was less nice. Chatting, not touching on any serious matters, gossiping about mutual friends, Celia, the state of Paris when Adele had left it, the state of London in the early spring when Lord Arden had last seen it. He had been charming, attentive, and fun; she could see why her mother liked him so much. No mention was made of Oswald Mosley, of his incarceration in Brixton Prison, or of Lady Mosley's in Holloway. He had appeared perfectly unsurprised that she had managed to acquire a place on the boat; she presumed he must have realised how desperate she was and guessed that she would go to any lengths to achieve what she wanted.

'Anyway, I'm here and I never thought I would be,' Adele said to Venetia, as they reached the outskirts of London, with the children both asleep in the back of the car.

'Didn't you?'

'Well – I did and I didn't. It all seems rather – surreal now. But at the time, it was hard to believe we'd get through. Especially when we were being shelled. And we ran out of petrol, of course . . .'

'I just can't believe how brave you are. How you could even have set out on your own like that.'

'Well – I was so terribly hurt and angry. About Luc. Though that did seem less and less important as time went by. And of course I had no idea how bad it was going to be. Lots of people turned round, started going back to Paris; I did even consider that at one point. But – well, I'm glad I didn't.'

'And – Luc?'

'I'm trying not to think about him,' said Adele after a silence. 'About any of it. There's obviously going to be a long separation. I've got time to sort things out, decide what I want to do. I suppose – I suppose there's nothing from him?'

'Nothing. We've tried and tried telephoning Constantines, but the phones are dead.'

'Constantines' phones are dead? But why, I don't understand—'

'All the phones are dead. It seems. We presumed they'd just taken over the telephone system. Certainly for international calls.'

'Yes, of course. They would have done.' Adele's voice was very low and flat. 'How naive of me to assume things would just stay the same. It's the first thing they'd do. And letters – nothing from Luc?'

'No. But even if it was possible to send one – why should he write to us? Why should he think you were here?'

'Because I told him I was coming. In my letter that I left for him.'

'Oh. Oh, I see. Well—' Venetia was silent; wondering what comfort she could possibly offer. 'Well, I just don't think anything, anything at all would get through. I mean surely they'd just – stop, take over control of the post office. Wouldn't they? That's what we assumed.'

'I don't know,' said Adele fretfully, 'I don't know what's happening there. Nobody knows. It's all rumour. Oh, Venetia, I'm so frightened for him. So frightened. Whatever he's done.'

'Of course you are. Of course. It's the most terrifying situation. I – I just wish I could be more helpful.'

'I should have stayed,' said Adele, and her voice was very shaky now. 'I should have stayed, shouldn't I, given him a chance to explain. It was wrong of me, rushing off, taking the children, his children, terribly wrong, I – just think of what might be happening to him now, and I took his car, his only chance to escape. Oh God, Venetia, how could—'

'Listen,' said Venetia gently, 'you did the best possible thing. You got your children away, you got yourself away. You were in real danger, far greater than his. You know the French have signed an armistice, don't you? Just – capitulated?'

'Oh, yes, we got some news on the ship. How did everyone take that here?'

'They were terribly shocked. I don't think anyone expected it really. One headline described the British government's "grief and amazement". That just about summed it up. But think, Adele, what that means. You were the enemy, you would have been – well, I can't bear to think about it. You needed to escape. If you'd waited, who knows what might have happened, he could have refused to let you go, persuaded you to stay, even. As he has all this time. That was so wrong, you know, that should make you feel less guilty, he shouldn't have done it.'

'I know. And the change of heart, the sudden urging me away, that was all because of – well, what was going on. Pretty shitty really, I have to keep telling myself that.'

'Yes, you do. He'll be all right, Adele, of course he will. And you certainly shouldn't start fretting over things like the car. I'm sure he could get another car quite easily.'

'Maybe. But the children, what right did I have to take them with me—'

'You could hardly have left them, could you?'

There was a long silence: then, 'No. I suppose not. But –' she sighed, '– well, maybe he will be all right. Dear God, I hope so. He's – well, he's a great survivor.'

'He'll need to be,' said Venetia soberly, after a careful check that the children were properly asleep. 'Do you still feel – in love with him? Guilt and everything apart?'

'I don't know. It hurt so much. When I found out. So maybe I am. But I don't think I could ever trust him again. And that's the most important thing, isn't it?'

'Yes,' said Venetia, 'yes, it is. Much the most important thing.' And she pulled the car over to the side of the road and burst into tears.

'Venetia, I'm so sorry. How stupid, how tactless of me. I just didn't think. Oh, darling, don't, don't be so upset, and anyway, you've done the sensible thing at least, drawn the line—'

'There's more to it than that,' said Venetia, blowing her nose.

'What do you mean?'

'Than – doing the sensible thing. Getting divorced, drawing the line.'

'What? There's something the matter, isn't there? Something more than – than all that. I know there is. What is it?'

'I'm pregnant,' said Venetia.

'I'm really sorry. But I'm going to – go.'

She smiled at him; saw him dragging his mind from his petition – that blessed petition about the purchase tax on books that was keeping him and Celia so busily occupied – watched him smile back at her. He had such a lovely smile; she had always noticed that smile, its sweetness, ever since the first time she had met him, when Celia had brought her to Cheyne Walk and introduced them to one another. Even then it had made everything much less frightening; it still seemed to work.

'Go where, Barty?'

'Wol, you know where. To join up. Don't look like that, I've simply got to. I'm getting more and more miserable now, not doing anything useful. I've just got to.'

'But—'

'Look.' She pulled a chair up to his wheelchair, took his hand. 'Giles is here, quite safe, in England. For a while longer, Helena says. Adele's come home. I know Kit is still – in danger. But you must be feeling better. Both of you. So I want to be released from my promise.'

There was a long silence as he looked at her. Then he said, 'Well, you only promised to stay for a while. You were very careful about what you said.' He smiled again. 'As you always are. Dear Barty, you mean so much to me, you know. Don't look at me like that, I just wanted to be sure you knew.'

She felt the tears, hot and sudden. 'Oh, Wol. Of course I know. And you mean so much to me. That's why I've come to tell you first. So you can get used to the idea.'

'You mean before Celia gets going. Bless you. Yes, of course we feel better and of course you must go. What are you going to do?'

'I'm joining the ATS.'

'Really? Why?'

'I like the idea. It's real soldiering. And you know how I love machines, well, cars and things, anyway. I just feel it would suit me. Goodness knows what exactly I'll end up doing.'

There was a silence; then Oliver said, 'Whatever it is, it will be very well done. We can be sure of that.'

'Thank you.'

'Don't thank me. Will you be going for a commission?'

'Haven't even thought about it. Honestly. I'll see what happens. Anyway, look how brilliantly Giles is doing. You must be so proud of him.'

'I am. Desperately proud. God knows I wouldn't have asked for it to happen as it has, but this war has really put Giles on his feet. Extraordinary, isn't it, how things turn out. Anyway, back to you: when – when will you go?'

'I'm not sure. I can only tell you I've passed my medical. They said I'd hear when they were ready for me. Should be quite soon.'

It was – very soon. Ten days later, an envelope came for her from the MoD. She was to be at King's Cross Station with an empty suitcase the following Friday.

She stood, smiling down at the letter, feeling a rush of excitement and relief. At last. Something she could do; something she could offer; and something to distract her from the sense of futile misery and emptiness that had haunted her so relentlessly for what seemed to her now most of her grown-up life.

There was a story – no one knew if it was true – of a German pilot's parachute getting caught on an RAF wing – and the pilot wriggling frantically to set himself free. That must have been very strange, Kit thought; to have the Luftwaffe, that great, impersonal machine, become a man, an ordinary man in dreadful danger. Because that was the whole point really. People, girls usually, often asked him how he felt when he hit someone; not much, he said, it was planes you were fighting, not a person. You didn't think about that person, baling out from a plane on fire; you'd silently wish him well and hope he'd escape. You didn't feel any animosity towards him, none of them did. Why should you? You were doing what you were trained to do, you couldn't let yourself do anything else. You were fighting for freedom, for your country's life. If you thought too much you got the jitters. It was the same as when your friends were killed; you'd feel a tremendous sense of loss, but you didn't let yourself dwell on it. It affected you too deeply if you did.

Keeping ahead of the game, hitting before you were hit, that was what counted. And concentrating; nothing could be allowed to distract you from that. One of the oddest phenomena was the way you could be in a sky full of planes, Spitfires, Hurricanes, 109s, Stukas, and the next minute, you'd be fighting just one other plane and the sky would seem quite empty.

They had become the heroes, the darlings of Britain, all of them; idolised for their courage, their dashing charm and looks, their extreme youth, their careless, irreverent lives. They'd walk into the pub in the evening, and everyone would buy them drinks and of course the girls were tremendously friendly. If it hadn't been for Catriona, he could have had a different girl every night.

They'd laugh off the day's struggles, talking about them as if they'd been playing cricket. If you got hit, they'd say airily, downing the third or fourth pint, you got down as fast as you bloody well could and then went straight up again in a new plane. (No one even discussed the loss of planes: literally hundreds of them. There always seemed to be more.)

They'd spend the evening in the pubs; or go haring up to London in overpacked cars, four or five of them in each one. Kit's little two-seater MG had often held as many as five chaps. There was, after all, no shortage of fuel.

They'd go to a nightclub, the Kit Kat was a favourite, to dance and

442

drink and return at dawn, over-excited, wide awake; Kit had got into the habit of taking four or five aspirins, which together with the alcohol would get him off to sleep. And then in the morning, he'd take benzedrine to make him feel wide awake, keep him going. It all seemed to work pretty well. If you had a really bad hangover, the doc would give you a whiff of oxygen, that worked like a dream. And then straight down to dispersal for dawn readiness.

As long as you didn't think too much.

'But sometimes,' he wrote to Catriona, 'at the end of the day there's something special. You come down into the countryside, and it's so quiet and you have this feeling of tremendous peace. It's as if there's something with you. Perhaps there is. Actually I do like to think there is.'

She wrote often; sweet, tender letters, telling him how proud of him she was, how much she loved him. Just the thought of her there gave him courage when he needed it, made him feel he wasn't alone.

'The Battle of France is over; the Battle of Britain is about to begin.' So Churchill informed the nation; without actually saying so, he was admitting the acute likelihood of an invasion. The beaches on the south coast were all lined with barbed wire down to the low water mark, signposts everywhere had been pulled up or turned round, factories were working round the clock, seven days a week, restocking the British armouries, 'all lost, defending the bloody French,' as Lord Beckenham frequently remarked. Lord Beaverbrook, brilliantly in charge of building up the fighter force, put out a call for everyone to give whatever metal they could to aid the war effort: saucepans, old bikes, tin baths were willingly sacrificed, so that they could, by some magical process which nobody quite understood, become planes, tanks, guns.

A hundred Spitfires and Hurricanes a week were being built. They were needed; the Battle of Britain was still at that stage being fought in the air. All summer it went on: the relentless pounding of the coast by the Luftwaffe. Dover was known as Hellfire Corner.

In the middle of August, Kit was granted a forty-eight-hour leave; he came home to Cheyne Walk looking exhausted. Celia, looking at him, seeing his boy's face hardened, his intense blue eyes shadowed, wondered how he could endure it.

'Oh, you just do,' he said cheerfully, pouring himself a second very large gin and tonic. 'Nothing else to be done really.'

'Have you lost – many friends?'

'A – few. We've been pretty lucky, really.'

The veterans like himself had; the new boys often only survived a week. Training had been cut to an all-time minimum; there were stories of people learning to use radio information by riding bicycles round the airfield.

'Look at me: not a scratch. All this time. Guardian angel, I've got, out there on my wings.'

'But, darling—'

'Honestly, Mother, if you know what you're doing, you're pretty damn safe. The biggest danger is from G, not the Germans.'

'What on earth is "G"?'

'G-force. It's what happens if you cut the throttle to throw the plane into a turn. Usually because there's someone on your tail. The blood literally drains from your head. You black out, your eyesight goes, you can't use your arms or legs.'

Celia tried to envisage this happening in a small plane travelling at five hundred miles an hour with several guns trained on it.

'Kit! And you tell me it's not dangerous.'

'No, it is. I just said so. But somehow you still know what you're doing and you get away from the bugger. Sorry. Once you've done 180 degrees, he's in front of you and you're all right.'

'I see,' said Celia. She took a large swallow from her own gin and tonic.

'Let's change the subject. What news of Barty?'

'Oh, she's up in Leicester. Doing lots of drills, she says. Very happy.'

'I think it's marvellous. And have you met Tory, Jay's Wren girlfriend? She's a corker.'

'Is she indeed?' said Oliver. 'No, we haven't yet. He took her home to meet LM and Gordon, though, so it must be quite serious. They liked her very much. Jay's doing intelligence work, apparently.'

'Oh, yes?' said Kit. Something in his voice caught at Celia.

'Kit, isn't that right?'

'Mother, I don't know. How should I? If that's what he says, then I'm sure it's true. He's still in England, anyway. LM must be pleased about that.'

'She is. Oh now, here's Sebastian. He wanted to see you. I hope that's all right.'

'Of course.'

He stretched out his long legs and smiled at her, then stood up as Sebastian came into the room.

'Hallo, Sebastian.'

'Hallo, my boy. Good to see you. Still not a scratch, I see.'

'No,' said Kit, reaching out and touching the small table that held his drink.

Celia looked at the two of them, smiling at one another, chatting easily, and carefully fixed the picture in her mind as she always did at some particularly happy moment, allowing herself to hope that perhaps it was true, that as Kit had so often told her, if you'd survived a few weeks of flying, you'd survive them all.

'Darling, you've got to tell him.'

'I can't. I feel so stupid.'

'But why? I don't understand. Takes two to—'

'I know that but—'

'And if he really said—'

'Yes, he did, he did. But even so I don't know if he meant it for – well, for ever again.'

'And if he—'

'Yes, I think I would,' said Venetia carefully. 'Well, I know I would. I haven't thought about anything much else. I do still—'

'I knew you did. Does he write much?'

'Not a lot. Too busy. But when he does, very—'

'Well, there you are. He'll be thrilled. I'm sure. Have you been writing to him?'

'Oh yes. Just silly, light-hearted letters. Nothing – heavy.'

'But why not? If he's—'

'I just don't want to worry him. He's got enough on his plate, surely.'

'Have you thought it might cheer him up?' said Adele lightly.

'Not really. It's not as if we hadn't got any children. We've got too many—'

'But he loves them. He's a wonderful father.'

'I know, I know. But—'

'Tell you what. Wait for one more letter and then tell him. How about that?'

'Yes, all right,' said Venetia, visibly cheered by this plan.

'Yes, I'll do that.'

In the officers' mess of their training camp in the furthest point of the Orkneys, Captain Mike Willoughby-Clarke poured Boy Warwick another large whisky and then watched him slightly anxiously as he downed it at one go. He had seemed disproportionately upset by the news that his ex-wife had been dancing cheek-to-cheek at the Dorchester with a handsome young officer. Funny, really. They'd been divorced over a year after all.

Barty often said afterwards that the primary qualification for life at Glen Parva Barracks – 'and every other branch of the services, I daresay' – was patience. Patience for the queuing. It was hardly exciting. You queued for everything: for uniform, blankets, medical inspections, hair inspection – 'I have been pronounced lice-free, you'll be pleased to know,' she wrote to Celia and Oliver – eye tests, hearing tests, and worst of all, for endless inoculations. The further down in the queue you were, the blunter the needle; there was no question of changing one until it literally wouldn't puncture the skin. Lots of the girls reacted quite violently to the inoculations, with first large sores and then scabs appearing on their skin, but Barty had nothing to show for hers. She worried about it until the MO told her she obviously hadn't needed the jabs in the first place; remembering the excruciating pain of some of them, this was not entirely welcome news.

Her uniform was extensive: skirts, slacks, tunics, shirts (with detachable collars), leather anklets, two caps, tin hat, leather jerkin, something the MoD was pleased to call a corset (to hold her stockings up), a greatcoat and some hideous stout khaki knickers which some of the girls had bleached to cream. The uniform was worn at all times (their own clothes having been sent home); she felt her own identity leaving her along with her suitcase. She was now simply Miller – perversely, she rather liked it. It seemed an important part of her new life.

She was surprised to find herself relatively unaffected by the early ritual humiliations and brutality of the basic training, the things the other girls complained about: being endlessly shouted at and insulted by corporals for the most minor misdemeanours (shoelaces done wrongly, coughing on parade, insufficiently polished buttons and boots), latrine parade (one minute allowed inside), the issue also on parade of sanitary towels – 'one packet, size 2, if you want 1 or 3 you ask your corporal' – the instruction never to remove your identity discs – 'one goes to your next of kin, the other stays on your body, then they know which way to bury you' – and, of course, the disgusting food.

Somehow she took it all in her stride; it seemed to her to most closely resemble what Giles and indeed Sebastian had told her of early life at public school.

They slept in hideously uncomfortable beds under scratchy blankets (no sheets in Nissen huts), hot that wonderful summer, but clearly destined to become extremely cold.

Having spent her childhood being mocked by nasty little girls for not being posh enough, Barty was now nervous of being mocked by nasty big girls for being too posh. But from the moment they got in the railway carriage that first day, the comradeship was strong. She saw a few girls exchanging glances when she asked if a seat was free, and noting the quality of her leather suitcase; but a pack of Navy Cut handed round the compartment (Sebastian's tip – 'I was a private in the first war, my darling, I know all about it') swiftly established her as a good egg, and they were in any case all in the same boat, all nervous, and that did a lot to cut across any other barriers.

There was one girl called Parfitt (Christian names were sent away with the clothes), who had looked as if she might cause her some trouble; she was scrawnily thin, with a sharp, beaky little face, rather small eyes, and extremely colourful language. She asked Barty in a rather hostile voice why she wasn't joining the WRNS – 'That's where your sort usually go' – and pushed her quite sharply out of the way in order to get herself an end-of-row bed in the Nissen hut. But that night there was the sound of muffled sobs from beneath Parfitt's blankets; Barty went over to her and sat on her bed and learned that she had never left home or her mother for more than twenty-four hours.

Barty told her that homesickness was like seasickness: 'you suddenly get used to it', supplied her with a handkerchief and a couple more Navy Cuts (sold at a special rate of eight pennies for fifteen that summer), and responded to Parfitt's threat to fucking break her head in if she told any of the other bleedin' wimps with an assurance that there was nothing to tell.

In the morning, Parfitt swaggered out on to the parade ground full of bravado and the statement that she wasn't taking any rubbish from any bloody sergeant major, but not before winking at Barty and thanking her for what she called 'waking her from her nightmare' the night before.

Drill was surprisingly hard and they all had to take a great deal of rubbish from the sergeant major; they were marched in their new shoes until they got blisters. Barty – and Parfitt – were among the lucky ones, they learned quickly, but there were others who found it terribly difficult and would stand on the parade ground trying not to cry while they were shouted at and insulted by the male sergeant.

They did very little in those early days except drill and queue and attend boring lectures on documents, crime and punishment and messing; the one on how to avoid wasting fat being particularly memorable. As the month progressed they were asked what they would like to do. Barty and Parfitt both opted for anti-aircraft defence, and were given a great many more tests, eye tests, tests for steadiness of hand, for mechanical aptitude and even for finding planes in photographs flashed in front of them on the wall.

'Wasn't no fucking plane there, was there?' said Parfitt afterwards; Barty didn't like to say she had spotted several, all camouflaged in the trees, and feared that was the end of Parfitt's anti-aircraft training. But Parfitt was so good at the other tests that she passed; and the two of them were told, along with several other girls, that they were now being sent to Oswestry to a mixed, heavy ack-ack battalion; Barty felt as proud as when *Brilliant Twilight* had reached the New York bestseller list for the first time.

It was then that the selection officer sent for her and told her she thought that she should apply for a commission and train as an officer 'to train recruits and therefore release the men' .

Barty refused; it was the last thing she wanted to do. She wanted to be in the front line, or at least very close to it; teaching raw recruits hardly met that criterion. She could tell from the stunned response that she had blown her chances, probably for ever, of becoming an officer, but she simply didn't care, and she left with a sense of genuine excitement for Oswestry.

It was Tuesday, 20 August.

That was the day Churchill made his speech in the House of Commons in praise of the fighter pilots who were 'turning the tide of war by their prowess and their devotion'. Celia, reading it aloud to Oliver from the next day's paper, faltered at the words 'never in the field of human conflict was so much owed by so many to so few', and looked at Oliver, her eyes filled with a mixture of terror and desperate pride.

'That's Kit,' she said simply, 'one of those few.'

Venetia's voice on the phone was choked with tears.

'I've had this horrible letter. From Boy. I can't – Adele, I can't bear it.'

'Saying what?'

'Saying he's got some leave in three weeks, but he thinks it's better if we don't meet. And that he imagines I'll agree.'

'What! But why?'

'Oh, Dell, I don't know.'

'But what does he say?'

'Just that. That he's hoping to be able to see the children but he'd prefer to go down there alone. And that then he's got to see various people about his business affairs and then he's going straight back up to Scotland.'

'How – extraordinary.'

'Oh I don't know that it is,' said Venetia, blowing her nose. 'Leopards don't change their spots that easily, do they? He's probably found some wildly beautiful WAAF officer or something.'

'I'm sure there's no such thing.'

'Well, Wren, then. Everyone knows they're beautiful. Why should I think he's suddenly fallen in love with me again?'

'Because he told you so.'

'Well, he wanted to get me into bed, didn't he?'

'Venetia, I just can't believe—'

'Well, I can. Boy is a very practised seducer, don't forget. He knows exactly how to make one feel – well, you know, tender towards him.'

'But he – I don't know, Venetia. I think you should write to him and—'

'Adele, I am not writing to him about anything at all. I feel so stupid, such a complete and utter fool.'

'But you've got to tell him about—'

'I absolutely have not. It's the last thing in the world I'd tell him now. I don't want him even to know.'

'But he's got to know some time.'

'No, he hasn't.'

'Venetia, of course he has. Shall I—'

'No! You are most definitely not to. Can't you see how—'

'Yes, I can. Of course I can.' Adele's voice was suddenly tender down the phone. 'I'm so sorry. So very sorry.'

'The worst thing,' said Venetia, starting to cry again, 'absolutely the worst thing is that I feel a complete fool. Well, I suppose that's because I am. Oh, I must go, Mummy's coming. Bye, darling. I'll try and get down at the weekend. Love to the children.'

The war in the air had changed. Everyone felt it. Suddenly it wasn't just planes they were fighting, it was Germans. The change had largely been brought about by the fact that several of the pilots had been shot at while descending on their parachutes. As someone remarked, this was very dirty tactics indeed.

Fear led to anger, which led to more fear and then more anger; this, combined with an absolute exhaustion, brought them to the very edge of human endurance. Flying to heights greater than Mount Everest as they did day after day in unpressurised aircraft made the flying more exhausting still.

Every single day now, comrades were lost, usually the new boys; one night's drinking companions would not be there the next. Not just one either, but many, the numbers mounting endlessly; it was horribly disturbing. The dashing boys were becoming desperate men; there were stories of tantrums in the mess about over-cooked eggs, cold coffee, trifles that once they would have laughed at or ignored. They sought release from the fear in drinking; if you weren't flying you were plastered.

Kit was too exhausted even to write to Catriona any more; they were all too exhausted to do anything except keep flying. Go up, look for them, find them, fire at them, come down, refuel, go up again. Often when he was in the air now he found himself thinking, quite calmly, that if he didn't die today, he would certainly die tomorrow; it led him, with an odd calm, into greater and greater risks.

The girls working on the radios reported horrific experiences, of hearing the boys calling out in delight when they saw a German plane, of hearing the crackle of the machine gun – and then of hearing them go down as bullets hit the planes and the transmitters went off.

Five hundred planes were lost during those last two weeks of the mighty air battle to save Britain; one hundred and three fighter command pilots died. And still Kit rode the skies, alone in his face-to-face battle every day with fear, danger, exhaustion and death. He was wonderful about telephoning home, managed it most nights, usually from the pub, very often quite clearly drunk. 'Still fine,' he would say, and Celia could hear him laughing against the hubbub, 'absolutely fine. Just thought you'd like to know. Got to go, serious drinking to do.'

'Thank you for ringing. Bye, darling. God bless.'

She always said that; half amused at herself, Celia Lytton, so famously a non-believer: 'God bless'. There being nothing else she could say or do.

Indeed, 'God must be up there with him,' another equally famous non-believer, Sebastian Brooke, said when she told him, 'keeping an eye on him, keeping him safe.'

She allowed herself to believe in the notion, found comfort in it

450

even – for what else could be called into play against such dreadful, horrifying, hopeless odds? – and indulged in every other foolish fantasy, touching wood, wishing on stars in the briefly peaceful night skies, lighting candles in Westminster Cathedral, anything that might bring special favour, special protection, upon him, upon Kit, her brave hero of a son, to whom so many of them owed so much.

And then, finally, the stars faded and the candles went out; and at last God looked away.

Chapter 31

'Kit, come on. Here, take my hand. That's right. I'm going to take you for a little walk.'

Izzie smiled up at him encouragingly, at the person she loved best in all the world – apart from her father of course. 'You'll enjoy it when we get going. Promise. It's a lovely day.'

'I'd – rather not. If you don't mind.'

'I do mind. Very much.'

The doctor had said she must be firm with him; her father had said so too. Firm and very positive. And that was what she was trying to be. It wasn't easy, but Izzie had not been raised to ease.

'Now come on. You might need a scarf, it's cold.'

'I really don't care.'

'You will when you're halfway round and you're shivering. I'll get it for you. Wait there.'

She looked back at him anxiously as she ran to the utility room, where all the coats and scarves were kept. But he was doing as she told him, standing quite still, facing the window, his eyes fixed on the sparkling day.

He looked much better than he had even three weeks ago when he'd arrived; not so thin, much less pale. He wasn't quite the same Kit, who had always been so gloriously healthy looking, sunburned in the summer, red-cheeked in the winter, but at least he wasn't the shadowy wraith she had met on the doorstep of Ashingham when Celia and her father had brought him down.

In fact, he'd looked just the same, really, his face was a bit thin and his eyes were somehow sunk into dark shadows, but he was just as handsome – he was so handsome, as handsome as a film star.

Izzie knew about film stars, Cook let her look at her *Picturegoer* magazine every week. She'd hardly ever been to the pictures herself; she and Henry and Roo had been taken to see *Pinocchio*, which was lovely, although devoid of film stars – and Adele had said they would all go and see *The Wizard of Oz* when it came round – but she thought she would really like to see a proper picture, a romantic one, like *Gone With the Wind*, which everyone was talking about, or a Western, with Gary Cooper. Kit looked a bit like Gary Cooper, she thought: or even Leslie Howard. Everyone said he was as handsome as a film star; and when they heard about his plane crash, the first thing Cook said once she knew he hadn't been killed was, 'Pray God he's not been burned.'

And he hadn't been.

She returned to him now, handed him the scarf.

'You do it.' ('Get him to do things for himself,' her father had said, 'as much as you can, it's important.')

'No, I don't want to.'

'Kit, you'll be cold.'

'I told you, I don't care.'

'Then let me do it. Bend down. Towards me, no, towards me, that's right. There.'

She knotted the scarf carefully round his neck, tucked it in. 'Very good. Now you'll be all right. Come on, this way. Take my hand. Careful, mind the step. That's right.'

They walked out on to the terrace; he held her hand loosely, carelessly, as if he could hardly be bothered.

'It's a lovely day, Kit. Really lovely.'

'I thought you said it was cold.'

'It is cold. But it's frosty and sunny and the fields—'

'Izzie, I'm sorry. I know you mean well. But I can't quite – cope with this. Not today. Can we go back please.'

'But—'

'Izzie, I said I want to go back. Now. At once. Please take me.'

'All right. Yes, all right, Kit. Turn round. Now this way. Sorry. Careful. Didn't see that post.'

And then realised what she had said, what it must have meant to him to hear her say it. That she hadn't seen something. A post. Just a post. When she could see everything else. And he couldn't see anything, anything at all . . .

It was the G-force that did it; the thing he had described to his mother, the temporary loss of consciousness after a sharp turn.

He'd had this bloody great Messerschmitt 110 on his tail, came at him out of nowhere, and he knew a sharp turn was the only thing to do. He'd done it so many times, coped with the G-force perfectly OK, it would be fine.

Only it hadn't been; he'd blacked out for longer, lost a crucial extra few seconds – and fallen forwards, hitting his head on the controls with such incredible force he'd knocked himself out. And came down, he never remembered how, afterwards, in the sea. Some miracle – actually another pilot – had saved him from the Messerschmitt. Miraculously too, the plane had slewed into the water undamaged, rather than hitting it nose down – when it would have somersaulted – and he'd been thrown out of the cockpit. He'd come to, a bit confused, couldn't understand why it was so dark, but he'd managed to get out, somehow. He'd had his Mae West on of course, and he'd waited patiently, oddly calm (wondering if it was night-time), till he'd been picked up. Everyone said he'd been incredibly lucky.

Incredibly lucky. Not dead; not burned; not disfigured; just blind. Totally blind. For the rest of his life. All sixty or seventy years of it, if he was unlucky enough to live that long.

He wished, with a savage misery, that he had been killed; that it had ended. They would have grieved for a while, his parents, his family, Sebastian, and then they would have got over it. And he would be over it. Everything would be over. Instead of going on and on and on . . .

Now what would he do? What could he do? A blind barrister: very successful. A blind priest: hugely practical. He couldn't even finish his degree. He'd never have a job, never be able to do anything. He'd just sit and think; and go for walks, led by the hand, and hear people telling him what a lovely day it was.

And then there was Catriona.

She'd come down as soon as she'd heard, sat by his bed, holding his hand, telling him she'd always love him, she'd look after him, they could still have a life together. It had helped so much that: knowing that there was some hope, somewhere, at least one small slice of future safe.

He couldn't think quite how it would work, but just hearing her talking about it made him feel better.

He'd said, of course, that she mustn't feel she had to stay with him, that he wasn't going to be much of a husband for her, that she'd be looking after him for the rest of their lives. He felt he had to do that, paint an honest picture for her. And she'd simply squeezed his hand and said she didn't care, he was the husband she wanted, and she wanted to look after him.

'And to prove it, I'm going to tell Mummy and Daddy I want to announce our engagement, make it official.'

'Oh, darling.' Tears filled his eyes; his useless eyes. He wondered if they showed: yes, of course they did. 'Darling Catriona, I love you so much. So very much. But I do worry that I won't be—'

'Don't worry,' she said kissing his hand, 'I'll do the worrying for both of us. From now on. Now you tell your parents, and I'll tell mine. All right?'

His parents had been sweet; even his mother. She had liked Catriona, he could tell. She actually said she was charming.

Catriona's parents had been more difficult. Advised her to wait before announcing it, that there was no hurry after all, there couldn't be a wedding for a long time, they were both so young and, as her father put it, Kit had to re-establish himself.

She'd written to tell him that; Izzie had read the letter to him. He preferred that to his mother doing it. After all, she was only a little girl, she wouldn't understand or feel awkward about it.

> I would have come to see you again, but I couldn't get away, and it's so impossible to get on trains and things. I'm so sorry, darling Kit. Anyway, it doesn't mean I don't want to get engaged still, and I was very upset at first at their attitude, but I can see that in a way they're right, I mean we really don't know how or when we're going to manage it, and there are all sorts of rules about nurses not being married, so I might have to think about doing something else. But I will, darling, I will, and you're not to worry and I do love you so much and I'm going to be Mrs Kit Lytton, whether you like it or not.

He'd been too embarrassed to ask Izzie to write a proper letter, he'd just sent a short note saying he understood and he'd look forward to hearing from her again, and signed it just 'love, Kit'.

But he'd still believed her, even though he was – upset.

She did come to see him once more; in October. She'd been sweet, loving, assured him that it would be all right one day for them both. But there was no mention of the engagement.

After that, her letters got shorter, less intense; and it was difficult for him to write back.

Finally she did write: to say that although she still loved him very much and she always would, she just didn't think, after all, that they should think about getting married for a very long time.

> It's so true, what Mummy and Daddy say, there really is no way I could look after you and work, and if I don't work, then how

455

would we manage? I know your people are quite well off, but they won't want to keep us both, and possibly our family, for ever. Darling Kit, I will never forget you, I will always love you, but I am just trying to do the best thing for us both. And I think that is for us to just be friends. Loving friends. We're so far apart, and meetings are almost impossible, certainly while the war is on, that I just can't see how even in the longer term it could work. I so hate doing this, but I think I have to be brave and tell you, so that we can both face the future honestly. Please forgive me.

I'll always love you,
Catriona.

Izzie read this out to him in a voice which faltered from time to time. When she had finished she said very quietly, 'Would you like me to write an answer?'

'No,' he said, 'no, thank you, Izzie. I'd like to be on my own now, if you don't mind.'

'Of course,' she said and he felt her lips on his cheek, kissing him very tenderly, and tasted the salt of her tears; and then she was gone. And then he started to cry himself, quietly at first, then more loudly until it was a roar, a dreadful, racked roar; and Izzie, standing outside the door, biting her lip helplessly, listening to him, thought how exactly like her father he sounded.

Only this time there was no comfort she could offer; she knew that.

'No more news from that wretched girl?' Celia's voice down the telephone to her mother was terse.

'No. Izzie's been watching the post for it like a little hawk. No sign.'

'Little beast. How can she do this to him, when he needs her so much? It's – it's inhuman.'

'Celia, she's very young. She probably just doesn't know how to cope, what to say or do. And from what Izzie told me, I rather gather her parents have put a big spoke in things. Well, who could blame them? They're both children, helpless children. There really can be no future for them.'

'Don't say that, Mama. Of course there can. Well, certainly for Kit. He has a future. I know he does. I believe it as much as I believe anything. It's just a question of – of—'

'Of what?' Lady Beckenham's voice was unusually gentle.

'Of finding it. Finding the way.'

'Of course.'

'So – is he terribly down?'

'Terribly. We all do our best, but he's so – angry. Of course. As he would be. It's impossible to say anything that isn't trite or maudlin. Or both.'

'Oh, God. Well – maybe he should be up here. It's hardly fair on you. But I can't cope with two invalids.'

'No, no, he might as well be here. And he's no trouble. He just sits there all day, staring – or rather not staring – into space. I've tried him with the radio, but he doesn't seem interested even in that. The only person who can get through to him at all is Izzie, bless her. And she doesn't get much change from him. I found her crying yesterday, she said she didn't seem to be helping at all. I told her she was, of course, but—'

'Poor Izzie.' There was a silence; then, 'Sebastian's coming down this weekend again. On the train, he can't get any petrol. Could someone meet him?'

'I will. Of course. Tell him he won't get much of a greeting from Kit, though; he just won't make the slightest effort for anyone. Poor chap.' She sighed. 'I can remember Billy being like this, you know. With possibly just slightly less to be depressed about. It's dreadful what war does to young men. All those years ahead of them. I sometimes think—' There was a silence; then she said, 'How are things up there?'

'Awful. Bombs absolutely every night. We sleep down in the cellar, it's more sensible. Terribly difficult getting Oliver down, Brunson and I carry him between us. I do wish he'd come down to you, but he won't, says Lyttons needs him. He's a frightful liability, can't be left anywhere, in case there's a raid.'

'Which there is every night, you say.'

'Yes. The other night I got caught on my way home when the sirens went, had to sleep in one of the underground stations. It was vile. The stench, I can't tell you. No lavatories, of course. But it was quite amusing in its own way, there was someone singing and someone else telling jokes, and everyone was sitting in deckchairs, facing the line, rather as if they were on the beach.'

'Did you have a deckchair?'

'Of course not. But there were some camp beds and so on. I managed to get one of those. They don't like people using the underground as shelters apparently, but there's nothing they can do to stop them. London looks so frightful, Mama, you've no idea. Every day more streets reduced to rubble, shops with the front blasted off, you suddenly see a bus upended, animals running about looking for their owners, it's tragic. Mappin & Webbs is quite funny, they put a great grille over the windows before ushering everyone down to the shelter: not to protect the glass, but to stop looting.'

'Very sensible.'

'I suppose so. The manager told me. I got caught there the other day, spent a raid in their cellars, very fine indeed, shelves of treasures all carefully stored. The House of Commons has been hit, not too badly, and Buckingham Palace, but you'll know all that, and the East End is just rubble – oh, it's utterly dreadful. Dear old St Paul's is still standing, somehow it just goes on and on surviving. As it's so near us, I find that rather comforting.'

'I hope you're being sensible. Looking after yourself. I worry about you, you know.'

It was so unlike her to express any maternal concern, Celia was quite startled.

'Of course. One has to spend the night in the shelter, but the cellar at Cheyne Walk is pretty solid. We've got sandbags round the door, and there's a sort of reinforced bit, a Morrison, you know, but as there's not room for all of us in it, we don't bother. We're a bit short of sleep, that's the worst thing.'

'Of course. And how's Venetia?'

'Oh – all right. Getting bigger by the day, but insists on working still. So ridiculous all this, she's absolutely forbidden me to speak to Boy about it, and I have to respect that, but – anyway, working is a godsend for her. Keeps her mind off – things.'

'I don't actually suppose it does,' said Lady Beckenham.

Celia had thought she knew grief well; now she could see it had hardly entered her life. And even now it entered it slowly, insidiously, and was the uglier for it, for when she had first heard about Kit, had been told his plane had come down, but that he was not dead, not even disfigured, a sweet relief had swept her.

'He's all right, he's all right,' she had said to Sebastian, over and over again, 'he's alive, he's not burned, he's all right.'

And even as she said the words, as she saw Sebastian's eyes on hers, doubtful, incredulous even, she heard their own stupidity and fell into the abyss.

Kit was blind: her beautiful, brilliant, courageous Kit, blind, sightless, helpless, his apparently charmed life not over but stunted, maimed hopelessly almost before it had begun. All the things that had seemed his birthright, taken most carelessly for granted, a brilliant degree, a dazzling career, social accomplishment; admiration, popularity, fun, all snatched from him in one dark, vengeful moment.

She grieved, she wept, she raged; for the first time in her life nothing could alleviate her misery.

'It's so cruel, so desperately cruel,' she said to Oliver, pacing their room, far into that first night, 'how could that have happened to him, to Kit of all people?'

He was hers, he was at the very heart of her life, she cared about him more than anyone or anything in the world: he was so especially loved, especially precious to her. He was still all those things, but changed, dreadfully and most sadly changed, moved from his place in the sun into a dark, chill solitude that no one seemed able to enter.

She had gone straight away to visit him, had thought – absurdly – that she must look nice for him, he cared so much about such things, and then, in the first of a hundred, a thousand moments, had realised there was no point. He was sitting in a chair by the window of his hospital room, staring in front of him: his head erect, his face set in the new heaviness they would all come to dread.

She had kissed him gently, had fatally wept as she did so, and he had felt her tears, and brushed them impatiently away.

He was wretched, she had expected that, she had sat with him all day, trying to break into it, into his misery, but had failed totally. He had been numbed, silenced by it, not only by his blindness but his own reaction to it; he was frightened by his own grief. He refused to talk, answered her questions in monosyllables, responded to a conversation that became increasingly banal with terse nods, indifferent shrugs. After two hours she was exhausted; expecting to be able to ease his misery with tenderness, with gentleness, with love, she felt useless, rejected and by the end of her visit, felt a despair of her own.

It would ease, the withdrawal, she told herself, he was in shock, when he was home, when he was with people he knew and loved he would feel safe, more relaxed, would start to talk, but he did not, he sat in his own room as he had in the one at the hospital, remote, silent, discouraging visitors. Later the anger began, an all-encompassing sweep of rage that spared nothing and no one; all of them, Oliver, Sebastian, Barty, the twins, Celia herself, were subjected to it, to violent outbursts, railing against the cruelty and injustice of what had befallen him and his life.

Celia talked to him, wept with him, sat silent while he shouted at her, allowed him to blame her, as he blamed everyone, not for what had happened but for being able to see.

For three weeks he stayed there, in his room; she tried everything, she read aloud until her throat hurt, played music, talked endlessly. She met nothing but rejection; she had lost him, it seemed, lost him and his love as he had lost his sight.

It was totally exhausting; after a while she went back to work, but he would remain with her all day, a dark, painful presence. She telephoned him several times a day at first, she had had a phone installed in his room, but he discouraged her calls, saying they seemed pointless. 'I'm perfectly all right here, and I've nothing to say after all.'

She would arrive home at first with books, newspapers, flowers – 'I thought it would be nice for you to smell them' – but he would shrug off her offers to read, and disliked the flowers.

'I find the smell sickly, I'd really rather not have them, if you don't mind.'

She began to dread going up to him; entering his room was a dark, hopeless experience, comparable, she supposed, to his own life. She remained determinedly cheerful when she was with him, but alone or with Oliver she wept and raged helplessly.

Finally, exhausted and in despair, she asked her mother if she would have him at Ashingham for a few weeks: 'He always loved it there and I think the change might help.'

'It might help you as well,' said Lady Beckenham. 'You sound absolutely exhausted. Of course he can come down here, at least it will spread the load a bit. Poor chap,' she added, a tenderness in her voice that was very seldom heard.

Kit submitted to the suggestion with a shrug of disinterest, and said it made no difference to him where he was, after all. His only expressed interest was Catriona, in those early days when he had still thought she loved him, that he had a future of sorts with her; her letters were the only things that could reach into his apathy.

Nevertheless, there was one other person whom he seemed at least willing to tolerate: and that person was Izzie. She took up the role of his companion with a willingness and joy that touched everyone. She and she alone was allowed to chat to him, to tell him things that had happened that day, without being rebuffed and asked to leave his room; she and she alone was actually encouraged to read to him. Indeed Cook had reported seeing him smile one morning as they sat, the two of them, on the terrace; that this deserved mention was testimony to the absolute despair in which he lived.

But not even Izzie could ease him out of his new grief, that of losing his Catriona.

Life had settled down again: to a surprising degree. Really a very surprising degree. Paris was still Paris. It might be overrun with Germans, German signs might be on all the street corners, the swastika might be flying on the much-loved landmarks: but at least it was intact, not being bombed like so many other great cities. Two weeks after they had arrived, the city was behaving remarkably normally. Restaurants, theatres, cinemas, schools were all reopening. Especially restaurants. The Germans particularly liked French food, indeed Simone de Beauvoir herself had remarked that nobody had ever seen people swallow such prodigious quantities.

They were everywhere, of course, that was to be expected: but somehow no one had expected them to become part of the city. They were on the buses, at the theatre (in the best seats), in the restaurants (at the best tables), to be found photographing one another against famous French landmarks, chatting to pretty girls, sitting at the pavement cafés, drinking wine: and they were, moreover, polite and courteous. There was the curfew, of course, which meant that theatres and cinemas all started early, at about six; and there were other regulations, such as an obligation to carry a *carte d'identité* at all times. The clocks had been moved forward an hour to coincide with the time of the Greater Reich, there was food rationing, everyone had their *carte d'alimentation* in which there was a brisk black market trade, but so far nothing terrible had occurred.

The only thing that had caused Luc a sense of serious anxiety had been the publication of the First Ordinance on 27 September 1940, stating the exact definition of a Jew: 'all those who belong or used to belong to the Jewish religion or who have more than two grandparents that are Jewish'. And an announcement that a census of such Jews was to be taken, by 20 October.

Those who owned businesses were required to put up a sign in their premises indicating Jewish ownership. But – no more. It was not so terrible. Everyone kept saying that: it was not so terrible.

Far worse was the fact that he was unemployed. He managed to do a little freelance work for other houses, some editing, and write the occasional article for a periodical; but it didn't amount to very much money. Suzette was very far from pleased; having regained her comparatively well-paid husband, she found herself required to keep him on the salary she earned at Balenciaga.

461

She was not pregnant; she had told Luc, her black eyes earnestly sad, that it had been a false alarm, that very sadly she had been wrong. Luc was not surprised.

He had moved back into the apartment in Passy; there seemed no point staying in the St-Sulpice apartment with its attendant expense and memories. He had moved out without a word to Mme André – and taking only a few of the favourite books and ornaments which he had brought with him from Passy. Suzette received them back with an irritating nod, clearly indicating that they were restored to their rightful place.

But he remained desperate for news of Adele. And for contact with her. He had no idea whether she was alive or dead, whether she had reached England in safety, or was marooned in some southern French town. Or something a great deal worse. It was dreadful; he was haunted by visions of her being arrested, imprisoned, killed even, and the children with her. There were dreadful stories of what had happened on that road south; he woke sweating night after night from bad dreams to worse wakefulness. He tried to tell himself he would have heard if she had not arrived; but she was not his wife, and there was nothing to show that she was. The children were on her passport, her British passport; but that was worth nothing – or a great deal worse than nothing – in a country where the British were officially the enemy.

The Lyttons would almost certainly not have known she was coming, the phone lines had been impossible – and would therefore have had no idea of her whereabouts, unless she arrived. It became an obsession; he spent hours pondering the odds, making enquiries of friends, acquaintances, colleagues. And of course his letter to her, the one he had sent through the *Style* magazine courier, had never arrived.

They had said in any case that the consignment could not be sent direct to London that day, but were trying to get it there via the New York offices; months later Philippe Lelong told him there was no indication they had even arrived there. It was truly a nightmare, a living, ceaseless nightmare. Too late, far too late, Luc realised how very much he loved her; and how absolutely impossible it was for him to tell her so.

'Nearly got him,' said Parfitt with great satisfaction.

'Number One! You're not meant to hit the pilot.'

'Aren't I?' Her face was carefully innocent, as she turned to face the sergeant. 'Sorry, thought I was. Thought he was the enemy.'

'Of course he's not. He's trailing that windsock. You're meant to hit that.'

'It's not that bugger wot takes us for drill, is it? Because if it is—'

'Of course it isn't. Now for Christ's sake concentrate next time. Number Two, you next.'

They were numbers on the gun park, not names. Barty took careful aim; hit the windsock exactly.

'Bullseye!'

'Not bad. Number Three.'

They had been doing it for hours; firing at the windsock, trailed by a very slow, very old plane, piloted by an extremely brave man. If anyone got the Military Cross, Barty thought, it should be that pilot.

She stepped back, winced as her shoe caught a new set of blisters. God, this drill was a pain. Literally. They'd had to learn a new form down here; artillery drill rather than infantry. The rhythm was different, you counted differently; it was very confusing. They were all taking a long time to pick it up, partly because they were all feeling bolshie about it.

'We've learned to bloody march,' Parfitt had said, after the first morning, 'I'll give that sergeant ruddy gunnery drill, right up his backside. As if that was going to win the war. Bleedin' army.'

It did seem just a little unnecessary.

But they were still enjoying themselves.

They were doing proper training now; in Oswestry they'd learned to use the complex equipment, the height-finders and predictors, to use binoculars, telescopes, matching manually the information fed them by a complex mass of dials, adding in wind speed, bearing and range, all information that was relayed to the guns, telling them where to fire, how high a plane was, how fast it was travelling, what the wind direction was. And then there was the gunpowder: which was l'ke the dye in knitting wool, she discovered, no two batches behaved exactly the same. Calculations had to be adjusted for each one.

And every gun barrel behaved differently too, changing with age; and the wind speed and bearing affected the round in flight. It was all complex and difficult but enthralling. And wonderfully therapeutic; she realised one evening she hadn't even thought about Laurence for weeks.

Both she and Parfitt had passed out well and had been sent on to their next post – marching on their way through the town to the station. They were sent to Anglesey, to an actual gun park, based on the cliffs overlooking the sea.

They were addressed on their first day by a young and rather good-looking officer; he gave them a terrific talk, telling them that they would be treated equally, men and women alike, that they would work together, that they had a job to do regardless of sex and that they must be prepared to die together too. There had been a silence after that; even Parfitt looked subdued.

But it was the noise which was really separating the women from the girls now; and it was frightful. There had been 'gun shyness' tests: if you could cope with standing behind four 3.7 guns, all going off at the same time, you were all right. Barty found she could – just; but it wasn't only the noise, it was the closeness of it all, the heat of the smoking cartridge case as it shot out, the smell of grease and cordite, they were all part of an assault that seemed to go deep within her, confusing all her responses. She developed strategies to cope with it, bracing herself mentally as well as physically, but a few of the girls couldn't cope at all and developed something similar to the shell-shock Barty had observed in the men at Ashingham during the First War, a kind of withdrawal and even quite severe trembling. They had to leave, to do other work; Parfitt was very scornful.

They were all given rubber ear plugs, but mostly they didn't wear them; there was so much crucial shouting going on, shouting of orders, information, warnings, and you simply couldn't hear that with plugs in. Barty learned to manage without, and sent up silent prayers that she wouldn't suffer from permanent deafness.

Permanent deafness: better than blindness, though. Her heart ached so much for Kit that she sometimes felt it physically, a heavy throbbing of helpless sympathy. She had been given compassionate leave when she first heard the news, to go and see him; remembering his glorious looks, his joyful attitude to life, his burning inquisitiveness, she was shocked by what she found, a still, dull shell, hardly troubling to greet her, certainly not to smile.

She had expected to have to work hard, to be tactful, gentle, careful of everything she said and did, but it was far worse than she had feared. He patently didn't listen to much that was said to him, hardly answered her questions, shrugged off her enquiries as to his health, refused every offer, of a walk, being read to, the radio, the gramophone. After half an hour she had felt exhausted and made an excuse to leave, and went to find Lady Beckenham; she was brusque with her.

'Of course it's difficult. I should know, I'm dealing with him every day. But hardly surprising. Wouldn't you feel like that? I know I would.'

'Yes, of course. But – what will become of him? It's hard to see him getting any better at all, with this attitude.'

'Oh, give him time,' said Lady Beckenham cheerfully, 'amazing what that will do. And look at Billy, what a state he was in.'

'Yes, but you found him something to do, something to give him hope. I can't think of anything that might help Kit. What on earth can he do, for the rest of his life?'

'Can't imagine. But there was some composer who was deaf, wasn't there—'

'Beethoven,' said Barty. 'Can – can Aunt Celia get through to him?'

'Not really. She comes down every weekend, sits with him for hours, but he's just the same with her. Poor chap.'

'Doesn't he want to go home?'

'Not really. He's happier down here. Says it's more peaceful. And it's safer of course. Anyway, he'll come through. I'm sure of it. Just a matter of finding something. When you get to my age, Barty, you know that things usually do pan out. They have to. He can't sit there for the rest of his life brooding. It won't work.'

Barty smiled at her; and thought what an amazing woman she was. She must be over eighty, yet she still charged about Ashingham day and night, ordering everyone about, more than half running the school, helping Lord Beckenham when necessary in his Home Guard duties, overseeing her horses – and still riding herself. The doctor had forbidden it, saying that a fall could be fatal, but she told him that if she couldn't ride she'd rather be dead and that was the end of it.

'Izzie is being marvellous, she's the only person he'll talk to at all. That upsets Celia, between you and me. I did think Billy might be able to help, but Kit gave him very short shrift. Dear old Bill; wedding bells in the air, you know.'

'Yes, it's lovely,' said Barty, 'I'm so happy about it. She's such a dear girl. She really loves him. Well, I'd better go and have another try with Kit, and then I'll have to leave. I've got to report back tonight.'

'Enjoying it, are you? Beckenham is desperately jealous.'

'I absolutely adore it,' said Barty simply.

Another letter had come from Boy: equally cold, equally distant. He had a final leave before moving off with his regiment to another location; he could be away some considerable time and he would like to see the children again before he left. Again he would prefer her not to be there. He imagined she would understand. As far as he could gather from what Henry and Roo had said, she was very seldom at Ashingham, so he imagined it would not exactly be a problem. He would be staying with a friend in London, since she had closed the house up. ('And I can imagine the sex of the friend,' Venetia said bitterly to Adele.) He would be gone before Christmas, and would organise some presents for the children which he would have delivered to Cheyne Walk. Perhaps she would be good enough to take them down with her.

And that was it.

Thank God, she thought, standing up, pressing her hand into her aching back, thank God she had her work to distract her. Otherwise she'd go completely mad.

Barty was having quite a lot of fun now; the nearest town put on very good Saturday night dances. The first one had actually been a bit of a shock, they had got used to the army hops with everyone in uniform and had sat there, khaki wallflowers, in a line, miserable in their stout shoes and thick stockings, looking at the civvy girls in frocks and curls; 'bleedin' tarts,' said Parfitt, speaking for them all.

They had a few drinks at the bar, and had just decided to go and catch the bus back to barracks when a young officer came over to them, half bowed to Parfitt.

'May I have the pleasure?' he said.

'Charmed, I'm sure,' she said, and allowed herself to be led into a rather stiff waltz, winking at them over her partner's shoulder every time she faced them.

Barty watched her enviously; she thought the officer was rather good-looking, wasted on Parfitt . . .

'Wake up, Miller.' Parfitt was grinning at her. 'I brought you a partner over. Told him you was more his sort than me. Here you are.'

Barty shook her head, laughing; but, 'No, honest, he said he'd like to talk to you. Didn't you?' she said rather aggressively, digging him in the ribs.

'I – did, yes. That is if you wouldn't mind, Miss—'

'Miller,' said Barty, 'and I wouldn't mind a bit.' The more she looked at him, the more he seemed to look like Cary Grant.

He was stationed nearby; doing commando training. He was very young, just thirty, but, 'I was born middle-aged,' he said apologetically. 'Everyone always thinks I'm older. John Munnings, by the way, sorry, should have said.'

466

'And what do you do, John Munnings? When you're not a' – she examined the stars on his epaulette – 'lieutenant.'

'Oh – solicitor. There you are, you see. Dull. Middle-aged.'

'Well, at least you're not an accountant,' she said cheerfully. He grinned back at her; he had a very nice smile.

The band struck up again: 'You are My Sunshine'.

'I love this,' she said happily.

'You dance awfully well,' he said, unscrambling his feet for the third time.

'Thank you,' said Barty.

'I know I don't.'

'Well – you're not bad. And you know what they said about Fred Astaire?'

'No.'

'When he did his screen test: can't act, can't sing, can dance a little. Look what happened to him. You could get better.'

'All right. Will you be my Ginger for the next dance at least?'

'I will. With pleasure.'

She had seen him several times since then; she liked him more and more. And he was very good-looking. He was hating army life, he said, 'but we have to do it, don't we?'

'We do. Actually I love it.'

'You can't.'

'Yes, I can. It's so – different. So absorbing.'

'You're amazing,' he said. And then, rather awkwardly, 'I would have thought you'd be an officer.'

'I didn't want to be. I'm happier mucking in with the girls. It's more – I don't know – relaxing.' She smiled. 'It's funny, you know, Parfitt, the one you danced with first, she's the greatest snob I've ever met. Well, with a couple of exceptions,' she cast a mental glance at Celia and Lady Beckenham, 'she's so class-conscious, never stops going on about it.'

'But you like her?'

'I love her,' said Barty, smiling.

After the third dance he asked her if he might kiss her. Amused at his old-fashioned chivalry, she had said of course he could. It hadn't been – earth-shattering, not exactly – well, not in the least earth-shattering – but very nice. She liked him more and more. They had a lot in common, liked the same books, music, the theatre; they found a great deal to talk about.

Parfitt was hugely excited by what she called the romance.

'Obviously likes you, Miller. But you can't marry him.'

'I wasn't planning to,' said Barty, laughing. 'But why not?'

'"Change the name, but not the letter, change for worse and not for better." You must know that.'

'Not really.'

'Anyway, if you do get spliced, I want to be chief bridesmaid. Seeing as I introduced you.'

'All right,' said Barty, 'you can be. That's a promise. If we do.'

Even Venetia, with her lack of literary experience, could see that Lyttons were publishing a lot of the wrong things. Her father, Edgar Greene and a couple of the other elderly male editors were suddenly in charge again, virtually unopposed, offering the public historical biographies, earnest intellectual novels, books of collected essays. Celia did her best, but she was distracted, depressed about Kit and bereft of Barty, of Jay, and of the two new young editors she had hired; she found it hard to push her own ideas through.

'I feel like the army at Dunkirk,' she said to Venetia one day, 'stranded on the beaches. Without a landing craft in sight. What was the use of beating off the purchase-tax threat in order to publish all this dreary rubbish?' She sighed, pushed away the proofs of a new edition of her Queen Anne biography. 'This is not what people want. Or that dreadful pompous set of political nonsense that Oliver is so pleased with. We need lots and lots of popular fiction, things like *Rebecca* and *My Son, My Son*. Even really good, meaty stuff like *The Grapes of Wrath* – did you read that – no, of course you didn't.'

'Don't be horrid,' said Venetia equably. 'I loved *Rebecca*, though.'

'Oh, she's so marvellous, Daphne du Maurier. I do wish she was ours. You know Oliver turned her down, all those years ago. I can hardly bear to think about it. And you know that Macmillan's biggest problem is finding enough paper for reprints of *Gone With the Wind*. And Oliver tells me, with his eyebrows raised, that people don't want what he calls that sort of thing . . .'

'That's what we want,' said Venetia, 'an English *Gone With the Wind*.'

'A little unlikely,' said Celia briskly, 'but yes, something like that. Anyway, if we don't find something soon, we'll be in serious trouble. We need a really big seller. Lyttons is barely breaking even at the moment. Sales are abysmal.'

It needed a German bomb to drop on Venetia's hairdresser for them to find it.

°

'It's too awful,' she wailed when she arrived at Lyttons one morning, 'look at me, hair like one of those hedgehogs baked in clay Grandpapa's always going on about, stomach like an unexploded bomb, and I've got to go and see Christina Foyle about a lunch for Guy Worsley. She'll just show me the door.'

'I'm sure she won't,' said Celia, 'but you don't look quite your best. Why don't you go to Elizabeth Arden? They don't do a bad job. You could get your nails done as well, they certainly need it. I would, Venetia, you'll feel a lot better.'

It was very hectic at Miss Arden's; Venetia had to wait for almost an hour. She was sitting reading an article in *Vogue* on the new hospitality – 'offer a hot bath, far more welcome than gin' – when she realised someone was trying to attract her attention. She pretended not to notice; she really wasn't in a mood to be sociable.

But, 'It's Venetia, isn't it? Venetia Warwick. You may not remember me, I knew your sister. I work on *Style* magazine.'

Venetia smiled politely. 'Yes. That's me.'

'I thought so. How is Adele? I heard she was safely back in England. What a nightmare for her with her poor husband still in Paris. If she ever feels like doing any work—'

'I don't think she will,' said Venetia carefully, 'she's down in the country with her children.'

'Lucky her! Wish I could be. Still, some of us still have jobs to do.'

'Yes,' said Venetia, and then because politeness required some kind of response, said, 'I'm sorry, I don't remember your name.'

'Lucy, Lucy Galbraith.'

She did remember her now; she'd been married to someone called Tim Galbraith and there'd been a messy divorce, he'd gone off with his own sister-in-law.

'Yes, of course.'

'You must forgive me for bothering you. I hate it when I'm trying to read at the hairdressers. But I just wondered – well, it's a bit of a cheek, but nothing ventured, and all that. I've had an idea for a novel.'

'Oh, yes?' said Venetia. She struggled to imitate her mother's famous polite coolness. 'How marvellous.'

'Yes. Actually more than an idea. It's half written already. I suddenly got so tired of being a fashion editor, thought there must be more to life. And I know your family are in the publishing business, so I wondered if I could possibly persuade you to have a look at it.'

'Well, it's a bit difficult at the moment,' said Venetia, 'we're frightfully limited as to what we publish, paper rationing, you know,

469

and—' She suddenly stopped. She might be turning away the new *Gone With the Wind*. 'Er – what's it about? Your novel?'

'Oh, well, it's really quite jolly, I think. You probably won't agree. It's the memoirs of a lady's maid to a frightfully grand family.'

'I thought you said it was a novel?'

'It is. It's fictional. That's why it's, such fun. Personal maid to a duchess, she is. A frightfully grand duchess, well, I suppose they all are, really, duchesses, I mean, I've called her the Duchess of Wiltshire, anyway, she's a minor lady-in-waiting to Queen Alexandra. She knew Queen Victoria, went around to country house parties with Alexandra, and then knew Queen Mary, of course. So it's her own story, the maid I mean, with a terribly sad romantic bit, but absolutely masses of patriotic stuff about the royal family, you know how everyone loves them, especially at the moment—'

'They certainly do.'

'And all interwoven with scraps of riveting gossip and history. Like she nearly went on the *Titanic*, this duchess—'

'My mother nearly went on the *Titanic*,' said Venetia.

'No! Well, there you are. And then all the stuff about Mrs Keppel, and the First World War of course, and I thought I could touch on the abdication, and end it now, with the Blitz and the marvellous King and Queen going round the bombed East End every day, and saying how glad they were they'd been bombed too. What do you think?'

Venetia's judgement of fiction was very simple; if she wanted to read it, it was good. She would want to read this.

'You'd better come and talk to my mother about it,' she said.

'Oh, Venetia, it sounds dreadful. Real housemaid stuff. Quite literally. Can you see us getting that past your father?'

'I think we should try,' said Venetia firmly.

'But why? Why should it be any good?'

'Well, because she's already a writer.'

'A journalist!' said Celia derisively. 'That is not quite the same thing, Venetia.'

'Dell says she writes really well. I asked her.'

'I don't feel Adele's judgment of literary skill is any better than yours.'

'Well, just take a look at it,' said Venetia, unmoved by this insult. 'You've got to, anyway, I've fixed for her to come.'

'I wish I'd never mentioned all this to you,' said Celia.

She was in a very bad temper the day Lucy Galbraith was coming in. She had come back from a particularly difficult visit to Kit, and had set herself so firmly against the book that Venetia had almost been tempted to cancel the appointment. But she hadn't. The book might be as good as it sounded. And besides, she felt a sense of solidarity with Lucy Galbraith. Divorced women had to stick together.

'I have to tell you we're not looking for popular fiction,' said Celia. This was so patently untrue that Venetia opened her mouth to contradict her, caught her mother's eye and shut it again. Celia picked up the rather messy-looking typescript as if it was going to soil her fingers and flicked through it.

'And certainly not of this genre.'

'Why not?'

Celia wasn't used to being challenged; she stared at Lucy, her features frozen in disapproval.

'Because it is hardly fashionable. People want—' She paused.

'All sorts of things.' Lucy smiled at her sweetly. 'Like the poem by that American woman, what's it called, oh yes, "The White Cliffs of Dover". And then *How Green Was My Valley*. And I believe Collins are doing a picture series about the English countryside.'

'How do you know that?' said Celia sharply.

'I'm a journalist. We get press releases. And then *War and Peace* has been re-published, hasn't it? And of course there's *Gone With the Wind* . . .'

'I trust you don't imagine this is a new *Gone With the Wind*. We have received at least a hundred manuscripts whose authors have been labouring under that delusion.'

'Of course not. But this could be very popular. Cheer people up. And it's quite patriotic in its own way. Please have a look at it, at least, Lady Celia. Just a few pages.'

'I'm extremely busy. I can't do it now, you'll have to leave it with me.'

'Of course. Now I haven't told you my provisional title.'

'No, I don't think you have. Of course we always retitle books.'

'Well, you might like it.' She was a pretty woman, dark, with very large eyes; she fixed them earnestly on Celia. 'But of course you could change it if you published it. I wouldn't mind.'

'I really don't think there is the slightest chance of our publishing it. As I told you, it's not what we're looking for. But I will, as a favour to you as a friend of my daughters, ask one of our readers to look at it.'

'Thank you so much. I'll – well, I'll leave it with you, shall I?'

'Please do. Just put it down there. Venetia, could you show Mrs Galbraith out, please?'

'Of course. Actually we're going to have lunch.'

'Well, don't be long. There's a great deal of work to be got through before the end of the day.'

When Venetia got back from her lunch with Lucy Galbraith, an hour and a half later, she looked into her mother's office. Celia appeared not to have moved. She was sitting absolutely still, her face frozen in a mixture of concentration and a sort of fierce hunger, turning the pages of Lucy Galbraith's typescript, making pencil notes on the pad at her side as she did so.

She looked up at Venetia and frowned. 'You've been a very long time. I wanted to speak to you about this rather urgently. What was the title your friend proposed?'

'*Grace and Favour.*'

'I don't dislike that. We might use it. Tell me, how far has she got with the book? Is there any more, or is this all she's done?'

'I think that's all.'

'Well, she'll have to get a move on, if we're going to publish in the spring.'

'The spring! But, Mummy—'

'Well, we've got nothing else in sight. This will have to do. It's not bad, Venetia, not bad at all. Please ask Mrs Galbraith to come back and see me tomorrow.'

'And now it's like a love affair,' Venetia reported to Adele that weekend, 'Lucy can do no wrong. You should have seen them on Thursday, heads together, of course Lucy's very stylish which helps, and well bred too, thank goodness—'

'Not quite as well bred as she seems,' said Adele. 'Father was an insurance clerk. She's put all that polish on herself. With a little help from Tim Galbraith and his money of course.'

'Well, good for her. Let's hope Mummy doesn't find out just yet. They're going to Worth together tomorrow, what about that? Press show, Mummy's frightfully excited. Anyway,' she grinned at Adele, 'of course she always knew it would be a marvellous read, from the moment I first told her about it, it now turns out. Also it's really cheered her up, she seems to have got some of her old energy back.'

'Venetia, how on earth do you stand it, working with her?'

'Oh,' said Venetia, looking vague, 'I find it quite easy. I just don't take any notice of anything she says.'

'I wouldn't find that easy.'

'Well, I do. Anyway, anything that takes my mind off Boy is awfully welcome.'

Boy's silence since his last cold, distant letter, his departure without saying goodbye to her, had hurt her so badly she started to cry every time she allowed herself to think about it. The only thing that kept her going was the reflection that he was clearly every bit as much of a rotter as she had always thought, using her like that, on his last night, and then just disappearing, after those few first nice letters. It was obvious he'd found another woman. She was intensely grateful that he had no idea about the baby. The humiliation of that would have been unbearable. For him to have known, recognised her incompetence, her foolishness in allowing it to happen, and then been forced to stay with her against his will: that would have been absolutely dreadful. At least she had her dignity. If you could call being seven months pregnant and unmarried dignified. She could just have the baby, and probably by the time the war was over, she would have some story to tell him, some lover who had been killed in the war. He could afford to support it along with the other children.

She still found that hideous affair of his difficult and painful; and it had turned her irrevocably against Barty. She couldn't help it. It might not be her fault, well, of course it wasn't her fault, but she had known and not warned her about it, probably enjoying – just for once – a sense of superiority over her. And anyway, she hadn't quite been able to believe the story of how Boy had met Abbie. Just accidentally. It seemed a bit unlikely. Barty had no doubt thought Boy would like Abbie, clever, musical, talented Abbie, so different from his own stupid wife, and arranged for them to meet. Not with anything really wrong in mind, but it would just – amuse her, it would be a sort of mild revenge. She would never believe anything else. Sometimes, before Barty had gone off to join the ATS and she had looked at her sitting at her desk, working earnestly away, she had actually felt quite sick. Working at Lyttons was much more comfortable without her.

Venetia absolutely loved her job; it fuelled her these days, made her feel alive and what she could only describe as pleased with herself. Not in an awful, smug way, but after years of believing herself stupid, fit for nothing except having babies and giving well-dressed dinner parties, it was wonderful to feel her mind growing, flexing its muscles, moving into action. She was incredibly grateful to her mother for making it possible; at first she knew she had been, if not exactly a hindrance, not a great deal of help. But now she could see she was actually valuable, especially with LM doing less, and that, as well as providing Celia with some very valuable support, her section of the company was running sweetly and smoothly.

She seemed to have a natural instinct for business – God knows where that came from, possibly her grandfather, old Edgar. She could spot an opportunity from nowhere and then just make it work, persuade bookshops, department stores, libraries, that it was exactly what they wanted to do and justify it to them financially. Her children's book club was going extremely well, and she'd had this idea of a competition now, an essay competition, to be judged by Sebastian Brooke. Of course she had no editorial instinct at all (although she had discovered *Grace and Favour* and suggested the cookery list), but there were plenty of people with that, including her mother. Venetia had an idea that they wouldn't be working nearly so well together if she were trying to become involved in that side of things.

She dreaded stopping, going into purdah in the country to have her baby; she had decided to stay until Christmas at least. It wasn't due until near the end of January. Someone else might start muscling in on her job in her absence. And if that happened, she might get extremely nasty.

Afterwards she often thought how extraordinary it was that the news of her pregnancy had never reached Boy. She was, after all, working and extremely visible in London whilst visiting bookshops and department stores, even lunching and occasionally dining in restaurants. There were surely other wives to note her condition and gossip about it and letters being written to husbands in Boy's regiment. But it did not. And there was a good reason for it.

Conditions in the desert were appalling: desperately uncomfortable, military success negligible, morale at times shaky. A fierce comradeship existed among all the men. They kept their own and one another's spirits up by sheer determination and considerable effort, and unwelcome news from home could only work against that.

In fact, Sheila Willoughby-Clarke had heard of Venetia's pregnancy and indeed wild speculation about who the father might be, and had written of it to her husband. But Mike Willoughby-Clarke was very fond of Boy and had been extremely remorseful at the misery he had caused him by telling him he had seen Venetia dancing at

474

the Dorchester; he could see no point in reviving that misery with what might, after all, be malicious gossip. And so he kept the news to himself and when another officer in receipt of the same gossip asked him if he had heard anything of it Mike told him to keep his mouth shut as well. 'Poor old chap's very cut up about his divorce. No point making him feel worse. Keep quiet about it, there's a good fellow.'

And so Boy remained in an ignorance which, if not blissful, was at least not painful.

Adele was taking Noni for a walk to the stables when she found Izzie crying. She was crying very quietly – Izzie did everything quietly, so as to give the least possible trouble – but quite hard. She was sitting on a seat behind the Dovecot where no one could see her. Adele sat down quietly beside her and put her arm round her. Noni clambered up on the other side.

'What is it, sweetie?'

'Oh – nothing. Sorry, Adele.'

'Don't say sorry. And it obviously isn't nothing. Come on, tell me.'

Silence. 'Missing Daddy?'

'Oh – a bit. But—'

'Kit?'

Izzie looked at her; her brown eyes were dreadfully swollen, her little face blotchy, her long tendrils of hair bedraggled. 'It's Kit. I try so hard, and he's so miserable still. Half the time he won't – won't—'

'I know, darling. He's very – difficult. But you're doing much better with him than anyone. Anyone at all. We all think you're wonderful.'

'But that's just the point.' She drew in her breath, sighed, then suddenly collapsed into tears again. 'He just told me he really would rather I didn't bother him any more. That's what he said. Bother him. I thought I was helping, a bit at least, but it turns out I'm making it worse.'

'Oh, Izzie, how could you be?'

'Well, he says I am. He just wants to be left alone. He says all I do is disturb his thoughts. That I really get on his nerves. I feel so bad, Adele, so stupid.'

Adele felt a rush of rage at Kit; at so savage a rejection of this sweet, gentle little creature. 'You mustn't. He's obviously having a bad day.'

'They're all bad days,' said Izzie, her voice rising again, 'all of them. I feel so sorry for him, and I can't help. He doesn't want me to help. It's so horrible, Adele. What can I do?'

475

'I think the best thing for now is nothing,' said Adele carefully, 'just leave him alone. He doesn't deserve you.'

'Oh, don't say that! It's all so dreadful for him, we have to—'

'I know it's dreadful for him. But it's dreadful for lots of people at the moment. People getting killed, horribly injured, losing their homes, the people they love—'

She spoke soberly; Izzie looked up at her.

'It must be horrible for you.'

'It is quite.'

'We miss Papa, don't we, Maman?' said Noni, her almost-black eyes fixed tenderly on Izzie.

'Yes, we do.'

'But we have to be brave.'

'That's right. Now listen, Izzie, let's go and wash your face. Shouldn't you be in lessons?'

'Miss Parsons sent me out. Because I was crying. She's awfully stupid anyway. Most of them are.'

Adele looked at her; she was such a clever child, far ahead of most of the lessons she was being given. She couldn't stay here much longer, surely. Sebastian would have to find a boarding school in a nice safe place for her. Only – goodness, they'd all miss her.

'Well – come and see Billy and the horses with us then. And just leave Kit be for a few days. Give him time.'

'Yes, all right. Sorry.' She blew her nose.

'Don't keep saying sorry.'

That evening Adele went to see Kit; he was in his room staring morosely into the distance, as usual, smoking.

'Hallo, Kit.'

'Hallo.'

'How are you feeling?'

A shrug. 'How do you think? Pour me a whisky, Adele. It's just over there, I'm told, on a tray.'

'Please.'

'What?'

'I said "please". Little word, you know, makes people want to help you a bit more. Try it.'

He was silent.

'Fine. You can wait for your whisky. Now then. I found Izzie this morning, sobbing in the grounds.'

Silence.

'Because of what you'd said to her.'

'Really?'

'Yes. Really. Now look, Kit. I know you're feeling wretched, of course you are, we're all desperately sorry for you and you can take it out on us if you have to, but not on Izzie. She's such a dear little thing and she's tried so hard, it's simply not—'

'Oh, fuck off,' he said.

'What did you say?' Adele was quite shocked.

'I said fuck off. If that's all you can offer me.'

Rage filled her: hot, almost sweet. She walked over to him, pulled the cigarette out of his mouth, stubbed it out viciously.

'You are a monster,' she said, 'a selfish, self-absorbed monster. How dare you talk to me like that? How dare you? How do you think I'm feeling, just now? With my Jewish lover trapped in Paris, at the mercy of the Nazis? What do you think it's like for my children, losing their father, just like that? I saw people on that road, holding their dead children in their arms, old men weeping over the bodies of their wives, people fighting over crusts of bread. You're not the only person who's having a bad time. It might help to remember that.'

'It was your choice to leave Paris. Get me another cigarette.'

'Absolutely not. And if that's how you talk to poor old Shepard when you want drinks and so on, I shall tell him not to do anything more for you either. What is the matter with you, Kit, why can't you—'

'I'll tell you what's the matter with me,' he said, and his voice was savage now, shaking with violence. 'I'm twenty years old. My life is over. Finished. I'm blind. I can't do anything. I can't even go for a walk on my own. I can't read, I'll never finish my degree, I'll never have a career, I'll just sit here and rot. And just to compound matters, the girl who said she loved me, wanted to marry me, has fucked off as well. After a very brief display of loyalty. And you ask me what the matter is. I've said it before, Adele, and I'm saying it again. Just fuck off. Leave me alone. And don't let that bloody child near me again. I don't want to see her. I don't want to see anyone.'

Adele went to her room and burst into tears.

She was very unhappy. The euphoria of getting home had passed, leaving her lonely, wretched and consumed with guilt. How could she have done that? Just abandoned Luc, left him without asking him for an explanation or without giving him one. She should have talked to him, offered him at least the chance to go with her; if he was imprisoned now by the Nazis, it would be at least in part her fault. She longed to make contact with him, to know he was at least not in danger and all right; but as far as she could see, it was impossible. She had tried, again and again. The telephone network was in the control of the Germans, no letters from – or indeed to – England would be delivered. Her father had repeatedly tried to get through to Constantines without success; it seemed totally hopeless. And against all logic, the fact that he had made no contact with her hurt her dreadfully as well: surely there could have been some way, in those very early days, that he could have found of getting through, to find out what had happened to her. And if not her, the children at least. Or did that mean he was indeed imprisoned, sent away to some work camp – or worse?

And there was something else: the seduction of the captain of the boat, of which she had spoken so airily to Venetia (and to nobody else), had actually, as time passed, become more, not less, horrific to her. At the time, it had seemed sensible, an absolutely pragmatic act, one of many she was prepared to commit in order to get herself and her children to safety. Now, locked into that safety, with nothing to relieve the boredom and the guilt of it, she examined and re-examined what she had done and found herself increasingly disgusted by it. The speed with which she had suggested it – and committed it: the ease with which she had been able to set aside the physical repugnance she felt towards his fat heaving body, his slobbery mouth, his bad breath: the very real possibility of pregnancy, venereal disease and, worst of all, of risking everything and still not achieving her end: all these things rose before her night after night, in evil, foul dreams, and skin-crawling, sweating recollection.

Memories of her journey filled her head as well, the terror of the shells, the frightful things she had witnessed by those roadsides, people killed and worse, not killed, mothers searching desperately for their children, children screaming for their mothers, grown men and women fighting over water, food, a shelter for the night. She had brushed them off when she told her story to the family, hardly described them at all; now they were assuming vast proportions in her mind, increasing all the time in horror, adding to her guilt, the guilt of the survivor. For she had committed other acts of treachery against humanity, she knew, refused help to old people, food and milk to children, had fought only for her own and given way to a selfishness, a near-brutality which horrified her.

She fretted over what she had done to her children, making them witness such horrors, hear her saying no, don't give him an apple, don't share that bread; feared too what horrible sights and sounds were stored in their own small memories. Noni seemed all right; she cried for her father quite a lot at night, but that was healthy, and there seemed nothing she would not talk about or discuss. Indeed Adele had even heard her telling Izzie and Henry and Roo about their journey and adventures, with a certain gusto even.

She worried more about Lucas; he was only a baby, it was impossible to talk to him and therefore reassure herself, but he was quieter than he had been, clearly confused and distressed by yet more new surroundings, different people. He slept badly, waking to scream in the night (and disturbing the few blessed hours of escape she had), and could only be comforted by bottles of warm milk which he drank with a kind of fervour, and by his beloved toy cow which he still clung to as if to a lifeline. He would not even have a bath without it.

Visions of Luc being interned, sent to a concentration camp, haunted her; she imagined him dying without her having said goodbye. She was not sure any more what she felt for him: not sure if she loved him. She missed him savagely, if that counted for anything. Together they had laughed, cried, made love, conceived children; it simply wasn't possible for that to be obliterated, there had to be something, probably a great deal, left. Yet she had simply turned her back on him and walked away; depriving him not only of herself but the children he undoubtedly loved very much.

More and more it seemed to her a most terrible thing to have done.

Chapter 32

This must be what hell was like, Celia thought. Fire everywhere, even the puddles were hot; as she moved along the pavement she could feel the heat from the buildings, and what seemed like sheets of fire all around her. She had got used to the bombing, the noise, to fires, to gutted ruins, they all had, but this was quite unlike anything she had ever even imagined. And she was out in it, and it felt like being absolutely alone at the end of the world.

It was 29 December. It had been peaceful over Christmas; Hitler had given them a break. Everyone had shopped, Oxford Street was crowded – in spite of John Lewis being a shell, there were a surprising number of Christmas goodies to be found everywhere, Norfolk turkeys, fine chickens and beef, plenty of wine and spirits, and boxes of liqueur chocolates. The only rationing appeared to be by price.

They had spent Christmas at Ashingham again, to keep all the children safe; only this year Jay and Boy were both missing, Jay in France, Boy in North Africa. They had been joined by Giles and Helena and their children (who were actually living with the grandparents in the comparative safety of Surrey), and Sebastian was there too, to Izzie's great joy. Giles was due to leave England shortly after Christmas, he told them; he was quietly cheerful, Helena rather subdued. Only LM and Gordon had stayed in London; LM was very upset, Gordon had said, at Jay's departure, and wanted to be quiet.

Everyone made a great effort to be jolly, with the exception of Kit. Not even Sebastian could make him smile. He sat stony-faced through Christmas lunch and left the room shortly before it ended. Celia ran after him and returned flushed and tearful-looking five minutes later.

Venetia was also jumpy and tearful. A brief courteous note had come for her from Boy, telling her he was going to North Africa and wishing her a happy Christmas, but nothing more; the imminence of the baby's birth only emphasised her loneliness. She and Adele sobbed in one another's arms on Christmas morning, before going downstairs to present a cheerfully united front.

'If only, if only I could just have some kind of contact with Luc,' said Adele, wiping her eyes, 'just to know he's all right, I don't care how much he hates me, or how angry he is, I just want to know that, and to tell him I'm sorry. I just feel more desperate every day. It's like some awful, endless nightmare. Oh, Venetia, why did I do it, why did I leave him, without even saying goodbye? What a terrible thing to have done.'

The children had all had a wonderful time . . .

They were all playing a rather noisy game of charades with the children on Boxing Day when Shepard came into the room.

'Telephone, Lady Celia. Mr Robinson.'

'Thank you, Shepard. Please do excuse me, everyone.'

She came back into the room looking upset.

'Apparently LM is unwell. She had a dizzy spell before luncheon today, and the doctor is concerned about her. Nothing too serious, but she has been ordered to rest. Oh, dear, she won't like that. Well, that settles it. I shall have to go back to London first thing in the morning. Venetia, do you feel up to coming with me or do you think you should stay down here now?'

'Oh, no, I'd much rather come,' said Venetia. 'Honestly, Mummy, I've got nearly another month to go, I'll only get miserable and grumpy down here.' She carefully avoided Adele's pleading eyes, her suddenly bleak expression; much as she loved her, her helpless misery was simply adding to her own.

'Very well,' said Celia with a sigh. 'I wonder if we should leave tonight, the roads will be quieter and—'

'Am I to be included in your plans in any way?' said Oliver mildly. 'Or should I simply make my own arrangements?'

Celia looked at him.

'I really think it would be better if you stayed down here a few more days,' she said. 'You look awfully tired, and—'

'Oh no, Celia,' he said, and his eyes sparkled suddenly with a sharp amusement, 'I'm not letting you get away with things that easily. I'll find you've allocated half our paper ration to that dreadful book of yours.'

He was passionately opposed to the publication of *Grace and Favour*, having pronounced it below-stairs rubbish ('as he does anything that might sell well,' said Celia to Venetia), and was terrified that it would invite legal action with its semi-fictional approach to the aristocracy. Indeed, he had only been persuaded to publish it at all by the combined weight of Celia, Venetia and Sebastian, who had read it and liked it immensely.

'You've got to move with the times, Oliver,' he had said gently. 'Lyttons needs a big seller for the spring. I think it's marvellous. I should print – what shall we say – a couple of thousand – if I were you. No more than that, of course. And see what happens.'

'It'll sell by the bucket load,' he said privately to Celia, 'but no use telling Oliver that, nothing makes him more opposed to a book than thinking everyone's going to like it.'

They went up to London the next day; Venetia sank into her office with a sigh of relief. It was wonderful to have something else to think about other than Boy and his new woman; what on earth would she have done without her job? she wondered, leafing through the post. There was a fat package, in Lucy Galbraith's writing: that was good, she'd finished the last quarter. She must take it in to her mother as soon as she'd read it herself. She couldn't wait to find out what the wicked Duchess of Wiltshire was going to do, now that her lover had joined the navy . . .

In fact she didn't have time to read it at all that day. Celia was out visiting booksellers and Venetia had been dealing with a lot of her enquiries. The next day was a Saturday and she had felt – and clearly looked – so exhausted that Celia had most unusually made her stay in bed. The following morning, Sunday, she felt much better and insisted on going into Lyttons: 'I've got such a lot to do, and I'm only going to sit about here, reading the papers and feeling sorry for myself. I really would like to go in for a bit, get some work, and bring it back here.'

'I'd come with you,' said Celia, 'but I've promised Gordon I'd go and see LM. There are a few things I want too; I'll give you a list. Have you got any petrol? I haven't.'

'Enough. What will you do?'

'Go on the bus of course,' said Celia. She made much of her use of public transport, which usually led into reminiscences about how she and LM had travelled to work every day by tram in the First War. Her grandchildren knew this particular speech off by heart and recited it to one another complete with grand gestures when she wasn't listening.

'Well, don't stay there long, Venetia,' said Oliver. 'I can't believe there are going to be many more nights without a raid . . .'

'Nonsense,' said Celia, 'not even Hitler would bomb London on the first Sunday after Christmas. They'll start again tomorrow, I have absolutely no doubt of that.'

Venetia got to Lyttons at about two; she spent a very profitable two hours planning her promotional expenditure for the coming few months and then realised her back was aching rather badly – and that she ought to go home. It was also extremely cold; she was glad of her unfashionably long sable coat. The long Christmas break had left the offices icy. She went into her mother's office and gathered together all the things that she had requested, then pulled on her sable coat and went downstairs and out into the street with a great sense of personal satisfaction and virtue.

It was only when she was halfway home, pulling into Parliament Square, that she remembered; the manuscript of *Grace and Favour* was still sitting in her desk.

'Damn,' she said aloud, 'damn, damn, damn.'

Apart from the fact she had planned to spend the evening reading it, the manuscript certainly shouldn't have been left in her desk. All valuable paperwork – which included manuscripts – had to go into the big safe in the basement, it was an absolutely unbreakable rule. Normally she was very good about remembering; she supposed it was the combination of her backache, and an accompanying splitting headache, neither of which she normally suffered from – and a sense of slight disorientation at being all alone in the deserted city. Having remembered, however, she quite clearly had to do something about it.

The one precious copy of what her mother had repeatedly said was going to save Lyttons was sitting in a wooden desk, in her second-floor office, at the mercy of Hitler and the failing water supply of London; it was not only irresponsible to leave it, it was criminally unprofessional. Lucy Galbraith didn't make carbon copies; she had told her so herself. 'Such a mess when you rub out.' What was in her desk was the only copy of *Grace and Favour* in the world.

She told herself it would be almost certainly all right; that there was no reason why the bombing should start that night and that even if it did, there was absolutely no reason why it would target Paternoster Row. She found each argument horribly implausible. She would have to go back.

She rummaged in her bag and found a couple of aspirins for her back; she could take them when she got back to Lyttons. She swung her car round and drove back towards the City. She had just about enough petrol, she thought: it wouldn't take long; and she would still be home before six.

Celia got home just after six; Oliver hadn't expected her and was enjoying his first whisky of the day. This was a regular indulgence and a well-kept secret from Celia, who was very strict about his alcoholic intake; two measures a day were all that he could safely be allowed, she told him, and poured his two glasses of wine at dinner herself, while constantly reminding him that Dr Rubens had said he should have no alcohol of any kind. At which Oliver merely smiled at her sweetly and told her that he would rather have another stroke. This could be guaranteed to put Celia in a furious rage. He looked at her now rather sheepishly.

'Instead of wine, my dear. We're getting very low anyway.'

'Whisky is far worse for you than wine, Oliver.'

'Oh, I don't know. How was LM?'

'Not too bad. I have to say, I don't like the look of her, though, she's a bad colour. Gordon is worried, I can tell, only he won't admit it. Where's Venetia?'

'She hasn't come back yet.'

'Hasn't come back? From Lyttons?'

'No. I was just thinking it was looking pretty dark.'

'Well, of course it's dark, Oliver, it's well after six. Where on earth is she? It's too bad of you—'

'Celia, I really don't think even you can blame me for Venetia deciding to stay at Lyttons a little longer. I expect she became engrossed in what she was doing and—'

'Venetia doesn't get engrossed in anything in that way. Oh, dear. I do hope – is there any petrol in the Rolls?'

'I have no idea.'

'Oliver, you are so – so out of touch. How can you possibly not know whether you've got any petrol or not? Just because you don't drive yourself. It's absurdly irresponsible. I shall go and look.'

The petrol gauge in the Rolls was firmly set at empty.

Celia tried to tell herself that Venetia must be all right, that they would have heard if she was not, and poured herself a Scotch twice the size of Oliver's.

In fact, at that moment, Venetia was indeed perfectly all right. She had felt extremely tired on getting back to Lyttons and had decided to sit and read for a few minutes before leaving again. Her head and her back were both still aching severely.

She opened *Grace and Favour,* and was immediately engrossed; the narrative had begun with the mythical Duchess of Wiltshire's attendance at a party where the Prince of Wales and Mrs Simpson were present; there was much fascinating detail in the diary about Mrs Simpson's dress, and the way the Prince of Wales was so clearly devoted to her. A few pages later, the lady-in-waiting was to be found waiting anxiously outside the Albert Hall while her mistress attended one of Oswald Mosley's rallies. Honestly, Venetia thought, it could all be about her own mother.

Goodness, her head ached; she wondered if she could risk another aspirin. She looked at her watch: only an hour and a half since the last one. Maybe not: perhaps a tiny snooze would be a good idea. She would take the manuscript down to her mother's office, lie down on one of her sofas and have forty winks. As Winston Churchill did each day, apparently. If it was good enough for him, it was certainly good enough for her. She lay down and closed her eyes. And fell asleep.

There was nowhere she could possibly be, Celia thought, in a growing panic. Sebastian was still at Ashingham, so was Adele. Giles had come back – maybe she was with them.

But, no, their maid said, Mr and Mrs Lytton were with the Duffield Browns for the day, down in the country.

'In Surrey, do you mean?'

'Yes, Lady Celia.'

'That is not the country,' Celia said firmly, and put down the phone. Even in her anxiety she felt she must make such an important matter clear.

She tried phoning Lyttons: no reply. She held on for a long time, then asked the operator to try again. The phone rang on and on.

Up to the coast of northern France, and thence across the Channel, following their now-familiar itinerary along the Thames towards London, came a vast fleet of German bombers. The Christmas peace was over.

Venetia awoke with a jump to the siren, wailing through the still night, more alarming for the long spell of silence. And then following it, the dreadful, familiar roar. Increasing in volume; getting nearer.

Her instinct was simply to get home; it couldn't take long, there was always quite a delay between the first siren and the first bomb. Surely she could drive the short distance to Chelsea in that time.

She went downstairs carefully (wouldn't help to fall), and gingerly opened the door. And shut it again. They were everywhere, the planes; seemingly all round her, a great mass of sound. She looked at her watch; it was half past six.

'Right, Venetia,' she said aloud to herself, fighting down the panic, 'down into the cellar. That's the sensible thing. And take the manuscript with you.'

There were torches down there; the raid probably wouldn't last long, she could finish the manuscript and then leave. God, her back hurt.

She remembered suddenly that she had left her mother's papers in the car; damn. Should she get them? No, probably not. Her car might be – God, that was close. It had started. Keep calm, Venetia. Keep calm. The cellar is safe.

Nothing could happen to her there; even if the building was hit. It was like a fort down there. Fort Lytton, her father had called it. Grandpa Edgar had even reinforced with steel where the huge safe was kept, beneath the stairs, so great was his fear of a fire. They had sheltered there several times over the past few months; her father had always been so calm, smiling at her, telling her this was nothing, she should have been in the trenches. It had seemed very boring at the time; she longed to have him there now, boring her.

She went down the narrow stone steps. God, it was difficult with her huge stomach. And this awful backache . . . oh, it hurt. Another aspirin would be all right now, surely. She felt her face screwing up involuntarily at the horrible taste. What she needed was something to take it away; she seemed to remember a boiled sweet in her bag. And she'd left that – damn, at the top of the steps, so she could hold the banister more firmly. She turned – and slipped. Not badly, but enough to throw her off balance. She fell forward, grabbing at the rail, and just saved herself. She took a deep breath, trying to calm herself – and then looked down in horror as a rush of water appeared at her feet. And felt a harder, more purposeful stab at her back, which seemed to reach round to her stomach as well.

'Oh, God,' she whispered, 'oh, dear God, no.'

There was no doubt about it: she was in labour.

'Sebastian, it's Celia.'

'Celia! Hallo!'

'Have you heard from Venetia?'

'No, I don't think so. I'll ask. Just wait a moment.'

He came back. 'Sorry. She hasn't rung. Why, have you lost her?'

'I'm very much afraid we have,' said Celia. And she started trying to telephone the local fire wardens. Not surprisingly there was no answer.

Afterwards, everyone was shocked at how completely they had been taken unawares. It was partly because it was Sunday of course, and a Christmas one at that; the city was silent, the exhausted ARP wardens and fireworkers still enjoying the peace. There were one thousand, five hundred fires in the City that night; there were reports that they could be seen sixty miles away.

Certainly, even quite early in the raid, the sky was red as blood and the fires could be seen from the Chelsea Embankment, where Lady Celia Lytton was loading her cook's bicycle into the Rolls, reasoning that it must have a little petrol and would go some of the way and when it stopped she could start cycling. She borrowed Brunson's tin hat, which he wore for his Home Guard patrols, told him to sit with Oliver and set off to rescue her daughter.

She had a fairly clear idea of what must have happened; for one reason or another, Venetia had stayed too long at Lyttons and was now trapped. Hopefully she was in the cellar; but she could be trapped there for the night and she was extremely pregnant. She simply couldn't be left.

The petrol gauge was blessedly pessimistic; Celia had reached Ludgate Hill before the car juddered to a halt. She didn't waste any time trying to re-start it; she pulled the bike out, put on the tin hat and started pedalling furiously towards St Paul's, the wonderfully solid shape of its dome outlined against the sky. She was overtaken constantly by fire engines; she could see the searchlights now, scouring the sky. The noise was deafening, from the planes, from the bombs, from the great guns firing; there were fires ahead of her in the City now, appearing endlessly, like monstrous kindling in a fireplace; she was desperate for breath, gasping in the awful air, hot, smoky, somehow gritty. Afterwards she said she supposed she must have been frightened, but she had no consciousness of it, her mind absolutely focused on where she was going, on finding Venetia, on doing both with the utmost speed.

Venetia made herself as comfortable as she could in Grandpa Edgar's vault. She must not panic. She absolutely must not. A few contractions didn't mean a baby. Labour took hours, endless hours; when the raid was over, she could still get herself home. Or to hospital.

Only – oh, God, that hurt. She did always forget how much. The wrenching, tugging, pulling pain. And it didn't actually seem very long since the last one. Supposing – no, Venetia, don't suppose. Just stay calm. And – yes, she could time the contractions. That would give her something to do at least. Something else to think about . . .

As Celia reached Paternoster Square, a bomb dropped seemingly just behind St Paul's; in fact it was a mile away, just north of the Bank of England, but she felt the ground shudder, watched the sky light up. She could see Paternoster Row now, see Lytton House; her heart felt quite literally as if it were bursting.

She felt the bike vibrating, realised she had not just one but two punctures – presumably the heat and the grit – saw a bomb much much nearer, on the far side of St Paul's. Not St Paul's, please God, not St Paul's, that was the safeguard, it had become London's talisman, a great symbol, surviving with them; while it stood, they all felt in some strange way undefeated. The great dome stood steady.

Only ten minutes since the last one. Ten minutes. That was when the doctor always said stupid things like 'coming along nicely now'. It wasn't just the growing speed of them, either, it was the length. These weren't little twinges, curls of pain, they were quite strong breakers; she could feel them tugging, heaving in her. This was nasty. This really was quite a nasty situation.

Better now. She took a deep breath, relaxed. She must try to keep calm. If the worst came to the worst, she would need all her wits about her. But – delivering her own baby. With no help. Could she really do that? Was it even possible?

Celia started to run; as fast as she could. And yes, yes, there was Venetia's car, the jaunty litle bright red Austin Seven that had been the twins' eighteenth birthday present and that Venetia still drove everywhere in; she was inside, then, and safe; the building, the whole street indeed, was still standing. Celia found herself, almost to her irritation, sending a brief prayer to the Almighty, who did not seem generally to be greatly concerned with people's safety. But Venetia was safe; she could be with her in minutes. And then she realised she did not have the key.

It sounded like the bell: the great, pealing bell by the front door which was hardly ever rung. Venetia, seriously frightened now, so close was the noise, huddled in her corner in the cellar, in Grandpa Edgar's vault, clutching *Grace and Favour* as if it in some way offered her protection against the danger, and bracing herself for the next wave of pain (due in about one minute if she was right), decided she could only ignore it. To go upstairs now, with London falling around her, would be absolute folly; and besides, who could it be, who could possibly be ringing the bell? Some passing warden, checking that there was no one there, perhaps? Surely not? That happened after the bombs, in the awful, crumbling, collapsing aftermath; not while they were falling.

It came again; and then again. Endlessly, persistently, on and on. She looked up at the steps warily; should she go? Risk leaving her fortress? No. She shouldn't. All the advice was against it. Of course all the advice was also against driving round London in a small car at dusk during the Blitz.

'Come on, Venetia, come on.'

What was she doing, couldn't she hear her, was she in some way incapacitated, had she fallen? Or had she gone? Had someone rescued her already? Maybe that was the explanation, maybe she shouldn't stay here, risking her own life, just take Venetia's car, she had the key, and drive out of this hell. But – not just yet. Keep ringing the bell a while, Celia, just keep doing it.

She looked behind her; the whole of London, from every side, seemed alight. It was like a great continuous wall of flame, a firestorm. She could feel the heat now, beating at her out of the air; a fire engine went past her, splashing her with the water from the puddles. That was when she discovered they were hot.

The bell again. Someone must think she might be in there. But who? Who knew? And who would be brave enough and insane enough to try and find her? No one; no one at all. And then suddenly she did know: at once and with a rush of intense gratitude and love. She stood up quickly and another contraction hit her, so strong, so violent that she bent double with it, gasped with the pain. She couldn't move until it was over: it was impossible. She stood there, clutching the stair rail, enduring it, willing it to pass. And praying that the ringing wouldn't stop.

She must have gone, thought Celia. She must. Perhaps someone from the fire service had rescued her. She had been ringing the bell for over five minutes now. There was no way, frightened and desperate as she must be, that Venetia would not have come to the door. She would just have to pray she was somewhere safe, and that she could get back before the whole of London went up. Now where was Venetia's key? On her ring with the front door key. Which was – yes, here. Good. She looked at the little car, almost as frail a protection as Cook's bicycle, thanked God for her tin hat and was just going to run for it, when there was another bomb, horribly close. Celia huddled into Lyttons' doorway and, as she often did in times of great difficulty, started to recite A. A. Milne's 'The King's Breakfast'. She could never remember now quite why, except that it was quite long and didn't seem to end. But as soon as that last explosion, so horribly close, had settled, she would go.

Pain easing now: thank God. Venetia took a deep breath, and hauled herself up the stairs. She got to the top, and then half ran across the tiled ground floor, heedless now of the danger of slipping. She reached the door, fell against it and was just able to open it before collapsing, confused, against her mother. Who looked at her almost crossly and said, 'What on earth took you so long?'

Afterwards, she could see it was the stuff farce was made of; her mother standing there, silhouetted against the flames, the over-large tin hat slipping over her grimed face, still wearing a narrow black coat from Worth and her high-heeled shoes, irritable with her for not answering the door more quickly, as if she had been arriving for a tea party. At the time she could only feel relief, happiness and the absolute childish security of being with the one person in the world who could put things right, create order out of chaos, keep danger at bay. And then the pain hit her again, so soon, too soon, and she said through it, through clenched teeth, 'I'm in labour.'

'Well, come along,' said her mother, her voice very calm, taking her elbow, supporting her, helping her out towards the steps, 'we must be quick.'

'No,' Venetia said, even in her confusion and pain remembering, 'we must get *Grace and Favour*, it's down there still, in the vault, where I was sitting.'

'Get in the car,' Celia said. 'I'll get it. Only be careful, it's dreadful out there. Even St Paul's looks as if it might go at last.'

Neither of them could recall a great deal of the dreadful first stage of that journey; the bombs seemed to surround them, the heat beating at the windows, the explosions of fire lighting the sky in great terrifying sheets.

Venetia only spoke once; huddled into her seat, dreading another pain, she suddenly saw a great crater in the road, and only just in time to shout a warning at her mother who seemed somehow to have failed to see it. Even then the car lurched terrifyingly, seemed ready to tip over, but a second yank at the wheel righted it.

'Close,' was all Celia said.

She was astonishingly calm; even when a fire in front of them and one to the side apparently barred further progress; she backed up a few yards, swerved down an alley to the left, hardly wide enough to take the car. 'No entry that was,' she said as they reached the end of it, and smiled at Venetia. 'Hope we don't get prosecuted.'

They turned left at the bottom of Ludgate Hill; the Rolls was still there, oddly defiant.

'We can't leave it there.' said Venetia, finding her voice again, 'someone might steal it.'

'They can't,' said Celia, 'it's out of petrol.'

They reached the Embankment; the fires were mostly behind them now, the river on their left absurdly familiar and comforting. Then a huge explosion hit some buildings across Blackfriars Bridge; they felt the shock of it.

'Christ,' said Celia conversationally. Venetia stared at her; she had never heard her swear.

By the time they reached Parliament Square, they were feeling safer. 'Worst over, I think,' said Celia.

'Don't tempt providence.'

'I think providence has long since yielded to temptation. You all right?'

Venetia nodded, then, 'Oh, God. Oh, God. Another one. Can we get to the nursing home?'

Celia looked at her. 'In Harley Street? Through all this? I think we're better off getting home.'

They finally pulled up outside Cheyne Walk, looked up at its familiar shape in mild astonishment.

'We made it,' said Celia.

'Yes.' Venetia threw her head back, looked at her mother. 'Thank you so much,' she said simply.

'What on earth for?'

'Coming to get me.'

'Oh, don't be absurd,' said Celia, 'and anyway, it was the manuscript I really wanted. Now come along, quickly, can you get inside?'

'Of course. Only you'd better get Mr Bradshaw pretty damn quick. I wonder if he's ever delivered a baby in a cellar?'

'Sebastian?'

'Celia! Thank God. I've been so desperately worried. I was about to set out for London myself.'

'Extremely stupid of you,' said Celia coolly. 'You'd have very likely been killed.'

'And what about you?'

'Well – I wasn't. We weren't, I should say. And the worst's over, I think. With the raids, I mean.'

'What happened?'

She started to tell him.

'You are extraordinary,' he said, 'really extraordinary. Cycling through all that.'

'Sebastian, I had to,' she said, sounding half surprised. 'Venetia was in danger. You know one would do anything for one's child.'

'Yes,' he said quietly, 'yes, of course I do.' And then added, 'Kit's been very worried. He got wind of it.'

'Tell him we're safe. And Adele and Mama. Now I must go, poor Venetia's in labour.'

'What! Is she all right? Thank God you got her.'

'She's fine. Or will be. Fairly hard going at the moment. Old Dr Perring is with her, her obstetrician's away, wretched man. Best not tell the others yet. Adele will only fret more.'

'All right. But let us know, won't you, when you – when she—'

'Of course.'

'Thank you for telephoning. And, Celia – you do – know. Don't you?'

'Yes,' she said, 'I do know.'

The Warwick children were summoned to their great-grandmother's sitting room before breakfast the next morning. They stood in a line, looking at her, their eyes apprehensive. Such confrontations usually meant trouble.

But, 'You have a baby brother,' she said, beaming at them, 'born last night. Your mother is very well. So is he. And before you ask, you can't go and see them. But your mother will be down here in a week or two.'

Amy promptly burst into tears.

'Don't be silly, Amy, I know you're missing her, but she can't travel down here with a new baby.'

'I'm not crying because I miss her. I'm crying because I wanted a sister,' she said.

'I don't know what to call him,' said Venetia, smiling at her mother over the dark head of her new baby, delivered just as the last bomber left London and headed back to Munich.

'I do. I've just been looking it up in our names dictionary. Fergal. I like that. Fergal Warwick. Nice ring to it.'

'Well – it's all right, I suppose. But if you want it,' she added, 'you should have it. I think I owe you a name at least.'

'I do want it. It's Gaelic. And it means valorous man. He might or might not turn out to be valorous, but his mother and grandmother certainly are. Well done, Venetia. You were jolly brave.'

'Was I?' She sounded vague. 'Good. God, it hurts, doesn't it? Every time. And I've never had one without any gas before.'

Dr Perring had had no such luxuries with him; and he had agreed Venetia was safer having the baby at home than trying to get to a possibly fire-bombed nursing home.

'When I had Giles there was no such thing,' said Celia, 'and he took thirty-six hours to be born.'

'How ghastly.'

'Yes, it was rather. My mother got me through it. She just kept telling me it would be over. You know that's one of her mottoes. And whenever I so much as groaned she told me it was common. She was right of course. On both counts.'

'I think I sounded a bit common at times last night,' said Venetia, and giggled.

'Once or twice. Not bad, though.' Celia looked at the baby. 'He looks just like Boy,' she said.

'Yes, I suppose he does.'

'So – when are you going to tell him? Boy, I mean.'

'Oh, Mummy, I don't know. Never, probably. Let's not think about it.'

'Yes, well, there's certainly no rush,' said Celia soberly.

The devastation in the City next morning was dreadful; and many of the fires were still burning, it had not been possible to put them out. The reason was very simple: there had been too little water. The Thames was very low, the fireboats couldn't manoeuvre near the site of the fires, and the pumps were out of range of the water. So they had to burn out; hour after hour. Twice, Fire Brigade control centres had to be abandoned: the staff had escaped through the cellar network under the gutted buildings.

St Paul's was still standing, brooding over the devastation around it; twenty-eight incendiaries had hit it, one had even lodged halfway into the outer shell of the dome and began to melt the lead; then suddenly it fell outwards on to the parapet and burned out. Yet again it seemed inviolable.

The Bank of England survived too; and so did the Faraday building, the Cabinet's private refuge, although the flames were so close at one point that the Army contemplated blowing up the adjoining buildings to protect it. It proved unnecessary.

Countless other buildings did go, including eight Wren churches, the Guildhall was badly damaged and the Port of London reduced to a quarter of its capacity. Paternoster Row had become a smoking, charred ruin.

'It's gone, Oliver,' Celia said gently, taking his hand. 'I'm so sorry.' He had heard of the fire, had expected the worst; just the same, he sat staring at her, clearly shocked.

'Have you seen it?'

'No. I tried, but the police have completely cordoned it off. But I met Hubert Wilson – you know?'

'Oh, from the City bookshop?'

'Yes. He'd managed to get through. God knows how. He said it was unbelievable, the devastation. Not just us. Every building, reduced to – well, to shells. Gutted shells. Longmans, Nelson, Hutchinson – and Collins and Eyre & Spottiswoode, the list is endless. Apparently Paternoster Square is just rubble, the only thing recognisable is a pillar box. And even that below ground level.'

'Even the basements?'

'Even Grandpa Edgar's fortress. I'm so sorry.'

'So – we've lost everything.'

'I'm afraid so. The safe may have survived. We won't know for days, until people can really get in there. It's still red-hot in places, you see.'

'I see.' He was silent; contemplating the end of Lytton House, the end of the building which had been the centre of their lives for so long. She could see how much it hurt him, that loss; it was agonising, deeply personal, the beautiful building which had shaped his own history, which old Edgar had bought and fashioned into something entirely special and unique and then bequeathed to him. She watched him remembering, knew what many of those memories were, his own early struggles and triumphs, her own introduction to Lyttons, his office and indeed hers where so much had been discovered and fought over and celebrated and mourned. The lovely entrance hall, the great door, the fine staircase, the precious library, the priceless first editions, the elaborate original artwork, the superb bindings – all gone, senselessly and wantonly destroyed by a madman.

He sighed, a heavy, desperate sound, almost a choke. He looked at her, and she saw his eyes were filled with tears. And then he spoke very slowly, his voice suddenly stronger.

'It doesn't really matter so very much.' he said. 'I might have lost you too.'

Chapter 33

On a good day Adele looked as if she were in the throes of a serious illness; on a bad one, she looked as if she would never recover.

The excited, triumphant girl who had arrived home had become a distraught wraith, wandering about Ashingham all day and much of the night, her eyes huge and haunted in her white face. She was frequently in tears, she didn't eat, indeed she hardly did anything at all, she didn't read, she didn't talk to anyone unless she had to, and although she helped in the house when asked, it was in a dilatory, listless way, like an obedient, browbeaten child.

She still cared, and most tenderly, for her children, and indeed she had developed such an acute anxiety over them that if one was missing from her side even for five minutes she became dreadfully upset, crying and calling for them, tears streaming down her face. No one so much as took them out on to the terrace or up the front drive without telling her, and even then they risked her wrath: 'They have to be with me,' she would say fiercely, grabbing Noni's hand, picking up Lucas, holding him to her as if he had been threatened with violence. 'I don't want them separated from me.'

She felt desperately tired all the time; so exhausted, so achingly, throbbingly weary, not just physically but emotionally, that the effort each day of getting up and dressing herself and her children was so great she would often have to lie down and rest for half an hour or more afterwards, and again after giving them their lunch, and yet again after taking them out for the brief walks that were their only visit to the outside world.

She felt at her best when she was crying; released from the struggle to be brave, to make anything but the worst of her situation. She would set aside time each day to weep, looking forward to it rather as if she were about to have a meal or a glass of wine, and would abandon herself to the luxury of the release of quiet but violent sobbing, lying on her bed, her head buried in her arms, often holding Noni and Lucas to her as she did so. Afterwards, she would feel briefly better, calm and almost cleansed; freed for a while from the thought of Luc hating her for taking his children from him. She often wondered what he would have done if there had not been a war on, if he had been able to come after her; would he have taken them back, robbed her as she had robbed him, sought to remove her from their lives as she had removed him? And then it would start again, the churning, soaring guilt and misery and remorse that left her so absolutely confused and wretched. And terribly, terribly frightened at what she had done.

Cedric Russell had been away for Christmas and the New Year at a country house party given by his latest boyfriend, the artist Bertram Cullingford. They had met at the theatre one night on a rare visit by Cullingford to London, very early in the war; he was, at forty, a little older than Cedric could have wished, but he was handsome, charming and extremely civilised, and after all, Cedric told himself, if he had been younger he would have been at the front. Cedric himself had avoided the call-up; to his great relief and rather illogical joy, it had been discovered he had a weak heart – almost certainly caused, the MO had told him, by a serious attack of scarlet fever in his childhood – and he was therefore not fit for active service.

There was also the little matter of Cedric's sexual ambivalence; despite arriving at the call-up centre wearing one of his father's old tweed suits, his curls slicked down with Brylcreem, his voice and his mannerisms made it fairly clear that he was not quite what the army was at ease with; the Conscription Sergeant was greatly relieved by the news of the weak heart.

Cedric had wanted, nonetheless, to do his bit and found work instead as a porter and ward orderly in a large East End hospital, filled mostly with casualties of the Blitz; slightly to his surprise he enjoyed it. The patients all loved him, he cheered them up, sitting on their beds and chatting away, telling them jokes, and the young nurses thought he was wonderful, giving them advice as he did on their make-up and hairstyles and their love lives; the Sisters and Matron took a rather different view, but since he was very good at his job (chatting and time-wasting apart) and undoubtedly did a lot for ward morale, they put up with him.

'Just the same,' he confided in Cullingford, 'not quite what one has been used to. The food! Too awful. And of course one never sees anything stylish from one week to the next. Except perhaps for the nurses' caps: rather lovely, they are, I tried one on last week, it quite suited me.'

They had had a very good Christmas break, in Cullingford's country house in Wiltshire, but Cedric had had to report back on duty at 6 a.m. on 3 January – 'and besides, that dreadful raid the night before last, it will all be quite awful, so many casualties' – and he also wanted, he told Cullingford, a little bit of time on his own.

'My flat is in a fearful state, I can't get anyone to clean it, and I do find dust so grindingly depressing. And there's such a lot of it about, with all the bombs.'

Cullingford had a neighbour who was a major in the marines and who had some petrol; he agreed rather unwillingly to drive Cedric up to Chelsea where he lived in a studio just off Milborne Grove and belonged to the large set of actors and artists who frequented such places as the Artists' Café in the Fulham Road and the famous cake shop there, and who continued to make visits to Soho and Sadlers Wells as if there was nothing more to worry about than getting sugar in their coffee and a good seat in the gods. Life was indeed, as Cedric often said, one long party. Perversely for one so fastidious, he also adored nights in the shelter and was to be found leading sing-songs and telling ghost stories far into the night.

That night when he walked into his flat, a note had been pushed under the door. It was from a girl called Miranda Bennett, a fashion editor on *Style* magazine: 'Tried to get you at Bertie's to no effect. Obviously much too busy to hear the phone! Give me a ring: something a bit odd.'

Intrigued, Cedric telephoned her. 'The most extraordinary thing,' she said, 'a package arrived on Christmas Eve from Paris.'

'From Paris! But how could it? Was it from Philippe, is he all right, how—'

'He was all right – then. Don't know about now. The point is, Cedric, it's taken six months to get here, can you imagine. It went via New York, and God knows where else. Anyway, wonderful pictures of Paris in the days before the Germans arrived, one of a farmer on the Champs-Elysées with a flock of sheep. And empty streets, completely empty of cars. Just so strange.'

'Well, I'd adore to see them, darling, but why are you ringing me? Unless it's to tell me you have a love letter from Philippe or—'

'No, I don't. But there's something else. Why don't you come round here actually, have a drink? I've got some horrible sherry Mummy gave me.'

'What, to Redcliffe Gardens? Darling, no thank you, I've had the most exhausting journey up from Wiltshire, with a desperately dull man who clearly thought I was going to leap on him and start tearing off his horribly scratchy trousers. As if one would. Anyway, what is it?'

'If you'll just be quiet for one minute, Cedric,' said Miranda Bennett, 'I'll tell you.'

Cedric wondered whether he should phone Adele; she would be so thrilled, poor darling. She had been so down when he had last seen her, on a rare trip to London in October, so fearful for what might have happened to Luc, so racked with guilt at her departure from him. He had tried to persuade her to do some work for him, but she had looked at him as if he had suggested she take to the streets of Soho and said it was absolutely out of the question. It would be wonderful to be able to give her some good news. On the other hand, he didn't have her number at her grandmother's; which meant ringing her dragon of a mother and asking her for it. Maybe he would wait until tomorrow; or – damn. Sirens. Air raid. Could he be bothered to go down to the shelter? He really didn't think he could. He was so tired and he had a long day in front of him. They were still busy with the East End, they weren't going to bother with Chelsea. No, he'd stay here, and if it got really bad he'd get into the Anderson shelter under the stairs that Bertram had insisted upon. He'd be all right. He'd be fine . . .

Adele had made a decision; she was going to go away. She wasn't sure where, but she was finding life at Ashingham more unbearable every day, all those noisy, cheerful little boys, the Warwick children with their irrepressible high spirits always trying to include Lucas and Noni in their games; and then there were so many strangers coming to the house all the time, that was dangerous for the children, not to mention Lord Beckenham's endless drilling of his troops, which was a huge worry because it fascinated little Lucas so much and he wanted to join in.

Christmas had been so unbearable; even Venetia didn't seem properly to understand how she felt. She had been looking forward to her return with the new baby, but now she wasn't so sure. Venetia was so busy with her new role at Lyttons and so obsessed with what she was going to tell Boy and when, and she kept trying to distract Adele from her own troubles, as she called them, and Adele didn't want that, she only felt safe when she was absolutely concentrating on them.

Quiet was what she wanted: absolute quiet. Somewhere safe, not only from the Germans but from other people. She had spent hours poring over her grandfather's map and decided that Somerset looked like a good idea. It wasn't too far, and the journey would thus not require a great deal of petrol – she had been saving her coupons carefully in any case – there were hardly any large towns, so bombing was not a risk, and she could settle down quietly with the children, probably rent a cottage or something, and find some peace. Of course she would leave a note, so that no one would worry about her; only without saying where she was going.

Having formed her plan she wanted to go quickly; it had snowed over Christmas but the thaw was setting in now, the roads were perfectly safe for driving. She decided to leave on the Saturday: Saturday, 4 January. It was the busiest day, with tradesmen arriving all the time, the battalion's major drill of the week and the little boys all over the place, especially in the afternoon when there were no lessons. If anyone noticed her leaving, which was unlikely, she could just say she was going to the village to get a few things from the shop. It would be really easy. And by Saturday evening, they would be gone, away from the noise and the chaos and the intrusion, and no one would have the faintest idea where she was . . .

Planning the whole thing had quite cheered her up; the only thing was that surreptitiously getting together her belongings and stashing them into the little borrowed car in the barn in the evenings reminded her so horribly of doing exactly the same thing in Paris. Don't think about that, Adele; just do it.

You mustn't move. He did know that. If you did, you risked bringing down what was left of the building on you. You just waited. As still as you could. He seemed to be all right; it was very dark, but then it was the middle of the night. And the planes had gone, the noise had stopped. So it wasn't going to get any worse. It was just a matter of time. Of waiting for the morning; or for the sound of the wardens picking their way through the rubble, calling out, 'Is anyone there?'

He had seen that enough as he had walked through the shattered streets on his way to work. Very often it was an animal you heard first, usually a cat; cats always got out alive. They could wriggle through anything, the tiniest crack. Alerting people to their owners buried, hopefully alive, far below them. Well, he hadn't got a cat; but he had a loud voice. He would make himself heard when they came looking. And in the morning, he would be got out safely. It was just a question of getting through the night. He wasn't even hurt: as far as he could make out. The worst was definitely over. Definitely.

And then he could ring Adele. And give her the good news. Perhaps even take her the letter himself. Only he wouldn't have time. Well, he would persuade her to come up and get it. It would be wonderful to see her face when he handed it to her. Yes, he would take her to the Café Royal and they would have the most wonderful evening . . .

That thought got Cedric through several very long and uncomfortable hours.

Adele felt almost cheerful all that Friday as she contemplated her escape. It was so very good to have something to think about, something to do. She even missed out her after-lunch crying session, and took the children down to the stables to see the horses instead. Billy greeted her cheerfully.

'Afternoon, Miss Adele. Hallo, Noni, hallo, Lucas. Got a carrot for the Corporal, have you?'

The Corporal was the name Amy Warwick had bestowed upon the little pony Lady Beckenham had recently acquired for her. 'He's a bit corpulent,' she had heard her say to Venetia, 'but we can get him fit pretty quickly.' Corporal being a more familiar word to Amy than corpulent, and the pony's other name being the rather grandiose and unsuitable Orpheus, it had stuck.

'No,' said Lucas, 'no carrots.'

'Well, I got a few in the tack room. Come on in and we'll find you one.'

It was a measure of her temporarily improved state of mind that Adele allowed Noni and Lucas to follow him into the tack room.

'You took your time,' said Cedric plaintively.

He had been buried underneath tons of rubble, mercifully safe, entombed in the shelter his lover had built for him, for almost eighteen hours. He was miraculously unhurt, apart from a crashing headache and some nasty cuts and bruises; but he had had a lot of trouble not panicking, especially when he heard the rescue team moving about what sounded like miles above his head and then apparently abandoning him once more, actually to summon reinforcements.

'Sorry, mate. Lot of stuff on top of you. You was lucky, just take a look around you.'

Cedric looked; and felt very shocked. The whole building had gone; there was nothing left not only of his flat, but the two adjacent; the rest of the building was tilting crazily on its side, like a child's toy house, wearied of and kicked aside.

501

'Oh, my God. Anyone – well, badly hurt?'

He shook the dust off his shoes, stepped back to look better – and slipped, crashing to the ground, hitting his head violently as he fell. The new, handmade patent pumps, still shiny on the soles, that Bertie had given him for Christmas had done what the Luftwaffe had failed to do and rendered him unconscious. He lay, oddly incongruous in the rubble, his eyes closed. His rescuers looked at him then at each other.

'Better get him to hospital,' said the first, 'or at least the First Aid post. Silly bugger.'

'Bugger's the word, if you ask me,' said the second, 'just look at them shoes. Come on then. First Aid'll do. Hospital's got enough problems. Get him on the stretcher.'

It was almost lunchtime the next day before Cedric, quite badly concussed and in any case confused by his ordeal, managed to pick up the phone in Miranda Bennett's house where he had taken refuge and telephone Cheyne Walk. To his great relief, Venetia and not Celia answered the phone.

'Noni, come along, sweetie, we're going for a drive in the car. Just a little one. Don't look at me like that, darling, please.'

The one visible effect of her ordeal on Noni was an acute resistance to cars. She had to be bribed to go in one at all, even her great-grandfather's open-topped Rolls, the greatest treat for most of the children, and as innocuous a suggestion as a ride on the tractor with one of the farmworkers or Billy Miller sent her into paroxysms of distress. Adele had been prepared for this, and had a small store of sweets – already a considerable luxury – in the car, together with three of Noni's favourite books and her most treasured possession, an old rag doll that had once been Celia's and which Lady Beckenham had given her when she first arrived at Ashingham.

'Come on, sweetie. Lucas is already in the car, he doesn't mind.'

'Well, I do.'

'Noni—' Adele could hear her voice beginning to tremble; she simply couldn't cope with this. It was the perfect time, just after lunch on the Saturday, the boys were doing their cross-country running across the meadow in a long, noisy stream, and everyone else was in the house. 'Noni, please, don't be silly. Please.'

'No. I don't want to. I'm not going to. And you can't make me. No, no, no.'

*

502

Lady Beckenham was in the gun room, trying to find a pair of riding boots small enough for Amy to wear, when the phone rang.

'Grandmama? It's Venetia. Can I speak to Adele, please? It's urgent. Really urgent.'

'Well – I'll try and find her. It isn't easy these days. We're awfully worried about her, Venetia, I do wish you'd come down.'

'I am. Next week. But – please, Grandmama. I can't tell you how important it is.'

'What on earth's happened? I do hope Celia hasn't done anything foolish.'

'Of course she hasn't. No, this is good news.'

'Oh – very well. Where are you? I'll ring you back. It could take a while.'

It did; she was interrupted three times, even on her journey to Adele's room, first by Lord Beckenham, who had lost his sword, then by Roo, who was emerging from the cellar, strictly out of bounds to the children and so therefore he was in need of a reprimand, and finally by Kit, who was walking along the corridor without his stick, also strictly forbidden since he was still inclined to crash into things and people and cause both not inconsiderable damage.

'When the war is over, Kit,' she said firmly, 'you can do this sort of thing. Just now it's dangerous.'

'Good,' said Kit morosely.

'Don't be insolent. Come on, settle down and I'll get you a ciggie.'

She was rewarded with the slight softening of his expression that was the nearest these days Kit got to a smile. She sat him down in the dining room, lit him a cigarette, and told him she'd be back and that she was looking for Adele.

'It's important, apparently. Venetia wants her. If she comes in here, be sure you tell her, there's a good chap.'

'OK.'

She wasn't at all sure that he would.

'Hallo, Noni.' It was Izzie. 'I'm just going for a little walk. Want to come with me?'

'Yes, please.'

'No, Izzie, she doesn't. I'm sorry, we're just going to the village.'

'Well, you can go without her. She doesn't seem very interested in the idea. I'll look after her, don't worry, Adele.'

503

Her smile, as she looked at Adele, was sweetly innocent; to Adele it appeared patronising and almost insolent.

Adele glared at her. 'No, you won't. And don't interfere, Izzie, please. I've decided we're going and we are. Noni, get in the car.'

'No, I won't.'

'Yes, you will.'

Noni started to scream; Adele looked at her. This was becoming ridiculous.

'You are a naughty, disobedient little girl,' she said. She looked at Noni's furious little face, and then suddenly reached down, pulled up her skirt and smacked her hard on her bottom. The shock of it, the departure from her usual indulgent, over-protective behaviour, rendered both Noni and Izzie absolutely silent; then she picked Noni up, half threw her into the car and slammed the door. Noni looked at her through the window, an expression of such wild distress in her eyes that Izzie could hardly bear it. Her own eyes filled with tears as she looked at Adele. Adele glared back at her.

'Stop staring at me like that, Izzie. She has to learn to do what she's told. Now we're going.'

She got into the car, slammed the door, and set off at high speed down the drive.

This was agony. What on earth was her grandmother doing? Surely she could enlist help finding Adele. There were enough people down there. She'd scream in a minute.

She counted to twenty, then dialled the number again.

Izzie ran into the house, crying; the incident had upset her horribly. Emotional hardship she was accustomed to; physical violence was a new experience. Even seeing the little boys given the mildest thwack of the cane on the hand in lessons distressed her; despite Henry's constant assurances that he had been caned frequently and it had never done him any harm.

'Makes a man of you, Izzie. Father says he was beaten every week at Eton and it did him no end of good.'

Izzie had tried to believe him then and found it very difficult; the memory of Noni's frantic little face at the car window, seeing the red imprint of Adele's hand on her small white bottom, was making her feel sick. Noni was so quiet, so good, so gentle; Adele had no right to hit her, no right at all.

She flung herself into one of the chairs at a table and buried her head in her arms, sobbing, quite loudly.

'What on earth's the matter?' It was Kit, speaking from Lord Beckenham's big chair at the top of the table.

'Adele hit Noni,' she said with a gulp.

'Well, I expect she was quite right to. That's nothing to cry about. For heaven's sake, Izzie, you are so ridiculous. Anyway – where is Adele? Grandmama's looking for her.'

'Gone. Gone to the village. In the car.'

'Well, run and tell her, will you? It's important.'

'I—'

'Izzie, do what you're told. Or I shall smack *your* bottom.'

She looked at him in horror; but he was half smiling. Even in her misery, she felt faintly pleased. He must be feeling better.

'Yes, all right.'

She went out to the corridor; saw Lady Beckenham at the end of it.

'Adele's gone to the village,' she said, 'in the car. Kit told me to tell you.'

'Thank you. I'd better phone Venetia, tell her she'll have to wait. She won't be long, I don't suppose.'

'No. No, I'm sure she won't. She—'

'She what?' said Lady Beckenham, picking up the distress in her voice.

'She smacked Noni hard. And sort of threw her into the car.'

'Well, I expect she deserved it,' said Lady Beckenham briefly, walking into the drawing room and picking up the phone. 'Venetia? No, we haven't found her. And now she's gone out for a bit, it seems. Yes, to the village. Oh, she won't be long, I'm sure. And when she does— What? Good God. Oh, I see. Well – yes, of course, the minute she comes back.'

'Absolutely extraordinary,' she said to Kit. 'Apparently, after all this time, a letter's turned up for her from Paris. From that so-called husband of hers. Well, maybe that will cheer her up. I certainly hope so.'

Izzie decided she would go the village herself. She had some pocket money and although she'd had her sweet ration that week, she wanted some paper and some stamps, so that she could write to her father. And she could get Cook's *Picturegoer* at the same time. Cook would like that; she said it was her only pleasure these days.

She would take Roo's bike and go on that; he wouldn't need it, he was playing football. It would be much quicker. And if she did see Adele, she would get the news that much sooner.

'I won't stay in here. I won't.' Noni, unsilenced by her smacking, glared at her mother. 'I hate the car. I hate it.'

'Well, you're going to be in it for quite a while,' said Adele, 'so you'd better get used to it.'

'Why? I'm going to run away when we get to the village and go home without you: I know the way.'

'No, you're not.'

'Yes, I am.'

'You're not because we're not going to stop in the village. We're going on a long journey. Somewhere different, somewhere nicer.'

'What do you mean? Away from Ashingham?'

'Yes. Far away.'

Noni looked at her and saw she meant it; contemplated it, sitting in the car for hours and hours, leaving everyone and everything she had grown to love, the house, the garden, the stables, her cousins, Lord and Lady Beckenham – she especially loved her great-grandfather – and quite simply couldn't bear it. Panic rose in her, panic and a terrible violent sickness; she took a deep breath and threw up all over the back seat of the car.

Adele was sitting by the side of the road, crying, trying to clean up Noni with some grass when Izzie reached her. She looked at her rather desperately, all her anger gone.

'Hallo,' she said listlessly, wiping her eyes on the back of her hand.

'Hallo, Adele. Can I – can I help?'

That was brave of her; it was a horrible sight.

'No. It's all right. I think – well, I think we may have to come back and clean up properly.'

'I can get whatever it was you wanted in the village,' said Izzie.

'What?' said Adele. She sounded vague. 'Izzie, I'm sorry about that. Sorry I shouted at you. And hit Noni. I feel terrible. She's forgiven me. I hope you will too.'

'Yes, of course,' said Izzie. She hesitated. 'You seemed very upset.'

'I was,' said Adele, and she started crying again. 'I'm always upset and – oh, dear, it's very complicated, I'm afraid.'

They sat in silence for a moment; then Izzie remembered.

'There's a letter for you,' she said.

'A what?'

506

'A letter.'

'What, at the house?'

'No, I think it's in London. Venetia phoned.'

'Venetia phoned? About a letter?'

'Yes. It's from France, Lady Beckenham said. From – from your husband.'

Izzie never forgot what happened next. Adele stood up extremely slowly, as if she were dreaming, her expression sort of fixed and very, very pale. Then she said, 'From France? From Luc?'

'Yes,' said Izzie, very gently, because it was obviously so important and she didn't want Adele to start crying again. 'Yes, I heard Lady Beckenham telling Kit. And then she said that should cheer you up. Adele, are you all right?'

'Yes,' said Adele, still talking very slowly, rather as if she were asleep, 'yes, I think so.' And then she sped up almost visibly, her eyes became brilliant and her cheeks quite red. She pushed her hair out of her eyes and said, 'Izzie, I must get back quickly. Could you – would you mind very much – bringing Noni, pushing her on the bike? Or even walking with her? She's all right now. But I really can't make her get back into the car. I'd be so grateful. And as soon as I possibly can I'll come back for her myself.'

'Yes, of course I will,' said Izzie bravely, although it seemed to her the most awful thing she had ever been asked to do. 'That's perfectly all right, Adele. Don't worry, I'll look after her.'

Adele bent to kiss her.

'You're an angel,' she said, 'an absolute angel. I'll be as quick as I possibly can. Oh, thank God you were sick, Noni, thank God, thank God.'

And then she hurled herself into the car, swung it round so fast its wheels screeched, and roared off down the lane back towards Ashingham at what looked to Izzie about a hundred miles an hour.

Grown-ups really were very peculiar. There was just no other word for it.

Chapter 34

Kit heard the car drawing away and felt suddenly very bleak. It was Izzie and Henry, both leaving Ashingham for their new schools: Henry for Eton, Cheltenham Ladies' College for Izzie.

Henry he didn't care about so much, but he felt dreadful about Izzie; he'd been so rotten to her and the poor kid had only been trying to help. After the day he had sent her away, and Adele had attacked him, he had made a bit of an effort, but she still irritated him, with her determined cheerfulness and her constant suggestions about things he could do. He did submit to her reading to him with a fairly good grace; she read very well, without any of the rather tedious dramatic emphasis which so many people went in for. The worst was his mother: she seemed to feel she had to act every character in the book for him. Although she did manage to choose the ones he most enjoyed. He found the whole thing desperately irritating, he had always read so fast himself, and it was agony hearing something unfolding so slowly. Billy had suggested in his straightforward way that he might learn to read Braille, but Kit had been appalled at the very idea.

'I don't see why,' Billy said. 'You'd be able to read what you wanted that way.'

'I know I would,' said Kit shortly, 'but I just couldn't stand it. Don't ask me why.'

'OK then,' said Billy placidly. 'I just thought it would be a bit like my false leg. Helping out, if you know what I mean.'

'That's quite different,' said Kit. It wasn't, of course; but he wasn't prepared to consider it. It meant accepting what had happened and that was something he couldn't bear. While he was still angry, railing at fate, he felt he was still in some strange way denying it, was not a blind person, fumbling at strange hieroglyphics, but a sighted one who was temporarily unable to see. For the same reason, he absolutely refused to have a white stick.

Just the same, Billy was one of the very few people whom he could talk to; he was so easy, so straightforward, there was none of the dreadful tactfulness that everyone else went in for. His grandfather was another; Lord Beckenham would sit with him for hours, grateful for a captive audience, talking about his own military history, about the Home Guard, about life in general, with a complete lack of tact which Kit found for some reason rather soothing.

'Lovely morning,' he would say, 'just look at the sky, another scorcher coming up, don't you think?' And then add, completely unfazed, 'Sorry, old chap, keep forgetting. Anyway, blue sky, yellow sun, all that sort of thing. Very nice. Good day for an invasion, I'd say.'

Lord Beckenham had been deeply disappointed that no invasion had materialised; unlike most people, he continued to hope for it and drilled his troops ruthlessly. He slept with his rifle by his bed, his tin hat slung over the bedpost, and never sat down to a meal or retired for the night without patrolling the Ashingham defences.

'Can't afford to be taken unawares,' he would say. 'It's when we're least expecting them they'll arrive, you know.'

He joined Kit now, having waved the car off.

'I shall miss Izzie,' he said. 'Pretty little thing she's turning out to be, don't you think?'

Kit was silent; the usual pat on his knee followed.

'Sorry. Anyway, she is, you can take my word for it. She'll be breaking a few hearts in a year or two. Fancy a walk? I want to have a look at the trenches down by the barn. Come on, I need the company.'

There was a sudden disturbance of the still morning as a herd of small boys went past them on their cross-country run; they waved and shouted at them both. Lord Beckenham waved his rifle back.

'Lovely to have all these young ones about,' he said, 'cheers me up no end.'

'Does it?'

'Oh yes. I like children. Always have. So much common sense. Sometimes wonder if they wouldn't make a better job of running the world than we do. Watch out, old chap, bit of rough ground ahead. Here, let me take your arm, just for this bit. We can steady one another. Old pins aren't what they were. Oh, now there's young Bill. Wedding coming up soon, isn't it? Nice girl, very happy for him. He's a splendid chap. Don't know what we'd do without him.'

'No,' said Kit. And then greatly to his surprise heard himself say, 'He asked me to make a speech at the wedding.'

'Did he?'

'Yes. I don't really want to, of course, but—'

'Why not? You can still talk. And rather well, I should think.'

'I – just don't,' said Kit, and he lapsed into silence.

But he enjoyed the walk more than usual; and afterwards he sat down on the terrace in a spot sheltered from the wind and wondered why he felt just a very faint lifting of his depression. It wasn't just Lord Beckenham's company, or the pleasure, albeit limited, of sitting in the warmth of the sun: although he found the noise of the small boys shouting and laughing almost unbearable. It was something that had been said. What was it? Not about the speech – he really couldn't face that, standing up, hearing people laughing dutifully at his jokes, unable to see their expressions, visualising the appalling sympathy and embarrassment. No, it was something else. What had it been?

And then he remembered: this rather intriguing notion of a world run by children. For some reason that had seized his imagination. What would it actually be like? With children in charge of government, the law, education? What would they make of it, what would they do, what would they change? And how would they deal with the adults who had made such a hash of things? Banish them? Employ them? It was all rather – interesting. For some reason it stayed in his head, all day; occupying him, distracting him just occasionally from himself and his misery. It was a distinctly novel situation.

'Page proofs,' said Celia, placing them down on Oliver's desk, 'of *Grace and Favour*. They don't look bad, in spite of that awful paper. And the tiny typeface of course.'

'I don't suppose the readers are likely to notice,' said Oliver.

'Of course they will. I don't know why you persist in thinking that the only readers of this book will be the housemaid class, as you so charmingly call it.'

'Because it's housemaid's stuff.'

'Oh, don't be so pompous. Just thank your lucky stars that we didn't lose the whole thing six months ago in the fire,' said Celia. And then added, 'You look tired. Why don't you go home?'

'I am tired. But I don't want to go home. Where's Mrs Gould? I've got a lot of letters to write. And is LM in her office?'

'I think so. She looks worn out. It'll be a very good thing when Venetia gets back. LM's been landed with all her work, you know.'

'I do find it so noisy here,' said Oliver. He sighed. 'It's so – so frenetic. The street outside, I mean, not in the house.'

510

'So you say at least once a week,' said Celia. 'Perhaps you'd like to find us a different office – in between commissioning books and writing letters.'

'Oh, don't be absurd. I know it was very good of your parents to let us use it and at such short notice. That fact does not unfortunately make it an ideal location.'

She ignored him and walked out of the room, thumbing through the proofs. They did look very good. The art department had had the text set in Times Roman, so that it looked as if it had come straight out of the author's typewriter and had made a virtue of small font size and narrow margins – designed to save paper – by presenting each page as if it were a notebook. It read so well: sharp, acutely observed, and with a slightly staccato style. There had been much agonising over the cover, which Celia had wanted to look like a rather small, leather-bound diary; the art department and Edgar Greene had looked for something grander, more in keeping with the content. It was still under discussion.

She went into the room that was her office and that had been her mother's sitting room and sank down at the makeshift desk. She was tired; terribly tired. She had forgotten how tiring war was above all else: the perpetual anxiety, the broken nights, the complication of performing the most simple tasks, thanks to lack of staff, the breakdown of the usual channels of communication, the lack of transport, the restrictions on almost everything.

And of course they were still suffering from the loss of Lytton House, and all the things that had been stored there, practical things, manuscripts, ledgers, authors' and agents' contracts. That had been the most appalling revelation of those first few dreadful days, that there was nothing, absolutely nothing left that they could refer to.

Celia and LM had gone up to Paternoster Row as soon as they were permitted, hoping they would find Grandpa Edgar's safe. But even that was a burnt-out shell. Hubert Wilson's description of the 'cavernous glowing holes' which were what he called the 'crematoria of the City's book world' was hideously apt.

'How are we ever going to operate again?' Celia had said to LM and then, hearing no reply, looked at her and saw she was weeping.

'I'm sorry,' LM said, trying to smile, rummaging in her pocket for a handkerchief, 'just shock, that's all. Being brought here by my father was my earliest memory; it seems impossible that there is simply nothing left.'

'Of course,' said Celia quietly; but after a moment, LM rallied, and said, 'Now then, where can we start? We've got orders to meet, we can't let people down.'

'Well,' said Celia, who had already spent the morning desperately trying – and failing – to work out how Lyttons could physically fit into Cheyne Walk, 'the first thing we need is an office. More space than our house can possibly offer, although I do think we could manage there for a few days. I've made a few phone calls and a list of where we have work in progress, manuscripts waiting to be set, galley proofs waiting to be sent to us, pages waiting to be bound, that sort of thing. And there are hundreds of our stock books of course, stored at various printers round and about the country. Mercifully Venetia had the manuscript of *Grace and Favour.* Paper will be our biggest problem, everyone will be after it and we'll just have to take whatever we're offered, a few hundred sheets at a time. But I have found one source, a printing works near Slough. Because it's quite near Mama, I can get Venetia to – oh, my God!'

'Yes?' said LM. She smiled at her; she had known Celia a long time, she recognised an idea in her voice.

'Curzon Street. My parents' house. They're not using it. I wonder if – well no, I don't wonder, I'm quite sure – they'd let us use it. It's quite large enough, the drawing room would make a general office and the dining room an art room, and we could use all the smaller rooms – yes, it's a brilliant idea. We can even set up a small counter in the hall. Oh dear, Papa would have a fit, we must make sure he never sees it. But he doesn't need to. Come on, LM. Let's tell Oliver, he'll be thrilled.'

The Beckenhams did give their permission – albeit slightly unwillingly – and a skeleton staff moved in two days later. But three or four hundred separate works that had been in print were lost for ever, together with several manuscripts, and the financial cost was considerable. They had been insured, but most of the losses were incalculable, and the loss of all the records had led to months of chaos and constant argument and wrangling with authors, agents and booksellers.

That was the day the book trade changed for ever. Lyttons was not the only house which adapted its systems to expediency, stopped the costly and cumbersome procedure of shipping books back from the printers to their own offices and then shipping them out again. The central distributor, working for all the publishing houses, was born: 'If Hitler knew he'd actually helped us become more efficient, think how furious he'd be,' said Celia happily to Oliver. He was unable – as usual – to share her optimism.

As she sat looking out on to the back garden of Curzon Street – surprisingly large and lush – that lovely spring day, there was a knock on her door and Sebastian walked in.

'Hallo.'

'Hallo, Sebastian. What are you doing here? You should be at home working.'

'Tired. Wanted to talk to you.'

'Of course. I'd offer you a cup of tea, but I think we're completely out of milk.'

'That's all right. The last cup of tea Janet Gould made tasted more of cabbage than anything else. Celia, do you know where I could get hold of a dictating machine?'

'Oh – one of the department stores, I should think. Army and Navy probably. Or a big stationers possibly. I could ask Janet, she'll know.'

'Would you? I want one.'

'They're very expensive.'

'I don't care.'

'Who's it for?'

'Kit,' said Sebastian. 'Best news since his plane went down.'

And he sat down on one of Lady Beckenham's priceless John Adam drawing-room chairs, which Celia had sworn to her parents were stored safely in the cellar, and told her about it.

'Wake up, Miller. In that little world of your own again, are you? And I know who with and all, don't I?'

Barty jumped, and smiled rather feebly at Partfitt.

'Of course not. Pass the salt.'

'Of course you are. I can – oh, gawd. Alarm. Here we go again.'

If the alarm went off at mealtimes, the routine was simple: you just dropped everything and ran down to the gun park, taking your gas mask bag on your chest – also used by all the girls for transporting their make-up – and pulling on your tin hat as you ran. It happened a lot at night now – they had been posted to Crystal Palace – but lunchtime was more unusual. As they ran, the firing began; there was no way but forward. Barty fixed her eyes on the encampment in the middle of the gun park and just made for it; she had always been a very fast runner and that day it saved her life. As she looked back from the comparative

513

safety of the encampment, banked up with sandbags and turf for camouflage, she saw pits and dust all along the path where she had been running.

'Phew,' said Parfitt, grinning at her rather shakily, 'that was close. Best get to work.'

It could be disorienting, looking down into the instruments when a raid was in progress. With all the noise and disturbance you could somehow lose a sense of where the plane actually was. Not that it mattered; your job was to report what you saw in the instrument. But there had been occasions when Barty had actually seen a plane opening its bomb doors; it took a lot of control not to look up, see exactly where it was in relation to her.

The raid that day was savage; the target was a huge ammunition dump for London. How did they find out these things? Barty wondered. One of the great balloons had been sent up and they were going for that. She hauled her concentration back; it was not her job to think about such things. She had to find the height of the plane and inform the guns, while Parfitt read the speed and wind direction; the information was passed on by the oldest form of communication known to man, the shout. It was fast, crucial work; oddly, she was seldom frightened. But seeing the dust on that path today had rattled her: just a bit.

Her romance with John Munnings was troubling her deeply. She liked him more and more; he was so gentle and thoughtful, so good to talk to, and they had an enormous amount in common. Despite his rather old-fashioned air he shared her views on politics, on women's rights to a career and a proper place in the world. And he was extremely good-looking, there was no doubt about it, with his dark brown hair and his dark eyes and what she could only describe to herself as a sweetness of expression. He was interminably good-natured, nothing panicked or irritated him, and it showed in everything he said and did; he had a calmness about him which she found immensely engaging. He had had very few girlfriends; he had told her that with commendable honesty.

'The thing is, unless I really like someone, I simply can't be bothered to spend a lot of time with them. It seems such a waste, going through all that rigmarole if there's no point in it at the end.'

This was so exactly in accord with Barty's own views on relationships that she leaned over and kissed him.

Fate also seemed to be taking a hand in their relationship; just as she had been posted to London, so had he. He would be going abroad, probably quite soon, he told her, but he was still in training with his regiment, and had a little free time.

He was now enjoying army life: 'Everyone said I'd hate it, but it's such a marvellous change, so much excitement and challenge, and I really get on rather well with both my brother officers and the men. I like the spirit of the army, it's so – uncomplicated.'

Barty said that was how she felt exactly: marvelling yet again at the closeness of their views and experience.

They were able to meet at least once a fortnight, sometimes more often; London had settled down again, with the easing of the Blitz, and there was much to enjoy: the lunchtime concerts at the National Gallery, the West End plays – *Blithe Spirit* actually opened to an audience dressed in dinner jackets and long dresses – the Proms conducted by Henry Wood – where every single seat was sold and the ballet, with wonderful performances by Fonteyn, Helpmann and Ashton, albeit to music provided only by two grand pianos.

Barty was so delighted by John's liking for ballet that tears filled her eyes when he revealed it: 'You are only the second man I have ever known who wanted to see a ballet. Oh – it doesn't matter who,' she added quickly, trying not to think about it. About him.

What she was enjoying with John Munnings was a romance: and she wasn't sure it was any more than that. Happy, sweet, intensely enjoyable. But with Laurence, Barty had experienced passion: an experience so intense, so powerful she could still absolutely recall it, both physically and emotionally, and it was something she was quite unable to set aside or forget.

She could also, of course, recall the pain in exactly the same way.

'This is getting ridiculous,' said Adele. 'You can't go on denying the existence of your own child to your own husband.'

'I'm not denying it exactly. Just not telling him.'

'That's splitting hairs.'

'Not really. We don't exactly enjoy a close correspondence. Two letters in the last six months.'

'Yes, and your letter was all about the children.'

'Well, that's what he'll want to know about.'

'Exactly. Venetia, you're being so perverse. If you're not careful I shall write to him myself.'

'Don't you dare. Just because you're feeling better doesn't mean you have a right to take over my life as well.'

Adele was feeling better: immeasurably so. Reading Luc's letter, absorbing the love, the remorse, the genuine grief at his loss of her, she had felt rather like some half-dead animal brought in from the frozen, threatening outside world. She had been tempted to tell Venetia to read it all over the phone, indeed had instructed her to begin, but after the first few words, 'My beloved, my most dearly beloved Adele', she had said she must stop, must bring it instead, knowing she could wait from this first wonderful spring of happiness for the torrent that would surely follow.

Venetia had arrived four days later with her new baby and the letter (the post being so extremely unreliable); it had, after all, taken six months to reach her; it could surely take another few days. Adele had paused only to admire Fergal and kiss Venetia before taking the precious envelope up to her room and reading it, over and over again. Each day she read it, at first several times a day: its generosity astounded her.

She had expected at least some reproach, some anger even; instead she found only acceptance of what she had done, and love, and a desperate concern for her safety.

It may be months before I know how you have fared and I can only pray, knowing of the dreadful dangers on that road, that the news will be good. I cannot telephone England, and there can be very little hope of a letter from you reaching me, at least for a while. God knows how things will settle down. But for the time being all is well. They have not yet arrived, but are certainly almost here; there are the usual rumours, but I have chosen to hear none of them. The offices of Constantine are closed; Guy is moving to Switzerland. No doubt in due course he will communicate with your father. This letter comes to you, quite quickly I hope, via a special courier service to *Style*. I shall wait impatiently for news of you.

With all my love, *ma chère, chère* Mam'selle Adele,
Your adoring Luc

That he had not behaved as if he adored her, that she would not indeed have left him if he had, that he had most steadfastly refused indeed to become her husband, that he had misused her dreadfully, that he had been ill-tempered and critical of her, that he had been a bad provider, that his own pride had refused to allow her to add so much as one franc of her own money to the family budget – all these

516

things were as nothing to Adele. She only cared that he said he loved her, that he forgave her, that he prostrated himself before her with remorse at his behaviour, that he had never been so unhappy, that his only happiness indeed had come from her and their children, and then again, that he loved her, more than life itself, and that whatever became of them, she was to know and understand that and believe it for the rest of her life.

Illogically, knowing that he still loved her, that he felt no anger or desire to blame her, made her feel less remorse, more happiness; 'And so you should,' said Venetia, with whom at least some of the contents of the letter had been shared, 'he's admitting he was wrong, that he deserved for you to act as you did. It's not as if it was in a fit of pique, or so you could run off with someone else.'

'I know, I know. But I should still have given him a chance to explain, to make me understand.'

'In which case you'd still be there.'

'Yes.' Adele was silent; thinking then of the dangers of still being there, with her children. She would certainly have been imprisoned, and possibly all of them; as it was, they all lived free and happy in the English countryside. She felt sad still, she missed Luc and she feared most dreadfully for his safety; but in days she had changed; she became easy, smiling, released her children from her suffocating care, helped in the house, sat with Kit, and helped her grandmother with the farm, which she discovered she loved.

In her darker moments – and they came more frequently than anyone knew, with the exception of Venetia – this idyll would be punctured by fears for Luc and by her impotence at being able to contact him. She longed to write back to him; had indeed posted several letters (while knowing how hopeless an initiative it was), had telephoned Cedric to ask him (while knowing it was fruitless) if the courier service between Paris and London was still running, albeit via New York.

He had rather specific news of Paris, gleaned from messages via New York; that couture was still alive, despite German endeavours to move it to Berlin, that *Vogue* had ceased to publish along with *Style*, that the fashions were of necessity modest, minimal even, in their use of fabric. News that at another time, in another life would have fascinated her, but now meant nothing, nothing at all.

But, in spite of her frustration and her anxiety, she was deeply happy; released from guilt and restored most surprisingly to love. Love and a state of grace.

517

And then, a few weeks after the arrival of Luc's letter, Helena had telephoned.

'Adele? I have some news for you.'

'For me?'

'Yes. It's about getting messages to – well, to your – your—'

'To Luc?' said Adele helpfully. She was constantly amused by the difficulty Helena had with such matters. And then she realised what she was actually saying. 'What, Helena, how—'

'Apparently through the Red Cross, you can send a written message. It's quite easy. Well, not exactly easy but it does more or less guarantee the person getting the message in due course.'

'Oh, my God—' Adele's voice was shaky, very quiet.

'Yes. You go to the Citizens' Advice Bureau where you fill in a form, saying whatever it is you want to say—'

'You mean I can write to him?'

'Well – not exactly. Not a long letter, anyway. There's a limit of – let me see, I wrote it down for you . . . oh, yes, twenty words—'

Twenty words. Enough. Enough to tell him she was safe, that she still loved him, that she had only just got his letter to her.

'So how, what—'

'I've got all the details here,' said Helena, her bossy voice more clipped than usual. 'As I said, you go to the nearest Citizens' Advice Bureau. That twenty words does exclude name, address and relationship, incidentally. Then it gets transcribed on to a Red Cross form—'

'You mean they get to read it?'

'Yes. Apparently it's against the censor's regulations for the sender to fill in the Red Cross form.'

'Oh, oh, I see. Well—' That seemed an outrage; then she realised that set against Luc's assuming she must either be dead or still absolutely hostile to him it was nothing, nothing at all. 'Well, go on.'

'After that, they get posted to the International Red Cross Committee. And they send them on to the person to whom they are addressed. Via their own Foreign Relations Department.'

'Oh, God.' Adele suddenly couldn't even hold the phone, so weak with shock and relief did she feel. She put it down on the hall table, buried her face in her hands.

She could hear Helena calling her but could do nothing about it; finally she managed to pick it up again, and said simply, 'Helena, I don't know how to thank you for this, I really don't.'

'It's not my personal scheme, Adele,' said Helena, her voice almost a reproof, 'but I'm very glad if it will help.'

518

Adele cycled into Beaconsfield that very afternoon, after playing for hours with her twenty words, working out how she could make them say the most; handed them over in all their raw love and concern, watched, feeling oddly exposed, as a coolly emotionless woman read them carefully, nodded at her, took her sevenpence, checked the address and said she would see it went off with the next bundle.

'And then – how – how soon will it get there?' she said, hearing her voice shake.

'It's impossible to say. They often have to go by a fairly roundabout route, as I am sure you can imagine. But you can rest assured it will arrive.'

'Even – even in Paris?'

'Of course.' She gave her a slightly superior smile. 'Try not to worry. Good afternoon.'

'Good afternoon,' said Adele. And cycled home, her heart singing. She tried to believe that Luc would receive the letter within a few days. Or at the very most weeks.

She buried her anxiety and her frustration in helping her grandmother on the farm: and there was a great deal to be done. The young men had all gone; in their place was a small group of land girls, not quite the smiling, sturdy creatures of the posters, many of them townies, unused to physical work of any kind, let alone the backbreaking toil of hoeing, planting, lifting potatoes, making silage, repairing fences. A couple were dreadfully homesick, even took to their beds; surprisingly, Lady Beckenham's brisk sympathy, her watchful eye on the more serious problems of injured backs, strained joints and, on one occasion, a septic cut sustained from a rusty scythe, and her willingness to work alongside them at all but the heaviest tasks, did more for their morale than anything.

They liked Adele too; she was always the last to come in at night, working into the long summer twilight – made even longer with the establishment of double summertime – little Noni often sitting beside her in the tractor, her small face burnt dark brown, her large black eyes brilliant with pleasure.

Lucas, sturdy and sunburnt too, spent much of his time at the stables with Billy; he would sit for hours on a manger in the yard, watching the horses, allowed to help mix their feed and even, when Joan managed to find him a small enough broom, sweeping out the stables. The horses were working now: with the shortage of petrol, horsedrawn ploughs were being brought back into service; and Lucas

519

would trail along on his short legs behind Billy as he drove the two great shires over the fields.

Tucking them up in bed each night, after going through the small, sweet ritual she had evolved of looking out of the window and sending their love to their father, she managed, slightly to her own surprise, to find considerable happiness for herself. And to believe that she had after all done the best thing. For all of them.

It was high summer now; and that evening, Barty and John were going to see what John had warned might be a rather limited production of *Arsenic and Old Lace*; 'And then maybe supper somewhere?'

Barty was looking forward to it; but she was also anxious. He had told her there was something he wanted to talk to her about; and she knew what it would be. Commitment from her, in the event of his going away. She had a decision to make and she owed it to him to make sure it was the right one.

The play was better than they had expected; supper in a small Chelsea restaurant surprisingly good; the inevitable rabbit was a strong feature of the menu, but they both ordered it, cooked in cider, and agreed it was almost indistinguishable from pork. After it, they sat unusually silent, but comfortably so; finally John said, 'Barty, there's something—'

And then, as she tensed herself for the question, probed her own consciousness for the hundredth time for the answer, it happened: the siren went.

'Everyone was right then,' said John cheerfully, standing up, holding out his hand. 'It's starting again. Hitler was just biding his time, waiting for us to get lulled into a sense of false security. What shall we do, public shelter, underground station, what? It's up to you.'

He might have been reacting to the need to shelter from a light shower of rain; Barty looked at him: so level, so physically calm, with no sense of panic anywhere in him, and felt a wave of gratitude and admiration. And something else too: a desire to show her gratitude, and to stay with him, not to allow the evening to disintegrate into the squalor of the shelters.

'We could – go to my little house,' she said quite casually. 'It's very near here. I – well, I'm not sure if I mentioned that.'

'You didn't actually,' he said, 'no.'

'Oh, well – anyway, we could go there. And I have a Morrison shelter, so if it does get near – but of course you may prefer the underground.'

'Barty,' said John, smiling his sweet calm smile, 'I would far prefer to share your Morrison shelter.'

'Not as safe. You do realise that?'

'Of course I do. I prefer the risks as well.'

'Come on then.'

They walked to the Mews, just a few streets away. A few people were running in the direction of the shelter, but there was a general air of calm. Barty suddenly remembered she had left her house in a great rush, that her clothes were in dreadful disarray all over her small bedroom, and the remnants of her lunch were on the kitchen table. She hoped that John would not be too offended by it.

He didn't seem to be.

'This is charming,' he said, looking round her sitting room – that at least was tidy – 'how very nice for you to have such a welcoming place to come to.'

'I'm glad you think it's welcoming,' said Barty, 'that's what I aimed for when I did it up. Having grown up in a rather grand house, I wanted exactly the opposite. Somewhere anyone could walk into and feel – well, unthreatened.'

'No one could feel threatened by this. And yet it's delightful. I like the colour scheme, all that white, it's so unexpected these days.'

'Well, it suited the house, I thought. The whole point about mews houses is that once they were stables. They don't ask for a lot of dressing up and fuss. And then white is such a marvellous background to colour, which is why I was quite bold with it. I mean, some people are shocked by those scarlet curtains, but I love them, they cheer me up.'

'They cheer me up as well,' he said, 'they're an incredible colour, like poppies. And that's a beautiful little figure there.'

'Present from Celia Lytton. When I moved in.'

'The famous Lady Celia. What a very grand family you belong to: I feel quite overawed.'

'But I don't belong to it,' said Barty almost fretfully, 'it just took me over.'

'And made you part of it. You can't deny it, Barty. When it's done so much for you.'

'I know, I know all that. But that's exactly the problem, that it's done so much for me. I had to be so grateful for so long and now gratitude is an emotion that has the ugliest connotations for me.'

'Oh, I can understand that,' he said, 'although in quite a minor way.

My godmother paid my school fees. Very kind, of course. But never a week passed without my having to express gratitude and to prove that I was working hard.'

She smiled at him; 'Then you will exactly understand.'

'But it's not quite the same thing as being brought up by Lady Celia, educated by her, and very expensively it must be said, and then given a job in the company.'

'I earned it,' she said sharply, and then felt ashamed of herself.

'Of course you did. But the opportunity, that was a gift for you to make the most of.'

'Well – yes. But—'

'Barty, it was. You shouldn't, you cannot deny it. And I don't see why you should.'

She stared at him: suddenly seeing she must agree with him, wondering at his gift of simplicity and straight-forwardness, and his ability to pass it so quietly on.

'You're right,' she said, 'of course you are. And—'

She was interrupted. The noise had suddenly begun; the incessant, growing roar, louder all the time.

'Come on,' he said, calmly sensible, 'I think it's time to stop philosophising. Where's this Morrison of yours?'

There was no raid on Chelsea that night; West London bore the brunt, with several bombs on Acton. They sat in the Morrison for an hour or so until the All Clear went, and then wriggled out.

'Well, that was fun. I enjoyed it.'

They had; they had taken in two of the Meridian books with them which John had never read. He had been spellbound, apparently oblivious to the noise and the danger; Barty, who had been given the page proofs of *Grace and Favour* by Celia, had read equally oblivious.

'Good,' she said, smiling at him, 'mine wasn't bad either. Clever lot, those Lyttons. It was Venetia who discovered this one apparently.'

'So she works there, does she?'

'Not really, at the moment. She had a baby just after Christmas, she's down in the country with him and all her other children. But Celia says she's got to come back soon, they're so short-staffed.'

'You're not tempted?'

'Goodness, no. I'm like you, I'm enjoying my war. Anyway, women are about to be called up, I heard. So not a lot of point me going back.'

'We shouldn't really, should we?' he said.

'Shouldn't what?'

'Be enjoying it. When so many people are suffering so horribly.'

'I know,' she said soberly. 'It worries me.'

'Me too. But – it doesn't stop me, well, liking what I've got. Although—' He stopped, looked down at his hands, then took a deep breath, leaned forward, looked at her very intently. 'I was going to tell you earlier. But I have to anyway now. I'm – going away, Barty. In a week's time.'

'Going away?' she said stupidly. She had felt so safe, so secure in the isolation of their relationship, that she was shocked at the notion of it ending.

'Yes. Being sent abroad.'

'Where? Do you know?'

'Not yet. Really I don't. But – it will be for some time. And so—'

'Oh, John,' she said, and found her eyes stinging with tears. 'I—' and then stopped and blew her nose hard.

'You what?' he said gently.

'I – I don't want you to go.'

'I'll tell my CO,' he said, smiling. 'I'm sure he'll understand, change the arrangement.'

'Sorry. That was such a stupid thing to say.'

'Not stupid,' he said, 'and very welcome. I would have been most upset had you seemed pleased or relieved.'

She managed to smile. 'Oh dear. I shall miss you.'

And realised, as she said it, exactly how much; she felt new tears rising and sat staring at him, letting them roll down her face, unchecked.

'I shall miss you too,' he said gently, 'terribly. It's been such a happy time, Barty. Really so very happy.'

'It has, hasn't it?' she said, blowing her nose again. 'Very happy. I've loved it.'

'Well – that's why I wanted to talk to you. Because I've loved it too. And I – love you, Barty. I didn't say so before, because I wanted to be sure. As you know, I'm a cautious sort of a chap. But – well, I do. Love you. I think you're very lovely and very special and I can't believe how lucky I am.'

She was silent; a raw illogical panic slithering into her.

'And what I wanted to say was—' He stopped, clearly looking for courage, and the right words, then slightly loudly and with gathering speed, 'I wondered if you could consider – a promise. Not an engagement as such, that would be too formal, perhaps too soon, but if I knew you were here, waiting for me, I'd be a lot less—' He stopped.

'A lot less what?' she said, playing for time as much as anything.

There was a long silence; then he said, his voice low and shaky, 'Frightened.'

Barty looked at him: moved beyond anything she would have believed by this confession, the courage of it, a further revelation of everything she liked and admired about him. All of a sudden, doubt flickered and died; she felt strong, happy, almost certain.

She put out her hand, took his, kissed it gently.

'I like it so much that you said that,' she said.

'What, that I was frightened?'

'Well – yes. It's not an easy thing to say.'

'It was easier than the rest,' he said, smiling at her now. 'I was very frightened indeed of that.'

'What of asking me to – be waiting here for you?'

'Yes. I've never said anything like that before.'

'Haven't you really?'

'Of course not,' he said, and he looked quite indignant. 'I told you, I've hardly ever cared for anybody very much. And certainly not enough to ask them such a tremendously important thing.'

'Oh,' said Barty. She felt very humble.

'I'm not going to ask you about your past, because I suspect there is something quite – big there that you will tell me about if and when you want to.'

She was silent.

'But I would like an answer. To my question.'

'May I think about it? Just for a little while?'

'Of course.' He smiled at her; she could see that even this had hurt him, that she was not sure enough to answer immediately. 'But I would like to know before I go.'

'You shall know then,' said Barty, 'of course. And – John—'

'Yes?'

'Would you like to stay now? For the rest of the night, I mean?'

He looked at her, clearly astonished; then he flushed and was quiet for a moment. Finally, 'I would love to,' he said, 'really I would. I can't think of anything more wonderful. But I would prefer it to be when – if – I know. If that doesn't sound too ungrateful.'

'It doesn't sound ungrateful at all,' said Barty, 'it sounds absolutely right.'

He left quite soon after that; she kissed him goodbye and went up to bed, feeling surprisingly peaceful and calm. And happy. It was so wonderful, the effect he had on her. She wondered how there could be any doubt at all as to what her answer would be.

Giles had come home on a few days' leave: fit, lean, happily confident as Helena could never remember him. He was about to be sent away, he said; but he had an important bit of news. Very important. He thought she'd be pleased.

'It's too marvellous,' said Celia to Oliver. 'Giles has just phoned, he's home for a few days, and he's been commissioned. He's a lieutenant. Isn't that thrilling?'

'It is very good news, yes,' said Oliver quietly.

'You don't sound terribly pleased.'

'Of course I'm pleased. But I don't feel I could possibly be any more proud of him than I already was. In my view that was a far greater triumph.'

'Well, he's thrilled,' said Celia slightly crossly, 'and Papa will be terribly excited. And so will Mama.'

'Now that really is important,' said Oliver.

'There's a letter from Daddy,' said Venetia. She made a huge effort to smile, to sound pleased and excited; but the tone and content of the letter hurt her so much that she felt as if she had received some physical blow.

'Let me see.' Roo grabbed at it.

'Roo, don't,' said Lady Beckenham. 'That is your mother's letter, there may be private information in it.'

'Oh, no,' said Venetia cheerfully, hoping they would not see the tears standing so dangerously in her eyes, 'nothing in the least private. In fact it's for you children really. You can read it aloud, Roo, then Amy and Elspeth can enjoy it too.'

'OK, thanks. Shut up, Elspeth, I'm reading it, Mummy said.'

'Dear Warwicks, I am very glad to tell you that the war is going well out here. It is like one enormous beach, sand everywhere, and awfully hot. So hot that you can fry an egg on the mudguard of a truck. Imagine that. The only really bad thing is the flies which are a dreadful nuisance. We wear special hats with sort of veil things to protect ourselves from them, and we look pretty silly, I can tell you, and the men have competitions to see who can swat the most flies. We play football a great deal and do a great deal of digging. Water is not too plentiful, and we only have a few cups a day for cleaning our teeth and shaving and so on.

525

There is another hazard – or rather two – scorpions and vipers, but if you are careful – and I am very careful – you are perfectly all right.

'We have had some very exciting battles, driving across the desert in our tanks, and have seen the enemy off several times. The other strange thing is a sandstorm; the air is literally a great mass of sand, and it gets very dark. You can't possibly go out in it, so we just have to stay in our tents and wait for it to pass. The food is very dull, we have bully beef fried, bully beef broiled, bully beef stewed. All served up with something that looks and tastes like dog biscuits.

'I think of you all so much. Henry will be enjoying Eton by now, and I hope Roo is behaving himself' – 'Of course I am,' said Roo indignantly – 'and that Amy has not broken anything yet, falling off her pony. Seriously, it's all jolly good fun out here, and we are being very successful; you shouldn't believe anything you might be reading in the papers, about the Germans' victories under Rommel (who is known as the Desert Fox, incidentally, he's so cunning). He might have won a few skirmishes' – a few skirmishes, thought Venetia, when Rommel's recapture of Tobruk in April had sent morale plummeting lower in England than it had been for months, and there had been reports of thousands of English dead. She had waited terrified for days for a telegram; it had not come.

'I think that's all for now. Love to everyone there, and all of you be good for your mother's sake. Tell Great-grandpapa I could do with a few military tips and ask him if there's any way he could get out here' – 'For heaven's sake, don't,' said Lady Beckenham, 'or he'll be chartering a plane' – 'and tell Great-grandmama that riding a camel is a lot less comfortable than a horse. I'll write again soon, but as I have no idea how long these letters take to get to you, you must be patient. Certainly don't worry about me. I'm fine. Just a bit warm.

'Lots of love,
'Daddy.'

How could she possibly write and tell him he had a new baby? Venetia thought wretchedly, escaping to the safety of her room and able finally to cry, when he had not even written her a letter of her own, merely included her in a message to his children. It was absolutely impossible.

＊

Adele would have given anything for a letter, however cool the tone. Six months now since she had sent her message to Luc: and nothing. Excitement changed to anticipation, and then to disappointment and finally despair, she tried to fight away the despair. She had gone into the Citizens' Advice Bureau several times; each time they had told her the same thing: that if there was a letter for her, she would have received it, that it could take many months for a message to reach its destination, travelling as it might a route of incredible complexity and then, of course, the same would apply to a returning one; and that there was of course a risk of a message being mislaid or delayed, but it was very rare, that from the United Kingdom alone countless thousands of messages had already been successfully sent and received. None of which was a great comfort to Adele. For some reason, it did not occur to her to ask what might happen if the address was incorrect.

Chapter 35

'For richer and for poorer, in sickness and in health, forsaking all others.'

The lovely words of the marriage service sang in Barty's head. As always on hearing them, her eyes filled with tears; only this time, of course, the emotion was deeper, richer, sweeter. She longed more than she would have believed that her mother could have been here: to see her much-loved son, for whom life had seemed so hard and for whom it had now become so very rich, finally married to his beloved Joan.

He stood at the altar gazing at her, unsmiling, his eyes filled with love; and she smiled up at him, her round, pretty face framed in white lace, fresh pink roses in her blonde curls. She was dressed entirely in white: several of the villagers had given some clothing coupons so that she could buy the material, and she and her mother had been making the dress all through the summer, of parachute silk, tight-fitting over her fine bosom and slender waist and then flaring at the hips. The small bridesmaids – six of them, Elspeth and Amy Warwick, Noni Lieberman and Joan's own three little nieces – were in pale blue and Izzie Brooke, grown tall and slender, her lovely golden brown hair put up for the first time and studded with roses like the bride's, was chief bridesmaid in palest pink. Sebastian had come down for the wedding; as Izzie walked into the chapel, so suddenly grown-up, he smiled at her with such intense pride and love and at the same time terrible sorrow that Adele, standing next to him, felt tears in her own eyes, reached out, took his hand, and held it tightly.

In the front pew stood both the Beckenhams. Lord Beckenham, blowing his nose repeatedly, Lady Beckenham, wearing her sternest face, lest some quiver of emotion might betray her. Next to them Celia, and in the aisle in his wheelchair, Oliver. Beside Billy, smiling valiantly, was Kit Lytton, who had most surprisingly a month earlier agreed not only to make the speech at Billy's wedding but to be his best man, in the absence of his youngest brother who had suddenly announced that he would not after all be coming to the wedding. Billy had been so distressed by this, had been so near to tears as he told Kit about it that Kit had heard himself almost against his will offering his own services and Billy, blowing his nose and pumping him by the hand at the same time, had accepted the offer so effusively that it was impossible to inflict further pain by withdrawing it again.

The speeches made later at the reception (held in a marquee in the paddock, a happy compromise between the bride's own tiny garden and the grandeur of the terrace at Ashingham, offered by Lady Beckenham) were all in their way splendid, Kit's extremely amusing (there was none of the polite laughter he had been dreading), loud, joyful mirth filled the air and could be heard up at the house; Lord Beckenham's was heartwarming, as he recalled Billy's arrival at Ashingham and paid tribute to his skill and determination as potential husband, head groom, and recruiting officer of the Ashingham battalion, and Billy's own touching as he thanked the Beckenhams for all they had done for him, the Barbers for producing Joan, and Joan herself for agreeing to take him on.

As the late summer dusk fell, the dancing began, the music played first by local fiddlers, and later, as the older generation retired, by Venetia's gramophone. Izzie, entrusted with playing the records, from a selection made by both Billy and Venetia, enjoyed herself so much that she quite forgot to worry about either Kit or her father, her major preoccupations for most of the time. They were both, in any case, perfectly happy, chatting and laughing together, and perhaps the biggest surprise of the evening came when Sebastian suddenly rose to his feet and whirled his daughter round the floor to the strains of 'Deep in the Heart of Texas'.

'Your mother was a wonderful dancer,' he said to her, holding her away from him and studying her almost in surprise as she stood flushed and breathing heavily at the end, laughing up at him. 'It's a talent you seem to have inherited.' And then gave her a kiss.

It was a moment no one could have begun even to dream of five years earlier.

It would all have been quite perfect, Barty thought, if John could have been there; she longed for him to meet her family and her extended family and for them to meet him and approve of him as she knew they would. They would all love him, everyone loved him, for his gentle charm, his courtesy, his genuine interest in everything, his infinite capacity for making the best of everything. Even Celia, she thought, would like and approve of John; and he would of course find much to admire and like in her, while dismissing with dutiful care what he did not.

She missed him a lot; it was not the savage, aching misery that had accompanied missing Laurence, it was a sweet, sad, but oddly comfortable emotion which had more to do with a basic happiness and contentment, mingled of course with anxiety and fear.

She had made her decision – as she had known she would – to wait for him; 'I cannot imagine doing anything else,' she said, giving him her hand, smiling up at him. 'There is simply no alternative. I shall wait and wait and hope and pray and when you come home again, I will be there for you.'

He had kissed her, gently at first, then with more passion; an hour later they were in bed. And that too had been exactly as she might have known it would be: tender, sweet, careful, infinitely loving. It was not, of course, emphasising the 'of course' repeatedly to herself afterwards, not sex as she had known it before; there had been no savagery, no turbulence, no calling out, no abandonment of herself to pleasure so violent that it was almost pain. This was different, and like the relationship itself, peaceful, gentle, deeply loving. And pleasurable – infinitely so, moving from one range of sensation to another, each of them richer and deeper than the one before. They shared everything that first and last night together, talked of their whole lives past and the one to come, if that was to be granted to them; only somehow Laurence became in the telling a brief, wild affair, a folly of her youth, a rite of passage. Of the fact that he had taken her over, in every single possible way, possessed her, led her into a knowledge and experience of herself and him that had shaken her beyond anything she could ever have imagined, of that fact she spoke so very little that it amounted to nothing at all.

And now John was gone: to Italy, he had said, and for a long time. 'I will write of course, and so will you, I know, but if you hear nothing, you mustn't worry. I am told that the bad news always travels very fast; if letters are slow, then be grateful for it.'

She was back at her post by this time in Croydon; and like millions of people all over the world at that time, they waited and endured the waiting and learned to live constantly with fear.

Grace and Favour was inevitably a great success despite being published several months late. There was an immediate demand for a reprint; in an agony of frustration, Celia struggled and failed to find enough paper for the three thousand copies she had orders for, and only managed to send out fifteen hundred. Lucy Galbraith was much fêted; there were not many new novels that winter, indeed not many books published at all. Readers were driven to the public libraries, where there were long waiting lists for books. The classics were most in demand: Trollope, Dickens, and the work of those very English poets, Tennyson, Shelley and Keats and, of course, Rupert Brooke, in a rush of patriotic sentimentalism. Against this background, *Grace and Favour* sat most charmingly; and the slight audacity of writing real people into a fictional framework made it much talked about. Lucy Galbraith was several times asked at readings in bookshops if she was related to the Duchess of Wiltshire herself; after a very short while, she said she was, which increased the demand for signed copies considerably. Oliver Lytton was distinctly shocked by this, and wanted it stopped, but both Celia and Venetia told him he should be grateful, Venetia adding briskly that as far as she could see, bookselling was increasingly a form of show business and this was a wonderful scenario.

Lady Celia Lytton was not alone in struggling to keep a literary salon of a kind going. She was often to be found in the company of John Lehmann, editor of *New Writing*, in his exquisite deco flat in Carrington House, Mayfair, or of Cyril Connolly, the editor of *Horizon*, in Chelsea, surrounded by such literary luminaries as the Sitwells and T.S. Eliot, engaged in the kind of conversation she liked best, a combination of gossip and books.

She was also on the guest list of all the great London hostesses, and indeed remained one herself; in doing so she easily outdid most of her rivals. Emerald Cunard had been driven from her near-palace in Grosvenor Square to what her enemies described as lodgings at the Dorchester, and Lady Colefax was so hard up that although her Wednesday dinner parties continued, she was forced to make a small charge.

Dinner parties at Cheyne Walk still retained a certain glamour, despite the food; somehow rabbit omelette (made with dried egg) became quite ambrosiac when eaten in the company of Edith Sitwell or Cecil Day Lewis, with Celia and Oliver Lytton at either end of the table, she as beautiful as ever, he as intellectually challenging and original – and the lovely and surprisingly brilliant Venetia Lytton, rumoured now to be her parents' true choice as heir to their company, set among the guests, a newly discovered jewel in their crown.

531

Lyttons had another potential literary success which it was agreed should be published in the spring – there being no paper available for the ideal time, which was Christmas; a book of such charm and originality, written with so sure a touch, and endowed with so much humour that all those reading it were comparing it – in quality although most certainly not in style or content – with that other great contemporary classic, beloved by both adults and children, the Meridian saga.

The new book, at once an intriguing and exciting children's novel, and a study of an England, a peaceful England, leading the way to a peaceful world, was called – rather simplistically – *Childsway*. Every child and every adult who had so far been permitted to read it had been not only entertained and enchanted by it but uplifted as well; the adults reading it far into the night and the children doing the same thing, only under the bedclothes and by torchlight.

Its author was a young pilot called Christopher Lytton tragically blinded in the war.

'Adele! Telephone.'

She couldn't help it of course: every time. Thinking, hoping, praying. Of course it wasn't Luc. But it was the next best thing: Cedric's lilting voice.

'My darling, we need your help.'

'Cedric, I've told you, I can't—'

'No, darling, not up here. Down there.'

'Oh. Oh, I see—'

He was doing a shoot for *Harpers*: 'I'm still no use to the hospital, with this wretched leg, so it's back to normal work. The new tweed suits, darling, desperately dull, I just can't put the girls in a studio. I remembered you telling me about your wonderful work as a farm labourer—'

'Not quite accurate, Cedric,' said Adele tetchily.

'Oh, darling, you'd look divine down a coal mine. Anyway, I want to get these girls into the fields and the woods, that sort of thing, mowing hay or whatever you do—'

'The harvest's in, Cedric, I'm afraid.'

'But the fields are still there, surely. I just wondered if we could come down and shoot it there. And if you could get together a few rustic bits and pieces. A plough, that sort of thing.'

Adele said she'd have to ask her grandmother, but she was sure she wouldn't mind.

'And I can't think of anything more wonderful.'

They arrived a week later, three models, a fashion editor and Cedric and his assistant. Adele had booked them into a hotel in Beaconsfield.

'I'd love to have you here, Cedric,' she told him on the phone, 'but the house has been turned into a school and it's absolutely full of little boys . . .'

'My darling, how cruel. Sending me away.'

'I hadn't thought of that. All the more reason for the hotel, I'd say.'

'Will they be around while we're shooting? They could make wonderful props.'

'I think it would be much better, Cedric,' said Adele severely, 'if you confined your props to tractors and ploughs.'

The thought of what Mr Dawkins might make of Cedric was alarming to say the least.

His rather flamboyant pale-blue Bentley arrived at Ashingham the next morning; he leapt out, a dazzling figure in cream slacks and blazer.

'Cedric, how do you manage to get clothes like that still?' said Adele, laughing, throwing herself into his arms. 'And petrol to run that thing?'

'We get a little extra, as our work is considered essential. And everyone chipped in with their coupons. I'm glad you like the clothes. Aren't they lovely? Bermans, darling. I have this chum there, and occasionally they sell things off. This was filthy, but I had it cleaned and it's come up beautifully, as you see. This is its first outing. Pure who's-for-tennis, country-house comedy, don't you think? I thought it would be so suitable for today.'

Adele caught a glimpse of Mr Dawkins peering out of a window, staring transfixed at them.

'Utterly suitable,' she said. 'No fashion editor?'

'The poor thing's ill. Utterly poleaxed at the hotel. Said she ate something last night. I think she drank too much. Anyway, when she heard it was you, she calmed down.'

'Well, I'm very flattered,' said Adele, 'but it's years since I did a fashion shoot.'

'Doesn't matter. Your eye is peerless, darling.'

'Well, I'll do my best. Now come on in, Grandmama is dying to meet you. She said were you one of those pixies. I presume she meant fairies. I said yes.'

'Darling, you're so cruel.'

533

The shoot went well at first; the girls sat on tractors, leaned out of stables, walked in the woods. Adele was happier than she could remember being for months, putting outfits together, adding scarves, belts, overcoats from the gun room, and, for one picture of a girl sitting laughing on a gate, one of the little boys' caps.

And then it happened.

Cedric, who had been growing quieter and quieter as the morning went on, suddenly turned extremely pale and disappeared behind a hedge; he came back grass-green.

'So sorry. Shouldn't have said that about Loretta. I did think that meat was a tiny bit suspect. Just give me five minutes and I'll be all right.'

But he wasn't; half an hour later he had to be helped inside to lie down; even the sight of ten small boys walking from one classroom to another failed to penetrate his misery.

'It's frightful, Adele, too frightful. We have to finish today and we've got three shots to do still. Maybe in an hour or so – oh dear. Darling, where is the lavatory—'

He came back shaking, lay down. 'What are we going to do? We're behind our deadline already. I just don't think – oh dear.' He closed his eyes, his hand on his brow; then opened them again feebly. 'Darling, you'll have to do it.'

'Me! Cedric, I can't.'

'Of course you can. It's really not very difficult. Jason will do the light readings for you, all you have to do is style the pictures. And compose them of course. He has no vision. And you have so much – oh, God, I must leave you again—'

It wasn't really very difficult; she couldn't have managed the light readings, but her eye was superb, and she had spent years studying what made a picture work, how to lift it out of the ordinary, give it what Cedric called 'the magic'.

She was particularly excited about the last picture she did; the three girls shot against the light in the late afternoon, walking in line behind one of the great Shire horses and the plough. They were wearing check tweeds from Worth, very sharply cut, with felt hats, and on their feet were not shoes but heavy wellingtons, again borrowed from the gun room; it was a bold piece of accessorising, but she knew it would work.

Cold, tired and hugely excited, she went to find Cedric, who was feeling a little better.

'I think they'll be all right,' she said.

They were more than all right; the art director loved them, phoned to tell her that he was leading with the Shire horse shot across a spread – 'those wellington boots, an inspiration' – and moreover asked her if she'd like a credit.

'A credit?' said Adele. 'What, a styling credit?'

'Adele, don't be dense, dear. A photographic credit. You certainly deserve it.'

Adele said that would be very nice and wondered if there was anyone at Ashingham who would properly appreciate the importance of this piece of news. She decided rather sadly there was not.

Chapter 36

'I'm going to tell him. I've decided.'

'You can't. You know Mummy said it would just worry him, we weren't to tell him, that it would be a lovely surprise when he got home. And it's not your secret.'

'It's not even a secret.'

'Yes, it is.'

'Roo, you're being ridiculous. How can a baby be a secret? And I think he'd like to know. He likes babies anyway, he told me when Amy was born. And Fergal is quite big now. I mean, he's one, not even a baby any more. It's so nice to know they like each other again, don't you think?'

Roo was silent; a lifetime of at least appearing to defer to his elder brother had taught him discretion. Henry obviously meant what he said. He had that look about him. And maybe he was right; after all he was almost grown up now, really tall, and his voice had broken. He looked very like their father; Roo, who missed Boy dreadfully, would sometimes almost think it was him if Henry came unexpectedly into the room.

Roo had joined Henry at Eton now; when the two of them went off together for the first time from Ashingham that spring, waving slightly grandly from the car, oddly handsome in their tailcoats, Joan Miller was not the only person to cry.

'It just doesn't seem possible,' she said to Lord Beckenham, who was standing next to her, openly wiping his eyes. 'Seems only yesterday they were running around in short trousers.'

'It does indeed, my dear. And I shall miss young Roo terribly. The cadet corps' gain is the battalion's loss. Damn fine soldier he'll be.'

'Anyway,' said Henry firmly now, 'I'm going to write tonight. And if you tell Mummy I'll break your neck.'

'I don't see her enough to tell her anything,' said Roo slightly sadly, and it was true. Burying her personal unhappiness, Venetia was working increasingly hard, and had spent most of Roo's final weeks at Ashingham in London. She had more or less taken over LM's role, dealing with budgets, promotions and sales; booksellers loved her, appreciating her blend of slightly scatty flirtatiousness and tough bargaining ability. Nor did she waste their time; like her mother, she had an instinct for how to present books, varying approach to content and audience, enthusing over a book to one shop where she would scarcely mention it in another. Her task was in any case not difficult; business was booming and the public could not get enough books. The bookshops that had survived the Blitz were desperately busy, and publishers found themselves in the novel situation of rationing their supply.

Venetia was inevitably successful; which did much for her self-confidence. She and her mother worked extremely well together; delegation was one of Celia's talents and she trusted Venetia absolutely. Their problem was Oliver, increasingly anxious over their approach, and their commercialism, resentful of their closeness.

As always he said very little, but won what battles he felt to be absolutely important with a stubborn and largely silent negativism; 'I cannot and will not agree to that,' he would say, and they would look at his closed face and know that time spent arguing would be put to better use on something else. He also felt physically disorientated; he had been deeply shocked by the loss of Lytton House, and found it hard to come to terms with working in Curzon Street, for reasons other than practical ones. He felt he had lost his past, his heritage; Lytton House had always been as much part of his life as his own home. He had spent long hours there from early childhood, absorbing its legends, its history and its atmosphere; the books that had lined his walls had also been the background to his life, and if he were set down in any part of the building blindfold, he could have told you exactly where he was simply by the sound and feel of it.

The loss of all the records had upset him too, increased his sense of confusion. He had always liked to be able to trace the history of a book, from concept to publication, it gave him authority. He had loved browsing through old contracts and letters, they were as personally important to him as the children's birth certificates, first locks of hair and shoes were to Celia. Curzon Street was providing a base for Lyttons; but it was in no way its home.

And he missed LM dreadfully, her unspoken and unquestioning loyalty, the history they had shared. She was a staunch, if discreet, ally, she understood how he felt about books, how distasteful he found the rampant commercialism Celia and Venetia were employing. But LM was seldom there, a two-day week was a full one for her now, and even then she would come in late and go home early. She insisted there was nothing wrong, but she was clearly not well; nobody quite knew what was the matter with her, both she and Gordon parried questions with skill and brevity, but she was a bad colour and painfully thin; and she had a weariness about her that was absolutely at odds with her old forceful self.

She insisted it was sleeplessness and worry about Jay, a just-plausible explanation which Oliver and Celia clung to. The real reason was something which she and Gordon had agreed to keep to themselves for as long as possible: she had cancer of the stomach and in the doctor's considered opinion, since she was brave and insistent enough to ask for it, could be given a maximum of six months to live.

'Adele! Letter for you.'

'Thanks.'

From *Vogue*, no doubt, they said they would pay her. Well, that would be nice, she could do with—

'Oh, my God.'

'What? Whatever is it?' said Lady Beckenham.

But Adele had gone: to her room, holding the precious envelope, small and brown like a telegram envelope, with its *Deutsche Rotes Creuscz* printed within the large Red Cross symbol. Impossible to look at that, at the German gothic lettering on the postmark, without a shudder. But – for God's sake, Adele, open it. Open it. She pulled it out: not only words, but in Luc's own handwriting, not copied out coldly as her own had been. Words, wonderful, wonderful words: '*Mignonne*. Message delayed. All well with me. Write again, will collect from Mme André. *Je t'aime, je t'embrasse, je t'adore. Luc.*'

It had come via Geneva, and then the Red Cross in London: and from there seemed to have been posted in the usual way, for it had an English stamp on it. She looked at the date; it had taken five months. Five endless, painful months. And it was a year since she had written to him.

It took some time to digest, to work out what must have happened. He had left the apartment; she should have thought of that. But it explained the delay, his apparent failure to reply. Dear Mme André must have forwarded her letter to him or he had been back to the apartment. And he was still alive, still all right . . .

538

She went back into Beaconsfield that afternoon.

This time her message was shorter. There was really so little to say: when very much more was impossible.

'*Je t'adore aussi*. Mam'selle Adele.'

She handed it over with her sevenpence, her eyes streaming.

'Thank you so much,' she said again; and went to sit outside in the autumn sunshine, reading again and again her own message from Luc, tears streaming down her face.

My dearest,

I know this is rather – premature, but I do love you so very much. And I wonder if you would consider becoming engaged to me: when I finally get home again. Those days and weeks together and that last wonderful night were not just the happiest of my life, they were beyond my wildest imaginings. I think we could be so happy together and make such a very good life. Please, Barty, take time to think about it and don't feel in any way pressured to answer. We have plenty of time – I fear. Or perhaps I hope.

Your very loving
John

Barty read this with the mixture of happiness and panic that followed all John's declarations of love and requests for commitment. She kept hoping that the panic would ease, but it rose up to reach her, snaking its way into her head and her heart, disrupting her pleasure, giving her no rest.

It was absurd, she would tell herself, she loved John and he loved her, they were absolutely right for one another, they shared views, pleasures, ambitions, were absolutely at ease with one another. She could imagine so well and so happily a life together with him, having children with him, could see that at no time would he stand in the way of anything she wanted to do, resent her career, or envy her success.

It would be a peaceful, fulfilling life, each of them adding to the happiness and fulfilment of the other, she would go into it joyful, confident, absolutely secure. There would be no fear, no jealousy, no deceit, no violent demands on her attention; she would not have to pause before every action, however small, to wonder if it would find acceptance; she would know absolutely where she was and within the constraints of all that seemed to her to be important about marriage, she would be free, free to be herself.

And yet, yet the panic would not go away.

'Letter for you, Major Warwick.'

'Thanks, Corporal. Let's see – oh yes, it's from my eldest son, judging by the writing. He's a pretty good correspondent.'

Better than his mother, Boy thought, ripping open the letter. She hardly wrote at all, and when she did, only with news of the children or her job with Lyttons which seemed increasingly to occupy her. She implied she was practically running the place. Some kind of inflated secretarial job no doubt, handed to her on a plate to keep her occupied. And give her an excuse for being in London rather than cooped up in Ashingham with her children.

He began to read:

Dear Father,

I hope all is well with you. We enjoy your letters very much and are so proud of you. When we read about the 8th Army retaking Tobruk we were incredibly excited; we were home at Ashingham on an exeat and Great-grandpapa went through the whole thing with us, drawing maps of the area and the Qattara depression. He said it was a bit like a boxing ring in which both sides were facing one another. It sounds jolly exciting.

Everything is fine here; Roo is enjoying Eton and is already in the rugby and cricket teams, and he likes boxing. Also he's the star of his year in the corps. I've kept a pretty close eye on things and I don't think there's been any bullying. Of course you can't always tell, but he certainly hasn't said anything. Amy and Elspeth are both at St Christopher's now, keeping the Warwick flag flying. They both say they wish they could go to a girls' school.

GGP's Ashingham battalion goes from strength to strength and the reinforcements round the place are really fantastic! He now does a dawn patrol in addition to all the others, although everyone says an invasion is very unlikely. He's very disappointed, but still hoping of course! He really is a dear old chap. He had a letter in *The Times* the other day, about utility suits. These are the cheap, basic men's suits tailors now make to save cloth. GGP discovered that they have to have waistcoats and sent off a furious letter to *The Times* about it, saying of course they shouldn't have waistcoats and no one needed a new suit anyway, he hadn't had one made since 1925. He was terrifically pleased with himself.

Joan Miller, you know, married to Billy, Barty's brother, is having a baby in September. She says she thinks it's twins.

Amy's riding is really fantastic, she can take really quite big jumps. Great-grandmama is so proud of her, they ride together all the time. GGM is amazing. Adele was saying the other day that she's over eighty, yet she still works on the farm for a few hours every day. There are a whole lot of landgirls there now, jolly pretty, some of them.

Adele is very excited, she took some fashion pictures at Ashingham and they were published in some magazine and she's been asked to do some more.

Apparently Uncle Giles is in Sicily. We don't see much of Aunt Helena. Jay is still in England – I think! A bit hush hush, all that. We met his girlfriend, Tory, at Christmas, she's an absolute corker. Barty is still enjoying the ATS, what she does sounds really interesting.

Everyone is very excited because Kit has written a book. He's certainly cheered up! Apparently it's awfully good. I haven't been able to get hold of a copy yet because it's in proof form – note technical publishing term! Maybe I shall join Lyttons one day! I think I'd rather go into banking like Grandad. Maths is definitely one of my strongest subjects. And history. I also rather like art. Bit of a cissy subject, I know, but still! I'm also playing loads of rugger, but I'm not in Roo's league. Bit embarrassing to be beaten by your younger brother, but I'm getting used to it.

Mother came down to take us out last Sunday, it was lovely to see her. She works at Lyttons in London all the time now, bit risky I'd have thought, although there isn't that much bombing these days, and she seems to enjoy it. She was looking jolly pretty.

Anyway, there's a bit of news. I've thought quite hard about telling you this, but I've decided I should because no one else is going to. I know GGM and Grandpapa both think you ought to know, I heard them talking about it, and they said LM thought the same, and I do too. Mother said no one was to tell you because it would be something more for you to worry about, but I honestly think that's a bit ridiculous. Anyway, here goes: the news is, Mother's had a baby. Well, not exactly a baby, he's a year

541

old now. He's a nice little chap, quite jolly, looks a lot like Roo. His name is Fergal. I imagine Mother will be pretty fed up with me when she finds out I've told you, but it can't be helped. I tried to think what I'd want if I were you, and I decided I'd really rather know, worried or not. Anyway, he's at Ashingham with Nanny and everyone, so quite safe. No need to worry at all in fact!

Well, that's all for now. Quite enough, I expect you're thinking. Write soon, if you can. Look after yourself.

Your loving son,

Henry

Boy read this letter several times; growing angrier each time. How could Venetia have done that to him: had a baby, for Christ's sake, and not told him? It was monstrous. He was astonished no one else at Ashingham had told him.

Well, she hadn't wasted any time. Interesting there was no mention of any man in her life; no doubt she was keeping that very quiet. Presumably he was away. Working in London must be very convenient for her. She had probably led the children to think that the baby was his. They would assume that anyway of course, they'd never quite grasped the concept of divorce, especially as he'd been at the house so much and they'd both worked so hard at being nice to one another in front of them. Lucky for her the baby looked like Roo – who in turn looked exactly like his mother. If he'd had blond hair and blue eyes she'd have had a bit more trouble explaining it. And Fergal – what a bloody silly name.

God, it was a shock. That she'd just got together with this chap, almost as soon as he'd left, and gone on her own sweet way. The baby was a year old. That meant – Boy did some ferocious calculations – only two or three months after that last night together. It had obviously meant a lot to her, that night. Christ, he felt a fool. An absolute, bloody fool. Saying all those things to her, about how he still loved her, wanted to be with her again. Thank God nobody had really known about their reconciliation. Their extremely short-lived reconciliation. Who the hell had Willoughby-Clarke seen her with? He'd been too proud to quiz him at the time and now the poor chap had copped it. God, he'd lost some good friends over this past eighteen months.

Filthy business, war was. Absolutely filthy. He was so utterly sick of it, the heat and the filth and the flies, those fucking flies. Morale was up a bit now of course. Auchinleck, the new General, was a good chap, and the retaking of Tobruk and Bengazi had done a lot for them all, but just the same the men were tired. Sick and tired. And that was how he felt. Sick and tired and unutterably miserable. It wasn't what you needed, when you were giving your bloody all for king and country, to hear that your reconciled wife had not only cheated on you weeks after swearing she still loved you, but had had a baby by her new lover. And not had the guts to tell you.

Boy looked at his watch; an hour before dinner. He needed a drink. Several drinks. And then he'd write to Venetia and tell her – Boy stopped, motioned to the mess sergeant to fetch him another whisky – tell her what, exactly? After all, they were divorced. Technically, she had every right to have a relationship and indeed a baby with whomsoever she chose. Maybe he ought to be a bit less emotional about this. She might have said she still loved him that night, but she was probably only trying to be kind, to send him off to war happily. He'd been a fool to believe her, but apart from that, she hadn't actually done anything wrong. He'd provided the grounds for their divorce after all, from their very first year. He'd do a lot better, look much less foolish, if he played it cool. Just wrote and congratulated her, made it plain he couldn't be less concerned, wish her well even. He might suggest that she tell the children the truth – no, that would be difficult for them at the moment, time for that after the war when presumably she'd want to marry this chap.

God, what a mess: what a bloody awful mess.

He ordered a third whisky and then walked rather unsteadily into dinner.

Chapter 37

'I think that if possible he should be got home now.'

'It could be difficult.' The voice was heavy.

'Obviously. But she is going down much faster than I feared. If he is to say goodbye to her—'

'Of course. I'll see what I can do. First thing in the morning.'

'I think that's wise. You go back to her, I'll see myself out.'

'Thank you. For everything.'

'I wish I could do more. I've told the nurse: as much morphine as is required.'

'Thank you.'

That had been the one thing Gordon had feared: that she would die in dreadful agony. As it was, she was torpid, only half conscious most of the time, but in very little pain.

And calm, serene, her only anxiety being Jay. Jay, and not being a trouble or a worry to him. Or indeed to anyone else.

She had forbidden them to tell him. 'How can he possibly do whatever it is if he's worrying about me all the time? There is simply no point. If he comes home, then he'll have to know. But for now – please don't tell him.'

And Jay, deeply in love, eager to spend what meagre leave he had with Victoria, had not been home for months.

He had hardly taken in that his mother had moved to Ashingham, had accepted that it was safer there, that she was more or less retired anyway, that Gordon had always loved the countryside, that it made perfect sense.

LM had been surprised herself at her desire to go there; it was hardly home, she and Gordon had been very happy in the house in Hampstead. But as her illness progressed, her pain and weakness increased, she felt a profound longing for the place.

'I'm sorry if you feel it is a rejection of you,' she said, placing her hand in Gordon's. 'It is of course nothing of the sort. But it is where I feel my roots are, especially now that Lytton House is gone. Jay and I lived there when he was first born, as well as through his childhood, after – well, after I had met you. And—'

'My dear, there is no need to say any more. I understand. And besides, some of my happiest times have been spent there in your cottage.'

'Well, that is occupied by the landgirls,' said LM, 'and I don't think we should disturb them. But the Dovecot is probably available. You could perhaps ask Lady Beckenham for me?'

'Of course.'

And Lady Beckenham listened as Gordon made his request, his voice heavy with weariness and pain, and remembered Celia making the same request of her, twenty-five years earlier, and agreed with the same reassuring lack of fuss, 'Of course. Whenever you want it. Just let me know.'

She didn't even ask why.

She knew of course; they all did. Gordon had come to Celia and Oliver and told them. They had both been shocked, both in tears, amazed by his calm courage.

'If she can be brave, then surely so can I,' he said. 'She asked me to tell you on my own, because she was afraid we would all become emotional. She wants everything kept as calm as possible, not a lot of histrionics, as she puts it.'

Celia had managed to smile. 'Not quite LM's style, histrionics. Of course. We'll tell the others.'

'Not the children yet. And I see no point worrying poor old Giles and Boy.'

'Jay?' said Celia, while knowing the answer.

'Not yet. Not until she feels it's time.'

They had moved down to Ashingham in May; spent a happy summer there, LM sitting on the terrace much of the time, watching the little boys, listening to Lord Beckenham, talking to Kit, admiring Amy's horsemanship. Celia came down whenever she could; shocked each time by the speed with which LM was deteriorating. Eating had become impossible, she was put on first a liquid diet and now was being fed intravenously. A full-time nurse had been engaged, and a small room had been found for her in the house. If she found LM's insistence on staying at the Dovecot with all its inconvenience irritating she never said so.

And it was inconvenient, there were no cooking facilities, and if LM needed her in the night she had to be fetched and to walk across – all right on a fine night but disagreeable if it was raining. But LM was happy there, reliving, as her morphine-induced confusion increased, the infinitely joyful time she had spent there after Jay was born. When she became too weak to make her way to the terrace, Gordon had a chaise longue set up in the walled garden and she lay there, cocooned in warmth, reading, chatting easily to her visitors.

Kit was one of her favourites; he was gently amusing, telling her endless anecdotes about the happenings at the house and never minding when she lapsed into silence and asked him to do the same. He was excited about his book; he told her it was very odd, not having been able to read it, but it had been read to him in its final edited version and he was delighted with that.

'I would like to see the cover of course, but Mother's described it to me, and it sounds very clever. A globe, held by a small child. Or perhaps you've seen it.'

'No, I haven't,' said LM, 'but your mother said she'd bring it down. She's so proud of you, Kit.'

Celia was: intensely, joyfully so. As much by the change the book had wrought in Kit as of the book itself. He seemed to have grown up suddenly; the wretchedly brooding boy had become quietly content, if not exactly happy, and as surprised as everyone else by the discovery of his unexpected talent. He smiled more, laughed quite often, and clearly – to everyone's delight – was looking forward to publication and the ensuing fuss.

'He's obviously a born celebrity,' Oliver said to Celia, adding with one of his sudden, sharp smiles, 'I wonder where he gets that from.'

And the fuss was well deserved, LM thought; the book was brilliant. She was only sad she would not see its publication, which had been delayed until Christmas that year.

'But it is – superb,' she said, 'and you should be so very proud.'

'I'm certainly – pleased,' said Kit.

'You should be more than that. Very pleased with yourself. Very – pleased—' She was tiring now; he could hear it in her voice. He waited, then leaned over and gently kissed her cheek. She smiled and said, half asleep, 'Your – father must be so – so delighted—'

'I think he is,' said Kit. 'He is publishing it after all.'

'Yes. Yes, of course. Yes, Oliver too.'

And then she was gone, drifting away from him. Her words did not strike him as in any way strange. Or at least any stranger than any others that she spoke during those last weeks . . .

Barty was shocked by LM's illness: and desperately upset. She had loved her from the first time she had met her, had found in her the directness and common sense that the other Lyttons had lacked. Barty's closeness to Jay, springing from those early days at Ashingham, and her reading to him from Meridian the night he nearly died, had created an unbreakable bond between them. Life without LM's down-to-earth wisdom, her slightly dark humour, her steady affection, was unimaginable; Barty visited her whenever she could and, considerably to her own surprise, told her about John.

'He's just – perfect,' she said, on the first visit to the Dovecot, 'in every way.'

'Then you're very lucky,' said LM, 'very lucky indeed. You must hold on to him.'

'Yes,' said Barty. 'Yes, I – I suppose I must.'

LM looked at her sharply. 'If he's perfect, what's wrong? Doesn't he think you're perfect too?'

Barty smiled. 'Oh, yes. He thinks I'm a lot more perfect than I am. He – well, he's asked me to become engaged to him.'

An interesting choice of words, LM thought: not to marry him, but to become engaged.

'And? What did you say?'

'I said I was thinking about it,' said Barty carefully.

'But, Barty, why? If he's so perfect?'

'Oh – I don't know. I want to be sure.'

'Well, if you want to be sure then you're not,' said LM.

Barty looked at her. 'Do you really think so?'

'Yes, I really do.'

'But – he makes me happy. It's so strange. I don't understand myself.'

There was a silence; then LM said, 'It's this other fellow, isn't it? The one in America?'

'I – suppose so. I can't—'

'Forget him?'

'Oh, I'll never forget him,' said Barty, 'that would be impossible. Of course. I'm sure you haven't forgotten Jay's father.'

'Of course I haven't.'

'No, it's more than that. I can't – let go of him.'

'But he was a rotter, wasn't he?'

'Oh, yes,' Barty spoke calmly, 'an absolute rotter, as you put it. And a little mad as well. Well, quite mad. And he certainly didn't make me happy. But – oh, LM—'

'Only you can decide,' said LM, 'and you must be sure. But I can only tell you there is much to be said for security, Barty. For the kind of peaceful happiness that you say your John gives you. I have found that with Gordon. Absolute peace and happiness.'

'And – with Jay's father?'

'Oh, a lot of that was sex,' said LM. 'There now, that's shocked you.'

'No, it hasn't,' said Barty, laughing. 'I was just – surprised.'

'Of course you were. Young people always think they've invented sex. Anyway, Jago was very exciting. He was a rough kind of fellow, you know.'

'No, I didn't,' said Barty. She was hugely intrigued; LM had never talked to her about Jay's father before, she couldn't remember her mentioning his name.

'Yes, he was a builder. Oh, I absolutely adored him. And he was very intelligent. We had a very good life together. Although we never actually lived together. I don't know that that would have worked. Anyway, as I say, I absolutely adored him, but as a marriage I don't know that it would ever have worked. We'd have had terrible differences over bringing up Jay, for a start. Whereas with Gordon – well, I have been blessed. Very blessed indeed. It has been a truly shared life. I hate the thought of him being alone.'

'We'll all look after him,' said Barty, leaning over and giving her a kiss. 'I promise.'

It was the last lucid conversation they had; a month later, when she was able to visit again, LM was incapable of anything but the briefest exchange.

Barty looked at her, lying with her eyes closed, holding Gordon's hand, looked at the love and absolute trust with which she smiled at him – and went back that night and wrote to John, telling him she would very much like to become engaged to him.

'I'm sorry I have been a while telling you,' she wrote, 'but I wanted to be quite, quite sure. And of course I am. And I love you very much.'

She posted it next day, praying it would reach him quickly and that it would not be too late. That was what haunted them all these days: that letters would be too late.

Boy had written to Venetia; a cool, extremely brief note, congratulating her on her new baby, saying he looked forward to meeting him when he came home. That was all. She sat and read it, staring at it in disbelief; that he could be so disinterested, so harsh about his own child. Whatever else, he had always been a loving father. Clearly his new woman, whoever she was, had absolutely taken him over.

Adele tried to comfort her, to remind her what Boy must be enduring in the desert, that the news of Fergal's birth must have been a shock – 'Who told him, anyway?'

'Oh, I don't know. He just said he'd heard. I suppose it was inevitable, all our friends knew.'

'Well, there you are. What news to get, out of the blue.'

'I wish you were in London more,' said Venetia miserably. 'You do make me feel more – sane.'

'Well, I'm coming up for a few days next week. I've been given another job by *Style*.'

'Dell, that's so thrilling.'

'Isn't it? I'm adoring it so. I feel a bit of a fraud, but I've got lots of books out of the library about photographic techniques—'

'I thought that was exactly what you were good at.'

'Not the technical stuff. The shutter speeds and so on. But it's quite easy once you get the hang of it. Lighting's more difficult, that's why I'm coming up for a bit longer, so I can play around in Cedric's studio.'

'Isn't he jealous?'

'Only a bit. He's been very sweet, actually. He's found some new boyfriend, so poor old Bertie Cullingford is being given the heave-ho and he's far more bothered about that. Anyway, I'm sure this is all just a nine-day wonder. But it's so marvellous to be busy and using one's brain again. Or whatever it is I'm using. It's distracting me wonderfully.'

'Good. Well, you deserve it. How's LM?'

'Not good. In fact – well, they say only a very short time now. But she's happy. Extraordinarily so, actually. Funny, isn't it?'

'Not quite the word I'd use. Let me know, won't you, when it's—'

'Yes, of course I will.'

Jay had just left for France; he had never told his mother what he did, had never told anyone in the family. He had been trained for glider operations, sent repeatedly on raids into occupied France, with a mission to destroy crucial roads, bridges, communication centres. That done, he and his fellow soldiers, often helped by members of the French Resistance, would make for the coast, where they would be met and transported at high speed back to England. It was exciting and it was extremely dangerous; he had more than once almost run out of his famous luck.

His commanding officer was sympathetic when Gordon phoned, but unable to do very much.

· 'If only we'd known yesterday. We can't do anything now until he's back. Lives would be endangered, you understand.'

Gordon said that of course he understood.

The doctor said that she still had several days, but that it was impossible to be precise. He hoped that Gordon understood.

Gordon said again that he did indeed understand. He went and looked down at her, at the beloved wife who had come to him late in his life and enriched and enhanced it beyond anything he would have believed.

She lay, quite peaceful, hardly recognisable, so thin had she become; her thick hair grey and wispy, her brilliant dark eyes closed. He had not thought she heard him; but her eyelids flickered and she reached out for his hand, too weak even to hold it for more than a moment.

'I think,' she said, 'I think perhaps I would like Jay to come now.'

So she knew.

'Of course. It may take a few days. But – hopefully no longer.'

'Good. Very good.'

And then she had drifted away again. It was frightening; each time he feared she would not come back.

The raid had gone well; Jay and his companions, the five of them, had successfully demolished a stretch of crucial railway line near Valognes and had safely made their rendezvous with two Resistance workers, who had driven them to the coast and dropped them in a small cove near St Vaast; their patrol boat was promised in an hour. The whole operation had taken just thirty-six hours.

'Piece of cake,' said Jay cheerfully, settling down on a rock, pulling his combat smock round him. 'Be home by breakfast. Could do with a bacon butty. Expect you chaps could too.'

They agreed that they could.

Celia came into the drawing room looking exhausted; Venetia and Oliver were reading.

'That was Gordon. He says –' she paused, dreading the bleak, dead expression on Oliver's face, knowing she must be the cause of it '– he says we should think in terms of going down there tomorrow. The day after at the latest. The doctor says she's sinking fast. Such an extraordinary expression that, I always think,' she added with a quick, bright smile. And then sat down next to Oliver and took his hand.

He gripped it tightly, looked away; she knew why, he hated to be seen in tears, was embarrassed by it. There was a silence.

'Of course,' said Venetia, taking over the conversation, 'can we manage any petrol?'

'There's enough in my car,' said Celia, 'but that means we can't take your wheelchair, Oliver.'

'Doesn't matter. There's the old one at Ashingham.'

'Right.' Venetia stood up. 'Well, I'm going to try and get hold of Barty. And Sebastian, of course, we must take him—'

'If we're not careful,' said Celia, misery making her irritable, 'this is going to turn into a grand opera. It's the last thing LM would want.'

'Celia,' said Oliver, and his voice was suddenly very strong, 'there will be no question of a grand opera, as you call it. Rather the reverse I would say.'

'Bloody long hour,' said Jay. 'Bloody long. It's cold too. Hell of a wind out there. Where is the wretched thing?'

It was a rhetorical question: nobody had the faintest idea. In any case the boats were often delayed. This was the hardest part of the whole thing; the adrenalin stopped pumping, they were tired, hungry, often cold, and beginning to get edgy.

'Can't be much longer,' said Mike Driffield, his second-in-command, 'bloody well hope not, anyway, it'll be getting light in an hour. Don't fancy a day here.'

'We won't be spending the day here,' said Jay confidently.

'Hope not. Jerry'll be looking for us soon. They're not going to be terribly pleased about our night's work.'

It was half-light now; still no sign of their boat.

'I reckon it's the weather,' said Jay, 'big sea getting up. Look out there, waves are bloody enormous.'

'Oh, great,' said Mike, who was a bad sailor. 'Can't wait.'

'You're going to have to. They've obviously been delayed. And then they'll need to send in a dinghy for us. Shit. This could get quite uncomfortable, chaps. One way or another.'

The Lytton contingent arrived at Ashingham at midday. Lady Beckenham came out to greet them. She looked tired and pale.

'Good to see you. Come along in. Oliver, Beckenham's coming round with your bath chair.'

The bath chair was something of a joke; one hundred years old, complete with klaxon horn. The twins had used it in the First World War as a cart until Lord Beckenham forbade them.

'That thing's an antique. Not to be played with.'

Oliver rather liked it; it had a stately, almost throne-like quality and Lord Beckenham usually enjoyed pushing him about in it. But today neither of them had much spirit for it.

'Bad business,' said Lord Beckenham sadly, helping Oliver settle himself. 'Hate to see the young 'uns go.'

Even in his distress Oliver was faintly amused by LM being one of the 'young 'uns'.

'What news of Jay?' said Celia to Gordon quietly, as they sat in what was known as the parlour of the Dovecot.

'Nothing yet. His CO was expecting him back today at first light. But I don't know the details. He's been delayed, I believe.'

'How – how long?'

'No idea, I'm afraid. Could be a couple more days, apparently.'

'And—' Celia nodded in the direction of the bedroom.

'It's impossible to say. Last night we were very fearful, today she seems a little stronger. She wants to see Jay now, very much. She keeps asking when he's coming.'

'Oh dear,' said Celia.

They had been picked up: by a farmer, quite an old man, taciturn and almost surly, in a large farm vehicle, and taken two at a time to his house down the road.

'It's not good. They're looking for you. We heard on the radio the sea was very bad. They turned us over yesterday, God knows why, so we should be all right today. We can keep you just until tonight, then you'll have to go, they're bound to get here. So, pray for calm weather.'

'Thanks,' said Jay, 'sorry.'

'It's our choice.' He spat out of the window. 'Two of you can stay in the house, and the rest in the hayloft.'

The farm was about two miles out of St Vaast, a turning inland off a long straight Normandy road. It seemed a long way to have to travel: and travel back again. Mike said as much; their rescuer shrugged.

'Unfortunately, we don't have a farmhouse nearer the sea. It's this or the cave. You can take your choice.'

'It's extremely good of you. Thank you,' said Jay.

The farmer glared at Mike. 'Better get those things off. In case we're stopped. In the back are some overalls. One at a time, change.'

The two farm labourers sitting on the back of the truck wearing blue overalls, with Gauloises hanging out of their mouths, gazed morosely at the German jeep which sat behind them hooting; it was Lucky Lytton who grinned cheekily at the driver when they finally pulled over so that the jeep could pass. And Lucky Lytton who got a good-natured grin back.

Barty arrived at tea time, distressed at a long delay on the road behind some tanks, fearful she was too late.

'It's all right,' said Celia, who had gone out to greet her, 'she's doing better today. She's asleep now, but Gordon and the nurse both feel she's had enough visitors for a while. She seems to know us all, we've each had a little while with her. She was asking for you, earlier.'

'Was she?' Barty half smiled. 'Well, perhaps in a little while.'

There had been no further news of Jay; Gordon was wretched with anxiety and remorse.

'If only I'd called him home earlier,' he said to Lady Beckenham, 'but she wouldn't let me, it would have alarmed her so much—'

'Of course. You're quite right to trust her judgment. Something about being close to death makes people very – sure. Oh, I'm not a believer in the afterlife, all that stuff about heaven and harps, very boring, and besides—' she stopped, grinned at him rather shamefacedly.

'Go on,' he said, smiling back.

'I've always thought one might find oneself with some rather unsuitable companions.'

'Absolutely. Anyway, you're right. She's been so confused until today and now she's absolutely on the button. I just pray she can hang on. It will be so dreadful for both of them if she can't.'

Lady Beckenham looked at him.

'If there is a heaven, Gordon,' she said slightly gruffly, 'you certainly should have a place in it.'

'Dear me,' he said. 'I hope not. I rather agree with you about it. Very boring. Unless of course there was a really good train layout running somewhere between the clouds.'

'There's a message about your boat.' The farmer had come into the kitchen; it was dusk. He glared at them; he really didn't seem to like them at all. 'You're to be there by midnight.'

'How's the weather?' asked Jay.

He shrugged. 'All right.'

'Good.'

'You have to make your own way. Farm vehicles out in the lanes at night, it's asking for trouble.'

'Of course. Look, we'll go now, or the minute it's dark, get off your premises.'

Another shrug. Then, 'Best wait a while longer. Till it's really dark.'

'OK. If that's all right.'

'It's all right.'

'Mr Robinson—' The doctor hesitated.

'Yes?'

'I'm afraid she may not last the night. She's very weak.'

'I see.'

'There's no news of the son?'

'No. Nothing.'

'She's waiting for him. But—'

'Waiting?'

'Yes. It's amazing how they can. Sheer will-power.'

'Yes, I see.'

He went back into the room, sat down, took LM's hand. 'Hallo.'

The eyelids flickered; a half-smile. 'Jay here?'

'Not yet.'

'He's a long time.'

'He's coming as fast as he can. It's not like just driving down from London, you know.'

'No.' She sighed. 'So tired. So tired, Gordon.'

'Rest, my dear. Just rest. I'll be here.'

'And bring Jay—'

'The minute he arrives.'

A long silence. Then, 'I love you, Gordon.'

'I love you, too, LM.'

'Right. Go. You're lucky, no moon. You're sure of the way?'

'Quite. Thanks. Thanks for everything.'

'Good luck.'

They went out at the back of the farm, then had to follow a footpath round the huge fields to a lane which ran parallel to the road. It was very quiet; owls hooted through the darkness, there was an occasional rustle in the hedges from foxes. Or badgers maybe. They were still in their blue overalls; it had seemed safer. It was very, very dark: no moon at all, and the sky was overcast.

'Doesn't look too good,' said Jay, pointing to the wildly waving trees. 'Still pretty windy, I'm afraid.'

'Great,' said Mike Driffield.

'Right. Let's get a move on.'

They moved silently round the field, keeping low; found the lane, began to run along it.

And then suddenly, they came: a convoy of trucks – three, four, all heading down the road towards the farm.

'Down,' said Jay, and they hurled themselves into a ditch, lay there, breathing heavily. The trucks passed them by, drove, headlights blazing, into the farmyard.

'Just in time,' Jay's voice was awestruck. 'Another five minutes and—'

'We're not out of it yet.'

'I know. But we'd have been like rats in a trap there. Poor devils, I hope to God they don't—'

They could hear a lot of shouting, searchlights everywhere, on the buildings, the barns. The horse, frightened, was whinnying wildly, the dogs barking, the cows mooing. It was like an absurd film, a comedy: only it wasn't funny. Then there was the sound of shooting.

'Christ,' said Mike, 'not them, please not.'

And then absolute stillness; they lay in the ditch for over half an hour, drenched in mud, envisaging questioning, torture . . .

'I've told John I would like to marry him,' said Barty gently to LM. She thought at first LM had not heard her, but after a few moments she managed a smile.

'I'm glad. He sounds –' a long silence, then '– right for you.'

'I know he is,' said Barty. Even at this moment, wondering about it.

'I want you to be happy,' said LM, 'you – deserve it.'

'I hope so.'

There was a long silence; Barty watched her. Thinking of the vivid, forceful woman she had been: thinking how sad that she had left them. And then thinking she was still there, that woman, she lived on, in Jay of course, but also in everything she had done, all that she had been. While they remembered her, she would be there; for all of them.

The trucks had swung round now and were facing the field, their headlights roaming it; 'Christ, they're coming for us,' said Jay.

'Do we move?'

'No, they'll see us. We'll wait. And pray.'

They watched; could see the lights coming at them, straight at them, it seemed, could hear shouting, laughing and then shots, over and over again, shooting wildly in every direction.

'What are they doing?' said Mike.

And then suddenly Jay knew: knew absolutely. And looked at Mike and started to laugh, a great grin of relief on his face.

'They're shooting rabbits,' he said, 'that's all. Best fun in the world, at night.'

'I'm glad you think so,' said Mike.

Finally the Germans went; driving off, shouting and singing, without stopping to collect their kill.

They waited until they had vanished absolutely, until not even a pinprick of light could be seen – and then ran. Ran and ran, along the lane, across the road, through the village, down to the sea.

'Christ, I hope we haven't missed them,' said Jay, throwing himself down on to the sand, fighting for breath.

'Course we won't have missed them. Not with you around, you lucky bastard. How many members of His Majesty's forces have heard enemy gunfire and then found it aimed at rabbits?'

It was a long night; Celia spent it in the parlour in case Gordon fell asleep. The doctor came at the nurse's urgent call at midnight: prescribed extra morphine, told Gordon that LM was unlikely to see the morning.

Three times they thought they had lost her; three times she rallied, grasping Gordon's hand, almost visibly hauling herself back to life through his strength and her own will-power.

She was waiting for Jay; Jay who arrived at six in the morning, just as the sun rose, and despite the shock, despite his own exhaustion, despite the almost unbearable strain of his journey from Dover, he came into her room with his wide grin, sat down on her bed, kissed her, and said, 'Hallo, Mother. I'm here. Safe and sound. Didn't I always tell you I was lucky?'

He sat and held her hand, with his dark blue eyes, Jago's eyes, fixed on her face, and she raised his hand to her lips and kissed it very gently and said, suddenly lucid, her voice quite strong, 'Yes, you did. And your father always said the same.'

'Well, there you are. Runs in the blood.'

'It does – seem so,' she said. And then reached up for his face and touched it, her dark eyes suddenly very bright, a smile curving on her lips; and then her hand fell again, her eyes closed and she gave a little faltering sigh.

Jay had come safely home; and so she could go.

Part Three
1943–1946

Chapter 38

Barty had known they were there of course. Everyone did. You could hardly open a paper without a photograph of them, the Americans, usually surrounded by a crowd of pretty girls, or the endless stories about the nylon stockings and chewing gum they handed out as bounty, or the resentment they were causing our boys, on account of being paid four times as much as they were and therefore being able to steal our boys' girls. 'Overpaid, over-sexed and over here' was the expression on everyone's lips. But – somehow she didn't think any more about their arrival than that.

Barty was low: quite low. She was tired, of course, everyone was; but there had been a lot of good things. The tide of the war was turning; and after the great battle of El Alamein the victory bells had rung out through England for the first time; and then John had come home on leave at Christmas quite unexpectedly, for a time of extraordinary love and happiness, their engagement officially acknowledged, with everyone's blessing and approval; Kit's children's book was a triumph, selling as many copies as they could get paper for, with interviews with him in all the papers and magazines (for it was a wonderful story, the dashing flying ace and his courage in defeating not only the enemy but his own blindness and despair; initially embarrassed by such mawkishness, Kit had become first resigned to it and then rather reluctantly pleased); and then Barty's own war work had been recognised and even rewarded by her promotion to sergeant, something of which she was inordinately proud; so with all these good things in her life, why did she feel – depressed?

She supposed it must be LM's death; which had been one of the most painful experiences she could remember, along with her own mother's death and the loss of Laurence. Life seemed darker, more tenuous, less secure, the thread of constancy slackened. She talked to Sebastian about it; he sighed and agreed.

'LM was the old guard; and a very fine example of it. The opposite of self-seeking, whatever that might be. It's a rare quality. And besides

561

it is very dreadful when you lose someone who's in the front line as it were. You feel yourself move forward into it.'

Barty had not thought of that before; it made her feel worse.

Of course she was terribly happy and excited about her engagement; and even more so about being married, although she and John had agreed they should wait until after the war.

'Marriage to me is being together; while that is impossible, it is more than enough to know that you are there,' he had said and she had, yet again, marvelled at how much they thought and felt the same way about everything, both great and small.

They even shared culinary likes and dislikes; they both hated eggs – 'even fresh ones' – loved fish and had a passion for treacle tart which she had promised she would cook for him every Sunday when they were married.

They seemed to have everyone's blessing and approval: 'Charming, Barty, charming, you're a lucky girl,' said Oliver; 'Top-hole chap, darling, almost good enough for you,' said Sebastian, and even Celia had paid him the compliment of flirting with him.

Billy too had given John the thumbs up; a family man himself now, with a large and bouncing son born in September and Joan already pregnant again, he had adopted a slightly superior attitude towards Barty.

'It's time you found someone to look after you,' he said, as if he had been married for eighteen years rather than eighteen months, 'and I think John is the man to do it. I like him very much; he seems a very genuine sort of a person.'

'Jolly good chap,' said Lord Beckenham, 'enjoying the war, he told me. That's the way.'

'He might not be quite out of the top drawer,' said Lady Beckenham quietly to Celia, 'but he seems very fond of Barty and one can't help liking him. I think it's a very suitable match for her.'

Kit said John was a splendid chap, 'He talks more sense than anyone I've met for a long time.' Adele and Venetia were both sweetly and genuinely delighted for her (while agreeing privately how inevitable it was that Barty would have found someone to marry who was too good to be true): 'Ten out of ten. He obviously adores you,' said Venetia, 'and he's what I'd call truly charming.' (Barty knew what that meant; that John had shown a great interest in her. Just the same, she was pleased.) 'He's so absolutely sweet,' said Adele, giving her a kiss, 'and you suit each other so well, I can't imagine anyone being more right for you.'

She had been worried about what he would make of the twins: in spite of all that had happened to them, they still, especially when together, had a great capacity for silliness; but he was enchanted and fascinated by them and told Barty he could have sat looking at them all day.

She was pleased, of course: no, not just pleased, delighted, it was wonderful that they all liked him so much, all thought he was so right for her. It was, as everything to do with John was, too good to be true. But – that was exactly it. It was stupid, perverse, childish of her even, but she just couldn't help feeling it might have been more interesting if someone had voiced just the slightest criticism of him. So that he wasn't so ten out of ten, so absolutely right, so sensible, so genuine.

And why, for heaven's sake, should she want that? Knowing the answer, she crushed it firmly, ruthlessly into the bottom of her heart. And had a wonderful Christmas with John; they spent Christmas and Boxing Day at Ashingham, 'we'd better get it over', and then escaped to her own little house.

And then he was gone; after a last, sad, tender night, full of promises and statements of love.

She was so lucky; so, so lucky. And she did love him: very, very much. Maybe she wasn't really depressed. Just – tired. That was it; weary. Of restrictions and rationing – stricter than ever now. People complained about tea rationing most – two ounces a week didn't make many pots – and sugar: 'Just as well you're not getting married now, Miller,' said Parfitt cheerfully when they met one night in London, 'you'd have to have a cardboard wedding cake. That's what all the brides are doing now, my mate had one last week. She was going to wait like you, but she got in the club. Not careful and sensible like you.'

Maybe that's what she should do, Barty thought: get in the club. So that everyone would think John wasn't quite such a fine fellow. Or fine in a rather different way.

God, what was the matter with her? What on earth was the matter?

Izzie was growing up; everyone noticed it. She was thirteen now, tall and slender, her figure developing, her face no longer a child's. Sebastian's attitude towards her was interesting; at once proud and fiercely defensive, he tried to deny her maturing, glaring at her small high bosom, tutting when she loosed her lovely hair from its plait, reprimanding her fiercely when she came down to supper one night at Ashingham in a silk cocktail dress she had borrowed from Adele.

'What do you think you've got on? You look ridiculous. You're still a child, you've no business dressing up like that.'

'Sebastian, that was beastly,' said Adele, when Izzie had fled the room, flushed with misery. 'She's thirteen years old, of course she wants to look pretty and a little bit grown up.'

'Well, I don't want her to. And she is exactly that, thirteen. A child. And I don't like you encouraging it either.'

'Oh, for heaven's sake, Sebastian,' said Lady Beckenham. 'You're living in the Dark Ages. Or rather you're not,' she added with a grin. 'My grandmother was married at fourteen. I think it's lovely that Izzie's growing up so charmingly.'

'Well, I see it as precocity,' said Sebastian, 'and I'd prefer you didn't interfere. Isabella is my child and she has no mother to guide her. I have to do it instead.'

'Well, I would say you're not making a very good job of it,' said Lady Beckenham, and she went to look for Izzie. Whom she found sobbing on a window seat in the library, with Kit beside her, one arm around her, his other hand tenderly stroking her cheek.

'Oh dear,' said Lady Beckenham, retreating into the corridor, her face oddly concerned: and then again, 'Oh dear.'

Giles had been injured: quite seriously. He was in a field hospital just north of Naples, waiting for a hospital ship to take him home to England. He had been involved in some very heavy fighting at the Garigliano river, and his company commander had been killed; Giles was extremely lucky to be alive. Helena felt almost relieved; if he was in hospital, he was safe. She had no real idea what his injuries were, or indeed their extent, information was extremely sparse, and she waited for further news in a mixture of hope and dread, but at least the state of permanent fear she lived in was eased.

Adele would have given anything to know Luc was coming home or was safe in some hospital: the messages, arriving at roughly six-month intervals, were an agonising form of torture. Knowing that they meant nothing, except that when they had been written he had been safe, and that the very next day, the next hour indeed he could have been in terrible danger.

She thanked God for her work; she couldn't imagine now how she had survived before without it. It distracted her when she was most afraid, soothed her when she felt most panicked; she knew it was absurd that such acute fear could be eased by the contemplation of frocks and models, lighting and background, colour and style, and indeed she was almost ashamed that it was. She only knew that she felt lighter-hearted, braver, more hopeful.

She went to London at least once a week, usually staying overnight at Cheyne Walk, for meetings with fashion editors and models, art directors and designers; at first she worked in her old capacity of stylist as well as taking photographs, but her sure eye, her capacity for directing as well as recording a shot, the swift rapport she established with the models, thereby enabling her to persuade them to do difficult and unexpected things, and in particular her skill with lighting, ensured her more work than she was willing to do. One of the most famous shots in her portfolio was of a girl wearing a fur coat, picking her way delicately through the giant vegetable patch and smallholding that Hyde Park had become in the effort to feed London; it became a classic, well known among art directors, and she was constantly asked for 'another allotment shot, darling'.

She had no desire to move back to London full time, she knew her children, more vulnerable than most, still needed her badly; but a few days each week without her did them no harm.

From being bored, anxious and restless, she changed, became her old self, confident, witty, happily absorbed in what she was doing; and she began to see her old friends again, to have a social life, albeit limited, to take an interest in her own clothes, to look pretty and even chic again; Venetia was delighted, took her everywhere she could with her: 'The Lytton twins are back,' someone had said to them as they lunched together at the Ritz one day, and they looked at one another and laughed and agreed that, yes, indeed, it was true.

And then it came, on one lovely spring day, when she had been playing in the garden with the children: the now familiar Red Cross envelope.

The message was in English. She sat outside in the sunshine, reading it, and felt the morning grow dark and chill: 'My darling, I may not write again for a while. Don't be afraid for me, I am quite, quite safe. I love you. Luc.'

Somehow, reading those brave words, she knew they might well be the last.

Venetia came down to the dining room at Cheyne Walk, ready for her journey to work. She cycled to work these days; it was the easiest and quickest way and she enjoyed it, unless it was raining, her expensive handbag thrust into her bicycle basket, her briefcase strapped on to a carrier on her back mudguard. But it did mean you arrived with your hair in a mess, and your stockings often laddered – not that she wore them often, she had resorted long ago to colouring her legs with make-up, and drawing seams up her calves with an eyebrow pencil, a piece of ingenuity brought in by the factory girls but seeming, to both her and Adele, hugely sensible. Celia said it was extremely common.

London was full of bicycles: they were lots of people's preferred mode of transport. It was one of the many things which had changed the appearance of the city. The poet Charles Graves had remarked that 'apart from the uniforms you see in the streets, London might be at peace with the world'. Venetia would not have agreed. London might have been patched up, the worst of the rubble cleared away, but everywhere was dreadfully shabby and decayed. The windows of the bombed buildings were boarded up, their fronts looking somehow like so many toothless smiles; the beautiful terraces in places like Regent's Park were for the most part empty and seemed to be literally rotting away, the grass in places like Leicester Square had been worn to dust, and buses were no longer uniformly red, but brown or green, many of them borrowed from the provinces.

More acceptable but even odder was the profusion of flowers and trees; many bombed churches had been turned into gardens, the ruins around St Paul's – where Lytton House had been – were covered by London rocket, and someone had counted four different types of willow and a poplar tree growing on a bomb site on the corner of Bond and Bruton Street. Butterflies fluttered round the heart of the city, and a friend of Venetia's, who lived in Thurloe Square, reported a Peruvian plant growing which 'everyone presumes has been blown here from Kew'.

There were allotments everywhere; in the great parks, the residential squares, the forecourt of the British Museum, even in window boxes; and strangest of all, perhaps, there was wheat growing on the roof of New Zealand House.

There was very little to eat: nobody went hungry, but there was hardship. Two ounces of butter a week, four ounces of bacon, ham and cheese: mealtimes were not bountiful occasions. Food was an obsession, everyone complained about it all the time. The rich did better than the poor by the simple process of eating out. 'You can still have a very good four-course meal at the Berkeley,' Celia Lytton was heard to remark, 'or, of course, at the dear old Dorch' ('Let them eat cake,' Adele murmured to Venetia with a nudge). The government

566

sought to regulate this by putting a maximum charge of five shillings on a meal; but all the big hotels simply instituted a charge of six shillings over that for the privilege of dining on their premises, an extra five shillings and sixpence for smoked salmon, and two shillings and sixpence for dancing.

And then there were American servicemen, many of them black, all over the city, in their neatly pressed fine-wool khaki uniforms. Their wonderful rich accents, only ever heard before, by most people, in the cinema, and a seemingly endless supply of money to spend in bars and restaurants and ballrooms gave them an automatic glamour.

There were women everywhere: driving buses, delivering milk, manning ARP stations, delivering letters, driving ambulances. And running companies, Venetia thought, as she flicked through her diary that morning, checking on the day ahead. The war had done considerable good to the female sex in general; and had also succeeded where Venetia's mother had failed, teaching her that there was a great deal more to be got out of life than what her friend Bunty called Domestic Prostitution.

'You sleep with them, and in return you get board, lodging and, if you're lucky, a few nice frocks.'

Venetia could not now imagine what she would do without her job: or why she had refused to do one for so long. She was also rather painfully aware of the vapid, aimless creature who had been married to Boy: and how extremely unsatisfactory he must have found her. She buttered herself a piece of toast and went to see if there were any letters for her. There was one: from Boy. Telling her that he was coming home on a fortnight's leave in 'roughly a month' and saying that no doubt they should meet to discuss various matters, including the ongoing care and welfare of their children.

Venetia read it twice, which didn't take her very long since it was so extremely brief, and then put it down on the table and burst into tears.

Barty was on sentry duty; she absolutely hated it. She felt such an idiot, standing outside the gate with her rifle and its bayonet; she had five rounds in her pocket but was forbidden to load the rifle in case she shot someone. The whole thing was such a nonsense. And every time she said 'Who goes there?' she felt an insane desire to giggle; in fact, the first few times she *had* giggled and had been severely reprimanded for it by her commanding officer. She was actually doomed as a sentry; she had once waved a dispatch rider through, without demanding his

ID, thinking she recognised him; he was actually doing a security check. She had been put on a charge for that; she often said she would not be surprised to be confronted by the first invading German of the war, disguised as Winston Churchill, and to find herself waving him through as well.

Now it was raining, dripping steadily through the collar of her rubber raincoat, and although it was April, it was cold; she had a headache and her feet ached. And she was tired, so tired, she felt in danger of falling asleep as she stood.

Still, after this, she was off duty for forty-eight hours; she was going to go home. It was the marvellous thing about being stationed at Croydon; she could go home even for the shortest leave.

A letter had come that morning from John; she had it in her pocket, was saving it until she got home. His letters were always so long, and so amusing, as well as loving; he had a great talent for observation. It was odd; he wasn't exactly witty but he could make a funny story out of anything.

This was very tedious; very tedious indeed. She looked at her watch; still-twenty minutes to go. Her head hurt dreadfully; she thought longingly of her kitchen and a cup of strong, sweet tea. Workman's tea, Celia called it; she drank her own tea – usually Earl Grey – very weak with lemon. And no sugar.

A car pulled up at the gates; she straightened, said, 'Who goes there?' and tried to ignore the icy water now dripping off the bottom of her mackintosh and running into her shoes.

She didn't get home until after ten; she felt dreadful. Shivery and hot at the same time. Maybe she had flu. A hot bath would help. She boiled the kettle, swallowed two aspirins and made the tea; then she carried it into the bathroom, together with her letter from John, and settled into the bath. Oh for a pre-war bath, deeper than the regulation five inches. It was such a measly depth, hardly covered your legs; there was no possible opportunity for wallowing in hot water. Even the King had announced that he had had a line painted five inches from the bottom of his bath, as a discipline.

She settled into the bath, splashing herself repeatedly with the hot water to keep warm – her house was very cold – and leaned back against the bath pillow that Venetia had given her for Christmas – 'they're heaven, you've no idea, for reading in the bath' – and pulled John's letter out of its envelope. She felt warmer, happier, better, straight away.

My dearest,

I wonder what you are doing as I write this. (He would be amused, Barty thought, if he knew; the last night he had been home they had tried to share a bath as a romantic gesture, and the five inches of water had proved so inadequate they had given up, laughing; he had stayed in, and by the time it was her turn the water was cooling fast.) I am sitting in a highly uncomfortable truck, stuck in an endless line of such things, on the road to somewhere or other. A small dog has just lifted its leg against the feet of a man standing at the side of the road, watching us (this is a local sport); he has not yet realised the fact and the dog has made off, clearly feeling there might be some retribution. I like dogs; I think perhaps when we are married and have our house, garden and apple tree (last discussed on 1/1/43 at 0300 hours, you know how I like to be as precise as possible), a nice golden labrador might make a most welcome addition to the family. What do you think?

Oh, I miss you. I miss everything about you, but particularly at this moment you—

The phone rang out shrilly; Barty frowned. She was already cold; but getting out of this shallow, tepid water was going to make her colder. Maybe she should just let it ring. It was probably only Celia. Or maybe Parfitt. And they would both phone again, thinking she was not yet home.

It stopped abruptly. Good. She settled back to her letter. John was missing her: what, especially? He was rather good at finding odd, unexpected things, like her ears, which he said he found particularly sweet, or her near-photographic memory for dates, or her capacity for laughing at his jokes: but they were all things he had told her about before and he was also very good at finding new ones . . .

The phone began again: damn. She would have to answer it. She put John's letter on the cork stool, got out of the bath, then realised she hadn't brought her dressing gown into the bathoom and, moreover, had left the towel in the tiny airing cupboard so that it would be warm when she wanted it. Oh well. No one could see her.

She walked across the sitting room quickly, shivering; she would have to ring whoever it was back. As she picked up the phone, she glanced up and saw herself in the mirror over the fireplace, thought how absurd she looked, stark naked, her hair falling down from where she had pinned it loosely on top of her head, her face rather flushed.

Maybe she had a temperature; it certainly wasn't the warmth, in fact, she was shivering quite violently.

'Hallo?' she said rather uncertainly, meeting her own eyes in the mirror. And then watched herself move into shock, saw her own face blanch, her eyes grow somehow hollow and dark, her body at once become absolutely still.

'Barty? I presume that must be you. Yes? Hallo, Barty. How are you? This is Laurence.'

Chapter 39

So it had happened. All of it. As she had known of course that it would. She had said all the right things: and done all the wrong ones.

She told him not to come and see her: not to open the bottle of champagne he had with him because there was nothing to celebrate; not to touch her, certainly not to kiss her; not to so much as suggest there was anything to be discussed by either of them; not to even think of asking her to have dinner with him and certainly not to go to the Grosvenor House and dance; not to dare to propose that they meet again the next night, one night might be just about acceptable, a meeting between old friends, but that must be the end of it; not to ply her with stories of his failed marriage, his endless unhappiness ever since she had left; not to express his bottomless remorse at all the unarguable wrong he had ever done her; not to assure her that he was changed, reformed, a different, better and stronger person now; not to try to persuade her into bed with him; and, most of all, not to think for a single moment that she now felt anything more for him than she would for any man she had once known and been rather fond of, five long years ago.

And had let him into her house, weak, frail with shock at what she felt, just looking at him standing there, staring at her absolutely intently in the way she had never forgotten; had smiled rather feebly as he passed her the glass of ice-cold champagne – 'So difficult to get anything iced in this country of yours, how do you stand it?' – had allowed him to kiss her, albeit briefly, a light dusting on her lips, and to hug her warmly, nicely, a brotherly hug; had changed into the only really good dress she had, a black sliver of silk, piled up her hair, and gone to dine and then to dance with him at Grosvenor House. She had stood, stock-still on the dance floor with him, her head bowed, her eyes closed as the old violent sensations invaded her, and agreed to meet him the following night – 'Shall we try the Savoy? I'm told it's not too bad, and that they even have ice' – listened to, while struggling not to believe, the story of his disastrous marriage – 'I only married her because I couldn't have you, you know that' – and tried to believe that he was changed, reformed, a better and stronger person; and finally and most inevitably of all had allowed him home that night, to her house and into her bed, and remembered, as he took her and invaded her and moved in her and loved her, how strange and strong and perfect his love-making could be.

The next day when he was gone and she was dressing herself in her neat, proper, virtuous uniform, she reached into her drawer for a handkerchief, and pulled out with it the letter from John which she had been reading when Laurence telephoned. She had put it there in her haste, as she rushed round tidying up, finding something to wear, for he had only been five minutes away, and had simply forgotten about it. All about it. And now she sat, weak with distress and shame, staring at it, lacking the courage even to finish reading it, reading words of love from a man she had promised to marry and had betrayed with a speed and thoroughness of which she would not have believed herself capable.

Laurence was based in London; that took care of any hopes that he would be whisked off to the north of Scotland or Ireland, both established bases for the Americans, or that he would disappear from her life again. He was not strictly a soldier at all, although he had been given the honorary rank of colonel in order to simplify matters; he was on Eisenhower's staff, working in Military Intelligence as a translator.

'I was too old to be an ordinary Joe,' he said to her, 'but I got in this way. It's fascinating work.'

He had an astonishing gift for languages; he could speak several perfectly, including Russian, and could even get by in Japanese: 'But it's my German and possibly my French that they're interested in.'

Barty said she was surprised he had volunteered at all. 'You surely didn't have to. You must be – what?'

'I'm forty-five,' he said, 'unbelievably.'

'Then . . . ?'

'I wanted to,' he said. 'I thought it would be a tremendous adventure.'

That made sense: it was part of his obsessive search for new experiences, his restlessness, his careless courage.

'And anyway,' he added, smiling the strange, reluctant smile she had never forgotten, 'I wanted to come and find you. I could hardly come as a tourist, now could I? Death seemed a far smaller hazard than never seeing you again.'

She was silent; then she smiled at him and said, 'Is it really that dangerous? What you're doing?'

'Not at the moment. But – it might get more so.'

'How?'

'Oh – interrogating prisoners. Close to the enemy lines.'

'I see. And – how did you find me?'

'Oh, that was easy,' he said. 'I just phoned Lyttons. They said you were away, fighting the enemy, and they asked who I was; I said I was a long-lost cousin, one of the American Lyttons, and the very nice girl I was speaking to told me where you lived and gave me your telephone number.'

'I see,' said Barty, resolving to speak to Vera Martin, the new receptionist, so different from the wildly discreet Janet Gould.

'And you know the rest. Anyway, what about you? Is what you're doing dangerous? It sounds as if it could be.'

'Not often,' said Barty. 'In fact at the moment it's quite dull.'

If only, she thought, the rest of her life was as dull.

He looked exactly the same, had hardly aged at all; his hair was still the same bright red-gold, his eyes the extraordinary blue-green, he was a little thinner, but still very muscular, radiating health and strength, perfectly dressed. He had arrived in civilian clothes, wearing a dinner jacket, and had taken her out to dinner the next night in his uniform – 'I had it made by my tailor, the one they gave me was horribly ill-fitting.'

He told her she looked just the same too, studied her, remarking on it. 'Your hair, I like it longer, your wonderful lion's mane of hair – it was Lady Celia who had described it like that, wasn't it, yes, I thought so, I do look forward to meeting her now, and your eyes, those beautiful eyes, and your neck, that long graceful neck, I have dreamed of your neck, Barty, you know – well, yes, you are changed, and I'll tell you how, you're more beautiful, far more beautiful than ever.'

He had talked a great deal abut his marriage, about the years without her: 'They were hell. Absolute hell. An unhappy marriage is a prison cell. Worse. A prison cell shared with someone you can't stand.'

'You didn't have to marry her,' said Barty.

'I had to marry someone.'

'But why?'

'To show you how desperate I was.'

'Laurence, that is completely ridiculous.'

'Not at all. You knew how much I loved you. How much I wanted

573

you. It was the ultimate declaration. Designed to make you see how desperate I was, what I was prepared to do.'

'You do talk absolute nonsense,' she said. 'And besides, what about your poor wife? Pretty hard on her, I'd have thought.'

'Not at all. She wanted my money. And a fine household. And babies of course.'

'Ah yes. The babies. How many—'

'Two. A boy, nice little chap, called Bartholomew—'

'Bartholomew?'

'Yes. After you. Do you like it?'

'You called your son, by another woman, after me?'

'Yes. I rather enjoyed the idea. A sublime piece of perversity, don't you think?'

'I don't – know,' said Barty slowly. She felt quite shocked. 'It's just – extraordinary.'

'Well, you may think so. I didn't. Anyway, we call him Bif. And then there's a little girl, Catherine. Kate. She looks just like her mother, behaves like her too, very spoilt.'

'Not like her father at all, of course.'

'Barty,' said Laurence indignantly, 'I have never been spoilt.'

She didn't argue: there was no point.

'I love you,' he said, suddenly serious. 'I love you so absolutely. I can't believe I've got you again.'

'Laurence, you haven't got me.'

'Oh, but I have,' he said, his extraordinary eyes fixed on hers, taking her hand, kissing it. 'I've got you and this time I am not letting you go. There is simply nothing to be discussed. You must agree. You do agree. I can see.'

'Laurence—'

'Oh, be quiet. Let's not waste time. If you have to leave in an hour and a half, we have some very important things to do. Starting with both of us removing every vestige of clothing—'

'Laurence, I don't really want to—'

'Of *course* you do. Of course you do. I always know when you're prevaricating, Barty, you fiddle with your hair.'

'Do I?' she said, genuinely astonished.

'Yes. And when you're nervous, you stroke your nose. And when you're reading you clear your throat a lot. And when you're hungry, you get quite irritable. And when you're late you tend to be rather clumsy and rush round knocking into things. And when you feel sexy, you get stiller and stiller. It's very lovely, that stillness.'

'You know me so terribly well. Better than anyone in the world.'

'That's true,' he said and he leaned forward and started to unbutton her dress, 'and all these years without you, I have recalled everything carefully and consciously each day, ticked it off like a list, so that I shouldn't forget anything, anything at all . . .'

'Oh dear,' she said helplessly. She felt helpless: all the time.

She sat on the train going out to Croydon, watching the evening light on the dreary suburban houses and thinking how beautiful they looked, her body singing with remembered pleasure, her head in a turmoil that was at once joyful and dreadfully, horribly distressed.

What was she going to do? In the name of heaven – or hell – what?

It was midsummer: Izzie was home for the holidays.

'It's so nice to be back,' she said to Kit as they sat on the terrace after tea. 'I do like Cheltenham, in fact I love it, but there's no peace there. I do like peace and quiet.'

'I get a bit too much of it,' he said.

'Really? I thought you were happy here.'

'I am happy. Of course. I couldn't be better looked after, I love chatting to the little boys, and all the Lytton children, and Grandpapa and Grandmama are both so marvellous to me. But the fact remains I'm twenty-three, Izzie, and I'm living the life of a middle-aged man. Sometimes I do wonder what will become of me.'

'You'll find some lovely girl,' she said, 'who will fall terribly in love with you and you'll get married and have lots of babies.'

'Which I'll never see.'

'No,' she said, meeting this with her steady courage – she was still one of the very few people he bared his heart to – 'no, that's true. But you'll have them, and they'll love you, and grow up thinking how wonderful you are. And they'll be terribly clever and terribly brilliant, just like you, and frightfully handsome, just like you.'

'Am I?' he said, sounding surprised. 'Am I really? Wandering round here with my stick . . .'

'Kit, of course you are. You haven't changed. You look exactly the same. I suppose it is hard for you to believe. You're the most handsome man in the world. I always thought so. Except maybe for Father, of course.'

'Yes,' said Kit, 'yes, I do remember him being wonderfully good-looking. The twins always said when he was younger that he looked like a film star.'

'That's quite true, he did. I found some pictures of him the other day, at our house at Primrose Hill, when he was really young, I've brought them down to show Adele, I thought they'd interest her, they're just snaps, but in a sort of sepia tint. Anyway, there's one of him playing tennis and another of him sitting in a boat somewhere or other, in white trousers and a cricket sweater, a cigarette between his teeth, laughing, really laughing. He doesn't do much of that these days, I'm afraid.'

'No. But he used to. I remember. I'd like to see—' He stopped, sighed. 'I still say things like that. So stupid, isn't it?'

'Not at all,' she said. 'Not at all stupid. Your brain's the same, just like your face is, it thinks the same, it's bound to.' She stopped, then said, 'Your new book is so lovely, Kit, you must be terribly excited.'

'It is wonderful,' he said, 'to have something to do, something I can succeed at, be proud of. I enjoy it enormously. And funnily enough, I can't imagine actually writing those books. In some strange way, dictating them somehow makes them more vivid, more alive.'

'Well, there you are. Oh, hallo, Noni. How are you?'

'Very well, thank you. GGM' – they all used this nickname for Lady Beckenham – 'said to come and tell you it was sherry time.'

'Oh, dear,' said Kit, 'the sherry gets worse and worse, more like cough mixture every day.'

'Don't drink it, then,' said Izzie.

'Oh, no, she'd be fearfully upset. Lead the way.'

'I will. Just hang on a minute, I've got something in my eye, I've got a hanky somewhere in here—' She rummaged in the leather satchel she had brought out, containing some books and magazines she had promised to read to Kit. A couple of photographs fell out.

'Oh, now those are the ones I've brought to show Adele, old ones of—'

But Noni had picked them up, was looking at them.

'These are really funny,' she said. 'Kit, I didn't know you could row a boat.'

'Kit? They're not of Kit,' said Izzie, smiling at her, 'they're of my father. You know, Sebastian. When he was young. Just about the same age as Kit is now.'

'Well, he looks like Kit,' said Noni, 'really exactly like him. Are you sure it's not him?'

'I'm absolutely sure,' said Izzie, dabbing at her sore eye. 'That's better. Now put them back in my satchel, Noni, and let's go and have this sherry that Kit's looking forward to so much.'

Kit, listening to this conversation, waiting patiently for Izzie to take his hand, was scarcely aware of it consciously. But something deep within his mind, some blurry memory, that had meant little to him at the time, shifted, moved further forward, into focus. He wasn't even sure what it was. But it stayed there, waiting to be examined further: when the time arrived.

'Boy's coming home next week,' said Venetia. 'I'm really dreading it. I just don't know what to do, what to say to him, what to tell him.'

'Want me to—'

'No. No, thank you. I've got to deal with this on my own. He's suggested lunch at the Dorch on Wednesday. Nice neutral ground. Oh dear.'

'Are you going to take some pictures of Fergal? Just in case?'

'Oh – I don't know. Yes, I suppose so. He's going down to Ashingham the weekend after, to see all the others, they're all there, so he'll meet Fergal then. Oh, it's such a stupid, ridiculous mess. I should have told him right at the beginning, shouldn't I, and then—'

'If you say that once more I'll scream,' said Adele cheerfully. 'Now look, can you think of anywhere at all I might find a full-length mink coat? In this day and age?'

''Fraid not. You've asked—'

'Oh yes. And Grandmama. I might have to declare myself beaten on this one. Shame. It's for the most heavenly new art director. At *Style*. Cedric's really cross this time, he wanted him all to himself. Not that he seems the sort to fancy Cedric.'

Boy wasn't enjoying his leave as much as he had expected. The first few days had been marvellous, simply waking up to cool mornings – even the warmest English summer day seemed chilly – and the unbelievable luxury of having a bath whenever he wanted it, albeit only five inches deep – the last he'd had had been on leave in Cairo – the absence of sand in everything, the air no longer thick with flies . . . all that sort of thing.

But he very shortly began to feel lonely. He was staying at his flat in Pont Street, and although that too had seemed wonderfully luxurious for a while, he was beginning to long for companionship. For so long now he had been with people more or less twenty-four hours a day, all with the absolutely common aim of beating the enemy, enduring so much together, the heat, the discomfort, the triumphs and the defeats, the loss of friends – they had become his family, his fellow officers and his men, closer to him in many ways than his actual family had ever been.

It seemed absurd to be nostalgic for warm beer and the eternal bully beef, shared in fierce discomfort, but after a few days that was almost what he felt. The desert war was said to have been a very personal war, shared intensely by its protagonists; they had been so far removed from the rest of the world, he had often thought, it was like being alone in the universe, especially at night, so huge was the sky, so great the physical solitude.

He had seen a few friends in London of course; but everyone was so busy, so distracted with their own lives, even the women seemed to be doing some kind of work, and there was so little common ground. Somehow conversations about deprivation and difficulty seemed shallow, set against what he had known and endured; he became visibly irritable one night when a woman who had very kindly asked him to dinner complained constantly about the problems of stretching her petrol ration and doing much of her own cooking. She would not be asking him again, he thought, and felt remorseful.

He was looking forward to seeing his children; but even that was overshadowed by the prospect of a forced meeting with this new baby. And he was frankly dreading his encounter with Venetia; he felt so angry with her, so resentful, and so – what? Foolish, he supposed: cuckolded. It was deeply unfair, of course, when he had cheated on her so much, and under far more serious circumstances, but he couldn't help it. He really couldn't. He didn't know how he was going to approach her, what he was going to say, whether he should leave her to broach the more difficult matters or raise them himself . . .

He was beginning to regret having suggested the Dorchester; somewhere quieter might have been better, there might be friends there who would interrupt their conversation, make references even to Venetia's new lover, whoever he might be. On the other hand, it would be better than a one-to-one confrontation with no distractions of any sort. Which was precisely, of course, why he had suggested it in the first place.

Well – it was only a lunch. And then, with luck, they could part on a constructive and friendly basis.

'You look tired, Miller.' Parfitt looked at her consideringly. 'What you been up to? Lover boy's not home, is he?'

'No. No, of course not,' said Barty hastily. Thinking how shocked

Parfitt would be if she had known what unspeakable things she had been up to.

While she had been with Laurence, she had thought of nothing but him; he had always done that to her, forced her to focus absolutely on him, driven all other demands and considerations away. But now, removed from him once more, from the pleasure and the pain, it was as if John were with her, beside her, shocked, hurt, absolutely betrayed.

How could she be doing this? She, so clear in all her moral choices, so firm in all her moral judgments, how could she be deceiving a man she had promised to marry, declared her love for, a man so good and so kind and so gentle he deserved not so much as a frown of irritation, the slightest suggestion of sharpness from her? How could she, after the mildest, most unconvincing of protests, the slightest, briefest of hesitations, have gone to bed with a man she had left in a fury of rage and grief, a man with no morals, no integrity, so unstable and obsessive that he had gone to the lengths of marrying another woman purely to distress her? How could she have allowed herself to be seduced by him with such pathetic and distasteful ease?

There was no hiding place for her, no possible excuse. She had not been lonely, neglected, ill-treated, she had been loved, cared for, admired; she thought remorsefully of Adele, waiting literally for years now for the man she loved, and Venetia too, both of them displaying infinitely more virtue than she was capable of. She was not bored or deprived, she was deeply involved in something she enjoyed, she was warm, well fed, comfortable, surrounded by friends.

Wherever she looked she found the same: a treacherous, self-seeking, self-indulgent woman. And she was ashamed to be her.

She wondered if there was something wrong with her, some severe psychological flaw in her make-up, hitherto unsuspected, that she could behave so badly; she felt physically sick, and so disgusted was she with herself that she couldn't sleep, couldn't eat, and was distracted and miserable. Until she was with him again, when she became wildly, helplessly happy, and so incapable of keeping the promise she continually made to herself – to give him up, to send him away, to tell him it could not, must not go on – that the very idea was laughable.

She did try once; and he smiled at her and said, 'Do you really think I would allow that to happen again? I've lost too many years with you already, Barty.'

And he did seem to have changed; he was just slightly less demanding, just a little more conciliatory. He listened to her more, considered what she said; he even acknowledged that she might have some grounds for feeling some guilt and emotional discomfort: 'Although how you could promise yourself to another man, I really cannot imagine, when it was me you really loved.'

'Laurence, that is so outrageous. You married another woman, had children by her.'

'I've told you, that was only to distress you.'

'You're mad,' she said, and then saw that he was smiling.

'I love you,' he said, 'so very, very much.'

She was silent; he looked at her, the smile gone.

'Barty?' he said. She knew what he meant. Said nothing. 'Barty?' he said again.

And then she did say it: slowly, painfully, fighting the truth of it, knowing she had to give in.

'I – do – love you,' she said, her voice very low.

'Good,' he said, his own voice changed, quite brisk with satisfaction. 'That is settled then. So when shall we be married?'

'Married! Laurence, I'm not going to marry you.'

'I don't see why not. I'm here, you're here, I love you, you love me, we are both free. Of course we must get married.'

'Laurence, of course we must not.'

'But – why not?'

'Well—' She stopped. There was indeed only one reason; and it was not a good enough one. For him.

'Give me time,' she said, 'please. It's – it's not right. Not yet.'

'It's very, very right,' he said, kissing her, 'but I will give you a little time. If you really want it.'

'I really want it.'

And she went back to her torture chamber, more distressed even than ever before.

'Mrs Warwick? Mr Pickford of Gamages here.'

'Oh – hallo, Mr Pickford.'

'Mrs Warwick, I'm in the vicinity, I wondered if I might come and see you. I am told you have the first bound copies of Mr Lytton's new book.'

'Mr Lytton's?' said Venetia stupidly. She was so nervous at the prospect of seeing Boy she hardly knew her own name.

'Yes, indeed. Christopher Lytton's. What is its title? It escapes me for a moment, but I do know that Hatchards have seen the book and—'

'Oh, you mean *Seen and Heard.*' She was rather proud of that title, she had thought of it herself.

'Yes, of course. I presume the title is based on the well-known quotation?'

'Yes. That children should be seen and not heard.'

'Very good. Well, anyway—' He paused.

Venetia looked at her watch. She should be leaving in a quarter of an hour: leaving for the Dorchester and lunch with her husband. Or rather ex-husband. Still, it was only a short walk away.

'Well – it would be very nice to see you, Mr Pickford. But I'm afraid I don't have very long, I've got a luncheon appointment.'

'Oh dear me, it won't take long. Just enough to have a look at the book and the cover of course, and to discuss how many we might take. The last one was a great success, we could have sold twice the quantity we did.'

'Of course,' said Venetia. There was no point, after all, in losing an important order. She was going to need her career in the future. In fact, the lunch with Boy was little more than a business meeting itself. What was it he had said? To discuss future arrangements. Well, then.

Mr Pickford was late: he didn't arrive until ten to one. And then the girl who was manning the reception desk had been engaged on a telephone call when he arrived, and so it was almost five to one before he was in her office.

Even then, he was painfully slow, considering the cover, debating (again) the title, discussing the price (five shillings), deploring the paper quality (so thin you could see the print on the other side), calculating aloud the number of copies he might take.

Venetia looked at her watch: almost ten past one.

'Mr Pickford,' she said, 'I really do have to go. It's—'

'Of course, of course,' he said, 'how very remiss of me. I'm so sorry, Mrs Warwick. Thank you for your patience.'

He reached the door, then turned round, smiled at her.

'While I'm here,' he said, 'I'd like to know how many copies of *Grace and Favour* you may be able to let us have this autumn. It's still selling extremely well . . .'

She was late. Very late. Twenty minutes now. No doubt making a point. Or perhaps she was with her lover: discussing with him what she might or might not say to Boy, whether he was still to be allowed the easy custody arrangements of before, what arrangements there might be for the new child.

He had phoned Lyttons that morning, spoken to Celia; she had been initially delighted to hear from him, welcomed him home, congratulated him on the victory at El Alamein, and then became rather – odd with him. It was hardly surprising under the circumstances, he supposed, she must be embarrassed, must know who the father of the baby was. In reply to his invitation to luncheon later in the week, she had said that, yes, it would be very nice but she was extremely busy, the war was creating so many problems, and she would prefer to leave it for a while.

He had asked her if Venetia was there, and she had said, yes, but she was busy all morning with meetings – she was clearly playing the same game as Venetia, and inflating her job into something much more important than it actually was; he said he was having lunch with her that day and wanted to check that she was still available. Celia said that she would ask Venetia's secretary to telephone him if she was not.

Venetia's secretary! Some filing clerk, no doubt. Well, she was certainly playing hard to get now: or something. He had already drunk one gin and tonic, had another one on the table; he had learned the menu almost by heart – God, people didn't know they were alive, it was like a dream, gulls' eggs, quails' eggs, chicken; he had read the leader page of *The Times* as well as the letters, where there was a series running, to which Lord Beckenham had contributed, on the deterioration of manners during the war, and was aware that two couples at least, happily sharing a meal and some wine, were looking at him and commenting on the failure of his companion to appear.

He would give her ten more minutes and then he was going to leave: he was simply not prepared to be made a monkey of like this. He'd been away for over two years, he was due at least a little common courtesy . . .

'Excellent. I'm delighted. Thank you so much, Mrs Warwick, for showing me the *Grace and Favour* poster. Delightful. Good gracious me, I have made you very late. Can I escort you to your luncheon appointment? It's the very least I can do, I feel. And I could even, perhaps, explain to your companion the reason for your delay.'

'Oh – no, thank you.' Nothing could have been more agonising; and besides, she simply had to put on her hat, some perfume and her lipstick before she left. And Boy would wait, he'd have to. He'd guess she'd been held up. And he wasn't going to walk out on her today: not even Boy would do that.

Well, that was it. Twenty-five to two. Outrageous. He'd go, leaving a message with the head waiter that he hadn't been prepared to wait any longer.

Boy drained the glass of its rather warm gin and tonic and stood up, glaring at anyone who might be watching. It was – well, it was unforgivable. He would—

'Boy! Hallo! How lovely to see you. You're not going, are you? Come and have a drink.'

It was Jay.

'I'm waiting for Tory. My fiancée,' he added with a slightly embarrassed grin. 'She's always late. Worth waiting for, though.'

'I hear she's an absolute corker,' said Boy, 'according to my eldest son, that is. I didn't know you were actually engaged, Jay.'

'Pretty recent development, actually. Yes, she is a corker, Henry's quite right. He's grown up a bit, hasn't he, since you left? It must be awfully sad, not seeing them all grow up.'

'It is.'

'It's so good to see you, Boy. I hear you've been having no end of a caper in the desert. Pretty good show at El Alamein, though. Is Monty as good a chap as everyone says?'

'Marvellous,' said Boy, 'quite marvellous. He has a sort of magnetism about him, hard to explain – anyway, how are you, Jay? What have you been up to? I'm so very sorry about your mother. You must have been very upset.'

'I was. I had no idea she was so ill. you know, she wouldn't let anyone tell me. And then I nearly didn't get there in time, you know.' His eyes were heavy; he sighed, looked into his glass.

'I'm so sorry,' said Boy again.

'Well – at least she wasn't in any pain. I do miss her, though. She was a remarkable old bird. And we were always pretty close. Still . . . I suppose that's life. Or rather death.' He sighed, drained his glass, waved at the waiter for another. 'Poor old Gordon's pretty cut up. But I've tried to spend some time with him, we're building a new train layout and we've done a bit of bird watching and so on. And Tory is very good with him, he likes her a lot. How's Venetia?'

'I – don't know yet,' said Boy shortly. 'I'm waiting for her now. She's terribly late.'

'Everyone's always late at the moment, Boy. There's a war on, you know. Anyway, she's looking marvellous and going great guns at Lyttons. More or less doing my mother's old job.'

'Really?' said Boy, surprised.

'Yes. Frightfully good at the whole thing. Of course Lyttons have moved, you know that, don't you? Bombed into extinction, the old place, Venetia almost had her baby there that night, only got out just in time, I expect she told you all about it.'

'No,' said Boy shortly, 'she didn't.'

'Really? I'm surprised. If it hadn't been for Celia, God knows what would have happened to her. Anyway, you must be looking forward to seeing her. And Fergal, nice little chap, you'll approve, I'm sure. We were all – darling! Hallo. You look marvellous as always. Boy, this is Victoria Halifax. Tory for short. Tory, Boy Warwick, my – what are you, Boy, cousin by marriage, I suppose – anyway, Venetia's husband, you know.'

'Ex-husband,' said Boy lightly. 'How do you do, Miss Halifax.'

'Call me Tory, please.'

She smiled at him, an enchanting smile, sat down; her short Wrens' skirt revealing astonishingly good legs. Henry had been right: she was a corker. But then Jay would get a girl like this: it was all part of his famous luck.

'It's marvellous to meet you,' said Victoria. 'I've heard so much about you.'

'Really?'

'Oh yes. And all your heavenly children. I think—'

'Boy, hallo.' It was Venetia; breathless, flushed, looking – well, looking beautiful, he thought, he had forgotten quite how lovely she was. She looked as chic as always in a perfectly cut jacket and skirt, her hair longer than he had ever seen it, almost on her collar – it suited her – her dark eyes brilliant.

'Hallo,' he said. He stood up, leaned forward, kissed her briefly, formally.

'I'm so sorry I'm late, I – hallo, Jay! And Tory. How lovely. What a nice surprise.'

'Hallo, darling,' said Jay. 'How funny we should all be here. The last time you and I were here, Venetia, was that night we had dinner and danced, remember? Got a bit carried away, I'm afraid, Boy. Very cheek-to-cheek, weren't we, Venetia?'

'Very,' said Venetia quickly.

'Now hang on,' said Tory, 'I'm not sure I like this. You mean you've been dancing with another woman, Jay?'

''Fraid so, darling.'

'He spent the whole evening talking about you,' said Venetia, laughing, 'showing me your picture and absolutely drooling over you. Except when we were dancing.'

'That bloke was there too, wasn't he?' said Jay. 'Someone from Boy's regiment. We had to hide behind our menus, remember?'

'No, not really – oh – oh, yes, I do. Mike Willoughby-Clarke, it was, Boy; how is he?'

'He's – he was killed,' said Boy. He spoke very slowly, his voice strained.

'I'm sorry,' said Venetia.

'Yes. Bit of a shock.' He was absolutely silent, staring at her as if he had never seen her before. They all looked at him, unnerved by the silence.

'Well,' said Tory finally, 'shall we all have lunch together?'

'That'd be fun,' said Jay.

'Er – no, I don't think so,' said Boy, still in the same, strained voice. Jay laughed awkwardly then shrugged.

'Well – that's fine by us. I suppose you two have a lot to talk about.'

'Yes, we do rather,' said Boy, 'an awful lot.'

'What on earth is going on?' said Tory. 'They seemed rather – odd.'

'Well, they haven't seen each other for over two years. And they are supposed to be divorced, although she's had that baby. But anyway – yes, I agree, a bit odd. Anyway, darling, let's go in, I'm starving.'

In between enjoying their lunch and planning their afternoon and evening, much of which was to be spent in bed, Tory and Jay watched Venetia and Boy: watched them, clearly hostile at first, talking fiercely, almost angrily; then leaning forward across the table, listening to one another with immense attention; then visibly beginning to relax, and to smile; and finally starting to laugh: and then they saw Venetia reach into her bag and produce some photographs, observed Boy leafing through them, smiling, asking questions, and then suddenly reaching out and touching her face, stroking it gently. And watched Venetia slowly and very gently, her eyes fixed on his, take his hand, and kiss it.

'I would suggest,' said Tory thoughtfully, 'they might be spending the afternoon a little bit as we plan to. What would you say, Jay?'

'I'd say I don't really care what they're going to do,' said Jay, 'I'd just like you to finish that disgusting-looking trifle so I can get you out of here and out of that uniform. I know it's awfully smart, but you do look a whole lot better without it.'

'What a very impertinent observation,' said Tory.

'So Daddy and I are going to get married again,' said Venetia, 'and after the war we'll all go back to our house together.'

'I never thought you weren't married,' said Elspeth.

'Nor did I,' said Amy.

'But we told you, we explained—'

'I know, all that stuff about liking each other but not being able to live together,' said Roo. 'It seemed pretty silly to us, specially as you had Fergal. You must have lived together for a bit to get him.'

'Roo, really!' said Venetia.

'Oh, Mother, I know about all that, Henry told me. He said I needed to before I went to Eton.'

'Oh, I see,' said Venetia weakly.

'Anyway, you're quite right,' said Boy. He was sitting on a sofa in the library, with Fergal on his knee and the girls on either side of him. 'We do still like each other quite a lot, and we think we can live together after all.'

'Good,' said Henry. 'It will certainly make life much simpler. I do think, though,' he added, 'if you don't mind my saying so, five children is probably enough. I mean Fergal's quite jolly, but I don't really fancy another baby now, yelling all the time. None of the other chaps at school seem to have babies in their families.'

'It's true,' said Roo, 'it's a bit embarrassing.'

'All right,' said Venetia meekly, 'no more babies. If that's what you want. Now listen,' she added with visible relief, 'there's the lunch gong. Why don't you go and see if you can help GGM?'

Boy smiled at her over Fergal's head when they had all gone.

'I never thought I'd have to listen to a lecture on birth control from my own children,' he said. 'It's clearly time we grew up and became a bit more sensible and responsible.'

Venetia giggled. 'All right,' she said. 'I suppose we can try. I just can't help thinking it was a bit more fun the other way.'

Chapter 40

She had written to him and told him.

That she had made a mistake, that she was desperately sorry, that she didn't think, after all, they should get married, that she wasn't good enough for him, that it couldn't possibly work, that she would always love him, that she would never forget him . . .

And then imagined his grief and pain as he read it, grief that he would carry into battle with him, perhaps die with – and so she had torn it up and thrown it away.

She had done that four times now.

She longed for someone to talk to about it; and yet couldn't think who that person might be. The thought of confessing to any of the Lyttons that she was betraying John – John, who was so good and kind and whom they all loved so much – was horrific; it meant she had to confront her own bad behaviour, and, what was more, confront them with it, say look at me, I am not the good, loyal, intensely moral person you imagined, I am bad, duplicitous, unscrupulous, self-serving.

She almost hoped they would find out, that one of them would see her with Laurence; it was quite likely after all, she had had a long-overdue fortnight's leave, had been in London, they had been out a lot together, as Laurence wanted to see London, wanted to experience what it had to offer. But each night, as they entered the Berkeley or the Ritz or the Mirabelle, the theatre or even the cinema – Laurence had a childlike passion for the cinema, and insisted on seeing *Dangerous Moonlight* four times and *Mrs Miniver* five – she would look round half fearfully, half hopefully, for a familiar face – and find none. You'll get no help from me, fate seemed to be saying, you'll have to do your own dirty work; only of course she couldn't, she lacked the courage. Lacked the courage! She, who had always been so unhesitatingly, so determinedly, brave.

Parfitt did guess that something was up, had observed her hollow-eyed exhaustion, her jumpiness, and said, with a knowing grin, a tap on the side of her nose and a certain admiration in her voice, 'You've been up to no good, haven't you, Miller, you dirty devil.'

But she didn't understand. She thought Barty had simply been out dancing or even to supper and then for a smooch, as she put it, with someone else, she had no idea, and indeed how could she, of the violent, dreadful betrayal which was taking place, and her advice was rough, ready, absolutely pragmatic.

'You don't want to worry too much,' she said. 'You have to take your pleasure where you can. There's a war on, you know. And what the eye don't see the heart don't grieve over.'

Thinking of how John's heart would grieve if his eye had got the faintest glimpse of what was going on, Barty could only smile at her feebly and say nothing.

Laurence, patient, by his standards, for a few weeks, was pressing her now for a marriage date.

'I simply don't understand you. It will be wonderful. And we may not get the chance again for a long time. I have the licence, look, here in my notecase, all ready.' And indeed he had, and all she had to do, he said, was follow him into a registry office and do what she was told.

'But, Laurence, I can't, not yet, you don't understand, I have to tell John and—'

'Barty, how long does that take? Five minutes. It can be a perfectly nice letter after all, just telling him you're going to marry me instead of him—'

'I don't know how you can be so – so stupid,' she said, crying and laughing at the same time at this sublime insensitivity. 'Think how desperately hurt he'll be, what it will do to him.'

'You did it to me.'

'That was quite different.'

'Why?'

'Well – because you'd done something terribly wrong, I had a good reason.'

'Not terribly wrong,' he said, and his genuine indignation frightened her, it was such a clear indication of his blindness about himself, 'misguided, of course, I grant you that, but no more; I said I was sorry and—'

'Laurence, please!' cried Barty. 'Please, please try to understand.'

'I am trying.' he said, and clearly he was, his expression an absurd mixture of anxiety and bewilderment. 'I'm trying very hard. I just don't see why he'll be so upset.'

'Because he loves me.'

'Not really,' he said, playing with some tendrils of her hair, twining them round his fingers, 'he doesn't love you as I do. He's not consumed by you, you are not his entire life. He'll be a little upset, of course, I can understand that, but then he'll recover and find someone else. And be much happier. You could never go back to him now, after all. That would be really dishonest.'

And that was the only thing he said which was true, the only thing which was unarguable. She couldn't go back to John now.

Giles had been awarded the Military Cross.

He had been home for almost two weeks now; the almost unrecognisable wraith who had come off the hospital ship, thin, exhausted with pain, and running a constant temperature as a result of the infection in his leg, was slowly becoming himself again, but the leg had stubbornly refused to heal. There was a fear of gangrene; they had given him the new wonder-drug penicillin and initially he had improved, but the pain and the infection had returned: 'Must be something in there still, old chap,' the surgeon had said, patting his arm encouragingly. 'Hoped they'd got it all out, but we'll have to have another look.'

They had warned Helena that if they didn't find the cause of the trouble, or indeed if they found indications of extensive tissue death and therefore a real risk of gangrene, the leg might have to come off.

But the leg had been saved; the surgeon had found some shrapnel buried deep in it and removed it and although there might be some wasting and muscle loss, he should make a very good recovery. Helena sat holding his hand as he lay, nauseated and groggy with anaesthetic, and told him that as soon as he felt better, his commanding officer wanted to come and see him.

The purpose of that visit proved to be the news of Giles's decoration.

'Who would ever have thought it,' Celia said, reduced to tears by the news, 'that Giles of all people – it's so wonderful.'

Oliver said that he would have thought it of Giles of all people: 'After all, he nearly got decorated after Dunkirk. And from the very beginning of the war he has shown extraordinary courage. Not least on insisting on enlisting in the ranks. I think we can both be very proud of him.'

'I am,' said Celia, 'very, very proud.'

'Venetia, you are never, ever going to believe this.'

'Believe what?'

'I was walking out of Cedric's studio today, with my arms full of cabbages, don't ask me why—'

'Why?'

'Don't be annoying. When I saw Barty.'

'What's so astonishing about that? She's been on leave. She came in the other day, to see Mummy and Daddy.'

'It's not that. She was—' There was a long pause. 'She was with someone.'

'What, you mean—'

'Yes. I do mean.'

'Not—'

'No, of course not, he's in Italy, poor darling.'

'My God. My God. But – I mean, are you sure she was – well, really with him?'

'Of course I am. They were walking into a cinema.'

'Well –' Venetia's mind roamed frantically round for an explanation, while not being sure why it wanted one '– well, maybe he was an army colleague or something.'

'Venetia, what is the matter with you? He had his arm round her.'

'Was he in uniform?'

'Yes. Yes, he was.'

'Well, then—'

'Oh, for heaven's sake.' Adele's voice was taut with exasperation. 'It was an American uniform.'

'Oh, my God. Do you think it was – you know?'

'Well – I don't know. I've never seen a picture of him. But it seems possible. He was divinely handsome. Sort of reddy blond hair, quite tall, didn't see much more. He looked rich, though.'

'They all look rich,' said Venetia, 'I could quite fancy one of them myself.'

'Me too. Anyway, he was terribly attractive, I can tell you. Clever old her.'

'God,' said Venetia again, 'I can't believe it. Saint Barty. With poor old John out there fighting for king and country.'

'I know. And he's married, isn't he? If it is him.'

'Worse and worse.'

'Or better and better,' said Adele. 'It's just so – unlikely. How can we find out, do you think?'

'Goodness knows. She'd never tell. I feel so sorry for lovely John, don't you?'

'Terribly, terribly sorry. And him so perfect.'

'Like her. Only she's not at all. I absolutely must tell Boy. He was always a bit – cool about Barty. Said he knew she disapproved of him. He'll be so shocked.'

They took him out for a drink to tell him; he was not shocked, but he was amused.

'Well, well, well. How extremely intriguing. But I suppose we shouldn't leap to conclusions.'

The twins looked at one another and raised their eyebrows.

'Boy! You, of all people!' said Venetia. 'Of course we should. The blessed Barty is having an affair with one man, a frightfully rich and wicked man, if Maud is to be believed, while she's engaged to another—'

'Who? Oh, Maud. Well, you really don't know that it's him. It might be some other American she's met. There are an awful lot about, one and a half million, I believe.'

'Well, this is one in one and a half million,' said Adele. 'I saw him and he could have been Maud's brother. Same colouring, same sort of – look.'

'Well, time will tell,' said Boy. 'Is one of you fiends prepared to confront her with it?'

'Of course not,' said the twins in absolute unison.

Adele told Sebastian about Barty. She hadn't meant to, but she did. The whole business had actually upset her; so absolutely faithful to Luc herself, so completely determined to wait for him, she found Barty's perfidy shocking and distressing. It was another certainty destroyed for her in a world increasingly devoid of certainties: that Barty could behave so badly. Barty, who was so famously moral and good, betraying the man she was supposed to love and who most emphatically loved her. What was happening to the world she had once lived in, the world of love and fidelity, of promises kept and commitment absolute? Did war destroy ideals and integrity, along with everything else?

It brought home to her, too, how little she had in her life that was certain, that she could actually wait for. Everything about her future, her past even, was under question, any cause for happiness infinitely frail, any reason for hope arguably foolish. Luc might have survived, he might be living in Paris safe and well – although the messages had stopped completely, for longer than at any time, over nine months now. But it seemed so very unlikely. A sense of failure had settled upon her; she felt increasingly abandoned, increasingly alone in the world.

If it hadn't been for her work, she would have gone quite mad; even with it, even with her increasing success and satisfaction and the undoubted fun it brought her, she felt, beneath everything, depressed, a failure.

She had had offers from men, old friends home on leave, to take her out to dinner, to dance – even to go to bed. She had enjoyed the dining and the dancing, but had always refused the bed, despite considerable temptation at times; that was for Luc, as long as there was hope, any hope at all. She felt she must wait, until she knew. And so she remained lonely, and beneath her gaiety, her courage, her blithe determination not to give in, desperately sad.

And Barty's behaviour had increased her sadness.

It was Sebastian who found her tearful one afternoon, sitting alone in the entrance hall of Curzon Street; she had arrived to see Venetia, to invite herself to dinner, and had found her leaving for the day, going to meet Boy for the theatre and dinner.

'He's going off again soon,' Venetia had said apologetically, adding, with a half-heartedness that even Adele could hear, 'Do come with us.'

'Don't be silly,' she had said brightly. 'Play gooseberry, me? No thanks! Have a lovely time.'

And had sat down to try and work out what to do with herself that evening; she found it so dispiriting that when Sebastian asked her if anything was the matter, she turned a quivering face to him and said, yes, something was.

He was very good; he lent her a handkerchief. 'I always used to have to keep your mother supplied with the things,' he said, then gave her a cuddle and invited her to have supper with him at his house.

'I'm lonely too, we can cry on one another's shoulders. Come along, it'll do you good.'

And sitting there, eating Mrs Conley's excellent rabbit pie – far better than the rabbit pie at Cheyne Walk, she told him with a giggle – she did try, falteringly, to explain how bad she felt. He was so understanding, so patient, that she found herself telling him more and more. About her own remorse and sense of failure: and after that, and after he had told her how foolish that was, she had somehow – and she really hadn't meant to – told him about Barty and how angry and resentful that had made her feel. He was very sweet, very reassuring, had promised to say nothing to anyone. More importantly, he had understood.

'Nothing worse than seeing bad behaviour rewarded,' he said, the old mischievous grin suddenly appearing. 'Especially when one is struggling to be good. I'm surprised at Barty, I must say. Although knowing her, I'm sure she's in torment.'

'I hope she is,' said Adele fiercely, 'poor, poor John.'

'Maybe she's told him.'

'He still can't be feeling too happy.'

'Of course not. Anyway, he's not our main concern. Let's concentrate on you.'

'Yes, let's. Why do I feel so bad about it?'

'Oh, other people's happiness, especially when it is ill-won, is hard to bear when you are unhappy yourself,' he said. 'I should know.'

'I suppose you should,' said Adele, smiling at him wearily. 'Oh Sebastian, when does it get better?'

'It doesn't,' he said almost cheerfully. 'Sorry. You just get used to it, that's all. I still weep when I remember Pandora and how much I loved her, or when something brings it forcefully back.'

'Poor Sebastian. Poor, poor you. That was so cruel, so unfair. And—' She stopped.

'And what?'

'Oh – I was going to say something a bit stupid.'

'Well, go on.'

'Let me guess. Seeing Isabella growing up to look so exactly like her mother must bring it back more forcibly than anything.'

'Well – yes. It's true. It is very painful. But she is not like Pandora as a person. She is more serious, and more vulnerable, I fear. There was quite a tough little person behind Pandora's sweet face. Isabella is going to be hurt a lot by life. I wish I could save her from it.'

'You can't, I'm afraid. No one can save anyone from life. She is the dearest girl, though. My children absolutely adore her. I suppose she's doing terribly well at school?'

'Terribly well,' said Sebastian, 'and that's another thing, she's terribly ambitious. Always a danger, especially in a woman. It leads inevitably to trouble in my observation.'

'What does she want to do?'

'Oh – all sorts of desperate things. Run her own publishing company. Have her own school in the slums of London, bringing joy and enlightenment to deprived children. Write Nobel-prize-winning novels . . .'

'It all sounds quite harmless to me,' said Adele, laughing. 'Goodness, she and Kit adore each other. I mean she's always loved him, but it's certainly mutual these days. They spent absolutely hours, days on end, in the holidays, just talking and laughing, going for long walks, and she reads to him endlessly. I'd say you might have trouble on your hands there in a year or two, Sebastian.'

'Oh, nonsense,' he said lightly, 'it's just a brother and sister thing, for heaven's sake.'

'We-ell. Yes, of course, at the moment. But I'd say there's a case of puppy love developing in a big way. Kit's very young for his age, don't forget. He's only had one important girlfriend ever and I'm sure he's never slept with anyone. Sorry, Sebastian, it's this lovely wine talking. You look quite shocked.'

He did for a moment: drawn and startled. Then, 'No, no,' he said, smiling easily at her again. 'No, Adele, nothing can shock me. Now then, have another glass of the lovely wine, and then I'll run you home. I presume you're staying at Cheyne Walk? Your mother will be wondering what's happened to you.'

'I don't think so,' said Adele, laughing, 'she'll just assume I'm working at my job, you can practically hear the inverted commas when she uses the word, she disapproves of it so much.'

'She's a very silly woman at times,' said Sebastian, 'dearly as I love her.'

'Brave words!' said Adele.

'Come along, darling. Let's go. And don't think too harshly of Barty. I would hate to see a family feud developing.'

'Oh, of course there won't be,' said Adele. 'You need something dangerous in a family's history, surely, to create a feud. We may all be a bit – mad in our different ways, but there are no dark secrets to rise up and divide us.'

'Well, that's good to know,' said Sebastian lightly.

Chapter 41

'Bad news, I'm afraid. He's died.'

The voice was so brisk, so matter of fact, that Celia could not relate it to a human tragedy.

'Who's died, Mama?'

'Beckenham, of course. Who did you think I meant?'

How dreadful in that first pre-grief shock to want to laugh; to say she had thought it must be a horse or a dog.

She did in fact smile; then felt her mouth start to quiver, felt the tears rise into her eyes, sat down suddenly, dizzy and disorientated. Her father: dead. Her immortal father, so old, so brave, so sadly deprived of the final glory of his life, an invasion of Ashingham. Her fine, good-looking, sweet-natured, badly behaved father. A lifetime of courage and hard work and loyalty to king and country and pursuit of pretty women finally over.

'Oh, Mama,' she said, 'Mama, I'm so sorry. When, how, I mean—'

'Oh, just about an hour ago,' said Lady Beckenham, in the same brisk tone. 'Silly old fool, it was his own fault. Went out to check the defences last night. I told him not to, it was pouring with rain, and he slipped and fell, knocked himself out. Shepard brought him in, God knows how he managed it, I thought he was going to die as well. Anyway, your father never recovered consciousness. We got the doctor of course, severe concussion followed by a stroke, he said. He wanted to take him to hospital, I said he was doing no such thing, I wasn't going to have Beckenham dying in some horrible place surrounded by a lot of ghastly people. He had a heart attack in the early hours and – well, that was that.'

'Are you all right?'

'Of course. Why shouldn't I be, nothing wrong with me.' The voice was sterner still. 'All for the best, really, and it's what he would have most liked, short of the invasion. He had his sword with him, and he looks really perfectly fine. Anyway, come down if you can.'

'Mama, of course I'll come down. And I'll bring Oliver and Venetia. When – I mean – I don't suppose you've thought of it yet—'

'The funeral? Friday. Eleven. All right with you?'

'Perfectly all right,' said Celia, 'of course. We'll be there this afternoon.'

'Jolly good.'

She had laid him out herself. He lay in the great bed they had shared for nearly seventy years dressed in his infantry uniform, his medals pinned to his chest, his sword at his side, oddly docile as he had never been in life.

Celia stood there, staring not at him but at her mother, so indomitably controlled, her own great age brought suddenly into focus by this life-shifting event. She had never quite known how old her mother was: but she must be in her late eighties.

Lady Beckenham smiled at her quickly. 'I know what you're thinking. What am I going to do now? Same as I've always done. Only with no housemaids to worry about. Only worry is James, of course. We never got on, and I certainly don't like that wife of his. Still, we'll work something out, no doubt. I'll leave you with him for a bit, shall I? Then we can have a drink.'

It was proof of how much everyone had loved Lord Beckenham that they all came to the funeral: they stood in the chapel, a great mass of Lyttons and honorary Lyttons, all grieving, even Helena, even George and Mary. Many of the children were in tears, and not only the grand-children and great-grandchildren, but the small boys at the school, who had been so fond of him, and who had sat in small phalanxes at his feet on the terrace as he told them his unsuitable stories of battle and death and gore, and drilled earnestly with him whenever they were allowed. 'You can't start too early,' he had said, 'you'll do far better in the corps when you get to your public schools if you've some idea about drill.'

Sebastian was grim-faced, Kit ashen, Izzie between them, holding both their hands.

Billy and Joan Miller stood behind the Lyttons, Billy fierce with grief, Joan weeping openly, and next to her was Shepard, who had joined Lord Beckenham as his valet just before the First World War and had risen to the position of butler in the twenties, his white head bowed throughout, clasping Lord Beckenham's sword.

Oliver, in his wheelchair in the aisle, was close to tears himself;

Celia, looking at him, knew what he was thinking, of the first time he had stood in this chapel with Lord Beckenham, the unsuitable bridegroom for his daughter but treated with courtesy and kindness nonetheless. Remembering those things herself on that difficult, joyful day she smiled at him and, understanding, he smiled back.

Barty was there, granted compassionate leave, pale and very thin; Boy had asked her if she would like to sit with them and to her great surprise, as the tears rose in a flood and she fought to control them, she felt him take her hand and squeeze it.

Jay and Gordon had come together, both pale and clearly shaken by this new loss, and little Noni, so close and beloved a companion to Lord Beckenham, in the absence of her own father and grandfather, was sobbing silently as she clung to her mother's hand. The twins were both weeping, so much in fact that Lady Beckenham frowned at them in disapproval: the frown was enough to instantly stop their tears. She herself was dry-eyed, absolutely controlled; her frequent assertion that public displays of emotion were ill-bred and uncalled for had never been so forcibly demonstrated.

As the prayers ended, Kit stood up, was helped forward by Sebastian; he stood there, a pale, courageous figure, and began to speak.

'I know you all loved Lord Beckenham and I am also aware that some of you may wonder why it is I standing here, not one of his sons. The answer is that I was asked to by Lady Beckenham, as she felt I had spent more time with him than anyone else over the past few years, and could best speak of the man he had become, as well as the man he was. The simple answer is that I do believe those two men were the same: he was indeed very old, but he was still sharp, amusing, brave, vigorous – and, above all, optimistic. That was the lesson he taught me. In my darkest hours, it was Lord Beckenham who made me laugh, dared to challenge my depression, to speak of what I had lost with simplicity and frankness and to show me that I still had much to be grateful for. It was he, indeed, who inspired my books, he who was responsible for driving me to write them. When the news came that my first book was a success, he reminded me quite forcibly, and with some self-satisfaction, that if it had not been for him, I would never have written it. Indeed, he became quite pressing about taking a share in the profits' – a few reluctant smiles, even a murmur of laughter, went round the chapel at this – 'and it is with some shame that I tell you that, despite my good intentions, I never quite got around to making the necessary arrangements with my father.

'He was, quite simply, an inspiration to all who knew him: as a fine soldier, as a successful and compassionate landowner and as a family man, a marvellous husband, a devoted father and a deservedly beloved grandfather and great-grandfather. The world will be the poorer without him; but we must not let him go. We must continue with all he taught us. It is more necessary than ever in these difficult times to be as he was: brave, hopeful, compassionate, open-minded and, above all, merry-hearted.

'I wish him farewell, as must we all; but in the knowledge that we are the better for having known him. Thank you.'

'Oh Kit,' said Barty later, linking arms with him as they walked back from the graveside, 'that was so lovely. So very lovely. It couldn't have been done better by anyone.'

'I hope so. I didn't want to let Grandmama down.'

'You didn't. Do you know she even had to blow her nose after that? I thought for a moment she was actually going to cry.'

'So common,' said Izzie, who was walking with them, in an exact replication of Lady Beckenham's voice, and they all laughed; she looked round nervously. 'Is it all right to laugh at a funeral?'

'It's absolutely all right,' said Barty firmly, 'in fact it's the best thing to do sometimes. Think how pleased Lord Beckenham would be, he wouldn't have wanted everyone crying: "Lot of snivelling," he'd have said, "can't stand women who snivel." '

'Unless they were very pretty,' said Izzie, and she giggled again.

It was after tea that things went wrong.

They were sitting round the large dining table, in the awkward, post-funeral cheerfulness. Clearly exhausted by the day, and by the strain of remaining in control, Lady Beckenham asked them to excuse her while she went down to the stables.

'Surely not necessary, Mama,' James said. 'Miller can see to that for you.'

'James,' said Celia in the voice which chilled the hearts of all the Lyttons, 'James, Mama wants to go.'

James's heart remained patently unchilled: 'But, Celia—'

'James—' she said again. This time he was silenced.

'Well,' said Jay, into that silence, 'we should be getting back. I've got to report first thing in the morning. And—'

'Where are you based now?' asked Venetia.

'Oh – up in Scotland,' he said vaguely, 'training, you know.'

'Still with the gliders?'

'Yup.'

'I'm off early too,' said Boy, clearly grateful for this opportunity to escape gracefully, 'so perhaps we should—'

'Could I beg a lift, Jay?' said Barty. 'Or if you haven't got room—'

'Oh, we've got room. For a little 'un. Haven't we, Gordon?'

'Of course. You're certainly very thin, Barty. I hope you're eating enough.'

'Of course,' said Barty.

'I mean there you are, in the front line, marvellous, I think it is, for a girl, slip of a thing like you—'

'Well – I'm not the only one,' said Barty, aware she was sounding foolish, anxious to deflect attention from herself.

'Yes, of course. There's young Victoria as well. Marvellous girl. But you're the only lady fighter amongst us today, that's why I mentioned it. Jolly good, jolly brave.'

Something snapped in Adele; bloody Barty, getting the praise again, doing it right, as always. The distress of the day, her sadness at losing her grandfather, rekindling other loss, other grief, made her reckless, careless of what she said.

'Oh, Barty's absolutely wonderful, aren't you, Barty? Practically winning the war single-handed. We all admire her so much.'

'Adele,' said Sebastian gently. She ignored him.

'How is John getting on out there in Italy, Barty? He's all right, is he? You must be missing him quite dreadfully.'

Barty looked at her; she was very white, and her eyes were wary.

'Of course I am,' she said, 'yes.'

'Or perhaps you haven't heard from him lately. That's terrible, not hearing from people. I know that myself of course. Even though I'm not in the front line.'

'Yes, of course it is,' said Barty.

'You imagine the worst, all the time. And you get so lonely, that's the thing, isn't it? Although I suppose you have all the other girls' company. I don't have that.'

'No, it must be very – difficult.'

'Oh, not difficult exactly. I wouldn't say that. Just lonely.'

'Yes.'

'Or have you found anyone to make you feel better? Anyone who can really cheer you up?'

'Dell—' said Venetia. 'Dell, why don't we—'

'Because I haven't,' said Adele, ignoring her, 'no one at all. And I

599

wouldn't. Wouldn't want to, while Luc was alive. I think it's pretty awful, what some women are doing, betraying their husbands, or their fiancés of course. What do you think about that, Barty?'

'Adele, can we not have this conversation now?' said Barty. 'It isn't the best time or place.'

'Well, what would be? Somewhere quiet and private, I suppose. Where you could tell me about it and nobody else would hear? Or know? Would you prefer that?'

'Adele,' said Boy. 'Adele, darling, please—'

'Adele, darling, what? Shut up, not upset Barty, not let people know about her, that she's not the perfect person we all think—'

'Adele!' Celia's voice was cold, absolutely authoritative. 'Adele, stop this at once. It is outrageous to behave so badly at such a time. I have no idea what you're talking about but—'

'Well, I'll tell you,' said Adele, her brilliant, tear-stained eyes turning to her mother, 'I'll tell you all about it. About your beloved Barty, and—'

'No, Adele, you will not. You will be quiet. If you want to talk to me then you can do it in privacy. I am going to my room, I don't want to endure any more of this. You may join me there, if you wish.'

'I don't wish,' cried Adele, starting to sob, 'I don't wish anything. Anything at all. Except to have Luc back. And to know he's safe.'

'Come along, darling.' It was Sebastian; gentle, firm. 'Come for a walk with me. It's been a funny old day, we could all do with some fresh air. Isabella, would you like to take Noni and Lucas down to the stream.'

It was more an order than a question; Izzie, trained to absolute obedience, stood up at once.

'Of course. Come on, you two. I'll show you how to build a dam.'

'Sebastian—' It was Kit. 'I wonder if you'd be good enough to take me to my room. I'm a bit tired.'

'Of course. Here, take my arm.'

'So who else knows?' said Barty. Her voice was heavy, exhausted.

'Oh – only the twins,' said Sebastian. 'And Boy, I believe. Adele told me about it. She was very upset.'

Barty ignored this. 'And – how do they know?'

'Adele saw you. With this fellow, whoever he is.'

She was silent. Sebastian looked at her.

'Is it—'

'Yes. It's him. Laurence Elliott.'

600

'Ah.'

She started to cry; then hauled herself back under control. 'It's so dreadful, Sebastian, so awful. I just don't know what to do. I feel so ashamed, so terrible about John and yet I can't, can't—'

'Help it?' His voice was gentle, his eyes, as he looked at her, almost amused.

'Yes,' she said, 'I mean no. That's exactly it. I can't help it.'

'One can't,' he said simply, and sat down on a tree trunk, patted it. 'Sit down. Come on.'

She shook her head, stood staring down at him. 'You seem to know what it's like.'

'Of course I do. I've led quite a dissolute life, Barty. I've lived through most of life's dilemmas.'

'I see. So who, when—'

'Oh, this is not the moment for chapter and verse from me. It's you we're talking about. Worrying about what you can do.'

'I don't know what to do,' she said, and she started to cry again. 'That's the worst thing, I don't know what to do.'

'Well, let's look at the options. Give this fellow up?'

'I just don't – don't seem able to.'

'So you – love him?'

'So much, Sebastian. So very much. And he's so – so wrong for me in so many ways. He's quite – dangerous in his own way. Obsessive. Even a little mad. You know all the things he's done, bad things, frightening things, I've told you.'

'Yes, indeed.'

'But – he's all I want, I'm afraid. He's not good like John, not gentle like John, I don't share things with him like I do with John. But he makes me—'

'Happy?'

She shook her head. 'No. Not happy. John makes me happy. Well, Laurence does make me happy, wildly happy; and excited and all those things. But – oh, it's so hard to explain. When I'm with him, I feel sort of – settled. No, that's too comfortable. I feel as if I've discovered myself. Who I really am.'

'I see. Well, that sounds pretty serious. Isn't he married?'

'Not any more. Divorced. He wants to marry me.'

'And—'

'Well, of course I can't marry him,' she said fretfully.

'Why not? When he makes you feel yourself?'

'Because he's not right for me.'

'It sounds as if he is. I'm sorry to play devil's advocate, but – in lots of ways he sounds very right for you.'

'But, Sebastian, he's quite – wicked. And devious. And controlling. And terribly awkward. And—'

'Barty, love is not convenient. It doesn't fit comfortably into our lives. The people who are right for us in theory are often not so in practice. It could be that Laurence is what you do need. God knows why. And that John, for all his kindness and gentleness, is not.'

She was silent. Then, 'So what do you think I should do?'

'Oh, my darling, I can't tell you that. No one can tell anyone that.'

'And what about John?'

'Oh, you mustn't marry him,' he said firmly.

She stared at him.

'Why not?'

'Because he so clearly is not right for you. Even if you do both like Beethoven and hate boiled eggs or whatever. You wouldn't be behaving like this if he was. It's as simple as that. You're too honest, too loyal.'

'Hardly,' she said.

'Yes, you are. If you really, really loved John, as Adele loves that wretched Luc for instance, then nothing would have persuaded you to—'

'Cheat on him?'

He grinned at her. 'If you like. I was going to say to go back to Laurence. He is clearly the great love of your life, however disastrous. Now then,' he stood up, held out his hand to her, 'I said I wouldn't tell you what to do. I won't. But if you do decide that John is not the man for you, then you must tell him.'

'But, Sebastian, he's out there, fighting, risking his life, how can I? Can't it wait till he gets home?'

'I would advise against waiting,' he said.

'But why?'

'Because this is a small world. A lot of people know you, and I would say a lot more people know Laurence Elliott. I'm sure he is not being nearly as discreet as you are. If John were to hear from someone else, and it seems entirely possible, it would be a double betrayal.'

'You mean I'm not only a two-timer, but cowardly with it?' She managed a smile. 'Very attractive.'

'You said it. I could express it more charmingly, but that's about the size of it.'

'Oh, Sebastian,' she said, taking his arm, 'I wish I was as wise as you.'

'Darling Barty,' he said, 'I do assure you, no life has been less wisely lived than mine. Now come on, or you'll miss the lift with Gordon and Jay. You don't want to have to go back with the Warwicks, do you?'

'Not terribly,' she said.

'That was very well done, Mama,' said Celia. She smiled at her mother. 'It was a splendid day. Papa would have approved.'

'I hope so, I did it for him.'

'You look all in.'

'I feel pretty much all in. You wouldn't like a short walk, I suppose?'

'Of course I would.'

They walked out on to the terrace and then into the meadow and towards the woods.

'It's going to be pretty rotten,' said Lady Beckenham, 'without him. Sixty-eight years is a long time, I'd got quite used to him. Even the housemaids.'

'You were a marvellous wife to him.'

'Yes, I think I was,' she said, 'and in the end he wasn't such a bad husband to me. I really don't like James very much, you know,' she added, a note of surprise in her voice. 'He's so high-handed. And he treats the servants so badly. I can see trouble for Billy, for a start.'

'Why?'

'Well, because of Bill's history, he tends to be a little familiar. Perfectly polite always, but – easy. Natural. I don't see James understanding that.'

'You don't think he'd try and get rid of him?'

'Not while I'm here, no. But there could be some clashes. I might warn Bill.'

'Good idea. Will you – will you stay in the house?'

'Of course. It's my home.'

'It will be Sarah's and James's now as well. And their dreary offspring's.'

'I am perfectly aware of that,' said Lady Beckenham coldly, 'and it's most unfortunate. My goodness, that girl is dull. She makes Helena look quite interesting. Anyway, I shall take over some rooms for myself for the time being. And then I might move down to the Home Farm if things get difficult. Take it over and run it. The new man is having trouble with it, I think it's too big for him. And it's a nice house, I could be very happy there.'

It was a very nice house, a Victorian farmhouse; but quite large. Celia looked at her mother in alarm.

'Mama, you can't live there alone. And talk about running a farm.'

'Why on earth not? I'm not in my dotage yet, you know. And the stables are marvellous, better than ours in some ways.'

'Exactly how old are you?' said Celia curiously.

'No business of yours. But – not far off ninety. Not far enough, in fact. Oh, dear.' She pulled a handkerchief out of her antiquated coat, blew her nose fiercely. 'I'm going to miss him,' she said, 'I can tell you that. Probably don't want to go on too much longer.'

'I'd back you for at least another decade,' said Celia.

They had reached the woods now; they paused at the gate, Lady Beckenham looked out over the parkland and the farmland beyond it. It was hard to see where the one stopped now, and the other started; the parkland had been ploughed up to grow wheat and barley. But in the spring evening light, it looked glorious, a great sweeping sheet of land meeting the sky, heavily grey with approaching rain, great red and gold banners of sunlight just pushing through. Lady Beckenham lifted her face and sniffed the air, like an old warhorse: 'Marvellous smell,' she said, 'spring countryside. So sweet. Nice old place this, I must say. Glad he brought me here.' She blew her nose again, then said, 'Ah. Yes.'

'What?' said Celia, intrigued by the change of tone.

'That.'

'What?'

She pointed: it was Izzie and Kit, wandering through the bottom meadow, talking intently, his hand in hers as she led him carefully along the river bank.

'I've been meaning to talk to you about that. They're inseparable these days. Could be a bit of a worry.'

'Mama, Izzie's a child.'

'She's fourteen. Growing up. If you've got any sense, you'll keep an eye on it.'

'Yes, all right,' said Celia, 'if you say so.'

She spoke lightly; but her heart was suddenly and horribly chilled.

Chapter 42

'It's just so bloody unfair. Rotten. I'm finding it almost unbearable.'

'Giles—' Helena looked at him helplessly. 'Giles, try to—'

'Don't start that.'

'What?'

'Trying to make me feel better. I really can't stand it. Boy, Jay, even Barty, all off, all doing their bit. And me – the marvellous lieutenant, with his MC, confined to—'

'Barracks?' She smiled, she couldn't help it; he glared at her.

'Helena, it's not funny.'

'I know. I'm sorry. Very sorry. But at least you're at the War Office. You have got a job—'

'Oh, sure. A wonderfully important job. Bloody admin. I'm not a cripple, Helena, I'm perfectly fit, perfectly capable of leading my men.'

'Giles, that isn't quite true.'

'Of course it's true. Oh, what's the point of talking to you. You can't have any idea how I feel. I'm going out.'

'Well, take care. It's nearly dark. We could have another raid.'

'Good. I hope one gets me.'

He stalked out of the house; Helena watched him as he went. She did understand – or she thought she did – how he must feel. To be forbidden to take part in the invasion of France, in the biggest combined military operation of the war, for a man who had proven himself so fine and so brave a soldier – this was clearly agony for Giles. After a life that had been, if not a failure then certainly not conspicuous for its success, he had found it, found his way, and gloriously so. Only to have it barred to him at this incomparably historic hour. It was very cruel. But – and Helena could see this very clearly – he was handicapped by his leg. He might have worked himself into a state of health and fitness by sheer determination and physical effort in the gymnasium, but the fact remained he could no longer run, at least not run fast, it was more of a scuttle, the bad leg pulling along behind him. There was no way he could go into battle.

'You'd be a handicap, old chap, to your men and your fellow officers,' his commanding officer had said. 'Know how you feel, of course, but the company must come first. Sorry! We'll find you something, don't worry.'

'Something!' Giles had roared at Helena that night. 'Bloody something! Pen-pushing at Whitehall, I daresay.'

And it had gone on; his fury had not abated, and much of it seemed to be directed at her and the rest of his family.

'This is it, then.'

'Yes. I'm afraid it is.'

She managed to smile at him, to stay brave. 'Take the greatest care of yourself.'

'I will.'

'It could be awfully dangerous.'

'Oh – phooey. This is Lucky Lytton you're talking to. Give me a kiss. And you take care of yourself, Victoria Halifax. Shortly to be Victoria Lytton, jolly shortly now. Just the minute we've got this lot on the run.'

'I will.'

'London's got a bit dodgier lately. I want you to remember that.'

'I could hardly forget it.'

It was true; the bombing had begun again. It wasn't quite like the Blitz in size and intensity, but it was serious. Ever since January, there had been raids, the sirens wailing through the night again; people were back in the shelters and in the underground, and anyone wanting to find accommodation out of London was offered free rail travel. There had been a great deal more damage done. Whole streets had been destroyed once more, both Wormwood Scrubs and Wandsworth prisons seriously damaged, Horseguards Parade badly hit, even Number Ten had had its windows blasted out; and – especially sad to Lyttons and the rest of the book world – in February, the London Library was hit, with 20,000 books lost.

Jay was off to Scotland, for some intensive training. He was still flying, training for a large-scale airborne operation – of which he did not yet know the details. He was still a lieutenant (but earmarked for promotion to captain) and a platoon commander.

As he travelled up that night on the train, there was talk, endless speculation, of when it would be: next week, next month, in May, June . . .

And of course nobody quite knew when: not exactly. Not even Eisenhower, Supreme Commander of Operation Overlord, as it was called, and his team, not even Mountbatten, not even Churchill.

But the country was getting ready: everyone joined in the endeavour with a passion which was somehow felt and shared.

'I'm going to work in the munitions factory in Slough,' said Adele to Lady Beckenham. 'I feel I just have to do my bit, rather than taking stupid photographs.'

'Quite right. They'll be glad to have you, I'm sure.'

'If it's all right to leave the children every day . . .'

'Don't worry about the children. They need victory more than anyone.'

She rather liked the factory work: she wished she had done it before. Sitting there, in the vast building, with hundreds of other women, the sheer energy of the operation impressed her. She was making shells; the noise was incredible. Lost in it somewhere, 'Music While You Work' and other entertainment were transmitted through the loudspeakers. She could not imagine how anyone could hear it.

They had taken her on gratefully. Every factory was working at full strength. Later, she learned that thirteen thousand aircraft, seventeen thousand tanks and millions of bombs and shells were being turned out in those few frantic months. She only knew that, as she sat there, the noise of the machinery throbbing through her, she felt, for the very first time since she had been on the road down through France, a part of something vast and infinitely important.

Every day, as she travelled to work on the bus, people talked about the clearing of roads and railways for the invasion traffic, of how people in Sussex and Kent were being moved out of their homes, of how every building was being commandeered, of the millions of troops being moved into place. The air itself during that lovely spring throbbed with energy, with a physical excitement.

And there was something else too, Adele thought: the invasion of France, if successful – and how could it not be, with so much now on their side – would free Paris; and free Luc. It might not be so very much longer. At the very least then she would know . . .

'Goodbye, my darling.'

'Goodbye, Boy. Take great care of yourself.'

'Of course. No one else to do it.'

'Boy, it's not funny.'

'I know. But it is exciting. Get them on the run at last. God, I can't wait.'

'How much do you know?'

'Not a lot. Only that it'll be soon. End of May, early June. And that's an educated guess. We'll be told a bit more when I get there. Although not much. After all, as Mountbatten said, your most crucial weapon in an invasion is surprise.'

'And you'll be—'

'Oh, God knows. Somewhere in France. On a tank. Riding high. Don't worry, darling, I'll be absolutely fine.'

'I do hope so,' said Venetia soberly.

He was back with the Grenadiers: a company commander, on one of the armoured divisions. There was to be a great deal of training, on beaches and in rough waters: 'Almost as dangerous as the real thing,' his CO had said with relish. He imagined that either Normandy or the Pas de Calais would be their target. He rather hoped Calais; the Normandy beaches would not exactly offer a lot of shelter.

The thought of it all ending was almost unimaginable. He viewed with a certain astonishment the world where he had passed his days, on golf courses and at race meetings, even when he had been running his own auction rooms. God knew what he would do when the war was over. It would certainly have to be pretty absorbing. The more so since his wife, his empty-headed, idle wife, had become a dynamic, single-minded, powerful executive, with the entire economic running of Lyttons resting on her narrow, elegant shoulders. She was going to take some living up to. It was a slightly disturbing thought.

Well, it wasn't over yet. They had a few little dust-ups to get through first. He had asked Giles for a drink at the Reform the night before he went; it was a mistake; Giles was morose, almost hostile.

'I feel so absolutely bloody useless,' he said. 'And angry. I just don't know how I'm going to get through it.'

'You shouldn't feel angry,' Boy said. 'You've done your bit and more. And you'll be doing something pretty useful, from what you've said.'

'I'm sorry,' said Giles, glaring at him, 'but it's awfully easy for you to say that. Off to the front line, seeing the thing through. While I sit in Whitehall twiddling dials. Or my thumbs. It's so bloody unfair.'

'Giles, old chap—'

'Don't old chap me,' said Giles, 'I'm a bloody good soldier—'

'No one's doubting it.'

'And how does one slightly gammy leg change that? Change my ability to inspire, to direct, to lead—'

'And run, Giles?'

'I'm sorry?'

'This is going to be an appalling battle. Really appalling. A bit like our fight out in the desert, a killing match, as Monty put it. Anyone not absolutely one hundred per cent physically fit is going to be a serious liability. You must see that, Giles—'

But Giles had gone, leaving his whisky and soda half drunk, the door of the club door banging furiously. Boy stared after him, feeling, for once, a certain sympathy with Helena.

'We're being moved down to the south coast,' said Barty, 'to Rye.'

'Oh God. God, I wish you didn't have to do this dangerous thing.'

'Well, I do. And I'm glad.'

'When are you going?'

'In a week. We'll be in tents, apparently.'

'Tents. It sounds horribly vulnerable.'

'Yes, well, there certainly aren't any underground shelters there. Apparently we'll have Morrison shelters.'

'In the tents?'

'Yes.'

'Oh, Barty. I wish I could stop you.'

'Well, you can't. Any more than anyone can stop any of it.'

'And – do you get any more leave?'

'Yes. Twenty-four hours. Sunday to Monday.'

'Thank God. I'll be waiting for you.'

He had a key to her house; he had filled it with treasures for her. Fine furniture – but perfectly chosen, nothing large, nothing ostentatious, some exquisite chairs, a Regency table, some Persian wall rugs, a French mirror, some paintings.

At first she was angry: 'This is my house, how dare you take it over?'

'Barty, why not? It's ours now, everything is ours, life is ours, this is mine and my houses are yours, it's so simple, why can't you see?'

And later, when she had recovered from the shock, she was touched, touched by the care and thought he had put into his choices. Later, other more personal things were waiting for her, a diamond watch from Cartier, a mink coat, silk negligees, a drawer full of nylons, Chanel scent . . .

'It's disgraceful,' she said, sitting on the bed, laughing, 'we are

609

supposed to be frugal, not spending our money on luxuries. How did you get it all anyway?'

'I never can quite see that, you know. How not spending money can help to win the war. Anyway, I brought some from New York, the jewellery and the lingerie. Knowing that I would see you. And the rest – well, you know there is a black market, you can get anything in this benighted country of yours if you can pay for it. Now, I would like you to put that negligee on. And then take it off again. I chose it especially.'

She had had a pregnancy scare; God knew she had been going the right way about it. Her period was very late, and she felt nauseated all the time. It was a dreadful prospect. At least – well, yes, it was.

She saw her doctor, organised a test. Three weeks went by, three long, dreadful weeks. Then the result came through: it was negative. That afternoon her period arrived.

'Told you,' said Parfitt, who had told her no such thing. 'Always holds it up, worry does. Well, what a relief.'

'Yes,' said Barty, 'yes, what a relief.'

Yet against all logic, part of her was disappointed. She had told Parfitt everything; she had been unexpectedly supportive.

'I never thought that John was right for you, Miller. Too – soft. You're a toughie, underneath all that gentility.'

'Oh dear,' said Barty, laughing, 'genteel's the last thing I want to be.'

'Well, that's what you are. Sorry. Anyway, I told you, change the name and not the letter and all that. What's this new one's name?'

'Elliott,' said Barty.

'Barty Elliott. Very nice. You going to marry him?'

'No,' said Barty firmly.

'Not even if you're preggers?'

'No.'

'Why not? Thought you said he was rich?'

'He is.'

'And mad about you?'

'He is.'

'Well, then—'

'It just wouldn't be a good idea,' said Barty.

'You're barmy.'

She hadn't told Laurence of her fears. But she had to explain that she had been ill, had fainted on parade twice more, had been in bed for several days, because it meant missing a forty-eight-hour leave which she had arranged to spend in London with him.

He asked her immediately if she was pregnant, his voice hopeful.

'No. I'm not.'

'Are you sure?'

'Quite, quite sure.'

'I want it more than anything,' he said, 'anything in the world. For you to have my babies. Well, there's plenty of time.'

'Laurence—'

'Now then, when can we—'

'Laurence, I've got to go. Sorry.'

She put the phone back on its rest, leaned against the wall feeling faint again. Faint with distress – and with fear. It was the fear that was making her ill: nothing else. He was not going to be fobbed off for very much longer. And there was no knowing, no knowing at all, what he might do.

She had written to John again: and finally posted it. The same short, sweet, dreadful words: that this time he would read. She had been prompted, not only by Sebastian's wise, calm, words, but by Laurence's threat to write himself.

'You wouldn't.'

'Barty, I would. It'd be a kindness, put him out of his misery. And me, come to that.'

'You don't know where he is.'

'I'd find him.'

She believed that: Laurence's obsessional determination and the full weight of American Intelligence would make a powerful combination.

She waited after that for some kind of peace, of relief, but it didn't come. She felt as wretched as ever: her dilemma over, but imagining every moment John's horror, his rage, his grief, waited for a letter back, the vituperative letter she deserved, castigating her. That didn't come either.

And she told Laurence she had written to him.

She did that by letter; there was no question of seeing him for several weeks and she had thought, in any case, it was the easier way.

She was wrong. He wrote demanding that she marry him at once, that there were no further obstacles, and when she said she couldn't, he unleashed an assault on her, a savage assault, of demands, assertions, accusations, a bombardment of letters, day after day, some so passionately loving that she felt the power of them physically, some

611

so angry and abusive she felt distraught and afraid. Followed by others, often the same day, remorseful, self-abasing, begging her to forgive him.

That was what had frightened her: those letters. She would sit reading them, the first absolute proof that he had not – of course – changed, had not become easy, more reasonable, less manipulative.

And every day, she wondered why and how she could love him so much: and what on earth could become of the pair of them.

'And what of you,' she said to him now, 'in this endeavour?'

'I don't know yet. I'm hoping to go with them.'

'What? On the invasion?'

'Yes.'

'But, Laurence, this is going to be the most dreadful of battles, surely they won't take you—'

'On the contrary. Information will be crucial to us. Any high-ranking prisoners could hold extremely vital information. No, I expect to go.'

She said nothing, assuming, hoping, that he was as usual exaggerating.

'What's Eisenhower like?' she said.

'Extraordinary. A superb soldier and a most remarkable man. He has the ability to strike up such rapport with people. He doesn't think of himself as an American, or indeed as British, or Canadian or French or Polish. He's just a soldier, doing that job, and determined to do it so well that we win. I admire him enormously.'

There were very few people Laurence admired.

She managed somehow, by pulling rank, exaggerating her ill-health, to wangle a last two days' leave. London was strangely empty.

'They've all gone,' said Laurence, 'all the military anyway. And a good few others as well. People are scared. It's all you hear – what hell it's going to be, when the invasion starts, that London will be bombed night and day, we shall have to live in the shelters . . .'

'But you're still here.'

'I'm still here. And so are you. So what else matters?'

'Nothing,' she said feebly. 'Nothing at all.'

'Good. I have plenty of plans. And, you know, suddenly you can get taxis, the restaurants are empty, so are the nightclubs, we are going to have a marvellous time.'

°

He was adamant still that he would be going 'over with Eisenhower'.

'Are you sure?'

'As sure as I can be.'

'Oh,' she said staring at him, and it was a moment of absolute revelation, of how very much she loved him, 'oh, Laurence, no.'

'Won't you be proud of me? Because that's what I want.'

He was like a child, she thought wearily, a demanding, spoilt child.

'Ye-es. But—'

'Oh, Barty,' he said, his voice impatient, 'you're very hard to please.'

'It's not that,' she said. 'Of course I'll be proud of you. You know that. But—'

'But what?'

'I shall be frightened,' she said very quietly, 'so frightened for you. So frightened I shall lose you.'

There was a long silence; then he said, his voice gentler than she had ever heard it, 'That is very good to know.'

'It's true.'

'But—' he added, suddenly brisk, 'I shall be perfectly safe. I'm not going to have to fight my way in, you know. VIP treatment and all that sort of thing.'

She was silent: knowing he was, to an extent, a large extent, lying.

'I love you, Barty. Very, very much.'

'I – love you, Laurence. Also very much.'

He smiled at her. 'This has been the most extraordinary time,' he said, 'I shall never forget it, as long as I live.'

'Nor shall I.'

She stood there, looking at him, thinking of it, of the strange, difficult, joyful, wretched time, of what he had done to her and to her life. Then, 'Tell me what plans you have for the next two days,' she said.

'They were quite extensive. Now I think I would like simply to stay here.'

But she made him tell her; and agreed they should do at least some of it.

There was still no word from John.

She was billeted near Rye in the last week of May; they were under canvas and sleeping in tents of four, pitched in a cherry orchard. The promised Morrison shelters, protecting them from the shells, formed a sort of tunnel inside the tents. There were two camp beds in each, into which they had to crawl every night.

Their steel helmets had to be worn at all times, even down to the village on their evenings off; every morning they would count the chalk marks on them to see how many hits they had notched up in the night. They were working now with magnetic ammunition, so the strike rate was much higher.

She could truthfully say they were all too busy to think about what might happen to them, too busy even to notice the noise and the sight of the shells. As long as you could shout and could hear someone and as long as they could hear you, that was all that was required.

The security was ferocious, so great was the terror of discovery. Barty had had to sign a certificate declaring on her honour that any mail she sent (limited to the most urgent) related only to 'private and family concerns'.

Ten years later, Barty edited a history of that week, the week of Operation Overlord, when the south coast seemed to contain nothing but troops, troops drilled, exercised and trained into absolute readiness; when the great mass of trucks, tanks and lorries that had filled the roads in an endless line for weeks had finally come to a halt; when every hotel, every building, every house had been requisitioned; when every beach was covered with great rolls of barbed wire; when every field was khaki coloured with army tents; when every port was filled with naval vessels, and with assault and landing craft; when a temporary pipeline was already in place under the Channel, to carry a million gallons of petrol daily to France; when the extraordinary half-constructed Mulberry Harbours were loaded on to landing craft, ready to be towed on to the French beaches and provide shelter for the great armada of invading ships; when an elaborate set of fake preparations were in force, for an attack on the Pas de Calais; when the whole country was becalmed, holding its breath: and when General Eisenhower and his staff sat helplessly waiting for a go-ahead from that most capricious of enemy tyrants: the English weather.

They still had no knowledge of the actual day: it was impossible. Decent conditions in the Channel were an absolute necessity; hourly forecasts were brought to Eisenhower by the Met office. They needed a day to give the go-ahead, to set the thing in motion when there was a certainty of a day of calm to follow. And there was no such certainty. A classic early June brought a severe depression, rain and high winds. A second depression was following on its heels.

It seemed hopeless. The men waited; waited on their ships, in their tents, in a long silence which fed their fear. They read, they smoked, they played cards, they wrote letters to their wives and sweethearts. And began to think they would never go: even High Command began to fear the whole thing would have to be called off.

And then the miracle happened; there was a break in the weather. Or rather one was coming. It would arrive late on Monday, continue through Tuesday. Early on 5 June it was decided.

Eisenhower said to his driver as he came out and got into his car, 'D-Day is on. Nothing can stop us now.'

And so it began.

Jay Lytton, with D Company under the command of Major John Howard, was one of the first to leave from Dorset, in his glider fleet, on the evening of 5 June, their objective being an air assault on a vital bridge over the Caen Canal, immortalised afterwards as Pegasus Bridge. Its capture and that of its neighbour was essential to the entire D-Day exercise; they carried a lateral road vital to the supply of ammunition, fuel and rations to the beachhead. The cloud was thick, and the conditions frightful; their towing tugs, the Halifax bombers, were flying almost three hundred feet ahead of them, at 6,000 feet, to delude the German radars into thinking this was just another bombing raid on Caen. Every possible skill was called into play. Precise landing position was crucial: too high and they would smash into the roadway embankment, landing short would alert bridge defences, and to top it all they had to navigate a belt of fifty-foot trees. They had studied the landing ground from a precise scale model for the past three days; Jay was in the lead glider, absolutely focused on his task, pushing through the clouds, waiting for the release 8,000 feet over the Normandy coast, felt nothing at all, no fear, no excitement even, only a white-hot concentration. They were released three miles short of the French coast; the angle of descent was horribly steep. They managed it with extraordinary accuracy, their parachute brakes marvellously silent, their only obstacle a herd of cows, disturbed in their cud-chewing slumber and stampeding, mercifully quietly, away from the planes.

Jay's crew was the only one of the three to land in the right place; but the courage and savagery of their attack made up for their missing numbers. They landed at 12.16 and only ten minutes later, the bridge was in their hands, the first vital objective of D-Day achieved. And although later there was extremely heavy fighting, the bridge was held.

But then, as Jay told Victoria later, Howard had had an unsuspected weapon: quite apart from his own remarkable skills, his superb equipment, the courage of his men, he had Lucky Lytton in his company.

It was as well they had not been aware of the odds: losses of glider pilots were estimated at six or seven out of ten. Gordon Robinson did not, of course, know that, but he knew of the appalling danger, and as he sat all that day listening to the radio reports, with no idea where Jay was, or whether he was alive or dead, he was thankful for the very first time that LM was not with him.

Boy never told Venetia very much about that dreadful day; rather as he had with his desert experiences, he buried the worst of it deep within himself.

He had survived the horrors of the crossing, the vile sea, the small boats lifted six or seven feet on the waves, the seasickness, the ghastly terror of the landing, had witnessed the craft just in front of them running into an underwater mine, and somehow made it inland. He managed three miles that first day, losing many of his men on the way. Later, he listened to tales told by the Americans, who had undoubtedly got the worst of it; it was said that on Omaha you could walk on the dead from one end of that beach to the other. Of the one hundred and thirty thousand troops ashore that day, nine thousand were dead.

But Boy survived, had witnessed the incredible gratitude and relief of the French as they made their way inland, while feeling deeply sickened by the slaughter of the small towns they passed, their grey stone houses and brightly flowered squares turned to blackened skeletons.

It was something quite different that haunted him, though, and more than the rest, and something he did tell Venetia: it was the sight of pretty young French girls weeping, some of them literally collapsed in grief as their German lovers were taken prisoner and marched away. That, he told her soberly, had brought home to him, more than anything, the absolute stupidity and futility of war.

Three days after D-Day, when the grim news was easing into optimism, Barty was walking exhaustedly back from the canteen after breakfast, when she was told the CO wanted her.

'Someone to see you, Sergeant Miller.'

She knew who it was immediately; and yet she knew it couldn't be, knew it was absolutely impossible, no one could do that, not even Laurence.

616

It was Laurence.

Somehow, he had pulled strings, pulled rank, talked, argued, charmed, eased his way in; and, more incredibly, eased her out.

'Only for the day, Sergeant. Back at 1800 hours.'

'How did you do that?' she said, laughing and crying at the same time as they walked down the lane. 'How could you possibly have done it?'

'Oh – you know. Colonels, even in the American army, have a certain amount of influence.'

'But you're not even a real colonel.'

'Do be quiet. Nobody knows that here. Anyway, I told them that you were my wife.'

'Oh, Laurence,' she said. 'Laurence, how could you—'

'And that I had some bad news for you. Which I wanted to deliver personally.'

'Now that is really naughty. You shouldn't lie about such things, when there is so much—'

'It's not a lie,' he said, and his voice was very gentle, as she had hardly ever heard it, 'it is bad news, I'm afraid. This came for you. I – well, I knew what it must be. So I opened it.'

Too shocked, too afraid to be angry with him, she took the envelope. An army envelope. From it fell her letter, her letter to John. And a letter from his CO deeply regretting his death. And the fact that her last letter had never reached him.

'I don't know why I feel so sad,' he said, holding her tenderly while she wept, 'but I do. So very sad. For you and with you.'

'No,' she said, 'no, I don't either.'

'I would have expected to be feeling something quite different. But I'm not.'

'Well – thank you. Yes. Oh, God. Oh, Laurence. Well, at least he never—'

'No, he never did.'

They were in a hotel in Playden. She was still confused as to how he had got there at all.

'I got a train, they wouldn't let me get off at Rye, I had to go on to the next station. And I walked back. It was only a few miles. It didn't seem like anything at all.'

'Oh, Laurence. Thank you so much for coming.'

'Now let's not get carried away,' he said, a smile beginning to appear. 'It wasn't the only reason I came. It was so clearly a God-given opportunity to see you. Besides, I have some other news.'

'What?'

'I am going over tomorrow.'

'To France?'

'Yes. It seems they have work for me to do.'

She was too exhausted, too shocked to feel anything; she sat silent, looking at him, then put out her hand to touch his face.

'I mustn't ask anything, must I?'

'Oh, you can if you like,' he said cheerfully. 'I hardly think you're going to get on the phone to Nazi HQ. Go ahead.'

'No,' she said, 'I don't think I want to. I think I'm going to pretend you're still safely in London. In my – our house.'

'Very good! I like our house. I like all our houses. Now. I have a few surprises for you. I didn't want the whole day to pass in a vale of tears. First is – well, wait there.'

She waited; he reappeared after a few minutes bearing an ice bucket and a bottle of champagne.

'I brought the champagne with me, I didn't quite trust them to have it here. But they managed to put it on ice. Now. Take a glass. Here's to us. What shall be the toast? What would you suggest? Mr and Mrs Elliott?'

'Laurence—'

'Now, I have something else for you. Here. I would have given it to you before, but I've been having it sized for you. Give me your hand.'

She held out her hand. He smiled at her, excitedly, like a child, produced a small box from his pocket, opened it.

'Laurence! Oh, but it's – what is it? I know it's a ring, but—'

'It's more than that. It's something very special. It is – it was my mother's. My mother's engagement ring, given her by my father. Now I think – yes. Perfect. I stole one of your rings, gave it to Cartier – to size it. Your hands are very thin,' he added almost severely, 'you should eat more.'

'I – don't know what to say,' she said.

'Yes, you do.'

'I love you. Will that do?'

'It'll do.'

The ring was not the huge solitaire she might have expected; it was a flower of jewels, an aquamarine, set in a circle of small diamonds, on a narrow pink-gold band.

'My father said, apparently, that he chose the aquamarine to match her eyes. She had extraordinary eyes, my mother—'

618

'Like yours,' said Barty.

'Yes. Greener, though.'

'Like Maud's?' She spoke without thinking.

'Can we not spoil the day?' He was the other Laurence suddenly, scowling, dark; Barty leaned forward, kissed him.

'I'm sorry. I didn't mean—'

'I know,' he said, clearly with difficulty.

'Laurence, I love it so much. And it's so – so wonderful of you. To give it to me. Your mother's ring. I can't think why – I mean, I know what it means to you. I can't even begin to thank you.'

'Well, there is no one else in the world,' he said, sounding slightly impatient, 'who could possibly have it.'

'Maybe. I'm very, very, truly, truly overwhelmed. Oh dear, I'm not sounding very articulate.'

'I love you,' he said, 'however you sound.'

'And I shall never, ever take it off. As long as I live.'

'Now that is a very good promise.'

She sat, alternately staring at the ring on her finger and then smiling at him; and then suddenly found herself crying again, crying with the loss of John, who in her way she had loved, though with a gentle, lesser love, with the cruelty of his death and with relief that he had never had to know of her betrayal: she told Laurence so.

'Do you think that's very wicked?'

'Don't ask me,' he said, 'it's you who are the good one. I am so absolutely wicked I can't possibly be expected to tell one act from another.'

'You don't really think that, do you?'

'What?'

'That you're absolutely wicked?'

'Oh, yes, I do think so,' he said, sounding almost complacent. 'I've known it since I was a very young man.'

'Laurence—'

'Yes, Barty?'

'You are not absolutely wicked. I can't let you say that. So much of you is good, generous and kind and thoughtful and – and loving. It's a nonsense for you to deny it.'

'Not bad and mean and cruel and hateful? Surely that is what you think? You've told me that. And more than once.'

'I wish you would forget it.'

'I can't forget anything you've said to me,' he said. 'I remember it all, all you said from that first night in New York, and onwards from there. Some of it good, some of it bad, some of it foolish, some of it interesting. But it is all here, in my head.'

'Oh, dear,' she said with a sigh.

'Don't you remember everything I have said? I shall be very upset if you don't.'

'Of course. Every single word,' she said smiling at him. 'What else can I say? I certainly don't want to upset you. I know how dangerous that is. But – Laurence, what are you doing?'

'Drawing the curtains,' he said, 'and then locking the door. And then I am going to ask you to remove that hideous tunic. I am getting tired of this philosophical talk. I have never found it amusing. Now, we don't have very long, remember, only a day. Your commanding officer said so. Only a little over half a day now. Not very long at all. Come here, Barty. Come to bed with me.'

Afterwards, she could see what they had been doing: learning one another by heart. So that for the rest of their lives, and for however long that might be, they would remember, remember the feel, the sight, the sound of one another. That time, that day became always; not one afternoon but a lifetime.

Slowly, sweetly, they explored one another, as if it had never been done before: as if it was the first time. They looked, touched, smiled, wept; joined, moved, rose, cried out with pleasure – and afterwards laughed with joy.

'That was love,' said Laurence, holding her, kissing her, 'that was love, here in this room, we had it, we heard it and we saw it.'

'Yes,' she said, smiling into his eyes, 'that was most certainly love.'

Lying there, they talked: a great deal. They contemplated their lives, and what they had accomplished with one another, all that they had enjoyed and achieved, the things that they regretted. They told one another things hitherto unshared, with anyone; looked at each other, astonished, at these new discoveries; and it was a long journey they took together, back into their troubled, difficult past, and thus forward to their hopeful present, their tremulous future.

'I regret only a few thousand things,' Laurence said, lifting one hand, kissing the fingers one by one.

'A few thousand? So many?'

'Yes. The few thousand days I have not spent with you. Everything else is unimportant.'

'Yes,' she said, 'yes, I think it is.'

◦

620

Finally, the time spent, they left; he walked her back to her camp, kissed her briefly, told her he loved her – and walked away. And she watched him and she was still so full of the happiness and the pleasure of him, she could not feel anything else.

Not even afraid.

Chapter 43

It had been forbidden when they were small: it was felt to be in some way unsuitable. They had done it just the same of course, had been punished for it if they were caught, smacked quite hard on their small bare bottoms by the first nanny – the one who had done other bad things, so bad in fact, like ill-treating Barty, that she had been sacked, without any notice – and then been forbidden sugar on their porridge, stories at bedtime, threatened with their mother's wrath by the beloved second nanny.

It had all been quite useless. They had wanted, had needed even, to sleep together, in each other's arms, curled into bed like puppies, for quite a long time, and had gone on doing so in times of trial right through their childhood. And tonight, Adele had needed that and Venetia had known it and welcomed her with wordless sympathy and held her all night long, sleepless, weeping, grieving with her, the letter lying between them on the coverlet of the bed.

It came one day early in October; she had been waiting for it so long that she hardly recognised its credence as it lay on the hall table at Cheyne Walk. It seemed like yet another figment of her imagination, a fragment of hope, a piece of a dream.

But it was real. It was absolutely real.

She had read everything about the liberation of Paris of course, had devoured it, not so much the triumphal entry of the Allies, the pretty girls climbing on to the tanks, kissing the American soldiers, the ecstatic crowds, the bursting doors in the metro, the dancing in the streets, de Gaulle's proud march the next day up the Champs-Elysées, the service of thanksgiving at Notre-Dame, the replacement of the swastika by the *tricolore,* and of course the rumours that the sewers had been mined, that General Choltitz had been ordered to first torch Paris, then to blow it up as he left (but disobeyed).

It was the darker things that haunted her: the rough justice of the witch hunts, the acts of revenge, the punishment of the women guilty of the *collaboration horizontale,* of sleeping with the Germans, the shaving of their heads (referred to with harsh Parisian irony as *la coiffure de 44*) and the branding of swastikas on their breasts as they were paraded through the streets; the execution of the black market-eers and informers and corrupt government officials, and of Georges Suarez, editor of *Aujourd'hui,* and Jean Herold Paquis, the 'radio traitor'; the brief arrest of Coco Chanel, famous for her anti-semitic views, and the longer detention of Sacha Guitry the actor, and that of the actress Arletty, who had had a German lover, but who was released (her head shaven, or so it was said) to film *Les Enfants du Paradis;* and perhaps most of all the establishment of the Bichot Hospital at the Porte St Ouen, where survivors of the camps were being sent.

Was Luc there? Was he still in hiding? Was he not in hiding at all, had he managed to survive those years? Was he in one of the detention camps? Was he alive anywhere at all?

She tried: she wrote to Mme André, she telephoned their apartment endlessly, she tried writing to, cabling, telephoning the Constantine offices, while knowing it was pointless, useless, that they had gone before the fall of France.

She was restless, wretched, more unhappy still than she would have believed. She couldn't sleep, and when she did, she had wild dreams, in which she saw herself waking with a start to see her bedroom door opening and Luc walking in, or running to the telephone and hearing his voice. Only, of course, in reality, she saw nothing and heard nothing.

Nothing at all.

She had left the factory and returned to do some occasional photographic work in London; but a sadness pervaded her work, she had no relish for it and it showed. She still spent most of her time at Ashingham, keeping her grandmother company, taking her part at least notionally against the pompous, heavy-handed new Lord Beckenham. Lucas had no idea, of course, that Paris had been freed, that their father might now be restored to them, but Noni could read the papers and had asked her several times if they could now go home. Home! That was so much part of her trouble: she had no idea where it was.

And then the letter came.

It was from a neighbour of Luc's – he said. Although she did not recognise the address, in the thirteenth arrondissement, far from the Place St-Sulpice or even from Passy.

Nor did she recognise the name: Bernard Touvier. But it was addressed to her at Cheyne Walk, presumably given to him by Luc as the surest way of finding her.

It was in French. She had come in from a long day, working with *Vogue;* she was tired and she felt strangely calm as she took it into the morning room, even pouring herself a glass of sherry, before beginning to read.

Dear Mam'selle Adele,

Forgive my calling you by this name; but it was how Luc always spoke of you, and it will persuade you that this letter is truly from a friend.

I am afraid there is no easy way of saying this; I am so very sorry to have to tell you that Luc is dead.

From the autumn of 1942, he was in hiding. He and the friend and colleague with whom he had been lodging, Jean Marc Triolet, together with Monique, Jean Marc's wife, moved down into the cellars running beneath their street. They were not alone down there, there was another family in another section of the cellar, although I did not realise that then. There were many such hiding places set up by Jews at this time: and many brave people helping them. I would like to tell you I was one of those, helping Luc and Jean Marc, but I was not; although I did from time to time procure food for them, and books and newspapers, so essential to people in hiding. They had a very good friend, a shopkeeper called Edouard leClerc, who occupied another apartment in the building; it was he who took them food each day, and other necessities of life. He was part of a large Resistance organisation, working within Paris.

Luc and the Triolets had been there for nine months when they were betrayed. I believe it was the concierge, as it so often was; if so, she has now met a deservedly appropriate fate and has been imprisoned herself.

It happened one Sunday morning, it was 24 June, I think you would wish to know the date. The scene was one we came to know well. I only witnessed it because I had been suffering during the night from a severe headache and had decided to go out for a walk and to get some fresh air.

The Gestapo arrived, in three lorries. They gained access to the building easily, and then we heard them beating on doors, shouting. They always did it in areas by buildings, and streets.

They would have a list and work through it. Usually at night, sometimes like this, early in the morning. After only a few minutes, there were many people on the street, all wearing their yellow stars; families, couples, old people on their own. Luc was not with them, or Jean Marc, I thought perhaps they were safe. But then there was some delay and suddenly they had Luc. And Jean Marc and Monique too. They were all very quiet, very controlled.

The Germans started pushing people into the truck; Luc was at the side of the group. A man and his wife were told to get in, and as they did so, they glanced back. The Germans did not see that glance, they were too busy hustling people into the trucks, checking off names, but I did and so did Luc; there, almost hidden in the doorway, was a small girl, perhaps five or six. Her parents had obviously hidden her when they heard the Gestapo coming and she had been told to stay where she was, but was too small and too frightened to obey. There was a small truck just by the door; a truck with a tarpaulin over the back. I looked at it, and I noticed so did Luc.

Suddenly, there was a diversion; another truck-load of Gestapo arrived, shouting, obviously with orders or instructions for the first; Luc was still standing on the street on the edge of the group of prisoners, they were all looking at their lists, shouting at one another, counting, almost relaxed, sharing cigarettes.

Everyone was distracted just for a moment; in that moment he did it. It was so brave, so futile and yet it could – perhaps – have worked.

He moved backward, picked up the child in the doorway, and threw her into the truck, under the tarpaulin. All in one swift movement. He might have got away with it even then, had she not screamed; but they heard that and realised what he had done.

They shot him: there and then. The only comfort I can offer you, Mam'selle, is that he died at once. His fate might have been much worse. I am sure it is hard for you to accept that, but from what we have learned since of the conditions at Drancy, where the Jews were sent, and worse, after Drancy, I can say that with confidence.

He loved you very much, Mam'selle. I never had a conversation with him that did not lead to you, his Mam'selle

Adele. More than once he asked me to notify you if anything should happen to him. So I am sorry to bring you this news, but I fear I must do so.

If you ever come to Paris in the future, do please visit me.
Your friend,
Bernard Touvier

She read it once more, then sat in the growing dusk, waiting for Venetia to come home.

Venetia understood it all so very well: there was no need to explain anything, not so much her grief, but her rage, her furious impotent rage; and after that, her pride in Luc,

'That is what you have to feel the most,' she said, holding Adele while she wept and railed, 'you have to feel proud. It was so brave, what he did, so amazingly brave, and you must make sure the children know that too, how brave he was.'

'Oh, yes,' said Adele, her voice raw with pain, 'that will make it all all right, won't it? "Now listen, children, I want you to know that your papa was very, very brave. You'll never see him again, he's dead, but he was very brave. And you never said goodbye to him because your *maman* saw to that" – Venetia, how could I have done that, how could I have not even let them say goodbye to him?'

'Because if you had, you'd never have gone. And if you'd not gone, you'd have been imprisoned within weeks. And your fate would have been as bad, worse than his.'

'But that's not the point. I didn't leave because the Germans were coming, if I had we would have said goodbye, I left because I was so angry with him and so hurt and all those absurd things. I behaved as if I were just having a fit of pique and would go back when I felt better or he sent some flowers, instead of taking his children away from him for ever.'

'But, Adele, it doesn't make any difference why you did it, you did it, the result was the same.'

'It does, it does make a difference,' said Adele, her voice rising to a wail, 'it makes a difference to me and it made a difference to him—'

'Dell, darling, you did have a reason, he was – cheating on you.'

'Oh, so that's unforgivable, is it?' Adele sat up suddenly, her face odd, twisted with rage. 'Your husband never cheated on you, I suppose, your husband, your suddenly wonderful husband, he never had a mistress or lied to you, did he? You forgave him, and I would have

626

forgiven Luc. I did forgive him. Over and over again I forgave him.'

'And he knew. He knew you forgave him.'

'No. Well – yes. Yes, I suppose so.' Her voice was quieter. 'I hope so. Thank God for those messages, if it hadn't been for them—'

'Them and his letter, the one that came from New York. They all told you the same thing. That he loved you and forgave you. And that he knew you'd forgiven him.'

'I can't believe,' said Adele, settling back with a great sigh, 'how people can be so wicked. How does it happen, Venetia, how do people get that way? Do we all have that potential for evil? Is it some kind of ghastly disease that runs through a people, could it have happened here, those awful, dreadful things?'

'I don't know. When you see the power Mosley had here, just in that short time, you wonder. Maybe we're herd animals, all of us, maybe under the skin we do what the herd and its leader do, and the weakest go to the wall.'

'It's such a horrible thought. That Lucas, for instance, sweet, gentle little Lucas could grow up to be a bully and a thug. Just because some situation, some threatening, dangerous situation could command it.'

'Oh, no,' Venetia suddenly smiled, 'he won't. He wouldn't. Because he's Luc's son. And it didn't happen to Luc, did it? He was in a threatening, deadly dangerous situation, and he didn't go under, he didn't give in to it. He died trying to save a little girl. Knowing he would possibly – probably die. So – think of that, keep thinking of that. Be proud of him. Make your children proud of him, tell them as much as you can, as soon as you can.'

'Yes,' said Adele, and for the first time she smiled, 'yes, you're right. I will.'

She decided to hold a little ceremony in the chapel at Ashingham. Her earlier thoughts of converting to Judaism herself, and bringing the children up in the faith, had gone; she could only cling to what she knew and found comforting herself. She wanted only the children there and Venetia and Kit, who was still living there. She would have liked her father to come, for he had always liked Luc, but she did not ask him, for she was adamant she did not want her mother. Perversely, the old hostility towards her had revived with Luc's death; Celia's dismissal of the persecution of the Jews as so much fantasy haunted her, she could scarcely bear to tell her what had happened, accepting her condolences with cool courtesy and going out of her way to avoid her.

But she wanted Lady Beckenham there, for apart from Venetia she had been more help to her than anyone, with her lack of fuss, her slightly brusque sympathy; she said she would be delighted to come and asked if she would like her to invite the organist to play: 'Not hymns or anything of course, just something to lift things a bit.'

Adele would not have thought of that and the music was greatly comforting, easing a silence which could have been bleak.

They sat in the front pew and said the Lord's Prayer and Adele said the prayer of St Ignatius; she had been afraid of feeling foolish or, worse, breaking down, but as she said the lovely words 'to give and not to count the cost, to fight and not to heed the wounds', she heard her own voice growing stronger, almost happy. The children brought flowers and lit candles, and Venetia made a little speech about Luc, about what a lovely man he had been and how brave, about how he had died saving a little girl's life and they must always remember him and be proud of him. Lady Beckenham said a few words too, about how courage was never wasted as long as it was remembered, and that fighting evil was the most important single thing anyone could do.

Adele had felt it was important for Noni and Lucas to have Luc's passing marked, however simply; while he had been alive, or certainly while she had thought he was alive, she had continued to talk about him, to remind them of their lives together, to reassure them that he was busy and happy and working in Paris and that when the war was over, they would hopefully all be together again. Lucas could hardly remember his father, but little Noni could, and she certainly remembered loving him very much, and knew there was a loss in her small life.

Adele had told them he had died, that they would not be seeing him again, had sat and held them and answered their questions; Lucas had listened politely and then asked if he could go and ride his trike, but Noni had sat with her for a long time, thinking and shedding a few tears which Adele imagined to be at least in part dutiful. And after a while she said, 'I know we haven't got him any more. But if we remember him, he won't quite go away, will he?'

'No,' said Adele, smiling at her, 'no, my darling, he won't.'

That was when she thought of having the ceremony. And afterwards, although it hurt no less, she felt eased, some order had been created in a small way out of her chaos, and while not hopeful she felt at least no longer hopeless: and able at last to look to the future just a little.

As time went by, as she learned of the worst and most dreadful excesses in the concentration camps, she was increasingly able to be thankful that Luc had died as he had.

'Imagine knowing that, knowing someone had endured that. Someone you loved. How could you bear that, how could you not go mad?'

And Venetia, as shocked and disturbed as Adele herself by the reports of three million Jews – women and children as well as men – starved, beaten, tortured and finally sent to their deaths in the gas chambers, simply by virtue of their race, agreed that you could not.

Only one thing remained now for Adele to do; and she knew it must wait for a while. To go to Paris, with the children, and to find not only Bernard Touvier, but also Mme André, and to thank them for all that they had done, and to let them know that while Luc might have died, he still lived on in his small, brave, *très chère famille*.

Chapter 44

'It's a girl, Mrs Miller. A beautiful little girl.'

Well, they would say that, wouldn't they, Barty thought, collapsing feebly back on to the bed, they were hardly likely to say she was an ugly little girl. She was mildly surprised at herself for having such a rational thought, after the long, exhausting, painful hours; thirty-six of them altogether, twenty-four in the nursing home, six strapped up in some dreadful sort of stirrup arrangement. And that had been with the best possible attention, kindly nurses and midwives, an excellent doctor. She thought of her mother, enduring the same experience – what was it, ten times? – in a tiny basement room with only the local midwife, usually unqualified, to see to her. How had she borne that? How had she borne any of it?

'Let me see her,' she said, and they handed the baby to her, wrapped in a blanket, this tiny new person, with hazy-blue eyes and a fluff of red-gold hair.

She looked down at her, at her daughter, and thought how entirely wonderful and astonishing and extraordinary it was that two people should make love, no more than that, and then that nine months later those moments of pleasure should become flesh and blood, a human creature, with a brain, a will – formidable in this case, no doubt – and the capacity to laugh, to cry, to hate and to love. And in that moment, thinking that, Barty knew, as of course she had known before, but without fully understanding it, that her life was changed for ever now, indeed it was no longer her life but their life, hers and her daughter's, to share, and to make of it what they chose.

Something else came in that moment, something she had feared might not, a great sweep of love, not love as she had known it before, with herself at its centre, but a new emotion altogether, fierce, protective, and absolutely exclusive. Whatever she did now, wherever she went, she would have this child with her and even if she was not with her, then the concern and the love would be. The universe had shifted, upturned even, and all her certainties, all her wishes and hopes had changed, refocused on this minute and absolutely important being which lay in her arms, tentatively moving and stretching itself and giving an impression at least of staring at her through her father's brilliant eyes.

'What are you going to call her?' asked the nurse, and, 'Jeanette,' said Barty firmly. 'After her grandmother.'

'That's a pretty name.'

'To be absolutely truthful,' said Barty, stroking the baby's small face, 'I don't terribly like it. But I know that's what her father would have wanted, more than anything in the world.'

The nurse clucked with sympathy.

'It's so very sad,' she said, 'to think he'll never see her. It happens all the time at the moment, we have so many of you young women here.'

'Well,' said Barty, 'it's a lot better for me than not having either of them.'

'That's true. Sad but true. Now you give me little Jeanette, I think you need a good rest. Don't look like that, she won't be far away. If you want me or her, just press this bell.' She walked to the door, then turned. 'Here's an idea for you,' she said. 'I had a cousin called Jeanette. But she was known in the family as Jenna. Maybe you could call her that.'

'Oh,' said Barty, smiling at her, suddenly sleepy. 'Oh, yes, I like that. Thank you.'

And Jenna the baby became, from that moment on.

She was of course so much more than a baby. She was all that Barty now had of Laurence; a reminder, a demonstration of love, a continuation of his line. She was a cure for loneliness and an easing of grief, she was sense, order, a promise of happiness.

Her greatest regret was not that Laurence had never seen her, but that he had not even known of her existence; the memory of his voice telling her that more than anything in the world he wanted her to have his babies had helped her immeasurably through a bad pregnancy, a difficult labour. If only, if only he had known. But they had never spoken again, never written even, after that last day; he had been killed three days later in an ambush on the approach to Cherbourg.

She had been given that news by her CO: oddly gentle.

'Apparently he left careful instructions that you should be informed as soon as possible. I'm so sorry.'

And Barty, staring at her, dry-eyed, too shocked to feel anything at all, said only, 'Thank you very much,' and went straight back on duty.

They said she could have some leave, but she refused; she felt oddly safe there. It was as if the pain was kept away, barred from her by the appalling noise, the undoubted danger. The Germans had a deadly new weapon, unleashed shortly after D-Day, the V1, known as the doodlebug, a flying bomb carried in a pilotless plane; in a country euphoric after the success of D-Day this was the revenge weapon, bringing with it a dreadful effect on morale.

They came over in their hundreds, the doodlebugs, with their very distinct noise, a stuttering, deep-throated growl; it was well known that if the noise stopped and the engine cut out, that was it, you could count fifteen and then it exploded. And they flew over exactly where Barty was, over Doodlebug Alley, as it was now known, on their way to London. The damage there was appalling, the Blitz all over again, five thousand civilians killed in June alone.

But somehow Barty was grateful: not for the bombs, but for the challenge they presented her with, the challenge of concentration, of fighting exhaustion, of keeping calm, of not giving in. And by the time the worst was over, she knew she was pregnant, and with that the worst of her grief ended too.

Many years later, she was to say that there could have been no happy outcome for her and Laurence together; that his ferocious selfishness, his obsessive demands, a personality so quixotic it verged on instability, could have created nothing but distress for both of them. But at the time, so possessed by him and by her love for him, it was almost unbearable.

She raged, she wept, she occasionally even screamed with grief; Parfitt, proving herself the very best of friends, bore the brunt of it, listening to her hour after hour, walking with her round the camp, even occasionally shouting back at her, asking her who she thought she was, that she was not the only one who had lost their man, there were three more in the camp alone. And then taking care of her when she began to be sick, covering up for her when she fainted, and finally, against all Barty's wishes, reporting her pregnancy to the CO and having her removed from the front line.

'I'm sorry, Miller,' she said, as Barty shouted at her, her face contorted with rage, 'but you're nothing but a liability, and we got a war to win. This ain't no place for you.'

Later that day, Barty apologised to her; it was a lovely day, they had the afternoon off and they were lying in the field looking up at the great ceiling of barrage balloons above the cherry trees in their orchard.

'I'm sorry,' Barty said, reaching out, taking Parfitt's hand, 'so sorry. Of course you're right. And you've been such a good friend. Forgive?'

'Yeah, all right,' said Parfitt cheerfully, 'long as you give me me hand back, people'll think we're bloody lezzies.'

She had gone back to her house in London; there was nowhere else apart from Ashingham, and she couldn't face that. Not yet anyway.

Walking in the door, the sense of Laurence hit her like a physical blow; she felt faint, staggered, had to sit down. There was a letter on the table propped against a last gift from him, an exquisite French carriage clock with decorative panels: 'This is to mark our lifetime together,' he wrote. 'I know we have said it many times but just in case you were in any doubt, I do love you to a quite extraordinary degree. Look after yourself, won't you? I need you. Laurence.'

And she sat there, holding the letter in one hand, the clock in the other, crying and wondering. How was it possible to hurt so much without failing to function altogether? And then she was reminded quite forcibly of the need to carry on: for as she sat there, she felt the most extraordinary sensation. A creeping, a fluttering, like a tiny, captive bird; which became still and then after a moment, began again; and she realised suddenly what it was, it was her baby, Laurence's baby, alive, moving, exploring her, exploring its boundaries, and she sat there, staring down at her still-flat stomach in a shock and a delight which was the first pleasure she had known for four months. And from then on things were never so bad again.

She had to tell the family of course. Celia was, as she had known she would be, calmly supportive. She made no enquiries as to who the father might be, simply said that if Barty began to feel lonely or vulnerable, she would be very welcome at either Cheyne Walk or Ashingham, and then said that if she would like to do a little proofreading it would be extremely welcome. Of all the help offered to Barty over the following few months, that was without doubt the greatest. She found work the most marvellous antidote, both to grief and her sickness, which never eased; as she said, when Jenna was finally born, not many women were still suffering from morning sickness in the final stages of labour.

In the final two months, she did move down to Ashingham; she began to feel vulnerable on her own, and the thought of giving birth in the middle of an air raid – as Venetia had done – did not appeal to her.

She moved into the Dovecot, and had the baby at the nursing home where LM had had Jay; 'I wish she had been here,' Celia said, visiting her the day after Jenna was born, 'she would have so liked the thing of history repeating itself, right down to living in the Dovecot, that's where she was before Jay was born, you know.'

'I do know. And I know what you did for her that day, too,' said Barty, who had been told the story by Adele.

Adele had come to her very remorseful, shortly after Barty left the ATS, and asked her to forgive her for her outburst after the funeral.

'I'm so sorry. It was unforgivable. I really don't have any excuse.'

'I think you do,' said Barty, smiling at her, 'every word was true, I was behaving very badly.'

'It must be fun to behave badly,' said Adele, slightly wistfully, 'I've forgotten what it's like. I'd quite like to do it myself. In theory. Only in practice there's absolutely no one who appeals.'

'That's because you loved Luc so much,' said Barty. 'I'm sure no one will ever appeal to me again, either.'

She was very clear, however, on what did appeal to her: and it was not a life lived out in the nursery. Even after Jenna was born, and she was swept up into this new, demanding life and love, she did not change her mind. She was as determined as Celia had been to continue with her career; it was as intrinsic to her as breathing.

Celia told her that her job at Lyttons was waiting for her as soon as she wanted to resume it; 'several jobs, as a matter of fact, we are woefully understaffed. More so than in the last war, so many young women have gone this time, Lyttons is beginning to look like a home for old gentlemen.'

It would not have occurred to her to include herself among the more elderly of the staff.

Barty planned to return to London in the early summer. The war was virtually over, it would be safe, what appeared to have been the last bomb had fallen in March; there was an easing of blackout regulations, the shelters were being closed, the barrage balloons brought down, the fire-fighting services were being cut. And, 'At last, thank God,' said Celia, visiting Ashingham one weekend, 'people are beginning to dress decently at the theatre again.'

Adele winked at Barty across the table.

'Thank God indeed,' she said.

In any case, Barty wanted to leave Ashingham. Life there was not entirely happy. Lady Beckenham's fears about the behaviour of the new Earl had proved well-founded. He was arrogant, pompous and charmless, worried the tenants, upset the staff and complained so much about the small boys that even the mild-mannered Mr Dawkins told him he would not be sorry to return to the school's old premises for the summer term.

And he had several run-ins with Billy Miller, culminating in Billy's refusal to saddle up one of the horses for a ride one morning.

'I'm sorry, your lordship, but it would be wrong. The horse is lame and you are quite heavy.'

'You bloody well do what you're told,' said Beckenham, 'and saddle that horse up. And don't make personal observations.'

'I can't saddle her, I'm sorry,' said Billy. 'My decisions about the horses have never been questioned, and if you don't believe me, ask her ladyship.'

'Her ladyship, as you call her, is no longer my mother, but my wife. And my wife would certainly agree with me that it was not your place to query my decisions. You're a damn sight too full of yourself, Miller, and this is not the first time I've noticed it. Now, do what I say.'

Fortunately for both Billy and the horse, Lady Beckenham had been in one of the stalls herself and heard this exchange.

'James,' she said icily, 'a word please. Billy, go up to the house and fetch my crop, would you?' She watched him walking heavily out of the yard, then turned to her son. 'How dare you speak to Bill like that? For the very first time, today I feel glad that your father is no longer alive. The grief and embarrassment that exhibition would have caused him is almost unimaginable. Not to mention the complete lack of concern for your horse.'

'He's paid to do what he's told,' said James.

'Not at all. He's paid to do his job. Which is look after the horses. You seem to be under the misapprehension that the servants are in some way inferior to you. An extremely vulgar point of view and one you would be well to rid yourself of if you are to run this place with any success.'

'Oh, for God's sake, Mama. I would have thought you were the last person to have subscribed to this newfangled "we're all the same under the skin" rubbish. Miller has a very strange manner. Something to do with being Barty Miller's brother, I imagine, and what's more, with that handicap of his, I'm not sure he should be running the stables. Not sure he's all that able.'

'He is extraordinarily able,' said Lady Beckenham. 'He has more of a feel for horses and stable management than you will ever have. And no, of course I don't think we're all the same. We're quite different. But that certainly doesn't make one class better than another. Each has something to offer the other. I don't believe with mixing socially of course, but that's another argument. We should respect one another. That is how I have always run this house and this estate and that is how your father ran it.'

'Well, I would say it's led to a great deal of sloppiness,' said James, 'and, I might say, Sarah is of the same opinion.'

'Which does not surprise me in the least. Her grandfather bought his title, as I recall. And if you go out on that horse now, James, you will regret it. She is lame, Bill is quite right. Up to you of course, but don't blame either of us if you have to keep her in for the next six months.'

Three weeks later, Barty found Shepard sitting outside the back door almost in tears. He stood up suddenly in his embarrassment and knocked the cup of tea she was holding out of her hand.

'I'm so sorry, Mrs Miller,' he said (along with the other servants he subscribed to the view that the birth of Jenna had wrought a change in Barty's marital status), 'so sorry.'

'Shepard, don't be silly. It doesn't matter.'

'I'm afraid it will to his lordship.'

'To who?' Barty found it hard to accept the existence of a new Lord Beckenham.

'To Lord Beckenham. He just told me that he was finding my deafness very hard to cope with. I know, of course, it can be a problem, but his lordship, that is, the – the—'

'The real Lord Beckenham?' said Barty, her lips twitching. Shepard was too distressed even to smile.

'Indeed, Mrs Miller. He always was careful to speak clearly, and of course he understood it resulted from my time in the trenches and so was patient about it. As is her ladyship, of course.'

Barty patted his arm. 'Don't worry about it, Shepard. We all understand. And I have never known you unable to hear me, even on the telephone.'

'That is good news,' said Shepard. 'Of course, you do speak very well.'

'Well, thank you. Now off you go and get yourself a nice cup of tea and you can bring me one to the Dovecot to make up for the one we smashed between us.'

She reported this conversation that night to Lady Beckenham, who said she would see what she could do.

Adele had decided it was time to move back to London. Ashingham had been a wonderful refuge for her, but with her grief fading, her sense of despair ended along with the years of uncertainty, she felt she needed to return to real life.

Her career as a photographer was developing fast; she could have worked five days a week had she accepted all the work she was offered. And she loved it, really loved it, it was where she felt her future happiness lay. She had started doing reportage work, along with the fashion; she would walk miles with her Leica camera, across London and into the countryside as well, indeed some of her best work was done there; fine landscapes, country people working, a woman on a milk round, a whole series of a blacksmith's day, a group of children playing soldiers, drilling in the lane, a dense crowd of the new evacuees, fleeing the doodlebugs, on the platform of Amersham station.

To her great delight she had had several photographs published in *Picture Post,* and her most cherished possession was a letter from the American *Life* magazine, regretting that it could not use her shot of barrage balloons over Slough, but encouraging her to submit more work.

The children would settle in London; they were small enough to move. Noni loved Ashingham too, but she loved her Warwick cousins more. Lucas too; he was proving a brilliantly clever child – 'Like his father,' Adele said to Venetia – and was more fascinated by books than anything else. She started looking for a house – 'something like Barty's would do beautifully' – and took on the lease of a studio in Soho. Her mother put up the capital: 'I can see it's a good investment,' she said to Adele, 'and I'm very impressed by what you're doing.'

Adele was so astonished by this change of heart she could hardly stammer out her thanks; later she realised that she had become rather high-profile in the heady world of magazines and advertising, and that for the first time in her life, her mother was proud of her.

'It's made me feel quite proud of myself,' she said to Venetia.

Venetia was worried over Boy's future. 'He's having a wonderful time being a war hero at the moment' – there had been a photograph of Boy in one of the newspapers at the Liberation of Brussels, at which he had been at the forefront, with pretty girls all over his tank, throwing him flowers and kissing him – 'but to be honest, I think he's going to miss it dreadfully. Running some silly antique business just isn't the same.'

'Maybe he could work at Lyttons,' said Adele. 'You know Mummy thinks the sun shines out of his every orifice.'

'No, thank you. That's my little kingdom. I don't want him muscling in on it. Anyway, what would he do? Only the same sort of thing as me. Maybe it'll be the bank after all. But I can't quite see it. And then there's Giles, another worry.'

'Well, he'll be back at Lyttons. Obviously.'

'That's exactly it,' said Venetia. 'He will.'

'I think,' said Lady Beckenham to Billy, one lovely morning, as she gazed from the terrace across the intensely green dew-drenched landscape, 'I think the time has come for me to move on.'

'Move on, your ladyship?' said Billy in horror, visions of being left alone at Ashingham with the new Earl rising before his eyes.

'Yes. Oh, don't worry, I'm not suggesting taking a bungalow in the village.'

That seemed even less likely than joining Lord Beckenham.

'Well, I'm pleased to hear that,' said Billy. He had had another fight with his new employer the day before, had even told Joan he thought he might have to leave.

'I'm going to move into Home Farm, Bill. And run it. Buy James out, if he agrees, which I think he will. He can't cope with it and he needs the money. Beckenham left me a few pence. And I shall take my own horses and Shepard of course.'

'Yes. Yes, I see,' said Billy. He felt a leaden weight somewhere in his stomach. Lady Beckenham looked at him, a gleam in her dark eyes. 'Want to join me? I might be able to use a little help and support. You seem to understand farming as well as horses. You could come in as a stakeholder if you like.'

Billy flushed deep red. 'I haven't got any money. Otherwise I'd be very interested.'

'I've been thinking about that. I've left you some money in my will, you know.'

'Me!'

'Yes, you. I don't know many people who deserve it more.'

'Oh, my good Lord,' said Billy. He felt faintly dizzy.

'Yes. Seems to me it'd be more use to you now. Less death duties to worry about as well. So you can have it, if you like. I've admired the way you've got on with life, especially recently, not easy coping with the new era down here.'

'No, your ladyship.'

'So, what do you say? It's not charity, mind, you'll have to work hard, damned hard, but I know you will. And I think we'd make a good team.'

'I'll have to ask Joan,' said Billy, 'course. But it sounds – well, it sounds grand to me.'

'Good. Jolly good. There's a lot of wasted potential there. I know we have no option at the moment with all this arable, but building up a herd of really good cattle, Herefordshires for instance, would be a marvellous investment, and a really exciting thing to do.'

Billy sat staring at her, his face even more red. Then he got out his rather grubby handkerchief and blew his nose very hard.

'It was a lucky day when I lost my leg and came down here and that's a fact,' he said. 'I don't know how ever to thank you, your ladyship.'

'By working hard,' said Lady Beckenham, 'and never pretending to agree with me. I'll need frankness from you, Bill, more and more as I get older. Promise me that.'

'I promise,' said Billy.

'It's over then,' said Kit.

His voice was flat; his face expressionless.

Izzie looked at him, switched off his radio. She had thought it might upset him: the endless reports of the crowds outside the Palace, never less than a thousand strong, of Mr Churchill first walking from the service of thanksgiving at St Margaret's, Westminster, back to the House of Commons, of him standing on a balcony in Whitehall as he said, 'My dear friends, this is your victory', and of the crowd singing, 'For he's a jolly good fellow' to their hero, this short, stout, ageing gentleman. There were stories of people running with his car that day, of fathers holding up babies so that they could boast in later years they had seen the great man on Victory Day. And then the stories of revellers climbing lamp-posts, or up on to window ledges, of the royal family on the balcony, waving to the crowds, sharing in the moment . . .

All people for whom the war had ended well.

'Yes,' she said, 'yes, it's over.'

Kit sighed. 'Well – good.'

'Kit—'

'What?'

'You helped, you know. You helped win it.'

'Do you really think so? Do you really think without Kit Lytton, today would not have happened?'

'Of course not. But without lots of Kit Lyttons it wouldn't. You were a symbol, Kit, you and the others, of courage and hope, of never giving up—'

'Oh, sure,' he said, 'I never gave up. It gave me up, though.'

She knew this mood; there was no talking him out of it.

'Let's go for a walk,' she said. 'Come on, it's a lovely evening.'

She had chosen to spend the day – a school holiday – there, rather than in London as her father had suggested; 'Kit might be a bit down,' she had said, 'I'd like to be with him.'

'But what about me?' he said. 'I might like you to be with me.'

'Father, there are lots of people you can be with. Kit has only me.'

They walked slowly down towards the woods: their favourite walk. She held his hand, as she always did.

'I'm sorry,' she said.

'What about?'

'What you must be feeling. It must be hard to be – totally pleased.'

'Yes, it is. Apart from the tiny matter of my losing my sight, there are millions of men and women and even children dead. So we've won the war. At what price.'

'Yes. But there's no point going down that road, Kit. We're English, and we – you – fought for that, for Britain's freedom. That's what matters now.'

'I suppose so.'

'Careful, this is the bumpy bit.'

'Let's sit down,' he said suddenly.

'Why?'

'Because I want to say something. And I want to concentrate on it, not have to worry about bumpy bits.'

She helped him sit down, sat waiting quietly.

'I – want to thank you,' he said.

'Whatever for?'

'For helping me so much. For being so patient when I was being such a pig. For being so understanding. Always. For being here today.'

'I knew it would be hard for you today,' she said.

'Exactly. Who else thought of that? Certainly not my mother. Or my father.'

'Well, I do think about you an awful lot,' she said.

'Yes, I know. And I appreciate it an awful lot.'

'You did a lot for me too, once,' she said smiling.

'I did?'

'Yes, when I was little and Father wasn't quite so – so kind to me.'

'That's an understatement,' he said, 'he was horrible.'

'Well, I can understand now. Just about. You knew my mother, didn't you?'

'Yes, I did.'

'Was she very pretty?'

'She was lovely. I think about her a lot,' he said suddenly.

'Why?'

'Because everyone says you look exactly like her. So that helps me imagine you. It's awful, not being able to see you.'

'Why, especially?' she said.

There was a long silence; then he said, 'Izzie, I know this may be a bit – a bit of a shock. But – well—'

'Yes, Kit? What?'

'I – that is, I think that – well, the thing is, Izzie, I probably shouldn't be saying this. But I – well, I love you. Very much. And I know you're only just fifteen – I have a birthday present for you, by the way—'

'Oh, Kit, you didn't have to—'

'Yes, I did. Anyway, I've been thinking about it a lot. And you may not feel the same way at all. But if you do – well, Izzie, all I'm saying is, next year you'll be sixteen. And I thought we could tell them all then.'

'Tell them what?' said Izzie. It was not a foolish flirtatious question; she hardly dared breathe, certainly didn't dare believe what she might be hearing.

'That one day – maybe when you're eighteen, my mother was eighteen after all when she got married—'

'Married! You're asking me to marry you?'

She felt dizzy, quite faint; she closed her eyes.

'Yes. Yes, I am. If you felt you could take me on. I know I shouldn't be asking you at all, certainly not yet, and it is asking a lot. But I do love you so very much, I couldn't have got through these past few years without you, and I can't imagine being able to get through the rest of my life either.'

'Oh, Kit.' Izzie discovered she was crying; crying and smiling at the same time.

'Is it such an awful idea?'

'Awful? It's wonderful. I think – well, ever since I could think of such things at all, I've kind of imagined – dreamed about it. About how lovely it would be, how happy we would be. And just put it out of my head as a bit of silly schoolgirl nonsense.' Without quite realising it, she had imitated her father's voice exactly; Kit smiled.

'Well – not such nonsense. But it is asking an awful lot; I mean here I am, a chap who can't see—'

'A chap who can write wonderful stories, a very successful chap, actually.'

'Well, let's not argue about it. And of course you must go to university or whatever you want to do, I wouldn't dream of stopping you—'

'Kit! Do you really think I'd go to university and leave you if we were married?'

'We could live in Oxford, in what used to be your mother's house, maybe. I thought of that. Oh, I've worked it all out.'

'Yes,' she said wonderingly, 'yes, I can see you have.'

'So – what do you think?'

'I think it would be heaven. I've never felt so happy.'

'But – not a word to anyone. Not till you're sixteen. Otherwise they'll all start flapping and fussing.'

'Not a word. Of course.'

'Izzie—'

'Yes?'

'Can I kiss you? I mean really kiss you?'

'Of course you can. But maybe—'

'Yes?'

'We should move into the woods.'

'Why?'

'Oh, Kit,' she said, half exasperated, half amused. 'If this is going to be a secret, we can't have everyone watching us kissing, can we? And we're rather visible here.'

'I hadn't thought of that,' he said, 'but then I wouldn't, would I?'

'No,' she said, 'no, you wouldn't. Of course.'

She lay awake all night: staring into the darkness, sometimes smiling, sometimes very solemn, awed by her own happiness, by this miraculous realisation of her dreams.

Kit loved her! Really loved her. Loved her so much he wanted to marry her. It was so amazing. It was all so amazing.

And really – what was to stop them? Why should anyone want to stop them? Certainly if they waited until she was eighteen. When he would be – what, twenty-eight. Of course, he was ten years older than her. Funny, what a long time that was when you were a child, and how short when you were grown up.

Her father had been much older than her mother, she knew that. Oliver certainly looked much older than Celia. Ten years was nothing. Nothing at all. And they could wait. Even if they made them wait until she was twenty-one – which they wouldn't, loads of girls married at eighteen, even some of the sisters of her friends at school.

Oh, it was so, so wonderful. Kit, her hero, her beloved Kit, so handsome – she wondered if he knew how handsome he was – so brave, so clever. In love with her. In love! No one at school was in love yet. Well, not in her class. They mooned over film stars, over Clark Gable and Cary Grant, but not over real people. Although Joanna Humphries had said some boy had kissed her at a New Year's Eve party. Well she was sure he hadn't kissed like Kit. It had been amazing, his kissing; she'd felt so much more that she'd expected to. All kind of fizzy inside. And it had been really nice, not slobbery like you thought it might be, watching film stars. And standing there in the woods, in his arms, her arms round him, it had felt so right, so wonderfully right . . .

Goodness, she was lucky. So, so lucky . . .

She was going to be happy now for the rest of her life.

Chapter 45

'It was a heart attack, Lady Celia, I'm afraid.'

'A what?'

'A heart attack. Without doubt.'

'But' – she looked at Oliver, lying still and pale, apparently peaceful – 'but he's – I mean he isn't—'

'Oh, I know. He's alive. And doing pretty well on the whole. Thanks to you, in no small measure. All that insistence on his exercise regime, keeping him on his diet. For a man of his age, and after what was a very major stroke, he's doing very well. But there's no doubt that's what happened. It was a minor heart attack, and a little calling card from mother nature.'

'Saying what?'

'That he needs to slow down. Finally. Stop going into Lyttons every day, take things easy. The two of you could have a very nice time now, you know, enjoy yourselves, have some leisure. It really can't be necessary for you to carry on working at the pace you do.'

Celia looked at him in horror. Of all the things that appalled her in life, the prospect of a great deal of leisure was the greatest. Work to her was the purpose of life: it gave it its colour, its inspiration. It dispelled depression, fought despair, increased joy, created energy. Leisure was a tedious commodity, welcome, for occasional brief interludes, while she recovered from some particularly arduous task or other, and then to be left behind, abandoned like a dull guest at a party.

All her life she had worked: worked hard and passionately. It had been her happiness; when all else failed her, she had turned to it with a joyous relief, knowing that in it she would find satisfaction, fulfilment, and an absolute release. She would listen as politely as she could to people as they told her – as they often did these days – how much she might enjoy doing at least a little less, suggesting she travel, take up some hobby, spend more time with her children and grandchildren, while finding it hard to comprehend properly what they were saying. It was as if they were speaking in some foreign

644

language, or at least in some complex dialect; it simply made no sense to her. Life was about work and success and, to a lesser extent, personal glory, and if she could not have those things, then she would quite simply rather be dead.

Oliver, she knew, saw things just a little differently. And she was very afraid of the consequences for herself . . .

Oliver had been growing weary. He hated the new building – a modern one just off Oxford Street, very near the rebuilt John Lewis. Lyttons occupied the lower three floors; an engineering company the top three. He felt utterly miserable there, displaced indeed; he hadn't liked working from Curzon Street, but that at least had some style. This building, with its square rooms, devoid of cornices, picture rails, fireplaces, its plain corridors, its dreary entrance hall, shared with the engineering firm, seemed to him an absolutely unsuitable home for a publishing house. He had wanted, desperately, a lovely house in Grosvenor Square, but it was three times the cost.

'It's just out of the question, Father,' Giles had said. 'Things are very tight as it is, and really what difference does the building make? It certainly won't affect the quality of the books we put out.'

'I wouldn't be so sure of that,' said Oliver.

He grieved for Paternoster Row as for a person; his heart was still there, he would think about it, about his days there, over more than three decades, the tears rising in his eyes. He had made enquiries about rebuilding there, but it was as yet unplanned.

Boy Warwick had found the new building; property was now his business. He had come home from the war, uncertain what to do, bored, restless, had gone for a walk one day exploring the ruins of London, had noticed the feverish rebuilding going on – and begun to buy. Quietly, carefully, a few houses here, a couple of buildings there, sometimes developing them, sometimes just holding on to them. He was particularly skilful, Venetia told Adele, at spotting what he called development potential; 'that means he'll buy some place in between, maybe, two others, and sit and wait. A bigger firm will come along, wanting to develop the row, and he'll hold out for a bit while their price goes up and then sell. Very clever.'

Venetia had actually been with her father in wanting the building in Grosvenor Square; she hated 45 Clarice Street herself, but she had a greater regard for a balance sheet than he did and had allowed herself to be talked round.

Giles, on the other hand, liked Clarice Street, he said it was modern and streamlined, and suitable for a modern, streamlined business.

Only of course Lyttons wasn't modern and streamlined at all.

The book trade altogether was finding life difficult; the end of the war had not brought an end to wartime problems. Paper rationing continued; indeed the quota had been reduced still further. There was a wave of strikes, as people returned from the war with higher expectations than the country could afford; the cost of paper, along with other overheads, soared, and production slowed.

It was generally accepted that it now took a year for a book to pass from manuscript phase to publication. The public, requesting particular books from booksellers, was very frequently disappointed. Also, the War Economy standards for books still held, so that British books had a shabby utilitarian appearance; this affected exports, and American books in particular, so much glossier and more attractive, were in high demand.

The boom in books during the war years was over too; people needed to escape less, were more discriminating. Stock piled up in warehouses and on booksellers' shelves.

But these were difficulties Lyttons shared with other publishers; their greatest problems were peculiar to them.

The worst was the constant conflict: the over-cautious reactionary approach of Oliver and Edgar Greene, set against the high-risk instinctive impulses of Celia, backed by Barty and the young women editors. New books by promising authors were either rejected or over-debated by Oliver and Edgar and snapped up by other publishers with more foresight and faster reactions.

Schemes dreamed up by Venetia for deals, promotions, advertising campaigns were rejected by Oliver and Giles as vulgar, distasteful, over-costly.

The great money spinners for Lyttons in the old days, the Meridian books, the Buchanan saga, were no longer in such demand. There was a new gritty realism in literature, and the world which had made *The Snake Pit*, Isherwood's *Berlin Stories* and *Cannery Row* bestsellers did not have a place any more for the gentle nostalgia and humour of *Grace and Favour*.

Barty, working again at very much full strength, the small Jenna cared for by an excellent nanny, had found two books which she had longed to buy, one a black comedy of a thriller, the other an intensely raw story of a family struggling to come to terms with post-war life, but she had been voted down both times.

'I'm so sorry, Barty,' said Celia, 'in the old days I would have paid for an advance from my own money, but it just isn't possible any more, the amounts are too large.'

Two of the younger editors were intensely demoralised, finding no outlet for their energies and brilliance; one had an offer from Macmillan and one from Cassell. Celia had managed to persuade them to stay, but with great difficulty.

Jay was not yet back; he was not due for his demob until Christmas at the earliest. But his return, Celia could see, would create more conflict still, another young impatient talent pitting itself against the old guard.

And then there was Giles. He had come back to Lyttons after leaving the army early, because of his leg, filled with his new confidence – but still with all the old resentments.

He spent his days raging, sometimes silently, sometimes more openly, at what he saw as the swift, easy progress of Venetia, and of Barty, backed by Celia's determination for Lyttons to pursue her own editorial policies. He had some support from his father and Edgar Greene, but he was aware this was not in itself a permanent solution. These were the old guard, he needed space and backing for his own progress.

He had done his time as an apprentice at the firm, he was forty now, he had had a superb war, he had proved himself as an inspirational leader, and he had a right to do so again. He was used to a chain of command, to decisiveness, to absolute obedience from those below him, and he found the dithering and arguing that went on at Lyttons almost unbearable. The solution seemed to him perfectly simple; his father was an old man, clearly no longer able to run Lyttons, and it was time he moved over and made way for him, as his heir. Every time he heard that Venetia had pulled off some brilliant new deal with a bookshop, or Barty had tied up some wonderful young author, and every time he heard his mother say how much she was looking forward to having Jay back with them, he felt angrier and more impotent – and more ill-used.

And none of it made for a very happy ship: and Oliver, feeling it, and feeling unable to do anything about it, was unhappy too.

'I think actually he's quite relieved that he's got an excuse to go,' said Celia to Sebastian, 'but of course at the same time he doesn't want to go.'

'Of course not.'

'And it means either handing over to Giles, which even he can see is a mistake, or causing terrible problems, splitting the company up.'

'Which he can do?'

'Oh, yes. Oliver can do what he likes. He owns all – well nearly all – the shares.'

'Oh, I know. I always thought it was outrageous. You only having ten per cent.'

She shrugged. 'I never thought it mattered. What mattered was running Lyttons. The only time I was scared was when he wanted to sell out to Brunnings. Remember?'

'I remember everything about that time,' he said, his eyes very intense as he looked at her.

'Yes, well. We survived.'

'What about LM's twenty per cent? Didn't Jay get them?'

'No. They reverted to Oliver. That was how Grandpa Edgar set it up. He was terrified of the power becoming diluted, of the firm falling into other hands. His father had founded it, and his son was going to own it and that was that.'

'It's feudal.'

'I know it is. But – somehow it hasn't mattered before. I haven't minded, Venetia has plenty of money . . .'

'And a very hard-headed businessman of a husband. I doubt he'll be happy to see this going on indefinitely.'

'Maybe not. Anyway, decisions have to be made. And Oliver knows it.'

'What about you? Are you going to retire? All right, all right, I'm only teasing. They'll need you there more than ever.'

'Well, that's another thing. Oliver doesn't approve of my editorial judgment. He never has.'

'Even though it's made Lyttons famous and successful.'

'Even though. Anyway, they must all get an equal share. With me as caretaker for a bit. Well, for a long time. Only of course Oliver would like to have me at home with him.' She sighed, visualising the new pressure of a lonely, bored Oliver demanding her presence, jealous of her continuing involvement with Lyttons, a fretful shadow hanging over everything she did.

'What about Barty?'

'Well, that's a difficult one. She's terribly clever, hugely talented, the best all-rounder, I'd say, but – well, she's not a Lytton. And there would be terrible trouble if Oliver tried to give her a share. Certainly a sizeable one.'

'That doesn't seem fair.'

'No, I know. It isn't. But – they all resent her in their different ways. Always have. For different reasons. I just can't see a solution to that one.'

'And do you think Oliver will try to force you to retire?'

She stared at him. 'Why should he?'

'That's not the point. Could he?'

'Of course not.'

'In theory he could. He could compel you to sell your shares and then vote you off the board.'

'Don't frighten me.'

'I'll try not to. Anyway, it wouldn't make for a very happy retirement situation.'

'No. It's simply nonsense. Now, Sebastian, there's something else we have to talk about. Isn't there?'

He sighed. 'Yes. Yes, there is. I did have one idea—'

'Isabella, I've been thinking.'

'Yes, Father?'

'How would you like to go abroad for a year?'

'Abroad? I'd absolutely hate it. I hate abroad.'

'Don't be silly. You've never been. You don't know. Travel broadens the mind, especially at your age. I was thinking of America.'

'America!'

'Yes. We could go together. I thought we could spend a year there, I'm always being asked to give lectures there. You could meet the American Lyttons, Robert, Oliver's brother, and Maud, whom you've heard so much about—'

'Father, I told you, I'd hate it. I'd hate it and I'm not coming.'

'You are if I say so, Isabella, and that's all there is to it.'

'That went down very badly. She became practically hysterical. I'm afraid there may be something in all this. We shall have to go, I can see.'

'Barty's going over there after Christmas.'

'She is?'

'Yes. She wants to show Jenna to her American relations – those of them who will welcome her. I think Maud will still resist. And visit the New York office. She still feels a certain interest in it. She did very well there.'

'I remember. Incidentally, whatever happened to the shares in Lyttons New York, the ones Elliott owned?'

'Oh – he left them to the wife. Oliver was speaking to Stuart Bailey the other day.'

'Really? She shown any interest yet?'

'No, none at all apparently. She'll probably sell them. But it's a terribly complicated will apparently, as you'd expect. Nothing's been properly sorted out.'

'Father wants me to go to America.'

'America! Why?'

'I don't know. He says it will be good for me or something. Broaden my mind. I'm not going, Kit, I won't, I won't. Imagine not seeing each other for a year. I'd rather die.'

'I can't imagine it. Don't worry. I'll think of something. I love you, Izzie.'

'I love you too, Kit.'

'Now, Oliver, we really have to talk about this properly. It's terribly important.'

'What's that, my dear?'

'Your retirement. And who's going to take over.'

'Oh, there's plenty of time for that. And I'm awfully tired.'

'You're tired, Oliver, because you're not well. You know what the doctors have said. They all agree. You've got to give up properly. What you're doing at the moment just isn't fair. To any of us. Everyone knows you're going. You've got to make it official. However you do it. Have you got any ideas?'

'Plenty, my dear. And I would like to talk to you about it. Very soon, I promise. But as I say, not now. I really don't feel up to it. Tomorrow, perhaps.'

He was a genius at avoiding confrontation. It was something Celia had lived with all her life: at times to her great advantage. But she had also learned there was absolutely nothing at all that could be done. Until he chose it.

They all spent Christmas at the Warwicks'. Celia, who had always found Christmas difficult, had been viewing this one with its attendant family and family politics with dread. Spending it at a non-Lytton household might help. They were to be a big party; Adele and her children, Lady Beckenham and Sebastian and Izzie were joining them, and so was Jay, demobbed in time for Christmas, and Tory – a spring wedding planned – and Gordon Robinson. Barty accepted for herself and Jenna at the last minute.

'I did think of spending it alone,' she said to Sebastian when they discussed it, 'but it might have been a bit bleak. And if you're going to be there . . .'

'We certainly are. You might try and get Izzie interested in the idea of New York. Talk it up a bit.'

'Whatever for?'

'I want to take her there for a year. Do her good.'

'Would it really? I thought she was doing so well at school, talking about going to Oxford and everything.'

'Well, I think she's getting too serious,' said Sebastian vaguely. 'A year off will do her good.'

'Sebastian, I'm not sure that it would. What's this all about?'

'Nothing.' His dark-blue eyes were blank suddenly. 'Nothing at all.'

He picked up Jenna, who was sitting at his feet, playing with his shoelaces. 'You're a pretty little thing, aren't you? Looks like her dad, does she, darling?'

'So exactly,' said Barty, 'same hair, same eyes—'

'They are a gorgeous colour. Exactly the colour of that ring of yours.'

'Yes,' said Barty, smiling at first the ring and then him, 'apparently that was the idea. It's a nice story, I'll tell you.'

'You seem happy,' he said.

'I am happy,' she said, sounding surprised. 'Most of the time I'm really happy. Occasionally I get angry, or lonely, or long for Laurence to have at least known about Jenna, but generally I'm – yes, happy. It's marvellous being back at work, although it's a bit – difficult there at the moment.'

'So I gather.'

'I'm looking forward to the break. I do love New York, I often feel it's where I really belong. Silly, I know, but – anyway, let me tell you about the ring.'

'Funny old thing, inheritance, genes, all that sort of thing, isn't it?' he said when she had finished. 'Some children look so exactly like their parents, or one parent – like Izzie could be Pandora now, couldn't she? And the twins, their mother all over again.'

'Yes, and Giles, too, in a way. I often think it's a bit sad for Oliver, not one of them really looking like him.'

'Kit does, surely. Blond, blue eyes—'

'Well – yes. But that's all. He's a different build, and his features are different. Apparently he's much more like Grandpa Edgar than anyone. Celia says, anyway.'

'Does she now?' said Sebastian.

Christmas was not entirely comfortable. Most people made an effort, but Giles was morose, Helena edgy and Izzie noticeably quiet, sitting close to Kit and not even responding to Henry Warwick's teasing, which she usually enjoyed.

Henry was seventeen now, tall, extraordinarily handsome, easily charming – 'I feel so sorry for whoever he marries,' said Venetia to Adele with a sigh. Roo was shorter, less good-looking but extremely funny, with a huge talent for mimicry. Between them they made the day fun, especially the after-dinner charades. Roo being a caterpillar in the style of Frank Sinatra, the new teenage girls' heart-throb, had everyone crying with laughter.

'Do you like Frank Sinatra, Izzie?' asked Henry.

'Not particularly,' she said, slightly primly, 'I don't like that sort of music.'

'Why on earth not?'

'I just don't.'

'Well, you ought to,' said Sebastian firmly, 'at your age. You're turning into a little old lady, Isabella. A trip to New York will do you good. You might even see him in person.'

'I don't want to see him in person. I don't even want to go to New York,' she said. And got up and left the room.

There was an awkward silence; then Helena said, 'I really think we ought to go.'

'Oh, Mother. It's such fun,' said Mary, 'just one more game.'

'No more charades, for God's sake,' said Boy, 'it's too exhausting.'

'Let's play one of those round the room memory games,' said Amy. 'I like those.'

'Boring,' said Elspeth.

'No, they're not. I like them too,' said Sebastian unexpectedly. 'I went to market, that the sort of thing you mean?'

'Yes.'

'Oh, I love that,' said Tory. 'I'm rather good at it.'

'Come on, then. You start.'

'All right. I went to market and I bought some cucumber.'

'I went to market,' said Roo, 'and I bought some cucumber and some itching powder.'

Izzie came back into the room. She sat down quietly next to Kit. 'What are we playing?'

'The memory game. You like that. Come on—'

They went round the room once; everyone managed it, then people

652

started dropping out, forgetting things. By the end of the third round only half a dozen were left in: by the end of the fourth only five: Kit, Izzie, Oliver, Tory and Sebastian. The list was now extremely long; Sebastian embarked on round five with relish: the end of it saw Oliver off.

'My memory's too old. Tory?'

But then Tory was out; the remaining three of them sat laughing, playing on and on, their memories apparently flawless.

'This is getting boring,' said Henry, who had been out in round two. 'Let's change.'

'No, we have to finish,' said Sebastian. 'Izzie, come on.' But as she sailed through the next round, and Kit the next, they gave in.

'Extraordinary,' said Gordon Robinson. 'Jolly clever. Photographic memory, isn't that what it's called? Absolutely identical brains, obviously, the three of you.'

There was a brief silence; then Sebastian said quickly, 'Oh, it's just a knack. I just remember the first letters of everything and make a word out of them. A nonsensical word. Easy.'

'That's funny,' said Kit, 'that's exactly what I do. Exactly.'

'We really must go,' said Helena.

Lying in bed that night, thinking about Izzie, worrying about this trip to America that her father seemed so bent on, Kit suddenly found himself focusing on the slightly odd business of the memory game. That he and Sebastian used exactly the same technique to remember something. He supposed it was a fairly standard thing. Although he'd never heard of anyone else doing it. And then he heard Gordon Robinson saying, 'Absolutely identical brains, the three of you.' And then something else stirred in his head: another memory, in some way relevant . . . What was it, exactly? A photograph, something to do with a photograph – they'd been sitting on the terrace at Ashingham and little Noni had said something – no, he couldn't remember that either. And LM, there'd been something she had said – oh, God, he'd had too much of Boy's red wine. The room was beginning to spin a bit.

Kit fell asleep.

Chapter 46

'Oh, I love you, I love you. You darling, darling little thing.'

Felicity Brewer looked at Barty over Jenna's red-gold head. 'She's just heaven. You clever, clever girl.'

'Not really,' said Barty, laughing, 'it was actually quite easy.'

'Has Robert met her yet?'

'Of course. He's a man in love. He says she looks exactly like Jeanette.'

'She does too. Only more beautiful. And Jamie, what does he think?'

'He seemed to like her too.'

'I can't wait for you to see Kyle. He's been so looking forward to your coming.'

'How is he?'

'Oh, pretty well. Over his divorce at last. It was pretty amicable. Lucy just – well, I guess she didn't love him enough.'

'Her loss, I'm sure,' said Barty lightly.

'Of course. Anyway, dinner here tonight. Robert, Jamie, everybody, it's all arranged. And this little angel of course. Now then, any time you want to go to visit Lyttons, anything like that, you know she'll have a very good babysitter right here. And of course my housekeeper can't wait to get her hands on her either.'

'That's very nice of you,' said Barty, smiling at her, 'and just once or twice, it could be very welcome.'

She had forgotten how easy, how enveloping Americans and their hospitality could be. That was what she liked best about them, what made her feel so at home here. In hours she had been caught up into it all, felt she had never been away. She had been afraid that New York without Laurence would be painful, but it was not; or certainly no more than anywhere else. She felt him more strongly, of course, in the restless, relentless energy of the city, and occasionally she would be taken by surprise and shaken by some small memory – a café on the

Upper East Side where they had had a coffee, a bench in Central Park where they had sat and argued about whether they should go and see the latest Busby Berkeley (her choice), or *Modern Times* (his). Needless to say it had been *Modern Times* . . .

But for the most part, she found it all perfectly easy; she could sit in the Palm Court at the Plaza enjoying tea with Felicity, drive up Park Avenue, past Elliott House, glance into the Colony, all vivid with memories, but touched with only a drift of sadness. Every day she remembered him more happily; it was a surprising and lovely thing. He had been the most important thing in her life, and she had loved him absolutely, and he had made her terribly happy and terribly unhappy, and she would be quite a different person without him, and she would not have missed a day of him, not even the most wretched, but now she could simply enjoy what he had given her and be glad of everything that they had shared.

Most of all, Jenna.

Barty would not have believed it was possible to love anyone or anything as much as she loved Jenna. She had listened to the twins, to Celia, to other women saying that you didn't know about love until you were a mother and she had not believed any of them. But it was true. Jenna was more important to her than anything in the world, and she knew that had Laurence lived, even he would have been relegated to second place. Or certainly to a different one. And thought, wryly, that that would not have pleased him very much either. And as Jenna grew and developed into an inevitably wilful, difficult, determined and entirely charming and enchanting child, Barty watched herself and her pleasure in her in amazement and every day wondered at the appalling and unimaginable emptiness there would have been in her life without her.

It was wonderful to be in New York, after London. In a city that had no bombsites, no boarded-up buildings; a city where the streets were lined with dazzling store windows, filled with wonderful, almost unimaginable things, silk dresses, fur coats, fine shoes, luxury perfume. Where you could have anything you wanted to eat, and as much of it as you wished, where you could fill your car with petrol as often as you wished, book vacations wherever you pleased . . . Set against the grim reality of London it seemed like a fantasy city, and she couldn't imagine ever wanting to go home.

She had booked into a fairly modest hotel in Gramercy Park, near Lytton House, where she knew Jenna would be welcome; but Felicity wouldn't even hear of her staying there, made her check out the first day and move into their guest suite.

'You don't have to think you'll be putting us out or be in the way, because you won't be. You can come and go as you like, but when you are here and you have time for us, then that will be wonderful.'

In the three weeks she was there, they saw all the shows; *Annie Get Your Gun, Carousel, The Magnificent Yankee*, ate in all the best restaurants, shopped endlessly, and went dancing with Kyle Brewer and Jamie and his wife Lindy (American as apple pie, Felicity had described her, laughingly) in Greenwich Village.

Her only sadness was Maud, who refused to see her, having heard of her reunion with Laurence and the birth of Jenna. She was married, to another architect, and they lived in a town house on the Upper East Side with their two children.

'I'm sorry, darling,' Robert said, clearly embarrassed. 'She says she just can't accept you.'

'It's all right. I understand. Really I do.'

She did, but it hurt.

She visited Lyttons New York several times; it was a fierce contrast to Lyttons London. Busy, energetic, successful, 'making a lot of money,' Stuart Bailey told her, 'there's quite a little boom in publishing over here.'

He had aged very little; still rather stern-looking, with his iron-grey hair and patrician features, but lean, fit, full of enthusiasm. She thought of Oliver and the sad contrast between them, and then felt dreadfully disloyal.

'Your Geordie MacColl is still a big success,' Stuart told her, 'one of Lyttons' bankrollers. That was a great discovery of yours, Barty. We keep him firmly under lock and key, I can tell you. They've all been after him in their time, Doubleday, Random House, Macmillan, the lot, but we'll never let him go. You should have him over to London, do some promotion for him there. He has a new book, *Opium For the Few*, coming out in May, his usual thing, but very topical, about a GI returning from the war; why don't you publish it over there? We'd want quite a lot for it, mind you, but—'

'Yes,' she said, 'yes, we might.' She wondered how any such idea would get past the blundering dinosaur that Lyttons London seemed to have become.

Just the same, she had lunch with Geordie; she took him to the

Colony, knowing he would like it, testing her courage, laying yet another ghost.

'We won't get a good table, I'm afraid,' she said, laughing, when she telephoned to invite him. 'Definitely not in the first enclave.'

'I don't mind that,' he said. 'I love it there anyway. And, you know, lots of people prefer the back now. It's become quite smart. A lot of movie stars, they like the privacy.'

In the event they got quite a good table. 'About halfway there,' he said smiling at her, 'well done.'

She had a suspicion it was his name rather than hers that had procured it.

He was just the same, with his boyish WASP good looks, his slightly diffident charm; he'd been through a divorce too.

'It's all the rage here,' he said, smiling at her. 'Really you're no one, no one at all without at least one under your belt. And certainly not at the Colony.'

He was working already on a new book, he told her: 'I'm quite excited about it. It's about the New York Mafia and the way they're infiltrating the charity thing . . .'

It sounded rather complicated to Barty, but she smiled and said she couldn't wait to read it.

As they were finishing their meal, Kyle Brewer appeared at their table.

'Hallo. Nice to see you, Geordie. Telling Barty you're coming to join us instead?'

'Sorry, Kyle, no. I like Lyttons.'

'Hey, that could be a slogan. You can have that for free, Barty.'

'Thank you. I'll give you a drink for it. Come and join us.'

He sat down and chatted; then, 'Is Barty getting you over to London? That new book is a natural for England, with the war background.'

'She – might be,' said Geordie, giving Barty his quick, sweet smile.

'Well, if you do, mind you insist on staying *chez* Lytton. What a dynasty. There's Oliver, almost a parody of the English gentleman, his wife, the Lady Celia, so beautiful and so witheringly clever, you scarcely dare speak. And then there are the twins, I shall never forget those twins. Absolutely identical and so lovely. They were the most ravishing little girls. Maud has various pictures of them still, one that was in *Style* that shows four of them, in a double mirror.'

'Oh, that one. Yes, it did cause something of a stir. Well, they're still ravishing,' said Barty. 'Venetia works for Lyttons, very important, she is—'

'As important as you?' said Geordie.

'Much more important than me. And anyway, she's a Lytton.'

'And what does the other one do?'

'Adele is a photographer. A very successful one.'

'And if I do come to London, shall I meet these extraordinary creatures?'

'If you want to, I'm sure it could be arranged.'

Barty cabled Lyttons that afternoon, asking them if they were interested in Geordie's new book: accustomed already to New York efficiency and enthusiasm, she was at first outraged, then resigned as no reply came for three days, and then only a suggestion that she bring it back with her so they could 'have a look at it'.

This was a book that was being bid for by five major English publishers; Barty felt a wave of despair.

'We should have bought that book of Barty's. The one by that MacColl fellow.' Jay came into Celia's office looking distressed.

'I know, Jay. But – well, you know. I did my best. There was nothing I could do. It's a terrible shame, we need a bestseller desperately for the early autumn. Have we definitely lost it?'

'I think so. Hutchinsons offered a very high figure. That was the last I heard. Celia, what is happening to Lyttons? It seems to have lost its ability to function—'

'Jay, I know. I would like to say we're going through a rough patch, but—'

'Well, if we don't look out, we won't be here much longer. The place seems to me to be dying on its feet.'

Jay went back to his office to cable Barty personally and tell her it wasn't his fault they hadn't got hold of *Opium*, as it was called in the trade. Barty cabled back: 'Didn't think it was. Hold on to your hat. Barty.'

Now what on earth did she mean by that? he wondered.

'Isabella, there's a letter from Barty. And a few postcards, the Statue of Liberty, look. Doesn't that make you feel excited?'

'No. It doesn't.'

'What, not even the thought that we're going to see it?'

'I don't want to see it. And I'm not going.'

Sebastian's temper was never particularly level; worried as he was, it soared. 'Don't be insolent. And go to your room. We're going to New

658

York at the end of your term, and that's that. Most girls your age would be over the moon.'

Izzie stared at him in silence, then got up and walked out of the room, slamming the door behind her.

'I've been thinking,' she said to Kit on the telephone that night, when Sebastian had gone out to dinner, 'I've got an idea.'

'What's that?'

'I daren't say it on the phone. But – it's quite exciting.'

'Could you come down here tomorrow?'

'What, to Cheyne Walk? Yes, I think so. I've got to go to the dentist at two o'clock. I could sneak off after that.'

'Good.'

She arrived breathless and excited; Kit opened the door himself.

'Is anyone here?'

'No. Well, Father's asleep. No one else.'

'Good. Come on, let's go and sit down.'

They went into the drawing room and she closed the door.

'Ready?'

'Yes.'

'Well, listen. This is it—'

She left half an hour later, with a passionate kiss. 'I love you.'

'I love you too,' he said, 'more than ever. It's a marvellous idea. As marvellous as you.'

'I'm sorry, Father, I was so rude yesterday. Of course I want to go to New York.'

'Good.' He smiled at her, patently relieved. 'I'm glad. So do I. Want to read Barty's letter now?'

'Yes, please.'

'Now then, I've been thinking about your birthday. It's an important one, isn't it? Sixteen. What would you like to do? Would you like a party?'

'Oh – I don't know. I'm not a terribly party person.'

'Well – a family party. How about that?'

She thought for a bit. 'Yes. Yes, that might be very nice. Here?'

'Yes, I should think so.'

'And could Henry – and Roo of course – come?'

That should put him off the scent.

'Well, they're certainly family. As long as they're not at school.'

'If it was a weekend, which it would have to be, or I'd be at school too, it would be all right. They could get an exeat.'

'Fine. Well – what about the weekend before? Your birthday's on a Wednesday, I think.'

'Oh – no,' she spoke quickly, 'no, I'd much rather it was after. Otherwise I wouldn't feel properly sixteen. I'd feel I was cheating.'

'You're a funny one,' he said, smiling at her. 'All right. Afterwards.'

'Good news,' he said to Celia, 'I think we're winning. Not only has she given in to the idea of the American trip, but she's specifically requested Henry Warwick comes to her birthday party. So it looks like – touch wood – it was just puppy love. As I always thought.'

'Good. Thank God for it.'

'Well – we're not quite out of the woods yet. But – anyway, while we're about it, could you put down the date in your diary? Saturday, 18 May: Big family party. Lyttons, Warwicks, Liebermans, the lot.'

'Of course.'

A few days before she left New York, Barty took the bus out to Long Island. She had to go; she had to lay this last and most dangerous ghost.

She took Jenna; it was rather a long bus journey, but they could spend the afternoon on the shore. Jenna had never seen the sea, at least never experienced a beach; the South Shore had been Barty's own first introduction to the beach, it could be Jenna's too.

The bus stopped at Southampton; she put Jenna in her folding pushchair and set off down the track towards South Lodge.

It seemed much longer than when she had been driven down it in Laurence's Packard.

South Lodge was set at the very end of the track; she turned the corner, and there it was, just as she had remembered. She had visited it in her memory day after long day, night after sad night, imagined the steep, curving drive, the wisteria-covered stone walls, the pillars flanking the front door, the walled gardens to the side of the drive . . .

Barty caught her breath, found she was crying, crying quite hard. Jenna turned her head at the unaccustomed sound, looked up at her, her small face intrigued.

Barty smiled quickly, brushed her tears away; this was too much, she shouldn't have come. She knew why it was hurting so much: not just because she had loved it so much, had been so extraordinarily, if briefly, happy there, it was where she had finally left Laurence that day, where they had spent their last night together, where they had had the last desperate showdown, where her life with Laurence had ended. Or so she had thought.

She looked up at the house thoughtfully; it seemed to be completely empty. The windows shuttered, the great gates closed, no sign of life anywhere. She began to walk up the drive, towards the gates, slightly tentatively as if she might at any moment be stopped, ordered back. But she was not.

She reached the gates, peered through; she felt a little better now. She could hear the roar of the ocean; the shriek of the sea birds. What a ravishing place it was. The lawns were still perfectly kept, the shrubs cared for. Obviously someone had given orders for it to be kept in perfect condition.

And then it happened; a gate to one of the walled gardens opened and a man came out. It was Mills! Mills, Laurence's driver, the one who had driven her in and out of Manhattan that dreadful day. He caught sight of her, stared for a moment, frowned, then smiled uncertainly as he recognised her.

'Miss Miller! Is that you – surely not—'

'Yes, it is. It is me. Hallo, Mr Mills.'

'Well, in the name of all that's wonderful. Here, let me open the side gate, let you in. How very very nice to see you, Miss Miller. And – who is this little one?'

'Oh, it's – she's my daughter,' said Barty hastily.

'So you're married?'

'Well – yes.' It was simpler that way.

'Hallo, little 'un. My word, she's pretty.'

Don't notice, please, don't notice, don't say she looks like Laurence.

He didn't. 'You come along in, Miss Miller. Now would you like maybe some tea? And where's your car?'

'I came on the bus, Mr Mills.'

'The bus!' If she had said she had come by flying saucer he would clearly have found it less astonishing. 'You came all that way on the bus! Well you'd certainly better come in.'

'Is – is there anyone else here, Mr Mills? I mean . . .'

'Well, no, of course not, Miss Miller. Didn't you know – hadn't you heard – oh, dear—'

'Mr Mills, of course I know. I know Mr Elliott was killed. In France.'

'Well, that's right. Why should he have wanted to go, Miss Miller,

661

that's what we kept saying, he didn't have to, there was no need, he was far too old. Risking his life and – well. It was so terribly sad.'

'I think he was just very – brave, Mr Mills.'

'Very brave. Very, very brave.'

'Anyway – I just wondered if – well, you know, if anyone was living here now?'

'Nobody's lived here, Miss Miller,' he said, looking surprised, 'nobody's lived here for – well, for several years.'

'Oh, really? But I thought – when Mr Elliott married—'

'He never brought her here, Miss Miller. Never. Oh, except for just once, when they took photographs for some magazine or other. He never would let her come here. Never. I think she wanted to, well, I know she did, I heard them fighting over it more than once, but he just said no and that was that. You know what he was like, Miss Miller. Very determined.'

'Yes. Yes, I do know. Very – determined.'

'We had to keep it up, take care of it, the house had to be kept absolutely spick and span, but she never came. He did, from time to time, on his own, but he never even brought any of his friends here ever again. After – well, after you, Miss Miller.'

'Oh.' Barty felt very odd: confused, shaken.

'Are you feeling all right?' he said suddenly, looking at her intently. 'You look terribly pale. You really shouldn't have come all that way on that terrible bus. With the little one. Come along into the kitchen, sit down here, I'll make you some tea. Mrs Mills isn't here this afternoon, she'd be able to look after you better. Here, now, that's right. Does the little one want a cookie?'

'She'd love one,' said Barty. 'Thank you.'

And she went on sitting there for a long time, staring out of the window now, down the great sweeping lawn, across the tall grasses and out at the sea. Wondering at this extraordinary man, who had hated her so much he had sent her photographs of his fiancée, and reports of his wedding, just to hurt her, and loved her so much he had never allowed anyone to visit this house, this special house which he had told her was the only place in the world where he felt properly safe – and which they had made their own for however brief a time.

Mills insisted on driving her back to the city: 'I couldn't possibly let you take that child back on the bus. And what Mrs Mills might say I cannot imagine.'

She kissed him gently when she said goodbye, to his huge

embarrassment, and said she hoped she would see him again and sent her love to Mrs Mills.

'It's been a wonderful day, Mr Mills. Really wonderful. Thank you so much.'

'It's been an absolute pleasure, Miss Miller. And she is just the cutest little kid I ever saw. You know there's something about her that reminds me—'

'I must go,' said Barty hastily, slithering herself and Jenna out of the car, 'and there's a cop bearing down on you, Mr Mills, watch out. Goodbye, and thank you so much again.'

She felt quiet that night; they had all been going out to dinner, and she was more than relieved to hear it was cancelled.

'John has a client come into town unexpectedly,' said Felicity, 'and I'm tired; maybe you and I could eat alone together, if that wouldn't be too dull.'

Barty said nothing could be nicer than a dull dinner.

She liked Felicity very much; she was so gentle and yet so dynamic, travelling all over the country, giving her poetry readings, writing at least four long mornings a week while still entertaining tirelessly for John.

'I'm just an old-fashioned wife,' she said slightly apologetically to Barty that evening. 'I guess I think that's what we're for. Looking after the men. It must sound very strange to you, having grown up in Celia's household. But then, you see, I came to a professional life rather late. Celia always worked, from the very beginning of her marriage.'

'Yes, she did, and I'm not entirely sure Oliver wouldn't have liked an old-fashioned wife himself,' said Barty, laughing.

'Oh, surely not.'

'No, I mean it. He gets so exasperated with her, never having any time for him, always under pressure, always too much to do, always out – she is very exhausting to live with.'

'But she's done so much.'

'Yes, she has. And of course Lyttons wouldn't be the same without her. She's brought so much to it.'

'Of course.'

'But especially now – he's not so well, poor old darling.'

'Yes. But it's not serious, is it?'

'Well – not desperately serious. But he's not so young, he's been in a wheelchair for over ten years, he's just had a minor heart attack—'

'I didn't realise that,' said Felicity slowly.

'Oh, it was very minor. But the doctors all say he has to ease up, stop working every day, hand over at last—'

'And if he does – will he be all right—'

Her voice had an odd note to it; tremulous, deeply anxious. Barty looked at her; she was pale and her eyes were brilliant. She felt a need to reassure her.

'Oh, yes,' she said quickly. 'Yes, I'm sure he will.'

'I was – I am – so fond of him. Well, we both are. He stayed here once or twice when he came over without Celia on a business trip. He used to talk so fondly of you, of all the children of course. But I think he had a very special feeling for you.'

'He did?' Barty was pleased, touched. 'Well, it's mutual. He was so good to me. There was one night especially when – well, let's say I was all set to run away.'

'Why was that?' said Felicity gently.

'Oh – something happened. I – found out about something. Something in my childhood. Which upset me dreadfully.'

'And what was that?'

She almost told her, almost began to talk about it; then drew back. There was nothing to be served; it was not her secret, not really, it was Celia's, and it was better buried. Buried with the baby, her sister, the baby who had died, so long ago . . .

'I can't tell you,' she said quickly, 'it's too personal and too painful, and – well, anyway, Wol was marvellous then, so kind and gentle and – and steadying, somehow. I love him very much.'

'I – can understand that,' said Felicity. 'He's a very unusual person. Do send him my – my special love, won't you?' She too seemed on the brink of saying something more; then, like Barty, she pulled back, clearly thinking better of it.

She stood up suddenly, smiled at her, her sweet, brilliant, warm smile. 'It's been so lovely having you here,' she said, 'I'm so sorry you're going. Are you going back to Lyttons or have you finished with them now?'

'Not to Lyttons.' said Barty. 'I have just one appointment in the morning.'

'With—?'

'Oh – nothing important.' She smiled at Felicity. 'Just – just tying up a few odds and ends. And then I'll be ready to move off around two. We sail at five.'

'You will come back, won't you? I'd hate to think this was your last visit.'

'Oh, Felicity,' said Barty, 'it absolutely won't be my last visit. I promise you that.'

Chapter 47

'What did you say?' said Jay.

'You heard.'

'Yes, but—'

'Jay, don't argue. We've got it. Got *Opium*. Just be grateful and start putting some plans in place for it fast.'

'Yes, but how, I mean the price was going sky-high—'

'Let's say I – entered into a little arrangement with the author,' said Barty lightly, 'who'll be coming over, incidentally, to promote it in the autumn.'

'I see. And does Celia know?'

'Of course. She's going to tell Oliver.'

'I still don't understand—'

'You don't need to,' said Barty, 'not at the moment anyway.'

Jay went back to his office feeling more hopeful than he had for weeks.

'Barty—'

'Yes, Giles.' She smiled at him.

'Barty, what is this I hear about this book you've bought?'

'Acquired, Giles, acquired.'

He frowned. 'Whatever. *Opium For the Few*, anyway. By this American chap?'

'Geordie MacColl, yes. He was a discovery of mine when I was working in New York. Every book a bestseller. We published a couple over here.'

'Very American.' This was a clear criticism.

'Well – they would be. That hasn't stopped other books being successful after crossing the Atlantic, Giles. Like a few of Mr Hemingway's works, *The Grapes of Wrath*, *Gatsby*—'

'Yes, yes, I don't need a lecture on American literature, Barty.'

'Of course you don't.'

'The thing is that you seem to have acquired this book, as you put it, without reference to me. Or my father.'

'That's true. But you were taking such a long time to make up your minds, Celia and I and at least one other editor thought we should have it, and we were going to lose it. So as it hasn't actually cost Lyttons anything—'

'That's not quite the point, Barty. As I see it.'

'And how do you see it, Giles?'

'My father is in charge of Lyttons. Everything has to be approved by him—'

'That's not quite true, though, is it? Editorial decisions have always been made by Celia. Celia and her editors.'

He hesitated. 'Perhaps. In the past. But we're working in different times now. This is no longer a small cosy family business—'

'You could have fooled me, Giles. Actually.'

He ignored this. 'Publishing, like everything else, has to move into the modern world. Decisions can't be made on an individual's whim. A company's development must be based on strategies, there has to be a chain of command—'

'Giles, this is like being back in the ATS, listening to my CO. We're talking books, not battles.'

'There has to be order in everything. I learned that above all in the army. It works. Now I've talked to my father, and we have agreed that in future no book is to be bought or – acquired – without a full, careful assessment by us. Taking into account cost, potential . . .'

'All right, Giles. I get the idea. And of course I'll bear it in mind. But that's the future. *Opium For the Few* is now. Fortunately, in my opinion. Now I must get back to work, if you'll forgive me.'

Celia came in quietly a few minutes after Giles had stalked into his own office and slammed the door.

'Well done,' was all she said.

'Not long now. Only – let's see, a month and three days.'

'Three and a half.'

'I've got the – you know.'

'Well done.'

'Just think. Going up there, through the darkness, into our new life.'

'I am thinking. I don't think of anything much else.'

'Well, you should. You should be thinking of your new book. We're going to need that.'

'Of course. Although whether my father will publish it after – well, afterwards, I really don't know.'

'He will. He'll need to, from what I've heard. Lyttons are not doing terribly well at all.'

'How do you know?'

'Kit! They are Father's publishers, I heard him talking to your mother. On the phone.'

'Oh dear. Well, anyway – got to go. Bye, darling, I love you.'

'I love you too.'

'Did you enjoy that, Oliver?'

'What?'

'The wedding, of course. Didn't Tory look absolutely wonderful? Jay is a lucky young man. Although she's lucky too of course.'

'Oh – I suppose it was all right. Not really for me, that sort of thing.'

'Oliver, really. No one can say weddings aren't for them.'

'Celia, you asked me and I answered you. I'm sorry if my answer was the wrong one.'

She looked at him and sighed. 'You look so tired.'

'I feel so tired.'

'Oliver—'

'I know, I know. Next week, my dear, I promise. I have to have some meetings with the bank first.'

'With the bank? Shouldn't I be there?'

'Not the lawyers, Celia, the bank. When I see the lawyers, of course you must be there. Now I'd like to go to bed. Could you call that rather bossy young woman you've hired and ask her to take me up?'

'Yes, of course,' said Celia.

She sat alone in the drawing room, looking at the river, brilliant in the spring evening, thinking about the wedding, about how glorious Victoria had looked as she came down the aisle, about how Jay's face had lit up with love as he made his vows, about Gordon Robinson's sudden look of savage sadness, and how she had understood it and shared in it, in the sadness that LM had not been there.

'I've made my decisions, Celia, I would like to discuss them with you, naturally, since they affect you. And I have asked the lawyers to come in to see us tomorrow. But there is something else I think you have to know.'

'Yes, Oliver?'

'Let's have a drink first, shall we?'

*

668

'Father's called the meeting for tomorrow.' Giles's voice was casual; he poured himself a large whisky from the decanter. Helena always set out a tray for him for his return in the evening. It was an important time for her, for them both, while he relaxed and told her about the events of the day. The children were not allowed to disturb them, the closed door at that time was as unassailable as their bedroom door.

'The meeting?'

'Yes. The one where he is going to announce his plans for the company. And for his own retirement.'

'Well,' said Helena, 'at last. Thank God. After all these years.'

'Yes, indeed,' said Giles.

'Tomorrow,' said Venetia, 'tomorrow's the day. Give me a drink, darling, would you? I'm done in.'

'What day?'

'When Daddy announces his retirement. And tells us what's in store.'

'It had better be good,' said Boy.

'Well – to be honest, Boy, I've slightly lost interest. Just for now.'

'Oh, don't be absurd. I've never seen a woman so driven.'

'I know. And of course I do care – terribly. But just at the moment I've got something else on my mind.'

'What's that, darling?'

Venetia looked at him. 'Boy, what did I ever have on my mind? Apart from you and work, that is?'

'Clothes? Parties?'

'Oh, do stop being so dense. You know—'

'Oh, my God,' said Boy. 'Oh, God.'

'Aren't you pleased?'

'I – think so, yes. Bit of a bombshell.'

'I know. It was for me too. Nice, though.'

'Very nice. But – how on earth are we going to tell the children?'

'Tomorrow's the day,' said Jay.

'Really? Darling, how exciting. Well, it had better be good.'

'I'm not over-hopeful. Giles is walking round looking like a turkey cock.'

'A rather foolish turkey cock. No, you deserve something and you ought to get it. And we'll need some money because I've found the most divine house. In Chelsea. It's so lovely, Jay, I can't wait to show you.'

'Within our budget?'

'Well – not exactly. But much too nice to lose. I can see us being so happy there. So – if you don't get what you want from Lyttons, you'll just have to go somewhere else.'

'Tomorrow is a very important day,' said Barty. She tucked Jenna up in her cot, smiled down at her. 'Very important indeed for your mummy. And for you.'

Jenna looked at her. 'Mummy.' she said and smiled back, put her thumb in her mouth and closed her eyes. It seemed to indicate a certain confidence in her, Barty thought.

'I've bought a suitcase.'

'Oh, darling. How marvellous you are.'

'Kit, it wasn't very difficult.'

'I didn't mean that. I meant planning it all. Now how are we going to get to the station?'

'In a taxi.'

'Yes, but how will we get one?'

'I'll order one. You can do that, Father does it a lot now he doesn't drive any more. He's got an account, I can use that.'

'You're so special.'

'What you've got to do is make sure you're here early. I mean by about five. The party's due to start at seven. And we'll be leaving at six. So they'll all be frantically busy, organising, laying tables and things. You can tell them you want to help. Or – oh, anything. You're the imaginative person.'

'I think you're pretty imaginative yourself. I do love you, Izzie.'

'I love you too, Kit. Isn't it marvellous?'

'Marvellous.'

'Right. Thank you all for coming.'

As if they wouldn't have come, Giles thought, looking round the room, all of them so hopeful, so expectant. He didn't know what they were all hoping for: a few shares, he supposed. Well, that would be all right. He could agree to that. Bit high-handed of his father to do it this way, though. Without speaking to him first. But then, he always had been one for the indirect route. Not like his mother. He looked at her, still so beautiful, gazing out of the window, her large dark eyes thoughtful. She was wearing a light-grey tweed suit and some very high-heeled shoes. He could never remember her looking anything other than fashionable. Fashionable and glamorous, whatever happened. A bit like

Venetia. Although Venetia didn't look quite herself today. Tired and slightly less sleek than usual. She'd been working very hard; it was surprising Boy allowed it really. All those children, she really needed to be at home, running the household. But Boy seemed quite happy about it, in fact he never stopped saying how proud of her he was.

Young Jay was looking pretty cocky too. Much too full of himself. The way he talked these days, you'd think he'd been in the publishing business for decades. This will do well, those need more promotion, we really should try and get hold of that . . . and his mother and Barty and Venetia too, all listening to him as if what he was saying must be really important . . . Time he was taken down a peg or two . . .

What was his father saying? What? He couldn't be. He *couldn't*. It must be a mistake, a suggestion that he had rejected. He must be running through possible scenarios, yes, that was it, it obviously wasn't the final plan. He must listen more carefully, stop letting his mind ramble . . .

'So I hope that will be acceptable to you all. It will take effect from the next quarter day, 25 June, Until then, I shall remain in overall control. Celia will of course be here for some time to come. So you will have plenty of wisdom and experience to draw on. The lawyers have drawn up articles of association which you all, as shareholders, must sign. It only remains for me to wish you well and to ask you to care for Lyttons as Celia and I have done, and my father before me. It has been a major decision and a very big step to break up the shareholding in this way but, as I have explained to you, it seemed the only equitable way to arrange things. Thank you.'

'I just don't believe it. It's outrageous. After all these years, all your hard work. Not even a majority share. Oh, Giles, it's dreadful. You have to query it, you have to. I absolutely insist. It's – well, it's unjust. Apart from anything else. He was handed Lyttons on a plate—'

'Not quite true. LM had a twenty per cent share.'

'Yes, which meant he had eighty. What have you got? Twenty-five. And twenty-five for your sister. And twenty-five for Jay! Jay, who's had virtually no experience at all. It's totally unacceptable, Giles, and you have to contest it. And if you won't I will. Did – did Kit get anything?'

'No,' said Giles, 'no, Kit didn't get anything at all.'

'Or Adele?'

'No, nothing. The remaining twenty-five per cent my parents still hold jointly. That's all.'

'Barty?'

'Of course not.'

'Well, I suppose that is something to be grateful for. God, it's so, so unfair. I mean what justification did he give for it exactly, why—'

'I told you. He said we all had very different strengths and talents and he wanted that to be reflected in the structure of the company. He said it would be unfair to give a majority shareholding to any of us.'

'Unfair! He has no concept of what the word means. He's led you all these years to think—'

'I know, I know. And I will talk to him about it,' said Giles, 'of course. But I really don't know what good it will do me.'

'Well done, darling. You must be pleased. A quarter share, eh? Congratulations. Well, you certainly deserve it. Sit down and put your poor old feet up – pretty shoes – and have some champagne. No? Maybe later. Oh, darling, you look ghastly. Here, let me help you up to your room—'

'Jay, that is such good news. Congratulations. And it means so much, you can make decisions, really get Lyttons moving forward. I'm so pleased. And it means we can get our house, doesn't it? Oh, whoopee – let me give you a kiss. Or even more—'

'Well, Jenna. We're on our own. As usual. Not terribly fair but – well, I'm not a Lytton, you see. Never will be. And Wol did try to explain, make me feel better. Said how much he valued me and what I'd done but he just couldn't give me any shares. Just some stupid title. Which doesn't mean anything. And a rise, which I don't want. It's not fair, it's not fair, I should have some shares. You don't even know what shares are, do you, angel? You will one day, Jenna, I promise you that. Anyway, here I still am, Barty the foundling, the charity case. Still, even now. Oh dear—' She started to cry; Jenna reached up, trying to catch the tears with a chubby finger as they rolled down her mother's face.

Barty sniffed, managed to smile.

'Silly Mummy. It's not as if it mattered. Not really. What would I want being on their stupid board anyway? And at least I haven't got to be grateful. Oh, Jenna. I feel so – so lonely. So absolutely alone. I wish your daddy was here. I do, I do wish that. So very, very much . . .'

Chapter 48

Only two more weeks. And then she'd be sixteen. Grown up. Old enough to be married.

Married! And she was going to be. Actually married. To Kit. Whom she loved so much. It was just – well, it was almost too much to bear, she felt so happy. So excited. And it was all going to be so easy . . .

Of course they wouldn't be too pleased at first. It would take a bit of getting used to. They'd say she was too young, and that Kit wouldn't be able to look after her properly. But it wasn't true. She wasn't too young, she hadn't been too young to love Kit all her life, and help him through all his unhappiness, to be the only person who really understood how he'd felt all those years. And of course he could look after her; they'd be looking after each other anyway. He was making quite a bit of money with his books now, they did very well, he'd just written a third and it was a bit like Sebastian, he was asked to give talks to children at school and in libraries and bookshops and after the first few when he'd been a bit feeble, he said, he'd proved really good at it, just as Sebastian was. He was always very nervous beforehand he'd told her, but once he stood up and got going, he quite enjoyed it.

Anyway, they'd be all right, they'd be fine. And they wouldn't need much, not a big house or anything, the smallest cottage would do. Of course later when they had children it would be different; but they'd talked about that and agreed it should be a long way into the future. Kit seemed to know all about that sort of thing; Izzie was relieved. She was a bit hazy about it, the nearest she'd got to finding out exactly what happened was by way of a slightly garbled version from the girls at school. But she was sure that when the time came it would be wonderful. Judging from the way she felt when Kit kissed her, it certainly would. He was terribly good at kissing.

It was all arranged. She'd bought the train tickets, and kept them in the one place she knew they'd be safe, in the drawer in her room where she kept her underwear and her sanitary towels and things like that. Well buried, of course, but there was no way her father would ever ever look in there. And she had put her own laundry away ever since she was six or seven; Mrs Conley just put things on her bed for her. Anyway, Mrs Conley was so short-sighted now that she'd hardly know a train ticket from a magazine. And come to that, the same could almost be said of her father.

She hadn't booked the taxi yet, she thought it was best to leave that until the day before. You never knew, her father might ring up and they might refer to it in some way.

She'd packed her case though, not much of course, a few jerseys and skirts and a jacket. And some underwear. She'd actually bought a beautiful grown-up silky nightdress; it had taken a lot of her coupons, but she had plenty, because Venetia had started to give her lots of her lovely clothes when she got bored with them. And she had wanted just one thing for what was after all going to be her honeymoon. She might not be going to have a wedding, well, not a proper wedding, but she was going to have a honeymoon. And she had also got some really lovely perfume, a new one by Schiaparelli called Le Roy Soleil which Barty had given her, brought back from New York. There was lots of everything, Barty had said, in New York, no rationing at all. She'd love it. Izzie had said, yes, she was sure she would.

Anyway, it was the most wonderful smell and very grown up, and she was sure Kit would like it. His sense of smell was very acute: like all blind people. So was his hearing. 'I could hear you coming all down the street,' he would say, or 'Listen! Front door' or 'Careful, someone on the stairs.' When she couldn't hear anything.

Anyway, her case was packed, and put casually on the top of her wardrobe, where she kept her school case in the holidays. She really didn't think anyone would bother to get it down and look in it. And she had some money, some cash. She had gone to the post office and drawn out most – but not all – of her savings. Kit had given her the money for the tickets; he had a bank account of course. She hadn't got one yet, but her father was opening one for her for her birthday.

She worried about her father a bit; he would be very upset at first. He did love her very much, she knew that, and now that she was older, he liked doing things with her, going to the theatre and to concerts and just talking to her over dinner. But once he'd got over it, they could all be friends and she could see lots of him. And he was so fond of Kit, he always had been, he'd forgive him in time, she was sure. Anyway, if there hadn't been all this stuff about going to New York, none of this would have been necessary. They'd been going to tell them when she was sixteen anyway. It was his own fault for treating her as if she were some kind of troublesome child, just announcing she had to go away with him without finding out if she was even remotely interested.

No, it would all be all right. It would all be wonderful.

'Mother's in the pudding club again. God, it's disgusting. Honestly, how can they? At their age.'

'How do you know?'

'Because she's written and told us. Here you are, it's to both of us. Listen, "I hope you'll be pleased to hear that I am going to have another baby. Due in October. I know you said you'd rather there weren't any more babies, but Father and I both feel that Fergal is rather one on his own and it would be nice for him." '

'Nice for him! What about us?' said Roo. 'Yuk, just think of it, it's hideous. I mean Father's forty, over forty, you'd think they'd have got over it by that age.'

'I know. And what are we going to tell the other chaps?'

'We could not tell them.'

'Don't be daft. She must be – God, four months already. She'll be all fat at the Fourth of June. She says the girls are really thrilled.'

'Well, they're welcome to it. Bad enough having Fergal all over our rooms and records and things, I'm just not going to have anything to do with it.'

'Nor am I.'

'So that will be – good heavens, Celia, ten grandchildren. How amazing you are. You don't look old enough to have even one.'

'Sebastian, don't be ridiculous. Of course I do. You above all people should know better than to flatter me. Now then, this birthday party of Izzie's. Do you need any help?'

'Oh, yes, please. Lots. Mrs Conley is getting far too decrepit to be any use at all. I've got a catering company doing the food, but—'

'What about flowers? Have you got enough chairs? Are you going to have a marquee? The size this family is now, especially the Warwicks, we just won't all fit into your house.'

'I told you I needed help,' he said. 'I hadn't thought of a marquee.'

'Well, start thinking. I'll give you some telephone numbers. They'll sort out chairs and tables for you as well.'

'Thank you. And certainly I can't do flowers. Can you do that? Or suggest someone who could?'

'I'll do them. It's the one domestic chore I like. And I'm tolerably good at. I'll come over after lunch on the day.'

'Bless you. It'll be quite a day, won't it?'

'It will, Sebastian, it will. Quite a day.'

'I've got something to tell you.' Barty's face was very serious as she walked into Celia's office.

'Yes?' Celia whipped off the spectacles she now had to wear for really close work; vanity made her deny their existence as much as she could.

'I'm – well, I'm going to New York.'

'Again? You've only just got back.'

'No, I mean, permanently.'

'I'm sorry?'

'I said permanently,' said Barty patiently.

'Oh, for heaven's sake. What are you going to do there?'

'Work.'

'Work where?'

'At Lyttons.'

'But – I don't understand. Why, for God's sake? Barty, you can't, not now, when—'

'When what, Celia?' Barty looked at her very steadily. 'When you might miss me rather? When my presence is more necessary than usual?'

'Yes. Precisely. I shall need all the support I can get, when Oliver goes and—'

'Well, I'm sure you'll get plenty. From Jay and Venetia and Giles of course and—'

'Ah. So that's it.'

'What?'

'You're leaving in a fit of pique. Because you didn't get any shares. Is that it? I'm surprised at you, Barty. I can understand Giles walking round like a bear with a sore head, although as I told him, he was fortunate to get what he did, but you . . .' She looked at Barty intently. 'Surely, Barty, you can understand—'

'Not quite, Celia, no. It's more important than that. I was very – hurt, yes. Perhaps it was silly, but I'd thought that – well, let's say it made me realise I would never be anything but an employee here. Which of course is up to you. But I want to get to the top of my profession, Celia, surely you can understand that. I don't want to work somewhere where I keep coming up against such a very low ceiling. I want to feel that one day I could be on the board of some company. Not made to feel an outsider.'

'Barty, that is so unfair. Nobody's making you an outsider.'

'I don't think it's unfair, Celia. It may be naive, but that's different. I know you've done everything for me, I know you've given me all the wonderful opportunities I could never have dreamed of, a marvellous education. And huge scope here to develop editorially. But I also know that I'm very good at my job. Very good. And there's this stopping point. And it seems so – hopeless. So, yes, I'm going. Sadly, of course, but I am determined.'

'I can't believe this, Barty. I really can't. And what Oliver will say I cannot imagine.'

'I hope he'll understand. As I hope you will in time. I feel – undervalued. I've done a lot for Lyttons, I know I have. And supported you in all your decisions, all your battles with Oliver.'

'For which I'm supposed to be overcome with gratitude, I suppose.'

'No, of course not. I of all people know how uncomfortable that can be. I just want you to recognise it. Not just verbally, but formally. And you know, it's a bit of a one-way traffic all this, I stayed on here when Wol begged me to, at the beginning of the war, I was considered family enough for that.'

'I didn't know that,' said Celia coldly.

'No, I know. But I did. It was when Kit first went and – well, never mind. I was happy to do it, even though I longed to go. And so many things since, and, God, I've just acquired the one big seller Lyttons is going to have this year—'

'Yes, Barty, how exactly did you manage that?' said Celia.

'I – paid for it myself.'

She hadn't actually meant to tell her that; damn. But the temptation to jolt her out of her complacency was suddenly overwhelming. She was successful; Celia's face was ashen, frozen into shock.

'You paid for it yourself?'

'Yes. Of course, in time I would want to recoup it. It must be built into the budget. But it seemed the only way of getting it, and I knew we had to have it.'

'But you haven't got any money. The offers for that book were very high—'

'Well, I – did have some. I'd rather not debate that now. The point is that I was prepared to put my own money, albeit temporarily, into Lyttons – as you have done more than once, Celia, as you've told me many times – and in return I've got no formal recognition of that. So

– I'm sorry. But I've made up my mind. I shall be very sad in lots of ways, but at least I shall still be in close contact with you—'

'And when are you going?'

'The week after Izzie's party. I was going to leave sooner, but she begged me to come.'

'And they have a job for you?'

'Oh, yes. Absolutely.'

'I can't understand it. How you can go off there, with a small child, uprooting her—'

'I feel her roots are more there than here.'

'And where do you think you're going to live? In a hotel, I suppose, initially. Your nanny won't like that.'

'I've got somewhere to live.'

'Oh, you're going back to the Brewers, I suppose. Very unwise. For more than a few days. She may seem very charming and pleasant, Felicity Brewer, but she's not all she seems. I would go so far as to say I find her a rather – what shall I say – an unreliable person. And not even entirely trustworthy.'

'Oh, really? I think she's absolutely marvellous.'

'Well, you are entitled to your opinion. As I just said, she's very good at dissembling. I think you would very quickly find yourself disillusioned.'

This was interesting, Barty thought; this hostility towards Felicity. Very interesting. It had always been there, a certain scorn whenever her name was mentioned, a dismissal of her wifely ways. She suddenly heard Felicity's voice saying that Wol was a very special person, to give him her special love; and wondered if perhaps once . . . What a thought.

She hauled herself back into the present.

'Anyway, I'm not going to stay with the Brewers. I have somewhere to live.'

'You do? Where?'

'Oh, Celia, you don't want to know that. Let's just say it's perfectly satisfactory.'

'Some wretched little downtown place, I suppose. Well, clearly you've thought it all out.'

'Yes, I have. And I'm quite determined.'

'Oh, Barty—' Celia sounded quite different suddenly; gentler, frailer even. 'I wish you wouldn't go. I shall miss you – very much.'

The dark eyes were suspiciously bright; Barty looked at her and for a moment, just a moment, she was tempted to change her mind.

She owed everything to Celia: to this difficult, demanding, autocratic, intensely generous creature. Without her she would probably be what her sisters were, overworked mothers with no prospects of any kind except further childbearing. Celia had given her a luxurious home, a superb education, and perhaps the greatest gift of all, ambition. She had not been easy, she had not been tender or gentle or patient with her, but she did undoubtedly love her in her own way; what sort of person had she become, Barty wondered, that she was rejecting her now simply because she had not been given any shares in Lyttons?

And then she steadied herself; it was not simply because of that. It was because she had a vision for herself, which Celia had also given her, and which she could not fulfil unless she broke away. In time, they would become close again, possibly closer; for the time being, she had to stand firm.

'I'm so sorry, Celia,' she said, 'so very sorry. But you of all people should understand what I feel. I'll go and tell Wol now.'

Jay was very upset, said he would leave too, would come with her, would resign in protest.

'Jay, don't be silly. You're doing so well, you have to make the most of what you've got here. You have such a good future; think how proud your mother would be. Anyway, there's nothing to protest about. It's my decision.'

'Yes, and everyone can see why you made it.'

Barty was upset; she had hoped the connection would not be so easily made. She felt less upset when he uttered the rider, 'Of course I know you're not a Lytton.' Even he seemed to feel it: the invisible barrier, behind which she had no rightful place.

Venetia was less voluble, but just as firm in her support.

'It's a terrible shame, Barty. Just when we're getting things going a bit, seeing our ideas pushed through a bit faster. Do you have to rush off so soon? Why not wait and see how it all pans out?'

'I can't, Venetia. Nothing's going to change for me, that's the thing.'

'Of course it will, you'll have more freedom, more flexibility, you'll have your grand new title—'

'But that's all, Venetia. I won't be part of Lyttons.'

'Yes, you will. Oh, you won't have shares of course, but—'

It was the 'of course' that told her yet again that she was doing the right thing.

Giles said very little; merely told her that he hoped she was doing the right thing and that he wished her well. His own misery was bleak; Barty felt desperately sorry for him. He moved through the days in a dark resentment that was almost tangible; for his sake and his alone she was glad she had no shares. That would have been much more than he could bear.

As she watched him, she contrasted this bitter, disappointed, angry man with the kind little boy who had been her friend, her only friend, with the sensitive young man who had told her he loved her, and the soldier who had been so brave and so visionary that he had not once but twice been singled out for high honours. And was sad: so sad.

Wol hurt her most, in fact: first begging her with tears in his eyes not to go, then telling her he would miss her unendurably, throwing in some of the emotional blackmail that was his forte – 'I thought we were very special friends, you and I, Barty' – but then, finally, asking her what she wanted and when she tried to explain, saying, 'But, Barty, how could that possibly be? You are not a Lytton, however much we love you. Surely you must understand that.'

Even Sebastian had been guilty of it: 'Darling, you must do what you want to do. And I'm sure you will be wonderfully successful over there. But we shall miss you so much. I don't quite see the need for it.'

She tried to explain: and he smiled his lovely smile and said, 'But, darling, what did you honestly expect? You're not a Lytton.'

And so: she was going.

She was not taking her nanny; she felt it would be too painful, too big an adjustment for the girl. She would invest time finding someone new; in the long run Jenna would benefit. In the short term, she was sure she could find someone to help. In fact she had one particular person very much in mind . . .

She would sail on Tuesday, 21 May. Immediately after Izzie's party. Very suitable really; her last gathering of the Lyttons. She felt quite sure it would serve to strengthen her resolve still further. Not that it needed strengthening at all.

'Celia, you know the matter I spoke of recently.'

'You speak of a great many matters, Oliver.'

'The financial matter? The loan from the bank?'

'Oh – yes. I thought that was all settled.'

'Unfortunately not. Despite the restructuring of the company, the projections we have done for the coming twelve months, they have refused the loan.'

'Well, that's very unreasonable of them. What reasons do they give?'

'Times are very hard. Money is short. Especially investment money. And our track record is not good at the moment. It is – rather worrying.'

'And what does it actually mean? In practice?'

'Oh' – he looked vague – 'it means we won't be able to do some of the things I – we had hoped. Salaries will have to be kept at the same level for some time. We won't be able to acquire any expensive properties. Of a literary nature, that is.'

'But – it doesn't mean another – well, another Brunnings?'

'Oh, good heavens, no. I wouldn't risk that twice in a lifetime. No, I'm sure we can get by. But it does mean we are going to have to keep a very wary eye on things. And find some money from somewhere.'

'Have you told Giles?'

'No. I haven't told anyone.'

'Well, I think you have to. They're shareholders now, they have a right to know.'

'Celia, the company isn't going bankrupt. Anyway, they're not shareholders yet. Until quarter day. Things may have improved by then.'

'Oh, Oliver, don't be ridiculous. Companies don't turn round financially in the space of – what? – under two months.'

'No, but there may be a larger light at the end of the tunnel.'

'This is a terrible time for the book trade,' said Celia firmly, 'for everyone, not just us. I'm sure we're not the only house having trouble paying the bills.'

But she knew, from talking to people at functions, from listening to gossip, from reading the trade press, they were one of the few houses without much in the way of new properties – or even bankable old ones. Indeed without *Opium For the Few* their autumn catalogue would have looked very sorry indeed. However Barty had done that, they owed her a great deal. Which they might not in real terms be able to pay. Well, no doubt the New York company, which was flourishing in a highly irritating way, would make it up to her.

It was tomorrow! Tomorrow! She had celebrated her actual birthday quietly at school, waking that morning to the happiness of being sixteen, old enough to be married, had accepted everyone's good wishes and cards, her father's letter, telling her how proud of her he was – that made her feel a bit bad – and enclosing a cheque for fifty pounds. 'To be placed in your bank account, of course, not for frittering away.' Fifty pounds! That would keep her and Kit for several months.

He said he had a proper present for her, which he would give her on Saturday, during the party. That made her feel bad too: to think she wouldn't be there. Well – it was his own fault. It really was – wasn't it?

She felt even worse when she got home on the Friday evening and saw all the preparations for the party. A marquee had been set up in the garden, filled with tables and gilt chairs; there was a vast stack of plates and glasses and silver trays and salvers in the kitchen; crates of wine stood in the pantry, including a large supply of champagne; ice buckets, neatly polished, were in the corner of the marquee.

'Henry and Roo have arranged some dancing for later, they're bringing a gramophone and some records. I couldn't be much help there,' Sebastian said. 'Oh, and I've arranged for Adele to take you shopping in the morning.'

'Shopping!'

'Yes. A girl has to have a very special dress for such an occasion. You haven't got one as far as I can see. I've told her no expense is to be spared.'

'Oh, Father –' tears filled her eyes '– Father, I don't deserve this.'

'Of course you do. I'm very proud of you, Isabella. As proud as can be.'

He was so seldom effusive, she felt physically quite shocked.

'Now then, Celia is coming after lunch tomorrow. She's going to do the flowers. You might be able to help her.'

'Yes. Yes, of course I will.'

All these people: all doing so much for her, and she was going to fail them: to run away. Perhaps—

But no. She wasn't running away because she was ungrateful and unhappy; quite the reverse. It was because she was terribly, terribly happy. And nor was she running away to some unspecified, meaningless place. But to Gretna Green, where she and Kit could get married. Without permission from anybody. They would understand in time. Of course they would. And be happy for her.

'Kit?'

'Yes? Be quick, the house is full of people.'

682

'Kit, your mother is coming here tomorrow after lunch, to do the flowers.' Oh, dear. Another wobble. Celia, frightening, beautiful, famous Celia, doing the flowers for her, for her party. It was a great honour. She took a deep breath, steadied herself. 'Come with her.'

'I'll see what I can do.'

'Bye.'

'Bye – my darling.'

It was the 'my darling' that did it. So much more grown-up and lover-like than just 'darling'.

They were grown-up. They deserved to be treated as grown-ups.

'Isabella, I'm just going out for a few minutes, to post some letters. When I come back, we'll have supper.'

'Yes, Father, that will be very nice.'

As soon as he'd gone, she shot into his study, telephoned the taxi company.

'I'd like to order a taxi, please. For tomorrow evening, at six. To go to King's Cross. Yes, that's right. Now, could you wait at the bottom of the street, my father's having a party and you might have a bit of trouble getting near enough to the house. Yes, just where this road meets Elsworthy Road. Thank you. I'll be there.'

She had been wondering about her suitcase. If they were seen leaving with that they'd be done for. If they just left the house everyone would assume they were going for a quick stroll. Well – she'd think of something.

'Mother, can I come up with you tomorrow to Sebastian's when you go to do the flowers?'

'You can, my darling. But wouldn't you prefer to come up with your father?'

'Oh – I've got something for Izzie. I want to give it to her quietly, before everyone's there.'

'Well, your father will be there in very good time. I really don't think it's the best idea, Kit, it will be pandemonium up there, and you'll just—'

'Get in the way? Be of no use? Well, thanks.'

His voice was bitter; Celia felt dreadful. There was nothing that distressed him more than such observations.

'Darling, of course not. But—'

'No, it's all right. I understand. I've got used to it, you know.'

'No, Kit, of course you must come. I'm sorry, I wasn't thinking. At about two. No later.'

'Oh – I don't know. Not if—'

'Kit—'

'Well – all right. Thanks. If you're sure it's not too much bother.'

'Kit, it's no bother at all. I'm sorry if I upset you.'

'That's all right.'

Well, he'd handled that pretty well.

'Isabella—'

'Yes, Father?'

'A little toast.'

They were alone in the dining room; in the late May dusk. Sebastian had opened the French windows; the sky was turning palest grey, settling over the pink haze of a London sunset. The gently brilliant colours of spring, of apple and cherry blossom, wisteria and clematis filled the garden; somewhere a thrush was singing its evening song, a pair of swallows swooped and rose again.

'Lovely, isn't it?'

'Yes, Father, it is.'

'Your mother loved this time.'

He scarcely ever mentioned her mother; it hurt him too much.

'Did – did she?'

'Yes. And this time of year. That's why she was so – happy that you were to be born in the spring.'

'Yes. Yes, I see.'

'You're so very like her, Isabella.'

'Yes, I know. I mean, people are always telling me.'

'I haven't been a very good father to you, I'm afraid.'

'Father, that's not true.' Tears filled her eyes, hot, dangerous tears.

'No, it is true. I've been rather – distant, I'm afraid. Certainly at first.'

She was silent.

'I just wanted to tell you that I know that if your mother could see you today, she would have been so very proud of you.'

'Would she?'

Not of a daughter who was going to run away: run away from her own birthday party, hurt her father dreadfully.

'Yes, she would. She was a remarkable person, your mother. Very free-spirited.'

'Yes. Yes, I see.'

Maybe that was where she got it from. Her free spirit.

'And brave. So brave.'

She was going to need to be brave.

'Anyway –' his voice changed '– anyway, I have something for you. As I told you. I was going to give it to you at the party, but it's a very personal gift. I felt it should be a private little ceremony. Here you are, Isabella, with my love. Happy birthday.'

He produced a jewel case, a rather shabby velvet one; she opened it nervously. Inside was a double string of pearls: luminescent, slightly pinkish in tone, perfectly graded.

'They were hers. Your mother's. I gave them to her. On our wedding day. She always wore them. Since – since she died, they've been in their box. Bit of a waste, really. So—'

'Oh, Father. Father, they're so lovely. So—'

She couldn't help it; she burst into tears. She wept copiously and for quite a long time and she knew why; not only because of this gift from him to her, a gift of such preciousness and personal generosity that only very few would comprehend it, but because it marked out her own betrayal of that generosity and of his love for her, his difficult, painful love.

'There, there,' he said, slightly embarrassed, patting her hand tenderly, 'don't cry. Here, put them on, come on, let me do them up.'

'No,' she said, putting them down, unable to allow this, the acceptance of the forty pieces of silver, 'no, not now, Father, I couldn't. Just – just let me keep them like this for a bit. I can see them better in the box.'

'You funny girl,' he said. 'All right. But wear them tomorrow, won't you? Promise me? I want you to wear them tomorrow, at your party.'

'Yes,' she said, 'yes, I'll wear them tomorrow. Thank you, Father.'

And she kissed him and then started to cry again.

'She was very – odd,' he said to Celia later on the telephone. 'I gave her the pearls and of course she was very pleased, very sweet, but she just couldn't stop crying. Extraordinary, I didn't know what to do.'

'Oh, she's probably getting her period or something,' said Celia briskly. 'I'm sorry, Sebastian, I know you don't like these reminders that she's grown up, but it's a fact that girls do cry a lot at such times. The twins used to sob endlessly, every month. Still do for all I know. I'm sure she'll be fine tomorrow.'

'I hope so,' he said, and his voice was concerned. 'It seemed a bit more than that. I hope she's not really worried about something.'

'Of course she's not. What could she be worried about? Now, I'll see you tomorrow at two. I'll have Kit with me by the way. He's in a bit of a funny mood too. Very touchy. Oh, and tell Izzie Adele will meet her at Woollands at nine-thirty. In evening dresses. That will cheer her up.'

They couldn't go. They couldn't. Not after that. She couldn't hurt him so much. He'd never understand, he'd never get over it, just like he'd never got over her mother dying. She'd just have to tell Kit they must wait, as they'd been going to. Maybe they could—

'Isabella, are you awake?'

'Yes.'

'Kit's on the phone. Something about some records for tomorrow, said only you would know what he should bring. Or shall I tell him to ring in the morning?'

'No. No, I'll speak to him. Thank you.'

She could tell him now: on the phone.

'Hallo?'

'Hallo, Izzie. How are you? Mother said you'd been crying.'

'Yes. Yes, I was. Kit—'

'I just wanted to say I love you. And to tell you that if something happened to stop us tomorrow I – just couldn't bear it. I'm sure you're nervous, darling, but there's no need. I'll look after you. Promise. Got to go. Love you, love you, love you.'

No, she must go. Kit needed her more than her father did. He'd had his life, and it hadn't all been sad, a lot of it had been triumphantly happy. He was famous, successful, he had lots of friends. Kit's life, changed so dreadfully five years before, was all ahead of him. And with her it would be so much better and sweeter. He needed her. As she needed him. More than anything in the world.

Chapter 49

'Oliver, I've been thinking. And I think we ought to tell them.'

'Tell who what—'

'You know perfectly well who. The children. And that there's a problem.'

'Oh, I don't think so. Why should we, why worry them?'

'Oliver, the company is on the edge of bankruptcy.'

'Nonsense. Wherever did you get that idea from? I told you, things are just a bit difficult . . .'

'That's not true. I've been looking at the figures.'

'You had no right to do that, my dear.'

'I had every right. Lyttons is mine as much as yours. And don't start getting technical with me, I know that's not strictly true, legally, although after quarter day – well, anyway, it's mine in spirit. Which is what counts.'

'Celia—'

'Anyway, I looked at the figures. It seems to me we're weeks away from going bankrupt. We're living on borrowed time, borrowed money, it's as bad as last time, probably worse—'

'We don't have an expensive libel suit hanging over us as we did last time.'

'No, that's true, but we don't have nearly as many assets either. Oliver, it's dreadful. You should have told me. We hardly seem to have the next quarter's rent.'

'We've got money coming in from sales.'

'Precious little.'

'Well, maybe I should look elsewhere for funding. I wondered about Boy—'

'Venetia was saying he's very stretched at the moment.'

'He can't be. He's as rich as Croesus.'

'Even Croesus had his limits. Boy's just bought half High Holborn as far as I can make out and there are several deals which he's waiting on to come through. None of them certain. And I don't think one should risk any more family money.'

'Good Lord. Well, there are other banks.'

'Exactly. I think we ought to look at them.'

'Very well. But I absolutely don't want the children to know there's any sort of problem. And I want this kept very much between us. Word gets round extremely fast and loss of confidence is far more serious than anything else in this sort of situation.'

'All right, Oliver. But we have to make some very serious enquiries about refinancing very quickly. You really can't delay it by more than a day or two.'

'I'll – see what I can do.'

'You have to do more than that. If you like, I could—'

'No, no, I want to deal with it myself. And I repeat, I don't want the children worried.'

What he really meant, Celia thought, going off to find Kit to tell him it was time to go up to Primrose Hill, was that he didn't want the children to realise the depths of his incompetence, incompetence that had led Lyttons into the financial disaster that was now staring it in the face.

'Such a lovely day. You lucky girl. Happy birthday.'

'Thank you.'

Izzie kissed her dutifully.

She did look rather pale, Celia thought; probably her diagnosis of the evening before had been correct.

'Now, have the flowers arrived?'

'Yes, they're in the marquee in buckets.'

'And did you and Adele get a nice dress?'

'Yes, it's beautiful. Really lovely. Adele's not here, she's gone back to Venetia's.'

'May I see the dress?'

'Well—'

'Oh, Izzie, don't be silly, dear. Let me come and have a look. Or better still put it on, I want to see how you look in your mother's pearls—'

So she knew about that. How did she know everything, was there anything her father didn't tell her? Izzie felt hurt, betrayed even.

'Go on, Izzie. I'm sure it's lovely. The one thing one can rely on is Adele's taste.'

'Oh – all right.'

It was a lovely dress, palest pink crêpe, very simple, with a round neck and a softly falling skirt to just below her knee. She put it on, studied herself in her looking-glass. She did look very pretty. Even she had to admit it. What a shame Kit couldn't see her. She put the pearls on, looked at herself solemnly again. They were such a wonderful colour, with that very slight pink tone; they made her skin look creamily rich. She suddenly saw her mother's face in the mirror. So familiar from photographs, saw how true it was how alike they were. Her mother would have approved of what she was doing, she felt more confident about it now: brave she had been, her father said, brave and a free spirit. She sprayed herself with her Yardley cologne – the Schiaparelli was in her suitcase – then piled her hair up on top of her head with a comb. She felt rather reckless. If she wasn't going to be on show tonight, she might as well do it now.

She ran downstairs, laughing; as she reached the hall, there was a ring at the bell. She opened it; Henry Warwick stood there, a box of records in his arms. He looked at her, whistled loudly.

'Wow, Izzie. You look absolutely superb. Congratulations. Here, Roo, come on in, look at the birthday girl. Absolutely gorgeous. Can I have a birthday kiss?'

She raised her face, for him to kiss her cheek. Roo demanded one too. Boys' kisses: not a man's, not like Kit's. Just the same, it was rather nice to be admired.

'That's a peach of a dress,' said Roo. 'Peach of a dress for a – a peach of a girl.' He blushed violently.

'Thank you.' She felt excited suddenly, excited and grown-up.

'Where shall we put these?'

'Oh – in the dining room. That's where the dancing will—' She stopped. Where the dancing would have been. If she wasn't going to spoil this wonderful event.

'Fine. Righty-oh. Can't stop, Father's driver brought us. See you later, Izzie.'

'See you later,' she said. And felt briefly bleak.

Celia admired the dress, said it was a little too long for her, and that her hair would look better down.

'No girl should put her hair up before she's seventeen. The pearls are lovely, aren't they? I hope you're pleased with them.'

'I am. Terribly.'

'Right. Well, you'd better go and change. Oh, here's Kit. Kit, Izzie is looking absolutely marvellous.'

'Of course she is.'

And he smiled at her, his lovely, gentle, loving smile, and she felt perfectly all right again.

'Izzie, dear, you'd better take that dress off again, you'll get it dirty. When you've changed, would you get some vases from my car? I couldn't carry them all. My car's right at the bottom of your road, well, it's Venetia's old Austin Seven actually, the bright red one. I couldn't get anywhere near the house.'

'Of course,' said Izzie. Perfect: she could put her case in Venetia's car. Celia never locked cars, she said it was common.

Only two hours: two hours before they went. Izzie felt sick. The marquee was filling up with flowers, with glasses, with silver, with champagne bottles. Oh dear. Oh dear.

She felt her arm squeezed.

'Hallo, Mrs Lytton,' said Kit's voice. Very quietly of course. In her ear. Mrs Lytton! In a few days she would be Mrs Lytton. Possibly tomorrow, even.

'Hallo,' she said.

'Isabella, I've got to go out,' said Sebastian. 'Get some more wine. The fools haven't sent enough red. Say they can't make a delivery now, it's too late.'

'Really,' said Celia, 'I don't know what the world is coming to. No concept of service at all any more. Take my car, Sebastian.'

'You know I can't drive. Or rather daren't. I'll get a taxi. Where's the number? Hallo? Yes, this is Mr Brooke. Elsworthy Crescent. Can I have a taxi immediately please. Yes. What? What other taxi? I haven't ordered a taxi. You must be mistaken. Just a minute—'

He stopped, looked at Celia and Izzie.

'They say a cab's been ordered for six o'clock. Mean anything to either of you?'

Izzie froze.

'No. No, of course not.'

'I thought not. Hallo? Yes, I thought so, you were mistaken. No, cancel it. What? Oh, hold on—'

'Father, I think Mrs Conley ordered it.'

Izzie felt her brain moving into sleek, calm order.

'Mrs Conley? What on earth for?'

'She's going out for the evening. As you know.'

'Yes, of course, but I thought her son was picking her up at seven.'

'Well, he – he probably can't. He's got to do something. So I expect she wanted a taxi.'

'Oh. Oh, very well. I suppose it can't do any harm, we can send it away again if it's not needed. Hallo, yes, leave that booking please. God, I never want to give another party as long as I live.'

You probably won't, thought Izzie, you almost certainly won't.

Oliver had arrived; delivered early by Watkins, who was then being dispatched to the Warwicks' to pick up Adele and her children. Adele was official photographer: she had been instructed by Sebastian not to miss a moment of the party.

Izzie greeted Oliver, gave him a kiss, helped Watkins push him out to the terrace at the back of the house.

'Happy birthday, my dear. Not ready yet?'

'No. I haven't had time. Going up in one minute. Can I get you a drink first?'

'Oh – a cup of tea would be nice. Or would that be very difficult?'

'Of course not.'

Why couldn't he have asked for something quick and simple like water, or wine . . .

A quarter to six. God. Oh, God. Everything prepared. Kit sitting in the dining room by the door. Case in Celia's car. Handbag stuffed into the hedge by the gate. This was it. Or nearly. Five more minutes—

'Izzie, help me carry these vases in, would you? No, one at a time. There's no great hurry. Besides, I want to decide exactly where they should go, you can help me.'

'Izzie—'

'Yes, Kit?'

'I've got a frightful headache.'

'Oh, Kit, darling, just go and sit in the garden.'

'Mother, it sounds like bedlam out there. I'd like a little walk.'

'Kit, we're all very busy—'

'Oh, I see. Well – I'm sorry. Sorry to be a nuisance. As usual.'

'Kit—'

'Kit, I'll take you for a little walk. If – if Celia could find someone else to help her with the flowers—'

'Oh, yes, I suppose so. One of the waitresses perhaps. But don't be long.'

'No, of course not.'

'I've been thinking, Oliver.'

Celia had joined him on the terrace.

'Yes?'

'And I don't know why we didn't think of it before.'

'What's that, my dear?'

'New York. The New York office. They're obviously doing extremely well. We could ask them to supply us with some finance. We own half of it, after all, and—'

'We do. But it is set up as a completely separate entity, surely.'

'I'm aware of that. All the better. They're more likely to be able to help us.'

'It would place things on a very different basis, Celia. Even if they agreed, which is by no means a foregone conclusion. They would be in control of us, rather than – theoretically, anyway – the other way round.'

'Oliver, that is better than our not being in control of anything at all. Which is the situation I see developing all too fast. I think you should telephone Stuart Bailey on Monday and see what he has to say. I would be perfectly willing to go over there to talk to him; or perhaps Barty could help. She seems to feel she is in a strong position there. I wonder if that isn't slightly wishful thinking. She's only worked there very much under your aegis. She may find things rather different now.'

'Possibly.'

'Anyway, don't you think it's an idea worth pursuing?'

'Very well worth it, my dear, yes.'

'Good. That's settled then. Now I'm going upstairs to change. Will you be all right?'

'Of course.'

This was it.

'Come on then, Kit. Take my hand.'

Out of the room. Out of the door. Down the path. Don't hurry, don't hurry. Talk, look natural. Get handbag. Out of the gate, slowly down the road. There it was, the taxi, waiting. Don't rush, don't.

'You all right, Kit?'

'Yes, Izzie, I'm fine.'

She could see him smiling.

Here was Venetia's car now: open it, take out the suitcase. Dangerous bit, this. If someone came out now, saw them, or was arriving—

'Kit, I've got the case.' Her voice sounded odd, shaky, panicky.

'Good. Don't hurry, Izzie. Just walk slowly. Keep calm. I love you. Deep breaths.'

Right. Here they were. Opening the taxi door.

'Miss Brooke?'

'Yes. Yes, that's right. To King's Cross, please.'

'Righty-ho. Here, let me help you with that case.'

'No. No, it's all right.'

But he had got out, was walking round the taxi very slowly.

'Can't let a young lady lift a great thing like that.'

'It's quite light. Look—'

God. This was agony. He smiled at her, picked it up, put it in the taxi.

'Better strap it in.'

'No. No, it'll be fine.'

'Don't want to lose it, do you? Feels like there's quite a lot in here. Right now, that's all done. In you get. King's Cross, wasn't it?'

'Yes. We have to catch the seven o'clock to Scotland. So—'

'Where you two going, then, Gretna Green?'

He laughed loudly at his own wit, got back into the car, started the engine.

'No, of course not,' said Izzie primly: too primly. He looked round at her.

'Beg your pardon, I'm sure. Right then, off we go.'

They'd done it; they were away. Nothing could stop them now . . .

'Where are Izzie and Kit?' said Celia. 'They've been a long time.'

'Have they?' said Sebastian vaguely.

'Yes. It's a quarter past six. Bit irresponsible, just wandering off like that. Especially when it's her party and everyone's working so hard.'

'Yes, well, I expect she was feeling a bit nervous. Edgy. I'm sure they won't be much longer.'

Five minutes later, Adele arrived.

'Hallo, Sebastian darling. You look awfully handsome. How are you feeling?'

'Oh – you know. I could do with a drink.'

'Me too. Let's get one. Where's the birthday girl?'

'Oh – she's gone out for a little walk.'

'A walk! But it's – goodness, twenty past six.'

'I know. Kit wanted to go. He had a headache.'

'Had she changed?'

693

'No. No, she hadn't. I'm sure she won't be long.'

'Well – let's get a drink and you can show me everything.'

'Celia, where's Kit?'

'I told you, Oliver, he went for a walk with Izzie. A few minutes ago.'

'Oh, yes. It seems longer than that. I wanted to ask him something.'

'Well, the minute he gets back I'll tell him. I wish he'd hurry, I've got to tie his wretched tie.'

'Mummy, I don't want to worry anyone, but I can't find Izzie and Kit anywhere. It's getting late, it seems a bit – odd.'

'Not odd,' said Celia crisply, 'but irresponsible. I shall be extremely irritated when they do get back.'

'I might pop out, see if I can see them and get them to hurry. They're probably having one of their heart to hearts.'

'Yes,' said Celia, 'very probably.'

'Celia, there's no sign of them. What on earth do you think they can be doing?'

'I don't know, Sebastian. It's – odd. Adele's gone out to see if she can find them.'

'They haven't slipped back, I suppose? Without us seeing them?'

'Unlikely. But I'll go up to her room.'

Izzie's room had the neat, unlived-in look of a room abandoned; not the untidy heap of a girl getting ready to go to a party. Celia began to feel sick. She looked at the dressing table: no hairbrush, no powder compact. She took a deep breath. Don't be silly, Celia, keep calm. She's a funny old-fashioned child, not a messy hedonist like your daughters.

She looked in the cupboard; the pink dress was hanging there neatly under its cover. Surely – surely . . .

'Sebastian—'

'Found her?'

'No, Sebastian, I—'

'Hallo, Sebastian. Here we are.'

It was Henry and Roo, absurdly grown up in their dinner jackets.

'Where is she? We're dying to give her our present.'

'She – she isn't here at the moment,' said Celia quickly, 'she took Kit for a walk.'

'What, just before her party? Bit rum. Well, never mind. The girls

694

are coming in and the aged parents are following in their car with Fergal.'

'Right. Well, you all go and have some fruit punch. Sebastian and I have things to do.'

'Want us to go and look for them? We can run jolly fast.'

'No, it's all right. Adele's gone. And it's only—'

Only twenty-five to seven. Three quarters of an hour since they'd gone. God. Dear God.

'Oh, Sebastian,' she said. She felt terribly sick.

'I can't see them anywhere,' said Adele, 'it's really odd.'

'Yes. Yes, it is a bit.'

'Mummy, are you all right? You look awful.'

'I'm – fine,' said Celia quickly. 'Um – darling, you go in and get your camera ready—'

'Mummy, what is it? Why are you looking so frightened?'

Celia stared at her.

'I think they – they might have run away,' she said.

'Well, we're here,' said Izzie.

'Yes. I can hear. Such wonderful sounds, steam hissing, trains whistling. I love stations.'

'Me too. Now then, just let me see if I can find a porter – ah, there we are. Yes, please. The seven o'clock to Scotland. Which platform is that?'

'Platform Six, Miss. I'll take you over. Here, put your case on this cart.'

'Oh – good evening, Helena.'

'Good evening, Celia. Are you all right?'

'Why should I not be?' said Celia icily. Even in her hour of terror, she was not going to have Helena patronising her.

'You look terrible.'

'Well, thank you for that.'

'No, I'm sorry, I mean you look marvellous. But a bit – pale.'

'Well, I've been working very hard all afternoon doing the flowers. Good evening, George and Mary. Giles, take them all through and give them a drink, would you?'

'Of course. Where's the birthday girl?'

'She's not here,' said Celia.

*

'Celia, keep calm, keep calm.' Sebastian was holding both her hands, staring into her eyes. 'It's probably perfectly all right. They've just gone on some childish expedition together. Very naughty, but not serious.'

'No, Sebastian. It's not that. I'm sure, I'm sure it's not. They've – they've run away together. And if they have—'

He looked at her; his face was drawn and almost grey.

'Yes,' he said, 'if they have . . .'

'Right. Here are our seats. You sit here, Kit, that's right, in the corner, and I'll sit next to you. Shall I take your jacket?'

'No. I'm a bit chilly, at the moment.'

He looked rather pale; he was shivering slightly.

'I feel shivery too. I suppose we're a bit – scared.'

'Yes. Still, once the train has started—'

'Mmm. And they have no idea where we are. So—'

'No. Here, sit down. Give me your hand. That's right. Better?'

'Much better.'

'Darling Izzie.'

'Darling Kit.'

'But they could be anywhere. Anywhere. How do we start finding them? I think we should get the police—'

'Mummy, they've only been gone for less than an hour. The police would laugh at you.'

'Venetia, please allow me to handle this in my own way.'

'Yes, all right. Sorry. Can Boy help?'

'No one can help.'

'We're here!'

'What – oh! Jay, Tory, hallo.'

'Hallo, Celia. Gordon's just parking. Sebastian, let me give you a kiss. You look terribly attractive, I can't wait to dance with you.'

'Yes, that will be very nice. Look – go and get yourselves a drink, will you? I'll be through in a minute.'

'Well,' murmured Victoria to Jay as they walked through the house, 'something doesn't seem quite right. I've never seen Celia looking so distraught. What do you think it is?'

'Probably just decided one of the waiters isn't quite the thing. Champagne?'

'Please.'

*

The party was already uneasy, pockets of silence in the noise, everyone wary, knowing that something was not right, not liking to ask what. Even Henry and Roo were unnerved. The waitresses stood with their trays of drinks, uncomfortable as well; not liking to start moving round this still, taut gathering. The younger children were in the garden, shouting, a backdrop of normality to the tension.

'I don't like this,' said Adele.

'Of course,' said Sebastian suddenly, 'the taxi rank. He said something about a booking for six o'clock. And Izzie said—' He stopped, raced upstairs to Mrs Conley's room. She was sitting dressed in her hat and coat.

'Mrs Conley, did you order a taxi for six?'

'A taxi, Mr Brooke? No, of course not. My son is coming for me, is he here?'

'Not yet, Mrs Conley, no.'

He ran downstairs again, into his study, asked for the number.

'Engaged, sir, sorry.'

'Keep trying.'

Barty arrived in a taxi, with Jenna.

'Hallo. Sorry I'm late, I – Celia, whatever is the matter?'

'We've lost Izzie and Kit,' said Celia. She had stopped pretending.

'Taxi rank?'

'Ah yes. Mr Brooke here. Look, we had a taxi at six today—'

'Yes?'

'Is he back yet?'

'Not as far as I know, Mr Brooke.'

'Well – do you know where the booking was for?'

'It was – let me see. Yes, King's Cross station.'

'King's Cross? But why there—'

'Mummy, Sebastian—'

'Yes, what is it?'

Adele had never seen her mother look like this, so absolutely shaken from her normal composure, chain-smoking, pacing up and down. It was – odd.

'I've been thinking. And I've got an idea. It's only an idea, but—'

'Yes, what is it?'

Adele took a deep breath.

'I think you should – well, have you thought about – about Gretna Green?'

697

'Surely the train should have left by now.'

Izzie looked at her watch. She frowned. 'Yes, it should. I wonder—'

A porter was coming along the platform; she let the window down by its leather belt, leaned out.

'Excuse me, has there been a delay?'

'Just a short one, Miss. Some problem with the guard. Apparently he's not well.'

'Oh, no! So how long will it be—'

'Not long, Miss. Shouldn't be more than a few minutes.'

'Oh. Oh, I see. Well – thank you.'

She sat down again, took Kit's hand. 'Did you hear that?'

'Of course.'

'Just our luck.'

'It's only a little delay.'

'I know that. But it could be dangerous.'

'How?'

'Well, suppose they've guessed. They might come after us. If the train's still here—'

'Izzie, don't be silly. How on earth could they possibly guess? Of course they won't. And even if they did, they'd never get here in time. Stop fussing and read me a bit of the evening paper.'

'Yes, all right.'

'I'll drive.'

Boy flung himself into his car, started the engine. Adele got in beside him, Celia and Sebastian in the back.

'What time is the train?'

'Seven.'

'Well, we won't make it. Can't. It'll take at least ten minutes. Even with me driving. It's five to seven already.'

'It's worth a try. Anything's better than just hanging around that place.'

Boy shrugged. 'OK. We'll try.'

'Of course,' said Adele, 'I may be wrong.'

'In matters of intuition,' said Boy, 'and in my experience, you and your sister are very seldom wrong.'

'And I am rather good at planning how to run away,' said Adele quietly.

George Riley, the guard on the overnight express to Scotland, swallowed his third Rennie tablet and stood up, then groaned loudly and sat down again.

'Bloody 'ell.'

'Bad, is it, George?'

'Bloody awful. The wife said I didn't ought to have had it. That pie. They never agree with me. Do for me ulcer. But I was so hungry and it looked that inviting – oh, lord. Excuse me.'

He rushed off in the direction of the lavatory; the stationmaster and the assistant stationmaster looked at one another.

'Looks like it's invited itself back,' said the stationmaster. 'Anyway, have to find someone else, I think. He can't go up to Scotland non-stop in that condition.'

'Excuse me. Any more news of the guard?'

'Yes, Miss. We've had to find a replacement. Mr Riley, that's the guard, has been taken ill.'

'Oh, dear. But – well, when do you think we'll be leaving now?'

'In about ten minutes, Miss.'

'You said that ten minutes ago.'

'I'm sorry, Miss. Can't be helped.'

'Thank you.'

Izzie sat down again; she felt sick. Suddenly it wasn't fun and it wasn't an adventure; it was scary, going wrong, and she didn't know how to cope with it.

'Don't worry,' said Kit. 'I told you, they'll never guess. They couldn't.'

'This is jolly exciting,' said Henry Warwick, 'better than having the party. I say, Roo, shall we ask that waitress for some more champagne?'

'Rather. Where's Mother?'

'Talking to Barty. Probably about babies. It's all the women in this family ever seem to think of.'

'Barty's pretty old as well, isn't she? I honestly don't know what's the matter with them all.'

'Platform Six, sir. You're lucky, it's been delayed. You might just—'

'Thanks. We've actually come to see someone off.'

'You'll need platform tickets then.'

Boy groped in his pocket, found a fiver.

'Will this do?'

The ticket collector looked at him with all the dignity of his calling.

'I'm afraid not, sir. One penny each, from that machine over there. Push your penny in, pull the slot out.'

'Jesus,' said Boy. 'Sebastian, for God's sake, have you got any penny coins?'

'Oh, good. There's the driver now, walking along, look, with his mate. That must mean – oh, there's our porter again. Have they found a guard?'

'Yes, Miss. Couple more minutes now and you'll be off.'

'Good. Kit, I'm just going out to the corridor, stretch my legs. I feel a bit—'

'Hallo, Kit. Hallo, Izzie.' It was Boy.

'Hallo,' said Izzie. Her voice was very quiet.

'Sebastian! They're here. Look, you two, I think you'd better get off—'

'We're not going to. Are we, Kit?'

'No. No, we're not. And you can't make us.'

'Kit—'

'It's no good, Sebastian, Izzie and I are in love. We're going to get married. We're going to Scotland. Where we can. And if you stop us this time, we'll just do it again. So you might as well—'

'Kit, old chap. Kit, listen to me.' Sebastian sat down now next to him, put his arm round his shoulders. Kit shook it off.

'Don't. Don't patronise me.'

'Kit, get off this train. And you, Izzie. Please. Just quickly and quietly. Otherwise there'll have to be a frightful row. We've told the stationmaster what you've done, they won't let you stay.'

'Why the hell not?' said Kit. 'We're not doing anything illegal.'

'Kit, please, get off.'

'No.'

A long silence; then finally Sebastian said, 'There's something I've got to tell you, Kit. Something which will – well, will change things for you. Which maybe we should have told you long ago.'

'Who's we?'

'Your mother and I.'

Kit was suddenly very still; it was as if a hot white light had flared in his head. The memories, the odd memories, making sense with each other and at last: LM saying, 'Your father must be so delighted . . . and Oliver too'; little Noni, looking at the photographs of Sebastian, saying, 'he looks like Kit, really exactly like'; the game

700

at Christmas, Gordon Robinson's voice, 'absolutely identical brains, the three of you'.

Sebastian's absolute determination to take Izzie to America: it all made sense. Perfect, ugly, disgusting sense.

He stood up and said, 'Let's get off the train. Come on, Izzie. It seems we can't go after all.'

Chapter 50

He never told Izzie. It was the bravest, most difficult thing he had ever done; but somehow he knew he must not. It was too ugly, too much for her to bear. One day perhaps; but not yet. Not while she was still a child, still so innocent. It was also a measure of how much he loved her.

It would have been easier to tell her. To tell the truth: to blame the whole thing on the adults. Rather than pretending first that he agreed to wait, and then that he thought it was better if they didn't after all think about getting married for quite a long time. Leaving her hurt, terribly, terribly hurt. But at least with her innocence, her faith in people intact.

They didn't ask him to do that.

Celia and Sebastian, his parents, said he must do what he thought best. They asked nothing of him: except to finish his relationship with Izzie.

At first, too angry, too shocked even to speak to either of them, he asked if he might go down to Ashingham and spend some time there, on the Home Farm with his grandmother.

That was dreadful – in its own way. Being there without Izzie, without her attention and thoughtfulness, her soft, pretty voice, her gift of bringing things to life for him, her hand taking his, her giggle, her slightly tedious jokes. It was absolutely dreadful.

He had to learn all over again what loneliness and isolation were. He sat scowling on the terrace, was morose and difficult with Billy Miller, sullen with his uncle James – or was he his uncle? God, it was so confusing. He couldn't work, he couldn't do anything. He didn't want to do anything.

How could they have done that: how? How could his mother, his brilliant, beautiful mother, have cheated on his father – on Oliver and to that extent? How could she have deceived him all those years? How could she have lived that lie, on and on? Telling everyone, simply by her silence, that he was Oliver's son. How could she have deceived her own children, presented him to the rest of the family as their brother, to the world as the youngest Lytton? And how could Sebastian – his father – have allowed it? Not just the deception, but the letting go, not claiming him, not saying 'this is my son'.

All for – what? Convention? Protection of themselves? Preservation of the status quo, the family, the name? Not a Lytton then; but a Brooke. Not even a Brooke: a bastard. All the ugly things, the ugly words: bastard, born on the wrong side of the blanket, out of wedlock, child of shame.

He couldn't bear it; he couldn't.

That first night had been dreadful; driving back in the car, Izzie clinging to his hand, crying, Sebastian and Boy silent.

Celia and Adele took a taxi back to Cheyne Walk. The party was hastily cancelled, the baffled waitresses cleared up the uneaten food, the undrunk champagne, while the younger children complained, begged to be allowed to stay, and the older ones understood only that something serious had happened, tried to find out what.

Roo and Henry Warwick heard a conversation, their ears pressed to their parents' bedroom door; completely baffling, completely unsatisfactory . . .

'It all makes sense suddenly,' their mother had said, 'well, a lot of things. Poor, poor Kit.'

'And poor Izzie.'

'And poor Daddy. That's who I keep thinking of. If it's true. Poor, poor, darling Daddy.'

And then their father said, very gently, 'I think, my darling, that Oliver is far better at taking care of himself than you realise.'

And then they couldn't hear any more.

Next day Adele came round: still more baffling conversation, in their stupid twin-talk.

'So do you think—'

'Oh, I suppose—'

'But if—'

'Yes, but then—'

'Poor Izzie.'

'Poor Kit.'

'Poor Daddy.'

'Will Mummy ever—'

'Shouldn't think—'

'Nor would I.'

'It's—'

'I know. But one shouldn't—'

'Of course not.'

And then their mother saying firmly, 'Not for us to judge, though', and Adele saying, 'Absolutely not'.

Both of them were clearly upset at lunch and then went for a walk together down the street, their arms round each other like stupid schoolgirls. When they came back, they were quite giggly and suggested they all play Monopoly.

'Should we ask Izzie round? Might cheer her up, she loves Monopoly.'

'I don't think so.' said Venetia carefully, 'not today. Maybe in a week or two.'

Izzie went to her room when they finally got back to the house, shot out of the car without looking at Kit, who was in the door; 'Don't come near me,' she said to her father fiercely, 'don't dare come near me. And don't send anyone else up either.'

She stayed there all the next day; in the evening she appeared in the drawing room white and hollow-eyed.

'I'm sorry, Father,' she said.

'Oh, my darling. Why sorry? None of it was your fault.'

She didn't quite understand why not.

'I'm sorry about the party,' she said, 'after all you did for me. Very sorry.'

'Oh, that,' he said. 'That doesn't matter. It couldn't matter less.'

'I think it did. Anyway, I just wanted to say that.'

He was silent; then, 'Would you like anything to eat?'

'No. No, thank you.'

'How about some cocoa?'

She hesitated. 'Yes. All right.'

'You're still wearing your pearls.'

'I shall never take them off.'

He seemed to have got off lightly. With Izzie at any rate.

Not with Kit, though. Kit stayed away from him, in icy, aloof isolation, refusing to listen to his stumbling attempts at an apology. Sebastian wrote to him; the letter came back unopened. Once or twice he called at Cheyne Walk; Kit refused to see him.

It was a double irony, a double tragedy: to have been acknowledged, however unhappily, by a son, and to have lost him, both in the same hour.

'Try not to be too upset,' Celia said. 'He'll come round. I know he will. He won't speak to me either. He's outraged, shocked, hurt, all those things. And he's very young.'

'He's twenty-six, for God's sake.'

'He's a very young twenty-six. As Adele once said.'

'And now – Celia, how – how many people know, do you think?'

'Oh – hardly anyone. Still. That's what Kit wants, clearly.'

'I suppose I'm relieved. But sad too in a way. I would so like to claim you at last. You and him.'

'Well, you can't,' she said, and told him what had happened that night when she had got home to Oliver.

She had gone into his room; he was sitting, staring out of the window, and she had said, 'Oliver, there is something, something I have to tell you.'

And he had said, looking at her with something close to amusement on his face, 'Celia, do you really think I did not know?'

Sebastian telephoned Barty the next day and asked her to come up to the house.

'Isabella's very upset that you're leaving, she wants to say goodbye. And I think she'll be able to talk to you.'

'Of course,' said Barty.

She found Izzie tear-stained, exhausted, but calm.

'I just feel so – stupid,' she said, 'I thought he loved me so much and – well, the first bit of opposition and he just crumbled. Fell at the first fence, as Lady B would say.'

'Haven't you thought,' said Barty gently, 'that he might have given you up because he loved you so much? That he suddenly realised, once he'd been made to think about it, what he was actually doing to you? I mean, I know you're very grown-up, Izzie, but – do you really think you're ready to be married?'

'Yes, of course,' she said, 'but anyway, it was all my idea. I thought of it, I persuaded him, not the other way round. You mustn't think badly of him.'

'I don't. No one could love Kit more than I do – what a stupid thing to say, you do, lots of people do – but he is quite a – a liability. Not just because he's blind, but because he's very self-centred—'

705

That was a mistake.

'He's not. He's not self-centred. He's incredibly unselfish, actually.'

'Izzie, that wasn't a criticism. It's all part of his blindness, his helplessness. In time, perhaps, he thought you would come to resent that, not be able to do all the things you want—'

'But I would have, we'd planned it all—'

'Of course. And I'm sure he would have been as helpful as he possibly could. I'm only saying that in many ways you would have had to look after him all your life.'

'But that's what I wanted. That's what we both wanted. Well –' her voice shook '– well, I thought it was what we both wanted. You don't understand.'

'Perhaps I don't. No. But I'm sure he must have realised what hard work it would have been for you. How much it would have – wearied you.'

'It wouldn't.'

'Izzie, you want to go to university, don't you? I've heard talk of you wanting to be a doctor. How could you have done that?'

'I could. He'd have helped me.'

'I think perhaps he realised that he couldn't have helped you as much as he would have liked. Or as much as you needed. I think he loved you so very much that he couldn't bear that.'

'It was a bit – quick,' said Izzie, scowling.

'It seemed a bit quick, I agree. But don't you think that underneath he did know it? And being – confronted – by what he was doing, made him realise it – quickly?'

'I don't know,' said Izzie, but she managed a watery smile at Barty. 'Thank you. Thank you for coming. I wish you weren't going away.'

'Come and see me.'

'That's what Father said. He still wants to go. Not for a whole year now, he said, but this summer. In the holidays.'

'Izzie, I wish you would. I've got – well, I've got a nice place to live. Not right in the middle of New York, somewhere much better. Come and stay with me, you and Sebastian, I'd love it. So would Jenna.'

'All right. We will,' said Izzie. 'It'll be better than being here, without Kit.'

'I think a bit better,' said Barty, smiling.

Sebastian thanked her, walked down the road to her car.

'She's very fond of you.'

'I'm very fond of her. As you know.'

706

'I don't suppose you feel very fond of me. At the moment.'

'Sebastian,' said Barty, reaching up to kiss him, 'if there's one thing I've learned over the last few years, it's that what people have done or not done doesn't seem to have much effect on how you feel about them. As I said to Izzie, you must come and stay with me in New York. I'd like that, very much.'

'Have you got room for us?'

'Oh, yes,' she said, 'I've got room.'

It was his grandmother who made some sense of it all for Kit.

She heard him one morning being rude to Billy; telling him to go away and leave him alone.

'Kit,' she said, 'I know you're very unhappy and with good reason, but that is no excuse for speaking to Billy like that. If you can't behave better, you'll have to go home.'

'And where's that?' he said. 'I feel I don't have one any more.'

'Oh, don't be so ridiculous. Here, take my hand, let's go for a walk. You've lost your companion, haven't you, that's very hard.'

'It's all very hard,' he said, and heard his voice shake.

'I'm sorry. Very sorry. I can only tell you you will feel better in time.'

'I don't see how you can know that.'

'I'm nearly ninety,' she said. 'I was married for almost seventy years. I know a lot about life and what it can do to you.'

'Grandmama, with respect, I don't think you ever had anything like this to contend with. I feel so – ashamed of them. Of them both.'

'Yes, of course you do. And it's a dreadful shock.'

'I admired Sebastian, you know. I thought he was marvellous. And we were very close. I – I shall never forget the day of Pandora's funeral. I think I really helped him.' He laughed, a harsh, heavy sound. 'Well, I now know why.'

'Oh, Kit. Does it matter?'

'I'm sorry?'

'Does it matter why you were able to help him, why you were so close? You were, you did, you loved him. All right, so he was your father. That doesn't invalidate it. A lot of people never get at all close to their fathers. It doesn't mean anything. Except that you helped him. A great deal. That's what mattered.'

'I just can't forgive him,' he said, 'I never shall. Or my mother.'

'Oh, I think you will.'

'Grandmama, I won't. That was a dreadful lie they lived all those years. It was an appalling thing to do.'

'Why?'

'What?' He stopped.

'Perhaps you should consider why they lived the lie. It wasn't – perhaps – what they wanted to do. But they did it for a lot of perfectly good reasons. To preserve the marriage. To keep the family together.'

'It's so hypocritical.'

'And what's so terrible about that? What would you have had them do? Your mother walk out on Oliver who loves her so very much, desert her other three children, disrupt everything, including Lyttons? Do you really think that would have been the right thing to do? That hypocrisy you disapprove of so much entailed great personal sacrifice on their parts.'

'Oh, for God's sake, Grandmama. They should have behaved properly in the first place, you speak as if they did nothing wrong—'

'Oh, we should all behave properly, Kit. All our lives, never make mistakes. Of course. Perhaps you will manage that. Although I wonder if you thought of the wretched unhappiness you would have caused if you had succeeded in your plan. Quite apart from depriving Izzie of her youth.'

'That's unfair.'

'It is not unfair. She is a child. She is totally unready for marriage.'

'But it was what she wanted.'

'Kit, she has no idea what she wants. She's very unsophisticated, absolutely unworldly. Far less so than the twins were at her age, certainly less so than your mother.'

'I feel so disappointed in my mother,' he said, 'so betrayed.'

'Well, that's natural. But – you will forgive her. I promise you. She loves you very much. She's a remarkable woman, Kit.'

'I don't think I can,' he said, 'forgive her.'

'Oh, nonsense. Good Lord, Beckenham did some dreadful things to me. As I did to him, I daresay. Have you not heard about it all?'

'A – a bit,' he said, a grudging smile on his face.

'Of course. Family legend now, quite amusing, the housemaids. But at the time, when I was a young woman, a bride, in love with my husband, it was appalling. He first got into bed with someone else a month after our honeymoon. I was pregnant with James, and he was having an affair with some woman, not a housemaid, I could have coped better with that, some woman in London. But – I did forgive him. The misery eased and I came to appreciate the other things, what he was, what he did for me. And then there were all the housemaids, think of that, under my roof, knowing the staff were watching, highly

708

amused by it all. A couple of illegitimate babies as well, to be dispatched, with their mothers, to cottages I had to find for them, with discreet financial allowances which I had to organise. Not easy, Kit, actually. But – I would say we had a pretty happy marriage. A pretty good one. Marriages don't stay in neat, tidy shapes, you know; they sprawl about, very messily sometimes. The important thing is not to let them get out of control. Which I think is what your mother did.'

'Oh.' He didn't feel exactly better; but there was just a slight easing of his misery. 'And then – my father. Or rather, Oliver, what could it have been like for him?'

'Oh, Kit,' she said, 'Kit, you really don't want to worry too much about Oliver. He is an extremely tough nut, far more able to take care of himself than all that vague, frail helplessness implies. He had his own way of dealing with the situation, I do assure you. I'm not saying he wasn't exactly happy with it, but – well, he hasn't been weeping into his pillow for the last few years. Why don't you talk to him about it? Mind you, you won't get much out of him. I have never known a man more able to avoid confrontation.'

'I – see,' said Kit. 'Well, I might – talk to him. One day. Yes.'

'Two things I'd like to say, and then we'll go back and have a stiff drink. I do admire you for keeping it from Izzie. Very brave indeed. I understand it was entirely your own wish. One day you may feel you can tell her, but she's much too young now. And the other thing is I never heard such rubbish about you not having a home. Of course you have. It could be argued you have two. Three, if you'd like to count this one in.'

'Thank you,' said Kit. And realised that he thought he rather would.

Chapter 51

'They've agreed in principle,' said Oliver.

'Good. I thought they would. After all, if it hadn't been for you, there would be no New York office. You have a half share in it.'

'I know that, my dear. So you have often said. Just the same, it was far from being a foregone conclusion. They're sending someone over to draw up the agreement. Go through our figures, all that sort of thing.'

'Oh, really? Who?'

'Stuart didn't say. Just that someone would be coming. And bringing a lawyer, of course.'

'It sounds a little – high-handed.'

'Well – I could hardly object. And they could have called one of us over there. They didn't.'

'Well – it would have had to be you. And they could hardly expect that.'

'And Barty is coming with him.'

'Barty!'

'Yes.'

'I'm surprised. I wouldn't have thought she was in a responsible enough position to attend such a meeting.'

'Well, I imagine she will make things easier all round. She knows us so well, knows the company and its history, and of course its plans, and now she's working there, she's familiar with the personnel—'

'Only the editorial personnel, surely.'

'Yes, I suppose so. Anyway, for whatever reason, she's coming. It will be nice to see her. I miss her.'

'Oliver, she's only been gone a little over a month.'

'I know. I'm allowed to say I miss her, aren't I?'

'Yes, of course.'

'I miss Kit too, I have to say. Very much.'

'So do I. Oliver—'

'I think I might have a rest now. And then I shall telephone our

710

solicitors and alert them to the date and so on, what we might need. I wish we still had Peter Briscoe. I liked him much better than this new young chap. I suppose it's a symptom of our age that we like the old chaps more than the young.'

'That may be so for you, Oliver, but I like the new young chap as you call him. Very quick, very smart. I always found Peter Briscoe a little – dilatory. When exactly is this happening?'

'Next week. Next Wednesday. The nineteenth. Just, inside our period, which is a relief. It will all be settled before quarter day. They're flying over.'

'Flying! Good God.'

'Well, it's much quicker. Takes about twelve hours. Rather than five days.'

'Oliver—'

'Yes, Celia?'

'You really shouldn't feel too badly about this. Lyttons may be going through a bad patch, but it is still one of the great publishing houses. And we did that. We made it that. We mustn't forget it, and we certainly mustn't let some upstart from New York forget it. They aren't bailing out some hapless incompetent company, they're getting a chance to be more closely involved with a brilliant publishing house, one with a fine past and a brilliant future. Just remember that, won't you?'

He smiled at her. 'You always were very good at stiffening my sinews, Celia. Anyway, you'll be there, won't you?'

'Of course.'

Celia felt unaccountably nervous as the day of the meeting arrived. She had cabled to suggest that Barty and the other two might stay at Cheyne Walk, but Barty had cabled back politely to say that they would be exhausted, and she would prefer to stay in a hotel so that they could go straight to bed and sleep off the journey.

'Maybe dinner Wednesday evening,' the cable had ended, 'love Barty.'

She didn't know why she was so nervous; she was more than a match for any publishing executive, and certainly for any lawyer. Their own solicitor, whom she had professed to like but actually considered quite dreadful, a pushy young man called Michael Talbot, was coming to Lyttons at two; the Americans and Barty were due to arrive at two-thirty.

She dressed with great care; in a dress she had ordered from Hartnell, a soft jersey sheath, swathed across the body, with one of the new clusters of tiny felt flowers pinned to the shoulder. Her hair was swept back off her face and piled up in a chignon; she spent twice the usual time on her make-up. When Celia's back was to the wall, she liked it to be elegantly clad.

Venetia alone knew that the Americans were coming and why; Celia had asked her to keep it to herself.

'Giles will start clucking about like an old mother hen, wanting to muscle in on things, and Jay will want to know exactly what, when and why. But come to dinner in the evening, will you, they're joining us, and Boy too.'

'Yes, of course. It'll be fun. Surely someone will see Barty, though?'

'They'll assume it's a social visit. Anyway, by the time she's been seen it will be more or less over.'

'I suppose so. Well, good luck.'

'I don't think we exactly need that,' said Celia coolly.

Michael Talbot was sitting in Oliver's office when the visitors' arrival was announced; 'We'll go to the boardroom,' Oliver said to the receptionist, 'please escort them there.'

'Miss Miller says she'd like to see you alone first. In your office, if that's all right.'

'Oh. Yes, of course. Please send her up. Mr Talbot, would you be kind enough to go along to the boardroom? We won't be long.'

'Of course, Mr Lytton. Now do please remember, we don't want to give too much away. You can always negotiate forwards, but never backwards.'

'I don't think there is any danger of our giving too much away. Now – Barty, my dear. How lovely to see you.'

She came in smiling, kissed them both. She was looking extremely chic: she must have spent most of her salary on that suit, a bright print tweed, Celia thought. If she hadn't known it was impossible, she would have said it was by Adele Simpson. It was certainly a very good copy.

'It's lovely to see you too.'

'How was your journey?'

'Oh amazing. It only took about twelve hours. We stopped in Reykjavik, to refuel, you know. Of course it's not fun, like the ships, but for just getting here it's so much better. And we had wonderful food, and some very nice wine, I slept like a baby last night, quite caught up with myself.'

'Where are you staying?'

'At Claridges.'

'Very nice.' They must think a lot of her, to be spending all this money on her. 'We're so looking forward to dinner tonight. Adele is coming, and Boy. I hope that's all right.'

'Of course.'

'We can catch up on gossip then. Is Jenna well?'

'She's absolutely fine. Loves it.'

'It must be very hot over there now.'

'Oh, no, it's all right. Where we are, anyway—'

'So your colleagues are in the boardroom, are they?'

'My colleague, yes.'

'Oh.' Celia frowned. 'I thought you were bringing two people. A solicitor and someone from Lyttons.'

'It's just me from Lyttons. And our lawyer, Marcus P. Wainwright.' She giggled. 'Isn't that a marvellous name? All Americans, American professionals anyway, have these terribly important initials. Which I sometimes think don't stand for anything at all.'

Celia ignored this piece of flippancy. 'Barty, I do hope this isn't all going to be a waste of time, we were expecting someone empowered to negotiate.'

'It won't be a waste of time. I can do any necessary negotiating.'

'Are you sure?' Oliver frowned. 'It's quite – high-powered, you know. Stuart led us to believe—'

'Wol, don't worry. I have full authority. Very full. Now, just tell me quickly, before we go in there, exactly what you need.'

'A – sizeable sum.'

'Ye-es. How sizeable?'

'Oh – Barty, is this really necessary? Now, without—'

'Yes, it is. I need to know. I really do.'

'Barty, I'm sorry, but—' Celia was becoming impatient.

Oliver interrupted her. 'Celia, I think we can trust Barty.'

'I'm sure we can trust her. But—'

'We need, I estimate, a quarter of a million pounds. To see us through this patch.'

'A quarter of a million? That doesn't sound enough to me. From what I've seen of the figures, I'd have thought twice that. If you're going to turn yourselves round, give yourselves room to manoeuvre, it takes time, you need—'

'Barty, I think we should go into the boardroom now,' said Celia. Her voice was very cold. 'This is not a discussion we ought to be having in here, on this informal basis.'

'Well – all right. In a minute. They can wait. I'm sure they're talking lawyer-talk.'

'I daresay they are. I was not concerned about them. More about us.'

'Look.' Barty stood up suddenly, walked over to the window, then turned to face them both. She smiled at them; silhouetted against the window, she looked faintly threatening. 'I have my own ideas on this. And they're very clear.'

'Barty—'

'Celia, please listen to me. I have a proposition for you. I want you to sell me the remaining half share in Lyttons New York. For a price that we can negotiate, but I would say in the area of two million dollars. That will give you plenty of working capital. Oh, and Marcus P. thinks we should have some shares in Lyttons London as well. But we can discuss that. In there.'

'Barty—' Oliver pushed his hand through his hair; he looked bewildered. 'Barty, forgive me, but I don't quite see – you say we should sell you the remaining half share in Lyttons New York?'

'Yes. Yes, that's what I said.'

'But – the forty-nine per cent or whatever surely doesn't belong to – Lyttons.'

'I didn't say it did.'

'I understood it had been left to – to Laurence Elliott's – that is to – to the wife.'

There was a very long silence. Then, 'Oliver,' said Barty, 'Oliver, there's something I haven't told you. Probably should have done. Sorry. I am – or rather I was – the wife.'

Epilogue

Autumn 1946

The Directors of Lyttons London request the pleasure of your company on Wednesday, 11 September 1946 at Lytton House, Grosvenor Square, to celebrate the launch of *Opium For the Few* by Mr Geordie MacColl.
Champagne.
6–8 p.m.

It was the first party in the new office; it was considered very appropriate. Not that anyone had spelt it out of course: that it was American money which had rejuvenated Lyttons and an American author who was to be fêted.

'Thank goodness,' said Venetia, 'we're not in that horrible Clarice Street. Imagine having a party there. If only I wasn't so huge. Do you know, I couldn't even get into my little car today.'

'Well, it's time you got rid of it.'

'I couldn't possibly. I love it far too much. We got that car for our birthday when – when—'

'Yes, I remember when,' said Boy, 'and you were nearly as beautiful as you are now.'

'You do talk rubbish, Boy. Oh dear, and I hear Geordie MacColl is terribly sexy. He won't have any time for me at all. Great sailing ship of a woman bearing down on him.'

'I think, Venetia, a woman who is eight months pregnant should hardly be worrying about whether a sexy man is going to have any time for her.'

'You will come, Boy, won't you?'

'Of course. Try and keep me away. And I think it's frightfully nice of them to ask the boys.'

'Isn't it? They're both terribly excited. You must read the riot act to

715

them about drinking. Roo was sick all night after Izzie's – well, after Izzie's evening.'

'I will. And I hear Izzie is coming.'

'Yes, with Sebastian. She telephoned me last night, so full of her trip, of Barty's house by the sea, Barty's wonderful office, Barty's other house—'

'Barty's other house?'

'Yes. There's this mansion on Long Island, which is amazing by all accounts, and then some palace on Park Avenue. Only she's selling that. Getting some little place in the city.'

'I do love it all,' said Boy, 'this Cinderella story. There she is, little Barty, rescued by your mother from the slums, the queen of Lyttons New York.'

'Well – yes,' said Venetia, who found the story slightly harder to love. Especially the fact that Barty could now be said to own a slice of Lyttons London.

'Don't be a puss in the manger. She's suffered for it, she's done her time. I think it's wonderful. When is she arriving? On Monday, I think, bringing the little princess?'

'I don't know, Boy. Sorry. I do hope this baby is a princess, incidentally. I don't think I could stand another boy.'

'I hope so too. I want an exact replica of her mother. Exact.'

'Jay, how do I look? Good enough for you?'

'Just about. Wow. You look terrific, Tory. Absolutely terrific. You look marvellous in any colour—'

'As long as it's black.'

'What?'

'Sorry. Being silly. Misquoting Henry Ford. Anyway, black's all right, is it?'

'It's perfect. I like that sort of tail thing, falling off the skirt.'

'Train, Jay, train. Oh, I'm really excited. I hear this man is terribly charming and attractive.'

'So am I.'

'I know, but I'm married to you. A girl likes a change. Just occasionally.'

'Tory! That's not very nice.'

'Sorry, darling. I just spoke to Venetia, she's so fed up. She says she feels like a beached whale. And told me never to get pregnant. I said too late.'

'Did you, darling? Jolly – Tory, what did you say? What?'

'I said I told her it was too late. That I was.'

'You're what? Really? Oh, Tory. Tory, my darling. Oh, heavens, how do you feel? Oh, God. Look, do you think you ought to come? You mustn't drink anything, when, I mean how long, I mean – oh, God.'

'Jay,' said Tory coolly, 'it's the woman who's supposed to turn into a mindless cretin when she's pregnant, not the man. Do calm down. In April. Or thereabouts. I feel fine. I plan to drink – in moderation. And I also plan to flirt monstrously with Geordie MacColl. It may be my last opportunity for a long time.'

'Maud! Oh, Maud, it's so, so lovely to see you. You look absolutely marvellous.'

'Adele! You look marvellous too. So chic. Is Lady Beckenham here? I'd so love to see her again.'

'No, she stayed at home with Kit. He – well, he doesn't like parties terribly.'

'I don't suppose he does.'

'Is that handsome man over there, with the grey hair, your husband?'

'Yes. That's Nathaniel. I'm glad you think he's handsome. So do I.' She smiled, the sweet, careful smile that Adele remembered from her childhood. She looked lovely: very elegant as always, in black draped jersey, her red hair drawn back in a chignon.

'I'm so glad you and Barty made it up,' said Adele impulsively. 'It was so sad when you – well, when—'

'I know. And I think I was terribly at fault myself. It's so wrong to be judgmental. These things are so very far from being one-sided. Anyway, now we're good friends again. Communicating really very well.'

She was so American, Adele thought, so serious and analytical.

'Good. Well, we're all delighted.'

'And I thought, what an opportunity for Nathaniel to meet all my English relations. When Barty asked us. So here we are.'

'Wonderful. You must excuse me, I'm supposed to be taking photographs. I'll see you later.'

'Yes, at your mother's dinner.'

'Giles, hallo. It's nice to see you.'

'It's nice to see you, Barty.'

He clearly didn't quite mean it; his jealousy of her was painful. His jealousy and anger.

'How could she have done that?' he had said to Helena. 'Not told us, not told us she was married to the man, that she had those shares, it was so devious—'

Helena looked at him; for once she was on Barty's side.

'Personally, Giles,' she said, 'if I'd had the chance to – hoodwink you all like that I would have done so. It must have been great fun.'

Giles hadn't spoken to her after that for several days.

He looked tired, Barty thought; tired and depressed. Poor Giles. His life was not very fulfilling.

'Have you met Geordie yet?'

'No, not yet.'

'Well, come and meet him. He's so nice.'

He followed her over; he had very little choice.

'Geordie, this is Giles Lytton. Oliver's eldest son. He and I grew up together. I told you.'

'Yes, you did. Lucky chap. I wouldn't have minded growing up with Barty. Was she terribly clever even then?'

'Yes,' said Giles shortly.

'Do please excuse me,' said Barty, 'I have to talk to the gentleman from the London Library.'

Geordie MacColl looked after her and smiled. 'She told me how it was you and her against the world quite often, and that you played the most wonderful games together. And she used to long for you to come home from school for the holidays. Count the days.'

'Did she?' said Giles. He was surprised; he felt better suddenly. That Barty had such happy memories of him, that she should have shared them with this person. She needn't have done that after all.

'Yes. She also told me about your war record. The Military Cross! My God.'

'Well – you know.' Giles shrugged modestly. 'Not a lot of use in civvy street. Peace time, that is.'

'It's a hard adjustment. I know. Of course it's a problem *Opium* addresses. Are you writing about it?'

'Writing? No, I'm not a writer, I'm a publisher.'

'You can be both. My father's brother was.'

'Oh, really?'

'Yes, he had a passion for travel. In his vacations he travelled and then the rest of the year, after hours, he wrote travel books.'

'Oh,' said Giles. 'Oh, that's interesting.'

He often said that; but this time he meant it. He had thought about the war so much, the extraordinary achievements of the most ordinary men and women, the power that patriotism, duty and training had to bring out such courage and endeavour. He had thought of writing about it, of writing a history of the Second World War from the ordinary soldier's point of view, interspersed with interviews; Celia had pooh-poohed it absolutely. Maybe he should just write it and present it to her; it would be something he would enormously enjoy doing, in any case.

'I – might think about that,' he said to Geordie MacColl.

'Do. Oh, now I have to go and talk to that lady, I believe, she's from the *Observer* newspaper. Excuse me. I understand we'll meet at dinner tonight. At your mother's wonderful house?'

He moved off. Giles looked after him. 'Nice chap,' he said to Barty. 'Isn't he?'

'He suggested I write a book. About the war. I had – thought about it, as a matter of fact. From the ordinary soldier's point of view. With interviews and so on.'

'Giles, that is such a good idea. I could give you some marvellous ATS people to talk to. Why don't you do it?'

'I might,' he said, and smiled at her. He suddenly felt a lot better.

'Could I take a photograph of you together? No, no need to move, just carry on talking. Thank you. That's wonderful.'

'Hey,' said Geordie MacColl, as the *Sunday Times* critic moved off, 'you're not the beautiful twin photographer, are you?'

Adele laughed. 'Well, let's see. I'm a twin. And a photographer. Don't know about the beautiful . . .'

'Oh, I do. Now then. Barty told me all about you. She said you were terribly talented. And famous even, pictures in *Vogue* and – did she say something about *Life*?'

'I did sell them something, yes. A series, actually. I mean they used them as a series. A day in the life of an English village. They seemed to like them.'

'My God,' said Geordie MacColl, gazing at her, 'that is something. That is *really* something. You must feel you can die happy now. Or something like that.'

Adele looked at him consideringly. Not many people reacted so appropriately to what had been the most important event in her life for many months.

'I do. That's exactly how I felt at the time, anyway.'

'Well, I'm very honoured to be in your camera. You know *Life* is the

719

Bible in the States. What am I saying, much more important than the Bible. Well, to some of us, anyway.'

'Oh, I do know,' she said, and laughed.

'Are you doing any more for them?'

'I hope so. Could I just take you over there, look, take a shot for the *Tatler*?'

'I didn't know they did literary pages.'

'They don't, I'm afraid. It's for their social pages. Would you mind?'

'Not for you. Like I say, it's an honour to share your lens.'

'A big success, Oliver.'

'Yes, it does seem to be. How nice to have Lyttons hosting a party like this again. I thought such delights were over. I suppose, strictly speaking, I shouldn't be here.'

'Of course you should. None of these people would be here if it hadn't been for you. Not even I.'

'Now that is ridiculous, Celia.'

'No, it's not. I mean it.'

'Well, I think you'd have made your name anyway. Incidentally, I didn't get a chance to tell you, I got a letter from Jack today. He's fearfully amused by the whole thing.'

'Really?' said Celia.

'Yes. He says he and Lily are coming home at last. Sick of Hollywood, it seems.'

'I'd like that,' said Celia.

'So would I. Nice young chap, MacColl, isn't he?'

'Very nice. Charming. Quite an old family, it seems.'

'Indeed. Don't sound so surprised, Celia. You know perfectly well they exist in the States. Look at Felicity, she—'

'I never quite believed in the age of Felicity's family,' said Celia coolly.

'Really?'

'No. You know, he seems rather taken with Adele.'

'Who?'

'Geordie MacColl. Every time I look at her, she's talking to him. That would be nice—'

'Celia, you sound like Mrs Bennett.'

'I hope not,' said Celia briskly, 'she was an excessively silly woman. Now look, I have to make my speech. I'll see you later. Don't drink too much, it's not good for you.'

❁

720

'And that is your redoubtable mother, is it?' whispered Geordie to Adele. 'She's very beautiful.'

'She is, isn't she?'

'You look very like her.'

'Thank you. You'd better be quiet, she gets furious if people talk over her speeches.'

'Sorry. I have to reply to it anyway, so I'd better listen. See you later.'

'Barty, this is such a nice party.'

It was Izzie, in her pink crêpe dress, her golden-brown hair drawn back, Alice-style, from her face.

'I'm glad you're enjoying it.'

'I am. Mr MacColl is so lovely. I really like him.'

'Good. Well, he told me he thought you were a very interesting young lady.'

'Really?' She blushed. 'Gosh.'

'Hallo, Izzie.'

'Hallo, Henry.'

'Enjoying the party?'

'Yes, terribly.'

'Roo and I are going to a jazz concert on Saturday. Would you like to come?'

'Oh – goodness. I'll have to ask Father.'

'Righty-o. It's perfectly all right, though, you can tell him. Chap used to go to Eton. Humphrey Lyttleton's his name.'

'Yes. Yes, I will. Thank you, Henry.'

'Can I get you a drink?'

'Oh – yes. Thank you. He's awfully good-looking, isn't he?' she said to Barty, looking at Henry's dark head as he moved through the crowd.

'Awfully. Just like his father.'

'Well, in a way, I suppose, but his father's really old. Oh – sorry, Barty.'

Barty smiled at her. 'It's perfectly all right.'

'Hallo, Adele, my darling. You've been working very hard.'

'I know. Well, it is my job.'

'Nice party.'

'Very. Are you enjoying it?'

'Oh – quite. I've had a bellyful of these things. To be honest, I only ever liked my own.'

'Sebastian! You're such an egotist.'

'I know. I've spent a lifetime developing my skill in that direction. Tell me, what do you think of our star author? He seems very keen on you.'

'I think he's very nice,' said Adele primly.

'Good. So do I.'

There was a pause; then he said, 'Adele—'

'Yes?'

'We've never talked about—'

'Kit? No. And I don't think we should. As Grandmama would say, it's grown-up business.'

He smiled. 'Wise old bird, your grandmama.'

'Very. She's done a lot for Kit.'

He looked at her very steadily. 'How is he?'

'Mending. Mending well. Working hard, too.'

'Good.'

'He—'

'Yes?'

'He said if I saw you, to say hallo.'

'Adele,' said Sebastian, giving her a kiss, 'that's the nicest thing I've heard all evening.'

'Hallo, again.'

'Oh – hallo.'

'Look – I wonder if you'd like to have lunch with me tomorrow? I don't often meet *Life* photographers.'

'Oh,' said Adele, 'well, it's very kind, but I have to take two models down to my grandmother's farm and photograph them with some rare-breed sheep she's just bought. It must sound very boring to you. Sorry.'

'Boring! Not at all. It sounds wonderful. Wonderful and eccentric. And I'd love to meet your legendary grandmother. My grandfather had a farm in Kentucky, bred racehorses.'

'In that case,' said Adele, 'my grandmother would love to meet you.'

'I couldn't come down with you, could I? If I promise not to get in the way of your camera. How far from London is this paradise?'

'Oh – a couple of hours. Yes, of course you can come. If you've got time.'

'I'll make time,' said Geordie MacColl.

'Well,' said Celia, 'what a good party.'

'Good speech, Celia.' Sebastian smiled at her.

'Thank you.'

'Barty looks lovely.'

'Yes, she does,' said Celia slightly coolly.

'Don't begrudge it to her, Celia. You of all people.'

'I – don't,' she said, 'not really.'

'Good.'

He looked at Barty intently. 'She must be terribly rich.'

'No, actually, not so terribly, it seems. He left her only the shares in Lyttons and a few more, a little portfolio as she put it. And his houses. Obviously worth a lot.'

'Yes, especially the one on Park Avenue, it's a mansion, I'm told.'

'Oh, the Americans would call any little house a mansion,' said Celia, 'they're so easily impressed.'

'Celia, have you ever been to the Frick museum?'

'Yes, of course.'

'Well, Elliott House is a little bigger than that, I'm told. And very similar.'

'Oh. Well, yes, that is quite – impressive.' Even she was silent. Then she rallied. 'Anyway, the rest of the money is left in trust. For his children. All those millions.'

'Did he know about Jenna?'

'No. But apparently there is a strong case to be made for her getting a share. As her father was married to Barty.'

'My God,' said Sebastian, 'clearly this story is very far from over.'